W9-BNA-028

VOID CITY LIMITS

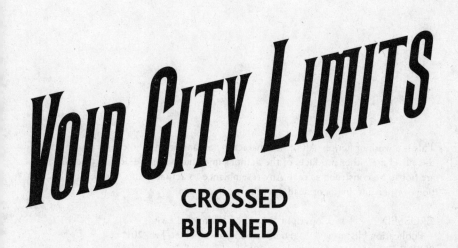

VOID CITY LIMITS

CROSSED
BURNED

J.F. LEWIS

SFBC
FANTASY

CROSSED   Copyright © 2011 by Jeremy F. Lewis
  Publication History: Pocket Books mass market, Feb. 2011
BURNED   Copyright © 2012 by Jeremy F. Lewis
  Publication History: Pocket Books mass market, Feb. 2012

First SFBC Fantasy Printing: April 2013

Selected by Rome Quezada, SFBC Senior Editor

Published by arrangement with
Pocket Books
A Division of Simon & Schuster, Inc.
1230 Avenue of the Americas
New York, NY 10020

Visit The SFBC online at http://www.sfbc.com

ISBN 978-1-62490-154-6

Printed in the United States of America.

CONTENTS

CROSSED

To my sons, thanks for teaching me (some) patience.
(Boys: No, you are not old enough to read this book, no matter what
year this is. Love, Dad.)

ACKNOWLEDGMENTS

VROOM!

The author would like to acknowledge every single person who made this book possible, but is quite certain (as always) that he's left someone out. If it was you . . . Oops.

My debt of gratitude to the WTF (Write The Fantastic . . . my writing group)—Rob, Mary Ann, Dan, Karen, and Janet—grows larger with each novel. Their mad baking skills have grown alongside their editing skills, and their constant support (and criticism) is more help than I could say.

Thanks are also owed to Mom, Dad, Alvin, Virginia, Rich, and Daniel for support and friendship above and beyond the call of duty, and to Mike McCrary for his keen eye and amazing attention to detail.

This time around, I feel I owe a special debt of gratitude to all those who were supportive about *the unpleasantness*. I won't go into it here, but if you Google "excommunicated" and "author" or "j f lewis," you'll probably find more information than you want. I'll name a few, but it's a really long list, so, in no particular order, to Jeff Carlson, Jackie Kessler, Jeanne Stein, Sherrilyn Kenyon, Ted Kosmatka, Alethea Kontis, Mary Robinette Kowal, Derek Tatum, The Gambers (Dan, Jackie, Ben, and Ellen), Sean Williams, C. E. Murphy, Michael Stackpole, Michael and Lorrie Mennenga, Summer Brooks, Mur Lafferty, J. C. Hutchins, David B. Coe, Gail Martin, Haley Elizabeth Garwood, Joy Ward, everybody on Codex, and a host of others: Just . . . thanks.

These acknowledgments would not be complete without mentioning two mighty women: my agent, Shawna McCarthy; and my editor, Jennifer Heddle. Without them, you wouldn't be reading this. I'd also like to thank Heather and Danny Baror, without whom these books might not exist in other languages.

Last, but never least, thanks to you, the reader. Without you, I'm reduced to a silly man typing stories in the dark and giggling to himself. ☺

I

◆　◆　◆

WEDDING BELLS

AS TOLD BY ERIC AND RACHEL

1

ERIC:

THE WEDDING DAY

I shouldn't have been doing what I was doing, but I was. I was supposed to be getting dressed, following the plan: slip into the monkey suit, get married, and fly away to Paris for the honeymoon.

Instead I was fucking the maid of honor, which while usually the objective for a single guy at a wedding, is less appropriate for the groom, even if he happens to be a vampire, like me. I could've blamed Rachel, the maid of honor in question, but it wasn't her fault. I already knew she had no morals. She'd demonstrated that in all sorts of ways, ranging from helping a demon try to steal my soul last Christmas to blowing up my strip club and setting my movie theater on fire—all to get herself out of a demonic deal that really hadn't been all that terrible in the first place. She was only the maid of honor because she was the bride's sister, and that was the picture Tabitha, my vampiric bride-to-be, had stuck in her head about the way her wedding day ought to unfold.

In a way, I'd spent my entire engagement to Tabitha waiting for the newness of sex with her little sister to wear off, but it didn't seem likely. As a tantric witch, if there was one thing in the world Rachel was good at, sex was it.

Sex between a human and a vampire is multilayered. For humans, it's about danger, the dark thrill of being with one of the undead, the idea that at any moment your lover will sink his teeth into you and you may or may not see the light of day again. For vampires, it's about getting to feel warm, being allowed to play with our food. It satisfies the primal urge to dominate the living I think we all have.

Sex with Tabitha wasn't bad, since she was a Living Doll—a vampire with the ability to turn her bodily functions back on—so she could feel warm and wonderful like a human, but sex with Rachel was on another level. Every time I slipped inside her, Rachel used her tantric magic to make me feel alive, literally, and each encounter was better than the one before, another heartbeat, or another true breath, not the stuff we do just to push air out so we can talk.

Then again, it wasn't just that either. I've always had a weakness for women in fancy dresses, their lipstick just right, all decked out to the nines . . . the way some of them still manage to look surprised that you noticed. In short, I was trying to stay faithful to Tabitha, but I was . . . less than successful.

I moved atop Rachel, her back pressed against the dresser, my eyes locked with hers. The butterfly tattoo on her left cheek caught my eye, a visible reminder of her thralldom. Any vampire more powerful than a Drone can make a thrall, but the amount of control and the strength of abilities passed on to the human participant is a variable, largely based on the power level of the vampire. Through me, Rachel was immortal—well, okay, ageless—but she was also bound to me. I could force her to obey commands.

"Are you sure you don't want me to release you?" I asked. "I still don't really believe in having thralls." I was such a hypocrite. Counting Rachel, I had six thralls, including a mage named Magbidion, a few ladies I'd rescued from a pimp down by the Bitemore Hotel, and Beatrice, a young woman who'd once been enthralled by another vampire named Lady Gabriella.

Rachel smirked and shook her head. "I'll keep the eternal youth, thanks."

I nipped at her neck, playfully, without the fangs.

"You already ate," she chided.

My eyes closed as I built toward climax, my fingers closing on her breasts, the metal rings in her nipples hard beneath my pressing thumbs. "So?" My breath blew cold against her neck, raising chill bumps.

"I want to try something." Rachel pushed me out of her body, taking me in her hand before I could protest. It wasn't how I wanted to finish. Rachel's lips blurred. Words that humans aren't meant to know or hear hissed at my ears. Rachel had lost her full mystic might when we'd killed the demon who'd given her magic, but the tantric side of her abilities had flourished. There are points on the body that funnel energy, or at least people who believe in that sort of thing think they do. They're called chakras, and just then all of mine got hot.

"What are you doing?"

Her eyes told me she didn't have time to answer, that for what she was doing the timing was vital. The pleasure built, a need to explode and then release, but with the release came something new, or perhaps old.

When you become a vampire, all of your bodily fluids are replaced with blood: tears, saliva, everything. Of course, an undead heart doesn't beat, but mine was beating. A vampire's blood doesn't flow, but mine was flowing. Taste buds become specialized, sensitive only to blood, but my mouth tasted like cinnamon; it was all I could smell too, a side effect of Rachel's twisted evil (and okay, awesome) magic. She held a single drop of the new side effect on the tip of her index finger.

"It worked," she howled triumphantly.

I counted heartbeats, felt the core warmth creeping back into my bones. While my fiancée can turn her body back on like that, make herself seem alive, and that's great and all . . . it isn't much better than average human warmth. Like most vampires, I crave *true* warmth, a sensation the living take for granted. Is it any wonder I kept sleeping with the one woman in the world who made me feel that way, despite the fact that she had almost gotten me and several people I care about killed to save her own neck?

The telltale cinnamon odor of her magic faded, overpowered by the scents of sex and sweat. My tux had a wet spot.

Shit!

Vampires have an excellent sense of smell, vampire fiancées included. Tabitha might not smell it while in her Living Doll state, because doing so dulls her vampiric abilities and senses. But she wasn't going to be the only vampire in attendance. I couldn't walk down the aisle smelling like Rachel, that was for damn sure. If I did, it would get back to Tabitha eventually—I was sure of it.

My "best individual" (apparently it isn't politically correct to say "best man" or even "best person" at a supernatural wedding), a Mouser named Talbot who'd been with me for several decades, ever since a particularly bad week or two in El Segundo, knocked on the door. "Eric? It's time." He opened the door a crack, looking dapper as hell, the custom-made tux perfectly fitting his massive muscular frame. Light from the hallway gleamed off his bald head and dark black skin. His kind can look human, but they're far from it. A cough preceded his next sentence. "And Rachel, your sister is wondering where her maid of honor has run off to."

"Do you want to see if it can get me pregnant? Want to be a daddy for real?" Rachel asked, beaming, ignoring Talbot completely. She'd put pink and blue streaks in her hair for the occasion—the wedding, not the sex—and that, combined with the current request, the twinkle in her bright green eyes, told me she'd given this much more thought than she wanted to let on. "You're up all night already so it isn't like you'll lose any sleep."

I gave Talbot a look that screamed "help," but he did not come to my rescue.

"I'll stall," he said before slipping back down the corridor into the chapel. *Coward.* As I thought the word, I recalled the image of Talbot in his furred-out super-cat combat form, eyes and mane glowing as I hurled him through the air after a demon that had been getting away. Killing demons are what Mousers do best and . . .

Rachel was still looking at me expectantly, still awaiting my answer. I looked at her finger and remembered the question she'd just asked me.

Double shit!

"Are you crazy?" I asked her, panicked. "No!"

Rachel laughed, licking the fluid in question from her finger, but she sounded hurt. "It's okay this time, but if you want to be really sure, maybe you should invest in some condoms, Master."

"Don't call me Master," I growled. "Think of something! I can't go out there like this."

"So don't go out there." Rachel slipped back into her pink dress. "Dominate her, or . . . hell, she's your creation. Tell her to get stuffed; leave her at the altar. You don't need her for anything unless you want to fulfill the whole '*ménage à trois* with sisters fantasy,' and even then, I can find you a pair of live sisters to do that. Fuck, baby, I'll find you twins."

Rachel is an enabler.

When I was human, I'd nearly gotten married. Instead of taking my vows and undergoing the big ring exchange, I'd gotten murdered by the man Marilyn, my then-fiancée, had been having an affair with . . . my best friend Whatshisname. It started with an R, I think. Ronald, maybe? Anyway, the important thing is that I rose as a vampire and also as a revenant, simultaneously, but I didn't rise remembering what had happened. My memory still sucks.

Old Whatshisname and I had both become vampires, and we were friends for decades after we died. It had been only a year or so since I'd figured it all out. Then, I trapped him in a little soul-prison that looks like a marble (a fate he'd intended for me) and gave him to Lord Phillip, the ranking local high society vamp who wound up sticking the Stone of Aeternum in my chest as a reward. The Stone can be used to raise the dead and other funky crap, but in my case it's supposed to make me a True Immortal (the living breathing kind) if I'm ever cured of my vampirism, not that I'm going out of my way to try.

Rising as two kinds of undead at once is supposedly what made me an Emperor-level vampire. Vampires are supposed to come in four different flavors: Drones, Soldiers, Masters, and Vlads. If they were beverages, Drones would be milk (no power to speak of and not worth crying over), Soldiers would be tea (a little bit of kick, but nothing that will keep you awake nights), Masters might be coffee (avoid before bedtime), and Vlads would be a concoction from Starbucks with an extra shot of espresso. But Emperors wouldn't even be a beverage— we'd be something like whole chocolate-covered dark espresso beans. Every now and then, the universe cuts you a break. Speaking of which . . .

Guests had been arriving at the wedding in transportation modes of varying impressiveness. Usually this meant some type of limousine with windows that had been thoroughly blacked out. I'd hoped that by holding the wedding during the day we'd get tons of polite regrets. Instead the vampiric elite had all taken it as a challenge to find a way to be awake and attend. I think most of them did it just to chap my ass.

Out in the vestibule, I heard Talbot greeting Lord Phillip, but beyond that, rapidly approaching, I heard motorcycle engines—not just one, but maybe a dozen. Needless to say, no one on the guest list would be showing up on a motorcycle. Then I smelled wet fur. Werewolves. The first thought that went through my head was: *I'm the luckiest motherfucker on the planet!*

"Attention, undead filth!" a voice rang out with the crackle and pop of an outdated bullhorn. "Marriage is for the living, not the dead! Till death do us part, not in death do we start! Now burn!"

"Get cleaned up," I ordered Rachel. Given her druthers, she'd have disobeyed, but that's the great thing about thralls. They can argue with you until you make it an order, but then they have to obey.

My vampiric speed kicked in and I ran out of the dressing room still zipping up my fly. My adopted daughter Greta, a six-foot blonde, met me at the chapel door. She was dressed as a flower girl in white, a basket of rose petals in her hand. I'd rescued Greta from a truly bad situation and adopted her as my own. She'd been human, only nine or ten years old, and though I'd turned her on her twenty-first birthday, sometimes when I look at her I still see that little girl, feel that need to protect her. Whatever was coming, it was *not* going to hurt my daughter. "I've never seen werewolves like this before, Dad," she said.

A Molotov cocktail burst through a stained-glass window, only to be deftly caught and flung out again by Ebon Winter, one of my guests. Imagine the most handsome man possible in all creation and you'll be picturing Ebon Winter. He has that effect on people. Winter is a gambler and an artist. He sings, he owns a really upscale club called the Artiste Unknown, he designs his own clothes, and he's one heck of an interior decorator. He's high society, and his pathological need to bet on damn near everything, up to and including social inter- actions and how long it'll take me to lose my temper, makes him a bit dangerous to hang out with, but otherwise not bad. I'd invited him even though he had told me he was betting against me in Paris . . . whatever the hell that meant.

"Phil," Winter called over his shoulder, "a little cloud cover for our combustible groom?"

Lord Phillip effectively runs Void City, the slice of urban America I call home, along with who knows how much of the rest of the coun- try. He's short, fat, and balding, but he's also the only vampire spell caster the Mage Guild hasn't destroyed. He's also in charge of the Veil of Scrythax, the magic what's-it that helps conceal the existence of the supernatural from Void City's more mundane inhabitants. Phil is rarely seen outside of the Highland Towers, preferring not to risk his unlife away from the ironclad protection of his mystic wards. My wedding was an exception.

"If you insist." He smiled and began to open an umbrella. "Tut, tut," he quoted, like a grown-up Christopher Robin gone horribly wrong, "it looks like rain," and suddenly, it did.

Phillip's clouds, black and rain-filled, rolled in so fast I scarcely made it out of the church in time to catch the last rays of vanishing sunlight and set myself on fire. Charbroiled and still sizzling, there was no way I'd have even a whiff of Rachel clinging to me. Not a drop of rain had fallen yet, but the werewolves were soaking wet, completely doused in water so holy I could smell the altar boys. They must have soaked themselves before the fight. *Lovely.*

The rain arrived right on cue, extinguishing my flaming carcass, and I laughed out of habit as the water washed over me, leaving me just as wet as the werewolves.

Werewolves usually look silly to me, but, even soaked to the skin, these guys were something special. Intricate patterns had been shaved into their fur like Celtic knotwork or henna tattoos. The flesh beneath had been inked in solid colors: black, blue, green, and red. I could tell which was the Alpha. I'd tangled with an Alpha werewolf not long be- fore, the first truly impressive lycanthrope I'd ever seen, and the leader of these guys gave off the same vibe he had. I can take on normal were- wolves in groups, but I'd never actually had to fight an Alpha, since the local Alpha, William, and I had worked out our differences at gun- point. First time for everything.

Most of these wolves had crosses etched or painted on their claws. The Alpha smiled at me with a mouth full of fangs that showed the same kind of detailing. His fur was black as midnight and he stared at me through angry eyes, one blue and one brown. I was still happy he'd showed up.

2

RACHEL:
LITTLE SISTER

Tabitha didn't even leave her dressing room, the stupid cow. Standing in her white dress, she peered eagerly past me into the hall, but made no move to go help her husband-to-be.

"What's going on?" Tabitha whined.

"Sorry, I've been ordered to wash up," I snarked. "No vapid bimbo chat time left."

I slid the frilly pink dress off over my head while waiting for Tabitha to react. Instead, she peeked out the door into the hallway, trying to get a glimpse of the excitement out front. Mom's imagined voice chattered inside my head, "Don't tease your sister, Rae, this is her special day." I slipped out of the light blue thong I'd been wearing and, as a second thought, wiped my crotch with it before following my master's instructions to wash up.

Cold water ran out of the tap and echoing raindrops spattered against the clouded glass of the restroom's single exterior window.

"Too bad Mom couldn't be here," I called into the other room. "She probably thinks you're still alive."

"I know," Tabitha answered.

"Want me to call her?" I teased. Mom had seen me buried. Before that, she'd watched the leukemia take its toll and break me until I was nothing more than a shell of myself, a pain-ridden harpy hurting everyone I'd ever loved because they got to live and I was a sick seventeen-year-old who was going to barely make it to eighteen and even that only if I was lucky. Tabitha could have saved me from the grave, from the sickness, from all of it. She'd been dating a vampire—Eric—even then, but as it was, I'd had to save myself, find my own way back to life.

You don't want to know what they do to little witch wannabes in hell. If you're strong enough, and willing, devious, and smart enough to play your cards right, you can work a deal to come back. First, though, you have to impress them. God, do you have to impress them.

"No!" Tabitha touched my back. "Don't you dare!"

"I think Mom and Lord Phillip would hit it off. With all the work she's had done, she still looks pretty fuckable."

I pulled several brown paper towels free of the wall dispenser and smirked, thinking about Father Ike. I still didn't understand how Eric had convinced a human priest to perform a marriage ceremony for vampires. When I asked Father Ike about it, the little old priest had laughed and cleared his throat. "I've been trying to save that wily old sinner since we served together in Korea. If he's still walking and talking, then I believe there is hope. If I can get him into a church for any reason, so much the better." Maybe if I'd met someone like Father Ike, back before I got sick, went to hell, came back . . . maybe it would have been different. Everybody ought to know a Father Ike.

"Rachel, please don't screw this up for me."

"Fine." I held the paper towels under the now-warm water just enough to get it damp and wiped Eric's scent off me. He was so paranoid. Tabitha's senses were dulled when she played human, and playing human was the only way she could stay awake during daylight hours. She was still as hard to kill as a vampire, but her other attributes became utterly mundane. He should have just let it go. Now I had to make him sorry. "Look, you're right," I said, smiling. "This is your special day."

"A little special for you, too," Tabitha said. She handed my dress back to me. "Who did you meet?"

"Some guy," I answered vaguely as I watched her reaction in the mirror, somehow disturbed by her ability. It takes insane levels of magic to fool a mirror. They reflect truth. "You don't know him."

That was true, too. She'd never really know Eric. You have to see terrible things, feel real pain and despair, and get angry enough to crawl out of your grave before you can see things the way he does. "You know what Mom would be worried about, don't you?"

"The fight?"

"Something old." I patted myself down with several more paper towels.

"Something new," Tabitha interjected. I let her help zip up the back of my dress.

"Something borrowed. Something blue," we finished together.

"I forgot all about that," Tabitha fretted. Thunder cracked and lightning struck out in the street. Lord Phillip was having some fun.

"Don't worry, Tab." *Slut!* "I can take care of everything." *Bitch!* I picked up my thong and waggled it at her. "Something borrowed and something blue all in one package." It was a pleasure to watch her recoil.

"But you wore those; they smell like sex," she whined, disgusted.

"It'll spice up the honeymoon too, the smell of me and you all mixed up together . . ."

Uncertainty was pushed gradually aside by her desire to please Master. I wondered if she even knew that she thought about him in two different ways, the vampire part of her recognizing him as Master while the human part still conjured images of Eric, her one true love, her knight in shining goddamn armor.

"Maybe."

Idiot. How he ever brought himself to turn you, much less propose to you I'll never know, I thought. *You can't be that great a lay.* "Or you and I could give him a three-way in the marriage bed. I guarantee you he'll never forget it."

She snatched the panties away with a sigh.

"No." She sounded exasperated. "You promised me that you wouldn't sleep with him."

"And I've kept that promise." Also true; we weren't sleeping. "But it doesn't hurt to offer. You know it's what he wants. Of course he might settle for permission to fuck me every once in a while."

"Shut up! Shut your filthy mouth!" The slap caught me by surprise, sharp and painful against my jaw. Anger had brought out a little of Tabitha's vampire strength, spinning me around so that I bounced off the sink and then to the floor, pink taffeta bunched up around my feet. That was the line she shouldn't have crossed. Eric could slap me if he wanted. As long as he got off on it I wouldn't care, because my magic would make it feel as good to me as it felt to him, but Tabitha? No fucking way did she get to bat me around. I think that's when I made my decision. How do you make a guy who doesn't care what you do to him sorry? How do you punish a good-for-nothing piece of shit big sister for knocking you around? Same way.

"God!" Tabitha moaned. "Why do you have to say things like that? Shit! I'm sorry. Are you okay?"

For the briefest of moments, I considered using some of the power I'd leeched from Eric and going toe-to-toe with her in my own minor version of Eric's uber vamp form. Killing her with his own power—power I wouldn't even have possessed if he'd been able to keep out of my pants—would have been epic in a *Fatal Attraction* sort of way, but I only managed to get a little bit of power each time Eric and I fucked, and to be honest, it was too precious to waste on her. No. She deserved a little trip on the Tantra Train. That way I could bat her around in my own special way while simultaneously gaining a tool to make Eric feel guilty as hell. Perfect. Frickin' elegant even.

All aboard.

I don't use Tantra the way others might. Brahma, Shiva, Kali Ma, all that is for humans. What I use is older. It's what a succubus might teach you in a Hadean back alley if she took a liking to you. Most forms of Tantra are about opening up to the energy that flows through us, tapping the creative force present in all life. Mine is about sex through power, for power, and of power—an unholy union. When I still had a demonic patron, I could tap into other branches of magic, like pyromancy—that sort of thing. Tabitha was going to wish that I had done just that: simply set her on fire.

I lay on the floor, unmoving. Tabitha stepped forward, the folds of her wide floor-length gown cascading over my arm. "I'm"—my hand went under her dress, touching Tabitha's *Muladhara*, the chakra between her anus and vagina; it controls survival instinct—"fine." *You have nothing to fear.* I forced a sense of safety less into her mind than into her being, her essence. *I'm your sister. I won't hurt you.* She would be surprised by the things I know about people. For example, Tabitha was never supposed to be a Vlad. She should have been a Soldier at best. Maybe she had enough hidden depths to be a Master vampire, but I doubt it.

When an Emperor vampire—like Eric—turns a human woman, that person is elevated to Vlad status whether she deserves it or not. Any members of the same sex an Emperor turns become Drones—it's why Kyle, Eric's son, was "born" an idiot while Greta, Eric's daughter, got to be a Vlad. It's un-nature's way of letting them keep friends around, but preventing those friends from becoming threats. The point is that Vlads usually get to be Vlads because they are incredibly strong willed and unique, which makes it harder for me to do my thing. Harder, but not impossible, and since Tabitha isn't a normal Vlad . . .

"Safe," she murmured.

Touching her through her gown was gonna work just fine. One chakra at a time, I manipulated the inner Tabitha: *Swadhisthana* over the groin to make my intrusion pleasurable, *Manipura* over the solar plexus to make what I was doing satisfy her hunger, *Anahata* over her heart to awake familial love and put her further at ease, *Vishuddha* at the throat so that I could still her tongue or guide her words. When I got to *Ajna*, the third eye, she was shaking violently, her spirit trying to fight me, shake off my control. Your spirit self knows things your brain doesn't, and hers knew that this was bad mojo.

My lips touched her forehead and I could sense her deepest desires. She wanted to taste. Her body could pretend to be alive in every respect but one: her taste buds still reacted only to blood. I gave her taste, filling her mouth with the cinnamon flavor of my magic. The pleasure built as I placed my hands on either side of her head and kissed the final chakra.

The crown chakra is called *Sahasrara*; it controls everything else. It's basically the doorway to consciousness. I took it last, stealing her mind. Normally when I do that to people I give them the most mind-blowing orgasm they'll ever experience in exchange, but not Tabitha. She didn't deserve it, so she got all the buildup without the release. *Nice.*

"Put on the panties," I told her. "It'll turn him on. Best not to think about why. He's a man. They get off on weird stuff."

"Okay," she said in a conspiratorial whisper. "Why not?"

"I mean, if he can't get kinky with his wife"—I straightened her dress, began to repair the damage I'd done to her makeup—"then he might want to stray."

"You're such a good sister," she said. One bloody tear welled within her eye and I dabbed it away with the paper towels I'd used to dry myself. She was still seeming human, so the tear should have been a normal tear, not a vampire's. I leaned in close, watched her eyes. I still had her in my power, and it wasn't like she was strong enough to put up any real resistance . . . or I didn't think she was, but it was almost as if I'd underestimated her, like she had hidden depths and was fighting my power. . . . *Odd.*

"No one else in the world has a sister like you," she said with a smile.

"You have no idea."

3

ERIC:
THE HAIRY BIKER REVIVAL

This isn't going exactly as I'd planned," I coughed between gouts of flame. Note to self: next time you wind up fighting one of the increasing number of werewolf zealots in the United States, and an ally of yours is nice enough to summon up a storm so you won't spend the whole melee on fire, don't let the werewolves bless the rain and force your mouth open. It sucks.

Not that the fight itself was going well. Based on the combat chatter, the lead werewolf's name seemed to be Deacon. He perched on my chest, hind claws cutting into my stomach, actively trying to rip my head from my shoulders. At least I could close my mouth.

"I'm coming to help you, Dad!" Greta's scream bit through the rain and storm.

"No!" I shouted back. "Even the rain is blessed. You'll be destroyed!" Greta's tough, but any holy wounds she receives don't heal unless I bleed on them. Of course, the way things were going, she'd be able to find my blood just about anywhere on the street.

My vampire speed just wouldn't kick back in, and strength alone wasn't cutting it. In short, my powers had picked a bad time to act finicky. Between the time I died and came back as a vampire, I'd been embalmed. Usually, that stops the turning process and you die for real, but not for me. I'd always thought that surviving my burial prep is what had screwed up my powers. Turns out I'd only been half right. Like everything with me, it was complicated.

The embalming didn't kill me because I didn't become a vampire in the traditional way at all. Like any other member of the Courtney family line who dies and is found "unworthy" of the big happily ever afterlife, I came back. Gotta love those family curses! As if that wasn't enough, I'd also been enchanted by Lord Phillip—magic elixir in the embalming fluid or something—supposedly to slow the development of my powers and to hide me from my sire, who apparently would eventually show up to kill me, not just for shits and giggles, but because I turned out to be an Emperor-level vamp, like her, and Phil didn't want that to happen too early for his Machiavellian plans, whatever they might actually be, to come to fruition.

Crazy, huh? Things got a little better recently, though. An Emperor's powers don't function properly until they create a *memento mori*: a repository for the more id-based portion of their power. Of course they can't die until they create one either, so if something happens which might normally kill the vampire portion of an Emperor (in my case, getting explodicated with shaped charges of blessed C-4), you create one when your body reforms. My abilities had become more reliable since then, but the further I am from my *memento mori*, the screwier they get. And they're screwy in the falling-out-of-the-sky *Greatest American Hero* sort of way.

Most Emperors use something small for a *memento mori*, the repository of their darkness—a ring or a necklace, something they can keep with them, something intensely personal—but since I'd created mine without knowing what I was doing and since it happened to be the closest of my personal effects that hadn't joined me in reduced-to-less-than-ashes land, I'd used my 1964½ Mustang convertible. It answers to "Fang." It feeds on roadkill. And since it is now, in effect, vampiric (with a few zombie-like tendencies), I try to keep it out of the sun—which is why I'd parked it a few blocks away on a covered deck. Parking closer might have been a good idea.

Ligaments in my neck started to pop. Skin sizzled with each drop of rain.

Then I heard it, the roar of one angry Mustang. I love my car, even more now that he's a twisted evil undead machine. My skin turned gray, then black, and I started to grow. Finally, I was about to get my uber vamp on! Holy stuff doesn't sting my Emperor form as badly as it does my normal vampire self. Even sunlight takes longer to kick in.

Behind me, in the church, I heard Winter say something about winning a bet and several vampires sighed while others applauded. Eight feet tall in my Emperor form, I flexed my leathery wings and clicked my claws.

"That damn vampire bets on everything," I growled.

"It's true," Deacon spat, which could have been an acceptable response to my statement, but the way his eyes widened as he said it made me think we were talking about two different subjects altogether.

"What is?" Was he talking about me being an Emperor? My uber vamp form? What? I threw him off me like a rag doll, but he didn't land like one. Spry and nimble, Deacon crouched on all fours, growling the opening of the Lord's Prayer in Latin.

"Form up, Apostles!" he shouted.

I hazarded a glance at the door of the church and the vampires crowding in under the awning to watch the show. Phillip held up a charred bit of metal, as if that would explain something to me about why he'd stopped tossing lightning bolts. More cautious vamps watched through the eyes of their human thralls. It's a trick that I don't know, but then again I prefer things up close and personal. Not one of them looked like they had any intention of helping me out.

Werewolves are good pack hunters. Vampires do well in ones and twos, but large-scale organization isn't our thing.

"Looks like you've got your hands full, boss," Talbot's voice caught my ear. He wouldn't help me either. Talbot only fights in self-defense or when he's hunting or when he damn well feels like it. There was no way he was risking that tux. Mousers are like that.

Twelve werewolves charged as one, wet fur glistening as they came. Time slowed for everything except me and Fang, raindrops slowing in the air, then freezing, motionless, like a wire-fu bullet-time moment from a huge effects movie, plus fur and fangs.

Two and a half tons of zealotry and claw looks dangerous no matter how fast it is or isn't moving, but the pause in battle gave me time to think. I wasn't facing just one Alpha wolf. This was a pack of Alphas. The other eleven didn't look like Alphas at first, because next to Deacon any other werewolf looked like a runt. Time returned to normal before it occurred to me that I ought to be hitting things, so I stupidly met the pack head-on.

Fang charged into the mass from the side, scattering them between us. One Apostle found himself being drawn slowly and inexorably beneath Fang's undercarriage, screaming as he went. Getting eaten by Fang is not a pleasant way to go, and the werewolf fought it, claws scoring the asphalt as he struggled. Everywhere I touched the wolves, their holiness stung. The blessed rain was taking its toll too, and I actually began to wonder whether I was going to make it without a little help. Covered in a mass of werewolves, I stumbled back against Fang, and then I felt them. The rats.

Once before, I'd summoned a cloud of bats to block out the sun. I had no idea how I'd done it then, but I'd seen the same sort of thing depicted in stained glass back at the Highland Towers. This time, it was rats, a plague of them. They crawled out of the sewer like they'd been massing underground waiting for my call. Surging out of storm grates, more rats than I would have thought could possibly have been infesting the area swarmed to my rescue, gnashing, biting, and paying no attention to the holy water.

Deacon grabbed the werewolf Fang was eating and hauled him out from under the Mustang with a horrendous rip like a cow tearing in half. That I know what that sounds like frightens me a little. Either way, the lycanthrope came free, though he was legless below the knees.

"Enough!" A voice like a nun's ruler on your knuckles cut through everything. I didn't see the speaker right off, but I knew his identity. Father Ike doesn't yell very often, but when he does, it demands attention. I'd ask him if he had a little touch of vampirism, but I know that's not where he gets the juice. He gets it from belief. The Apostles jerked up short, and a Semitic man wearing a priest's alb and preaching scarf over his single-breasted cassock stared at us all in a combination of disapproval and bemusement.

"Sorry, Ike," Deacon and I said together, surprising each other as well as our accomplices with our familiarity.

"Eric," he said, pointing at the rats. His gaze told me he wanted them gone. I transformed back to normal, wearing my standard "Welcome to the Void" T-shirt and jeans, the warmth of the newly formed clothes sinking into my skin despite the rain. With the uber vamp gone, the rats scurried like, well, like rats, back into the nooks, crannies, and drains from which they had emerged.

Pleased with my contrition, Ike and his glare moved on to Deacon. The sable fur vanished as Alpha werewolf was replaced by a tall blond man in his early thirties, heavily muscled, but proportioned evenly like a martial artist. I noticed the tattoos and other artwork weren't present in his human form and both eyes were brown. He had a chin you could crash a bus into, and the bus might come away with the worst of it.

Fang backed timidly into the shadow of the church, the ghost of John Paul Courtney (my great-great-grandfather—yet another recipient of the Courtney family curse that had caused my vampirism) appearing in the passenger's seat once the darkness covered the car. In life, he'd failed to do whatever it is the curse actually wants us Courtneys to do, but it turned him into a ghost and tied him to his magic revolver in kind of a Jiminy Cricket role to other cursed Courtneys instead of vamping him, which I guess is like being second runner-up or something when compared to the grand prize of being found worthy and actually being allowed to die.

What can I say? I've led an interesting death. So had John Paul Courtney. In his day, he'd been almost single-handedly responsible for scaring religion into the lycanthrope community. All the good little werewolves, the ones that said their prayers to God, Buddha, or the deity of their choice at night—he left them alone. All the bad little werewolves got a bullet from *El Alma Perdida* (the aforementioned magic gun) right between the eyes and had their furry little souls trapped inside. I don't think JPC realized that when he died, his spirit would be tied to the gun, too. Seeing him jogged my memory. *El Alma Perdida* was in Fang's glove box. I had a gun specifically for killing werewolves, a magic gun with fucking magic bullets, in my magic car and I'd forgotten all about the damn thing until the fight was over.

"Typical." It's no use being exasperated with my memory. As far as I know it's exasperated with me too and doesn't work correctly out of spite. I walked under the awning, glad to see I wasn't the only one who felt like a teenager caught fighting on the playground.

Heavy rain became drizzle as the wet werewolf in human form stood drenched and downcast before Father Ike. The Apostles shuffled clear, eyes averted, tails tucked between their legs. Sharp soft whimpers escaped their throats as Ike spoke.

"You know better than this." Father Ike placed a hand on Deacon's arm. "I expect better. You've come so far."

"But they're getting married, Father. The dead can't marry. It's evil . . . wrong."

"Oh, I expect they can in some circumstances." Ike patted Deacon twice, then moved his hand. "In China the dead may marry the living or each other. It isn't exactly the norm here, but then again neither is vampirism or lycanthropy. Would I refuse to marry two lycanthropes because they are sometimes wolves and, as animals, have no right to marriage or to heaven?"

"It's not the same, Father," Deacon growled.

"Not exactly, no." The sun peeked out from behind the clouds on Father Ike's smile. "But I expect it may be more similar than you are willing to admit. In death, I believe that there is no marriage, but the two souls I join together here today are neither exactly dead nor alive. I'm willing to let Him worry about the particulars of it all. Aren't you, Simon?"

"No," Deacon/Simon bristled. "No, I am not, but I will respect this place and I will respect you, Father. I'll come by later to repair the window."

"Don't worry about the window." Ike nodded toward the church. "It's been taken care of." It was, too. None of us saw it happen, but the hole was gone and there was no broken glass to be found. Every vampire parted the way as Ike walked toward us, each monster steering well clear of the priest for fear that even a careless touch might cause him or her to burst into flames. He stopped short before passing Lord Phillip.

"I won't have unnatural rain over my church again, Phillipus."

"*Mea culpa*, Isaac." Phil sounded whipped. It was a pleasant sound.

✦ 4 ✦

RACHEL:

ALWAYS THE BRIDESMAID

Ebon Winter sang "Agnus Dei" at my sister's wedding and I saw animated corpses with goose bumps and blood-streaked cheeks. If you check my iPod, you'll find a selection of Amy Grant (a very guilty pleasure if you're a witch). Her version of that song had been my favorite. After hearing Winter's, I had to delete it. He's like that. Once he covers a song, you can't listen to any other version without comparing it unfavorably to his.

If there really is a god out there, I mean besides something created by the minds of man, a glorified receptacle of group belief, I think she should have either struck Winter down for daring to sing a song like that or lifted him up and rewarded him for the act. I took the lack of chariot, flaming or otherwise, as yet another sign that she isn't there. Maybe hell made me cynical.

My sister walked down the aisle to a haunting rendition of "Here Comes the Bride" played on the church organ by Winter, and I tried not to sneer at how beautiful she looked. Tabitha's always been the pretty one, like Vivian Leigh's version of Scarlett in *Gone with the Wind*. Undeath agreed with her. It always takes off a few pounds and skinnies a person up a little. She'd been left with a wasp-like waist further accentuated by her ample breasts. Her long black hair hung down past her shoulders, and her dress was a marvel of white satin and lace. It was all I could do to stifle the urge to step on the six-foot train of her dress.

Eric's other female thralls stood in as bridesmaids. Beatrice's fiery red hair was done up in ringlets, cascading down her back, her startling blue-gray eyes reminding me of the storm clouds outside. She'd once belonged to Lady Gabriella, but she was happier with Eric. We all were. Behind Beatrice stood the ex-blood whores, three thralls Eric had rescued from a prostitution ring run by Petey and his gang, a group of child vampires out of what used to be Sweet Heart Row.

Gladys winked at Esteban, Lady Gabriella's lover, in a teasing way, curling strands of her recently dyed purple hair around her finger. Erin, the mousiest of the bridesmaids, elbowed Gladys when she noticed, only to find herself subtly rebuked with a withering glare from Cheryl, whose short brown hair and severe temperament remained unchanged for the happy occasion.

Tabitha was oblivious to it all and probably would have been whether I'd been controlling her or not. How fitting that she should be attended by whores and a hellion.

As if he could read my mind, Father Ike delivered a look of stern rebuke, which I returned with a lascivious smile and a mouthed "Eat me." The nerve of him, to look down his nose at me in a church full of vampires.

An arrangement of "Mama, I'm Coming Home" for pipe organ announced the groom. In jeans and tennis shoes, he walked down the aisle wearing his "Welcome to the Void" T-shirt like it was a tux, looking so hot it made me want to tackle him before he reached the altar.

Ike's frown vanished when he saw Eric. Was it because my sister had agreed to walk down the aisle first and let Eric follow? Or was it the strange hold Eric had over some people, Tabitha and me included? I couldn't hate him if I wanted to. Get angry? Sure. Get even? Absolutely. But stay mad? Never.

When Eric arrived at the altar, he winked at Tabitha and they kissed. Father Ike cleared his throat to the sound of amused chuckling from the audience.

"Sorry, Father," Eric murmured after the kiss.

Father Ike preached. He preached about love and faithfulness and he quoted freely from the Bible about the things love is, isn't, and must always be. I hadn't been to church since I was seven, but I found myself listening to him, feeling guilty about myself, and hating him for it. When he came to the part where they ask if anyone knows why the bride and groom should not be married, I couldn't say anything even though I wanted to. It was like his presence sealed my mouth. Eric didn't belong with Tabitha, he belonged with me. I gritted my teeth and surveyed the crowd. Talbot's eyes met mine and he shook his head ever so slightly. Then Eric raised his hand.

"Look," Eric coughed. "I have something."

If Tabitha had been completely human she would have shit herself. The vampire crowd ate it up just like they had the kiss: more polite laughter and condescension. Vampires don't get married. They hook up, abide together, but they usually don't have a ceremony. It's considered childish, naïve.

Eric took Tabitha's hand in his. "Sweetheart. I know why I want to marry you. I like sleeping with you." He glanced apologetically at the man in priest robes. "Sorry, Father." Tabitha squeezed Eric's hand, but he kept speaking.

"I didn't want you to leave; I still don't. I do care about you and I guess that's a kind of love, but even so. You'll still be marrying me." He emphasized the "me" as if the thought of anyone wanting to be his wife was unthinkable. "I'm not going to be faithful. I'll try, but we both know I'll fail. The only woman I ever managed to be faithful to was Marilyn, and she's dead.

"Be it on a hunt or with one of my thralls when I'm feeding, whatever . . . and when I do, I'm not going to feel bad about it. I might apologize to make you feel better, but . . . all I'm trying to say is that you know me. You know what you're getting. Don't go into this thinking I'll change. I may be wrong, but one day you'll want to leave me or something will happen to you and once it's all over, before too much time has passed, I won't even remember your name. Is that what you really want?"

No one will ever know what my sister might have said if I hadn't had her under my control. I almost amped up her nervousness, her embarrassment at his words. I think I could have made her dump him at the altar if I'd pushed hard enough, but Eric is my master and while I wanted him to feel bad, to get even with him for what happened before the wedding, I didn't want to have to deal with him pining over Tabitha, like he had over Marilyn, and trying to get her back.

So instead I concentrated on the change in plans I'd have Tabitha introduce—taking me with them on the honeymoon. I focused on being in Paris with Eric and all the time Tabitha would be asleep, the times where it would be just Eric and me . . . then I reinforced her love for him. It was already at an irrational, soul-encompassing level and I fanned the flames, quelled the doubts, and squashed her anger. To Tabitha, his outburst was romantic, a sign of affection, the act of a man who is experiencing love, true love, for the first time and, like a frightened child, is confused and lost.

"I do," she said without hesitation and with the sort of conviction that made me—her controller—glow inside.

"Really?" asked Talbot, echoing aloud the look on Father Ike's face.

"You still got the ring, best individual?" Eric snapped.

"Yes."

"Then shut up," Eric said through clenched teeth.

"Do you, Tabitha Elizabeth Sims," Father Ike broke in, "take this individual to be your lawfully wedded husband, to have and to hold, in sorrow and in strife? Do you promise to love, cherish, and obey him until you depart this world?"

"I do," she answered breathily.

"And do you, Eric—" Ike began.

"I'll do what I can," Eric interrupted, eliciting another round of chuckling.

"Then by the power vested in me by Almighty God, superseding the lack of recognition by the reigning government, I now pronounce you husband and wife." He put his hands on their shoulders, causing both of them to flinch as wisps of smoke escaped from underneath their garments. The touch was fleeting, but half the audience seemed ready to bolt. "Eric, you may kiss the bride . . . again."

Their kiss was inappropriate for a wedding, but I don't think those gathered expected anything less. After a few minutes, Eric had to forcibly push his bride away. What can I say? If he thought he wanted Tabitha, then Tabitha he was going to get. It was my duty to help him. That's what thralls are for. If she wanted Eric, then she was welcome to him as well, but only on my terms. I'd been willing to share. I still was, but Tabitha wasn't. She had refused to share Eric with me when I had lain dying in the hospital. He could have saved me from hell had she asked, replacing the struggle to return with the easy embrace of vampirism. And she refused to share him with me now that I'd made my own way back.

You know what happens to greedy sisters who won't share their candy, don't you? They get a stomachache. Or in Tabitha's case, maybe the term *heartburn* was more appropriate.

Since this was a vampire wedding, there were no photographers. A couple of hired artists roamed around, making sketches for the guests. A much more expensive one had been hired to paint an official portrait of the supposedly happy couple. At least there was cake, even though only the thralls could eat it.

During the reception, my master and his bride slunk off as night fell to hunt together for the first time as a joined unit. Tomorrow they would leave for Paris and the honeymoon, leaving the rest of us behind to watch after things and to look out for Greta in Eric's absence. Lord Phillip had been kind enough to arrange for their transportation and accommodations as a wedding present.

Or such had been their plan.

The plan would change now, of course; I'd go with them to make certain feeding didn't become a problem. Just in case. Tabitha would insist. And as for the marriage bed, she'd want me there too. Sisters share.

◆ 5 ◆

ERIC:
WEDDING NIGHT AFTERMATH

I can't talk about the wedding night. I promised I wouldn't and until I forget about that promise, I'll keep it. Three bodies were in bed with me when I woke up the next afternoon: one dead, one undead, and one alive. Two of them were related to each other (Tabitha and Rachel) and the third I didn't recognize, but her ghost loomed over me with an angry countenance.

"You didn't turn me," shouted the Asian ghost whose bleached blond hair looked more orange than any other color. Her spectral form was as naked as her corpse and had the same bluish pallor.

"Was I supposed to?" I rolled the dead girl off the bed, which isn't as gross (or unusual) as you think if you're used to sleeping with vampires.

Her slap would have connected if she'd been able to affect corporeal objects, but she wasn't anything special from a supernatural point of view, just your standard ghost. Enough will to hang around and bitch, but not enough juju to manifest physically. It happens. "She told me that you'd make me immortal." The ghost pointed at Rachel's sleeping form accusingly.

"No," Rachel said sleepily. "I said he'd make you immoral."

"But I thought . . ." Whoever the girl was, she started to look more panicked than angry. I'd met her before, but I couldn't remember her name. Kim? Mei? Chun-li? Something.

Rachel leaned up on her elbows and my eyes were drawn to the golden rings in her pierced nipples, the choker around her neck with its tiny golden padlock. "I can't help it if you were a dumb horny twat." She sniffed dismissively. "Eat her, Master."

"I think I already did, and don't call me Master."

"I don't mean her blood, Eric. I mean her essence, her soul. You have all the powers of a revenant and a vampire. Eat her soul so she can't make a return trip to get back at you. She's going to hell anyway; she had a foursome with two other girls and a vampire." Hands wandering along her own body, Rachel paused at her left nipple ring, twisting it casually. "Then come back to bed." Millions of years of evolution told me to do whatever was necessary to get back into bed and do more of what I'd done last night. Forty-odd years as a vampire told to me to sink my fangs into Rachel while doing it.

There are times when I do the wrong thing. If last night's corpse had been a little younger, she'd still be alive. Even when I'm out of control, I care about kids, feel protective of them. Somewhere around the age of consent, that need to defend vanishes. In the old days, I would have called a mage and paid to have the ghost moved along to its final destination, but if Rachel said she was hellbound (and Rachel ought to know), then wasn't destroying her doing both of us a favor?

The transition from angry vamp to vengeful ghost is quick, but far from painless. It no longer felt like I was being pulled apart so much as like my whole body had gone to sleep and was in the process of waking up: pins and needles everywhere, and I do mean everywhere. My vision blurred, rendering the world in muted watercolor tones, except for other ghosts. Spirits look alive to one another.

Her slap connected the second time, and the pain made me angry. I own up to my faults. My speech back in the chapel proved that. Rachel's voice sounded far away. "You're getting better at that, baby. Hardly any hesitation at all. Now eat her!"

If being a vampire was a world of cold punctuated by brief moments of warmth at feeding time, being a revenant was a world of ice with no relief.

The girl—Suzie was her name, I remembered suddenly—swung at me again, but when we made contact she screamed. Apparently soul sucking *is* like riding a bike: once you've done it, you never really forget how. Her spirit body pressed against mine, sinking into me, a vulgar intimacy.

"I'm never going to get to Paris, am I?" she asked.

"Seems unlikely," I told her, but she was gone. I watched a ghost get sucked into hell once. I tell myself I can't remember her name either, but I do. Marilyn is someone I'll never forget. I can't tell you which seemed worse—getting sucked into hell or getting devoured by a revenant. If given the option, I'd avoid both. "Is there anything in particular you wanted to see?" I asked the air.

"The Eiffel Tower," something whispered in my mind. The voice could have been hers. I like to think the scream that followed it wasn't, but I like to lie to myself, too.

"I'm not doing that again unless I have to," I told Rachel. My skin was freezing when I transitioned back. Mother Nature wanted to remind me that I was an undead monster . . . like I'd forgotten.

But you can't give in to that self-pity crap. Pithy little vampires that can't face the music piss me off almost as badly as those Doris Day "Que Sera, Sera" motherfuckers who think being dead is "da bomb" or however the hell they put it nowadays. I shook it off and let Rachel warm me up the way only she can, let the memory roll off into that place where forgotten things go. I didn't even remember her name. *Suzie Hu. She wanted to see the Eiffel Tower* . . . Okay, so I hadn't forgotten her yet. Give me time.

In the middle of round two, I got a call from William, the local Alpha. He and his pack live out at Orchard Lake and we have a semi-truce. I stay out of his area and he stays out of mine.

"I didn't know the Apostles were planning to crash your special day." He cut right to the point without a hello. "But you should know . . . I called my connections at the Lycan Diocese and they're not going to call him off. They aren't going to help him either. You're on your own, but so is he."

"Wonderful. So—" Rachel crawled back in bed next to her sleeping sister on the king-sized mattress and I lost my concentration. What the hell had I been saying? "So. Okay, so—are the Apostles something I need to take care of before I go to Paris?"

"You're going to Paris?" William asked.

I turned away from Rachel and Tabitha, focusing on the conference table and chairs that occupied the corner closest to the window. The ghost of John Paul Courtney sat in one of the three chairs. He was clad in the same checkered shirt he always wore, holding his wobbly head in place with one hand while he puffed a nearly expended spectral cigar that he held in the other. Cigar smoke drifted up through the bullet holes in his chest. His jaws clenched with disappointment in me, his descendant.

"That ain't right," he said. "What yore doin' with them two sisters ain't right at all. You keep testing Him like this and bad things'll happen."

"Yeah, I know," I said, answering both JPC and the werewolf on the phone. "It's for my honeymoon." *Plus,* I thought, *according to Lord Phil, the vampire that sired me lives in Paris and she'll be looking for me soon, so I might as well go looking for her and save us both the wait.* I wondered if she knew about the curse that had created me or if her sudden detection of me now that I had full Emperor powers was driving her crazy with questions.

"If he knows," William told me, "he might follow you."

If who knew? I thought. *Oh, yeah, Deacon.*

"Fine by me." I looked at Rachel. She'd seen me as a ghost before, and had noticed Suzie's ghost, but she gave no sign that she could see John Paul Courtney. Interesting. "I just don't want them fucking around with my stuff while I'm gone. I'm leaving Greta and Fang here with Talbot and the girls. Lord Phil has promised to look out for them, but . . . I don't know, maybe I should just cancel the trip."

William sighed on the other end of the line. "That's the last thing we need. If Deacon goes and pisses off that bloodsucking sorcerer, it'll start another Vampire and Werewolf War. I'll track Deacon down. He'll listen to me as long as I'm not trying to talk him out of ending you. Keep your eyes open. If he's going to France, then he'll have to start out in Lozère."

"Huh?"

"Vampires may flit willy-nilly across the globe, but werewolves are territorial. If you're a werewolf and you're going to France, particularly if you're going there to start trouble, you have to check in with the Alpha . . . and in France there is just one Alpha who is in charge of everything."

I covered the receiver and cursed. "Great. I don't suppose you know the man in charge."

"*La Bête du Gévaudan,*" he answered as if I ought to know, as if that should've rung a bell.

"That doesn't sound like English."

"That's because it's French. It means the Beast of Gévaudan."

"I guess I'd better bring *El Alma Perdida* then," I said.

"I'm not sure it will be any help if the Beast decides to come after you. He's the oldest werewolf in the world. Some say that he's truly immortal."

"Just peachy," I said. "Thanks for the heads-up." I hung up the phone and looked back at Rachel. "I'm going out."

"Tabitha asked you to force her awake before you left," Rachel said.

I got dressed without answering, resisting the urge to change into a bat and manifest my clothes. It would have been a waste of blood and I was already hungry. Hungry enough that I didn't want to feed on Rachel. The sun was still up, but I didn't care. I had to get away from my bride, her sister, and the dead body on the floor.

"I forgot," I said as I stepped out, bracing myself for the sun the way another person might have prepared himself to run out into the rain. "Get someone to take care of the body." I burst out the door, ready to dash for the shadows, only there was no sun. I was in the hallway outside the Honeymoon Suite at the Void City Hilton.

Rachel giggled behind me and I slammed the door. A few seconds later, I walked back in and carried the dead woman down with me to the parking lot so that I could feed her to Fang. Waste not, want not, as the saying goes. See how domesticated I am? Even taking out the trash. Isn't married life grand?

6

RACHEL:

LET'S MAKE A DEAL

One of the advantages of being enthralled by a vamp as kick ass powerful as Eric is that the deal comes with immortality that lasts as long as your master does or until he sets you free. And as masters go, Eric is the best. Since he doesn't "believe" in having thralls, he still treats us . . . well . . . like people (while most vampires seem to forget that after a while). He keeps his promises, too. Other vampires will offer to let their thralls go as a twisted-ass loyalty test. Not Eric. He means it. He used to have a seventh thrall, an ex-stripper named Ebony, but Eric packed her and her two kids up and sent them to live out at Orchard Lake with the werewolves, then released her from thralldom. All because she said it would make her happy.

Why she wanted out is beyond me. Being an Emperor's thrall has too many benefits. We're all a little stronger than normal humans, our senses are sharper, and we heal faster. But better than that is this: calories don't matter. Beatrice noticed it first. Do you know what it's like to be able to jump from twelve hundred calories a day to unlimited? And he wonders why we all want to jump his bones. I ordered up a Belgian waffle, two sides of bacon, hash browns, and scrambled eggs (with cheese). It's not the breakfast Eric would have ordered, but I wasn't eating for him.

If I'd been eating for Eric, I would have gone with T-bone steak (rare), three eggs (over easy), pork sausage (links, not patties), cheese grits (add salt and pepper), and a biscuit (split in half and buttered). Tabitha can't stand to watch people eat, because it's one of the few human things she can't enjoy, but Eric falls in with the rest of the vampire pack. He loves his food porn. Nothing explicitly sexual about it; in fact, Eric keeps it strictly compartmentalized, no eating naked or food

play in bed. When he's been really good, I choose cold pizza for breakfast. Pizza is his favorite.

I'd just started eating, when I got a text on my cell.

Where are you?—Andre

All of Winter's goons used Standard English when texting. So did
most of the thralls working for the vampiric upper crust. It's like they
were from another planet . . . which I guessed made Andre Winter's
chief ambassador to Earth.

AFK . . . fOOd

Before my attention was back to breakfast, my cell dinged. Another
text.

Winter wants to see you.—Andre

im nt h1s btch. I thumbed the letters angrily, then bounced my cell
off Tabitha's shoulder. It hit with a wet sound, and the smell of rancid
filth assailed me. Corpse sweat. Brown trickles of fluid had begun to
form on Tabitha's upper body, covering her skin with a growing sheen
of nastiness. Some vampires get it every night, but not Tabitha. It had
happened to her once before, just after she turned for the first time,
but as far as I knew it hadn't happened since.

I ran across and grabbed my cell before it got more yecch on it
and hurried to the bathroom to wash it off before the corpse sweat
dried there. I retched into the sink as the smell grew, less rotting body
odor than the unenviable scent of backed-up sewer. All thoughts of
breakfast forgotten, I grabbed my overnight bag and rushed naked into
the hall before the odor permeated everything.

Why the fuck was she getting the sweats now? She hadn't discovered any new powers (that sets it off sometimes). Getting married
hadn't . . . Shit. She was trying to fight my magic. Some inner part of
her wanted to shake free of the hold I had over her. How cute!

I slipped into a crimson thong, a pair of tight side-stitched low-rise
jeans, a white long-sleeved crop top, and my black Skechers.

So you're not interested in his deal then?—Andre

wht d3al?

The one Winter would like to speak to you about.—Andre

5p311 !t out, @55.

I'm afraid I didn't understand that last text.—Andre

Grr. Andre's inability to read a simple text message pissed me off no end. "Fine." My fingers jabbed the keys rapidly.

Spell it out, Andre. What deal?

I didn't wait in the hallway for Andre's next text message. I wanted caffeine even if Tabitha's stench-ridden protest had put me off my breakfast. A quick trip to the elevator and down to the hotel lobby took me to an embedded Starbucks. My Venti Mint Chocolaty Chip Frappuccino Blended Creme with Chocolate Whipped Cream and a double shot of Espresso was still in progress when my cell beeped.

Winter proposes a deal that will give you what you want. You want the issues between you and your sister over Eric to end. If you work with him, by the end of the game, you will no longer have to worry about the competition.—Andre

Before replying, I read the message twice more. Does he have a bet riding on the outcome? I texted. My drink vanished, barely tasted, while I waited. I bought a Raspberry Apricot Thumbprint Scone and ordered another Frappuccino, constantly checking my cell for messages. Ten minutes later, the response came in, a simple **Yes** without the **—Andre**.

WTF?!? Winter said he was betting against Eric in Paris... I stabbed Send and watched the little animation, a winged envelope flying into the distance, as my cell transmitted the message.

Meet him and talk about it tonight, Andre's message blinked back at me. **Just because Winter has bet against Eric in Paris doesn't mean he expects him to lose in Void City.**

When and where?

Meet him at the Iversonian. Sunset.

What? "Why the hell is Winter asking to meet at someone else's club? Much less a true immortal's club?" I murmured to myself. Iver Richardson a.k.a. the Iversonian, the club's owner, is a true immortal, a collector of the unique, both sentient and nonsentient. He rarely gives his acquisitions up, which is why others started calling him the Iversonian, and he has a massive control complex, which is why he named his club the Iversonian in some sort of weird bid to "own" the nickname. He's tangled with Talbot (which was a check mark in his favor as far as I'm concerned), but true immortals can't be ended—not really. Their essence can be absorbed by another of their kind, and under the right circumstances they can be freed from their body, transmuted completely to spirit, but even then, they are still present somewhere. *I wonder if a revenant can eat the essence of a true immortal.* The thought danced in my head, a tantalizing bit of curiosity.

Why not Winter's club? I texted back.

Discretion, he sent back.

"Discretion." I strummed my fingers on the tabletop in the Hilton's lobby. Fine. I'd go, but if Winter thought he was going to try anything funny with me . . . I'd saved up enough of Eric's imperial glory to defend myself. I tapped into a small sample of the power I sapped from Eric every time we had sex and smiled as my fingernails turned black and cold, extending into claws.

♦ 7 ♦

ERIC:
THE DEMON HEART—NEW AND IMPROVED

Fang drove me into the shaded lower level of the Pollux Theater's parking deck and I stared across the street at the newly refurbished and repurposed Demon Heart—or rather, Demon Heart Lanes Bowling Alley. What the hell had I been thinking? I'd traded strippers for synthetic Day-Glo balls, bowling pins, the sweet smells of griddle cakes and bowling alley pizza . . . Ah. That had probably been it. The pizza.

I took the short walkway from the parking deck to the lobby of the Pollux, my movie palace, and smiled at the improvements. The place had been gutted by fire several months ago, and Ebon Winter had restored it for me as a wedding gift.

Many things hadn't been changed at all, or if so, only subtly and with magic. The front was still four glass doors opening into a spacious area where, in times long past, moviegoers had purchased their tickets from a ticket seller inside a golden colored ticket booth. Winter had wired the booth with modern connections and credit card readers even though I wasn't likely to ever need them, given that I hardly ever show movies to the public. A state-of-the-art alarm system had been installed as well, with a full set of Guild-certified wards layered over it.

My chandelier was now self-cleaning, as was the mirrored entryway. The concession stand had been reworked too, only now there was a wine rack with a selection of blood wine from Lord Phillip's own stock. Vintages with which he had grown tired were no longer poured out or flung into the fireplace, but were instead used to restock my supply. I'm sure that was some sort of insult, but Phillip knew I wouldn't take it as one, and for that matter, he knew I just didn't care. I grabbed a bottle without looking at the label and headed through the theater doors, down the center aisle, right up to the stage.

Talbot was sitting dead center in the mezzanine, his heartbeat a steady thrum of calm composure, breathing in slow deep draws as if he were napping. We didn't speak. There was no need. I knew what had his attention.

I looked past the rows of new, more comfortable seats, let my gaze linger on the clever way that Winter had reworked the decorative hangings over the curtains concealing the organ pipes stage left and stage right to resemble the figures I'd seen squaring off against one another in stained glass at the Highland Towers. On the right, a female uber vamp with fierce red eyes, dark black skin, and engorged breasts glared at a vampiric knight in holy armor on the left. My gaze drifted further up to the apex of the dome's ceiling, where a magical painting of a night sky had replaced the old representations of Castor and Pollux that had been destroyed by the fire. The new painting showed the sky directly above the Pollux, but as it might have appeared if there were no light pollution—a clear perfect night sky that changed with the seasons. Winter has style, I'll give him that, but when I looked down at the stage to the same object that fascinated Talbot, that's when I felt a little shiver of excitement.

"The Mighty Wurlitzer," my theater organ, was well worth our attention. If you look it up on Wikipedia, they have a list of sixteen or so Wurlitzer theater organs that are still in their original locations. That number is one off.

My Wurlitzer really was original to the building, though it had been sold to a collector when I got blown up and had my assets seized while I was trying to re-form. Now, thanks to Winter, it had been returned to its place, stage left and in the upright position. I have a love-hate relationship with the damn thing. An organ like this should be treasured, should be played and maintained. An organ like this brings back memories . . . and memories and I don't get along.

I read somewhere that music and musical ability are stored in a different part of the brain than most data. The words might escape me, but I've always been able to sit down at something with the right number of keys and re-create a tune. When I died, I could still play, so apparently my muscles will never forget what to do.

At the start of every movie at the Pollux, back when it was open to the public, in addition to the cartoons, newsreels, and sometimes even local folks demonstrating their talents, there was always a sing-along and some organ music when the show was about to start and again after it was over. Ode to bygone days. Blah blah blah.

"Are you going to play it?" Talbot's voice was a study in restrained eagerness, his eyes focused on the organ.

"Why," I asked. "Want to hear 'Take Me Out to the Ball Game'?" I ran my hand along the top of the stage. Before the renovations, the floor had been too uneven for modern productions, but it was smooth now, up to code. I wouldn't have changed that.

"Is that what you feel like playing?"

"Sure." *No.* I looked up at him over my shoulder, momentarily surprised to see him wearing something other than a suit and tie. He wore a loose-fitting T-shirt, the sleeves torn or cut away to reveal his well-muscled arms to the best effect. A musky scent, sweat for his kind, clung to him. He'd been working out. *Why?*

"Then play it. Or not." His tennis shoes slid across the new carpet as he stood to leave. Just to make him show his real desire, I leapt onto the stage, crossed to the Wurlitzer, and turned the blower on. The subtle hiss of air whispered through the pipes. Talbot froze. In the good old days that sound had had much the same effect as the sound of a DTS test in front of the feature presentation in a modern theater. Talbot found his seat, waiting.

"Pick a song," I said.

"Any song?"

"Yeah, but I want a favor in exchange."

We both knew what he wanted. He wanted to see if it still worked, if when I played, he'd see the same sight that had made him my boon companion for the last twenty years. He wanted a song that could vanquish demons and save the world. He wanted me to be a hero, a golden soul . . . like in El Segundo. I swear to God, you save the world one fucking time and some people never let you live it down.

But then, I guess everybody has their little eccentricities. Talbot's is that he thinks I'm a hero. Whoever bought him DVD copies of *Angel* ought to be shot.

"*Stardust,*" he said quickly.

Fucking "Star Dust." It had been our song, me and . . . old what's-her-face, the woman whose name I'm pretending to forget: Marilyn.

"Don't you want to know my favor first?"

Talbot laughed. "You want me to find out what's wrong with Tabitha."

"How'd you know?"

"You walk in here the day after your wedding without taking a shower and think I don't know something's up? I smell Tabitha, Rachel, and some Asian woman, Eric." He gripped the rail of the mezzanine, leaning precariously over the edge. "You aren't the only one with a discerning olfactory sense. Mine tells me more about what you did last night than I want to know, but what I know about Tabitha tells me . . . I should look into it."

I looked down at the keys.

"It could be that someone magically 'spiked' the hotel room as a perverse wedding present. Just find out what happened for me."

Shoes hit the carpet on the mezzanine floor. Bare feet moved on metal. A glance showed me Talbot, perched on the rail at as close to the optimum acoustic center of the theater as he could reach without a rope.

"You comfortable?" I asked.

"Yes." I looked away before he grinned.

"I suppose you want me to sing it too?" I didn't look at him. I was fuming, but this was my fault. I'd offered.

"Please," Talbot answered.

So I did . . . and no offense, but not the Nat King Cole version. I like that one, too, but the first time I heard a song called "Stardust," it was sung by Hoagy Carmichael, just him and a piano, and it was spelled "Star Dust." The tune was slow, mournful even. That's how I heard it, how I think it should be played, and how I played it then.

It didn't sound quite right on the Wurlitzer, but partway through the song, I could feel that didn't matter. Playing the song hurt, singing it was worse. Drops of red stung my eyes before splashing down on the ivory keys. Something seized in my chest, but I ignored it, tried to shrug it off, make light of it.

"Well?" I asked as the last note reverberated through the theater. "Am I going to Hollywood?"

But Talbot couldn't answer. He was sobbing gently. During the song he'd transformed and I hadn't noticed. It was pitiful to watch, really, a massive furry demon eater, no longer perched like a predator but slumped over the rail, his silver mane glowing dimly in the dark. Luminescent tears illuminated the subtle texture of his smooth black fur as he gripped the rail with metallic silver claws. He stared at me through star emerald eyes, then a white glow flowed over him as he changed back to the human form with which I was more familiar.

"Even with her gone—" he said. His voice broke and he started over. "Even without her here, on this plane, your soul still shines like a star when you sing that song, Eric. I was right when I picked you."

"Stop looking at my soul, Talbot," I muttered as I shuffled off the stage, shaking. "Just go find out what's wrong with Marilyn . . . I mean Tabitha. Make sure it isn't anything permanent." The trembling started when I said her name, like an earthquake under my skin. I ached for

Marilyn. Playing the song brought it all back: the smell of her, the feel of her breasts, her tongue against mine, her voice in my ears. "Star Dust" was playing on Fang's radio out on the parking deck and I could hear it through the walls.

The world vibrated and my vision blurred from the tears, not water, but blood welling up within my eyes . . . and I howled in sudden pain. The Stone of Aeternum flared in my chest, bright enough to make shadows, shapes of my spine and rib cage visible through my skin. Fire lanced through the ring finger on my left hand and the band of gold, the wedding band Tabitha had given me, smoldered and hissed as it melted off my finger. I caught the drips of molten gold in my right hand, grinding my teeth as the hot metal seared my skin.

"What the fuck?" I blinked blood out of my eyes.

"True love . . ." Talbot whispered to himself. "Shit. He almost cured himself."

"How. Fucking. Romantic." I spat through the pain.

It didn't stop. The burning did. The gold cooled, and the light from the gem faded, but the memories of Marilyn kept coming. My fingers through her hair. Lower memories of sex came too, but mostly it was the sound of her voice young and old, the perfume she wore, the way she smelled fresh out of the shower, the echo of her heartbeat . . . even the ashtray taste of kissing her right after a cigarette.

"Too bad," I tried to say. "She's a corpse already. She's burning in hell where she belongs." The words wouldn't come. Instead I yowled, a low pitiful sound that turned into a scream. I've always said that I'd go crazy when I lost Marilyn and it occurred to me that was exactly what was happening—a full-on vampire meltdown. The wedding. The marriage night. The song. All together they'd been too much. I'd said good-bye, but I couldn't let go.

I felt the change coming and something else came with it. After I was blown up, when I reformed, I'd almost come back alive, but the Courtney family curse reached in and revamped me. It hurt like a bitch. This felt the same, like having swung close to being cured by or in association with the Stone of Aeternum, the curse was trying to swing the pendulum of me in the opposite direction.

When it rains it fucking pours.

The uber vamp roared, and it had a hunger that could not be sated by blood, could never be sated because it . . . I . . . wanted Marilyn and could never have her again, not even the hope of her, and I had dared to try and move on, dared to try to replace her.

My eyes closed and my mind touched the minds of every waking vampire in the city. They recoiled. Some of the sleeping vamps woke, their screams joining mine as if waking from a dreamless sleep that had somehow been invaded by a nightmare. My thralls. I sensed them, all but one, running toward me. Gladys's voice echoed dimly in my head. *I'm coming, baby. Hold it together.* But there was no holding things together. Fang's horn honked over and over again in the distance, engine revving, tires squealing.

Cool! Rachel's thought hit me as the theater shrank around me or I grew. I flexed my wings, preparing to fly out into the day and feed, feed until somebody stopped me, until someone found a way to put me down, but knowing that they wouldn't be able to, wouldn't stand a chance, not until the pain went away, and it never would.

Then there was blood in my mouth. It scalded my throat, but I drank it blindly. I'd had the blood only once before, in El Segundo, and it was one of the many reasons (all involving me) for which Talbot had been cast out, exiled by his people, willingly giving his "holy blood" to a vampire. And just as it had done then, it brought me back under control, damped down the rage and the loss. But this time I wasn't grateful.

When I change into a bat, it feels like I'm being forced into too small a space, the full-body equivalent of my balls retracting to protect themselves from the cold, but for the first time changing back into my normal human shape felt the same way. Talbot grabbed my face, forcing one of my eyes open, and I hissed at him.

"Hold still, damn it," he shouted, letting the claws of his left hand sink into my face to give him a better grip.

I hissed again and he swore. Smoke billowed from my cheek, but his claws weren't burning me, my blood was burning them. I don't know what he said, because it was in Cat, but it was definitely a swear word.

"Is he okay?" The voice was John Paul Courtney's.

"PMS," Talbot said, his eyes never looking away from mine. "Postmortem stress. Most vampires go through it within a few days of being turned, but Eric never has. It's why his eyes were still blue."

Were?

"Were?" asked the ghost. He reappeared closer, then shrank from what he saw. "They're going clear, washed out, dead pigment clear, like a normal vampire. That ain't supposed to happen. He's the last of the Courtney line subject to the curse, the one who c'n—" He caught himself as if he'd said too much. "It just ain't."

"Let. Me. Go!" Purple light covered my skin and I changed into the uber vamp again, hurling Talbot into the concrete base of the mezzanine. I could feel them, the bats, the rats, all the little creatures that would answer my call. They were mine to command. Others too: the vampires—the Drones, the Soldiers, the Masters, all the undead who weren't Vlads. I touched their minds and they quaked in their graves, in their beds, wherever they were.

Talbot rolled to his feet, claws reaching up toward the ceiling, and cut loose with more Cat-speak. It seemed important, incredibly earnest. He charged me again. At his touch, I was changed involuntarily back to my human form. I tried to push him away from me, but I was weak, too weak even to support myself. Warmth washed over my skin. My heart didn't beat, but the warmth spread, seeping into my muscles, my organs, and even my bones. I was core warm.

Talbot looked back into my eyes, his face beaded with sweat, and he smiled. John Paul Courtney stood next to him, hat in hand, worried.

"They're turning blue again," John Paul said with glee. "I don't know what you done, but you done good, cat."

"Thank you, Mother," Talbot said, ignoring JPC. "Sekhmet is kind to all her children."

"That some kind of cat religion?" John Paul asked. "You guys pray to some cat god?"

"Cats don't worship anyone," Talbot said as he lowered me gently into a seat. "I just needed a little help from my mother."

"You still think your mom's an Egyptian goddess," I said with half a smile.

"You still think she isn't," Talbot told me, "which is why I've never even started to tell you about my father."

"You're in deep shit now," I said, suddenly grateful after all. "You gave me your blood again. You worked your cat magic for me again. What does that buy you, like a hundred more years of exile?"

Talbot didn't answer.

Gladys burst in through the double doors, and Talbot stepped away. Gladys is the oldest of my thralls, older than me, but she doesn't look a day over twenty-five now. Her hair, recently dyed purple (thanks to an errant comment from me), brushed against my face as she sat in my lap, pushing my mouth against her neck in case I wanted to feed, then cradling me against her breasts when it was clear that I didn't.

Her breath tickled my scalp in calming bursts with each cooing shush that moved past her lips. "It's all right," she said. "It's all right."

Erin and Magbidion came next, followed at a restrained pace by Cheryl. Erin slid wordlessly into the seat next to me, her hand on my arm—her way of letting me know she was there if I needed her. She'd come out of her shell a lot since I took her and the other two away from Sweet Heart Row and made them thralls instead of blood whores, but she'd never be much of a talker. Blond bangs fell down over her face, mostly covering it. She squeezed my arm. Magbidion stood next to Talbot, shuffling his feet and looking for a place to stand where he'd be helpful and frustrated to find that the girls had it covered.

"You okay, boss?" That was Cheryl. She stood in the door, staring down at the other thralls with vague disapproval at the way they fawned over me. She likes me, she really does, but she doesn't like that she likes me, which is why she's kept her brown hair cut short when she knows I'd prefer it long.

"I'll be fine."

"You need anything before I go back across to the Demon Heart?"

"No. I'm good."

"Send one of them back when you can," she said. "I can't do everything by myself." She can, though, and we all know it, but that's just Cheryl being Cheryl.

"Mags," I said to the dark-haired man standing next to Talbot, "go help Cheryl. Gladys and Erin are going to tuck me in upstairs."

"You got it, boss." Damn, but he sounded chipper. I swear, you save someone's soul from a demonic loan shark and they go all puppy dog on you.

"And Talbot . . ."

"You're welcome," he said. "I'll go start work on that other thing as soon as I get cleaned up."

"Thanks."

He left, and Erin and Gladys helped me up the stairs to my bedroom. Winter had remodeled it, too, turning the space into a proper bedroom instead of a room with a bed against one wall and a sink against the other. He'd replaced the double with a king-size, put in a proper shower, even a fifty-two-inch projection screen on the wall. He'd extended the space into the storage area on the other side to make room for a walk-in closet. There was even a little fridge so I could store my magic ice sword without the condensation leaving wet rings on the floor. It was nice.

The girls took off my clothes, tucked me into bed, and lay next to me so that their body heat would keep me warm. Just before I fell asleep, Beatrice showed up and took Erin's place. She'd been over at the Highland Towers and it had taken her longer to make the commute. We didn't do anything because, despite my many indiscretions with Rachel, I was really trying to stay faithful to Tabitha.

It may sound funny, but to a man from my generation, especially from my family, wedding vows are important. You don't break them casually even if you cheated all through the courtship. Once you tie the knot, you stay faithful until the knot is cut. Even thinking about marriage made my ring finger ache. What the hell was up with that? I tried to put it out of my head and I actually slept again, which is a bit unusual for me. Weirder still, I dreamt.

8

ERIC:
A MIDSUMMER'S DAYDREAM

I hate dream sequences. I'm not fond of travel sequences either. The last one I had any respect for was in *Willy Wonka and the Chocolate Factory*, when they get on the boat and Gene Wilder sings, proving that Wonka is a complete nut job, but in a fun way. In my dream, though, I was having sex with a beautiful woman, a vampire I'd never met before, and she wasn't my usual type.

She was a classic beauty, rounded cheeks, well fed but not fat. She came from a time when women didn't exercise to excess, crafting their bodies into works of sculpted deprivation. Pale cold breasts overfilled my hands, unusually short thick nipples poking out from between my fingers. We were in Fang's backseat, top down, parked in the driveway of an abandoned house looking down on Void City. Nearby, in the remains of the two-story wreck, mice scampered, their tiny claws scrambling across the damp floorboards. Wet grass from a brief evening shower sent up a heady smell of life in contrast to my lack thereof.

"*Dites-moi*," she whispered, her voice urgent as she reached down and guided me inside her. "Tell me you trust me."

"Sure," I said, not wanting to lose the moment.

Moonlight caught on a necklace that was either gold or platinum. Eight strands of metal all hooked into a central jewel—a large emerald. An irrational urge to grab the necklace and tear it off, to run over it with Fang, rose in my chest.

"If you trust me, then tell me." She nuzzled my neck and I pushed her face away with my left hand. Her fangs flashed in the night; a frustrated hiss left her throat.

"I don't like to be bitten," I told her firmly. "If you aren't okay with that then we should stop right now."

"How can you say no to this body?" Her arms came up behind her head. Her tempo increased, the wet slap of our bodies drowning out the sounds around us. She was cute, but the pit hair was too much.

"Aw, come on! What the hell? Don't they sell Nair in my sex dreams?"

"Tell me where it is!" She dug into me with her nails, suddenly extending them into claws that tore through my shoulder muscles. I shouted an obscenity or seven. With the muscles severed, my arms wouldn't move properly and I growled.

"Get off me, bitch!"

"Tell me what it is, your *memento mori*! Tell me and this pain can end."

Sure, I could have told her that I didn't have clue one what she was talking about, and at the moment that was actually true, even though we were in my *memento mori*'s backseat. I was too confused, too jumbled up by what had happened with the Wurlitzer in the real world to recall the ins and outs of vampiric metaphysics, but I wasn't about to start explaining myself to an errant bit of S&M kink hanging about in my head, particularly one that hadn't even bothered to shave her pits.

So I popped my fangs; the vague pain as they forced my other teeth to move aside paled in comparison to the constant tearing of my shoulders as her claws flexed inside, flaying the meat. A vampire's pain receptors don't work like the living's. New pain hurts, but it's fleeting. Once the damage is done, the pain fades, unless the wound keeps tearing, then the nerves wake up again. The chick on my tip (oh, good grief, now I sound like a rapper) . . . the vampire on top of me knew how to keep her claws moving, stoking the agony to new life over and over.

Unable to get at her throat, I sank my fangs into the tenderest flesh available and jerked my head back like a zombie tearing into a fresh corpse.

That's not the worst bit.

Her breast came away, revealing rotted meat beneath. Decomposing flesh, the smell of it, filled my nostrils. Black blood seeped from the wound and I gagged . . . and came. That was the worst bit.

"*Non! Vous êtes mauvais! Très très mauvais!*" Above me, she began to grow. A black tinge crept across her skin, the same color as my uber vamp's.

"Oh," I spit the hunk of rotten meat out of my mouth, "that's not right. Who're you supposed to be? My sire? What? Do I get to have an Oedipus complex now?"

Wings, long and leathery, sprang from her shoulders. I'd seen her before, or a representation of her. A stained-glass likeness of her fighting one of my ancestors could be found hanging in a hallway at the High-land Towers. My ancestor had been a knight. He'd been turned into a vampire. And he'd asked for forgiveness. It had been granted and he'd run away, had fled all the way to America, where I had no doubt that his ghost was embarrassed by the lot of us, right down to his great-great-whatever John Paul Courtney, and me in particular.

"You'll pay for that, whelp!"

As the uber vamp, she still had hairy pits. I shook my head. "That just gets me. I know it's probably chauvinistic or something, but . . . doesn't that bother you?"

She was confused. So was I. This didn't feel like a dream. Every-thing was too real.

"The pit hair," I snarled. "Doesn't"—my skin turned black and I started to grow—"it"—the wounds in my shoulder closed around her claws—"bother you"—my wings sprouted, pushing me away from the car seat, shifting us forward—close to standing—"to be"—purple light from my uber vamp eyes washed across her body—"so fucking hairy?"

I gain an extra three or so feet in stature, but my legs and torso aren't the only parts of my body that get bigger. She grunted in ac-knowledgment. And, not to be icky, but so did I. We sagged against each other, momentarily overcome by the new sensation.

"It is true that I am your sire," she said in my ear. "I do not under-stand how you managed such a thing, and for that reason alone you must be destroyed."

I thrust in hard, bottomed out, and kept pushing. "How are you in my dreams?"

"Maybe you're in mine," she said, grinding against me.

"Shit."

She licked my neck with a long gray tongue.

"Are we fucking or fighting?" I asked.

"Must there be a difference?" Her fangs pierced my skin, and it felt like ten-penny nails ripping through my neck. I struggled, but it was hard for me to get any leverage. I flapped my wings, pulling us sky-ward, but she was already letting go, smoke billowing from her mouth as she fell away from me.

"What," she coughed, "have you been feeding on?"

"Mouser," I said.

We hung in the air, held aloft by our wings, glaring at each other in the night. She tried to lock gazes with me, but I kept my focus low, staring at her breasts. The one I'd bitten had already regenerated. As I watched, her flesh began to gray, her wings receding. Plummeting toward Fang, she screamed, more in frustration than fear. She landed on the hood, feetfirst, with a metallic *thunk* and a distinctly less metallic *snap*. Her legs gave and she fell to one side of my car.

"How is this possible?" She rolled away from the car, already trying to stand. "No vampire that has passed through the threshold of death and embraced undeath can—"

"Drink the blood of a Mouser?" I completed her sentence as I landed in front of her. "Yeah, I've never been much of a joiner."

Fang roared to life behind me.

"How?"

"If we're really in a dream, then anything is possible," I lied, hoping she'd believe that rather than figuring out Fang was my *memento mori*.

"Could the car—" she whispered, then interrupted one thought with another. *"Bien sûr que non.* I sensed magic from within his chest.

"Is that what you did, clever boy?" She slowly stood, her legs mending as we spoke. "Did you hide your *memento mori* in your own body?"

"Maybe." She sensed magic inside me? *The Stone of Aeternum,* I thought.

Last year I'd gotten into it with a demon and wound up with a magic rock that is supposed to make a vampire who finds a cure for vampirism immortal if he manages to find a cure while the stone is in his heart. I don't go for all that magic mumbo jumbo, but I'd held on to it, just in case it actually worked. The rock technically belonged to Lord Phillip, who wanted to use it for a magic ritual to make himself more powerful, but in the meantime, he'd been willing to let me hang on to it as long as I promised to hand it over on demand. I think he was more interested than I was in whether it would work or not. If the stone was powerful enough to throw Mommy Dearest off the scent of my real *memento mori,* off Fang, then I was even more pleased that I'd held on to it.

She smiled at me, and our surroundings faded. She had the information she thought she wanted, and I had an edge, a tiny one, but she'd been an Emperor (Empress?) for more years than I'd been on the planet . . . and I had the sneaking suspicion I was going to need every little break I could get to take her down.

9

RACHEL:

THE WRONG SORT OF PEOPLE

An hour before sundown, a gray Void City Department of Public Works van pulled up outside the Iversonian. A brown-haired man in a blue work suit stepped out of the passenger's side and peered out from behind the tinted lenses of his Bono-style sunglasses directly at my hiding spot in the open parking lot across the way. He was slightly tubby, but cute in a fun-to-hang-out-with-but-I-wouldn't-do-him sort of way, and seeing him brought out a sigh. I didn't need to see the little name tags sewed onto his work suit to know that his name was Melvin or that he worked for the Mage Guild.

He waved at me before yelling across the street.

"I'm just doing a standard sweep. Will I find anything?"

"Nothing of mine, but there's an assload of weird crap I don't recognize. Soul magic or some such."

"That'll be the Iversonian's work." Melvin worked his way across the road in grids. I watched him, admiring his attention to detail, his craft. Kind of a turn-on really, seeing him in action. Fifteen minutes later, he stopped on my side of the road, breathing a little hard, a thin layer of sweat beading on his forehead. "True immortals' powers range nearly as far afield as vampires'. The Iversonian is good with the trickier stuff, but none of this is leveled at Winter, only at folks who want to mess with Iver's place or who become violent."

"So Winter picked this place so he could take advantage of the Iversonian's well-laid protective countermeasures?"

"It's cheaper than paying the Guild for the same level of shielding." Melvin rubbed his nose with a well-worn square of faded cloth, then swabbed his brow with it. "I'm going to set a class nine detection web on the area, piggyback it on what's here in case someone decides to use any magic."

Damn it. "Go ahead," I huffed as if the precaution wasn't necessary, and looked up at the tiered signs of the Iversonian's self-titled club. "IVER," "SON," and "IAN" were staggered up the side of the massive white building. It looked better at night. "I wasn't planning anything, just showed up early to be certain Winter didn't have any strange ideas about a peaceful meeting."

"Fair enough." Melvin blew his nose on the cloth and squirreled it away in his jumpsuit pocket, putting himself right back into the "never in a million years" category. Not that I didn't watch him cast the spell. He worked magic like he'd been doing it all his life, and I realized that he had.

"How young?" I asked as he walked toward the van.

"My earliest memory is sitting in front of the High Magus and listening as he decided what to do with me. I think I was two or three." *Shit!*

"It should be safe to cast in this area in two or three hours, but before then"—he winked at me and climbed into the driver's seat—"I wouldn't."

Clouds of exhaust spat free of the public works van as he drove off. A guy like that could write his own check, be a member of the High Council. What the hell was he doing working jobs like this— routine service calls for a fricking vampire? I'd used him before when I'd tried to have Eric's soul captured, but I'd never realized how much he'd been worth the money.

My cell chirped. Another text. This one from Talbot.

Shenanigans, where you at?

Talbot was just as bad as the damn thralls, spelling everything out like textspeak was below him. And don't get me started on the stupid nickname.

FU cat.

Play it your way, Shenanigans. His message flashed up, vibrating even as I sent my reply. I hate it when he does that. **Eric wants me to find out what the hell was going on with the gang bang honeymoon. You have anything you want to tell me?**

"Fuck! Of all the times Eric picks to be curious!" I stabbed the number for the Irons Club into my cell. It wasn't really where I'd learned how to be a thrall, but I'd been there with J'iliol'lth and with Roger. People knew me there, and though they might not like the way

I'd gotten free of my contracts, my current master was more important than any of theirs, so they'd have to talk.

"Irons Club. This is Gregory speaking. How may I assist you?"

"This is Rachel Sims, thrall to the Emperor Eric." I heard an intake of breath, close to a gasp at the sound of Eric's name. Greg's a stuck-up ass with a limp, but he knows his place. "I need a gallon of werewolf blood and I need it in less than an hour."

He scoffed. "That is quite the—"

"Can you get it here or not?" I looked at the skyline. Dark was coming too quickly, sunset in progress. I needed to be done with the call before Winter showed. Why couldn't Talbot have texted me earlier?

"He's never asked for anything like this before, and I'm not sure where else to get it," I dissembled. "The Irons Club keeps a stock of exotic blood for when the rich and powerful with thralls to match want something out of season, right? Money is not—"

"We can provide it, of course, but the Irons Club is not a vending machine or a mercantile, Ms. Sims. We are a group of like-minded individuals united to assist each other in serving our masters to the utmost. You can have the werewolf blood to make your master happy, but . . ." He paused for a second, enjoying having me in a tight spot. "You will not receive our assistance in exchange for any level of monetary compensation. You will owe us a favor and you will respect the rules and regulations of the Irons Club."

I held the phone to my ear and considered that. Did I have other choices? Where else could I get werewolf blood? Back before I had double-crossed J'iliol'lth, I'd have tried contacting one of the local demons who dealt in that sort of thing: blood, body parts, etc. But now, most demons wouldn't work with me anymore, or rather, they weren't worth the trouble. In a way, getting out of a demonic contract the way I had bought me the respect of the demonic community, but realistically all that meant was they'd screw me to the wall at the first opportunity so they could be the one who got one over on the mortal who'd gotten the best of J'iliol'lth, used him up, played him, and gotten him eaten by a Mouser. I was out of choices.

"Fine. Leave it for me at the front desk of the Void City Hilton, and I'll play nice with the Irons Club."

"When we need you, if it doesn't directly interfere with your master's plans, you'll provide your assistance?" His voice rose at the end of the sentence like it was a question, but I didn't think it was supposed to be one.

"Yes." A powder blue Porsche Cayman S (I thought Talbot's car magazines said they only came in black) turned onto the street. Only one vampire would be caught dead driving a car like that. Only one vampire could pull it off. Winter.

"You're familiar with the rules?"

"Not as such, but I agree anyway."

"Your werewolf blood will be at the designated location within the hour. It will be under the name Marie."

"Good." I hung up as Winter stepped out of the Porsche.

My phone buzzed again. **Shenanigans?**

sum vmp s hsling me. brb. I tapped the message and sent it. When I looked up again, Winter was standing in front of me. Before I could saying anything, my phone was in his hands and he was scrolling through the messages.

"The cat calls you Shenanigans?" He laughed, handing back the phone, and despite my outrage, I felt a tingle down below. Winter was dressed for clubbing, in clothes so stylish I didn't even know what to call them yet. They were all Winter originals, and he always saved the best for himself. "Well?" Winter walked around me once, eyes raking up and down my body, not luridly, but evaluating me, as a designer might eye a potential new model. "Does the Mouser have your tongue as well as your dignity?"

"Talbot thinks I'm always up to something," I spat, "therefore . . . Shenanigans."

"I like it." Winter wrinkled his nose at me, those blue eyes of his sparkling. That he wore contacts was obvious only because I already knew him to be a vampire. "So. You're in a great deal of trouble and you'd like to get out of it."

"I've got a plan."

"Yes, I heard."

I doubted that, and my expression must have given me away.

"Vampire hearing, dear. Vampire hearing. You didn't expect Eric to notice that you'd hijacked your sister's volition? Or you thought he'd play it off?"

I nodded.

"He's married now, darling, and men like Eric, from Eric's time, the greatest generation, particularly the Courtney family . . . they take vows very seriously." Winter caressed my shoulder and the cool dampness surprised me. He'd been in mist form this whole time! Being able to turn to mist is a rare ability. As far as I know, the only two vampires in Void City who can do it are Winter and Lord Phillip. I was impressed.

"And you can convince him otherwise."

"No, but you can, and I'll tell you how. In exchange, I want your help."

"I won't hurt Eric."

"Of course not."

"Then what?" I stepped away from him, up onto the sidewalk.

"As you may already know, I've bet against Eric in Paris, but that doesn't mean I'm betting against him in Void City." A limo pulled up, and some of Winter's entourage began piling out of the car. I inhaled sharply, ready to use my magic, then I remembered Melvin's damn spell.

"All I want you to do is keep him in Paris for at least a week. Is that so hard? I'll even set you up with a little assistance." Winter followed my gaze toward his groupies. "Don't mind them. I've rented out the Iversonian for the evening. I can't exactly throw myself an anniversary of immortality party in my own club."

"All I have to do is keep him in Paris?"

"Yes."

"And you'll get me out of this?"

"Mmmm-hmmm. You won't believe that it will work, of course. So you'll only owe me if you do what I tell you to do and it works. I'll even be kind enough to renegotiate your debt to the Irons Club. You'll still be bound by the rules, but I'll let it be known that calling on you needlessly will make *me* needlessly pissy."

His entourage gasped in unison. The idea of a pissy Winter seemed like a bad plan to me too.

"What about Eric? He won't be hurt, will he?"

"Hurt? Yes. Destroyed or permanently altered? No."

"Fine. I agree. Tell me how to get out of it."

He whispered the answer in my ear, and I shook my head.

"Bullshit."

Winter stepped through me, his mist sending a shiver down my spine. "Think what you will, Shenanigans. But if you use my solution, you owe me. Paris. One week. Don't forget."

As soon as Winter headed into the club, I texted Talbot. Dn't no n.e.thng abt htl rm. We all hd fun. Whre r u?

Headed back to the Pollux to get Magbidion. Why?

No rsn.

Tabitha didn't rise until an hour after sunset. I still had time . . . if I hurried and if I didn't take any chances. I dialed information and asked for the number for Triple-T Waste Disposal. *Sorry, sis,* I thought to myself, *but it's you or me, and if Eric finds out that I put the whammy on you, I'm dead meat.*

10

ERIC:

". . . BUT I AIN'T STUPID"

I handed the cell back to Talbot. He took it calmly, slipping his precious iCall or uDial—whatever it was—back into the pocket of his suit coat. Magbidion stood on the other side of the hotel room, retching at the smell and made doubly uncomfortable by the purple glow of my eyes. Revenant's eyes. I hadn't transformed into uber vamp mode, but my anger was showing.

I hoped I was wrong. I hoped Rachel would be smart enough not to kill her sister in an attempt to cover up her little mind-control joyride, but when I know about something, I have to act. I'd rather not know. If my friends really hate me and are nice to me just because they get something out of it? Great! But I expect them to keep it to themselves.

Hell, I'd have forgiven Whatshisname for all the stupid crap he pulled: arranging my son's death, trying to steal my soul, wrecking my car, setting me up to fight William and his pack, murdering me . . . all of it, if he'd just said he was sorry and either stopped being an asshole or got better at concealing it. It's weird, but it's the way I work. Anybody can get a free pass, but they don't get many, and when they run out . . . they die.

The scents of rotten meat and sewage mingled in our nostrils, the final remnants of Tabitha's corpse sweat episode. Talbot and I acted as if it was no big thing, but even after I'd showered Tabitha off and sent her clothes, the bedding, sheets—everything that could reasonably be incinerated—out to be incinerated, the smell still threatened to bring tears (or blood in my case) to our eyes.

I looked at the bedside phone and shook my head. It was a test I wanted Rachel to pass. The chain of evidence goes like this: Talbot had suspected Rachel of doing something to Tabitha, Magbidion had been able to confirm the extent to which Rachel was doing something to Tabitha, and my text conversation with Rachel and my knowledge of just how scheming and low-down she can be filled in the rest.

I didn't know how Rachel was intending to do it, but if she was, there is one surefire body disposal method in Void City, Triple-T Waste Disposal, three *oni* brothers who won't report anything to the police for any price and who dispose of the evidence. I used them myself before Fang turned out to be almost as good. He leaves the bones behind and they don't, but . . .

"Shenanigans, huh?" From my seat at the edge of the bed, I put my cold dead hand on Tabitha's equally chilled one as she slept. She was safe, but if I hadn't woken up from the Lisette dream feeling paranoid, Tabitha might have been destined for *oni* cuisine. I may not be the world's best husband, but if anyone's going to kill my wife, it damn well better be me.

"I thought it was a good fit." Talbot paced the room. "You wanted to know, right? I know that you don't want to know a lot of things, but this?"

I took a deep breath and didn't let it out for a few seconds. It's a human thing. I still do a lot of human things for all that I'm dead.

"Yeah." The phone on the nightstand wasn't ringing yet. I wanted it to keep right on not ringing. "I needed to know. You did the right thi—"

Ring. I eyed the phone like it had betrayed a confidence, but that didn't stop it from ringing again. *Ring. Ring.*

"Damn." As the phone rang, I remembered the punch line to an old Cajun joke about a man who wins the lottery and tells his wife she can build any house she wants as long as he can have a "Hello Statue."

No. I want wanna dem tings what goes bring bring and have dat little ting what dat you pick up and say, "Hello? S'datch you?"

I picked up the "Hello Statue" with a laugh trapped in my throat, choking out a word. "Yeah?"

"She just called." The voice on the phone had a slight accent. It was Tiko, Timbo, or Tombo . . . one of the three. The *oni* didn't waste much time, straight to business. "We're supposed to meet her over at the Void City Hilton PDQ. She said we should head on up to the Honeymoon Suite and wait outside. Do we go?"

"Uh-huh. I'll hand you your check when you get to the room. I might even have a body for you to dispose of. Just don't let on that anything's up."

"Sixty grand, right?" You could hear the greed in his voice, like Scrooge McDuck thinking about his money bin.

"That's right." I hung up the phone. Hard. Plastic shrapnel scattered in all directions as my knuckles scraped the phone's inner mechanism. Pain flared, then faded too quickly, curlicues of torn skin weaving themselves back together fast enough to see. I killed the nightstand next, putting my fist through the alarm clock, an electrical jolt buzzing through my arm before the cord melted. I couldn't smell it over the lingering odor of corpse sweat, but I saw the sizzle and the smoke.

I put my fist through the television, too, and then stopped in my tracks, not from the pain, but from the searing memory of a house near the beach and a blond little girl whose foster father was not even worth biting . . .

"I'm not even going to bite you," I said under my breath.

"What, boss? You hungry?" Magbidion held out his arm.

"No." In my mind's eye, I saw my work boot on the back of the man's head, forcing his skull into the floor. "No. I'm fine. When's our flight?"

"You're supposed to leave at midnight." Talbot looked at his watch. "You've got plenty of time, even with airport security the way it is. After all, it's not like you're going commercial. Do I need to try and reschedule?"

"No." I squeezed my fist as tight as I could, watching as bits of glass, wood, and plastic rose to the surface, pushed out by my regenerative process. Two years ago, I would have thanked Lord Phillip for the use of his plane without a second thought, but nowadays, the idea that I didn't know exactly what was in it for Phil made me nauseous. But I'd promised Tabitha a honeymoon in Paris, and that's what she got. "Go back to the Pollux and make sure Beatrice doesn't need any help getting her stuff together."

"I thought Rachel was—"

I glared at him.

"Right. You sure you don't want me to stay?"

I shook my head.

Talbot left.

Ten minutes later, I heard heavy footfalls in the hall. Okay, to be fair, I heard the three *oni* talking to each other in the elevator on the way up too. Yeah. My hearing isn't quite at Superman's level, but it's good.

A check for sixty thousand dollars was sitting on top of the television. I got it, opened the door, and smiled at the three *oni*. For triplets, they sure looked different. Not one of them had the same number of horns or eyes, or the same skin color.

"What now?" one of them asked.

"Now we see if she's going to go through with it or not."

Three Japanese ogres waited in the hallway. A magician whose soul I'd saved waited in the bathroom. My wife waited, even though she didn't know she was waiting. We all waited.

Two minutes later, I heard Rachel's heartbeat outside on the sidewalk several stories down. It's not the sort of thing I usually notice, but I was specifically listening for her. Her heart was pounding; she was out of breath. Concentrating, I heard her exchange words with someone briefly. Was she checking for messages? Saying hello?

As the sun set outside, Rachel came up in the elevator.

"It's okay," I heard Rachel whisper to herself. "I've got time."

With a clunk and a swish, the elevator doors opened and I could smell the werewolf blood. *See? Now that's just clever.* Werewolves were out to get me again, so why not vanish her sister and make it look like the werewolves did it and Tab got a few good shots in before they took her down? Rachel could even guilt-trip me over the whole thing for not forcing Tabitha awake and taking her with me for the day.

"Okay, guys. We've got to do this fast. Like five-minute-meal fast."

She slid the key through the card reader, sending whatever magic codes were needed to signal the hotel's security system to unlock the door. Shouldering it open, she stepped into the room, looking over her shoulder at the *oni* and unscrewing the top of the blood-filled jug she was carrying.

"I can see why Talbot calls you Shenanigans," I announced, stepping forward into the patch of light that spilled through the open doorway.

Werewolf blood ran out of the plastic jug when it hit the carpet, creating a slick, growing puddle. Strong and bitter, the scent cut right through the other smells in the room.

"Lucy," said one of the *oni* in his best Ricky Ricardo imitation, "you got some 'splaining to do." The others laughed and Rachel tried to run.

"Stop." Though spoken softly, I made it a command, and Rachel froze with such violence that she looked like a dog that'd just run full speed to the end of its leash and had been surprised by the sudden stop at the end. Rachel fell backward into the blood puddle, the rich liquid soaking into her hair.

"No magic." Another command. "Don't move."

"I can explain. Eric. Master, I can explain."

Fang, I called for him with my mind and felt his engine start in response. *Get your undercarriage up here.*

"I'd like to hear all about it." My hand closed around her throat and I picked her up, carrying her across the room at arm's length. Ripping the window treatment down with my left hand, I broke the window with Rachel. Glass rained down onto the street and sidewalk below, some of it shattering into even smaller pieces as it struck Fang's windshield. Rachel's eyes widened at the sight of my Mustang rolling up the hotel's exterior wall in a tire-gripping defiance of gravity.

"No," she choked. "Please. Let me explain."

Bright light flared from the butterfly tattoo on her cheek, and I sensed her trying to pull free of my control. It's been decades since my sinuses hurt. Pressure built, but I fought back, reaching out for her along my link and holding tight. Her tattoo sizzled, the skin darkening like a brand. She winced against the pain and I stopped pushing.

"I turn a blind eye to a lot of shit, Rachel." Fang came to a stop over the window, and I wondered just what the Veil of Scrythax would make people think they saw. Would they simply believe they were seeing a movie stunt? A line of smiley-face stickers stared at me from Fang's undercarriage and someone (obviously Greta) had written "OK I LUV YOU BYE-BYE!" in blue sparkly paint pen underneath them. "I really do, but this? You think you can explain this? Tell me if I have it all wrong somehow, but you mind-raped my wife and forced her to engage in a . . . honeymoon gang bang and then, when you got caught out, you decided to feed her, your sister, to *oni* and blame it on the werewolves. Did I miss anything?"

"He was right," Rachel whispered.

"Who was right?"

"You." She stopped struggling even as I pushed her back against Fang, the line of smiley faces peeking out at me behind her shoulders. "You're right about everything. And I'm sorry."

"What?" I let her go at the word sorry, but she didn't drop. Her body clung to the metal, and I kind of wished Fang would go ahead and eat her, but he knows me too well. Apologies are one of my weaknesses. And like I said, I'll give anyone a free pass. Up till now Rachel hadn't used hers. I didn't even think she knew how to call it in, but—

"At the wedding, I tried to talk Tabitha into giving you a three-way, just once for your honeymoon as an extra special kinky surprise and she hit me with her vampire strength. It spun me around into the sink and when she walked over to me, I . . . I just reacted." Tears flowed down Rachel's cheeks. Crocodile or not, they were convincing. "I struck out and took her over with the dark tantra. I meant to let her go, right after, but you seemed to have such a good time that I thought I'd hold on to her until after the honeymoon. She's not hurt, just incredibly uninhibited and suggestible."

I turned my back on her.

"When I thought Talbot was going to find out, I freaked and decided to cover it all up. Magbidion's good enough that even if I let her go, I was afraid he'd figure out what happened. I wasn't plotting against you, Eric. I wasn't in league with anybody. I promise. I fucked up. I fucked up bad, but I'm sorry and it won't happen again. I swear. I swear to whoever you want me to swear to."

At the door, Tiko and the boys waited eagerly. "You're not going to let the car eat her, are you?" one of them asked.

"You can go, boys. Thanks for coming."

I shut the door and listened to the sounds of their grumbling departure, subconsciously amazed that the elevator was strong enough to hold their combined weight. *Oni* are heavy. Behind me, my sister-in-law sobbed and I did not smell cinnamon. With the window broken, the odor of Tabitha's corpse sweat was fading and I could detect the acrid scent of burnt electronics. In the bathroom, Magbidion was taking a piss.

I was going to let Rachel go. I had her dead to rights, caught red-handed attempting the unforgivable, but I was going to let her go because she said she was sorry. If you look up "gullible fucktard" in the dictionary, I'll be right there waving at you.

"You ever watch *Lost in Space?*"

"What?" Eyes red and puffy, Rachel blinked at me between sobs.

"I watched a lot of TV the first few years after I got turned. *Lost in Space* was on that first year. They had a robot and spaceships. It blew my mind, plus it had this gal, Marta Kristen, playing Judy Robinson. I lusted after that woman."

Rachel did that whole body shake and snuffle that happens to little kids when they've been all-out sobbing and have barely managed to stop and might start up again at any moment.

"But the character you remind me of is Doctor Smith. He was a constant pain in their ass, always getting them into trouble, trying to sell them out to aliens, the whole spiel, but Doctor Robinson would never kill him and he never let Major West kill him either, no matter what kind of shenanigans he got up to."

I pulled her off the car with a sound like tearing sheets of Reynolds Wrap apart.

"You have three choices." I held up a finger. "One. You can stop being my thrall and go do your own thing. If you do that, you need to leave Void City and stay the hell out of my business." She shook her head and I held up a second finger. "Two. You can stay my thrall, but no more of this crap, no hitting on me, no using the dark tantra thing on me or Greta or Talbot or Tabitha . . . or the girls . . . not even on Fang. No 'accidentally' letting me see you naked. None of it. And if I catch you out, just once, one sniff of cinnamon when there isn't any real cinnamon around, one slipup, and option three"—I pointed at Fang, still parked over the window—"is the last thing you'll ever see."

"Two," she coughed.

Yeah, I thought, *no shit option two.*

"What about Tabitha?" Rachel asked after a second. "What do we tell her?"

"Mags," I yelled at the bathroom. "Can you alter a vampire's memory?"

"I'd need help. Vlads are a little too strong for me alone." He looked at Rachel. "With her help, I could fix it."

I knew I was making a mistake, but I didn't want to have to tell Tabitha that I almost fed her sister to my car, and I didn't want to tell her about the first night of our honeymoon either. This way, I could pretend like it never happened. It was easy. Stupid, but easy . . . and I'm good at both.

"Help him, but no foolishness. I want her ready to fly to Paris with me and Beatrice."

Rachel bristled at that, but she was wise enough not to question it. "Eric?"

"Yeah?"

"Why don't you just order me to do all those things, like make it a master-thrall command?"

"Because then you'd be my slave and I don't do slaves. You have free will. Use it. Now get it done."

I walked out of the hotel room, out of the hotel itself, and met Fang down on the sidewalk. John Paul Courtney was sitting in the passenger's seat. "I'm prou—"

"Shut up!" I snapped.

Fang played "Born to Lose" by Ray Charles and I told him to shut up, too.

✦ 11 ✦

ERIC:

DA PLANE! DA PLANE!

Get on a plane and fly to Paris. Simple, right? It should have been. Everything was arranged. A midnight departure meant that with the twelve-hour flight and the seven-hour time zone change we ought to show up in Paris while it was dark outside. My not-so-blushing bride was all packed. I was all packed. Even Beatrice was all packed. Our passports had been taken care of (courtesy of Lord Phillip) and for the first time in four-plus decades, my identification even had the right last name on it. Rachel didn't show up to see us off, which got on Tabitha's nerves, but I thought it was a good call. Whatever it takes to keep you out of trouble, yeah?

I was carrying the last of the bags out to the limo (Phil insisted) when I heard motorcycles.

"Shit. Tabitha. Beatrice. Get your asses in the limo!"

Beatrice grabbed Tabitha's arm in an attempt to hurry her toward the limo, but Tabitha pulled away from her. "What is it? What's going on?"

"It's the holy hairy wedding crashers. I think they want to see me off. Get in the car!"

"No." She'd been seeming human, but still managed to pop her claws. As she got better at managing her powers, she'd discovered that anger helps her override the suppressive effect that seeming human has on her abilities, and the prospect of a honeymoon derailment provided more than enough of that particular emotion. "I'll help you."

"No, you won't." I locked eyes with her and pushed my way inside her head. "You'll get in the car, ride to the airport, and get on the airplane. If I'm not there when it's time to leave, then you can come rescue me. Now go!"

I'm totally going to have to answer for that when I get on the plane, I thought.

Fang rolled out of the parking deck as if he sensed trouble brewing. As the limo pulled out, I reached into the glove box and drew *El Alma Perdida*.

"Ah cain't believe it," said a certain dead man with a southern twang I recognized. "You actually thought to use my gun. Yer learnin', boy."

Greta came running out the front doors of the Pollux, a bloodied mouse in one hand. She dropped it and wiped her fingers clean on the back of her jeans. "Are we fighting something?"

"No." A thought occurred to me, the beginnings of an actual plan. *What? Even I come up with a plan from time to time.* "I'm fighting something. You're getting in Fang and driving to the airport."

"But, Dad!"

"No 'buts,' just do it."

I didn't have to make it an order. Greta's a good girl, and she knew I was serious. Without a word, she jumped into Fang's driver's seat and tore off for the airport, leaving tire tracks and the smell of burnt rubber in her wake.

I stood in the middle of the street, gun at the ready, until a car, hopefully not one of my customers, whipped by me, clipping my hip. It swerved and slowed, but didn't stop. And that's why when Deacon and crew came hauling ass around the corner, I was pulling myself up off the sidewalk. They were already wolfed out and ready to bite, which must have taken a lot of practice and explained why they rode such large frickin' motorcycles.

I didn't have a shot on Deacon, so I took the next werewolf in line, squeezing off a round that took him in the chest. In the movies, gunmen make all kinds of trick shots, but in basic training, just like in any other place where they're teaching you to use guns against people, Sergeant Shouts-a-lot taught us to shoot for the largest visible target. Usually, that means center mass. There was no spurting gout of blood, and I didn't stop to watch him die. I moved on to the next target because in war that's what you do, and anytime I aim a gun at a living thing and pull the trigger that's what it feels like . . . like I'm on enemy soil . . .

El Alma Perdida barked like thunder and my ears started ringing, all other sounds buried by the all-encompassing whine. Silvery flames poured out of the wound, and the werewolf tumbled from his hog, clutching at his chest. I've been shot more than once with *El Alma Perdida* and it's never been fun, but I didn't envy him the flammable fur coat.

My next round hit the fourth or fifth wolf in the bunch. He laid his bike down, skidding to a halt, flame trailing from his neck where *El Alma Perdida*'s bullet had struck home. By then I'd forgotten I was standing in the road out in front of the Demon Heart . . . My mind was far away and long ago in the mud of some other place. Bombs were falling around me in that else-when, but I kept on shooting, because that's what you do when you're at war.

"They're strong," Courtney offered. "Normal wolves go out like candles, once *Perdy* gets aholt of 'em." I looked at Courtney, didn't recognize him. He wasn't in my unit, but he didn't look German or Japanese and he didn't have a gun, so I told him to take cover and I took cover too, running for the Pollux entryway.

Both the injured wolves let loose with howls so shrill and terrible that it cut through the ringing in my ears. *Air raid.*

"*Perdy* got 'em anyhow."

JPC's voice came through loud and clear despite the fact that I could barely hear my own gunshots, but I didn't have time to ask why. Using the edge of the Pollux entry for cover, I got off one more shot before Deacon was on me. A third werewolf went down, flames licking up his chest and engulfing his head.

"That happens sometimes," Courtney said, "when you hit a vital organ. Must a' got that fella right in the ticker."

Deacon leapt straight for me, not even slowing to stop his motorcycle. We went backward through the glass double doors. Slivers of glass poked through my skin, drawing blood and eliciting a hissing yelp. A combination of the pain, the blood, and seeing the chandelier overhead brought me back to the present and I shoved Deacon off. I changed as he flew through the air.

Turning into the uber vamp was too easy. It felt natural, pleasurable, like putting on your favorite pair of jeans. Deacon hit the concrete, bounced back up, and charged into me. The hit carried us farther into the Pollux. We tumbled together in front of the concession stand, claws scrabbling for purchase in each other's flesh.

Sounds came out of his muzzle, but if they were words I couldn't understand them so I talked over him. "Three down. Nine to go, Deacon. You sure you want to keep doing this?"

Sharp pointy wolf teeth sank into my shoulder . . . always with the shoulder. He tore into the meat and I shouted an obscenity. A series of snaps and pops echoed in both ears complimented by a side of piercing pain and I could hear again, but something else was wrong. Fighting wasn't fun anymore. It was vicious and bloody and it hurt. I'd killed three werewolves and nobody laughed. Worse, I was tired of it all. I'd even had a flashback, for crying out loud. I hadn't had one of those since becoming a vampire, not one. If I hadn't known any better, I'd have said I was coming down off some kind of . . . high. And that's when I realized that I was.

According to Lord Phillip, I'd been under an enchantment that hid me from my sire and slowed the development of my powers since the very moment that I became a vampire. After the enchantment finally wore off at the end of the whole soul-stealing demon thing, I'd still had Rachel influencing me in subtle ways, making me happy. I didn't have that anymore because I made her stop. It was the magic. I was coming down off a forty (fifty?) year high and this was real life. This was real life and I was tired of playing games.

I turned into my revenant form and walked toward the street. Cold rushed in and the world went watercolor; the unreality of it made things easier. Deacon rushed after me, angrily clawing at spectral flesh he couldn't touch. A ghostly gun, *El Alma Perdida*, appeared in my ghostly hand (I guess because I'd been holding it before I changed) and I opened fire on the Apostles. They'd promptly formed a ring around Deacon and me, so they had very little chance to react. I'd say it was like shooting fish in a barrel, but it was worse than that.

"That's cheatin'!" Courtney's ghost appeared next to me, but I walked past him, reaching through the corpse of one of the dead werewolves to withdraw the bullet. It slid free of the flesh, a whole cartridge that looked as if it had never been fired at all. I popped open the cylinder, slid the cartridge home, and then snapped the cylinder back into place.

"I said, 'That's cheatin' and you shouldn't be shootin' those wolves anyhow. They're believers!'" Courtney scowled at me.

"This isn't a game anymore." I fired *El Alma Perdida* again and Deacon's claws swept through me without effect. "It used to be, and then I sobered up." The ice in my voice manifested itself on the asphalt as a spreading ring of frost. "This is war."

Deacon changed tactics, seizing *El Alma Perdida*'s grip with both paws. The silver cross on the grip burned his palms, but he refused to let go.

"Now there's irony for you," I said.

"I. Will. End. You." Deacon growled the words. I let him have the gun and grabbed him somewhere else, my glowing blue fingers sinking under the flesh and seizing energy that felt warm and alive.

"I don't think you will, Deacon." His eyes widened as he felt what it's like to have a revenant start to tear your spirit out of your body. It can't have been pleasant. "And I really wish you'd stop trying. I don't need to hunt anymore. I have thralls, willing thralls, to feed me, and I'm not going to make any other vampires. I'm done with that. In fact, I'm on my way to Paris to try and kill the vampire that created me. I probably won't stop at one."

"You're a monster."

"And you're dinner. Given a choice between the two, I'm more comfortable with my role in the scenario."

"You killed seven of the Apostles."

"If it makes you feel any better, they weren't the real ones." I let him go and he sank to his knees. I watched him shrink back down to human form, and he looked broken. Two of the remaining so-called Apostles grabbed him under the shoulders, pulling him away from me and to his feet.

They loaded up the bodies of their fallen comrades in a way that looked unsafe and illegal, and then they drove away. I didn't realize that they'd taken the other five bullets with them until the last were-wolf rode out of sight and John Paul started laughing.

"They're getting away with your bullets, Hoss. 'Course, if you knew the other way to reload the gun, that wouldn't be no problem, but I ain't fixin' to tell yeh how to go about that until you promise not to use *Perdy* on any more believers. And another thing . . ."

To say the least, it was a very long ride to the airport.

12

RACHEL:

SEE YOU IN PARIS

I should have been on that plane." The words left my mouth ten minutes after Lord Phillip's private jet took off. *Eric actually left me behind. Me.*

Me!

"Bye, Dad! Bye, Mom!" Greta sat on the hood of Eric's Mustang, still waving, still smiling, as if she had no intention of leaving, not until he came back to find her still smiling and waving. "Come back soon!"

"Bye!" Maybe she thought he would turn around if she waved long enough or called loud enough. Tears of blood rolled down her face. Talbot saw the tears and walked over. He went to put his hands around her shoulders and caught himself, putting both hands flat on Fang's hood instead.

"Let's go on back to the Pollux, Greta." Such a calm relaxing tone . . . A girl could forget he's really a cat. "We can get one of the girls to feed you."

"No!" She hit him with the palm of her hand. I think it was supposed to be a simple shove, but it knocked Talbot off his feet and into the air. He threw his body into a spin, rotating in the air, and struck the roof of the parking deck with his claws extended. Scratches trailed behind his claws, sparks popping from the needle-sharp talons as he used them to slow his progress. Inertia spent, he dropped to the floor on all fours with grace surpassing a cat's. Green flashes of light winked on within his cat's eyes, but he mastered his temper as he stood, and the light went out.

"I'm out," I said, and headed for the nearest exit. A trip in an elevator that smelled of piss and French fries took me down to the arrivals section without having to pass through security. I got into the first taxi I saw and texted Andre.

"Drive."

wht do i hv 2 do?

"Where to?"

I kept my eyes on the screen, ignoring the question, until I hit Send. "Give me a sec."

"I'm starting the meter."

"Whatever."

Andre's text came in fast: **You apologized?—Andre**

duh, I texted back at him.

"Head back into downtown," I told the cabbie, and we began to move. "I'm either going to the Artiste Unknown or the Demon Heart."

"The strip club?" The driver let out a whistle. "You a dancer? Aren't you a little young?"

"Fuck you." I tapped the screen of my phone and started a KenKen puzzle, impatient for Andre's reply. "First of all, it's a bowling alley now, and second of all, I don't even work there. I'm dating the guy who owns it."

"Don't you mean the vampire who owns it?"

I looked up as my phone vibrated, then glanced back down. On the second pass, the words made sense: **Meet at the Artiste Unknown. Winter is expecting you within the hour.—Andre**

omw. I sent the text and looked back up at the cabbie, really seeing him for the first time. He was dark haired, white, a little pimply, maybe mid-forties. "Take me to the Artiste . . ." I paused, suddenly noticing that the driver had little horns, a set of three on each side of his head, tiny horns, flat above his ears. "Un . . . known."

Horns.

Demon.

Shit!

I tapped into my magic, reaching out to his chakras before I realized what kind of demon he was. To an ancient Roman, a Gallus would have meant a castrated guy that served the goddess Cybele, but to a modern demonologist it means a sexless demon who serves as a messenger. While not physically very powerful fighters, the Galli have a knack of placing themselves in the future path of the people they seek. All they need is a photograph or a decent representation of the target. Once it's burned, they snort the ashes and in a matter of days, or even hours (depending on the strength of the Gallus involved and the distance from the target), they will run into the individual they seek.

They're perfect messengers. They don't eat. They don't drink.

They don't sleep. And they can't have sex, which makes my magic all but useless.

"You must be strong." He winked at me in the rearview mirror. "That tickles."

"Who sent you?" Below his eye level, I flattened my right hand against the back of the driver's seat and drew on some of the power I'd stolen from Eric. Swirls of black skin spread out from my wrist until the skin on my hand turned entirely black. My nails extended into claws. "I got out of my contract by the letter of the agreement and—"

"I'm not here to hurt you, Ms. Sims." His attention shifted to the road as he jerked the wheel to avoid a collision with a Honda Civic driven by a moron who needed lessons on staying inside the lines. "I do have a message, however."

"Who from?"

"One of the Nefario."

Nefario are lesser lords of the demonic political landscape. J'iliol'lth, the demon I'd sold my soul to, had been one of them before Eric fed him to Talbot. Like the Galli, they don't wield much direct power, but the Nefario specialize in giving power (some permanent, some temporary) to others, for a price . . . usually a soul.

"Which one?"

"Lady Scrytha, hatchling and heir of Scrythax." His tone changed as he got going, moving out of easygoing cabbie guy to sycophantic ass licker. "First-circle Nefario, potential Infernatti, and former overseer of the voided entity called J'iliol'lth. I bid you greetings on her behalf."

Holy shit! Jill's mom? Not good.

"Heir to Scrythax . . . as in Veil of Scrythax?" I asked.

"Yes, I believe a small portion of the former Infernatti's skin has been used on more than one occasion to alter the perceptions and minds of mortals." My driver pulled up onto the interstate just like he was really taking me to the Artiste Unknown. I let my hand revert to normal. "Even dismembered, Lord Scrythax is quite powerful. May he rise again in infernal majesty." He was in full dutiful servant mode, so much so that I wondered if he was transmitting the conversation back to his demonic mistress with a beacon link or Satan chime. I didn't see one, but that wasn't proof of anything.

"What does she want with me?"

"She wants to buy back your soul."

"No, thanks." I scoffed at the idea. "Doesn't she know how hard I worked to get the damned thing back?"

"Nice pun." He chuckled. "She understands the extent of your efforts very well indeed. And though my mistress, unlike her father, has no great fondness for humans, she has seen and admired your ability to deal with soul contracts. The Lady Scrytha also senses your imminent and utter destruction. If you would like to avoid the fate she has foreseen, my mistress would like to give you the opportunity to come and work for her as the Grand Madam of her succubae and incubi."

My mouth fell open. "Why the hell would she want to do that?"

"Perhaps she merely desires intercourse with you." The Gallus changed lanes, going all the way over into the outside lane. "I've never understood the draw it has for those with sexual organs, but—"

"Try again."

"The truth? No problem, as I'm authorized to tell it to you. Eric Courtney has diverged from his destiny, and this concerns Lady Scrytha."

"What destiny?"

"He is the last Courtney who may destroy Lisette and end the curse on the Courtney line. Eric's destiny was to do so, and then become human."

"And now?"

"Now, Lady Scrytha believes that he will not confront Lisette at all and will instead embark on a different quest, a quest that will be most disconcerting for the Infernatti."

"I thought you were going to say he was the chosen one or something."

"No." He coughed. "Eric Courtney is of no consequence in the grand scheme of things. Despite his previous exertions in El Segundo, he was destined to be little more than a mortal under a curse who redeems his family name and dies a bitter, lonely, and ultimately broken man."

"And now?"

"Now he does not die."

"So he sticks around for a few more years? So what?"

"Ever."

"Excuse me." I sat up straighter, all of my attention on the demon as he steered us off the interstate again.

"Eric Courtney never dies and in time becomes a hybrid of the man he once was and the thing he has become. If that is allowed to come to pass, then it will render countless prophesies incorrect."

"And how does she know all of this?"

"She *is* a Nefario."

"So." I ran the possibilities over in my head, chewing my lip as I did so. "She wants me to work for her to keep me from working for Eric?"

"And help you avoid utter destruction."

I gave a little grunt as he took a sharp turn into an alley, the inertia shoving me up against the door. He hit the brake hard, bouncing me off the back of the seat and bringing the cab to a screeching halt. I'd been so caught up in the conversation I'd stopped paying attention to the route. We were in an area of town I didn't recognize. It sure wasn't near the Artiste Unknown.

Two demons with dog heads, leather wings, and big axes stepped out of the adjoining buildings into the alley. After the first set came out, two more followed, and two more after them. "If I say no, then I get to play with the puppies?"

"Yeah." He looked back over the seats at me, back to easygoing cabbie guy. "Sorry about that. I'm just the messenger."

My skin streaked black, a sensation like lover's breath—no, more specific than that—as though Eric's breath on my skin, cool and steady, chased the black. I felt stretched open, as I grew. Uber vamp wings burst through the cab's rear window and I stood up through the ceiling, like shrugging out of an old jacket.

I killed the messenger first. A swift slash of my claws and he was headless, the violet glow that poured from my eyes turning his blood from light brown to muddied purple. Heat built up in my piercings, uncomfortable, but not as bad as the fierce sizzle I knew I'd get when I changed back. My uber vamp form isn't what it feels like to be Eric, but it's as close as I can get. Channeling this kind of power through a mortal body is like riding the devil's own stallion. It kicks and bucks. Too much sound and fury, but I'd practiced a time or two, so it didn't get away from me.

Faster than Eric, I took flight. Wind from my pursuers tickled the back of my neck and I knew where they were without looking. The uber vamp knew. We were like little kids playing tag—very scary, dangerous children. I was still human, still alive despite the boost, and I knew I'd be easily dispatched. Each beat of my heart felt as if it might shake me to pieces. *Thoom. Thoom. Thoom.*

An axe swung too close and I spiraled away. There was no need to fight them. A fight would have wasted precious uber vamp energy, and my supply was limited. I let them chase me through downtown, swooping in and around buildings until I saw the Artiste Unknown and turned on the speed in earnest. A block away from Winter's club, they broke off pursuit. Lady Scrytha could not buy my soul with threats. Winter and his cronies were set up on the roof as if in wait for me. I landed, then transformed.

They applauded, but not for me, and then I understood. They'd been waiting for me. He'd known. He'd bet on it.

"I won again," Winter explained.

I nodded, meaning to say something snarky, but caught up in the effort not to flinch at the hot-out-of-the-dryer warmth of my piercings. *Ow. Ow. Hot.*

"Now." Winter greeted me with a smile. "Let's talk about getting you to Paris. All you have to do is keep Eric there for seven days and we'll be even. Magbidion showed you how to alter a vampire's memory, yes?"

13

ERIC:

OLD BOLD SOLDIERS

When flying to Paris from abroad, the truly trendy undead traveler chooses to arrive at Orly. It's smaller than Charles de Gaulle International and since European cities don't use a Veil of Scrythax, as far as I know, I guess it helps to keep the supernatural under wraps.

"Isn't this awesome?" Tabitha kissed me on the cheek, the warmth lingering there long after she headed off down the aisle to disembark. I fumbled with Tabitha's suitcases, my single bag hanging around my neck dogtag style. Beatrice carried her own bag. She'd packed conservatively, like me.

"It's a better trip than last time," I said. Tabitha didn't hear me, but Beatrice did.

"You've been to France?"

"Yes." I tottered down the aisle sideways, crablike, trying not to bump the bags against the seats. Phil's flight staff hovered nearby, anxious to help carry, but I didn't want their help.

"Did you fly into Charles de Gaulle?"

"Didn't fly." My bag snagged on the arm of a seat, and I had to duck and swing my head to get it loose again.

"By boat? That must have been nice. I've never been on a cruise."

"Me either."

"But you came by boat?"

"Yes."

"Eric." Beatrice came to a stop, but I pushed on. Her breath caught in her throat, and I heard her heart rate increasing. "Were you alive or undead when you last visited France?"

"I was alive."

"And the ship you were on . . . it didn't land at a port, did it?"

"Not exactly." I reached the end of the aisle and looked down the steps. Tabitha was standing at the bottom talking to three humans. She still looked adorable in her yellow sundress and strappy white heels, but her mood had soured. I couldn't hear what she was saying because of the magic soundproofing Phil had layered onto his plane, but she wasn't happy.

"Where did you land?" Beatrice asked.

"Normandy." I walked down the steps. The three men weren't wearing uniforms. Halfway down, the sound kicked in.

"I'm sorry, mademoiselle, but you and your master will have to board the plane and return to America. Europe is closed to you."

The speaker was tall and dark-haired. He even wore sunglasses at night, just like that Corey Hart song. The earpiece in his ear made me think Secret Service, but his accent was French. Next to him, a blond in jeans and a "Born in the USA" T-shirt smoked a cigarette, paying more attention to the ground or a spot in the distance than to what was going on next to him.

I followed his gaze and saw a group of mercs clad in riot gear covered with runes and crosses, symbols from several religions. He gave them a subtle shake of his head, which I took to mean "not yet," and took another drag off the cigarette. His face was familiar, but I couldn't place it.

Up close, the third "man" was obviously either a woman dressing to minimize her curves or the most successfully androgynous man I'd even seen. A little closer and I inhaled her scent. Definitely a woman. She caught me sniffing and rolled her eyes.

"Just kill them." She had a German accent. I didn't like her.

"Already dead." I dropped the suitcases on the tarmac and unslung the bag from around my neck. "Besides, you can't destroy me."

"You may be an Emperor, but I assure you, we can destroy you. It may be difficult to figure out where on the plane or in your luggage you've hidden your *memento mori*, but—"

"I didn't bring it."

She scoffed. It was a very cute scoff. "Only an idiot or a madman would travel abroad leaving their greatest weakness and their greatest strength—"

"Then I'm an idiot." I dropped my bag next to the suitcases. "Now that we have that cleared up, why don't you explain to me why it is that I can't honeymoon in Paris?"

"Corey Hart" opened his mouth to say something, but stopped when the guy in the Springsteen T-shirt spat out his cigarette and shoved his way between his two compatriots. "No way in hell you're *that* Eric Courtney." He looked at me closely, sizing me up. His eyes glazed over, and the other two instinctively steadied him. "You are him!" Eyes refocusing, he shook off the others. "Thumper, how the hell did you wind up a vampire, you old son of a bitch?"

He took my hand and clapped me on the shoulder. This man obviously knew me, was glad to see me even though I was a vampire. I stared at his brown eyes and the tiny scar on his jawline, and knew that I knew him, too, but his name wouldn't come. I wanted to call him Carl, but that wasn't the right name.

"You know this vampire, James?" the tall guy asked.

"Hell, yes, I know him, Luc." He slapped my shoulder again. "I'm sure I've told you about Thumper."

"Thumper?" Tabitha gave me a quizzical look.

"They used to call me Bible Thumper." Finding the memory was hard, but it was there, buried deep under decades of misuse. "James must be from my old unit."

"But he looks young," Tabitha said.

"They're immortals," Beatrice said from the bottom of the steps. She stood there holding her bag. I wondered briefly what it felt like to be the only human in the bunch.

"What?" I looked at her. "Like true immortals?"

"Vampires may run the United States, Eric." She took a place next to the suitcases. "But the immortals run Europe."

"So you don't let vampires into Europe?" I rubbed my fingers over my eyes. "You'd think Lord Phillip would have mentioned that one."

"No," the German immortal said, "we allow vampires, but only under strict regulations. European vampires are allowed themselves and three offspring. After twenty-five years of unlife, unless their sire releases them earlier, Kings and Lords may petition the Council to establish their own households. After fifty years of unlife, Knights may petition to leave the service of their rightful masters, but they are only allowed one offspring."

She smiled a cruel smile. "Vampires that do not abide by these rules are destroyed. As you should be."

"So . . . what?" I looked at Tabitha, then back at Frau Krautenstein. "She look like three offspring to you?"

James shook his head. "No, Eric, but based on your aura, she is your fifth."

I counted them off on my fingers. "Lisa. Nancy. Irene. Greta. The guy . . . what's his name . . . K-something." I put that finger back down. "But he's dead so he doesn't count. And Tabitha makes five."

"One of your get has formally petitioned the council and been acknowledged in her own right," Luc told me, "but that still leaves you with four. If we granted you access to Europe, then you'd be bound by our laws and we'd have to attempt to destroy you." He sighed and gestured to Tabitha. "And as lovely as your new bride may be, we'd be forced to end her, too." Frowning, he turned back to me. "You would simply reform at your *memento mori*, true, but we have no desire for your honeymoon to end in such despair, so instead we are banning you from—"

"What happens if your sire has released you?" Tabitha interrupted.

James grinned. "If your sire releases you, and the Council acknowledges your independent status, you don't count against your sire's total. You still can't make any offspring until you've been around for twenty-five years and petitioned the Council again, but for now, both you and Thumper there would be in the clear."

"Then I guess I need to petition the Council, because Eric let me go back in Void City before we got married."

"I did?"

"You said . . ." She closed her eyes as if it would help her remember. "'That's bullshit. I don't own you and I don't own any of your crap. If that's what you're worried about you can tell everybody I said you're free or released or whatever high society pricks call it.'" Her eyes opened, and they were sparkling.

"Like he would acknowledge such a statement—" the German began.

"Are you saying I'm not a man of my word, Fritz?"

"Whoa, Thumper." James grabbed my shoulder, pulling me aside. "Ix-nay on the itz-Fray. Aarika's good people. She helped the Allies in the war. She's a cold fish, but you can't—"

"Gotcha." I pulled away from him and stepped toward Aarika. "Sorry." I held out my hand. "My bad. That was uncalled for."

She took it, but slowly. "Apology accepted . . . Thumper."

I laughed, just a chuckle, but enough to show there were no hard feelings. "Fair enough. Now how do we get my bride out of my tally so that I'll be back in compliance?" I slid my hand around Tabitha's waist and kissed her on the cheek. She flushed with warmth and I didn't let go. "My wife wants to see the Eiffel Tower and I have a sire to kill."

"You want to kill Lisette?" James started. "Okay, there are a few other rules you ought to know about." Great. Did every immortal in Europe know who my sire was? I wondered briefly if they knew what color underwear I was wearing, decided they probably did, and rolled my eyes.

14

ERIC:
CHARLEY V IS ALIVE!

I don't know what I expected, but riding in the back of a van (minibus to you Frenchies out there) from the airport to some ruined old castle at Vincennes wasn't it. Tabitha was glued to the window, but I was preoccupied by a growing sense of discomfort. Beatrice noticed, but didn't know what to do about it. She took my hand, holding it to her breast, not in a cop-a-feel sort of way, but in the feel-my-heartbeat-and-remember-I'm-here-if you-need-to-feed sort of way.

"Are you hungry, Eric?" Her blue-gray eyes were clouded, her face framed by fiery red tresses that made her look a little too much like Marilyn for comfort. Her skin was hot in the way that the flesh of the living is to us dead folks. She wore a peasant top that clung to her form and drew my eye even though I was trying not to notice. Keeping eye contact, she guided my hand between her legs to the flesh above her femoral artery, my favorite feeding spot.

"Yes, but not now. We don't have room and I'm edgy."

"I noticed." She left my hand where it was and began gently but firmly pressing her hands against my chest, trying to keep my body temperature up. Vampires are always in a better mood when we're warm, and if I wouldn't feed, Bea wanted to give me the next best thing. If it had been Rachel doing that, Tabitha would have gotten all pissed off, but Beatrice isn't into me like Rachel is, so there's no threat. Plus there's the whole not being her little sister thing.

"I brought some snacks if you want to watch me eat something."

I caught movement out of the corner of my eye, a human with a package, and my claws came out, abrading the tender skin under my fingernails as they grew. Beatrice winced as my talons scratched a line across her thigh. I hadn't drawn blood, but it looked painful.

A familiar double burst of discomfort in my upper jaw announced the deployment of my fangs as well, all for nothing more than a guy carrying a long thin package late at night. I'd read him as a threat, a man with a rifle. I'd almost shouted "Gun!"

Seeing James again, being back in France, being off the magic for the first time in fifty years—it all had me feeling the way I felt when I came here as a young soldier. I was jumping at shadows.

My pulse raced briefly, and Bea felt it.

"Eric?"

"I don't know." My heartbeat stopped. "I keep expecting . . ."

"What?"

"I keep thinking somebody's going to take a shot at me."

"Who'd take a shot at you?" Tabitha called over her shoulder, not looking away from the window, nose still pressed against the glass. She didn't want to miss a thing.

"Nazis?" Bea asked the question.

I nodded with embarrassment.

"Nazis?" Tabitha snorted. "That's stupid. Why would he be worried about Nazis?"

One moment I was on my own side of the car, the next I was fang-deep in Tabitha's jugular and the van was on its side. Bea was pressed against my back, unleashing a torrent of calming phrases ("Shhh. It's okay. It's okay. It's okay. Calm down, baby. She didn't mean anything. Shhh. Calm down."). Tabitha held very still, whispering a steady stream of apologies ("I'm sorry. What'd I do? I'm sorry. I'm sorry.").

The night air blew in through rent metal where something (I'm guessing the uber vamp's wings) had thrust through and forcibly ejected the doors and bent the frame.

"Gott in Himmel!" It was Aarika's voice and the air shimmered as she spoke. The van vanished and our surroundings changed. The city was still there, but it looked different, younger. *"Der Amerikanische Vampir ist bescheuert!"*

"What the hell was that, Thumper?" James stood transformed, still human but wearing a suit of all black modern body armor (helmet included). He wielded a sword two-handed, and from my angle it looked like the blade curved a touch near the end. There was a 9mm in a holster on his thigh, but I was more concerned about the two custom stakes with combat knife-style grips that were holstered on his belt.

I released my grip on Tabitha's throat, withdrawing the fangs as gently as possible. "I'm sorry," I announced to everyone, but mostly to Tabitha. "I have blackouts and I—"

"Get off." Tabitha pushed me with vampire strength, and I landed on my feet.

"I'll see to the minibus," Luc said. I turned toward the sound. Luc vanished, but I got a glimpse of metal armor, like in an old King Arthur movie, as he faded.

Aarika hadn't drawn any weapons at all, but her stance spoke of combat readiness: arms up in what looked like a defensive guard's posture; feet apart, in line with her shoulders. Her eyes were blue and angry, but I found myself staring past her at the buildings. What had been an urban metropolis now looked like something out of the fourteenth or fifteenth century. All signs of modern roadwork were gone. The grass was green and the air smelled better than it did back home, even in the national park.

"Hunh." Blood dripped from my lips. Tabitha's blood. "You okay, Tabitha?" The wound at her throat closed quickly. Flesh knit itself back together, and in three or four seconds her skin was marred only by a light coating of blood.

"What the hell is wrong with you?" She touched her hand to her neck and pulled it away, eyeing the blood, oblivious to the change in our surroundings. "You could have fed from me if you wanted. I wouldn't have cared. I *like* it when you feed on me. You didn't have to jump me and wreck the damn van!"

"Coming back here is traumatic for him," Beatrice broke in. She stepped between me and Tabitha. "The embalming magics used on him have worn off. He has forbidden Rachel to dull his senses, to use any magic on him or in his presence, and he is facing the world sober for the first time in his unlife, Lady Tabitha. Add to this that the last time he was in France was as a soldier in World War II, when, yes, being shot at by Nazis, bombed by Nazis, and otherwise fearing for his life was a very real concern . . . and one may see why your comment incensed him."

"That's not an excuse." I stepped around her.

"Like hell it isn't." Tabitha stared at me, angrier than before, cheeks flushed and eyes dimly lit with red. "Why didn't you tell me what you were going through?"

"Because it's stupid." I mumbled the words. "That was more than half a century ago, and anyway, bullets can't even hurt me anymore. There aren't any Nazis hiding in the bushes. I know that. It's dumb, but I still feel like they're there, waiting to get a shot off."

"Why did you confide in her, but not me?" Tabitha frowned, transitioning from hurt to sad. "I don't understand. We're married. I'm here for you. I—"

"I didn't tell her any of that stuff." I pointed at Beatrice. "She figured the war stuff out when we were getting off the plane, but—"

Tabitha and I both stared questioningly at Bea.

"I know you think Rachel is the most knowledgeable thrall you have, Eric, but I was Lady Gabriella's for quite a long time, and if there is one thing a high society thrall has to learn, it's how to find out every little thing about her master. If you know what's bothering them, what they want, what they're thinking about, you can be a better thrall and they treat you well."

"So you spied on him?" Tabitha asked.

"No, Lady Bathory," Beatrice said, using the most formal title for a female Vlad. "Well, maybe, but for me it's doing my job. Some of the information came from Magbidion when he got back from the Hilton. I wheedled a little more from Talbot when he came to make sure we were all packed up, and the rest I got by paying attention to Eric and asking questions. How else am I supposed to do my job?"

"Still—" Tabitha began.

Luc reappeared, and I nearly went for him out of instinct. His armor was gone, if it had ever really been there, and he was wearing the suit and sunglasses again sans earpiece. "I've taken care of the minibus. No one saw anything. It was late, and Aarika acted quickly."

"He should be deported." Aarika jabbed her finger in my direction. "He is too dangerous. He's an old soldier and I respect him, but let him return at another time, with his *memento mori*. Perhaps then he will be able to control himself."

"Let's get his wife's petition handled first," James said. He lowered his sword. "He can stay magic-side until that's handled and then we can let the Council rule on the issue of whether he can stay or not."

"Because he's your wartime chum?" Aarika asked. "For that reason we should ignore his control issues? He should be muzzled, not kept magic-side. He should be staked. It won't kill him."

"He will remain magic-side until the Council has ruled," Luc snapped. "And that"—he gave a pointed look, meeting the gaze of both other immortals, Aarika first, then James—"is final. Being kept here is restraint enough, I should think."

"Fine." She folded her hands over her chest. "I am not unreasonable. We are not in my country, after all. If the Treaty of Secrets is broken, it will fall at the feet of the Free French, not on Germany's head."

"Magic-side." I looked around. The surroundings were still vaguely familiar, similar to where we had been, but with a few hundred years of urban development erased. "Where the hell are we?"

"A Vale of Scrythax," James spoke first, sword still at the ready.

"That's not how the Veil of Scrythax works back home."

"V-A-L-E," James said, "not V-E-I-L." He had his hand over the lower portion of his face, mimicking a veil. "It's a pocket dimension. Think of it as being two quick steps to the left of the mundane world. We use the Vales instead of playing with people's memories. It works much better to keep the supernatural out of sight in the first place, and it keeps the European Mage Guild from getting the kind of stranglehold on the immortals that the American version has on the vampires."

"So why doesn't the U.S. use your kind of Vale?"

"We have a much bigger piece of Scrythax."

"Piece?" Tabitha asked. "As in body part?"

Aarika snorted. "Aren't you a little squeamish for a vampire?"

"Aren't you a little short for a storm trooper?" Tabitha fired back. *Score!* I laughed. Aarika frowned.

"I have no patience for the spurious accusations," Aarika began. "I am not a Nazi. I fought the Nazis. I—"

"She was making a *Star Wars* joke, Jerry." I flipped Aarika the bird. "Calm the fuck down and try to keep up with the times."

James opened his hands, and the sword dissipated into a cloud of silvery-blue effervescence that sank into his body. Interposing himself between Aarika and me, he held up his open palms. "Let's all stay friendly. Okay?"

Aarika considered looking to Luc for support—I could see it in her eyes—but I respected her for not taking it there. She backed down a little and so did I. God help me, but I was starting to like her, despite myself.

"Scrythax was a very powerful demon," she began, "the most powerful of the Infernatti. We're talking pose-as-a-deity powerful. In the Dark Ages, when the True Immortals and the other magic-siders went to war with each other, before the Treaty of Secrets, Scrythax stepped in on the side of humanity. Both sides united against him and he was torn apart for his trouble. In a weird way, though, he got what he wanted. United by a common foe, the magic-siders agreed that humanity and the supernatural needed to be segregated and that for the supernatural to endure, limits needed to be put in place on all sorts of things: vampire population growth, hunting practices of the therianthropes . . ."

"Over time," Luc picked up, "the various mystical properties of Scrythax's remains were discovered and he was parceled out."

"And which part of him alters the memories of humans in Void City, or dare I ask?"

"His skin," Aarika said. "Vampires stole," she emphasized *stole* like she was accusing me of doing it, "portions of his skin when the renegades who believed in less restrictive population controls fled to the Americas."

"Why would his skin do that?" Tabitha asked.

"Scrythax loved humans," Luc explained. "But his visage was terrible to look upon and his form was so . . . primal . . . that he could not alter his shape. Instead, he enchanted his skin to make mortals see him as something other than he was. He didn't much care what, just so long as they didn't run in fear. In the hands of the right mage, Lord Phillip of Void City for example, a piece of his skin can be used to make mortals see something other than what is and cloud their memory even of that."

"I wonder what his little toe does," I muttered. "So what piece do you guys have?"

"His h—" James began to answer me, but Aarika cut him off.

"A substantial one. Those the Council trusts can create a small pocket dimension which represents their present location as Scrythax remembers it. In this fashion, our differences may be settled away from mundane eyes and powers which might otherwise draw attention to our community may be exercised—"

"Without scaring the norms," Tabitha butted in. "So you guys have his head then, right . . . or an eye maybe?"

"I wish we had one of his eyes." Luc spoke up. "Either one is said to hold remarkable powers. There are stories of Scrythax restoring the dead with one eye while peering forward into the future with the other to ensure the world was a better place with the newly resurrected returned to it."

"I wouldn't want to be around if he decided the world was better off without me," Tabitha chimed in.

"No." James shook his head in vigorous agreement. "You wouldn't." One of the rules I was going to tell you about. In Europe, we don't allow supernatural combat in the mundane world. If you're a member of the community, you open a Vale of Scrythax and settle it there. Never to the death or destruction, either. Only the Council can grant permission for one magic-sider to kill another. Breaking that law is an offense punishable by destruction or permanent banishment into a Vale of Scrythax. You're lucky that you had your freak-out before I told you about it."

"Yeah, thanks for . . ." As I spoke, my heart beat . . . the first time I could remember that happening without Rachel around since I'd become a vampire. Then, the scenery shifted like air over gasoline or hot asphalt. Buildings rose up around us, winking into view to match the place we'd just left in the real world, right down to the wrecked mini-bus.

Luc glanced about, black hair falling down over his sunglasses. "*Alors!* Aarika?"

"We're still in the Vale of Scrythax, Luc. I don't understand. It should still appear as it did the last time Scrythax saw it."

My heart beat again, once, twice, and the magnitude of the effect expanded. When it stopped, the change stabilized.

"Hey, guys?" I asked. "The eye of Scrythax, the one that could raise the dead? What would it look like?"

"No one knows," James answered as Luc and Aarika went through motions very similar to what Magbidion does when he's looking at things through his magic. I guess they were gauging their surroundings. If what I suspected was correct, however, they'd have had more luck studying my chest. "Some pieces of his body crystallized into beautiful gems, others grew dull and black, like a rock or a piece of coal, and still others maintained their gruesome forms, like desiccated remains. Why?"

"No reason."

"We should get to the Council quickly," Aarika told Luc.

"This way." Luc gestured in the rough direction in which I'd seen the castle. "We aren't far. Let's press on magic-side. Aarika and I can maintain the Vale for all of us as we move."

Tabitha did what she always does—forgave me too much, too fast—and we set out along the road, my right hand in her left and my left hand in Bea's right, like I was a little kid or a sick old man who needed looking after. When we turned at the corner, the area that had been out of my line of sight before we transitioned to the Vale was still old-school.

Of course it is, I thought, *because I didn't see it in the real world and I've got an Eye of Scrythax, also known as the Stone of Aeternum, in my fucking chest, turning me into the mystic equivalent of those guys from Google Maps.*

Updates.

Jeez.

"I wanted to show you this anyway." James dropped back to walk with us while Aarika and Luc led the way. "We'll have to hurry to make sure we get there before you have to sleep, but the approach to the Château de Vincennes looks much better magic-side."

"I'm sure it does." I walked on, looking down at the ground in front of me. *And if you want it to stay that way, I suggest we leave by the same route.* Normal honeymoon? Yeah. Not so much.

15

RACHEL:

PARIS OR BUST

When you're young, hot, and a witch (particularly a tantric witch) you can soar through airport security—no broom required. Customs agents find it hard to do anything but pass you through when they're feeling unexplained pulses of sexual pleasure. The succubus who taught me magic calls it Blissing. "Any demon can punch their way through security," she used to say, "walk through all horns, scales, and hellfire, but it takes skill to ensure that when the hosts say serving you has been their pleasure, they're making a gross understatement."

Unlike my old teacher, I don't see the elegance of making someone cream their pants or experience an uncontrollable erection, but it sure is fun.

I walked out of Charles de Gaulle International Airport Terminal 2 with a garment bag over my shoulder and a small rolling suitcase trailing behind me. Springtime in Paris, and all I could see was pavement. I'd noticed from the air that the sections of Terminal 2 are shaped like eyes, with a road and TGV line where the eyelids would meet. The space where the iris would be is covered with ground-level parking, and the terminals make the eyelashes. I leaned back against a rounded section of the exterior wall, looking right toward the rest of the terminal. Even the roofline had little puffy parts that looked like eyes.

Businessmen and -women went on their boring little ways, hailing taxis and yammering away on cell phones, which reminded me to swap the SIM card in mine so it would work on the network here. I powered the phone back on, started downloading my messages, and began reading through them while I waited for the vampire Winter'd arranged for me to meet. The screen went black without warning and I stabbed the power angrily.

"Work, stupid fucking phone!" I looked up to see if there was a phone kiosk, thinking maybe the battery had gone bad, when I noticed the airport, the planes, the parking lots, the roads, the TGV line . . . everything . . . was gone. My surroundings had been drastically altered, going from *nouveau* French to rural farm, the bright lights of the city replaced by a panoramic starscape. I was leaning against a waist-high bit of crumbling stone wall.

"Oh, great! Somebody roofied me." It probably wasn't Kansas, but the surrounding area definitely looked like farmland. It wasn't modern farmland, with tractors and computerized irrigation, either. I couldn't put my finger on why, maybe it was the smell of French "fertilizer" or the too-clean country air, but the whole place seemed positively medieval, especially in the dark. "I'm probably being assfucked by some freako security kink and I'm not even getting any damn energy out of it."

A woman's laughter pierced the silence. In the starlight, I could see that her hair had been dyed candy apple red streaked with cotton candy pink and cut in a stylish pixie-cut with long bangs hanging down in a ragged edge over her left eye. Physically, she couldn't have been older than early twenties, but she had the washed-out irises of a vampire and hadn't bothered to hide them with contacts. Eyes once brown were now a faded gold. She wore blue lipstick and a mismatched ensemble of outerwear that meshed together perfectly. She'd abandoned modern trends, but she hadn't kept with the old styles either. Instead, she'd created a style of her own and it suited her.

"It's a cliché," she said as she extended needle-sharp fangs that appeared far more delicate than Eric's, "but you look good enough to eat."

"I am."

"I'll bet." Watching her move was hypnotic, each gesture out of time with her surroundings, too slow, then too fast. One instant she'd be looking straight at me, the next straight up at the sky, the next to the right or bent over, all with no intervening movements I could detect. In an eyeblink she was behind me and in another she was still walking toward me, until I felt dizzy as if she was approaching me from both directions at once.

Hands rested on my shoulders, caressed my cheeks . . . She was still walking toward me, but the touches were hers. Brief phantom whispers of touch cupped my breasts, curved along my pelvis, my lips.

"I can see why Eric finds you so tempting," she said when she finally reached me. Her hands were clasped before her, but they were in my hair, too, running through it.

"Your speed is impressive."

"May I taste you?" Cold breath carried the words into my ears. The scent of old blood mingled with wine in my nostrils.

"A little," I said.

Her bite was slow and lingering, the fangs pushing against my skin and sliding through painlessly. She went for the throat like most vampires do, but her tongue rasped against my neck, warm with my own heat, the suction of her mouth gentle yet insistent. I touched her chakras with my energy and gave her taste. I expected an increase in the urgency of her feeding, but it didn't come. She kissed me then and suddenly, inexplicably, my mind put a name to her face. She was Irene, Eric's Irene, the Irene of El Segundo. If I hadn't known before why Eric once loved her, I knew then. Her kiss was wild and unrestrained. Her fangs nicked me, but I didn't care. I'm not into girls really, but it was nice.

"You taste like cinnamon," she said. Her lips were slick with red, and I recognized the color. There's a peculiar thrill when you see your own blood on someone else's lips, and Irene knew it.

"I could drink you all myself." She stretched absently. The visual, like a movie with too many cuts made in it to repair the film, hurt my eyes.

"Then there wouldn't be anything left for later."

Her feral grin faded. "Just because you like candy doesn't mean you should always save a piece for later." She was behind me. "There *is* a certain joy in gobbling down the box of chocolates all in one go, to sit, greedy and full"—her hands, now warm, slid along my stomach—"and sick, with nothing but the memory to sustain you and the wrappers with which to play."

"Is that what humans are to you?"

She nodded. "When I was alive they had these little wax bottles, tiny things, with flavored liquid inside. You could pop the whole thing in your mouth." She mimed tossing a bottle into her mouth and chewing it up. "Or you could just bite the top off and," she mimed that too, biting the top off of an imaginary bottle and spitting it on the ground. A red trail of blood hit the ground. "Spit it out. That's all humans are: funny little blood containers. You walk and talk. You're fun to hold, fun to play with, but you're so close to fungible that one dead human hardly matters. There are billions more."

"Yeah, okay. You're all spooky or whatever." I opened myself to the magic and really looked at my surroundings. Was this an illusion? Glowing dots of demonic magic slowly separated themselves from the background. Pinpricks of power, combined and shifted, creating a bubble of reality? No. I studied the hue of the magic. At first it appeared red, but if I caught it at the right angle, a blue sheen came through. Memory? If Magbidion hadn't just worked with me on how memory magic worked, it might have been too subtle for me to notice. I opened *Ajna*, the chakra that controls magic, my third eye, and my view of the magic came into better focus.

"Where the hell are we?" Ice formed in my belly. "We're not in one of the hells, are we?" My voice cracked on the second sentence. I suppressed a shiver. This was Infernatti magic. Lady Scrytha! I knelt down, touching the field. Hot and cold at the same time. Very powerful. Extremely old. "No. Not a hell." I let out a long breath without realizing I'd been holding it.

"You're cute when you're freaking out. We need to get you some bad acid." Irene waggled her eyebrows, but the gesture was odd. "I'd like to watch that."

Thin lines of power thrummed beneath the palm of her right hand. It matched the power signature of the field around us, as recognizable as the brushstrokes of a master painter.

"You've taken an oath."

Irene followed my gaze and rubbed her palm self-consciously. "You can see that?"

"Who are you working for?"

"Oh, chill out, would you?" Her eyes were closed, then open again. Cords of magic unraveled, twisting and flailing as they receded back through her palm like one of those retractable leashes. "Every supernatural citizen in Europe has taken *that* oath. You can't use Vales of Scrythax without joining the Treaty of Secrets."

Old France faded and new modern wonderful France returned, the whole airport and all the beautiful city lights, along with my cell phone's power. Back in the real world, Irene forced herself to move at normal speed. Waves of irritation radiated from her. We took an escalator down to a well-lit open parking level in the iris framed by Terminals 2A and 2B.

"Tell me about this treaty."

"No. You tell me what we're going to be doing to Eric to keep him in Paris for seven days and why it's so important to Winter." A thin sheen of blood sweat began to form on her skin, and she jumped like another bad movie cut and was clean again. "You noticed?"

I nodded.

"I was tripping on X when Eric turned me." She paused, a bittersweet smile on her face. "The way I feel isn't the way I felt then. It isn't the same kind of trip, but in a way it's like I never came all the way down."

"You still remember what it was like?"

"Yes. Good times."

"Then you may like what I have in mind for Eric." I explained the details and Irene broke down into fits of hysterical laughter. She ran the plan back to make sure she'd understood and I assured her that she did.

"That's perfect." Her breath came in unusual spurts, not quite the way a human catches her breath. Vampires don't need to breathe, so I guessed she was actually trying to talk around the convulsions of laughter. Getting the air in to get the words out was the issue. "Winter used up a favor to get me to do that? Honey, I'd do that to Eric as a wedding present!"

Another round of laughter took her as we neared a yellow sports car. She gestured for me to get in. "Eric gave it to me back when we first got together. It's an Alpine A110. Roger made him buy it because he wanted Eric to get used to trading in cars."

"It's nice."

She shrugged. "I'm used to it. Now you have to tell me, before we get all this started. How did Eric finally get Marilyn to marry him? How tacky do they look together? She's what, eighty-something now?"

I climbed into the car which sped out of the parking space even as I buckled my seat belt. "Yeah, about Marilyn . . ."

◆ 16 ◆

ERIC:
DÉJÀ VU

"I would never have seen this if I hadn't become your thrall." Beatrice kissed me on the cheek. "This kind of thing is exactly why I chose you over Gabriella." She kissed me again. "I just—"

"Yeah, all right." I held up my hand, blocking the next outpouring of affection and gratitude. A quickly masked smile flickered across Tabitha's lips. She might be less jealous of Bea than any of my other thralls, but she pays attention to stuff like kissing. Still, I guess this counted as a special occasion.

We stood before a castle. A fortress. We stood within the walls of history.

"The *donjon* is beautiful!" Beatrice pointed at a stone keep that towered above the courtyard a good hundred and fifty feet or more. I wondered if the stone was naturally that pale or if it had been whitewashed. From where I stood the *donjon* seemed to consist of two circular towers connected by a wall the same length as if one of the towers were unrolled, but that wasn't the whole of it. A hint of another tower peeked over the rear, and the whole structure was surrounded by a wide wall, a moat, and other medieval castle-y shit.

"Dungeon?" Tabitha looked stricken. "I thought dungeons were underground."

"It's French for 'keep.'"

"We have no time for you to see sights." Aarika was getting on my damn nerves. "You are expected before the Council."

"In a minute."

The keep was set off center into the four walls protecting the courtyard, yet it was also held apart, separated from the courtyard by the same moat that surrounded the structure, a single bridge from the interior courtyard granting access. Smallish buildings were clustered around the base of the keep. Nine stone towers lined the walls and I only saw two entrances into the courtyard. We'd come in from the south and had a good view of a palace within the enclosure and a large chapel beyond it.

Bea was like a schoolgirl on a field trip overseas. She and Tabitha ran hand in hand about the enclosure, studying the façades, the gargoyles, the crenellations, all that architectural ostentatious crap. Luc put a hand on my shoulder and I shook free of him.

"Fuck off a second." Behind me, I heard James attempting to appease the other two immortals as I walked toward the chapel.

It was huge, like one of those gigantic Catholic churches back home. Children played tag atop my grave as I drew closer to the western façade. Windows ran along the sides of the chapel, broken up by little flat-sided pillars. I hadn't recognized anything else, but that chapel . . . it looked . . . so familiar. I stopped in front of it to examine the steps, the archway, and the patterned window over the archway, a *rosace.* Aarika pulled free of the other two immortals, crossed the courtyard, and spun me around to face her.

"You are wasting our time, vampire."

I turned into a revenant, my body going cold as the details washed out of everything but the people around me, rendering the world in impression very much like watercolor or . . .

"Stained glass." My memory works better in my spirit form. I'm not using my physical brain to think, and whatever's wrong with my underwhelming powers of recall is tied to the meat body. "It happened here."

In Void City there is an apartment building for vampires called the Highland Towers. Only the richest and most powerful bloodsuckers in the city can live there. I have some suites there I don't use, largely because the whole thing belongs to Lord Phillip. Among his possessions there, he has a magic stained-glass window, one of his many *objets d'art.* The story it tells is a piece of my family history.

It goes like this:

Once upon a time there was a dumbass among dumbasses, my great-great-great-great-great-grandfather or something like that. Dumbass the First was a moron from way back. He and the other heroic morons of his age were members of some stupid secret order that had nothing better to do than hunt supernatural what's-its . . . or that's what I assume they did. I know for sure that they wanted one particular vampire bad, and I mean write-her-name-on-a-bullet bad. They wanted this one vamp so bad they named their order after her. She called herself Lisette, *le Coeur-Démone*, the Demon Heart, so they called themselves *le Coeur de la Demone*, the Heart of the Demon.

So as the story goes, Dumbass and his homeys hunted Lisette all over the damn place and when they finally caught her, they wished they hadn't. I don't know exactly what happened, but that motion-picture-magic window of Phil's is all about their big showdown, really epic stuff.

Under the cover of darkness, a lone knight rides in on an injured steed and leaves his horse dying on the steps up to the chapel. He hesitates, tears off his helmet, and cowers before an immense cross above the door. Whoever did the stained glass got that part a little wrong. Here on the real church there was no cross, but the *rosace* behind the cross was unmistakably, though crudely, rendered on the stained glass.

Then again, maybe the cross depicted on the stained glass was intentionally symbolic, representing the power of God or holiness. Either way, the knight, baring small fangs to show that he'd become a vampire, gathers his courage and charges into the church.

Time passes, a stylized sun rises over the church, and the white clouds transform into a churning horde of black bats, blocking out the sun. A female vampire dressed in medieval finery flies into the image from the left-hand side. Thirty vampires on horseback follow her on the ground. She lands before the steps of the great stone church and French writing flies past on the scroll. I had Beatrice translate it for me once, but I don't remember exactly what it says . . . typical nyah-nyah-you're-one-of-us-now vampire crap. Periodically the stained-glass figure's lips part and she seems to laugh. *Mwahaha.*

A priest in brown robes comes out of the church. He holds a golden cross before him in both hands. They exchange words, your basic "depart now, foul beast"/"eat me, padre," bad guy/good guy exchange. The padre manages to piss her off and she transforms into an uber vamp similar to what I turn into, but with breasts (mercifully, the window leaves out the pit hair).

The vampire knight emerges from the church, snatches the cross away from the priest and pushes him back inside. Flames engulf the knight's gauntlets around the base of the large crucifix. The knight walks toward the uber vamp, stops at the center of the steps, and falls to his knees. His head slowly lifts up to the heavens and he prays to God to intercede. When that doesn't work, he recites the Lord's Prayer in Latin.

All of the vampires cast their eyes upward, and gold-lettered text of the prayer scrolls by. The knight holds up his cross defiantly. That much I had to give him. He had stones. Two angels with fiery swords part the horde of bats overhead. All of the vampires, the knight included, are bathed in the light of the sun. Wisps of gray smoke drift up off Lisette, but the thirty vampires with her explode, their horses with them. Lisette gives the knight some haughty Wicked Witch of the West garbage about hunting him down, hunting down his whole family, and then she exits stage-left in a huff.

The knight collapses in the sun but it doesn't burn him. His skin becomes less pale and he sits up, touching his chest, his teeth. He's alive again. More golden text flows by and it tells him that as long as his family remains faithful, the curse of vampirism will be spared them until the seventh generation and then, if the seventh generation is faithful, the curse will vanish completely. I'm lucky number seven, by the way. Yeah. Oops!

The priest comes back out of the church, looks at the knight, and falls to his knees in prayer, then everything resets to an image of the knight opposing the uber vamp and her posse. The knight's cross is gone and he holds a sword in its place, but that's just poetic license.

I walked up the steps and stood where Dumbass the First had stood, then looked across the enclosure at the keep. Resuming my vampiric form gave me a whole-body case of pins and needles, and I wondered if the immortals had their magic tree house in place way back then and if they had watched while my ancestor faced off with an Emperor-level vampire.

Anger hit me hard, and I went uber vamp so fast the sudden change in height made me nauseous, but at least I didn't black out.

"Motherfuckers probably sat there and did nothing while my whole family got cursed. Without the damn curse, I'd have died like I was supposed to. Sure, I might have risen as a revenant and killed Roger, but Marilyn—Marilyn might have been able to lead a normal life. She might have— She . . ." A cry of wordless rage ripped free of my throat and I took flight straight at the *donjon*. I didn't even have to ask where they were, because High Society freaks like these guys are always going to be at the very top.

"Eric?" Tabitha's question was just my name. Clueless. It's not her fault I didn't tell her about any of the Courtney family crap, but it left her with no way to come close to understanding why I was so angry. I don't care about what happened to the other Courtneys in the family line. I don't even feel bad for JPC. Even if Marilyn and I *had* wound up doing some lame Patrick Swayze/Demi Moore romancing like in *Ghost*, without the curse Marilyn wouldn't have died in some damn strip club. I'd have saved her from Roger and . . .

Bea was piecing it all together as my wing beats pulled me over the moat, and I heard her voice echoing my thoughts from minutes before: "It happened here." Bypassing the first five levels of the keep, I landed on the terrace. The prickle of a ward rushed over me, and I felt myself wincing in expectation. But nothing happened. Instead, I felt the ward part, accepting me, and words I'd heard before in a voice I recognized but couldn't place echoed in my brain: "You are expected."

17

ERIC:

FREEZE-DRIED DEMON

I was wrong, of course. There was no one on the terrace and the ceilings inside were so low that I had to move hunched over like a gorilla to make it through them as the uber vamp. On the fifth floor, a central pillar met the bones of the place and I realized that the king would never have walked up all those darn steps—servants would have had to do that. Winding my way down through the stone spiral stairs, I shifted from uber vamp mode to my normal height. The anger was still there, and I was spoiling for a fight, but the six-foot-or-so ceilings that cramped the uber vamp left my human form a couple inches of headspace.

Cold undecorated stone kept me company on the trip down. Floor-to-ceiling oak paneling greeted me when I got to what I thought was the second floor. Historians all over France cried in their sleep as I stomped angrily through a perfectly preserved royal bedchamber still decorated the way it was when Charles V lived at Vincennes. A fleur-de-lis done in gold on blue decorated each vault of the ceiling. Holy manuscripts were displayed in boxes in front of one of the windows. It was all very ornate and kingly, but what caught my attention was the floor.

"Nice tile."

Luc was waiting for me by the fireplace. Flames shifted within, changing from one static view of fire to another like a slide show of fire that emitted real warmth. "Everyone is waiting for you in the first-floor meeting hall."

"That's the first impressionist fire I've seen in 3-D. How artsy."

"Think of it as the memory of flames."

"Weird."

I crossed to one of the turrets and found the king's coffers. "No guards?" I reached out and touched a silver coin. It felt real, and I rolled it over in my hands.

"Most of this exists in a Vale of Scrythax," Luc explained, "as the demon would have remembered it; you can't permanently damage anything."

I bent the coin in half and dropped it back down.

Luc laughed. "Now turn away and look back. It won't be bent anymore."

He was wrong and I knew why. If my theory about the Stone of Aeternum being one of Scrythax's eyes was correct, I could have wrecked the whole damn historic fossil with a quick trip back into the real world. Let the Eye of Scrythax get a gander at the keep in modern-day France and these *Highlander* rejects would lose their little playhouse (or at least the grand historic version of it) but quick.

I picked the coin back up and tossed it to him.

"You have an unusually strong will. But you may trust me. If we were to leave and return, the coin would revert to its natural shape."

"Uh-huh."

"Think what you will. This way." He gestured. I followed, and we left the king's chambers and went down more stairs to a meeting hall.

It was a massive room with more vaulted ceilings and fancy detail work. Charles V would have been astonished to see their renovations. This section of the castle held mostly modern furniture and equipment.

They'd tried to match the stylistic sensibility of the historic site, but the laptops laid out on the U-shaped meeting table were a dead giveaway. Thirteen people I assumed were immortals lined the expansive room, not counting James, Luc, and Aarika. From their lack of reactions, it was as though I'd just barged in on a meeting of the Rotary Club at a garden variety municipal building, not the French Immortal equivalent of the Hall of Justice. I'd expected them to all look like Adrian Paul or Christopher Lambert, but they came in different shapes, sizes, apparent physical ages, nationalities, and genders, ranging from Aarika, who looked young and fit, to a man so old and fat I expected him to keel over at any second from a massive coronary.

At the center of the room, on a pedestal nestled within the curve of the meeting table, was the severed head of a demon unlike any I ever had the displeasure to meet. Curved asymmetrical horns layered the sides of its skull and it rested on them, the arrangement of horns holding it upright atop the stone. In places the skin had flaked away or had been removed, but in the spots where it was intact, it was more scale than flesh and had a metallic sheen to it as if the being to which it belonged were a combination of animal and mineral. Two rows of jagged fangs the size of varying calibers of ammo cartridges filled its mouth, though some had been torn away by force, leaving subtle cracks in the jaw. Beatrice and Tabitha stood on the far side of the table. The whole scene was lit by a dim golden glow emitted by portions of the ghoulish centerpiece. That side of the head had crystallized irregularly, revealing the cranial cavity, from which the semitranslucent light seemed to pour.

You didn't have to be a mage to feel power, electrical, spiritual, or otherwise, flowing around the room, from the immortals, the place, and especially from the head.

"His brain glows?"

As I came closer, I made out more details. Shrunken eyelids were closed, concealing the empty sockets beneath. Above the snarling mouth, three slit nostrils gaped, a tear in the central nostril linking it with the right. The head was twice the size of a man's and trailed off at the neck, revealing withered cords of muscle that would have seemed more at home in a robot than in a living thing.

"Guy looks like he was designed by H. R. Giger . . ."

And then it moved. Nostrils flared, gaping even wider, and the rush of air created by its sudden inhalation sent dust bunnies fleeing out from under its jaw. Its eyelids slowly opened with the sound of creaking leather to reveal empty sockets partially illuminated by the golden light pulsing within its ancient noggin.

My heart beat once and my vision shifted. Instead of feeling the energy moving through the room, I saw it. Ghostly streams of spiritual essence filled the room in a spiderweb of spirit and extended out through the doors. It flowed through the immortals, linking some of them, avoiding others. There was a separate strand tied to me, a deep line that ran from my chest to the head in the center of the room. As the immortals went into action, I watched cascades of spirit rise up from within them, manifesting into arms and armor. I realized that they weren't re-creating the items like I do when I transform. Instead, they had stored them, converted them purposefully to energy, and were bringing them back.

The demonic lips of the thing parted and a withered purple tongue with forked ends that had long since dried together rasped along the portion of the lips that were intact.

It spoke, and I recognized the voice. The same ghostly voice had spoken to me when the wards parted for me, both here in France and back in the States during the whole "let's trap Eric's soul in a marble" affair when it had let me through the wards at the Highland Towers.

"Does my nose deceive me," Scrythax asked, "or do I smell a Courtney?"

II

* ◆ *

IF ERIC IS IN PARIS,
THEN LISETTE IS IN . . .

AS TOLD BY GRETA AND TALBOT

18

GRETA:
DADDY'S GIRL

A walking dead man crossed the road at the corner of Fourteenth Street and Vicar Avenue. Shifting position on the roof of the old Greymont Hotel, I held a brass spyglass up to my eye so I could watch the expression on his face. His body looked young, but he wore it like an old man. It revealed him to be a vampire even before he was close enough for the death smell to give him away. Fresh from the kill, blood ran hot through his veins. High on life, but not for long.

If my dad were home I wouldn't have been able to do this, not actually make the kill. Daddy doesn't hunt vampires. He only likes to end them when they get in his way. Dad doesn't like it when I hunt them, either, but he went to Paris without me. He should have known I'd get bored. He even took Mom and Auntie Beatrice with him, but I wasn't mad.

My prey walked on, eyes on the open lot in which he'd parked. His car was safely stowed in the parking deck at the Pollux next to two others I'd stolen from him. Not seeing it, he panicked. I would have, too, in his place. Three nights running he had gone out, killed, and come back to find his car missing. This was night number three. He pulled out his cell phone and I took careful aim. Even with vampire strength, a .357 Magnum has a noticeable kick. Guns are wonderful. Bullets won't kill any vampire more powerful than a Drone, but they sound loud as hell to our preternaturally sensitive ears. That's why I was wearing earplugs.

Careful to squeeze the trigger, not pull it, I opened fire. My first shot trashed the tiny new Nokia; the second hit him in the left eye. I don't see with my eyes anymore, 'cause vampirism takes vision to a whole new level of mystic cool, but I'd watched this idiot for three nights and it was clear that he still felt human inside. He was still using his physical brain, the meat brain, and the meat body. That's why he walked like an old man. Only Daddy pulls that off without looking stupid. This guy was just some schmuck who couldn't comprehend what he had become.

Sliding the gun into my thigh holster, I leapt from my perch, propelling myself into range, and felt his power. Mom says that vampires show up like little holograms hovering in the air when she sees them, but for me, it's like a little dossier file opens in my head, complete with a short bio and a snapshot. His name was David. He'd spent the last hundred years as a vampire. He'd kept up with the times through about the seventies. He still listened to disco. I was unimpressed. David was about as strong as me. We were both Vlads, but he was outclassed. I've never met a vampire who can do the things I can do. Not even Daddy.

It's like some mystic law that Vlads and Masters can sense each other, but not me. Nobody senses me unless I want them to. When Dad is around I let people sense me. But when I'm hunting, I keep quiet, tightly drawn into my own head. They assume that I'm a Soldier or a Drone, because they don't get that telltale head warning. Sucks to be them.

I hit the asphalt, the impact forcing me down on one knee. He spotted me. Claws sprouted from his fingertips, dark little thorns of bone and blood. Mine are prettier, long sharp fingernails that gleam in the night. The black nail polish goes all the way down to the base. Hard to put it on that way, but half-done claws look trashy.

"Come to Daddy, little girl." He laughed, a low throaty challenge meant to make him seem menacing. My eyes glowed crimson, lit from within. Only Dad can call me that. It made me wish that I could've shot him with *El Alma Perdida*, Daddy's magic gun, but he'd taken it with him. The ghost inside the revolver doesn't like me anyway. I can't see him, but I can tell he thinks I'm weak . . . just like this vampire, David.

Underestimation is a powerful tool. I use it well. The more powerful the vamp, the harder they are to kill. Hunting Drones is no fun at all. Soldiers are okay if they've been around awhile, and Masters can be challenging if they're smart, but nothing beats going after a Vlad. It takes a hunter trial and error to find that one special way to send one of us to our final death, unless that hunter is me. All I have to do is read a Vlad on three successive nights and their special weakness pops into my brain like Christmas morning. It works on everyone, except Daddy.

This was the third night for David, here, and I now knew that he could only be killed by decapitation followed by submersion in running water until his body turned to ash and floated away. I didn't even need the sack I'd left on the rooftop or the flamethrower that I had stashed in the guard shack. Telly, the parking garage guard, was a smart boy. He didn't speak much English, but he spoke self-preservation like a native. I did what I wanted there and Telly never complained or said a word. He just smiled and nodded like a good human should. He had a cute butt, too. I wondered why he never asked me out.

I paid too much attention to Telly and David almost laid a claw on me. He was a better fighter than I expected, but far too slow, and he let my boobs distract him. I always dress to inspire when I'm hunting. Braless in a cut-off white T-shirt that's a size too small, I was deadly to the best of men that night. A pair of form-fitting black jeans revealed the top of my pelvic bone from the front and a flash of my thong from behind. I planted my combat boot upside David's head, sending him up and over the guard shack. Telly ran out of the booth and across the street. Part of me hoped he'd be back tomorrow. I'd been thinking of learning Spanish just so I could carry on a conversation with him while I was waiting for a mark.

David caught the edge of the shack with his fingertips, pulling himself gracefully onto the roof.

"Never cede the high ground, little girl," he told me.

Even blind in one eye and half-deaf, he was cocky.

I drew the Magnum and shot him in the crotch. As he fell off the guard shack, I fired again, splattering the back of his left knee. It wouldn't hurt long, but I didn't need long. He lay on his back screaming; I took the opening. My gun clattered to the ground. Before he could stand I was on him.

Straddling David's waist, I buried my fangs in his throat, tore out a hunk, and spat it onto the asphalt. Secondhand blood crossed my lips and it felt like I was stealing his kill, robbing him of the life he had taken tonight. Just like fruit, blood tastes sweeter when it's stolen. He struggled, so I put my thumb into his other eye. He shrieked like a baby when it popped, the wetness running out of the socket and covering my hand. It's good for the skin.

"Let me go and I'll do anything you want," he begged. Real men never beg. His daddy should have taught him that.

Blood ran down my chin when I let go of him. "I would," I lied, "but you did a no-no. You said 'Come to Daddy,' but you're not my daddy." I smiled sweetly, let my fangs retract, my eyeglow fade. I leaned in as if I might kiss him. "My daddy would crush you like a motherfucking insect!" Eyes aglow, fangs out, I slammed my forehead into his. Then I announced myself.

It's something vampires can do, a demonstration of power that only other vamps can feel. They see your power, your age, and in David's case, he cowered, a typical man, when he felt me. "You still use your meat brain, you useless ass. You still think like a human! You're a disgrace!" Slicing through his shirt with my foreclaw, I cut all the way through the flesh below, pulling it back, exposing the sternum and pectoral muscles beneath. There's a sweet spot in the sternum. If you hit it just right, you can crack it in half with one smooth motion. In humans, the good blood is in the veins, but vamps store most of the blood in their hearts. I don't know how it all fits in there, but it does. I think they do it with magic, the same way they make microwave popcorn.

Cracking his chest reminded me of shelling peanuts back when I was alive. His heart filled my hands and his screams stopped abruptly when I pulled it free of his chest. Still warm, the blood tasted like murder on my tongue. It's a messy business feeding on another vampire, but it's not that different from eating crawfish. You just suck the heart instead of the head. If you don't, you leave all the good stuff behind and it's hardly worth the effort.

I didn't notice Telly's return until he touched my cheek with a warm wet washcloth and started gently wiping the blood from my face. He babbled as he wiped the redness from my chin and neck, hesitantly at first and then with more confidence. Telly thought he had me figured out. What was I in his eyes, some dark goddess that hunts her own kind to protect the humans? It didn't matter. It would take David some time to repair the damage to his body without blood. I had time. Other nights I usually handed Telly a hundred-dollar bill or gave him a knowing smile; this night his reward got a bit more personal.

When we were done, he sawed David's head off for me, his eyes tracking me like a heartsick puppy as I hauled the body into the storm sewer to take care of my fellow vampire's final send-off. I held David under the polluted water. His flesh slowly disintegrated between my fingers and the guilt crept up on me. What Telly and I had done had been fun. It had felt wonderful and it had been a long time since I'd been with a man, but I shouldn't have done it.

It was the way he'd washed my face. Daddy usually does that. Impatient to get back aboveground and deal with Telly, it was hard to keep still. I shifted my weight from knee to knee, but David wouldn't come apart fast enough. As the last of his face sloughed away, I felt a contact pressing against my presence—another vampire, one I couldn't get a complete reading on without letting her detect me, too. She felt female, old, and more powerful than me.

"That's not right." David's skull bubbled away like an AlkaSeltzer, the bubbles tickling my fingers as the mass shifted and shrank, hard to hold on to. The only vampire that's ever felt more powerful than me is Dad. Did I dare reveal myself? The sensation faded before I made up my mind either way. Curious. I'd never hunt Dad. Never! But the idea of hunting a vampire as powerful as Dad . . . ?

Three words: Om. Nom. Nom.

David's remains drifted away. I watched after them, depressed that he was gone, the hunt finished. I felt hungry again, but not for blood. For the thrill of the hunt. I breathed slowly in and out, because it's something Dad would have done, then climbed out of the sewer to deal with Telly. He was such a nice boy and he worshipped me, but I picked my gun up off the ground and put a bullet in his brain.

I whistled for Fang, my dad's car—an undead 1964½ Mustang convertible. Fang's paint, candy apple red by night, black by day, didn't show any reflections under the moonlit sky. He rolled hungrily out of his parking space, my backup, just in case the mark has friends or is tougher than he seems. Fang rolled over Telly and I laid my head on the ground to watch. I don't know how Fang does it, but the skin ripped itself off Telly's body, followed by the muscle, then the organs. They flattened out against Fang's undercarriage, sinking slowly into the metal. The bones faded too, but I knew Fang hadn't eaten them and that they'd wind up in the trunk. I listened, cheek still pressed against the grit of the asphalt, waiting until I heard the muffled clatter of bones in Fang's trunk. It's nice to give Fang time to enjoy his meal. I lay on my back, the smell of oil and gasoline from the parking lot seeping into my hair, and frowned at the sky. Dark clouds rolled in fast, like a time-lapse video.

"Are you ready?" I reached underneath Fang and ran my fingers along his undercarriage, feeling the row of smiley stickers I'd applied. My hand lingered there against him, a shiver of excitement rolling up my spine complemented by a gentle tightness in each breast as my nipples hardened. It felt like putting my head in a lion's mouth. Fang crept backward, exposing the undamaged flesh of my arm, as if my excitement made him uncomfortable, and I sat up.

His engine revved and he let his tires squeal, leaving rubber on the asphalt. I liked watching the three-pronged centers of the simulated knockoff hubs spin, and he knew it.

"You *are* ready." I rounded Fang and the trunk opened. Telly's bones lay amid the debris, naked and unashamed. A splatter of water hit my arm as the rain began. I slammed the trunk and climbed in Fang's driver's side door. Telly'd had pretty pink lungs. I really liked him. I might learn Spanish anyway, in his memory, but I couldn't let a human come between me and my creator. It's like that old song that my grandmother used to sing, before she died and I went into foster care. "My Heart Belongs to Daddy."

19

GRETA:

THE NEW DEMON HEART

Rain came down in large heavy drops as I drove too fast through the city streets toward the Demon Heart. Midnight was a little early for me to turn in, but if I stayed out any longer I would kill again and I knew that I'd been doing too much stress eating lately. For the week I'd averaged two or three humans a night, plus one really stupid Vlad. And that doesn't even count pets, strays, or that lion I ate at the zoo.

My cell said that I had fifteen missed calls and a single voice mail. I thought that I knew what it said, but I checked anyway. Talbot's low grumble tickled the inside of my ears. "Phillip requests, and I quote, 'The pleasure of young Greta's company at her earliest possible convenience upon her return to the Highland Towers.'"

Uncle Phil was older than dirt, crazy powerful, and the only vampire wizard in the world. He owned the cops in Void City and most of the surrounding towns. The dirty cops were bought with greed and the good cops were kept in line with magic. He practically *was* Void City, so ignoring him wasn't wise, but I couldn't talk to him that night.

I hurt too much, my skin felt tight, and I was jumpy. Killing helped me focus, but it didn't last, and snapping at Uncle Phil was not an option. He and Dad had come to an agreement last year when Dad had killed Uncle Roger and the demon Uncle Roger had been in league with. It's a long story, but the short version is that Uncle Roger tried to kill Dad, steal all his money, and eat his soul. The demon tried to use Dad to get a magic rock, the Stone of Aeternum, from Uncle Phil. Bad career move all the way around. The demon wound up getting eaten by Talbot and Uncle Roger's soul was trapped in a fisheye marble, which is now on display in Uncle Phil's apartment. When Uncle Phil's in a good mood, we play catch. It drives Uncle Roger into wild fits of silent screaming. Pretty funny stuff.

"Can I put the top down?" Even with the "power" convertible top, putting the top up and down on Fang was a pain in the butt before his transformation. Now, he handles it all himself. Fang's top popped up and back, folding itself away and allowing sheets of cold rain to wash over my skin, each drop stinging as it hit. I laughed at the chill, at the newness of the sensation, and at the lengths to which I was willing to go to try and distract myself from the ache underlying everything now that Dad was so far away. I thought about my cell phone a little too late, the corners of my mouth making a downward turn as the screen died. *What message*, I thought to myself, smiling up into the rain. *I never got any message. My cell phone got rained on.*

I turned across from the newly restored Pollux Theater and left Fang in the no-parking area in front of the completely rebuilt Demon Heart. A new version of the same old heart-with-horns Demon Heart sign flashed on the roof, but now the sign beneath it said, "All Nite Bowling" in bright blue neon.

Dad had wanted to build a memorial to Old Mom. He picked a bowling alley. Dad's a little weird, but vampires are prone to eccentricity.

On the right, near the entrance, a picture of Old Mom as a young woman hung in a locked display case. Below it was a small metal vase containing what we'd been able to find of her body (mostly chunks of bone). A bronze plaque was mounted to the base of the case, dedicating the building to her memory. I resisted the urge to smash the case. Old Mom had slept around on Dad. If I'd known that when she was alive, she wouldn't have had time to get blown up. New Mom had slept around on Dad too, with Uncle Phil no less, but they worked it out before I had to murder her. She's so easy to kill, too, for a Vlad.

I pushed open the Demon Heart's double doors like I owned the place. The scent of junk food assailed my nostrils, my rain-slick blond hair matted to my neck and shoulders, and my soaked white T-shirt, not just wet but blood-stained, did not go unnoticed by our patrons. The only contestant in an unannounced horror-themed wet T-shirt contest, I curled my upper lip and struggled to keep my fangs in. It was a busy night and I wanted to eat all of them, to drain them dry and suck the marrow. Sizzling funnel cakes went into the fryer behind the snack counter; it was too loud.

Gladys smiled at me from behind the counter, but Cheryl's eyes widened and she shooed me away. Backing out of the Demon Heart, I turned and ran across the street to the Pollux. Fuck Cheryl! With trembling fingers, I typed the security code wrong twice before I got it right and the doors unlocked. I heard Cheryl jogging across the street after me, but I slammed the doors in her face.

The hole in my brain, where Dad's presence usually was, yawned empty in my mind, my heart, my stomach. I sank to the floor of the foyer and screamed. The emptiness crept further into my belly, my hunger spiked. It was all Dad's fault. He was too far away and I couldn't feel him. His absence was physical pain, like some strand of whatever passed for my soul was stretched from Void City, all the way to Paris. Magbidion and Erin, two of Dad's thralls, admitted that his absence was uncomfortable, but neither of them felt it as strongly as me.

Talbot walked down the grand stair and looked at me with pity. He's huge. Not that I'm short. I'm a good six feet tall, but Talbot picked me up and cradled me like a child. Dad had left him behind, too.

"Where's Rachel?"

Talbot was then taken by my question. "I haven't seen her. Why?"

"I was thinking I might eat her while Dad's gone. She's trouble. And he won't stay mad long. It's me."

"Yeah." He looked away as he answered. "I'm pretty sure he wants Shenanigans around a little longer."

My hand started shaking and I clamped it against my side, claws digging into my skin. "But I'm hungry." There was no blood flowing from the wounds.

"He's either got to come back or you have to go to him, Greta," Talbot rumbled. "Either that or . . ."

"I'm not making a thrall!" I roared. Bloody spittle landed on Talbot's cheeks, but he barely registered it. Having blood replace all of your bodily fluids is one of the many indignities that accompany vampiric immortality. Cheryl walked back to the Demon Heart, but she stood in the doorway, eyes drilling a hole in the back of my head right through the glass of the foyer. She means well, but she's not my mom.

I turned into a bat, my clothes falling through Talbot's arms to the floor as I flapped angrily toward her. Lucky for her Talbot is so fast. He snatched me out of the air, held me down like a wounded sparrow. My furry reddish-brown bat skin pulled smooth and taut when I changed back into a human. Talbot straddled my naked body. His heat was too much. It makes Dad horny, closeness like that. I'm not Dad. I get hungry. My fangs sank into Talbot's forearm.

"Greta, no!" His blood burned. He pushed me away, smoke trailing from my lips. "You've been through postmortem stress, Greta. You can't drink from me anymore."

"Hunt." I choked the single word, turning to leave, but he grabbed me again and then Cheryl's wrist was in my mouth. I bit down as hard as I could, worrying her flesh as I felt the bones crack. She screamed and Talbot hit me in the back of the head. Once. Twice. Three times. And then I let her go. She didn't run, she was too well trained for that, but her immediate departure took the form of a very rapid walk.

Talbot shifted his hold into a full nelson.

"Let. Go." My mouth was burned and speech was agony. It wasn't healing either. I could feel it not healing, the pain that should have faded and didn't, just like a wound inflicted by a cross.

"If you don't get control of yourself, Phillip is going to put you in storage until Eric gets back," Talbot warned me. "We've got to do something, Greta. Even you know it's getting out of hand. He hasn't been gone very long and you're already—"

Extending my claws, I raked his sides, but he didn't let go. "He told me to stay here and watch things. Dad put me in charge. Not you, Talbot! Not Magbidion or Cheryl! Me! If I want to kill everybody, then I get to kill everybody! I'm the boss! Me!"

"At least go talk to Phillip." Talbot's breath was hot against my skin. "Maybe he has some kind of magic—"

"Fuck Uncle Phil!" I bellowed. Tears of blood flowed down my cheeks, and I raked his sides again in frustration. Then I felt Phillip. He moved into range with such incredible alacrity that I had barely processed what I was sensing before he was standing right next to me.

"*Buona sera*, my dear," Uncle Phil said lightly in what I thought might be Italian. The diminutive chubby man was balding, but something in his bearing made spines snap to attention in his presence. Talbot let me go and I reached for my underwear, surprised when Phillip had the manners to avert his gaze. "Talk of the Devil and he is presently at your elbow, yes?" he quoted. Still pleasant on the surface, his voice contained depths of meaning for vampiric ears. Uncle Phil was playing nice, but he was pissed.

"I . . . I'm sorry, Uncle Phil," I said, slipping my jeans back on.

Dismissing my apology with a wave of his hand, he exhaled in perturbation when he saw Talbot. "Need his presence truly be inflicted upon me, Greta? I understand your father's reliance on his assistance, but surely you and I have no need of a chaperone."

"Go check on Cheryl, Talbot." I pointed at the doors. Dad once told me that it was never a good idea to be alone with Uncle Phil, but given the circumstances I couldn't see the wisdom in annoying him further.

Reluctantly, Talbot kissed me on the forehead, wiped his blood off my lips, and walked out the front door.

"Did you know that F-U-C-K originally meant 'Fornication Under Consent of King'?" Uncle Phil asked.

That's bullshit, I thought. *It's never meant that at all.* Fuck *has basically meant "fuck" for hundreds of years*, but I didn't say anything. Now wasn't a good time to correct Uncle Phil. I picked my shirt up instead, but it was too bloody to put on.

Before I formulated an acceptable answer, Phillip floated off. He examined the molding around the ceiling and the detail of the chandelier before landing gently on the gallery outside the mezzanine. He seemed quite interested in the restoration, making pleased little noises when he saw things that met his approval and tutting when he saw work that did not reach his standards. I held the ruined shirt over my head and wrung the last few drops of blood into my mouth, waiting for him to say his piece. The drops of blood eased my pain a little, which was a very good sign. I didn't want to have to wait until Dad got back for my mouth to heal. He'd thought to leave me some of his blood, in case of emergencies, but I'd been sneaking a little of it before bed each day and there was only a cup or so left.

"Did you know that I've not been inside this building in sixty years?" Phillip disappeared through the double doors of the mezzanine. Still half-naked, I followed him, leaping up over the balustrade, my feet slapping hard against the thin carpet. Just after I walked through the doors, I felt his hand on my arm. I counted to ten slowly, waiting for him to take his hand off my arm, but he started talking instead. "Greta is from German. It's a shortened form of Margaret, meaning 'pearl.' Such an apt name really, because you are a genuine treasure." Smile lines showed at the corners of each eye when he frowned. "Yet even the most precious treasures require care and attention. Silver and gold must be polished, and the most beautiful gems must first be cut in order to shine."

"Don't touch me!" I growled. Four long scratches appeared on Uncle Phil's face, jagged furrows that did not bleed like they should have. I thought I might have put them there.

Phil released his grip on my arm, momentarily stunned either by the idea that I'd actually hurt him or by the knowledge that I'd done it faster than he could turn to mist. I don't know which. He explored the wounds with his fingertips absentmindedly, as if it were a new sensation or a long forgotten one. The wounds healed, but not at Vlad speed—it was closer to a Soldier's or a Master's regeneration. *Duly noted.*

"What do you want me to do?" I sighed.

"Don't be like that, Greta. This is not a court. It is not as if you stand before your judge, jury, and executioner." He could have fooled me.

"*A buon intenditor poche parole,* as the Italians say," he continued.

"Which means what?" I interrupted.

"A word to the wise is sufficient," he translated. "You should study languages, my dear. A lively mind is such a charming companion to a beautiful exterior. Let me be blunt."

Let me get a T-shirt. I crossed my arms over my breasts and leaned back against the wall. *Or you could loan me your jacket.* But I didn't say any of that either.

"Okay." I nodded. Uncle Phil was never blunt.

"Do you know why vampires have children? Aside, of course, from your father, who is a very special case?"

He sat down in the front row of the mezzanine and patted the burgundy colored seat next to him. The seats were covered in real velvet. *So that you can eat them later?* "Because they're lonely?"

With white teeth bared in a sly grin, he turned to gaze at me. "I once thought the same thing." He put one hand on my knee and rotated further so that we were face-to-face. "Have you ever considered making Eric a grandfather?"

I already had. Not that it was Uncle Phil's business. Not that I'd even told Dad about his grandchildren. Who's to say he'd be the happy grandpa? Not me. And why the hell did Phil think making new vampires would settle me down? Had fatherhood settled Daddy down? If that wasn't what he was thinking, then it was just more talking, more controlling, more Phillipness, and I don't have a high threshold for men like Phil trying to make me do things I don't want to do. I didn't make it to ten that time. To be honest, I didn't even count.

"Hands off!" There is one advantage to thinking with your brain, like Dad does. I've gotten better when it comes to words, but actions . . . Using your brain puts a little extra cushion between the impulse to act and the action. With the cushion, I might have come up with a clever comeback. Without it, my fist (at least I kept the claws in) hammered into Uncle Phil's nose, bringing it flush with his skull. I was honestly surprised the punch connected. So was Phillip. We stared at each other, and Phil's charming façade vanished as he misted, maintaining his form, but with vapor trailing from the edges. I didn't like what I saw underneath that façade. He grew in stature, not unlike Ian McKellen's Gandalf in the first *Lord of the Rings* movie, you know, when he's really pissed at Bilbo?

"I have a thing about being touched," I told him carefully. "I'm not apologizing, but it's from before, when I was human."

I wanted to keep cool, not say anything else, but Uncle Phil just kept looking at me until I continued.

"I'll think about it, okay, but don't push me. It's my choice, nobody else's."

Phil nodded slightly, and vanished as swiftly as he'd arrived. No quip. No parting shot. Nothing. I was willing to bet that Uncle Phil's shit list had a new contender for *numero uno*.

20

GRETA:

OLD HABITS

An hour after Uncle Phil left, I was still sitting in the mezzanine and my hunger was back. It wasn't a thirst for blood, but a craving for real food: cookies, ice cream, the crap they served over at the Demon Heart, anything that was full of fat, sugar, or grease. I'd been dead for a long time, but stress still made me want to binge.

When Dad found me, I was tall for my age, over one hundred ten pounds, nine years old, and miserable . . . a fat little girl with floppy fat-girl boobs. I still remember it even though I doubt he does. Dad's memory is tricky. I think it's because he was embalmed. It makes Dad forget things, lots of things, so it's hard to know what Dad does or doesn't remember.

In a way, I hope he doesn't remember it. It was a warm summer night and the breeze kept it from being too humid. We were at the beach—well, at a rental house near the beach. It was the only vacation my foster parents had ever taken me on. Henry and Diane (my foster parents) got into an argument, which wasn't really unusual since they fought all the time, but Diane stormed out and left me with Henry. She'd never done that before. Henry had made it clear that all he was interested in was a government check, but Diane had been really nice to me. I expected her to come right back, but she didn't.

I don't like to think about what happened after Henry got drunk, but not a night goes by when I don't remember what happened later. Henry was passed out in the bed and I was lying there halfway under him, too afraid to move.

In my head I kept thinking about what I was going to do when I got my courage up. I told myself that I was going to get a pair of scissors and snip his bits off or find a kitchen knife and stab him in the heart. Maybe I would even set him on fire, or worse. Everything hurt, and more than anything else in the world, even more than I wanted revenge, I wanted to be brave enough to get up, walk downstairs, leave, and never look back.

Before it happened I remember stillness, a calm that came over the house and the beach. The gentle roll of the waves became inaudible and the breeze that blew the curtains stopped, leaving them hanging still in the night. Outside, a shadow crossed the open window, in front of the moon, and I got my first glimpse of Eric, my new daddy, the only real dad I've ever known. He was glorious, dressed in a leather jacket and jeans, with a white T-shirt. He looked almost like the Fonz in *Happy Days* reruns, but there was blood on his shirt. His boots hit the windowsill and, halfway in and halfway out of the window, crouched low and dangerous, he stared at the scene: me, Henry, the bed, the tangle of sheets, the blood.

"This better be the right fucking house," he snarled. "Is that Hank?"

I couldn't answer. He pulled a torn photo out of his pocket and looked at Henry. "Yeah, that's Hank." He dropped the picture and it fluttered to the hardwood floor of the house Henry had rented. In the moonlight, I could see the three of us—Henry, Diane, and me—standing in front of their house in Whedonville. There was blood on the photo, too.

Eric grabbed Henry by the feet and tossed him out of bed.

"Wha . . . ?" was all Henry got out before he hit the floor. Eric moved so quickly it was like a strobe light had been turned on. He was at the foot of the bed, bending over Henry. Henry choked, struggling for air, as Eric held him off the floor by the throat. Eric snarled, and moonlight caught the whiteness of his fangs.

"I didn't do nothing," Henry said between gasps.

"Who said you did?" Eric asked. "I'm not judgmental. I just want the ghost of your annoying little bitch of a wife to shut up." He let Henry drop to the floor. "She keeps going on and on about 'You've got to protect Greta. I never should have left her alone with him!'" he mocked in a whiny high-pitched voice. "It seems like every fourth or fifth meal has some sob story about unfinished business or how they can't believe you murdered them. And do you think there is a damn mage around here to send them on their way? Hell no! Not one that answers the phone anyway."

"I didn't do anything," Henry continued. "Just take what you want and—"

His sentence ended in a scream when Eric reached out and

grabbed his shoulder. Bones crunched under the pressure; I heard them from across the room. Bending down, Eric looked him in the eye. "Don't lie to me, Hank. I'm not your priest. I'm the executioner *du jour*. That's French for 'you were married to the wrong chick on the wrong night and now you get to die so that her ghost will shut the hell up'!"

"Okay, I was drunk and I . . . oh my God . . . I'm so sorry, please don't . . ."

Urine ran down Henry's legs and a wet spot blossomed on the front of his underwear, but his sentence ended when Eric punched him in the throat. "I'm not even going to bite you," Eric said as Henry choked to death. "You're rank, man. Christ!" On his knees, Henry gasped for air, but he couldn't draw any in.

I was still in bed, still staring. There was no fear, just adoration. For the entire time I'd been with the Reynoldses I had wished Henry would just drop dead and now he was going to do it, right in front of me. When Eric turned his gaze on me, the red light from his eyes washing over my body, I smiled. His fangs were out and the way they flashed in the moonlight made him look so cool.

"You can have me if you want. I won't fight you." I pulled the covers back and stood up slowly, limping. I'd recently gained a very clear understanding of what went on behind closed doors. Thanks to Henry, I wasn't wearing anything under my stained nightshirt, and a thin trail of blood ran down the inside of my leg. "You killed Henry . . . Hank . . . and that's just about the nicest thing anyone has ever done for me."

He recoiled from me.

"I can take a shower first," I offered. "So I won't smell like him. Or if there is anything else you want . . ."

He shook his head. "No, kid . . . Look, I'm glad you're not too upset and all but . . ."

"You're a vampire?" I asked.

He nodded.

"But he won't become a vampire, too?" I said, pointing at Henry.

"No, I didn't bite him and I'm not going to. There's more to it than that anyway . . ." Henry grabbed at Eric's leg and Eric batted him away.

"Will Diane come back as a vampire?" I asked. "Is that"—I nodded at his shirt—"I mean, you know, you bit her, right?"

"Nah, she's not coming back either, kid." He looked at the empty air next to him, tilted his head to one side, and then pointed at Henry. "But this jerk's not hurting anybody ever again. You see?" Crossing in front of me, he grabbed Henry by the hair and put his work boot on

Henry's head, pushing his face into the floorboards until the front of his skull collapsed, flattening to match the smoothness of the wood. Eric stood back up and looked at the same spot of empty air.

In the moonlight, if I looked just right, I could see Diane. Head lolling at an unnatural angle, her dress had been torn open and blood ran down a nasty wound on her inner thigh, but she was still smiling. She nodded once, then faded away, the first and only ghost I'd ever seen.

Eric let out a long breath and rested his forehead against the wall. "Finally," he sighed. "That bitch was driving me crazy. I don't know what she was clinging to anyway," he mumbled to himself. "Creep for an old man. Fat-ass kid lying around the house . . ."

As if he'd forgotten all about me, he straightened up and walked out into the hall. It was weird, like I had little control over my own actions, but I followed him. Diane and Henry were both dead, which meant there was no one left to tell me what to do. I should have been scared or angry, but instead, I was numb. I needed someone to tell me what to do, and the vampire was the only person around. He went directly to the kitchen and looked at the clock on the stove. "Three forty-five!" he exclaimed. "I've been wandering around the beach for four hours looking for this stupid house. It's not even *on the beach*," he said accusingly.

He brushed past me again and turned on the TV in the living room. Twisting the knob, he flipped through the channels before he put his fist angrily through the front of the screen. I screamed when it exploded. Sparks shot out across the carpet and Eric's arm caught fire. Calmly and with some annoyance he snatched up a sofa cushion and used it to put his arm out. "Now that's typical. No cable and I set myself on fire. That's perfect," he told me. "How am I supposed to know when dawn is if you don't have cable?"

"You could look in yesterday's newspaper," I offered.

"Do you have one?"

"Uh, maybe." I headed to the kitchen to dig through the garbage. Henry always read the paper, wherever we went. He read it and he threw it away. If Diane wasn't quick, she didn't get a chance to do the crossword puzzle. Something about Diane not being able to do the crossword puzzle disturbed me. My stomach rebelled and I fought back the bile. Parts of the newspaper were covered in coffee grounds, but not the pages he wanted. "Dawn is a little before six," I told him, "5:55 a.m."

"I should never have let Roger borrow my car," he said, sitting down on the sofa. "Everything just took too damn long." He stared at the broken television set and then looked at me. The smoke alarm hadn't gone off. I can't say exactly why I noticed, but it bothered me that it hadn't. "I'll just have to fly for it," he said, abruptly standing back up.

"You could stay here," I whispered.

He rolled his eyes at me. "I'm a vampire. I eat people. Why on earth would you want me to stay here with you? Shouldn't you be running away now?"

"You killed them," I said softly. "Not that I'm blaming you. I . . . you killed Diane, but you killed Henry . . . um, Hank . . . too, so that sort of balances things out, but it does mean that I'm out of a home now. I'm sure I'll get placed with another foster family and everything, but I'd rather not. Could . . . couldn't I just go with you?"

"Go with me?" he scoffed. "What're you, fifteen? Sixteen? What do you need me for? Just cash in on—"

"Nine," I interrupted, "but I'll be ten in a few weeks."

"Nine? Nine what?"

"I'm nine years old."

His blue eyes locked with mine and his pupils flickered reddish orange like the eye of a stove heating up. "Say that again." He cocked his ear toward me.

"I'm nine. I look older. I know. I've always been . . . big . . . for my age." I sniffled and wiped my nose on the sleeve of the stained nightshirt that smelled like Henry.

Little streaks of red appeared at the corner of Eric's eyes and ran down his cheeks. He wiped at them angrily with his palms. "C'mere," he said softly. Tentatively, I crossed the room. Crying, he looked more dangerous than before. Angry, he had seemed more predictable, but I wasn't expecting softness.

I was taller than him and I probably weighed more, but he held me just the same and I felt safe for the first time since my grandmother's death. Maybe I was in shock, but in his arms I felt utterly and completely at home. He had leapt through the window, killed Henry, and punched through the TV like it was all nothing. I couldn't imagine anything that could hurt him or anything that he couldn't protect me from. If he wanted to he could even protect me from death.

It's my fondest memory, that night when he first held me in his arms, platonically, like a real dad would. Sitting in the Pollux, thinking about what Uncle Phillip had told me, I wished that Daddy were home, that he could hold me again, rock me back and forth, and tell me everything was okay. He wasn't and he couldn't, so I stared at the stage and concentrated on the tenuous link between us, hoping that somewhere Eric . . . Dad . . . knew that I needed him and was on the way home.

Instead of Dad, though . . . I felt someone else. Another mind, searching for Dad. Questing. And then it hit me. I knew exactly who the other vampire was, the female vamp that was as powerful as Dad. It was Dad's sire. It was Grandma. He'd gone to Paris to find her and she'd come here looking for him. They'd missed each other.

Grinning, I grabbed my pillow, blanket, iPod, and a change of clothes from upstairs and took them back out to the garage like I had every night for the last few weeks. Making a pallet amid the bones, I climbed into Fang's trunk, turned into a mouse, and curled up inside Telly's skull. There, closed inside Fang's trunk, I felt safe, and the pain of Dad's absence lessened. I was about to start watching the next episode of *Tatsu 7* (it's a super robot anime I like) on my iPod when I felt her again. Still searching.

"She's looking for Daddy," I whispered to Fang. He revved briefly in response. In fits and starts, I gathered information from the Emperor vampire who sought my father. *Lisette.* The name popped into my head with a brief glimpse of her instead of a full dossier. She was fat. I didn't expect her to be fat. She was old, too, a hundred years or more. I couldn't tell exactly, because I didn't have a good frame of reference, but she felt old. After a few more passes, I had enough information for one night, enough to be sure.

A new hunt. The idea of it made me feel better, eased my tension. I crawled through Telly's eye socket (in through the right and out through the left, duh) and started the episode before retreating once more within Telly's cranial cavity.

"I'll kill her for you, Daddy," I muttered as the bombastic theme music began. "I'll kill Grandma. You'll see."

Om. Nom. Nom.

21

TALBOT:

JOBS NOBODY ELSE WANTS

Greta didn't know I was watching her. Most vampires don't. Vampires have excellent hearing and good vision, but a cat sees things in a way no human ever will. A Mouser sees them even better. I could see Greta's aura right through the trunk of the car. I sat on the roof of the Demon Heart and let the rain wash over me, soaking me to the bone. Dressed in a plain black suit that I'd bought off the rack and a green shirt from the same store, I wasn't worried for my wardrobe. The sun was coming up, but with the clouds, it was barely noticeable. Greta went still, completely still, and I crossed over to the parking deck.

"Tuck-in service." I needn't have said anything, but dealing directly with Eric's *memento mori* made me nervous. Fang essentially *was* part of Eric, the darkest part of him—not the vampire part. There is no "vampire" part per se. It might feel that way, to humans, but that's a coping mechanism. The "vampire" side is nothing more than survival instinct. Thinking differently makes some vamps feel better about it, makes those of them that dream sleep better at day.

On the other paw, Fang was also its own being. I couldn't be certain, but I didn't think it had all of Eric's memories. It could tap into them with Eric close by, but with him so far away, I expected Fang was taking most of its cues from Greta. Conceptually, very scary.

Fang's trunk popped open and I reached inside, tidying things up. Greta typically reverts to human form sometime during the day and I didn't want her to break her newest pet skull. Daikatana was screaming "Damn it" as he did at least once per *Tatsu* 7 episode when I turned off the iPod and stored it safe and sound atop Greta's neat little pile of clothes. I picked up the skull and gently shook Greta-the-mouse out into my hand. I positioned her near the middle of the trunk, tucked her in under a corner of her blanket, and arranged the rest of her things around her. Greta's pet skull fit nicely against the inner back of the trunk, next to the clothes, where she couldn't crush it accidentally. Clearing away the bones that might poke or prod her when she changed took all of a minute.

"All tucked in."

"Thanks, Kitty." She morphed back to human and I jumped, startled by her words more than by the change. Greta is notoriously hard to awaken, but she'd spoken like a sleeping child wakened by a dutiful parent straightening the covers. Being on fire had barely been enough to wake her last year, but . . .

Fang closed his own trunk, forcing me to jump back a bit or risk losing a hand. Still worried about Greta, I closed my eyes to the physical world and reopened them to the *akasha*. Greta's spirit writhed in agony, red and violet. It was hard to look at so I closed my eyes to the akashic light and waited, listening to Greta's sobs muted by the fall of the raindrops, the sounds of plastic pins being hit by proactive urethane balls, a selection of music best left forgotten, and the thousand other sounds that assailed my ears at any given second. I won't go into the smells.

It wasn't much better. So I opened my eyes to the *akasha* once more and resumed my vigil. I tried to explain it to Eric, once, the way cats (and Mousers) can see the world. This was before I knew him well. I went into the whole thing, the flow of life, souls, spirit. I touched on the *Panchamahabuta*, the five great elements in Hinduism, and tried to explain how *akasha* moves through every living thing, that it is present in earth, air, fire, and water, that it holds together and links all things. Not that I believe in Hinduism . . . I'm more of a *Book of the Dead*, born and bred, say hello to Sekhmet Egyptian mythos kitty myself, but at the time I thought the Hindu approach was easier for a vampire to grasp.

Eric listened to everything I had to say, looked me dead in the eye and said, "Don't give me that Surat Shabd Yoga bullshit. So what . . . you can see the Force. Can you make a light saber?"

Of course, I had no idea what he was talking about at the time; I thought he was a total moron. Later, when I saw *Star Wars*, my mouth dropped open. In his own way, Eric had nailed it in one: we see the Force. And the answer is no, we can't build light sabers.

Greta rolled over, reaching for her pet skull and cradled it to her breasts before passing out again. Her aura changed, mingling with Fang's. All of the emotions, the pain, died down to nothing and she lay there in the trunk of her father's car, just as she had every night since Eric left for Paris, a glowing spot of unlife where no life should have been. That—the ability to escape into a dreamless, painless state, free of all emotions—is one of the reasons all good little kittens hate vampires. Even when we're asleep, someone we know can walk up to us in the dreamworld and start chatting. Fights between spouses can carry right over into sleep. I don't hold it against vampires, though. I think it's cool. Of course, it's been a long time since anyone has called me a good little kitten.

Inside the Demon Heart, Magbidion was saying good night to the last customer of the evening, a redcap who works over at the Iversonian. I stopped at the front door of the Pollux, by the shiny new numeric keypad, and typed in the pass-code, paused, and reset the system. Something was wrong. Someone or something walked across my grave, turned around three times, and sat down. The scent slid into my nostrils and I wanted to hold on to it, to never let it go. Warm, musky, and magical, it . . . she . . . smelled like home.

"So this is how you spend your life now, Blackbird?" asked a familiar voice. "Playing nanny?"

"I prefer the term *manny*, Dezba," I answered, half sarcastically, as I turned toward her. She stood in the dry spot under the awning. Wide-eyed and beautiful, Dezba was an Egyptian Mau, and her silver coat was dappled with crisp black spots. No cat I'd ever met was as beautiful or as cruel as Dezba. Her chosen name was from the Navajo language and it meant "Goes to War." If I'd known she was coming, I'd have worn a better suit.

"As in a nanny, but still a Mouser, I hope," she sneered. "Or have you really been exiled so long that you would take pride in a title that labels you a man?"

I dropped to all fours, becoming a black cat, albeit a black cat with glowing star emerald eyes. "Don't worry, Dezba, I know exactly who and what I am. It's you who seem to have forgotten. I certainly didn't exile myself."

"You helped a vampire, Chogan! You went into the holiest of places and stole knowledge, then used it to help a vampire!" She'd used my Narragansett name, a name I hadn't heard in more than a decade.

"The vampire needed help defeating one of the Nefario," I said calmly. "And you know Eric is not just any vampire. You've seen him in the light of *akasha*, you know he's more than that." It would be easy to lose control around Dezba. For fifteen years every cat, Mouser or mundane, has refused to acknowledge me, has acted as if I were a human. A few had even attacked me. To have a cat, any cat, acknowledge me was so wonderful that it was almost impossible to keep up appearances. For that cat to be Dezba . . .

A momentary flash of paranoia overtook me and I glanced back at the parking deck. I could still see Greta's spirit. She was fine. When I looked back at Dezba, she laughed at me.

"Same old Chogan, my little Blackbird. No, I'm not a distraction."

"I answer to Talbot now," I said, angry with myself for letting her bait me. "I answered to other names before Chogan. I have no doubt that I will answer to other names after Talbot."

"So if a human threw a ball and said, 'Fetch, Talbot . . .'" She shook her head. "No, I'm sorry . . . Talbot . . . please forgive me . . . Talbot. I meant to say if a *vampire* said, 'Fetch,' then you'd just run out into traffic . . ."

I stood on two legs and became human again, turned, and punched in the security code. "It was nice seeing you again, Dezba," I said softly.

"Blackbird, wait." I felt a hand on my shoulder; it was soft, affectionate. "You know I can't help it. You know how I feel."

Her arms slid around me from behind in an embrace I hadn't felt for fifteen years. It froze the breath in my chest. She let her head rest on my shoulder, and I exhaled raggedly, overcome with sheer desire. "Something is coming, Chogan . . . Talbot. It isn't a danger to us, but then . . ."

"I'm not technically one of you anymore," I completed her thought.

"We can pull all of ourselves onto one plane."

"Oh." Mousers are creatures of more than one world. There are plenty of creatures capable of seeing into another plane than the one in which they normally exist. If you see a domestic cat staring at the air, that's probably what it is doing. With my kind, it's different. In exile, I was essentially straddling more than one world. To pull all of myself onto this plane would give the Ancients a good shot at making my exile permanent. "That."

Closing my eyes to the physical world and blocking out the *akasha,* I opened my other eyes, the ones set in a sable-furred leonine body resting in the dream world. The other part of me. It was a body with golden chains around each massive silver-clawed paw and around its great neck. All I had to do to escape the chains was pull myself all the way out of dreams. Six Mousers of lesser breeding stood ready to enact a Seal and bar me from returning if I did so. I closed those other eyes and became conscious of Dezba's touch again.

"You could snap the chains, Chogan."

"Perhaps, but not today. I deserve my exile."

Her arms vanished from around me, and when I turned toward her, she was feline again. "Be careful," she meowed at me. "Earthbound cats cannot escape if Lisette threatens, but you are still my Blackbird, and blackbirds can fly away. No one can enforce your exile, Talbot. We know that all too well." She turned, looked up to the moon, and leapt into the sky. I stared after her for a few minutes and then noticed Magbidion standing in the doorway of the Demon Heart, smoking a cigarette and looking straight at me.

"Did that lady cat just jump to the moon?" he asked.

"Don't be silly," I told him. "Everyone knows that's just a fairy tale. Besides, that was no lady cat; that was my wife." *Ba-dum-bum.*

I left him standing out there with his mouth open and went inside the Pollux. Once inside, I dried myself with a cantrip and for the first time in three years, I marked the threshold with my musk. If someone slipped in past the security, I would know. Eric never liked it because he could smell the musk, but it was becoming abundantly clear to me that Eric might not be back in time to handle the situation. I went upstairs, gathering Greta's trail of bloody clothes as I went, walked into Eric's bedroom, and dropped the clothes in the sink. I ran cold water over them to let them soak.

In my mind's eye, I could see what Eric would be doing at this time of night were he home. Greta would have fallen asleep somewhere in the Pollux, letting herself drop, not because she couldn't feel the onset of sleep, but because she knew it would make her father care for her. He'd drag Greta's corpselike body off into the shower. Hot water would rush out of the showerhead and sweep the blood from her skin. Some of it would have dried and he'd work on particularly crusty spots with the loofah sponge Rachel leaves in the shower. Her hair might need shampooing, so he'd take care of that before patting her dry, putting her in a clean T-shirt, and tucking her into bed.

As dysfunctional as Eric could be at times, he had never needed this much looking after. Greta required something that I couldn't give her, and if she didn't get it soon then things were only going to get worse around here. The clock on the wall read six thirteen. That made it after 1:00 p.m. in Paris. There was no way Tabitha would be up, but maybe Eric . . . I called the number they'd given me for the hotel in Paris and asked for their suite.

There was no answer. I tried Tabitha's, Bea's, and Eric's cell phones in sequence and left each of them a message asking them to call me.

22

TALBOT:

ANYBODY'S GUESS

Around 10:30 a.m. the downstairs phone rang. Everything seemed huge, too big, and that was when I realized that I'd changed shape in my sleep. Dezba's visit had gotten to me more than I wanted to admit. The last sweet memories of what I'd been dreaming slipped away from me. I shook off the cobwebs of slumber and glanced at my clothes dangling from their hanger on the door back.

"No time." I left them hanging and darted out of the room and down the stairs, where I reluctantly shifted forms to answer the phone behind the concession counter.

"Hello." I spoke brusquely, trying not to yawn into the receiver. You learn to keep strange hours when you live with the dead.

"Talbot?" The connection was bad, but the voice on the other end of the line sounded panicked and hurt. "Talbot, is that you? Damn phone. Hello?"

"Who is this?"

"Talbot! It's me, Tabitha." She sounded like someone trying to keep it together and act like everything is all right when it clearly isn't.

"What are you doing up? It's what, five-thirty over there?" Oh . . . right. She'd probably had Eric force her awake.

"Would you shut the hell up and listen to me." More crackling interrupted her speech. "My cell is broken and it keeps hanging up. Is Rachel there?"

"I haven't seen her since you guys left for Paris. Is Eric there? I need—"

"I don't give a fuck what you need, Talbot. Shut up and listen to me. Lisette is headed for you guys. She may already be there."

I glanced around. Through the *akasha*, people walking by outside or driving in their cars became visible, even through the walls. There was no sign of Dezba or any other eavesdroppers. "Where's Eric?"

"The fucking immortals lost him. And they made me do a lousy three-day initiation."

"I'd have thought Phil would have called ahead, cleared things—"

Tabitha interrupted. "Eric was kidnapped by someone with cinnamon-scented magic and a female Vlad."

"Damn. So you think Rachel—"

"Well, don't you think Rachel?"

"Probably." I sighed. "And Eric would want me to stay here and help Greta with Lisette." I hissed. "Do you know what the Vlad looked like?"

There was a jostling noise, audible even over the crackle of the bad connection. "Describe the other Vlad," I heard Tabitha say as the phone was passed to someone else.

A deep, yet female, German-accented voice obliged. "She was petite. Attractive. She'd been turned in her early twenties. The way she moved was distinct, as if she had trouble moving slower than her maximum vampiric rate. Eric seemed to recognize her."

Shit. Irene.

"Put Tabitha back on," I ordered.

Less jostling this time. "You know who it is?" Tabitha asked.

"It could be Irene," I said. There was no point in beating around the bush. Tabitha needed to know who she was up against. "She's one of Eric's children. He tried to kill her after El Segundo. She was involved with the demons there. To her it was a game."

"What was? El Segundo?"

"No. The end of the world," I said seriously. "You can't let him be around her, Tabitha. She's not right, and he's different around Irene. He'll kill for the fun of it, just because it turns her on."

"He'd do that for me," she said. Yeah, but the two of them were like apples and oranges. But how to get that across over a really bad phone connection?

"He lets her bite him," I said.

"That b—!" The static vanished along with the connection.

A dull throb settled in behind my eyes and I reached behind the concession stand, feeling around for a bottle of analgesic.

Something crossed the threshold of the Pollux. I felt it. It wasn't a nice something and it hadn't come to bring me breakfast. "Fine," I said softly to the dead line, as I hung it up. "Shenanigans went on a world tour."

I hopped over the counter and found the bottle of pain pills for which I'd been looking. After a brief fight with the childproof cap, I tapped two red and yellow capsules out into my palm and dry-swallowed them. "So . . . I'm going to Paris then. Guess I'd better take Greta with me."

Two seconds later and I caught the scent; it wasn't human, but it might have been human once. I couldn't place it. Whatever it was, it was male and smelled like cheap cigars and expensive cologne. Below the cologne I smelled dirt or maybe stone, faint but distinct.

I reached through the *akasha*, pulling a little more of the real me through to the material world. Vampires seem to find changes uncomfortable. My kind doesn't. A white glow spilled over my body as I clothed myself in fur and extra muscle, then vaulted up to the second-floor balcony, watching for the intruder, ready to pounce—if necessary.

The creature showed up through the *akasha* as sudden bursts of light, visible only when he moved. From the balcony overlooking the lobby, I saw a figure in a dapper brown suit and fedora gently tapping the rain off his umbrella. The suit coat bulged in the back, implying a pronounced hump, but he stood straight, which to me implied wings. He wore brown leather gloves, and his shoes squeaked when he stepped out onto the tile. I cleared my throat. The face that looked up at me was gray and goatlike. I fancied that if I took off his hat I'd find horns.

"*Bonjour.*" His voice was melodious and gentle, but the eyes were cold and hard: stone—and not in a metaphorical sense. "I hope you don't mind, but I let myself in. Could you tell me if the owner is in?"

Whoever he was, he took the sight of a battle-ready Mouser in stride.

"Maybe I'm the owner," I answered. He removed his hat and ran gloved fingers casually along his bald scalp. The horns were small, but they were there. This close, I picked up a new smell: pigeon droppings.

"That could be," he answered eagerly. He looked into the hat as he continued speaking, "but I was given to understand that the owner of the Pollux was a shorter individual, in his mid- to late thirties and with less fur—a man named Eric."

"Your information could be wrong," I told him as I walked down the stairs to meet him. "Perhaps the former owner passed away or sold the property. Maybe I ate him."

"Just so, I believe he did indeed pass away, some years ago, but if what I have heard about this man is true, mere death even via gastronomic interment would not preclude the requisite of his conversation with my employer. If he has indeed sold the property, however, you could perhaps suggest an alternative method of contact or a forwarding address?"

"Who wants to know?"

"I speak for my esteemed mistress, the Empress Lisette, *le Coeur-Démone*."

"I'm afraid that now isn't a good time." I flexed my claws, making sure they reflected the emerald light from my eyes. "*My employer*"—I took the stairs, continuing toward the concession stand where a stack of Post-its sat next to the downstairs phone—"is away on an extended honeymoon." Pen in hand, I made as if I were about to begin writing. "I'd be happy to have him contact you upon his return, perhaps give him the message should he call the office?"

He gave a cell number and shook my paw without flinching. "I do hope"—he made a point of looking up the main staircase toward the offices—"that your employer returns home soon from his . . . honeymoon, as you say it."

"I'll give him the message," I repeated.

"*Merci*," he said softly. I crossed to open the door, but it was unnecessary. It opened as he stepped toward it and closed gently behind him when he left. I watched him through the *akasha*. He took three steps forward before leaping into the air and flying away into the midmorning glare. Not taking the time to change, I dialed Rachel's cell again. And Eric's. And Tabitha's. I left messages at the hotel too.

"Get back here now. Lisette came looking for you. She's in Void City."

23

GRETA:

WINTERIZED

The next night, I broke one of the cardinal rules of hunting in Void City. It was a warm night out, the kind that only the dead appreciate. The flutter of Void City Music Festival banners flapping against the metal of the lampposts from which they hung mixed with the thrumming bass beat of bands and block parties, vibrating my abdomen and generating an increasing discomfort bordering on nausea. *Hungry.*

I tapped the underside of Fang's trunk once and it popped open. All the humidity made my hair completely unmanageable, so I put it up in a sloppy blond ponytail and said the hell with it, grabbed the clothes I'd laid out for myself, and changed in the parking deck. I wanted to head over to the Highland Towers and sense around for Grandma, but my hunger drew me out into the street.

There was food. In past years, the festival had never made it all the way down to Thirteenth Street and Eighth Avenue. I'd always thought it was to keep the revelers away from Dad, but the sudden expansion made me wonder if the real reason had been Dad's strip club.

Build a bowling alley and the norms come around to annoy you. What was I thinking? I imagined Dad might say something like that.

Car after car was parked in the deck, almost filling it. Way more cars than usual. I walked through the deck to the street exit and found Magbidion manning the booth.

"Why are all these people in our deck?"

Magbidion flinched at the question, unconsciously running a hand through his hair. "People kept asking, so I figured we might as well let them in and make them pay. I hope that's okay."

"Whatever." I glanced about. A full deck made me feel

claustrophobic. This wasn't their deck; it was Dad's. "It'll make hunting easier, I guess."

"You can't hunt during the music festival, Greta."

"Did Dad tell you to say that?"

"No." He wanted to lie. I could hear it in the way air caught in his chest. But he didn't. He wouldn't. He's Mags. "But it *is* tradition."

"Did Phil get Dad's permission to include *our* part of town in the festival?"

He looked down at his feet, but there wasn't a good lie down there either. "No."

I gave him a grin, fangs deployed and eyes a bright pretty red. "Oops." My eyes faded back to normal and I winced as my fangs retracted. "Why don't you get Captain Stacey on the phone? We're going to need him."

"Greta—" I walked away while Magbidion was still speaking. *I'm in charge.* As my feet hit the sidewalk, I heard Magbidion frantically dialing numbers on his cell.

People were actually swarming downtown despite the heat. Joggers were out in force, and a local jazz band was giving an impromptu concert. The vibe wasn't a normal Void City vibe. Everything was pleasant and neighborly . . . which just goes to show you that one hungry vampire can fuck things up for everybody.

I hit the sidewalk in a black sports bra, black track pants with a white zipper down each side, and my white Skechers. My whole ensemble was probably manufactured in some Chinese sweatshop by people who knew the value of a dollar more than I ever would. Magbidion was calling my name and saying something about Talbot and gargoyles, but the only voice I heard was the one in my veins chanting "Feed me" in time to the heartbeats of Void City's human inhabitants.

Two of those heartbeats stood outside the Pollux, looking at the summer schedule. We were supposed to start a summer film festival next week, beginning with *Casablanca*. Dad would be back by then. One of them touched my arm.

"It's really cool that you guys are reopening the Pollux," my potential meal told me. "*Casablanca* is my dad's favorite movie. He and Mom are planning a date night."

The blood was warm and young and there was more food nearby. One of them was a girl, but I couldn't tell which anymore. The urge to feed wiped out all the details, leaving a mass of veins pushing over a gallon of blood in a convenient, easy-to-open package. One of the food selections took a step back. Maybe it sensed something was wrong, but the other just kept on talking. "Hey, are you okay? You look a little pale." Forty hearts called my name, and this was number one, the chatty heart.

When I binge, I try to vary it up. Now, I knew I couldn't go killing a whole bunch of people every night without getting noticed or having to pay an outrageous fang fee, but I was really, really hungry. I was willing to pay the bill. It's only money, and I knew before I started that I wouldn't be able to stop with one. It didn't bother me really, it was just a fact.

But back to the cardinal rules.

Magbidion mentioned not hunting during the music festival, but that isn't a Daddy Rule, so it doesn't count. Dad has all kinds of rules about hunting. He even follows some of them himself. When I first turned, he made it clear that I ought to treat each rule like a holy law handed down by a very angry short-tempered god who would not hesitate to stake me and leave me in a freezer for a few months until I'd learned my lesson. The inside of a freezer loses its appeal pretty damn quick, let me tell you. It's the same kind of thing that Dad or Talbot tell all the new vamps Dad produces. Rule number one boils down to this: Don't get sloppy.

Rules or no rules, sometimes I got sloppy.

Dad has his sexy little favorite feeding spot on a human, but I like to mix it up. There are so many arteries available to a vampire, if you're willing to do the work to get at them and you don't care what happens to the human afterward. I grabbed Chatty's right wrist with my left hand and locked my right hand on his bicep. My vampire quickness didn't give him time to react or even process what was happening when I brought his elbow down on my knee with enough force to tear his arm in two. I held my greedy mouth over the wound the way a child does a drinking fountain, the arterial spray splashing over my face in a sudden wave. Two large swallows later and I dropped him to the ground. Screams came at me slowly, a drawn-out dull, guttural roar. You learn to parse it out in your head, force it to make sense when you need it to, or to let it remain incomprehensible gibberish. This night, gibberish was fine.

My claws lanced out, slicing through the neck of Chatty's companion when she turned to run, and stuck fast in one of her vertebrae. Blood from her vertebral and carotid arteries flowed around my fingers and I lapped at the wound.

One thing that I don't envy Dad are his blackouts. When he gets mad enough to totally lose control, he doesn't remember a thing and doesn't know what he's done. All he gets to see is the aftermath, and where's the fun in that? He misses all the good stuff. I gave a two-fingered whistle, and Fang's engine roared to life. He wheeled out into the street over the bodies of the two I'd just killed, leaving nothing to mark their passing, not even bloodstains on the concrete. My only disappointment was that, in killing the two as quickly as I had, there hadn't been time for their cries to be heard over the noise of the band on the corner. I wanted the people to panic and leave, but I'd done it all too fast and ruined things. Still, there was a crowd. I could always cut loose into them. . . .

"C'mon." I waved for Fang to follow. "I'm still hungry."

Fang honked.

"What?" I spun to face the Mustang.

Fang responded by hanging a U-turn in the street and popping his driver's side door open.

"But I don't like these people being here." I gestured over my shoulder. "And Magbidion is taking in all kinds of cash for the parking. We can pay the fang fee with that. It'd be like a free buffet."

Christmas music, completely out of season, began playing through Fang's speakers. Rolling my eyes, I started toward the car door to slam it shut, but then I heard the words. It was that Elmo 'n' Patsy song, "Grandma Got Run Over by a Reindeer."

"I know, and we will, but—"

Talbot burst out of the front door of the Demon Heart. "Cockblocker and Buzzkill"—I stomped to the car door—"the both of you. You're acting like a pair of old ladies."

"Damn it, Greta." Sweat glistened on Talbot's forehead, and his sweat smelled nice and tangy, like that lion I'd eaten at the zoo. "What the hell? I was clearing a jam on lane eleven and—"

"Don't worry." I walked past the open car door and lay down in the road. "Fang stopped me."

"What are you doing?"

"I'm getting all tacky and congealed." I kicked Fang's front bumper. "Fang's going to clean me up so I don't stink when I go hunting for Grandma."

Fang rolled backward a few inches as "The Addams Family Theme" interrupted the Christmas music.

"I don't care how creepy, kooky, or ooky it is, Fang." I never lose my temper with Fang, but I couldn't help it. He usually joined in with the fun. "You'll do it or I'm going to get up and have my Music Festival Massacre."

"He's going to what?" Talbot put his hand on the hood. "Now wait a minute."

"Do it, Fang."

Talbot stepped in front of Fang, his hands never leaving the hood. "Stay right where you are, Fang."

"Do it."

"Greta, get up." He looked down at me. His eyes showed genuine concern. "It's not safe."

"Do it! What are you, a Mazda or a Mustang?"

Talbot went flying as Fang rammed him, coming to a stop directly over me. I've crawled under Fang before to put stickers on him or draw, but never when he was angry. And boy was he angry. There wasn't much space separating me from it to begin with, but I noticed long ago that there seems to be more room under Fang than there should be. My cheek struck the line of smiley faces. It hurt, like a metallic slap. "Ow." I stretched against the metal, my body against him. "I trust you." I whispered the words, and as I said them, I felt myself drop a fraction of an inch away from the metal.

A tiny fleck of blood lifted from my cheek with a tingle not unlike a butterfly on my skin. It rose and flattened against the undercarriage, sinking into it. Fang worked his way across my face, tendrils of blood lifting off in tiny drips and drops. He went lower, his invisible hunger tickling my skin and tugging at my clothes. Butterfly touches caressed my breasts and traced warm lines along my rib cage. When he reached my groin, the excitement generated more blood and he was forced to focus on that area longer. . . .

I hadn't expected it to be sensual, much less sexual, so when pleasure built and I came, the orgasm surprised me and I lay back, relaxing in the grip of his power, not quite touching him and yet not quite touching the ground as the remnants of blood splatter rose from my legs, my socks, my shoes. "Far out," I said eventually, as Fang rolled back, revealing my clean skin, clothes, and hair.

Talbot hovered over me.

"Are you okay?"

I breathed in deeply, a nod to the very human sensations I'd just felt, and let it out in a dramatic postcoital shudder. I closed my eyes and nodded, waiting for my legs to stop shaking.

"I'm fan-fucking-tastic." I sat up, noticing the pavement beneath me, the way it bit into my skin. "And I have a totally new understanding of autoerotica."

With a satisfied sigh, I let Talbot help me up, then pushed past him and climbed into Fang. "To the Towers," I said. Fang pulled away, leaving Talbot behind, and I let my eyes close again. There was no music, just an uncomfortable silence. "Don't act all weird, Fang." I patted the stick shift. "It was nice, but I don't think we should do it again."

As if signaling his agreement, Fang's radio clicked on to Radio Disney. Someone who undoubtedly had their own show on the Disney Channel sang songs that were very pop rock and upbeat. I listened halfheartedly, wondering what would happen to Dad if I killed Fang. We hadn't actually had sex, so I guess it was okay not to kill him, plus Fang is a car and that would be like strangling a vibrator. Still, it might be interesting. It couldn't be too hard either, could it? As if triggered by the internal question, the LEGOs in my head snapped into place and I knew how to kill Fang.

He was a *memento mori*; all I had to do was melt him down or completely disassemble him. Knowing how was enough; Dad wouldn't like it if I killed Fang, and . . .

"Ow." When I'm stalking a vampire and figuring out how to kill him, it doesn't usually hurt, but this time pain stabbed through my sinuses like they were being cauterized with silver nitrate. I grunted, grabbing the bridge of my nose; my teeth gritted together.

More LEGOs fell into place, as if the idea of destroying Dad's *memento mori* and understanding how to do it was all I needed for the right pieces to click together.

I knew how to kill Daddy. I've read that there is a moment as a kid when you realize that your parents are going to die one day and leave you all alone. I'd never felt that way before. My daddy was an uber vamp. Not even the sun could kill my daddy. He was forever and he'd always protect me, just like he had from the moment I met him.

Destroying him wouldn't be easy, but it could be done. I punched the steering wheel. "Unacceptable!"

We'd barely made it two blocks from the Demon Heart when traffic came to a halt. Policemen were trying to direct traffic, but it was a complete snarl.

"I wonder if the buildings down here are close enough together for you to go off-road . . ."

"Now there's a possibility." The light, self-amused voice came from my right. I swiped at it without thinking. My claws passed through something cool and damp, yet ephemeral, and Fang accidentally nudged the yellow Mazda Miata in front of us. The vampire in the seat next to me gazed down at the point where my arm protruded from his chest without disturbing the straight lines of his unbuttoned dress shirt. I wrinkled my nose in confusion. He could do mist, and fast. The ability was rare—five or six in the world rare—and should have helped me figure out who he was. . . . Oh, yeah. Ebon Winter.

Other than my hand sticking through him, the only sign of his etherealness was a gentle blurring at the edge of his body. His hair, a shockingly vibrant blue, was done in tasteful spikes that appeared styled rather than horripilated. Delicate tattoos covered his face, but they added too much blue and didn't suit his look. It was close, but not quite right.

Like a scientist examining a bug, he focused on my reaction to his appearance. All sense of bemusement melted from his face, and it reminded me of a bird of prey.

"It's the tattoos." His smile returned with a degree of warmth that convinced me for a split second that it had never absented itself. "They don't work?"

I examined the subtle blue curves, wondering how they'd managed to do such a good baby blue. The basic pattern was designed to subtly enhance his features and complement the blue of his contacts. "They aren't quite right."

"I rushed him." The vampire casually pulled an old-fashioned silver straight razor out of the pocket of his jeans. "My own fault." He ran his left hand over his face one time and then again. "You'll have to excuse me for a moment."

The young girl driving the Miata had climbed out of her car. I only noticed because Winter glanced her way.

"What are you—"

He began to cut and my hand, still extended through his body, clutched convulsively, digging into the upholstery of the passenger's seat. Tracing the same lines his fingers had outlined, the vampire removed the tattoos, skin and all, with a series of cuts.

"Holy shit!"

Peeling away the skin on his forehead in one large rounded rectangle, he revealed a mass of uncut muscles like thin red cords. The vampire threw the now excess skin over the windshield past the hood and into the street.

The Miata's driver opened her mouth to scream, but Winter caught her eye and her mouth froze. In mid-scream, she closed her mouth, looked away, and got back into her car.

"The car will enjoy that," he said thoughtfully. I didn't see how Fang would enjoy the girl not screaming, but then I realized he meant his skin. Next he did the left side, flaying the skin next to his eyes and working down along the cheek, exposing the tissue beneath. The muscles there were less uniform than under the forehead, curving in circles near the eyes, yet cutting long straight angles at the cheek. He left the flap attached at the chin and let it fall loose, hanging from his naked cheek. There was no blood, not a drop.

"That's fucking awesome." I gripped the steering wheel tightly with my left hand and he began to cut again, on the right side, turning his head a little to give me a better view. He didn't flinch. His smile never faltering and his eyes never leaving me, he created an exact mirror of what he'd done on the left side of his face.

"The chin is the tricky part." He made an incision below his lower lip. "I tend to cut too deeply." Even as he said it, he made his final cut and I saw for the first time the way he would break into vampire speed, making adjustments and slicing away tissue as he pulled to give the illusion that he was easily pulling the skin away. Swapping just that much of his body back and forth to mist, cutting his face off while continuing to ignore my hand, still stuck through his chest, claws gripping the seat cushion. . . .

He tossed the rest of his excised skin to Fang and settled back in his seat. "Did I get it all?"

I nodded, and his eyes flashed red. An eruption of regenerative madness rolled across his skin and his face was whole sans tattoos.

"And you're just a Soldier?"

"Me?" He laughed between his words, and the sound warmed my stomach. "A Soldier? No, darling. I'm a King if anyone is."

"But I didn't feel you."

His eyebrows went up. "Is that all?" The sense of him hit me all at once, but the dossier was slimmer than what I was used to getting. His name I already knew. That he was a Vlad, I knew as well. That he could sneak up on vampires the same way I could—that was new.

"There," he said as I withdrew my arm from where it pierced his mist form, "now you've sensed me. Two Vlads in a *memento mori*, enjoying the night air. We're so cute together I may vomit."

Winter's voice tickled my ears and made my brain go fuzzy. It didn't really matter what he said, I just wanted the sound to keep coming out of his mouth.

"Don't drool now," he chided, "you haven't the time."

"Time?" *I'm not in a hurry.* What was he talking about?

"Of course you're in a hurry." He drifted sideways out of the car, straightening, and leaned toward me over the closed car door. His shirt fell open, exposing washboard abs. "You have to change into something appropriate if you're to be seen at my concert. And you'll need to bring your sire's *memento mori* with you if you intend to keep it concealed from Lisette. Who will, I might add, be there."

He ran his hand casually through his hair. "You need to read her on three successive nights in order to deduce her method of destruction, yes?"

"How did you—?"

"I have an eye for details."

I took another swing at him, but all it did was generate more laughter while sending portions of his shirt into swirls of mist. "Don't try to fight me, Greta. It's not something I do. If you truly try to end me, then I shall be forced to murder you . . . not a preferable course of events, though I find some of your practices revolting." He made a grand sweep, indicating Fang. "I mean, frotting yourself to completion against the car? Honestly. It's akin to masturbating with a matchbox car while wearing your father's underwear over your nose."

"I did not frot. It was an accidental thing, and—" I blinked. "You saw that?"

"I'm not the vampire who has thralls watching the Pollux and the Demon Heart, my dear." He leaned back against the car door. "But that's not what I'm here about. You're concerned that you've deduced a method by which your father may be destroyed. Now that he's created a *memento mori*, he's technically vulnerable."

"How did you know that?" I took a third swipe at him. Even at top speed, I caught nothing but mist.

"I'm very clever, and if you do that again, I'll skin you in your sleep and have my mage cast a spell to make the regeneration take a month."

Ow!

"Fine." I slumped back in the seat, arms crossed beneath my breasts. "What do you want again?"

"Come to my concert. Sense Lisette. And then I'll tell you how to make Eric unkillable again."

"Why would you do that?"

"Do you know which movie is your father's favorite?"

"Yes," I said.

"So do I." He murmured the words under his breath and then he was gone, shooting backward in mist form up into the air like a cloud. "Be at my concert."

"Where is the concert?" I asked myself, but then I knew. This was Ebon Winter. He'd be on the big stage at the Artiste Unknown, front and center. Where else?

What do you wear to a concert where the man who says he can make your daddy unkillable is performing? What do you wear to a place like the Artiste Unknown? The solution hit me like a bolt of lightning: Talbot would know.

"Looks like we're going to a concert," I told Fang. He pulled forward enough to devour Winter's discarded flesh, then turned toward the Pollux, much to the dismay of those in the lanes nearest us.

24

TALBOT:

AVERAGE EVERYDAY HERO

Every now and again I wish my dad had been a spider deity, his DNA granting me the ability to swing from rooftop to rooftop instead of the power to Devour. But I make do. From my perch atop the old Mandrake Hotel, I watched Fang driving up the exterior of the Void City Metro Bank building. Tired of the traffic jams from the music festival, Greta and Fang had clearly chosen that building because it stood taller than its neighbors and had widely spaced windows that aligned perfectly from top to bottom.

"That is physically impossible."

"Says the guy who can turn into a cat and eat beings larger than himself in their entirety without bloating up like a blimp." Magbidion chattered away in my ear via the Bluetooth headset of my cell.

"Touché, Magbidion."

"Here he goes. Watch him! Watch him!"

"I *am* watching him."

Fang reached the middle point of the building and gunned his engines. He lost traction on the slick exterior surface, smoke billowing free of his tires as he began to slide back down the wall, veering far enough to the right that I feared one of his wheels might plunge through the glass windows on either side. The Mustang drifted another four or five feet before lurching upward pedal-to-the-metal, rocketing up the side of the building with ever increasing speed, leaving tire tracks in its wake.

I switched over to the *akasha* and watched Fang's power build; a corona of brilliant purple energy flared out from his frame, centering on his engine. Violet sparks arced from the rapidly spinning prongs of his simulated knockoff hubs to the building and back.

"He's not slowing down." I caught myself standing up, leaning toward the scene without intending to do so.

"He won't." Mags's voice was excited. "He did the first time and they had to start over, but . . ."

The magician's words trailed off as Fang cleared the top of the building. Greta's whoop of exhilaration was audible even from where I was.

The car hung in the air, a fly in invisible amber. I counted under my breath . . .

One . . .

Two . . .

Three . . .

And the car exploded into motion, falling backward hood over trunk, headlights burning red, then purple when, tumble completed, the Mustang's wheels were once more oriented toward the ground and the fall slowed to a lazy crawl.

"He's—" I began.

"—gliding!" Magbidion broke in.

In the *akasha*, twin wings of magic like those of a gargantuan bat, the same purple as the car's aura, billowed out on either side of the unearthly vehicle.

"Chitty Chitty Fang Bang." My words were a whisper.

"That way! That way! That way!" Greta shouted from the driver's seat, her long blond hair trailing behind her like the tail of some golden comet. Her aura was still pained, but the joy, combined with what I interpreted as a renewed sense of purpose, was keeping her functional.

"Got any flight amulets, Mags?"

"I'm no good with that kind of working, Talbot. You could try the Mage Guild, but I think the going rate is upwards of four million bucks for something that really lets you fly at will."

"That much?"

"It's a luxury item with a sustained effect."

"Later then." I touched the button on my headpiece, ending the call, and stuffed the thing into a jacket pocket before rubbing my ear. I hate those things.

Eschewing the more mundane routes meant Greta and Fang would make it to the concert before me, but I was less concerned about beating them there and more concerned about . . . that! Breaking away from the roofline of a condemned Gothic-style church, a goat-headed being with gray wings took flight, cutting from building to building in short trips as if it wanted to remain unseen. Three minutes later and I'd counted half a dozen of them.

It would have been so much simpler if I'd staked Greta and left her in Fang's trunk until Eric got back. I looked down the side of the building and shook my head, picturing myself attempting to slide down the side of the thing using my claws to slow my fall. Maybe if I weren't banished and could make the leap into dreams like Dezba . . . Maybe if I were younger and had more lives left . . . Maybe. But not today.

I took the elevator down to the bottom floor and walked over to the deck where I'd parked my motorcycle. Straddling the bike, I donned my helmet, because even a Mouser can get in a wreck. I'm not much of a biker, but during the music festival, and really, any time there's a huge traffic disaster, it's easier to get around town on one. I test-drove a Hellcat Combat from Confederate Motors, but in the end, it seemed like a waste to buy a machine like that and only drive it a few times a year. Eric would have pitched a fit if I'd bought a crotch rocket, so when I decided to get a bike a few years ago, I went with American made: a 2008 Harley-Davidson XL 1200N Sportster.

The early evening rain was gone for the moment, leaving the normally intense city scents muted. Warm sticky air made my clothes cling to my skin. Pulling out of the parking deck, I looked up before heading out. The clouds told me the rain would return, and my nose for trouble advised me I'd be seeing the gargoyles too. Despite the weather, the crowd showed no sign of dissipating, and the music festival was in full swing. Somewhere up and to my right, Greta and Fang drifted toward Morne Park.

Void City has several small parks, but Morne is the largest of them all, the center of the festival, with most of the other parks hosting a smaller stage, and lesser bands playing on street corners throughout West and East Side. Ebon Winter often held a huge party at his club, the Artiste Unknown, but this year, he'd closed the club and agreed to play the festival. Belatedly, I caught myself wondering why.

Had he bet on Greta? On me? Against either of us?

How strange. An hour ago, I'd been worried about how to keep her focused, and now that she *was* focused, I was fretting about why she was focused.

Greta had come to me wanting to know what to wear to Winter's concert, and had been almost disappointed to hear that he'd be playing at the festival and not at the Artiste Unknown.

"Every woman needs a little black dress." I'd helped her sort through some of the other girls' things, most of which were too short for her. "Even the crazy vampire women." She donned the dress, an off-the-shoulder mini in basic black, and I flicked a stray bit of white string with my claw, removing it from the tight, body-hugging sheath.

In this kind of dress she'd have to be careful walking upstairs, bending over, or kneeling unless she wanted it to spontaneously transform into a T-shirt equivalent.

"So, do I look okay?" She'd let me get Erin to do her makeup, hair, and nails. Erin hadn't flinched when Greta insisted that the red nail polish be applied to her fully extended claws, too. The combat boots detracted, though.

"You'd look better if you were four-legged and furry, but as non-furry two-legged people go—"

"*Tal*bot." Greta had elbowed me so hard that not flinching required an effort.

"You look great."

"Not fat?" she'd asked.

"You're way past the amount of reassurance people can reasonably expect from a Mouser." I'd touched her chin—a dangerous test. She hadn't bitten my finger or snapped at me, which meant she had herself under control again. "You know that?"

"But do I look fat?"

"Why would it matter if you did?" I'd gestured at myself. "I'm not exactly a string bean."

"You're all muscled and stuff." Greta had poked my stomach. "Guys aren't supposed to be skinny."

"Are you sure you won't at least try a different pair of shoes?" I'd held a pair of open-toed black flats up for her inspection. "I understand that you don't like heels, but—"

"Is Dad going to be there?" She'd already known the answer and that had been her point. If Eric were home, she'd have worn whatever was necessary. In his absence, Greta curtailed her willingness to make accommodations.

"Why are you going to Winter's concert again?"

"I told you." Greta had pretended to admire herself in the mirror even though her reflection was a no-show. "It's a secret."

"You'll keep an eye out for gargoyles, at least?"

"Not really."

Her words played again in my mind as I weaved in and out of traffic, zipping past one of Void City's Finest as she directed traffic. I brushed her leg as I passed; I couldn't resist. Vampires aren't the only supernatural beasties with mystic speed.

I scanned the sky for gargoyles, but I should have been watching the ground. Running down the center lane two blocks from Morne Park, a stretch limo inched its way forward. I was zipping past the rear right bumper when the door burst open.

Completely unavoidable. Too stunned to react, I dropped into the backseat of my mind as if the body hurtling through the air was not my own. I saw the rear fender of a Lincoln Town Car and thought, *Other than that, Mrs. Lincoln, how did you enjoy the show?* I had time for only one more thought before I lost consciousness: *At least I wore a helmet.*

When I came to, there was an awful tightness around my throat and the feeling of being trapped. I blinked twice at the bleary image of a woman with full cheeks and a haughty nose. Her hair was done up like a modern Marie Antoinette, all ringlets and ribbons. Her hands were around my neck, and her claws sank into my throat, carefully, threatening, not ripping. She grew, skin changing from pale to black.

I found Lisette.

My own transformation began, but as the *akasha* flowed over me, Lisette slammed my head into the hood of her limo five times in succession, breaking my concentration. One hand reached inside my trousers and her claws touched my testicles.

"No transformation, Mr. Talbot." Her harsh voice cut through my head, increasing the headache that was already throbbing. "I wonder if you'd be willing to save us both a great deal of trouble by telling me where exactly in this city I can find Eric Courtney?"

25

GRETA:

FAT ASS GRANDMA

When Daddy's home, I never get to do this. Never ever. He has to save the day, because it makes him feel good. Happy. And I like him happy. He's more fun that way. And just as I was thinking about him, I thought I heard someone say his name. I almost didn't hear it—the sensation was more of a feeling than a sound, like when you could swear you heard someone say your name, but it's only the wind or someone saying something close to your name . . . that or they're lying to you and they really did say it, in which case it's perfectly fine for you to drain them on principle even if they *are* selling ice cream. Never mind.

"Did you hear that?" I didn't raise my voice despite the wind. The question was rhetorical, but Fang answered with an affirmative rev all the same. "I'll catch up with you at the concert."

"Eric Courtney." It had been Daddy's name, said by someone with a French accent. I crouched down across the floorboard so that when my clothes fell off they wouldn't blow away. Then I slid inward, like a sponge when someone wrings the water out: tight, dense, compact.

Daddy tends to transform into a vampire bat (which I totally don't get because echolocation gives him a headache, and he can turn into anything he wants, unlike the rest of us). Vlads usually get more choice in the matter, but it boils down to this: a vampire turning into an animal for the first time can *try* for anything it wants, but it has to be careful, because the less powerful a vampire is, the more likely it is to get stuck with the first animal it picks as its only option. Dad even had this vampire working in his old club that could only turn into a frog. Heh.

Tabitha had tried a bird and a cat and then gotten tired of doing either, preferring to focus on seeming human. I can only do three, but they're a really good three and I'm keeping two of them secret. The way I see it, every vampire should have a bat in its repertoire; it's a classic, but I did a lot of research before trying mine and went very specific. I turn into a *zorro volador filipino*, a giant golden-crown flying-fox, because they're fucking awesome! Plus, since they're the biggest bats in the world, with a wingspan of at least five feet, turning into one doesn't actually hurt much.

I clambered back up onto the seat, and Fang opened the driver's side door for me so that I didn't have to struggle against the wind so much when I took off. It's times like these that I wish vampires showed up on film so that I could see the whitish mask of fur on my face and how it mixes in with the reddish-brown fur. I've had Talbot describe it to me, even made a guy paint it once, but that's not the same as seeing it with my own eyes.

"He's not here." Talbot's voice strained, but I could still hear it as I cut through the air.

"Don't lie to me!" the French voice snapped.

Talbot grunted in pain and then, descending, I saw them. Smoke curled up from the remains of Talbot's motorcycle and a fat French lady who could only be Grandma stood in the middle of the street with one hand on his throat and the other down his trousers. *Grandma's a perv!*

Her hair was done up all fancy with ringlets and everything, and she wore this super cool renaissance-inspired dress with a corset. I didn't know how she'd crammed herself into the thing, but she reminded me of those hippos in tutus from *Fantasia*. A big gold necklace hung around her neck—eight strands of thick metal linked to a massive emerald that lay nestled between her breasts. It could have been pretty, but I couldn't help but think of an octopus when I saw it.

"That's a creepy necklace, Grandma." I landed barefoot on the asphalt. The overwarm air of the sultry evening clung to my skin and I wished I could do the whole bring-my-clothes-with-me thing that Dad and New Mom can do.

"You're naked," Grandma said, her lip caught partway between a smile and a sneer.

"Thank God you aren't." I stuck my tongue out. "I mean come on. Ew!"

"What did you say?"

"I said put the kitty down, Orca!"

"*Je ne comprends pas* Orca." Grandma cast Talbot aside with a hiss and he hit the side of a street lamp with his head so hard that it really did go *bong* like in the cartoons. "But I expect it is impolite."

"Yeah." I popped my claws. "Try these: Whale. Blubber butt. Fat ass. You look like an elephant in a tube top."

Grandma bared her fangs at me somewhere around "fat ass" and by the time I said "top" she was in motion. I backpedaled clear of her initial swipe. Her tiny curved talons failed to catch any skin, but my returning swipe scored a hit. A rent opened in her cheek where I'd clawed her; black ooze seeped out of the wound, its scent a mixture of rotted meat and spoiled herbs. Zombie blood?

"I can't eat zombie blood. Not even Talbot can stomach zombie blood. Ick!" My eyes flashed red, casting her face in crimson. "That's not fair!"

"Nor is life."

I heard the gargoyles before I saw them. Their wings cut the air with the heavy slap of sailcloth snapping in the wind. Grandma fell back into a stance of some kind, one leg leading the other, before going at me with a volley of kicks, alternating high then low in a hooking motion as if she wanted to trip me, but I was faster than her. I met the second high kick with a two-handed rake of my claws. She howled, but it sounded more like anger at her rent hosiery than pain. More black blood escaped her flesh, wrinkling my nose.

"I bet I can't eat you guys either." I pointed at the gargoyles, keeping my eyes on Grandma. "I hate fights where I can't eat the loser."

"You are always welcome to surrender." The speaker was a goat-headed gargoyle with a bowler hat and a dapper gray suit. On the ground, they looked smaller. Grandma's hand whipped by me, an open slap, easily avoided.

"Surrender?" I stayed on the defensive, getting a feel for Grandma and keeping an eye on the newcomers. It's hard to fight carefully, but I had to. Dad wasn't here to bail me out. Then again, he wasn't here to make me hold back either. "But there are only six of you guys, plus Grandma. You're toast."

"Silly child." Lisette grew, all of her clothes vanishing except for her necklace. Gray-black washed across her skin, her lips turning black and chalky as if powdered with coal dust. Her pupils faded to white, becoming dull and glassy like a zombie's. She licked her lips, leaving a trail of red blood in her tongue's wake. "I am an Empress."

"You also appear to be edible, after all." I gathered a smear of blood from her lips with a claw and licked it. It had the same heady tang that Dad's does—a distinct flavor. "Just hard to eat." I beamed. "Gourmet. Grandma, you're gourmet!"

Wings spread out behind her, drawing a chuckle from me. Wings are such a bad idea. Unless you're flying to or away from something, wings just get in the way. Grandma did neither, just stood in the street almost as naked as me. Her necklace matched the Empress form. Its gold chains had lengthened subtly. Transformed, there was a dim glow to the emerald on her necklace, the gentle green playing across her massive gray boobs. It stayed with her in both forms when her clothes didn't. That meant magic. But did that mean *memento mori*?

Only one way to find out: get it away from her and destroy it . . . melt it down or something.

"You like my necklace?"

"Huh?"

"Even in my Empress form, it captures your attention." Lisette reached back, unsnapping it with her claw-tipped fingers. "Try it on."

"Excuse me?"

"You keep calling me Grandma." As the emerald pulled away from her chest, the color swirled as if the gem were hollow. Then a dark crimson filled the space, changing the light from brilliant green to ruby red. "More properly *grand-mère*. You are my child's offspring, *oui*?"

"I'm adopted." Which answered the question, but didn't answer the question. Let her think I was a Soldier, just a really fast one. As I've said before, underestimation is a powerful tool. Just look at how people underestimate New Mom.

"I'd wondered. Imperial vampires create either Kings or Pawns. But—"

"But I'm not a Pawn." *Pawn . . . Pawn. What would she call Soldiers? Knights?* "And if I were higher than a Knight, you'd have sensed me and I'd have sensed you." *And I did sense you, too*, I crowed inside, *and tomorrow night I'll know how to destroy you. It'll be fun—a real moment of grandmother/ granddaughter bonding.*

"You're very quick for a *Chevalier*, my dear . . . ah?"

"Greta," I supplied the name for her, watching as she shrank back down to human size. Her clothes came back with her, warm and fresh-smelling, making me concentrate to avoid leaning toward their heat.

"I fight fast." I smiled. "But I can't do lots of animals or anything, and my clothes don't transform when I do."

"I'd noticed."

Lisette glanced at the limo and the driver stepped out, wordlessly stripping down to his Speedo and cap. He was about my height and trim, so the fit wouldn't be too far off. He offered me the clothes.

I slipped the pants on first, gouging an extra hole in the belt with the claw of my little finger. On the dress shirt, I buttoned only the bottom button, tucking it in so that it pulled tight against my breasts. Over that, I wore the jacket, using the bold crimson tie to replace the kerchief in the breast pocket. I was glad I'd had my toenails done, though, because though the ensemble worked surprisingly well, hardly anyone ever has shoes my size (I take a wide in a half-size).

As I dressed, several folks who'd been watching us and seeing whatever the Veil of Scrythax allowed, booed me (I guess it was because I'd put some clothes on), but Lisette silenced them with a twirl of her *memento mori*. It flashed blue and the whole crowd went slack-jawed for a few seconds, then went about their business. Interestingly enough, I felt the magic try to touch my mind too, and slide off.

I'm a little hard to control mentally. Dad says it's because most people don't know how to handle my mental landscape, which is odd, because I thought it had something to do with me being a little bit certifiable by human standards. Lots of vampires still have relatively human thoughts and feelings, but not me.

"Much better," Lisette approved.

"Even with the John McClane–inspired footwear."

She shrugged. "I'm not sure who that is, but it helps that you have attractive feet and know the meaning of the word pedicure."

"Cool."

"I feel we have had a misunderstanding, Greta, *ma chérie*." She held the necklace out to me, gripping the chains in a bunch as if she were holding a squid (or something else with tentacles). It was still overlarge and I realized it hadn't shrunk when she had. I didn't want that necklace to touch me. If Fang could strip a body down to the bones in seconds, who knew what Squidly was capable of. "I'm looking for my son. I have questions about how he came to be. I don't want to harm him."

I gave her the Spock eyebrow. "Really?"

"*Mais bien sûr . . .* but of course."

"Then why did you attack Talbot?"

"*Le chat noir?*" Grandma eyed Talbot's unconscious form. "How do you say in English? The Mousing?"

"Mouser," I corrected.

"I knew that he worked for Eric, but I knew not that he was more than a pet. How could I?"

"Well, it's just that Dad left me in charge of all his stuff while he's away and I think that includes employees and thralls . . ."

"Away?"

"Yes."

"Do you mind if I ask—?" She moved toward me, necklace extended.

W.W.D.D.—What Would Daddy Do?

I thought of so many ways to try and get more information out of her, to hide the idea that I know about *memento mori* and guessed that the necklace is hers. But Daddy wouldn't do that. He plays some things close to the vest, but not something like this. In UNO, he plays the special cards as soon as he gets them, throws them down with glee. So I do, too.

"Do you mind if *I* ask what your *memento mori* would do to me if I put it on?" I heard an intake of breath from Talbot at my comment and wondered how long he'd been playing possum. "Or do you think I'm a"—what curse word would Dad use—"motherfucking moron?"

My smile drew wide across my face as Lisette began to transform into her Empress form, throwing the necklace right at my head. Yeah. I thought that'd piss her off.

26

TALBOT:
CRUNCH. SLURP.

It's possible to see the *akasha* with your eyes closed, but it takes practice and things don't look the same. You catch it raw and uncut. Lisette's necklace, for example, active and in the presence of its Empress, snapped at the air with a sharp curving beak attached directly to the base of a massive gemlike eye. Lisette held it by eight of its golden tendrils, while two tentacles, more spirit than matter, wrapped around its creator's wrist.

More of a squid than an octopus.

I was still collecting my wits when Greta mouthed off to Lisette and the Empress threw the *memento mori*. Greta lurched to the right, dashing in at an arc to claw at Lisette's side, but Greta couldn't see the entire creature, only the material components, and one of the two spirit tentacles snagged her wrist. Similar things had happened with Eric in El Segundo. Vampires can't properly fight what they can't touch.

To be honest, though, I'd rather Greta died—much simpler that way—and at the hands of someone Eric was going to kill anyway.

"Ow," Greta said as the thing reeled itself in along the unseen spirit tentacles, and let the visible golden tendrils, which normally passed for necklace chains, take hold of her arm. "Get off, Squidly!"

I'd rather Greta died, but Eric loves her and he'd never forgive me if I let that happen, if I didn't pull out all the stops to save his little girl. . . .

I won't give you the whole spirit versus mundane versus magic speech, but suffice it to say that there aren't too many creatures that can exist in two worlds and touch both at the same time. I'm one of them (and to be exceedingly honest, I touch more than two). That Lisette's *memento mori*—Squidly, Greta had called it—could bridge the spirit and the physical worlds as well did nothing for my confidence level.

"Now you will have your answer," Lisette roared. "Let it touch you—"

"Damn." I don't curse a lot. Around Eric, there's no need. If something vulgar needs to be said, he'll say it, but every once in a while, I let one slip. Seems like that happens right before I get myself exiled or extend the exile under which I already find myself. "I am way too attached to that man."

I ignored Lisette. She and Greta could sort things out with the *memento mori*, but the gargoyles had to go. Two of them moved for Greta, and I shifted a portion of my spirit self through into the real world without thinking about it. When a vampire changes shape, there is no conservation of mass: it's pure physics-defying magic, but what I do is different. If I become a normal-sized cat, I shed the extra mass by moving it to the part of me that exists in either the dream-world or the *akasha*—the spirit world. If I go into full-out combat mode, I do it by pulling the bulk of myself into the physical world and leaving only a token presence behind, becoming something akin to a normal-sized cat there instead. If you're not used to being three places at once, it can get a little confusing.

There are methods and rituals I should have been doing in my mind to make sure I didn't lose my grip on the akashic realm altogether, but I didn't do any of them. I got lucky and pulled the right amount through without giving the other Mousers a shot at ejecting me completely, but it was a near miss, and I could feel them trying the entire time, like little kids tugging at my legs.

One step closer to the real me, in combat mode, as Eric calls it, I see the *akasha* more clearly. Demonic locus points show up nice and shiny, and the supernatural hums in my ears—a symphony of vibrations, not all of them good. The gargoyles were bad news. They were more than they seemed, too, creatures of three stripes: magic, mundane, and dream, almost like me in some respects, except that I have a paw in each of four worlds. In this form, with my spirit claws extending a few inches past my physical claws, I could see and affect the gargoyles, and the *memento mori*, in both worlds at the same time.

Using the same trick Squidly exploited to nab Greta, I jumped past the first gargoyle. It looked like a miss, but looks can be deceiving.

Gargoyles are tricky, because they are more energy than physical. They interact with the real world by inhabiting stone. If they are inside a statue, you can hurt them, but if they release their hold on it, what's left behind is wholly stone. You can't kill it, it's a statue with no more life than a brick. They are stuck though, usually able to interact with only one object at a time.

Destroy the statue and a gargoyle can manifest in another one. Call it insurance. If need be, they can easily flee to the spirit world, lick their wounds, and the next day, your statue of a little boy peeing in the fountain steps down off its pedestal and joins the fight.

To really hurt them, you have to hit the part of them that resides on the spirit plane, either when they are animating a statue or by using something that can affect them directly regardless of form. My claws, for example. Most humans can only affect the physical, which is why a gargoyle hangs between the worlds, balancing the protection of his stone skin against a stronger form that is more vulnerable to attack.

I inwardly laughed at the gargoyle's surprise when I sank my claws into the rest of him, the part of him hanging in the spirit world, little more than an aura to most folks. He let out an anguished shout as my claws tore his spirit and I took a bite that would never grow back because I'd Devoured it.

The closest one to me saw what happened and did the smart thing: he gave up the stone, going completely physical with blood flesh, hair, real horns, the whole nine yards. He lost the protection of the stone, but grew large with strength and gained speed in the bargain. His sinews groaned under the effort, but it was the best defense against what I'd done to his buddy.

"Does your heart weigh less than a feather?" I didn't wait for an answer, because I figured none was forthcoming. His wings tore apart under my callous fingers. "If not, I can eat you." He screeched like an eagle, then collapsed. Another gargoyle down.

"*Merde.*" That came from one of the remaining five gargoyles, but I couldn't tell which.

"Come on, boys. I—" While I spoke, one of the gargoyles shrunk in on itself, leaving a classic gargoyle statue lifeless in its place. It hung in the air at about head level just long enough for me to realize that he was breaking his own statue so he could interact with something else. Then the statue fell, hit the ground, and shattered.

Merde, indeed, I thought.

Another followed suit while a third pulled itself the rest of the way into this world and I found myself staring down two full-blown gargoyles with two unaccounted for and the fifth one grabbing Greta from behind.

Eric should be handling this.

Near the limo, Greta struggled to keep the Squidly off her chest, but the tentacles drew in ever closer, tendrils sunk deep into her shoulders for purchase. She had both hands gripped around the central gem/eye of the thing, pushing it away. Through the *akasha*, I could see its beak snapping toward her heart on the spirit plane.

"You want to play with the vampire or do you want to play with me?" I roared the question, hoping to draw the final gargoyle onto me, but he paid no heed.

Two rough-hewn hands made of asphalt thrust up from the road as one of the gargoyles created a new form for itself out of the street, which is something I hadn't realized gargoyles could do. I avoided one, got snagged by the other, and became a sitting target for two eight-foot goat-horned shaggy stink beasts hell-bent on turning me into cat tartare.

They were bigger than I was, but a lot of that was wing. Even so, it gave them a weight advantage to go with the numerical one. Each gargoyle also sported enough upper-body strength to flap those massive bat wings attached to his shoulders.

Blackbirds can fly away. Dezba's words went through my mind, and I came close to giving in. It would be so easy to cross back over to my homeland, leave the physical world and all this crap behind for a while. Sure, it would mean a helluva throwdown back home, but what were they going to do? Kill me? Here, maybe, but there? No way Sekhmet's favorite son goes down on his home plane. I remembered Dezba's body against mine, juxtaposed it mentally with the sensation of staring into Eric's aura, and the decision was made.

A swing, aimed for the head of a Mouser.

A punch, strong enough to knock out a Mouser.

A bite . . . Heh.

You'd be amazed at how wide a cat can open its mouth. Ever seen a lion roar? When I go silver-maned and furry, mine's bigger. And you can take that any way you want.

He screamed. Losing an arm up to the elbow will do that to a being. Gargoyles don't taste like chicken. There's a surprising similarity to turtle. I'd expected a muttonesque flavor, but turtle's not bad. A very earthy, gritty taste, but palatable. Thick claylike sludge oozed gray-brown from the wound.

Twin fists from the other all-in-this-world goat boy hit like hammers between my shoulders, driving me down in a serious face-meet-asphalt moment. I scraped the pads of my paws in a failed attempt to catch myself and did an excellent job of loosening at least one molar.

A bewitched passenger stared at me out the window of a Ford Taurus, the blank glaze on the man's face nothing like the Veil of Scrythax's effect. *Squidly,* I thought to myself, *that's some powerful flashy blue mind magic you've got there.*

Two more asphalt hands rent the street on either side of my throat. Wincing even as I did it, I swung both arms outward, smashing the earthen constructs at the expense of another road-face impact.

Strong but brittle.

Duly noted.

A swift kick to the asphalt hands gripping my ankle and I freed myself long enough for the other big gargoyle to land on my back, wrestling to get me in a full nelson. I hate it when they know my biggest advantage and effectively deny it to me. Eric would have been challenged, perhaps amused even. Not me.

Reaching up with both paws, I grabbed for the spot where the gargoyle's wings attached and found it. Metallic silver claws dug into the base of his shaggy brown wings. The left wing gave with an appetizing shredding of sinew and the sound of muscle ripping free of bone.

"*Non!*" From the voice, I could tell it was the polite gargoyle who'd showed up back at the Pollux. "*Pardonnez-moi!* I shall release you! I concede. Your forgiveness, I beg!"

Eric accepts apologies. It's in his rule book.

Crunch!

A single bite meant he'd never fly again. The rest of the wing, I shoved in like one of those creatures on *The Muppet Show*: no chewing—just one long thrust into my nigh-endless gullet. *Slurp.*

A cry of anguish more bleat than scream sounded in my ears. His grip went slack and I turned, free of him. "You concede? It may work that way in Europe, but in the States . . ."

But there was no need to finish. He was broken—in shock.

Taking advantage of the lull, I jumped onto the trunk of the Le Baron in front of Lisette's limo, keeping my feet clear of the ground. *Can gargoyles use metal too?* The thought froze in my head, stunned into repetition by the cacophonous thump of Squidly striking against Greta's sternum with a hollow reverberating sound like a *taiko* stick against a six-foot Japanese *taiko* drum.

Squidly's gem flared blue and Greta's eyes flared blue to match. Not to be repetitive, but . . . "Damn."

27

GRETA:

SQUIDLY

Water flowed in under the beach house door. Cold from the ocean, it tickled my feet, the salty sea smell filling my nostrils. A broken television glared at me from the midpoint of the wall, its screen ruined by Daddy's fist. I looked down to find myself still clad in a dirty nightshirt, thighs smeared with traces of blood and something else.

"Oh." I knelt down. Water lapped against me, soaking through the nightgown. I washed myself. Residue from my pre-Daddy life swirled away. "I'm in my head."

"Drown." The voice sounded thin and reedy, like Grandma's voice might if carried via tin-can telephone.

"I can't drown, silly." Water rose, lifting my nightgown. "I'm dead already."

I stood still. The water rose to my thighs. It felt foreign. Unwanted. Teeth set, I waited.

"You will drown in your own mind. And then you will be mine."

"You do not have my permission to fill my beach house with water."

"Drown."

Water touched my elbows, the cold making me shiver. My heart raced. Okay, so maybe, in this, my happiest memory, I was still alive.

"Do not make me go upstairs and wake him."

"Wake who? You are alone"—something touched my ankle under the water—"with me."

"You're not Grandma."

Rough squidlike tendrils wrapped around my legs. Fear, a treacherous sliver of it, gnawed at the back of my mind. What if I could drown? I couldn't move. Couldn't react. I knew where I needed to go—to the happy and safe place in my mind—but as the water rose over my chest, all I could do was scream.

But in my head, that's enough to bring him running. I didn't even have to call his name—just scream.

"Yes." Tentacles moved higher, a filthy caress across my belly and around my throat. "Scream while you can."

"What the fuck is going on down there?"

Daddy!

"How?" Water rushed in over me as the door exploded inward, and I knew that outside the beach house there was nothing but ocean. Tentacles wrapped around me, dragging me under even as the voice asked, wonderingly, "How can he . . . ?"

Daddy shouted my name above the water. His voice was muffled, but the concern in his tone still came through.

And then my awareness broke through in both places, inside my head and outside of it, simultaneously coherent like any other time a vampire has tried to control me. It's been done once or twice. Daddy can do it, because that's as it should be. Nobody can deal with the version of Daddy that's in my head. Most can't even deal with me.

"I'm not afraid, Grandma." Lisette stepped backward, eyes wide, frightened even in her Empress form. A quick glance showed me an older car idling in the far right lane. Six cars ahead of us, drivers had moved on, but for a half-dozen car lengths in all directions, the drivers patiently waited for Grandma's permission to move.

Grandma's *memento mori* writhed between my boobs, tentacles tightening convulsively around my neck. I plunged my hand through the sides of the car trunk, ripping it open to reveal a cooler, lawn chairs, and what I wanted: a tire iron. Auntie Rachel once stopped Fang by jamming a tire iron through his engine block, so I rammed the iron home, through the *memento mori*'s large gem, through my chest and deep into my own heart—which, based on the pain, will clean out sinuses if they're stopped up. I mean: fuckin' ow!

Grandma and her *memento mori* screamed in unison. Talbot leapt from the trunk of one car to the bed of a big truck, evading the grasp of the gargoyle that had been holding me before the *memento mori* got me. Two others lay on the ground trying to make the asphalt heal their wounds or something. Each of them seemed panicked and blubbery, mumbling to themselves in French.

"I think I left my stake in the car." I waved at Lisette. "Be right back."

"*Tuez-la!*" Grandma yelled in French, but I knew what she meant: Kill her.

In this part of downtown, newly refurbished buildings stood side by side with old ones, and the trees that once lined the streets were mostly gone, replaced by iron grids over sad-looking mulch. *Wood. Wood. Wood. I need wood.* I could punch through a wall, try to find a two-by-four. . . . I rolled through the glass of an abandoned furniture store with a lease sign in the window before I could change direction. I had a new plan . . . and it was much more fun.

The injured gargoyles came after me as expected. I ran out through the back, feet covered in cuts and glass, but they weren't holy wounds, so the pain was small and fleeting. The rear fire door wrenched free of its brick moorings when I hit it, and up the fire escape I went. One tiny jump for a vampire . . . At full speed, the edge of my vision blurred and I imagined a sonic boom (or maybe it was real, but I suspect it was only in my head). A series of rapid-fire jumps conjured a further image, one of Ricochet Rabbit from those old cartoons.

Gargoyles followed in slow motion. Each footstep hurt less and less as the particles of glass reached their maximum depth. Rooftops vanished below me as I raced back in the direction of Lisette, raised up my arms, and did a swan dive from about five stories up.

Her head came up at the final second, but she did the human thing: she reacted with surprise instead of moving.

"Qu'est-ce—?"

"No one expects the Spanish Inquisition!" See! Now why hadn't Dad been there to hear that?

I hit Grandma in the wings, driving her to the ground, smashing her face against the street. She threw her arms out in front of her. Bones snapped. Some hers. Some mine. Black ichor, zombie nastiness, flowed out from the wounds. It pooled at my knees and around her chest. I couldn't stop, couldn't give her time to heal. I forced her over onto her back, her left wing ripping as she rolled onto it at an unnatural angle.

I hit the sweet spot over her sternum just right, popped it, and went straight for the heart. Grandma's chest cavity was rotten on the inside. The obsidian flesh of her uber vamp body was full of rancid meat and pus. In the middle of it all, one organ was beautiful and full, untouched by corruption: her heart. It came free with a wet snap, more easily than a human's, and I leapt up, ignoring the pain in my knees, attempting to run on legs that'd broken.

"What on earth?" Talbot looked at me, eyes wide, nostrils flared, and smelling like fear. A grunt of annoyance passed my lips when my broken legs wouldn't support my weight.

Gargoyles hit the ground behind me and Talbot leapt forward to engage them, silver claws gleaming in the night.

"Greta, run!"

"I'm trying!"

Seizing Grandma's heart between my fangs freed up my hands, and I began to crawl. Her blood hit my tongue with all the heat of tobacco and none of the taste, kicking my regeneration into overdrive. Shards of glass pushed out of my feet as I stood on knees reknitting with audible pops and snaps. She tasted like Dad.

Now all I had to do was get Grandma's heart to a piece of wood so that I could impale it. If you can't bring Muhammad to the mountain . . .

A cry of rage broke through the night, and the street filled with the scurry and screech of rodents (winged and otherwise). Clumps of rats erupted from the sewer drains. Bats, a billowing cloud of them thick enough to block out the moon, descended upon the street. There was nowhere to run, and I could not get away. Vermin came from everywhere, tearing at my skin, gnawing, ripping, and biting. I struggled against the tide, smashing some with my arms and others with my fists, but there were too many. Vanishing under the wave of living fury, I smiled before my face was torn away.

Good girl, Grandma, I thought. *Very cool. You think you have me? Then come try to stake me. I need a stake anyway.*

Soon, my nerve endings gone, the pain faded and I waited. Rats fought over the tender morsels within my skull and it made me want to watch *Tatsu 7* something fierce. A hazard, I suppose, of watching anime from inside a human skull too many nights in a row.

Come on, Grandma.

The body is just an interface. Except for Dad, most vampires don't see with eyes or hear with ears, not really. They can, but if vampires adapt, if they give in, all of those senses are really activated by the magic that makes them undead. Maybe that's why I'm hungry all the time. Living like I do, always on when I'm awake, consumes the blood that powers me faster than other vampires. They let the meat be more than it is, and I don't.

Do you really think it's muscle that lets a vampire be super-strong, that human muscle, somehow supercharged by blood, lets us move so fast and grow claws? No, the body is just an interface. Since Grandma could still use her powers with her heart ripped out, I knew she knew, but what I was counting on was that, despite all that knowledge, she didn't truly understand. Hardly any of them do.

If I concentrated, I could feel little pieces of myself in a thousand different stomachs, catching glimpses of my nearly bare skeleton. I looked so . . . thin. Concentrating on holding back my regeneration and on keeping my bones together, concentrating on keeping her heart locked in my jaws (though the rodents refused to touch it), I waited.

If the rats noticed my bones didn't pull apart as they should have once the tissue was gone, they didn't say anything or give any warning in a language Grandma understood. I lost track of Talbot, but from the sound of things, he went toe-to-toe with Grandma and lost. I heard a scream like a skinned cat and assumed it was him. Poor kitty. He wasn't part of the plan, though. I didn't need him.

"*Avez-vous mon baton?*" Grandma asked. I barely made out her words over the screech and scrabble of my furry little diners.

"*Oui, madame.*" A single out-of-breath gargoyle gasped through clenched teeth. I couldn't hear any others. *Good job, Kitty.*

Vermin parted to reveal Grandma, one end of a wooden baton in her hand. She had transformed back into her human form again, but her clothes were ripped and torn. Her hand shook as she approached, baton held like a dagger. She'd broken it into a rude approximation of a traditional stake. Her hands blurred as she jabbed it where she thought my heart would re-form.

Poor stupid Grandma.

With skeletal hands, I grabbed her wrist, pulling the stake directly into my waiting mouth, right through her own heart, which I'd been holding so carefully for so long.

My mouth opened wide and the clamped cardiac muscle (and intruding stake) fell free, only to be caught in my still skeletal phalanges.

"I bet you weren't expecting that one, Grandma."

Her body fell backward among the scattering rats with a sickening *splurch.* I tried to smile, but couldn't, due to the lack of flesh. It produced an uncomfortable phantom sensation and perhaps, in the gullet of some rat or other, my severed cheek muscles twitched.

A lone remaining gargoyle stared as I pulled the tire iron from my cracked sternum, careful not to accidentally free Grandma's *memento mori*, and stuck it down into Grandma's still gaping chest cavity. My eye sockets flared red.

"Boo!" I took a step toward the gargoyle and it ran. With Grandma and her *memento mori* incapacitated, her hold over the crowd fell away and the screams started, first one, then another, and the crowd descended into panic.

I like screams . . . but they're *so expensive.*

My fangs sank into Grandma's heart once more and my flesh re-formed in a violent explosion of regenerative magic. I lifted Grandma's body with one arm and headed down the street toward the concert, still gnawing at her heart-on-a-stick. Six blocks down, a police cruiser waited, sirens blazing, lights flashing. Talbot stood there next to Captain Stacey.

In Void City, vampires and other supematurals have to pay "fang fees" if they pull stupid stunts the Veil of Scrythax can't cover up on its own. Captain Stacey is the person who hands them out, and he's a Mouser. He'll even do "off the clock" jobs for the right price. Last year, Auntie Rachel had paid him off to help her capture New Mom and Talbot during the whole demon-trying-to-steal-Daddy's-soul thing. He's much more fun to be around when he's just writing tickets and doing day job stuff. Captain Stacey pointed to a mage casting some sort of spell in the distance, and Talbot cringed. Both Mousers were shaking their heads. Talbot was writing out a check with a lot of zeroes in the amount.

Men and women in Public Works uniforms worked their way through the crowd, only a few of them bothering to look up at me as I approached. I dumped Grandma's body next to the police car, holding the heart-on-a-stick in one hand and the *memento-mori*-on-a-tire-iron in my other.

Now all I had to do was wait until tomorrow so that I could read Grandma a third time and figure out the one true way to kill her.

"Hey, cool," I said by way of greeting. "Do I get to ride in a police car?"

28

GRETA:

DEATH OF THE PARTY

An hour later, Grandma's body, her still-staked heart, and her pinioned necklace were safely ensconced in Fang's trunk. A dozen new pink "Welcome to the Void" baby-doll T-shirts sat on the back seat next to thirteen new shirts for Dad: ten black, two of the new white ones, and one royal blue, all purchased by Talbot from a lucky vendor. I was wearing one of mine along with a pair of low-rise jeans, decorative chains hanging from either side, a studded black belt, and a pair of pink Skechers. Talbot had sent Magbidion for my clothes when I'd decided I didn't want to put the dress back on.

Magbidion, Talbot, and I stood in the front row, waiting for Winter's set to begin. A thousand or more people crowded around the stage, some sitting on the grass, others in lawn chairs. Part of the grassy area at center stage had been cordoned off with blue velvet ropes overseen by a group of bouncers from the Artiste Unknown. Somewhere else in the city, maybe at the Highland Towers, maybe back at the Pollux, Lord Phillip wanted to speak with me again, but I didn't care.

"Can I eat that guy over there? The one with the nummy looking tats?"

"Not if you want to see the show." Talbot grabbed Magbidion's arm and held his exposed forearm in front of my face. "Do you need to take a hit off Mags?"

"Hey. Ow." Magbidion pulled halfheartedly against Talbot's grip. "Damn it, Talbot."

"No," I said. Talbot released Magbidion's arm. Mags breathed a quiet sigh of relief. "Not from there." And then I bit him. Sudden, hard, and fast, my fangs sank into Magbidion's throat. He started, but didn't struggle, so I kept things to a quick sip or two, following up with a bloody kiss on the cheek, leaving perfect red lip marks.

"Shit." A shortish teen with tri-toned highlights and a leash in her hand gave the collared girl next to her a subtle tug. "We're right next to a fucking vampire and her thralls." Her taller, thinner girlfriend— the one on the leash—nodded, heart speeding up, part thrill, part fear.

"Do you think she knows Winter?"

"Ladies—" Talbot wanted to warn them away or move them along, but I liked them. They smelled like grassy fields, sweat, sunlight, and the ghost of perfume applied in the early morning hours and worn away by the day's exertions.

"You like vampires?"

"Greta." Talbot's words had no wind to them, so dim they could have been a subvocalization. "I wrote a check for two million dollars to cover the excitement from earlier. Eric had that much liquid, but barely."

"Shhh." I hissed at him. "I know."

Two million dollars is a whole lot of money, but when I told Dad I'd killed Lisette for him, ended her forever, he wouldn't be mad. It was a great homecoming present.

Worried confusion flittered across the faces of the two foods . . . um, girls . . . young women.

"I asked you a question."

They looked at each other, then answered together, "Yes."

"Not lifestyle vamps." I ran a finger along the hot pinkish skin on the shorter one's neck and shoulders, leeching heat. "Real vampires?"

"Yes."

Smooth, well-lotioned skin passed under my fingers, the tips picking up traces of oil. Wending my way across her skin, up along her face, and down the jawline, past her neck, my hand stopped at her chest to feel her heartbeat through the reddened skin.

This is what it feels like when the tiger is the lady, I thought, *or when the tiger pets you.* Short girl's pet wanted to protest. Her tongue clicked in the back of her throat each time she began to speak, followed by the sound of teeth on teeth as she held her tongue.

"You have a sunburn."

"Yeah. I forgot—"

"And a nice heartbeat."

"Thanks."

"But you're fat." I didn't mean it as an insult exactly. She still lived. She could change. Just a fashion tip—like if you told someone they might look nice with a shorter hairstyle.

"I . . ." Eyes glistening, on the verge of possible tears, she reminded me of someone. Maybe Petey when I found him all hurt and mewling, before I turned him. Not Darla. Darla was never a crier. The girl on the leash was the one who reminded me of Darla . . . if Darla had grown up to be tall and thin. Making Petey and Darla had been my attempt at understanding the process, to know how Dad could care for me so much and then send me away for a year or so without ever even checking on me. I made them, I sent them away, and I haven't checked on them. . . . I still don't get it, but I keep trying.

"I'm not making fun of you." I touched her cheek with my free hand. "You're hoping to be a vampire one day, right?"

She nodded.

"Then you need to know about all of your physical flaws beforehand, so you can fix them, if you want to fix them." I leaned close, my lips touching her ear as I spoke. "I used to be fat, but my sire refused to turn me until I was toned and in shape. He wanted me to be in a body I'd never regret having."

She gave another slight nod, a subconscious one, and made a quiet "Oh."

"Forever is a long time to fret about a few extra pounds."

"Could you—" Leashed Girl spoke up. "I mean—" She looked away. "Are you looking for any new recruits?"

"I don't know." My answer was more for me than them—"We'll see." I didn't really want any more kids, but supposedly if I made a thrall, well, Mags seemed to think it would help me sense Daddy, all the way from here to Paris.

"Are you serious?" They said it in unison.

"If you're good. Thralls first and then—maybe—vampires."

"Thralls?" Leashed Girl asked.

"Humans who take care of a vampire's needs."

"What kind of needs?" Chubby Girl asked.

"All of them." I paused a beat while they exchanged looks that were equal parts trepidation and excitement. "I'm cold."

"I could get you a jacket . . ." Leashed Girl looked back over the crowd and at her watch, the doubt that she could make it to wherever they'd parked the car and back before the concert clear in her eyes.

"That won't help." Talbot's sudden utterance made the foods flinch. "Vampires don't have sustained body heat. Jackets, blankets, and such only help you stay warm if you're warm to begin with. They help you hold in your body heat."

"But feeding warms them up, right?" asked Chubby Girl.

"Some, but they start cooling again immediately. So unless you've got a heating element in your jacket, it won't do her any good."

"I'm. Cold."

"Um." Chubby Girl maneuvered herself around so that her back was pressed against my chest. A gentle tug on the leash told Leashed Girl to press against my back as well. The doubled heartbeat brought out my fangs, twin flares of fleeting pain heralding the deployment.

"I'm Rita, by the way," Chubby Girl said over her shoulder. "That's Peg on the leash."

"Don't be silly." I nipped her ear, drawing a single bead of blood. "I haven't decided what to name you both yet, but it certainly isn't Rita or Peg. Until I decide, I think I'll call you Apples, and Leash Girl can be Oranges . . . so I can compare you better. After all, I may not want to keep both of you."

Leash Girl . . . er, Oranges snuggled up more closely at that, nuzzling my neck. For all that she wasn't as large as Apples, Oranges put off more heat. *High blood pressure?*

Making these two thralls might work out, I told myself. Daddy tends to take beautiful women who want to sleep with him, make them thralls, and then refuse to sleep with them. Lesbians were the obvious choice for me if I wanted to do the same. They would want to sleep with me, but I wouldn't be inclined to have sex with them, because I don't like girls. Simple.

My cell phone vibrated in my pocket and I had Oranges fish it out.

"It says 'Uncle Asshat,'" she said before holding it in front of me.

"Turn it off," I told her. "And put it back in my pocket."

I rested my head on Apples' sunburned shoulders and smiled. If I were still human, I might be like these two, willing to offer myself to a stranger in the hope she might one day make me powerful and immortal. Daddy'd made me wait, but he hadn't strung me along. My eyes closed. Warmth surrounded me. Sweat and people, damp grass, the smell of cigarettes and beer all rushed through my senses. Thousands of conversations and conflicting music from various iPods built a wall of sounds around me both welcome and uncomfortable.

Winter was backstage, feeding. Gentle sucking sounds signaled the act of feeding through a plasma bag, but it wasn't human blood. Each time his lips left the tube, the smell reached me. Blood scent cuts through any other odors, a transcendent aroma. Cow's blood. Microwaved cow's blood! Why did he bother with animal blood when I knew he had thralls?

"Ow . . . um . . . Mistress?" Apples spoke, breaking my concentration, and the wall of sound tumbled as my senses contracted.

"What?"

"Your fingernails." Breasts make good hand warmers, and I'd been unconsciously cupping hers.

"Oh, my claws extended." I retracted them, the process unsettling but not painful, a phantom crawling of the nail bed. "Better?"

"Yes."

Winter hit the stage and the roar deafened me. There was no fanfare. No buildup. The spotlight hit center stage and he walked out into the light with a measured strut. He wore a white headset mike and said nothing. He stood. Waited. And the crowd grew louder. Apples and Oranges joined in, but not me. I'd always suspected Winter of using some kind of power to elicit this kind of reaction, but I couldn't feel one. They loved him. The living, the dead, and the "other" all worshipped him.

"Tonight—" The word was washed away by a cheer. Winter narrowed his gaze, cleared his throat once, and a hush fell over the crowd. "Tonight, I'll be doing something I never ever do. Tonight . . . I'll be taking requests from the audience."

The crowd roared.

"I'll be taking requests"—he spoke over the crowd, and they silenced themselves for him again—"but only from people who've done something very interesting today. Something weird or dangerous. Something touching or the very embodiment of hilarity. Andre will be waiting at the side of the stage with a microphone. But for the first two songs, I want a show of hands."

Thousands of hands went up, mine among them.

Winter's eyes sparkled like sapphires when he saw me.

"Void City's very own Greta Fleischman."

I hate it when people use my old last name.

"And what have you done this evening?"

"I ripped out my grandma's heart and ran a wooden stake through it!"

He beamed. Chuckles made their way through the crowd amid cries of "Bullshit" and "Me too" and "What did she say?"

"You'll sing anything?"

"Anything you want to hear, but it has to be a good song. One of mine or a classic."

"'Thriller!'"

He froze. It's something vampires who are really vampires can do. Go completely still, inside ourselves. "Michael Jackson's 'Thriller'?"

"That or David Bowie's 'The Laughing Gnome'!"

"'Thriller' it is, but if I'm going to sing it, then I'm going to do the dance." Hoots and hollers rose up from the crowd. "And if I'm going to dance it"—he pointed at the crowd starting at the left and sweeping right—"then you all have to dance it. And you'll have to be good or I won't take any more requests. Can you do it?"

They could, or they were willing to try. They'd do anything for him as long as he was onstage. Some performers are like that. Winter called a group of us up onstage to go through the dance routine and teach it to the crowd while he brought in the band one member at a time.

Before he started singing, Winter pulled me aside with a gesture, covering his mike with his hand. "You picked 'Thriller' to embarrass me?"

"No." I looked him in the eye, daring him to check. "It and 'The Laughing Gnome' are my two favorite songs. Next would be the theme songs to *Scooby Doo* and *Sesame Street*."

"I believe you," he said after a moment, his composure seeping back in. "I truly do, so I'll tell you something. Phillip has been trying to contact you tonight, yes?"

I nodded.

"You don't take down an Emperor in Void City without getting his attention. He'll want you to give Lisette to him. He'll offer you a lot of money or favors or both for her."

"And you want me not to do it?"

"I won't say what I want, but I will say this, make him tell you *why* he wants her before you agree or disagree. Do that and I won't hold your song choices against you."

I shrugged. "Whatever."

"Is that a 'yes'?" His eyes blazed red.

"Sure. Yes."

Talbot and my two foods came up onstage and Talbot read the Vincent Price part. It was the coolest version of "Thriller" I ever heard, and when Winter followed it up with "The Laughing Gnome," my heart sank. What did Winter think was going to happen? Why did he think he needed to sing both of my favorite songs when he so obviously didn't want to? The only reason I could think of was that he wanted to be on my good side or wanted me to put in a good word with Daddy.

In his final set, Winter sang a medley of the *Sesame Street* theme song and the theme to *Scooby Doo*. A chill moved over me, bringing with it an abnormal sense of dread. What did Winter know that he wasn't going to tell me? And why was he sucking up? Then and there, I made up my mind. I'd go see Uncle Phil tomorrow, *after* I killed Grandma.

29

TALBOT:

OTHER PEOPLE'S MESSES

"So what do we do now?" The dumpy faux redhead with control issues (the one Greta was calling Apples) stared at me with bleary eyes. Her taller, more attractive companion (Oranges?) snored softly, legs curled awkwardly to keep them from dangling off the edge of the circular sofa upon which she lay.

"Get some sleep." I paced the tiles in the salon-style sitting area outside the men's and women's restrooms in the downstairs area below the lobby and concession space in the Pollux. "Get Magbidion to show you how to tuck Greta in tomorrow morning once she's had a chance to introduce you to Fang."

"Fang?"

"You'll just have to meet Fang. There's no explaining him until you've met him." I flipped off the lights, purposefully allowing my cat's eyes to gleam yellow-green in the dark. "You can use this space for the day. The more private rooms all have Eric's thralls or me in them."

"You're not his thrall?"

"I'm not *his* anything, unless you mean friend, and even that is complicated."

"Complicated how?"

"I'm not human, for starters."

"Neither is he." Apples rubbed at her eyes.

"I'd debate that, but not with you."

"Why not with me?"

"You don't interest me." I enumerated my first point by extending a silver talon; it caught the light from my eyes and rendered Apples in shades of green—a Granny Smith. "And"—a second claw appeared to tick off my second reason—"you won't be around long."

"Longer than you might think." She rubbed her eyes again, and I knew she wouldn't make the cut. Oranges probably knew it too.

"Only if you kill Oranges in her sleep."

"I love Oranges." Her breath caught partway through the sentence. Watching her through the akashic field, I saw she told the truth. I saw other things too, which made the fact that Apples loved Oranges tragic and a bit too much information.

"I know. I can sense that."

"So, are you a were-something?"

"No." I made my way to the stairs and stopped at the bottom, backlit by the excess illumination from the light upstairs. "And don't ask questions about a being's supernatural heritage. Figure it out or wait until they tell you." I took a step up. "If you and your girlfriend are smart, you'll rest up and then leave before Greta gets up this evening. You won't, because you aren't. That's a pity."

"But she's going to make us thralls tonight! And later, she might make us vampires."

"It's possible." I let the eye glow fade. "Remotely. Anything she's seen Eric do . . . Greta might decide to do, but she's unpredictable, and unlike her father, Greta truly is a monster. Last night she started killing people in front of the Pollux for no reason other than she wanted to eat them. She's always hungry. Eric is good to the women and the men who serve him; he cares about them. But to Greta, humans are either food or toys."

"Immortality is worth it." Her voice faltered. "It's worth anything."

"You trying to convince me or convince yourself?"

She didn't answer. Her inner struggle played out visibly in the *akasha* as I watched. Reason lost out to envy, greed, desire. It wasn't a pretty sight to see. Oranges' aura shone bright and steady. She knew what she had to do, and she'd demanded the tools to accomplish it. Her lack of concern and desire to surrender her will to others combined with her genetic tendency toward thinness and her need, visible even in her sleep, to work out, to stay in shape. Oranges showed a streak of bleak resolve that might get her through this, but Apples seemed like dead meat.

"I'll send one of the girls down with a few pillows and some blankets."

Erin took them down for me, and I joined Magbidion in the parking deck. Mags had temporarily ensorcelled the side of his RV to be clear as glass and stood over the stove, cooking pancakes while keeping an eye on Fang.

"Want some pancakes?"

"No, thanks." I circled Fang, and the engine roared to life. "Calm down," I told the car. "I'm not going to try to open the trunk."

Greta's skeleton, rising through a mass of rats and bats, filled my mind's eye. The sight of her, standing triumphant over the body of an Emperor, *memento mori* defeated, the vampiric gender-swapped equivalent of David versus Goliath, was burned into my brain.

"Anything, yet?"

"Not yet." Mags flipped his pancakes out onto a plate, buttered them, and then poured a thick stream of syrup over the top of the stack.

"You sure you don't want pancakes? I already fed the girls and I still have batter left over."

"Thanks, but no."

"Fang?"

Eric's Mustang revved its engine once before idling down and turning off. Magbidion won't walk in front of the car when it's on, not since it advanced on him when he unwittingly helped Eric enliven it. The mage set his plate on his tiny kitchen table, stepped down from the RV, plastic mixing bowl in hand, and poured the batter directly onto the deck in front of Fang.

"Can it eat pancake batter?"

"I don't see why not." Mags scrambled back up into the RV and Fang started his engine, rolling over the batter, and then easing back into the parking space. "The contents of people's stomachs is never left behind. Neither are their clothes. So why not pancake batter?"

"Any word from Tabitha or Eric?" I paced the deck as I spoke, regretting my decision to turn down Magbidion's pancakes. He ate them with relish, pausing only to speak.

"No."

"Once we've resolved the Lisette issue, you know someone is going to have to fly out there and find out what the hell is going on."

"And leave Fang unprotected?"

Therein lay the rub. If we took Fang with us, Eric would be in danger. If we left Fang here, Eric would be in danger.

"Then I'll go to Paris." I adjusted my tie. "You can stay here with Greta and protect Fang."

He winced. "I'm going to have bacon and eggs next. Want any?"

"Sure."

"You like 'em scrambled, right?"

"Yes, please."

"Do you want ham or bologna in them?"

I don't remember what I told him, I think I said ham, but I wasn't concentrating on the eggs. Out of nowhere, I was thinking about Dezba, wondering where she was, what she was doing. I'd stayed nearby to help out, but Lisette was captured . . .

Through the *akasha*, I observed her. Lisette's spirit raged, as did her *memento mori*. Lines of violet and dark red burned through her spirit, etched with sharp yellow barbs of fear. Greta seemed confident she could kill Lisette when she woke up tomorrow, that she'd hit upon the method first thing, and I wondered if there was more to it than Greta was telling me.

"All those times Eric sent Greta away," I spoke the thought as I had it, "did you ever wonder what she was doing while she was running around without a chaperone?"

"She had a chaperone," Magbidion said softly, moving the eggs around in his frying pan. "Marilyn used to visit her every Tuesday. They'd talk on the phone most days, too, when Marilyn got home from work."

"How do you know that?"

"We were both smokers." Magbidion handed me my eggs. "You'd be surprised how personal chats get when you're standing outside, smoking in an alley."

I know he said "chats" but for a split second, I'd heard it as "cats." You'd be surprised how personal *cats* can get when they're standing outside.

"I didn't know that."

"You didn't know Marilyn was Roger's thrall either." Magbidion started frying bacon in the pan. "You've got good hearing, Talbot, and you see a lot, but how did you miss that one?"

"I didn't miss it," I said slowly.

"You knew and you didn't tell him." Magbidion dropped the skillet.

"I wanted to see how long it took Eric to figure it out." I looked down at the eggs and pushed them away. "And I know Eric better than you. He didn't really want to know. He rarely does. Besides, I do try to keep our laws."

"Laws?"

"Knowledge gleaned from the *akasha* is not for those who are blind to its light."

"You're a cold man, Talbot."

"I'm male, but I'm not a man, Mags."

After setting the hot bacon on a plate upon which he'd placed two paper towels to help soak up the grease, Magbidion cracked eggs in the pan with dexterity born of mystic gestures and precision that comes from working with forces that might blow you apart.

"So you're a cool cat then?" Magbidion asked with a grin.

"Maybe that." I picked up a piece of the bacon gingerly, taking careful bites followed by rapid chewing to keep from burning my tongue.

Once his eggs were ready, Magbidion spread mayonnaise onto two slices of bread and placed an egg on each one. He crumbled bacon atop each egg and looked up at me.

"Does it bother you that Lord Phillip hasn't sent a load of goons down here to take Lisette's body?" he asked.

"You have no idea." I stood. "If Eric calls, tell him I went to visit Dezba."

"Wait." Magbidion stopped, frozen in the act of cutting through his fried egg with a fork, the golden yolk spilling out onto the bread. "When are you coming back?"

"When you see me again, you'll know."

"But we're watching Lisette and—"

"And I'm bored, so I'm going out. Look it up under *cat*." Extricating myself from behind the little table took more maneuvering than getting behind it had. I caught a flash of red from behind Mags's back as I passed, energy from the blood tattoo that marked him as Eric's thrall.

Eric had once told me he could see the faces of other vampires when he looked at their thralls and concentrated. For me, the *akasha* makes thralls obvious even though it doesn't usually give me any idea to which vampire they belong. I rely on their convenient little markings to tell me the rest. Eric's thralls all have a butterfly tattoo. Lady Gabriella uses a rose. The glowing red tattoo I'd seen on Oranges' back was a stylized *P*.

A young man with a glow on his scalp, beneath his curly black hair, sat at a bus stop reading a newspaper. I'd seen him before, enough times to make out that the tattoo he had was in the shape of an ankh. He wore a pair of Oakland sunglasses with a yellow tint to the lenses and a subtle blue glow—a sure sign of magic. Possibly the same shade of blue Oranges' collar emitted, but it could have been different.

As I walked down the street, I noticed a group of people, all with various blood tattoos, sitting inside Carl's Diner, waiting for their breakfasts. Getting ready for another day of spying on Eric's business and reporting back to their various masters and mistresses.

I kept walking, leaving my car parked in the Pollux's deck and then, two streets over, I left my human form behind, too, padding down the sidewalk as a cat with star emerald eyes. Eyes that would have drawn attention in other places, but never in Void City. The Veil of Scrythax saw to that. Three blocks later, I broke into a run, the city blurring past me as I fled. It was different when Eric was home: interesting, fun, purposeful. But a cat is not a sheepdog. Riding herd on Greta . . . I couldn't do it anymore. When Eric came back, so would I . . . or maybe I'd even join him in Paris.

Or maybe, though I found it unlikely, maybe I knew what was going to happen to Greta and I couldn't bear to break the rules for her, but I was afraid I would if I stayed. What if, after I shared knowledge from the *akasha* once again, the other Mousers *did* find a way to exile me completely? Exile that I could end at any time, I could face for another century or two, but exile without end? Unthinkable, unless it was for Eric himself. And even then . . .

I closed my eyes, running sight-blind, relying only on the wind in my whiskers, the smells, the sounds . . . and then a hand closed around the scruff of my neck and I was jerked up into the air.

"Well, hello there. Running away from home?"

A man held me by my scruff in full sunlight, a man with Winter's features and Winter's voice, but . . . In. Full. Sunlight. And alive. He sat at a sidewalk table at a coffee shop and opposite him, applying cream cheese to a French toast–flavored bagel, was Father Ike.

"Winter?"

"Leave him be, John," Father Ike said with a disapproving tut. "He's one of God's creatures."

Winter dropped me on the plastic surface of the tabletop.

"There we are. No harm done. Can I pour you some cream?" He gestured to a cow-shaped cream pitcher sitting between Father Ike and himself.

"How?" I meowed.

"It's rather easy." Winter picked up his coffee cup and set it to the side, then poured cream into the saucer. "The milk comes out of the cow's mouth."

"But you're in full sun and you aren't burning."

"That's rich." Winter winked at me. "I'm sitting here not bursting into flame. Most people don't, you know. Billions of people sit around every day not bursting into flames." He reached out and skritched the fur under my chin. When he did, his spirit touched mine and I didn't breathe for three seconds. His spirit felt like . . . Eric's does each time he plays and sings "Stardust." "But it's the talking cat who asks, 'How do you do that?'" he continued. "That's rich. It really is."

"Maybe you shouldn't pet him, John." As much as Eric dislikes Winter, he likes Father Ike. Me, I find conversing with a soulless priest to be disconcerting. The edges of where his soul was torn free gaped like wounds in the center of his aura. The bright white edges brought the missing center into sharp and unignorable contrast. At some point, he'd sold his soul . . . for a noble cause, I'm sure, but still . . .

"Why? Because he could eat me? C'mon, Ike. That's exactly why I should pet him." His hands moved over my ears and he scratched behind the left one. I leaned into it. "Besides, I think he likes me."

"You're wearing blue jeans." He was! He was wearing blue jeans— normal ones—and a decades-old Void City Music Festival T-shirt, white, with the whole phrase "Welcome to the Void City Music Festival" on the front. I peered over the edge to check his shoes. *Crocs with socks!*

"So you're not . . . Winter?"

"I think that's a question better fit for a team of doctors, all with the word *psycho* in their title." He held out a hand. "John Hawkes. Nice to meet you."

"But . . ." He wore glasses instead of contacts and behind them, his eyes were a startling shade of blue that Winter's colored contacts only approximated. His blond hair seemed more golden brown in full sun, and his skin showed a light but noticeable tan. "But . . ." I held a paw in the air and he shook it lightly.

"Surprised?" John released my hand. "Winter is pretty upfront about Ebon Winter being a stage name."

"But you're human. Truly human. How?"

"Again." He chuckled, and the laugh was the same as Winter's but warmer, a living thing that could snare a person. People tell me I have a great laugh, but I don't. Winter has a great laugh. "Billions of people walk around being human . . . every day."

"What time did you say the movie started, John?" Father Ike checked his watch.

"Eleven."

"Then we'd best be going if we're going to finish our run and get cleaned up before we have to leave."

"Okay." John stood up and tucked a five-dollar bill under the edge of his coffee cup. "You want to come?"

"What's the movie?" I asked dumbly.

"It's a funny western with James Garner. Which one is it again, Ike?"

"*Support Your Local Sheriff,*" he answered. "One of my favorites."

"Wait. Wait." I trod in the saucer of cream by accident. "You two have coffee here every morning?"

"No." John shook his head. "We usually have coffee at the rectory, but Winter insisted we come here today."

"Why?"

"He said to stop the Mouser and shake its paw." John held out his hand to help Father Ike out of the white plastic chair in which he sat, but Ike waved him away.

"And then?"

"That's it. I've given up arguing with him if his requests don't seem too unreasonable."

Father Ike cleared his throat. "You coming?"

"What?"

"To the movie, Talbot," Father Ike intoned. "Are you coming?"

"Sure."

John reached into his jeans pocket and pulled out a small walkie-talkie. "Melvin?"

"Area secured," a voice called back after a hiss of static. "The path is cleared, Rockstar, you may proceed."

And so, we jogged.

30

GRETA:

AND THEN BAD THINGS HAPPENED

I woke, frantic to find Telly's skull. I'd gone to sleep holding it, but when I opened my eyes, it had vanished. After jumping out of the bed and stumbling as I caught my foot in the blankets, I looked around the floor of Dad's Pollux bedroom. Sheets and bedding hit the walls as I shook and discarded each article without finding the skull. I crawled around the floor on my hands and knees once before checking the obvious place. There he was, hiding under the bed.

"It's day three," I told him. "Now I can kill Grandma." I planted a quick kiss on his bullet hole and stowed him safely at the center of Dad's bed. Quickly pulling on one of Dad's "Welcome to the Void" T-shirts (one that smelled of him and of New Mom) I slipped into the same jeans I'd worn the night before and dashed barefoot down the hall to the stairs.

The two girls I'd met last night looked up at me from the lobby, struggling with a green futon frame between them. Oranges lost her grip. I rocketed down the stairs and caught the whole thing up over my head by one side, tearing it out of Apples' grasp.

"Don't you dare scuff up Daddy's floor with that crap!" Apples fell to the floor and Oranges took two steps toward the foyer. "Who said you could bring this in here?"

"Calm down," Apples spat from her spot on the floor. "Damn, we were just—"

I locked eyes with her and shoved a command into her head. "Exhale for two minutes!" Vampires can still command humans if we want, but we don't automatically win unless they're our thralls. It's a will versus will thing, and mine was stronger than Apples' hands down.

Unless a human knows circular breathing or is a freaking astronaut or something, even trying to exhale for two minutes will make her pass out. It took Apples way less than two minutes. Her face went red with strain, then her eyes rolled up and she went down. Oranges stayed put.

"I asked a question," I snapped.

"Talbot"—Oranges' voice was calm and steady, impossible to be angry with—"said if we put floor protectors on the bottom, we could bring the futon in and set it up in the sitting area for a couple of days, Mistress."

"Oh. Well, that's fine then." I carried the futon down to the sitting room and set it up against an empty wall. Oranges followed me down, then stood as if at attention, her thin metal leash hanging loose from the studded collar around her neck.

"How old are you, Oranges?" I took the red leather handle of the leash in my hand. Her eyes tracked the motion, but she made no move to resist.

"Twenty-one last week, Mistress."

"Do you want to live forever, Oranges?"

"If it pleases you." No fear. No hesitation. And no back talk. I could see what Apples saw in her. Oranges was shorter than me by a few inches, five foot ten at the most, with a lithe build that reminded me of Mama Irene, before Daddy tried to kill her. In the light of the fluorescent bulbs, she was strikingly beautiful. She had a fresh clean look beneath the makeup. Her black hair was now streaked with blue; the chemical smell still clung to it.

"Why were you afraid of me last night and not now?"

"I didn't know how to react last night, Mistress. Now, I do."

"Do you want to be my thrall?"

"Yes, Mistress."

"Even if I decide not to keep Apples?"

"She's a fat sow, Mistress." Oranges wrinkled her nose. "Do as you wish with her."

"Why don't you always say 'Mistress'?"

"I assumed if I said 'Mistress' after every sentence, it would annoy the hell out of you. Do you want me to say it every time?"

Oranges is fun without Apples!

"How about just when I give a command?"

"As you wish, Mistress."

"This is so cool!" I opened my mouth to give another command, make her do jumping jacks or bark like a dog, but the desire to be done with Lisette closed my mouth. "Okay. I'm going to go check something and then I want to feed. I haven't decided whether I want Apples' or

Oranges' juice for breakfast, so drag Apples out of the way and then wait for me at the concession stand."

"Yes, Mistress, but where are you going?"

"I'm going to kill my grandma."

That got Oranges' heart to thumping. It wasn't fear, not exactly. Dad's better at sussing out emotions than I am, but I know fear. This was close . . . maybe it could have been fear, just not of me.

"Don't worry, Oranges, she's not my really real Grandma." I bounded up the stairs. "I'll be back."

On my way out the front doors, I heard Oranges curse and the sound of a cell phone being dialed. Had I hurt Apples more than I'd meant to? Oh well. It wasn't as if I hadn't already decided to kill her when I came back in. Oranges was fun and in shape. Apples had cursed at me, which I'm pretty sure she shouldn't have done, not if she wanted to be my thrall.

Magbidion sat on a lawn chair, watching some horrid morning show featuring a bubbly blondish woman who should have been killed twenty years ago when she'd still been pretty and some old stocky guy with what might have been a hairpiece. They were interviewing the Blind Alley Rabbits, though, so I guess that made them kind of cool. He'd set a stool right next to Fang so he could keep an eye on Dad's car and the television.

"Hi, Greta. Good morning."

"Where's Talbot?"

"I'm supposed to say he went to go see Dezba."

"O-kay. Well, whatever then."

I tiptoed up to the trunk and rapped lightly on the metal. Fang opened up and there was Grandma, right where I'd left her, bundled up with her disembodied heart next to her face and the killer necklace (and the tire iron I'd run through the center of it) lying in her open chest cavity. I concentrated on the necklace first.

How do I destroy you?

The answer came through garbled, as if announced by a man with a mouth full of marbles, singing underwater, while being strangled.

"Damn."

"Damn?" Magbidion asked.

"I have to de-tire-iron it before I can get a good reading." I pulled Squidly out of the trunk. "I was afraid that might happen."

"What? Reading? What reading?" Mags jerked up out of his chair. "Wait! You've captured her. Why not wait until Eric gets back and let him kill her? Then you can figure out—"

I threw him the tire iron.

"Just jam that through it if I need you to."

"Kill you! End you! Make you mine!" Squidly's voice rang out in my head, but having fought it once before, the second time was easy-peasy.

It clawed and pulled at me with eight golden tentacle-like chains, and according to Magbidion, two more tendrils I couldn't see. I walked around to the front of Fang, to be sure it couldn't unstake its mistress with one of them, and focused on how to destroy it. Images of fire filled my mind, the necklace tumbled into a volcano. I could drive it to a smelting plant or something . . . but then I saw an image of Lisette standing at the lip of the volcano calling it back, the still bubbling metal sliding up the rock and re-forming. Okay, so just like a *memento mori* can call back its Emperor, the Emperor, given time, could call back his or her *memento mori*. Good to know.

Squidly was winning the physical battle, its gaping beak headed right for my chest again.

"Magbidion!"

He ran for me, tire iron over his head, and I felt the pressure decrease as Magbidion began to stick it and move as if he were avoiding the unseen tentacles, which had released me.

"Greta, it's stronger than I am. I can't."

"Fang—" I was going to tell Fang to do something, help Mags or something, but when I said the name, a new image washed over my thoughts like a cool rain. A *memento mori* could destroy another *memento mori*. Sweet!

I dropped to the ground, wincing as my head hit the concrete.

"Fang, roll over me and eat the necklace!"

Fang backed away.

"Do it or it'll get inside my head again! Please! If you have to eat me too, I'll be okay. That's not what it takes to end me. I—" Before I could even finish my sentence, Fang rolled over me.

Being eaten by Fang hurts like the dickens! I mean, serious serious owie territory. I felt pain in places I'd never been hurt before, places that I didn't even know had nerves. My head hit the undercarriage hard, splitting my nose and ramming Squidly into my chest, where its beak jabbed deep, piercing the sternum and my heart.

Squidly filled my head again, but this time, I took him to another memory. In my second happiest memory, Dad was on top of me. I was naked and his fangs pierced my neck. The mild disappointment that he wouldn't bite me in his favorite feeding spot was washed away as he thrust his wrist into my mouth and I died but didn't go away. The pain, which would have made me scream as my bowels voided themselves, didn't happen, because that's what high colonics are for. I hadn't eaten anything in three days, either, so the hunger that took hold of me when I transformed wasn't new, just a change in need.

Salt water blew open the door of Dad's bedroom at the old Demon Heart and then vanished, literally fading away before the wetness could hit me. Dad's eyes were filled with the flow of bloody tears, so much so he didn't seem to even notice the door or the water. I've never asked him, but I'm certain they were tears of joy.

And then I was awake again, in the trunk, a raw naked skeleton lying atop Grandma. I latched on to Magbidion's offered arm and fed, but not too much. I regenerated, clothing my bones in flesh, using Magbidion's blood, and smiled when he looked away, embarrassed by my nakedness. Once I had a nose again, it was filled with the smell of burning rubber.

Thin traces of new gold chased the rims of Fang's tires, and the power radiating from him was so strong even I could feel it . . . and technically I'm blind to it.

"What made you think of that?" Magbidion asked as he handed me his terry-cloth bathrobe. It was too short in the sleeves, but it felt hot—fresh out of the drier hot—so I put it on.

"What?"

"Feeding one *memento mori* to another." Magbidion cupped one hand to his eye like a tiny telescope. "Fang's aura is twice as strong. I've never seen anything like it."

"Now for Grandma." Fang's trunk was still open. I reared back a fist. "If she's part zombie . . ." I punched down through the side of her skull, shards of bone lodging in my knuckles. I spread the hole wider with my claws and scooped the putrid insides out, dumping them one glop at a time onto the concrete surface of the parking deck, then stomped each smelly pile flat, like Lucy and Ethel in that episode where they're in the big vat of grapes making wine.

An immediate change came over the body. The stink faded and the brains on the ground bleached into a healthier color, for all that they were flat and smeared. Dark black zombie goo turned normal organ color. Even the fluid and brain spatter that had covered the lower edges of Magbidion's robe, as well as my feet and legs, turned a more normal color.

"And now that she's just another Vlad," I whooped in Magbidion's ear, "I can totally end her sorry ass!"

A lightning bolt hit me when I reached for the stake. I tried to disconnect from the pain, but it followed me, equal parts physical and mental agony. Bolt after bolt struck, jerking my body so violently I couldn't control it. I never even felt the crossbow bolt tear through my chest and slam home into my heart.

A blur with metallic gold claws and white and orange fur whipped past my falling body and struck Magbidion, hurling him against the side of his RV with the sound a sack of melons might make if you dropped them off the roof.

By the time I hit the ground, Captain Stacey stood over Magbidion, glow fading as he reverted to his humanoid form. He already held a tire iron in his hand, the same one I'd used to impale Squidly, but from the sapphire gleam in his eyes, I expected he had a different plan for where to shove it.

Fortunately, Fang had other plans, too.

Captain Stacey lunged for the Mustang's hood and Fang shot into reverse, passing over me, lifting me up against its undercarriage, breaking my nose for a second time in under an hour, and proceeding backward through the winding center spiral, up, up, and up again toward the top of the parking deck.

"Stop that Mustang, Stacey!" Lord Phillip shouted. I could hear but couldn't see him.

As Fang's speed increased, the magical extra space that seemed to exist underneath him narrowed and soon left my back dragging the concrete, scouring away first the skin then muscle beneath it. Hair ripped free of my scalp, taking small hunks of skin with it. I knew Fang wanted to avoid eating me again or he'd have already done the deed. But I wished he'd get it over with. I might come out hungry again, but better one giant ow that goes away than this continuous scraping. I'm a rip the Band-Aid off in one go kind of girl.

When we hit the roof, the night air rushed over me, surprisingly cool, the humidity tolerable for Void City at this time of year. I fell away from Fang's undercarriage, and the crossbow bolt didn't come with me. It hung there from the bottom of the car, metal tip still lodged in my chest, but not quite deep enough.

"Good boy, Fang!"

I rolled out from under the car, holding the bolt in my hand to avoid accidentally re-staking myself, and tore it free of my sternum. Fang's painful trip had made a mess of Magbidion's robe, but as I climbed into the passenger's seat I found a new set of the exact same clothes I'd been wearing before, my jeans and Dad's T-shirt. They weren't warm, like Dad's clothes are when he remakes them, but they still had Dad and New Mom's smell on them, which was even better.

I whipped the shirt over my head as I regenerated and struggled into the jeans as Fang revved the engine and rammed the wall of the parking deck. He hit it once, twice, and on the third time, broke through. We glided free just as I heard the elevator doors ding open and saw Oranges step out, leveling a crossbow at me.

Captain Stacey was the one who worried me.

Every bit as fast as most vampires, he came running up the parking deck ramp and, without slowing, leapt after Fang, golden claws and sapphire eyes sparkling in the night. He landed on the trunk and I stood up in the seat, claws out, ready for a fight.

"Talbot's combat mode is cooler," I said, opening a series of bloody gashes in his chest. A blow I'd meant to get me a handhold on his vitals was reduced to mere flesh wounds by his speed. Damn Mousers.

"How fortunate His Highness isn't here right now."

He leapt at me and I took his charge, the two of us clawing at one another. Flames leapt up from my wounds and I hissed. His claws were holy, just like Talbot's. Why not?

Fang lurched down and then up, maximizing his gliding range. Stacey and I brawled wildly, a flaming furry whirlwind of vampire and Mouser. In short, Oranges' shot was miraculous. Staking a vampire with an arrow or a crossbow bolt is no mean feat to begin with. Old Mom was exceptionally good at it, from years of having to stake Daddy to calm him down, but the shot Oranges made—a shot like that would have given Robin Hood a hard-on. If the other bolt had still been in place, I'm relatively certain she would have split it in two.

My thought as Captain Stacey grabbed me, tore open Fang's trunk, and leapt back toward the parking deck with me and Grandma (one over each shoulder) was this: *Oh no! There's a hole in Dad's T-shirt!*

31

GRETA:

A PRAYER AT BEDTIME

Lord Phillip didn't say a word to me the first night. He had a debt to repay. After Phillip carried Grandma and me back to the Highland Towers with the VCPD running Fang interference, he had servants in bellhop uniforms come in to strip us, measure us, and bathe us both in blood. Then a second set came in and doctored our stakes. They cut Grandma's down so it was flush with her skin and then affixed a platinum stopper to her back and chest that completely covered the wood.

I couldn't easily see what they did to mine, but it appeared to be a similar thing with a golden stopper. Then, the first set of servants came back in carrying sets of clothes that might have looked more at home in a Victorian brothel than in modern-day Void City, and dressed us.

Phillip's study was the same as it had been the last time I was there, except that the curtains had been drawn back, revealing his larger-than-king-size bed, which, with the curtains drawn, dominated the room. It was a four-poster bed of some rich mahogany or maybe a darker-colored wood. Lavishly embroidered pillows lay on top of an equally elaborate comforter. Cords running from both the comforter and the mattress had been disguised to match the carpet, and I could barely make out where they snaked underneath the bed toward a wall socket even when the bellhops had me down on the Oriental rug working on my stake.

Once we'd been dressed, a third group of hired help (this time not in bellhop uniforms) came in, did our hair and makeup, and gave us each a manicure and pedicure. When they'd finished, the bellhops returned, arranging us by the fire in lush green velvet upholstered lounge chairs. Phillip's fantastical knickknacks lined the walls, and I could just make out Roger's soul prison in its ornate golden holder on the mantel next to the box of all the things Lord Phillip had used to ascend.

Grandma had been posed so she looked over my shoulder at the display case in which Percy was stored. Nobody knew why Percy was in there, but he was staked and displayed in doll collector fashion, with a plaque underneath him that read, "My dear Percy, who serves as a remembrance to all that I do not bluff, I do not make empty threats, and there are indeed worse fates than death." I used to make up stories about him and the things he must have done to merit that end.

We waited, the hands of the mantel clock counting down the hours, and waited.

And waited.

So, I got my own little dose of what it must have felt like for Dad to be trapped in the remains of the explodicated Demon Heart all those months when he was a ghost, but compressed into hours. Before dawn, Oranges came in with another group of bellhops. They moved our chairs in turn, taking us to the alcove where Uncle Phil stored his magic mirror.

The golden dragon worked into the frame seemed to leer at me. New Mom had mentioned the mirror once. She said it had a demon inside that let her see her reflection, but made her feel bad for all the horrible things she'd ever done. I don't know what she was talking about though, because I didn't feel anything bad. It was nice to know my burns had healed when they gave me the blood bath, though.

"Good girl," the demon within the mirror whispered in my mind. "What a precious thing you are. What a treasure."

"Do you know what Uncle Phil is going to do to me?" I thought at the mirror.

"A vampire like you, with your understanding, your composure?" It burbled at me. "No more than you allow."

Four bellhops traded me out for Lisette and when they brought her back, streaks of blood were running freely down her cheeks. I guess she'd been happy to see her reflection, too. It was a little weird she could still cry while staked, though. For that to work, she pretty much had to be connected to her body very closely and still be feeling things. What's the point in that?

The fire, I thought, *maybe she likes feeling the fire.*

And that's what I was thinking when the sun rose on my first day as a P.O.P. (Prisoner of Phil).

On the second night, the ritual repeated. They bathed us in blood, changed us into fresh skanky brothel-wear, and gave us each our turns in front of the mirror.

"Still here?" the demon asked.

This time, when he spoke, he brought me back to my first favorite memory, except that the mirror was there in the beach house, hanging over the burned-out television.

"I guess he's mad at me for something."

"Well, sure, Phillipus is like that, but I'd expect your father to have come for you by now."

"But he's in Paris." My memory self scowled at the mirror. "It's his honeymoon."

"True, but I thought he was only going to be gone for a few days."

"How did you know that?"

"You know it"—the eyes of the dragon frame seemed to glimmer— "so I know it . . . while we're together."

"Oh." I frowned. "Well it's not like he's been gone such a long time."

"But you expected him back yesterday."

I looked away as the mirror spoke and focused on the version of Daddy in my memory, asleep on his bed, exhausted from the act of creating me.

"Or you expected him to call."

"No I didn't."

"You can't tell fibs to me, Greta." The demon's voice took on an edge of friendly menace. "You haven't wanted to face it, but in the back of your mind, you expected him to show up tonight and save you, but he hasn't even called. Talbot hasn't come looking for you either. I wonder why? Maybe if you'd finished the job with Lisette . . ."

I opened my mouth to respond, but I was being carried away from the mirror. Demons lie. I knew that, but what if the stupid mirror was right? If *Daddy* was mad at me, if I'd been bad, then he might not come at all, not until I'd been punished. . . . It would have to be something worse than being locked in the freezer.

Grandma had her turn at the mirror next, and the moment she'd been returned to her spot, I sensed Lord Phillip. He was coming.

The door to Phil's apartments opened behind us and our chairs rotated to face the opening. A line of bellhop-clad girls filed into the room, with Oranges in the lead, her uniform differentiated by the collar and leash she still wore around her neck.

They chattered among each other, wondering why they were here, all together. I knew Uncle Phil ran a contest every few years to see who his next offspring would be and that the competition was fierce, but, like the girls, I didn't think it was time to choose a winner and I was too preoccupied by what the mirror demon had said to think about it too hard.

"Favete linguis," Phillip's voice intoned. From the reaction, I guessed he'd just told them to shut up, in Latin or French or something. He flowed into the room as a cloud of mist, materializing with his hand on Oranges' leash.

"Some of you may no doubt wonder why we have gathered here out of turn and you would be right to wonder . . . as it has happened only once before." He fiddled with Oranges' leash, towing her free of the line, and she followed willingly, a look of superiority clear in her eyes. "Every decade, I hold a contest to determine my next two children, one male and one female. Offspring in whom I see the potential for becoming beings who will keep my unlife . . . interesting."

"It's a cycle." He placed his hand on Oranges' waist and her lips jerked slightly down. "First I appoint my *nulli secondus* and then my *nulli secunda*. My young man and woman. My son and my daughter." He began to unbutton her overshirt, letting the air hold her leash in place through one of his little magic tricks, and the smile on her face vanished, replaced by a thin rigid line of null expression. "As the Latin implies: my second to none. Tonight I appoint my *nulli secunda*."

Alive with objections, the air filled with words and Phillip fed on it, grin widening like a jack-o'-lantern's.

He silenced them with a gesture.

"I could remind you of the old adage: *Perfer et obdura; dolor hic tibi proderit olim."* He looked directly at me when he translated, "'Be patient and tough; some day this pain will be useful to you.'" His hands twitched as if he fought the urge to applaud himself. "But that is no longer up to me. As Senator William Learned Marcy once said, 'To the victor belong the spoils,' or, in the case of my little competition . . . to the winner belong"—he looked down the line, spots of red sparking in his eyes—"the losers.

"Though you may object to the timing (I know you thought you had a few more years left in the competition), there is, as I've said before, a precedent. A young man came to me some few decades ago and made me a promise: Make me a vampire"—Phillip slid Oranges' overshirt off and dropped it to the floor, revealing a white undershirt—"and give me thirty million dollars instead of the usual ten. Do this and I promise that you will be destroyed within fifty years' time.

"Do you know how rare it is to find a human with such gall?" He reached around Oranges' waist, unfastening her black belt, a belt that reminded me of Dad's, and let it fall. "You all know the human who made that deal as the vampire Ebon Winter. He"—Phillip paused as he struggled to get a grip on the pull tab of her zipper—"has yet to make good on his promise, but every oracular method with which I am familiar assures me of two things: He is working on his plan and"—his hands gripped the fabric of her pants tightly as he dragged them down—"whatever the plan may be, it might work."

If I'd been Oranges, I would have gone with panties, especially if I'd been dumb enough to make a deal with Uncle Phil to begin with. Fear radiated from Oranges. Heartbeat, breath, pheromones—all of them were out of control. If I could have looked away, I would have, because I had an inkling of what was coming next.

"That's what I like to do," Phil continued, "and he understood. Winter knew that what I really want in unlife is to have a good enemy, someone to plot against. Wendy here, or Peg, or Oranges as I believe some have come to call her . . ." He tore the shirt from her back, a stylized *P* tattoo visible briefly before he spun her about, revealing her naked front. My view of her chastity piercing was both excellent and unfortunate. ". . . may not have come to such an astute conclusion, but she did make herself an excellent example of *qui audet adipiscitur.* She who dares wins.

"Not unlike me at that level of mortality. When I was a human wizard, no vampire would embrace me, so I sought magical means to become immortal. Unfortunately, the ritual I used left me a lowly Drone—barely immortal—but I have in time been able to advance my status, one excruciating level at a time, through the use of magical items and the sacrifice of vampires of the level of power I desired to next attain. It was a long climb to Vladhood and the wait for an Emperor-level vampire with whom I could bear to part has been even longer.

"Enter Lisette and, by virtue of her willingness to aid me, Oranges. She agreed to keep an eye on Greta"—he gestured to me as he fondled Oranges—"to infiltrate her good graces and to inform on her should she come close to destroying Lisette. You see, I need Lisette. She's the only Emperor vampire I've ever experienced who bored me completely, a perfect sacrifice to fuel my final ascension."

Uh-oh.

"If not for our Wendy, or rather, my Wendy, Lisette would likely have been destroyed. For that reason, her prompt action in both calling me when the time was right and in exercising her skill for exceptional archery (which I hope may be aimed at me one day soon) I declare her the winner of this round and promise to make her a vampire and render her reward to her this very night . . ."

Oranges relaxed, but she shouldn't have.

"As soon as a final bit of hazing has been endured."

"Hazing?" Oranges asked.

"Oh my dear." Phillip ran his hand along her body. "It is quite clear how to make you hate me forever, and the most wonderful thing about it is it's something I do to all the winners anyway."

As her former competitors/future property looked on, Lord Phillip tore her piercings out and changed shapes. He started out as a wolf when he first mounted her, transforming as his foul pleasures required. After an hour or two, he called three other vampires to his suite to join in. If I'd ever had any doubts Uncle Phil was a freak, he erased them.

It was wrong, all of it. Sure, I like to play with my food from time to time, but this was excessive, pointless, and cruel beyond even acceptable vampiric levels. And let's face facts, if I thought it was too much for a vampire to get away with, that's saying something. No wonder Dennis had left town after winning.

Phil kept his promise though, eventually, pausing long enough to make sure all her wounds had healed, then forcing his blood down her throat and strangling her with it. A person doesn't have to bleed out to be a vampire. As Daddy says, it's just more efficient. Act (or acts) completed, he removed her collar and leash, then, well and thoroughly spent, he had the bellhops take her to her new quarters to await her rising . . . and her pleasure the next evening. Which left us alone with him.

Wearing only bloody smears and the various secretions Oranges would never have again, Uncle Phil pulled up a stool, opened a bottle of blood wine, and leered at us in the firelight, holding the wine in one hand and the leash and collar in the other.

"Enjoy the show?" Phillip asked. He guzzled the wine, draining half the bottle in one go. "Your Oranges wasn't particularly enthusiastic, and I thought her screams were a bit exaggerated, but it's a pleasant way to spend an evening while creating what will undoubtedly be an inferior foe." Tipping the bottle back, he took another long drink. "Which is, I believe, entirely your fault, Greta. You forced my hand, and I do not enjoy being forced."

"But in the end"—he stood, reaching for a pair of opera glasses that rested on the mantel by the clock—"I managed to gain you"—he touched Lisette's cheek tenderly—"my first expendable." He looked through the opera glasses at Lisette. "Empero . . . No!"

Oops.

"How?" Frantically twisting and turning the focusing knob on the glasses, Phillip howled.

Not to be impatient, I thought, *but this would be a good time for a rescue, Dad.*

"I . . ." He yawned. "I . . ." Uncle Phil's sleep pattern had always been unpredictable, and I felt a flare of hope.

That's right! Fall asleep now, Uncle Phil.

No such luck.

"You did this." He seized my chin between his thumb and forefinger. *"J'accuse!"* He looked into my eyes, and I made contact. For three consecutive nights, I'd been in Uncle Phil's proximity. Being staked had blocked it until that moment, but suddenly I knew Phil's secret death condition, and boy, was it a doozie. *Anything* could kill him. He'd used magic to become a vampire and magic to increase his power, but when it came to destruction, deep down he was still just a Drone.

Unstake me, Uncle Phil. I pushed the command home. He'd had half a bottle of blood wine. He was tired, on the verge of collapse, but his mind, unlike his body, was every bit as powerful as I'd feared.

"Everything I did to Wendy," he snarled, "I'll do to you. And it will only be the beginning."

Un. Stake. Me.

Phil pushed into my head, expecting the usual mind-to-mind contest of wills, but that's not how it works in my head. I took him to the beach house, let him see little girl Greta, let him smell the blood on my thighs.

"Oh my. How delightful." He adjusted more quickly than most and appeared wearing his usual dapper attire. The pants were tented with his obvious excitement. "It never occurred to me to create a mental library like this, a realized space inside the mind, a place to retreat. Shall we play?"

My head. My rules. His hand went for his belt and I swapped memories.

Beach house became Pollux bedroom. Little girl Greta vanished and vampire Greta, newly born and ready for blood, appeared behind Phil and sank her teeth into his neck. I won.

UN. STAKE. ME. NOW! YOU FUCKING BASTARD!

It worked.

A golden knob hit the floor. Next to it, the remains of a bloody crossbow bolt glistened in the firelight. The hole in my chest snapped closed with a zipperlike noise. A blow to both temples crossed his eyes and kept him from using his magic. One hand lanced to his throat, choking him. I shoved the other into his mouth, intent on removing the top of his head.

Glass shattered. Another vampire's presence filled my mind. He was old—younger than Grandma, but only just, and he was more powerful than me. A sharp pain. And I was immobilized. With nothing to support me, I tumbled to the ground, a marionette with its strings cut.

Percy stood over me and Phillip, his eyes narrowed as he adjusted his glasses.

"Terribly sorry to interrupt." His voice was pleasant and rich, an accent I felt Lord Phillip had been unconsciously trying to mimic. "But at the last moment, I couldn't bring myself to permit it."

"Percy?" Phillip's voice quaked with fear. "I can explain. I'm sorry."

"Your apologies are quite unnecessary, Phillip." He reached out to offer Phillip a hand, but Uncle Phil backed away from him, scuttling across the floor. "You did nothing beyond that which I allowed."

"But you were staked."

"Well." Percy brushed glass away from his clothes. "I suppose that's true, but now you know *my* little bit of unique flair. All Vlads have them. I can't seem human or eat food, can't turn to mist or become a virus, but a stake through the heart does nothing to me."

"So all this time . . ."

"Oh, a stake through the heart makes me seem dead, renders me undetectable by other vampires, but I could have left the box at any time."

"Then why did you stay?"

Percy adjusted his golden-rimmed spectacles.

"We all have our little eccentricities, my boy. Our ways of keeping ourselves entertained. You like to create opponents. I do something similar. I pick a human, give them a taste for immortality, let them fall in love with my power, if not my body, and then I deny them in all ways to see how they react. In other words, your quirk is that you like to torture." He leaned down and kissed Phillip full on the mouth. "Mine is: I like to watch." Percy indicated me with his hand. "It's your third act, Phillipus. You've been rescued. There is only a little time left before your swan song." Percy's fangs extended. "Show me something worth watching."

Phillip advanced on me again, and I waited for Dad to come. I'd given it a good try. I had. I'd almost killed Phillip and had been robbed by fate or circumstance. Phillip tore at my clothes, and I decided not to let it happen. Not again. Maybe Dad was waiting so he could show up and avenge me as he'd done when we first met, but I couldn't let this happen, not again, not even for Dad.

One of the reasons I scare people is because they can't control me. Not really. I do what Dad tells me because I love him, but I'm nobody else's girl. Phillip leaned down to lick my neck, but I didn't feel it. For vampires, the body is an interface. To use it or not use it is a choice. I decided not to use mine anymore and let it go, leaving Phillip in a rage, staring at my body as it aged from twenty-one to forty something, my true age revealed just as happens with other Vlads when they finally meet their ends.

    Oh, Dad, I thought as the world faded and the scenery changed, *I wish you'd been on time.* Phillip ran to a drawer and fetched out a soul prison, but it was too late. I was already moving beyond his reach. I stuck out my tongue and gave him the bird before I lost sight of him. With that, I sniffed the air to see if I could find her. After all, if Dad couldn't rescue me, then perhaps Mom could comfort me. I caught her smell, ashes and smoke over a layer of clean old Marilyn, and, like a bloodhound, I followed the scent into the gathering dark.

AN AMERICAN
VAMPIRE IN PARIS

AS TOLD BY ERIC AND TABITHA

32

TABITHA:

MEANWHILE, BACK IN THE HALL OF JUSTICE

(Seven days before Greta dies)

After Eric posed for a few seconds on the steps of the chapel and then inexplicably flew off to the top of the *donjon* in a huff, Luc motioned for us to follow him into the castle. I was much more interested in the castle than in whatever Bea claimed "happened here." Even when I became a vampire, it never in my wildest dreams occurred to me that I'd get to go to Paris, meet immortals, and visit magic castles.

Before my trip to the Château de Vincennes, the only castle I'd ever been to had been the one in Disney World. It was a few years before Rachel died. Mom and Dad took us there for three days and I remember not being able to feel like we were really, really going until we were inside the park and I saw Cinderella's castle.

In my head, I'd been afraid it was all going to turn out to be a big joke. Dad had come home late that Thursday night. We'd already been in bed and he'd made us get up and pack in fifteen minutes. In the back of the van, Rachel had complained about forgetting her pillow and her toothbrush, but Dad wouldn't have any of it. He had driven all night, and for the longest time, I'd watched him. Rachel had slept on my shoulder. Mom had dozed in the passenger's seat. Miles Davis had played on the CD player, hypnotic music that made my eyes want to close. I've never been a fan of that sort of jazz, but Dad was, and instead of sending him into the lethargic state to which it often sent me, the music worked its way inside Dad, brightening his eyes, making him alive, making him smolder like the end of the cigarettes he used to smoke before Mom had made him quit.

"We're heading to Florida?" I'd asked. A rhythmic pattern had set up as we'd crossed onto a rough section of highway. *Ba-thump ba-thump ba-thump. Ba-thump ba-thump ba-thump.* Rachel had squirmed against me in unconscious irritation at the vibrations that shook the car with each jarring *ba-thump.*

Signs suggesting attractions at Disney and at Universal Studios had sprung up, punctuated by "We Bare All" signage and ads for Sea World.

Eventually, I'd slept. We'd stopped for gas once, the lack of motion pushing me awake. "Wha—?"

"If you're awake you can have something." Dad had looked back at us from his position near the gas pump.

"Can I have a Coke and a candy bar?"

He'd nodded. When he had come back, he'd presented us with two bottles of Coke and two Zero bars.

"They had glass bottles." He'd been proud and excited. "Coke tastes so much better in a glass bottle."

We'd talked about stupid stuff and had sipped our Cokes while he drove. I didn't remember being awake very long, just long enough to eat the Zero bar and talk a little. Dad never talked about anything of real consequence, not with me or Rachel. We were just girls to him, as if "just" being girls was a bad thing.

He'd made the drive in eleven hours, and even when the stop-and-go of the Disney World traffic had woken me up again, I'd still been convinced we were going somewhere else. We'd parked in Minnie 37. That was the parking section. Dad had told me to remember it and I still did.

Waiting in line at the ticket booth, I'd heard how much money the tickets cost and my mom had begun to complain that we couldn't afford it, but Dad had bought us all five-day Park Hopper passes, the kind that never expire.

I remember having seen a topiary shaped like Mickey Mouse as we headed to the Ferry Boat. I'd been sure something bad was going to happen. The boat would sink and we'd all die in the Seven Seas Lagoon. But we hadn't. Rachel had leaned over the side, smiling down at the water, and I'd walked up to the top level, admiring the palm trees and eyeing the resorts in awe.

When Eric asked me to marry him, and when I said yes, when I asked him where we were going for our honeymoon, I think I was hoping he'd say Disney World and that we'd stay at the Polynesian or the Contemporary Resort. Little did I realize when he said Paris that, in a way, it was the same thing.

As we'd passed through the turnstiles and walked under the train station, I had broken into a run. I'd ignored Main Street USA completely, running by the re-creation of old-time Americana, and had stumbled. I'd caught myself on a bench and run into the street, darting past a horse-drawn trolley. Mom had called my name, anger clear in her voice, but Dad's laughter had spurred me on. I'd passed the ice cream parlor, heading into the square, and I hadn't stopped until I was standing in the little park area where Main Street makes a circle, and I'd been able to see the whole thing.

"Well, what do you think?" Dad's hand had touched my shoulder.

Behind him, farther back, I'd heard Rachel complaining. "We're just going to have to walk back to get our picture taken."

"It's okay." I'd been so full of teenage cool. Embarrassment had colored my cheeks at the thought of how I'd raced across the park. Going ga-ga for fantasy castles didn't go with the black polish on my nails.

"Okay, huh?" Dad said.

He'd hugged me and, despite a plaintive cry of "Da-aad," I'd hugged him back.

James, Eric's war buddy, touched my shoulder as I eyed the real thing. The so-called dungeon looked more like a sand castle than a Disney castle. The outer wall was made from sections of small stone divided by narrow sections of larger stone in a pattern that looked a little like columns. I would have done that bit with seashells. The wall was topped with a roofed walkway, which stuck out a bit, and had a round tower with a cone-shaped roof at each corner, even though the base of the thing was square. On the side closest to me, four towers framed the drawbridge, with two short guard towers in front, and two taller towers set into the main wall behind. I couldn't really see the moat yet, but from the gap between the guard towers and the entrance towers, I guessed it was wide. Inside the wall, an impressively large keep rose at least fifty feet into the air. As a sand castle, it could have been built tall and rectangular, and then had a big round tower placed around each corner. It seemed to me that King Arthur might have designed Camelot to look something like this. . . . It wasn't ornate and lacy like the chapel, but it was pretty in a functional way.

I crossed the courtyard, walked the edge of the moat, and looked down into the murky water, not yet ready to cross the bridge into the stronghold proper. "What do you think?" James asked.

I watched Eric disappear over the edge of the *donjon*, surprised to see his reflection in the water. Magic water. Magic castle. Why shouldn't it show a vampire's reflection if it wanted?

"It's beautiful, the second most wonderful castle I've ever seen."

"Where was the first?"

My lips drew into a smile. "Disney World."

We crossed the bridge and I saw a man sitting atop the wall. He wore a long leather duster and had a polearm of some kind slung over his shoulder and a pistol on his hip in a holster strapped on over his jeans. Long black hair hung in a braid that draped over his right shoulder down to his waist. His face was one of those movie-star faces, eyes hidden behind dark sunglasses with silver frames. Casually smoking a cigarette, the man let his feet dangle over the edge at the top of the covered walkway that comprised the top section of an exterior wall protecting the *donjon* proper. Next to him, a trumpet gleamed in the moonlight.

"Who is that?"

"Christian," Aarika answered. "He's Lord Isaac's paladin. He's maintaining the wards this year."

"What do you mean? He's powering them?"

"Maintaining." Luc broke in when it was clear Aarika wasn't going to answer my question. "The wards themselves are powered by Scrythax. A maintenance person guides them . . . acts as a controller."

"What would have happened if he hadn't let Eric through?"

"I don't think he *did* let the vampire through." Aarika nudged James in the arm. "When was the last time you saw Christian smoking?"

"Maybe one of the Elders overruled him." James studied Christian for a moment. "He doesn't look happy."

"Ho, Christian," Luc called up at the immortal. Christian responded with a simple nod and a gesture to "come ahead."

Moving through the wards felt like walking through a fine mist. Gooseflesh rose on my skin, subsiding as we passed through the doors into the courtyard. The stone bridge continued beyond the wall, and my view opened up on the interior courtyard. Steep stairs led down from the walls to the lower courtyard, but the bridge led only one way, straight into the *donjon*, and we soon entered the meeting room.

Then I saw the head.

Three catlike faces were all attached to the same oversized head. The angle of feline faces allowed the head to be held level by the jaws of each open mouth. Its eyes were closed, the lids sunken in as if there were nothing left behind them. The tan fur was matted and tangled, even missing in spots, laying bare the shriveled muscle underneath. Dried blood was at its base where the head had been severed from the trunk. The gruesome thing was displayed on a stone pedestal in the center of a U-shaped table upon which laptops were scattered in various stages of active, screen-savered, or hibernating.

Several normal-looking guys and gals were standing about, broken up into little cliques—not a very united front. They stopped talking as we entered and turned to face us.

"Wait a minute." I stopped, forcing Beatrice to halt as well or ram into me from behind. I walked up to the edge of the table, not wanting to walk into the open space and stand too close to the decapitated head. I pointed. "You want me to touch that?"

"Upon the conclusion of a three-day assessment, assuming you are found acceptable by the Council." One of them, a fat man who looked like he belonged at a nerd convention, stepped away from the slight, swarthy brunette with whom he'd been conversing.

"Acceptable?"

"Do you agree to undergo a thirty-six-hour assessment, at the end of which you will, if found acceptable, be allowed to swear the Oath and join the Treaty of Secrets?"

I thought about it. If I said no . . . no honeymoon in Paris. Back to Void City. "What happens if I fail?"

"Luc, if you wouldn't mind escorting our errant Emperor down to join the rest of us?" An Asian boy, who looked like puberty might hit any day, gestured up at the ceiling. He wore a white T-shirt with some kind of robot dragons on the front, camo pants held up by a studded leather belt, a black hoodie, and a pair of those *Tatsu Ne* sneakers from Onmyoda that I only recognized because Greta had asked for some and had been mad that this exact shoe didn't come in pink.

"Of course, Se Fue." Luc bowed and took off at a fast walk.

"Se Fue?" I whispered over my shoulder to Beatrice. "What is that, Japanese for 'little brother'?"

"It's Chinese for 'teacher.'" The young boy stepped toward me and smiled. "Not all of us become immortal at the same age, and few of us find it uncomfortable to dress according to the age of our bodies."

"Do I have to call you Se Fue?"

A smile broke across his face. "Only if you want me to teach you how to fight. In twenty-five years, you'd have mastered the basics."

"No thanks. I'm on my honeymoon."

"Then you may call me Ji."

Beatrice slipped past me to get a better look at the head. "Why does it look so human?"

"What?"

"The head." Beatrice gestured at it. "It's just a decapitated human head. Why is it so powerful?"

"The Head of Scrythax is actually quite alien-looking." Aarika crossed the room as she spoke, moving closer to a blond man wearing a tailored business suit. "It takes remarkable concentration for even a supernatural being to see it as it actually is. It took me years."

"Or a being who is truly noble at heart," Master Ji corrected her. "Such beings cannot be fooled by Scrythax's *huan xiang*, his illusions. One of the tests we administer early on is to see what appearance Scrythax takes for you. It—"

All of the immortals looked up at once, stepping back to their places.

Eric came into the room, Luc trailing behind him. "His brain glows?" Eric squinted and kept walking, sparing the assembled immortals little more than a glance.

I looked at the head more closely. *His brain?*

"Guy looks like he was designed by H. R. Giger . . ."

Who?

And then it moved.

The noses sneezed in unison, sending puffs of dust out from under the head and out of its nostrils and mouths. The eyelids of each face opened with the sound of squeaky shoes on tile to reveal empty sockets. People moved around me, but Beatrice and I stared openmouthed at the head as the cat lips closed and opened in unison. The withered pink tongues became moist and supple again.

"Does my nose deceive me"—each word seemed to come from all three mouths—"or do I smell a Courtney?"

33

ERIC:
SMELLS LIKE COURTNEY SPIRIT

Great," I said as I tried to pop my claws and went uber vamp instead, "the fucking decap-a-Muppet is talking to me." Once again the transformation from human-sized to extra-large felt good, natural, like slipping on a favorite jacket. But that's not how it's supposed to work. My body should have felt like it was expanding, like an overfilled balloon, and that fundamental wrongness worried me as much as the talking head.

My wings knocked Luc down, taking him in the chest and hurling him back into the wall. He'd been standing too close. Immortals shifted left, right, and sideways, donning their combat armor. Weapons appeared, flowing out of the coalesced energy I'd seen surrounding them all. The Asian kid stood out the most, going from punked-out anime clothes to a Hello Kitty *gi* and a yellow headband. I can't say which got me more, the *gi* or the fact that his hair was dyed a vibrant shade of blue.

"You've got to be shitting me." I was talking about the kid, but it was the demon who commented.

"Quite unlikely, as I'm currently unaware of the location of my anus." The inner row of teeth moved independently of the outer row; it made my flesh crawl to see it. The immortals were frozen in place. Of course they were. They swore oaths on a demon head. "Now . . . I've taken the liberty of halting our—"

"I'm not talking to you," I said.

"Excuse me?"

Tabitha backed away from the table, claws out. She took a position in front of Beatrice, instinctively protective of her. "Eric, what's going on?"

I wondered if she guarded Beatrice because she was my thrall, because she was human, or because she was a possible food source.

"Eric?"

How do you explain to your twentysomething wife (vampire or otherwise) that you're sober for the first time since you met her and nothing makes sense the way it used to? That you're still you, but you're also something that went to sleep a long time ago, something that woke up when the magic went away. That you're a vampire, but you're also a boy who went to war, a man who went back for more, and a guy who just married the wrong woman, because the right one died? That you have a piece of a demon in your chest? That the magic castles and the immortals don't feel like magic—they just make you tired? Is there any good way? I looked for the words and the only thing that came was this: I could have told Marilyn.

Oh, boo-frickin'-hoo, I told myself. *Why don't you go cry all over Scrythax?*

"Eric, are you okay?"

"Yes, Mr. Courtney"—double jaws clicked and clacked, flashing as the demon spoke—"are you feeling well?"

My heart beat twice.

"You felt that quite well, I would imagine."

So my theory about the thing in my chest being the Eye of Scrythax seemed pretty likely if he could use the damn thing to make my heart beat.

"Stop it." A leap and a series of wingbeats brought me to the center of the room. Despite the pedestal, my uber vamp form towered over Scrythax. "You want your eye back? If you tricked me into bringing it to you, then fine. Tell me how to get it out and you can have it."

"Tricked?" The demon's eyelids narrowed, a glimmer of light visible between the slits. "No. I have tricked no one. Nor do I desire the return of either eye at this time."

"You have one of this thing's eyes?" Tabitha continued backing away from the head, making sure I was between it and her.

"Then what do you want?"

"I want many things, but mostly I desire a conversation with one of my champions."

"Who the hell are your champions?"

"Why, you are, Eric; you and one other from Void City." Its horns skritched on the stone pedestal, skittering like the legs of a centipede, moving it back as if it wanted a better look at me.

"I'm not your champion, Scrythax."

"Of course you are. You're a Courtney. You are all my champions. Did you not stop the plot in El Segundo and save the world?"

"I barely remember that."

"You could always turn into a revenant. Your noncorporeal form is not possessed of the same ailment your physical body possesses."

"What ailment? I've got a bad memory. I was embalmed and—"

"Embalming had nothing to do with it, Eric. True, Lord Phillip's counter-enchantment, the one that hid you from Lisette, also played merry hell with your powers, but surely we both know full well your problem is altogether different—or do you truly not recall that even in your last few years of life, you'd begun to have difficulty recalling your personal history, keeping facts straight, remembering little details?"

No, I didn't remember that either—which didn't exactly prove any-thing. "So what's your diagnosis, if you know so damned much?"

"You have what humans refer to as early-onset Alzheimer's, Mr. Courtney, or something very much resembling it." I must have looked stricken, because the demon frowned as much as its features would allow. "I apologize if it comes as something of a shock, but I thought you knew."

"That's bullshit. I was embalmed. I—"

"Embalming stops the resurrection process. Having survived it, a vampire of your stature shouldn't have had any further side effects."

"I don't have Alzheimer's." I shrank to human size; the transforma-tion hurt, like cramming your feet into a pair of shoes that don't fit. "Tabitha"—I looked back at her—"you don't think I have Alzheimer's, do you?"

Her face told me everything I needed to know. It was the oh-poor-baby look. "What's my maiden name, Eric?"

"Smith."

"Sims," she corrected.

"That doesn't prove—"

"What was Marilyn's last name?"

"Robinson."

"Perfect." She winced. "Hers you remember. What about this one? How did Kyle die?"

"Who the fuck is Kyle?"

Tabitha touched my cheek. "Your son? You made him at the same time you made Greta."

"No, I didn't. I didn't make any—" A sound on a telephone, a rush of air, like a vampire being dusted. I remembered that sound and at-tached it to a name. "Kyle. Damn. Was he the one who died out front of the Pollux, the one who set me up?"

"No, that was Roger."

"No, Roger was my best friend . . ." Roger yelling at me outside of the Pollux, so bitter and angry that it was easy to let it wash away once he was gone.

My face must have said it all, or maybe Scrythax was using his eye to read my mind. "Now you remember."

I dug around in my pocket for my cell phone. "Beatrice, how do I call the States?"

"Talbot programmed it into your phone." She stepped out from behind Tabitha. Her heat hit me like the opening of an oven that's kicked up to baking temperature. "Why?"

"I need him to fly out here and eat this asshole."

The demon's laugh was clear and brilliant. "And the other Infernatti wonder why I find live humans to be so wonderful."

"I ain't alive."

"Yes, you are." Scrythax's eyelid closed, the eyebrow ridges rising on the left side and flattening on the right like overexpressive eyebrows expressing sly thoughts. "A tiny little light of life, to be sure, but it's there. It had to be there for you to be an Emperor, and it will remain until you undergo postmortem stress and surrender to undeath completely. You are two kinds of undead at once, which can only happen when the soul is in flux at the point of death but not wholly beyond. This is why you've continued to age, albeit slowly, and why . . . What does he answer to now? Talbot did you say?"

He clucked that putrid tongue of his and sighed a happy sigh, sending more dust pouring off the pedestal. "This is why Talbot has gone to such lengths to ensure that you do not undergo true postmortem stress. He's afraid it would ruin you. I know better, of course, but it's very sweet."

"What do you want?" I brushed an errant dust bunny off my shirt.

"From you?"

"No, from the fucking Easter Bunny." I uber vamped again without meaning to, and it felt so nice I almost hit a knee. "Yes, from me."

"Nothing." I opened my mouth to refute that, but he kept talking. "Or rather, nothing that you aren't already intending to do. You see, I would never dream of giving orders to my champions. I choose beings who will already do my bidding whether they know it is my bidding or not. Your great-great-grandfather John Paul served me against the shifters."

I expected JPC to pop up and call bullshit on that play, but he didn't, which made me wonder if he was barred from Scrythax's Vales or if he was still too pissed off about me shooting the Apostles with *El Alma Perdida* to pay attention to what was going down in the material world.

"When he was active, lycanthropes in America were on the verge of a return to the old ways. Some hunted humans. Others merely preyed upon them in other fashions, but John Paul provided a unifying threat—a boogeyman, if you will, who would only kill the naughty little shifters, only the ones who didn't . . . say their prayers at night."

"And me?"

Scrythax opened its mouth to speak and coughed instead, showering me with more dust bunnies. Wiping at them angrily, I took two steps back.

"My apologies." He hacked for a moment before continuing. "I was attempting to evade that question by answering questions you hadn't asked."

"Well, that didn't work."

We waited in silence, and Tabitha went out like a light. Dawn. I caught her reflexively and shifted her over to Beatrice's care for a minute.

"I can't tell you."

"Excuse me?"

"I can't tell you, because if I told you what I wanted you to do, you might refuse to do it simply because I wanted it done, even if you might otherwise have done exactly as I wished had you simply not known I wished it."

"That almost made sense." My nostrils flared, the light from my eyes growing brighter. "So why talk to me at all?"

He laughed again and, if he'd had fingers I imagined he would have put his index finger to his lips before answering. The pause was there, but it lacked something without the gesture. You could tell he was a being who spoke with his hands. Big expansive gestures and tiny ones providing nuance for every sentence.

"How could I resist? You are a Courtney. The only human family I have directly influenced in four centuries. The instant you landed, I felt it and just as certainly as I knew they would bring you here, I knew I had to say hello."

"What do you mean, influenced?"

"Oh, come now, Eric, do you really think that God would return a man's humanity and hold it over the heads of the next seven generations of his kin? Do you actually believe he would part a bat horde and let the sun shine down in such a grandiose fashion, proclaiming what he had done so that all could hear?"

I bumped into Beatrice, only then realizing I'd been backing away from the demon.

"But why?"

"Because I love humans." Scrythax's lips quivered, the slits of its nostrils flexing wider for a brief instant. "Why else would I have let the supernatural community unite against me, disembowel me, scatter my parts . . . ? Because in doing so, I brought them under control. The vampires accepted population control. The therianthropes agreed to hunting limitations. All so that they could band together with the immortals against me. And with the big three working together, how could the other beings hold against the proposed treaty? The Fae had already been reined in by the spread of metal tools. All they needed was a common threat, one that could wipe them all out."

"If you love the humans so much," Beatrice asked, "why didn't you wipe out the supernaturals?"

"Because they have souls too, most of them." If he'd had intact eyeballs, they'd have looked up at the ceiling. As it was, the eye ridges carried off the gesture pretty well. "And like all demons, I do have a weakness for the ensouled."

"So you're saying that you're the one who—"

"Helped Dumbass the First?" He smiled, showing both rows of teeth. "Yes. But in my own defense, they were keeping me in the chapel at the time, under the altar, and he was praying so fervently. The priest didn't seem to know what to do. All those heartfelt prayers and confessions. And it had been so long since I'd pretended to be a god . . . I couldn't help myself."

"So why the strings, then?" I walked toward him again. "Why fuck over the next seven generations?"

"Because I'm a demon, Eric . . . Mr. Courtney, and no matter how powerful we are, in order to accomplish good with our powers, there must be a price. We all must answer to Fair Practices and Equitability." His eyelids lowered, a centimeter or so from closing, then sprang wide. "An unpleasant prospect, even for me."

"So what about your eye?" I tapped my chest.

"Oh, it will do everything Lord Phillip said it would. Find a way to cure yourself and my eye will make you a True Immortal as surely as it could allow Phillip to become an Emperor were he to have an Emperor to sacrifice in his stead . . . as surely as my other eye allows its possessor to peer into possible futures." He sounded wistful. "Though I might have preferred you remain unadulterated by it. I have no doubt you'd have found a way to become human again eventually, and humans, once touched by magic as powerful as you've been touched by, rarely die properly . . . so I fancy you'd have become immortal in the end. Just like Dumbass the First."

"He's still around?"

The horns tapped out unnerving patterns on the stone, and Scrythax spun his head around to face the stairs, where Luc lay unconscious.

"You Courtneys are always so splendidly dense. Did you fail to notice the family resemblance?"

I looked at Luc and I saw it all at once. He looked a lot like my uncle Robert.

"Shit." Light from the demon glittered off the blackness of my claws. I extended a hand to Beatrice. I kept my gaze on the head, then shifted my focus to the ladies. Beatrice had gotten up and was craning her neck to get a better view at Luc. "We're going."

"Don't leave on my account," Scrythax purred. "It's been lovely chatting."

Then the immortals were moving again, and Scrythax wasn't.

♦ 34 ♦

ERIC:

GANG BANG

What's wrong with this picture? A group of really old immortals swear an oath on a demon's head to work together with vampires and other paranormal whatnots to hide from, and in some ways protect, humans. A vampire shows up and the head starts talking to him, so they attack the vampire, not the head. On second thought: What's right with this picture? If your answer is "nothing," then we're on the same damn page.

"Oh for fuck's sake." I didn't see which one of them produced the bow, but the arrow hit my chest with the solid thunk of metal on stone.

"He's unstakable," one of them said.

"He is?" I spotted the bow. Fat Boy had it. About the time I finished focusing on him, he loosed a second shot, hitting me in the left eye and robbing me of my depth perception. "Now there's a new pain." Nothing feels quite like a poke in the eye with a sharp stick.

Despite being all uber vamped, my speed wouldn't crank up. None of the immortals appeared to be as quick as a vampire, but with me not being as quick as most vampires either, the fight wasn't as much fun as it ought to have been. Killing things makes me feel better, and I'd been cutting back, feeding mostly on my thralls.

I held up one hand to protect my remaining eye and someone chopped into it with an axe, cutting through the muscle and lodging the weapon deep into the bone. A sword pierced my stomach. Something long and thin (a spear maybe?) went in through my shoulder. Gunshots exploded around me, sending bursts of agony through my chest and wings.

I ghosted to break free. The weapons stayed where they were, but in the light of my ghostly senses, they blazed with energy and I took it in, throwing open the gates of hunger. The immortals screamed. A Ray Parker Jr. song ran through my head. Weapons were pulled away, but I wouldn't let them go. Tunnels of spirit ran through them and I sucked the energy down. Anime Boy's foot hit me square in the chest, knocking me away from the group of immortals centered on me.

He swatted the weapons clear with lightning-quick blows, never making contact long enough for me to try to feed on him.

"A revenant," Anime Boy observed. "That makes you the second or third most powerful Emperor I know."

"That means a lot coming from a Final Fantasy reject."

He set his feet and thrust his hands against my chest as I spoke. I felt my strength ebb, the power flowing out of me into his hands. Pulling back seemed like the best option.

"Final Fantasy is a good game." He gritted his teeth. "I prefer Three." The ebb flowed then stopped.

"I prefer Seven." It was a standstill.

"Stop, or we end your wife. She'll never get to undergo her three-day trial—never be pronounced free by the Council. Think about it—such a poor end to your trip abroad." Luc's words had the wrong effect.

Ji knew it was a bad plan, the thought "Idiot!" showed clearly in his eyes, but it was too late. I hadn't seen how Luc got over there, but there he stood, stake ready to plunge into Tabitha's heart. James held that big damn sword of his to Tabitha's throat, and the blue glow of my spectral form went purple.

Without Rachel to help me control them, without Talbot to intervene, and without Marilyn to calm me down, my rage blackouts were back. Akira Ifukube's *Godzilla* score might as well have been playing in the background. The air around me crackled. My surroundings, already blurred by the ghost vision, twisted. Walls and tables became smears of color, like staring into a twirling fun house mirror. Words faded in the dull rush of a deep sustained roar. Icy waves of cold flowed out of me. My vision faded. Sound fell away. And then there was nothing.

✦ 35 ✦

TABITHA:
HOSTILE HOSTAGE SITUATION

Aline of frost hit the blade at my throat, the chill burning my neck and shocking me awake as the blade froze. Luc muttered a curse, and I knew he felt it, too. Corpses don't shiver, but I did. Across the room, Master Ji's hands were locked against Eric's chest while Eric clawed at the immortal's throat, leaving angry welts that went from purple to black, spreading across his skin an inch at a time.

Normally I couldn't see Eric in his ghost form, but now he was clearly visible, surrounded by a road-flare corona. I tried to pull away from Luc, but his fingers locked down, digging hard into my skin. Was this guy using me as a hostage?

Seeming human helps me stay awake, but it saps my vampiric abilities. A little anger helps me overcome that so I can be awake and vampire-strong. Eric's voice played in my head. He'd once called me a moist warm tightness, but now that I'd won and he'd married me, the memory wasn't as effective. He'd said it to push me away, because being with him is dangerous. In a sad, twisted way, his resorting to comments like that had been a sign of how much he'd let himself come to care for me—a sign of affection. I thought of Rachel instead, searching for a memory that would make me angry enough to push past the seeming-human power dampening and get my vampiric abilities going. I closed my eyes, picturing her with Eric, hearing her voice in my head. "Hi, slut! Where ya been?"

My abilities came back so quickly I felt like a revved engine. My body shook, but I couldn't tell if it was from the cold or the rush of power.

"Waking up?" The condensation from Luc's breath blew past my face, a white cloud. "I don't want to have to kill you just to make a point."

He *was* using me as a hostage!

"You bastard!"

I grabbed the sword, half expecting the frost to peel the skin from my fingers, surprised when shards of brittle frozen metal clung to my skin as the sword came apart in my hand. Bits of it clung to my neck, my dress, even my arms as the metal fell. Luc began to shift his grip (reaching for another weapon, maybe?), but I was close to full speed and he let the spectacle of Eric's glowing purple fury distract him. I grabbed his throat with both hands. My claws extended directly into the muscle as I lifted and pulled, thrusting my butt backward into him to shift his balance and leverage. My fangs pierced his jugular while he was still in the air and I followed him down, drinking long droughts of warmth so hot and strange it sent tingles through my tongue.

"Christian!" the fat immortal bellowed, calling the name of the guard outside. "Apply the wards to the vampires!"

My skin tingled and I squinted my eyes against the pain I felt sure was on the way, but the tingle faded with a hideously shrill shriek from outside. Several of the immortals moved toward the gate, suddenly ignoring me, Eric, and Beatrice completely.

Aarika didn't.

Beatrice shouted a warning, and I twisted Luc's head from his body. That probably wouldn't kill him, but I hoped it would put him out of the fight. Without Luc to worry about, I saw Aarika lunge; she had abandoned her blade and was wielding wooden stakes in either hand.

"We should have done this at the beginning." Aarika was fast. One stake rammed home just above my right breast, punching through my sternum and into my lung. The other would have been on target, but I smacked her arm away, the bones in her forearm giving way with a definite snap.

We winced together. Even though it had been brief, the pain in my chest was enough to rip a howl of pain from my throat. The urge to scream generated a desire to breathe, forcing my lung to collapse and summoning more agony. She twisted the stake in my wound and I tried to bite her neck. Aarika slung her left arm (the broken one) out hard as if she were slinging mud from her fingers. A low sound like the crack of two billiard balls against one another, combined with the smile on her face, informed me that the arm was no longer broken.

While I watched her eyes, she responded with a savage knee to my abdomen. My mouth dropped open as she jerked the stake from my chest, but the thought of being staked brought me past the pain. Talbot had once tried to explain to me that since I'd gone through PMS (postmortem stress), my body was an interface for my essence. Supposedly, once I got better at it, I'd be able to shut off pain more efficiently. I wasn't good enough yet, but I was still a Vlad.

I caught the stake, my hand closing on hers with such rapidity that I could have sworn I saw admiration in her eyes. The snap, crackle, and pop of finger and hand bones breaking and giving way sounded beneath my fingertips.

"How do you like that, bitch?"

Her other arm shot up, and I snagged her wrist. She smiled through the pain. "I've had better."

I never saw the stake coming. James rammed it in from behind. Bloodied, but unsplintered, the tip of his custom stake jutted out at an angle between my breasts. Aarika had maneuvered me into position, arms wide, completely preoccupied with kicking her scrawny ass. It was a good tactic.

"Sorry about that." Eric's war buddy shifted me around, using the stake as a handle to move me as he wanted. "Normally this is not how I treat the wife of a friend." He locked eyes with me and I felt a connection, not unlike the one forged when vampires locked eyes with each other or with humans, but I couldn't push my will across it.

"Damn it." My lips didn't move, but I heard myself say it.

"Who did Eric bring for backup?" James's lips didn't move either. "Who's out there fighting Christian?"

Telepathy. Real telepathy, not push-me-pull-me mental dominance. I laughed, the sound ringing loud in my mind and James's. Before I convinced Eric to turn me, I'd believed becoming a vampire would let us have some sort of lovers' telepathy. I heard the crack of a gun, and the side of James's head vanished in a spray of gore.

"Somebody grab the fucking thrall." James's voice was clear in my head even though his body was already falling to one side. With no one to support me, I fell. On my way to the floor, I caught a glimpse of Beatrice, holding one of James's guns in both hands, like someone in a cop show. Aarika was on one knee, flexing her fingers to get Bea's attention while reaching for a boot knife with her right hand.

"Put the gun down, thrall." Aarika snarled the words. "Do you wish to see how quickly you heal from a broken neck?"

"Enough!"

It rang through my head, vibrating my skull, a jet plane roar of communication before the doors exploded inward, the bodies of the immortals who had rushed off to reinforce Christian flying in after the pieces of the ruined doors.

It was a wolf—not a werewolf, but a wolf wolf, a giant one with black fur and blazing eyes. It stood easily as high at the shoulder as Eric, if not higher. Werewolves with Celtic patterns shaved into their fur walked with it, three on either side.

All of the combatants scattered save for Eric and Ji. Beatrice let the gun tumble from her hands, and it seemed to take forever to hit the ground. She might have moved to unstake me, but either the wolf terrified her in some primal way or else it did something to her, because she collapsed as it drew near. Frost covered its nose as it padded closer to Eric, out of my range of vision. As my anger turned to curiosity and fear, sleep took me, and my last thought was from a terrible movie Eric had made me watch—something about a wolfman and 'nards.

36

ERIC:

LA BÊTE GARNIER

Anvils of pressure landed on my chest. Ribs cracked, and I heard the Asian kid grunt. He had a giant black-furred paw on his chest, the well-trimmed claws digging into his pectorals. You'd have expected a musky scent, but the fur had a nice clean shampoo smell. I looked up and saw nothing but dark black fur. There was a wolf the size of a Clydesdale standing on top of me. Its paw covered my chest, restraining my shoulders, and all I could think was: *When the hell did that thing get here? And wasn't I all ghosted up just a minute ago?*

I tried to ghost myself, but got a bodywide electric shock instead, which numbed my teeth and crossed my eyes. The wolf's tremendous head bent low. Clean white teeth the size of small countries filled its mouth, and a wave of mint assailed me.

"Stay put, vampire." I couldn't help but make a comparison to James Earl Jones. This guy sounded just like him, but the delivery was much more "This is CNN" than "Luke, I am your father."

Pressure eased on my chest. My ribs healed as the massive paw lifted, but Asian Guy winced at the unavoidable pressure increase that resulted.

"You smell nice for a big dog." I rubbed my chest, but made no move to rise.

"Garnier," he answered. "Now be quiet."

Deacon stood to the wolf's left in balls-out werewolf fashion. Even so, he looked cowed. The surviving Apostles were with him (two on his side of Megawolf and three on the other side).

"Master Ji." Megawolf lifted his paw, and an unrestrained wheeze escaped the man's throat. "Explain."

"The vampire charged the Head of Scrythax." He coughed, but it was a spark of energy, not blood, that escaped his lips. "We couldn't let him take it."

"I was only talking to the damn thing—"

A gargantuan wolf paw to the chest shut me up. "Why are you speaking? I asked Ji."

"Impossible." Master Ji was looking better by the second. His ribs had healed, shifting back into place without any outside assistance. Neat trick. "We did not hear it speak. Scrythax is all but dead; he could not have—"

"And yet"—Megawolf didn't actually have to stomp Ji to get him to quiet down again; a simple shift of the leg was all it took to make Ji's mouth slam tight—"I believe him."

The wolf shifted its gaze to the other immortals, who were slowly regrouping near the pedestal. "Oddvar!"

The old, morbidly obese immortal stepped forward. "*Oui, la Bête?*"

"Convey my apologies to Isaac. I ingested his paladin."

The fat man cringed. "Did you—?"

"Soul-battle? No." The wolf chuffed. "He will re-form. Digestive processing is unpleasant for immortals, but survivable. Ask Master Ji."

"This thing ate you once?" I tentatively moved to rise, making it a slow, deliberate motion. I do understand the idea of respecting power, and as far as I could tell, this thing had single-pawedly slapped me down in full-blown raging blackout uber-vamp mode, and I really didn't want to make it mad. I would if I had to, because I'm me, but still . . .

"Twice." Ji looked away, face blanched. The tang of fear rose off him in waves, and the Megawolf loosed a barking noise that could have been a laugh.

"Unnecessary fear, Ji." Gripping the immortal gently with his fangs, the wolf pulled Master Ji into a standing position and gave him one brief lick on the face. "No need to repeat the lesson. You understood on the second pass."

"*Merci, la Bête.*" Ji bowed low.

"What's a soul battle?" Beatrice asked that one. The immortals flinched.

Aarika opened her mouth to explain, but Megawolf's response silenced her.

"No." He held his head high, puffing himself up in a way. "My time is not for wasting." He turned his head to Luc, who was in the midst of reattaching his own head. *La Bête* waited while the flesh melted together and the wound healed. "Explain."

"Explain?" Luc asked, rubbing his throat and testing the mobility of his newly healed neck.

"Oui."

"Explain what, *la Bête?*"

I'd compared Megawolf's roar to a thunderclap, but the rumble was reminiscent of an earthquake. It shook the walls. "Idiots!" The creature's teeth receded painfully, blood flowing from its open mouth in a thick stream. Bones cracked and reknit themselves, filling the room with a sound like oaks creaking in a hurricane. He roared again as its hair withdrew in random patches. Its muzzle shortened and its digits both grew proportionately longer and shrank, bulging awkwardly as the claws receded, forcing the skin to stretch to accommodate it and only then shrinking.

When it was done, a male in human form knelt where the wolf had been. He rose, revealing himself to be quite tall, close to seven feet. Nude at first, he covered himself as an after-thought, summoning what looked like some sort of historical hunter's attire, all leathers and fur, the same way I'd seen other immortals produce arms and armor. There was still a wrongness. In the same way that normal werewolves look fake, he felt wrong. It took three seconds for me to find the source of the problem. His shadow wasn't human. It still matched the size, proportions, and shape of his Megawolf self.

Deacon and the other Apostles averted their gazes.

"Do I have to wear your form"—the words came from his mouth this time—normal words, yet accompanied by a telepathic echo of the voice I'd heard before—"and speak with this?" He gestured to himself with obvious disgust. "Must I draw out my meaning and make puzzles in your minds so that you can comprehend what should be obvious?"

"Mea culpa, la Bête," Luc began.

"The next man who names me, I will eat." Megawolf crossed the room and seized Luc by the throat. "I feel it when you name me. It touches my spirit. I will not be defined by words. I am not words. I am form and spirit and hunt. Do you understand, Luc?"

"Oui." He barely caught the *"la Bête"* but he kept it in.

"Now. In words that will pass these ears"—he tapped the side of Luc's head with an index finger—"and be understood, here"—he thumped Luc's forehead. "Why did you allow an Emperor vampire to enter Paris?"

"You do not wish him to remain?" That was Aarika. "We'll remove him at once—"

Megawolf cut her off with a look.

"I expressed no such opinion." His gaze shot to me and then back to Luc. "I already know why *I* allowed it. Now, I want to know why *you* did and why you brought him to your beloved demon-god."

"He has a right to be in Paris."

"No." Megawolf's spoken words were soft, but the matching telepathic message was a shout. "No more Emperors. I said as much when Lisette was accepted. Did you think my mind had changed because a few thousand moons had passed?"

"But he wants to kill Lisette," Luc protested. "Surely that—"

"Close." Megawolf grinned and the expression overstretched the natural boundaries of his lips. "If you had said you did it because he is kin, because of your family curse, Luc, then I would have understood."

"Family? Curse?" True bewilderment touched Luc's eyes. He really didn't know. "He's no relation of mine. The seventh generation of Courtneys would have died off years ago."

"You are a poor ancestor, Luc," he snarled, "and a blind one. Can you not see the touch of Scrythax on his spirit? What magic is as old and pure as the curse of an Infernatti? Do you not see the piece of Scrythax which blazes in his heart?" Megawolf paused. "I see that you do not. Ah, you swore on the demon's head. It has altered your senses. Of course it would."

"Can you go back to being all shut the fuck up and eatin' people?" I shook my head, struggling to stand, "'cause I was interested when you were a Megawolf. But the Tall Hairy Guy who runs his mouth and acts all pissy is just annoying."

Maybe it's that I've never been the tallest guy in the class. Maybe that's where my mouth came from. Could be that I was just too brain-addled to keep my mouth shut. A trickle of cool went through my body, leaving traces of warmth in its wake, and it didn't feel like Rachel's magic. It was cold and pure. Scrythax. The stupid demon was trying to calm me down, but that had been my problem all along. Sober, I overthink things. I worry about details. But buzzed—altered—I might do damn near anything.

"I'm talking to the immortals, vampire." Tall Hairy Guy gave a dismissive wave as if he were flicking me away with his hand, which put him just within arm's reach.

"Round two." I had no vampire speed, no red-eye glow. It wouldn't come. But my strength is always there. I grabbed his wrist and yanked him off balance with a good solid tug. Eyes wide, Tall Hairy Guy gave me a satisfying "oof" as I folded him over my knee with a sharp knee spike to the stomach. I rammed the knee home once, twice, three times, my strength giving me the power to overcome his larger shape.

I let him drop to his hands and knees, then followed up with a kick aimed at his head. He caught my leg. Which was fine with me, because who wants a one-sided fight? I wasn't even particularly mad at him. I was frustrated and tired of the talking and I wanted to beat on somebody. He'd drawn the lucky number.

"It's been a century or more since I fought in human form." Tall Hairy Guy shoved me backward. His position gave him superior leverage, and I didn't even fight it. I saw a smile vanish from Deacon's face as Tall Hairy Guy began to fight back. So Deacon didn't like *la Bête du Gévaudan*? If he wasn't happy, then maybe I was attacking the wrong person.

"Shall we make things interesting, vampire?" *la Bête* asked.

"In what way?"

He stood, ducking to the side to avoid a jab I'd launched at his face, and followed with a punch of his own. I felt like a guy in one of those disaster movies where they know the asteroid is going to hit Earth and it's too late to do anything but take it on the chin and hope you make it. In human form, he wasn't as strong as I expected, but a good solid shot to the cheek, just under the eye, is never fun, and in boxing, it's kind of the sweet spot.

Blood sprayed out of my mouth, but the pain was brief. From a pure endurance standpoint, vampires have the edge in hand-to-hand combat. Even so, I saw spots before my eyes.

"No claws. No fangs. No powers. No shifting. Hand-to-hand."

"Speed?" I put the question out there and let it hang.

"I said no powers."

"Yeah." I caught myself talking with my hands. "But I don't always have a good handle on controlling mine."

"If you can get it to work this far away from your *memento mori*?" He gestured, too, weighing the options in his hands as if they were physical things. "Sure."

"I'm in."

Around us, stunned immortals looked on. Beatrice knelt by Tabitha, and I smiled when one of the immortal crowd responded to her unspoken request for help moving my day-struck bride. They carried her to a set of chairs I hadn't seen and laid her across them. While I was watching that, *la Bête du Gévaudan* hit me with a combo of rabbit punches followed by an uppercut that lifted me into the air like a cartoon boxer and sent me sprawling toward the pedestal.

A human throat shouted, "You idiots!" My back struck the pedestal and I felt the thing begin to topple. Time slowed, and the common inrush of breath sounded low and slow to my time-dilated perceptions. It was the sound of immortals getting ready to act. My heart sprang to life, and Scrythax spoke in my head.

"Interesting." If he'd been a cat, I'd have accused him of purring.

"You've learned to draw on the Stone to assist you in the absence of your *memento mori*."

"Yeah." I grabbed the head as it fell from the podium. "I'm all clever and shit." I think I meant to set it back on the pedestal and tell the immortals to chill out. Instead, my lips drew into a hard tight smile as I shifted my grip from a horn to the base of the skull, and I threw the Head of Scrythax at *la Bête du Gévaudan*.

37

ERIC:

TIME OUT FOR BAD BEHAVIOR

Time stopped again, and in midspin the Head of Scrythax decelerated into a languid roll. He smiled at me, the rows of teeth clicking shut in a disconcerting lack of unison. "Better?"

"Dude." I tossed up my hands. "I'm just trying to fight a fucking hairy-ass immortal werewolf here. I threw you at him. Why can't you just hit him like a normal decapitated head?"

"Very well."

Time sped up again and Scrythax slapped against Megawolf's chest, one horn digging into his flesh. Did that count as a weapon? Fuck!

"Wait. Shit." I made a *T* with my hands, signaling a timeout. "Decapitated demon heads count as a weapon. My bad." I held my arms out to either side of me. "You get a free shot with the Head of Scrythax."

"He certainly does not," Oddvar (I think Oddvar was the big fat one) shouted. "This has gone far enough!"

Megawolf burst into uncontrollable fits of laughter, rapid bark-like bursts, punctuated by huge inhalations of air. "Fine." He wiped his eyes, still laughing, struggling to speak between chortles. "Take him and"—he withdrew the head, shaking with laughter, close to dropping it—"put him back on the pedestal. Protect the demon god, Oddvar. By all means."

"Maybe we should take this outside?" I suggested as Oddvar stormed across the room and took the head away from Megawolf. The immortal brushed past me and set Scrythax reverently back in his spot atop the pedestal.

"No." *La Bête* grabbed Deacon's shoulder. "No, I think we'd best leave things as they are. I must resolve my business and be on my way. Apologize to the vampire," he commanded the werewolf.

What?

"I apologize." Deacon choked on the words.

"For what do you apologize?" *la Bête* prompted as I opened my mouth to ask the same sort of thing.

"I apologize for invading your territory." He looked at *la Bête* as if he might challenge him, but thought better of it and shifted his gaze to the floor again. "On two separate occasions, my disciples and I disregarded the truce between you and William, the governing Alpha. We did so without rightfully challenging him to claim the territory. We did so like lone wolves, like packless rogues, without the proper authority or direction of the holy and righteous Lycan Diocese." He and the other Apostles knelt as one, became human, and offered their necks. "Our lives are yours, Eric Courtney."

"Fuck off."

La Bête nodded at my words and the Apostles jerked to their feet, changing forms as one. "You do not accept?" Deacon shouted now that he was all wolfed-out and tough again. "You mock me?"

I've never met a big guy with such a clear-cut case of short man's syndrome before. But that was Deacon through and through.

"He mocks you because it is his right," Megawolf snarled. "Just as it became my right to rule on this when you lost your head and chased a wronged party into *my* territory. I do not like vampires—I never have—but your discourteous lack of gratitude astounds me, Deacon. This vampire spared your lives when I delivered them to him as payment for the rules you knowingly broke, and you have the gall to object to the words he used when doing so?

"I would almost offer you up again if I were not certain you would shame me with a further demonstration of your disrespect."

"Forgive me." Deacon dropped to the ground and rolled onto his back, arching his neck up toward *la Bête*.

"Return to him what has been stolen."

Deacon reached into his pants pocket and withdrew a small leather bag, then stood and walked to me, dropping the bag into my hand. "The bullets of *El Alma Perdida*."

"I took the liberty of releasing the spirits of the werewolves encased within," said *la Bête*.

"Whatever." I emptied the contents of the bag into my hand. Each bullet felt lighter in my hand, a tiny difference, yet a noticeable one. *Wasn't it supposed to be glowing or something? Recharging?* I dropped the bullets into my pocket, wishing I'd brought Magbidion with me so he could give them a once-over. "That was JPC's deal anyway. Not mine. So? Now what?"

"I grant you three nights' time in my territory."

"Well, fuck you, too."

"Explain."

"Fucking?"

"No." *La Bête*'s eyes narrowed. "You're rude and uncouth, but you usually have a reason. Why do you disdain my generosity?"

"Because I'm here on my honeymoon and you just basically said that as soon as my wife is done with the stupid three-day ritual these assholes"—I indicated the immortals—"insist she completes, she has to leave without getting to spend any time in Paris at all."

"Oddvar, can this ritual be waived without difficulty?"

"The moment she agreed to it in front of the Head of Scrythax, the ritual began." He shook his head. "If she leaves early—"

"Then she disqualifies herself," *la Bête* interrupted. "You and your rules. I cannot deny they've kept the vampires largely in check."

"If you were to agree to swear the Oath—"

La Bête's form exploded, chunks of flesh and gore spattering the room as his wolf form erupted from the human one. "I will not swear any oath by a demon!" Megawolf's massive paw caught the fat immortal in the stomach, knocking him flat. The wolf's teeth drooled blood onto Oddvar's cheek as he growled. Flecks of cast-off skin dotted Megawolf's black fur and he howled, even as his telepathic words filled our minds.

"Five nights then," Megawolf decreed. "As the ritual will still be kept, you shall be welcome here for five nights, during which time you and your bride may hunt and kill three humans each. I decline to allow you into the Treaty of Secrets. This should save you the trouble of refusing to swear on the demon head yourself. On the basis of my own authority, I decree that you shall have free rein to destroy the vampires of Europe as you see fit."

"That is not acceptable," Aarika began.

Luc joined his voice to hers. "Be reasonable, *la*—" He caught himself again. "You know the Council of Immortals cannot condone this."

"You broke your word to me." Megawolf swelled up and howled again. *This,* I thought, *must be what it's like to argue with me when I'm angry.* "I said no more Emperor vampires! And you let one in. Shall I take that act as dissolution of our agreement? Shall I interpret it as an act of war? Because I am ready. Are you?" His snout jutted toward Luc: "Are you?" At Aarika: "Are you?" And on and on to each of the immortals until every immortal in the room had turned away, unwilling to fight.

"You didn't ask me." I couldn't resist baiting him.

"You'd say yes." A hint of amusement accompanied his telepathic utterance. "Besides, I'm being magnanimous. You've been wronged and I'm making it up to you. Now, shut up.

"I decree," Megawolf repeated, "that Eric Courtney and his bride shall have free rein to destroy the vampires of Europe as they see fit. And the vampires of Europe shall have free rein, if individually attacked, to respond in kind, but only upon the Courtney who attacked them. As Eric is not an Oath-sworn citizen of Europe, the responsibility for keeping the mortals unaware of his and his wife's presence shall fall upon the immortal community, which is to grant them both all courtesy as the Courtneys are their guests . . . and mine."

"What happens if I'm still here on the sixth day?" I asked.

"Then we shall meet again on less friendly terms, Mr. Courtney." *La Bête*'s breath washed over me, still smelling of mint and hot as a sauna.

"I shall . . . deposit . . . Christian in the countryside in approximately six to eight hours' time," *la Bête* thought at the others, "and then I shall return to Lozère. Good day to you."

He left the room and the Apostles followed him. Once they were gone, I smiled at the immortals.

"So." I clapped my hands together. "Do I get conjugal visits with Tabitha during the stupid ritual thing?"

"The sire must not have any undo—" Aarika began.

"That's fine," I cut her off. "In which case, I'm leaving Beatrice here to feed and look after Tabitha and I'm going sightseeing. Which means I'll need a guide, someone to watch over me and make sure I don't get seen, and . . . seeing as how I can only kill three humans, I'll need a lucky volunteer to play the role of snack food. Any takers?"

Luc scowled. "I will go. It is my—"

"I don't bite guys, Dumbass."

One by one, the men turned to Aarika.

"I vill kill all of you vun day," she said resignedly, her irritation bringing out a little more of her accent than I'd heard before, "und I vill enjoy it." She offered me her arm, the very model of stoicism. "Shall we go?"

Of course, if I'd known any number of things about what was going on back home, or would go on, or even that Rachel had come to Paris to mess with me, I'd have jerked Tabitha out of her whole "make me my own vampire" testing and flown straight home. But I didn't know any of that, so Aarika and I walked arm in arm out of the castle and into the sun . . . where I caught fire, because I'm good at it.

Once I'd doused the flames in the moat, I ghosted, becoming

corporeal once I had moved to the shadow of the castle. Aarika was laughing at me.

"Oh, yeah," I growled, "you and I are going to get along famously."

"And to think," she said between guffaws, "I thought I would not enjoy this assignment at all."

I turned into a mouse. "Put me in your bra."

"That will not happen."

"I have to be protected from the sun somehow." I batted little mousey eyelashes at her.

"First"—she bent over and picked me up—"I am not wearing a bra, *und* second . . . a pocket will suffice." She crammed me in her right pocket next to her car keys and off we went again, this time sans the fire. Seeing Paris with a German. I could hardly contain my enthusiasm. . . .

◆ 38 ◆

TABITHA:

NONE OF THE ABOVE

Two number-two pencils, a desk, and three Scantron sheets. Master Ji leaned against the castle wall, dressed like an anime character. Strawberry Pocky in one hand and a bottle of sugar-free Bawls in the other, he looked up from the book he had on autoscroll on his cell phone and then back down when I didn't ask a question. He'd taped a sign to the stone next to him, but it was in Japanese or something and I couldn't read it.

I sat at the desk, looking at question number one on my test:

1. You are very hungry and it is close to dawn. There are too many people around for you to reliably use a Vale of Scrythax to separate a human from the crowd without risking the notice of the other mortals. There are a few rats nearby upon which you could feed, but you find that distasteful. Choose the best option from the following list:

   a. Go to bed without feeding in hopes that you can hunt better tomorrow. You think you can handle the thirst without losing control.
   b. Try to ensnare a mortal anyway, using a Vale of Scrythax. You might get lucky.
   c. Feed right out in the open and try to convince the crowd it's a scene from a movie.
   d. Feed on the rats.

"You guys must really think I'm special ed." I looked up at Master Ji. "How did I even get into this dumb hypothetical situation to start with? Why am I not hunting with Eric . . . and if things are all that bad, why don't I just feed off a thrall?"

Ji took a sip of the soda, the tangy scent of the taurine forcing me to blink my eyes against the fumes each time he opened the bottle to take a sip.

"Just fill it in," Ji said.

I put an X in the oval on the Scantron sheet that contained the letter d.

I sighed. "Am I going to see my husband at all today?"

"Fill it in. Neatly."

"Where's Beatrice?" I thought I heard her, off in another building, but I couldn't be certain.

"You'll see her later, after the day's testing."

"But I'm cold."

"You're a vampire," Ji told me. "Cold is your natural state. If you're to be trusted as a free individual, you'll have to demonstrate your ability to function without the presence or assistance of thralls or your sire."

I carefully filled in the bubble for d, erased the portions of my X that overlapped the marked edges of the oval, and blew the tiny pinkish gray bits of eraser off the sheet.

Question two:

2. You've just made your first thrall. S/he is good at his (or her) job, but you decide it was a mistake. You've already killed your quota of mortals, so you cannot slay the thrall. What do you do? Choose the best option from the following list:

   a. Kill the thrall anyway and hope the immortals don't sense it.
   b. Get another vampire to kill the thrall for you and promise you won't hold it against her or him.
   c. Lock the thrall in the basement and forget about him or her, or command the thrall to carry out a meaningless task that might attract attention.
   d. Learn to live with the thrall and remember the lesson for the future, then deal with the thrall appropriately when you are allowed another kill.

I filled in d and rolled my eyes at the next few questions, answering d to all of them. It was simple stuff, the purportedly correct answers obvious based on tone, if not context. An idiot could pass it.

"Is this one of those tests where I can just go through the whole thing checking *d*?"

"Believe it or not . . ." Master Ji set down his drink, took a bite of his Pocky, and continued speaking. "There are many vampires who do not pass the written portion of the test."

"Why?"

"They've changed too much." He picked up the exam and flipped through it. "Some find it impossible to give the same answer over and over again. Others have become arrogant predators who find the idea of even pretending not to do what they want to do unfathomable. Others refuse to finish it or to take the testing seriously at all. They believe they are more important than the billions of mortals living in Europe, that they are somehow better just because they are longer-lived and more of a burden on their fellow beings."

"Oh." Was I guilty of thinking myself more important than normal people? Probably. "May I have my test back, please?"

The papers rustled as Ji returned them, and I set my mind on the task of completing the test. The answers weren't all *d*; they changed to *b* halfway through and then to *a* at the three-quarter mark. The answer to question two hundred and fifty was *c*.

"What next?"

"The essay." He provided more paper and let me sharpen my pencils. "Please write an essay explaining why you haven't asked me what this means." Ji tapped the sign he'd taped on the wall. I said Eric's favorite words and started writing.

"Master Ji?" I asked.

"Yes?"

"Is it all going to be like this?"

"Not all of it," he said. "Tomorrow night we're going to watch an educational video."

I bit my tongue and went back to the essay.

◆ 39 ◆

ERIC:

WHY ERIC WON'T ANSWER THE PHONE

I spent my first ten minutes at the Louvre trying to understand why some dumbass put up a glass pyramid and the next ten staring at the thing while Aarika tried to explain it to me. I don't understand; I probably never will.

I'd used my tour guide and my free time running about Paris to find places Tabitha would like so that I could do them with her once she was all free and clear, since we'd only have two nights. Yeah. I know. I'm a total fucking sweetheart. Once Aarika understood the concept, she'd actually been fairly helpful.

Oh, and by the way, France sucks. How vampires put up with everything closing so damn early, I'll never know. Nightclubs and restaurants are open, but what if you want to buy a CD, a book, or a DVD? You're SOL, that's what. You'd think they'd have used their pull to push back the closing time on the city. Not so much.

One thing I do like about France is the scenery. You can't buy a plasma screen television at 8:30 p.m., but the city will entertain you with her architecture alone.

Then again, I like old buildings. It's humbling to stand on top of a structure older than your country. Okay, humbling for some people. But, to quote one of my favorite movies: "I ain't people."

"Eric!" Aarika shouted at me from the lower platform. I pretended I couldn't hear her, but she knew I could. "Eric, get down from zere."

I stood on top of the Eiffel Tower, on night number last of Tabitha's big test, attracting attention to myself and watching *Singin' in the Rain* on my iPod. Gene Kelly danced across my tiny screen and I mimicked his movements. Only an American would be standing where I was, right on top of the tallest antenna. Well, okay, I do know a Swede who might do it, but he's crazy and I'm pretty sure he's dead.

Gene swung on a lamppost; I jumped up and down on the television mast, playing havoc with everyone's reception and trying not to break any of the antennas. Not showing up on security cameras is a real benefit sometimes.

"Come and get me, bitch!" I yelled into the night, more to Lisette than Aarika, but my immortal tour guide didn't have to know that. *"Voulez-vous coucher avec moi ce soir?"* That's the longest sentence I know in French. I was tired of being on top of the Eiffel Tower, tired of being in France, and even more put out that no one was showing up to play.

My plan had been simple. Fly to Paris. Spend a night or three taking Tabitha to all the little romantic spots that tourists can go at night. By night four, big badass uber vamp was supposed to show up and fight me or talk or I don't know—something! On night five Tabitha and I would make love in the Eiffel Tower after it closed and then we'd fly back to the good old US of A on night six or seven. Here on night three, my sire's failure to appear was pissing me off, and Tabitha's stupid exam had almost completely ruined our supposed honeymoon.

Vampires can "announce" themselves mentally to other vampires. Or did I already tell you that? Well, either way, I had been doing it every night in different parts of the city, basically anywhere Aarika and I went, and still no dice. Eventually some local vamp would come along to either fight or to ask me politely to fuck off. *La Bête's* grant of free rein to kill vampires was the only thing keeping me sane. Speaking of which . . .

A dead guy popped into my head. Two Drones, five Soldiers, and a Master vamp landed at the bottom of the television mast before shouting up at me in angry French. One of them said something about a futon, and his groupies laughed.

My eyes flashed (they do that a lot) and I ghosted, flying down past Aarika (but not without giving her a wave and a smile as I flew by), and materialized in front of the Master vampire. He dressed better than I ever would, and he looked like he thought that made him better than me. Other vamps feel the powers and ages of other vampires in different ways. I think Greta actually gets birthdays and stuff, but I get more of a comparative feeling. For example, this guy's felt like Bruce Dickinson's announcement that he was leaving Iron Maiden, but before he did the Raising Hell farewell concert. In other words, somewhere around seventeen years or so ago, Jean-Philippe had impressed someone enough for them to make him immortal.

"Verdammt vampires!" Aarika bellowed as she waited on the elevator. I paid her no mind and neither did my new friend, Jean-Philippe.

As Aarika neared, the air wavered and a shimmer spread out from me and my fellow combatants. She'd opened a Vale of Scrythax. Vales were supposed to show the area as Scrythax remembered it, but thanks to the Eye of Scrythax I had buried in my chest, each Vale I entered got a happy little update. I had a feeling Old Headless could pick and choose, but had decided to be annoying.

"*Parlez-vous anglais?*" I asked the Master vamp.

"*Non,*" he lied. I punched him in the face, showed him my fangs.

"Sure you do," I said. I swept his feet out from under him, tagging him again with my right fist on his way down. "I only asked to be polite."

Having thralls was just chock-full of benefits. If I remember to check (and I rarely do) I could tell where my vampiric offspring were and how they were doing. I could even sense when they got themselves into trouble. It juiced up the old vampire early warning system, too.

Vlads and Master vamps can sense other vampires, whether or not they announce themselves. Before my first thrall, I got faces, names, and relative ages. With practice, I learned to get a whole lot more. During my short time in France, Aarika'd taught me to weed out the bloodsuckers that spoke only French from the ones that just didn't want to let on that they understood English.

Jean-Philippe was one of the latter. He and his goons sped up. Vampires in France were faster than the ones back home, but they also weren't as strong. His goon squad tore into me, and my own speed increased. Every other vampire I know can speed up at will; it's decision based, like diving for home or going from a walk to a run. They're just always that fast if they want to be.

My powers are a little less fickle than they once were, now that I have a *memento mori*. The closer I am to Fang, the more reliable my powers. QED, the farther I am away from him, the more flaky they are. And since from Paris to Void City is about four thousand five hundred miles . . . I think you get the picture. Total flakesville.

They ripped and tore at me, but despite the pain I wasn't concerned. It's hard to kill a Vlad if you don't know how, and even harder to kill an Emperor like me. I could remember being staked, beheaded, burned alive, dowsed in holy water, and even blown up by blessed charges of C4 by people and things with a much greater desire to see me dead than these fashion victims. No, I wasn't worried. I caught two vampires by their throats, one in each hand, and roared as I squeezed, fingers sinking through the flesh to touch the bony spine beneath. A sharp, high-velocity flick of the wrist sent their heads right off onto the metal floor. *See? There's the speed! It worked for a whole second.* Anger seems to help. So much for *Singin' in the Rain.*

Twin jets of blood splattered the Eiffel Tower's brown girders. Jean-Philippe went into instant retreat, turned into a bat, and flew. One thing I had learned about French vampires was that they didn't try to kill each other. It was about skill and who was better, not like in the States. Compared to them we're animals, unless you count some of the nonfatal punishments they come up with to entertain each other. It wasn't surprising that Jean-Philippe would run once he realized I was the crazy American vampire that *la Bête du Gévaudan* had given a free pass. It came as a total shock that his five remaining buddies tried to cover his escape.

I locked eyes with one of the Drones and ordered, *"Allez!"* I hadn't been able to kill a Drone since the werewolves killed . . . I don't know . . . somebody important. A guy, I think? Name starts with a K? I couldn't remember his face, yet all of their faces reminded me of his, the dull little gleam to their eyes, the light that had gone out rather than burning brighter . . . I just couldn't do it. The first Drone ran and the second one went with him before I'd even sent the order. That left me and the last three Soldiers.

They fought well, and they were used to working together. One of them favored some kind of freaky kickboxing. It was cool and deadly. I've had very little martial training since Korea. Fortunately for me, turning into the uber vamp is something of an equalizer, even if it does take a little bit for the old uber vamp juice to get flowing.

My skin went gray, moving steadily toward black, and I grew in size. Fancy-Footwork Boy kicked me off the Eiffel Tower (my fault for letting my mind wander) and the transformation sped up. Purple-eyed and grinning, I flew back toward the three Soldiers. In France they call them *les Chevaliers.* Even with the fuzzy state of my brain, I remembered that it meant "knights." I also recalled the name of the kickboxing style Soldier Number One had been using on me. It was called *savate.* It's funny, the things I remember. He kicked me in the head and it crossed my eyes. Not that I haven't taken an injury like that before.

This time something was different. There was a pop and a hiss, followed by a strong odor, gunpowder and something else and then more pain, hot and burning all through my sinuses, as if someone had lit a pair of bottle rockets and shot them up my nose. *Pop. Hiss. Ow.*

I felt another vampire, a Vlad. She was on Aarika in seconds, moving with impressive speed. Aarika armored up, but even as her weapon manifested, the new Vlad was taking it away from her and pinning her to the Eiffel Tower with it. The new Vlad reminded me of "99 Luftballons" by Nena. Then again, that could have been Aarika, because she's German. Something about the newcomer reminded me of the last episode of *M*A*S*H*, too.

Stars flared in front of my eyes. The Vale of Scrythax was dissolving around us. The Soldier I was fighting tried to use the opening to leave, but the new Vlad broke his neck from behind and pulled his head off. His body rotted so fast, it looked almost as though he'd just turned to dust, a swirl of particles in the night. My face felt hot. Beads of red ran down my forehead and I touched one and the gunpowder smell melded with a sweeter one—cinnamon. I closed my eyes. The fight went on without me, but the newcomer didn't need my help. In my head she blew me a kiss. She seemed so familiar.

Pixie-cut hair of candy apple red with lighter streaks of cotton candy pink hung down in a ragged edge over her left eye, barely obscuring eyes the autumn gold of a maple leaf. Needlelike fangs peeked out from behind lips painted dark blue and twitched into a confident smirk. A white shirt with overlarge armholes swung wide as she fought, revealing flashes of her small breasts, nipples erect from the thrill of combat. She laughed as she fought, her speed so great that she seemed to pop from place to place, appearing as a sequence of still poses, like photo frames.

Irene?

Two more puffs of rapidly dusted vamp, one after another, and the two remaining Soldiers were ended. Gone forever.

The cinnamon scent grew stronger, overwhelming me, and I tried to form a command. "Rachel, sto—" I hit the ground, nose smashing into concrete, my fangs cutting my mouth. And it was all gone. How I'd gotten there, where there was, who I was fighting and why . . . Gone.

However long I lay there, when I came to, I leapt to my feet, claws out. I sensed something near me: the other vampire. I spun toward her, when I felt another flash of pain, this one full and throbbing in the back of my skull; my vision went to shades of emerald. The taste of wintergreen filled my mouth.

"I would've preferred mint," I mumbled. And then it was worse; like someone put my memory in a blender and hit puree. My eyes closed for what felt like a few seconds. When they opened again, my vision was back to normal, but the last thing I remembered was Roger saying that we needed to go to El Segundo. What the hell was I doing in Paris? That's where I had to be, right? Where else do they have a life-size Eiffel Tower? How the hell had I let Irene talk me into this?

Irene helped me up, concern clearly showing in those washed-out

brown-turning-to-gold-colored eyes. They'd once been a rich chocolate, but time had changed Irene. "Are you okay, babe?" she asked me.

"I think so." I ran my tongue around the inside of my mouth. *Had I
tasted something for a second there?* "What happened?"

"I think that vampire kicked you a little too hard in the head," she
teased. When had Irene dyed her hair red? She wore a white silk
blouse with no bra to cover her pert little breasts. Another woman's
scent wafted up from her groin. Some living girls spray perfume in
their underwear drawer to cover up the odor that Irene was cultivat-
ing, but vampires can be . . . different. Irene would usually make one
of the girls at the Demon Heart wear her underwear for a few hours
before she put it on to make herself smell alive. I didn't recognize the
woman's scent, which meant she'd likely been Irene's dinner.

The idea appealed to me for an entirely different set of reasons,
but I didn't think it would be wise to enumerate them for her. Instead I
slid my hand up her thigh beneath the matching white skirt. She was
still warm from feeding or a kill.

"When did we get to Paris?" I asked.

She kissed me hard, letting her bangs rest on my face. Irene had a
few inches on me in height even without the four-inch spike heels she
was wearing. My hand slid farther up her leg, brushing the space between.

"We can do that in the limo," she whispered in that husky voice
she has, nipping playfully at my neck. I'd had a no biting rule with all
my other girlfriends, but Irene was always an exception. "The sun is
coming up soon. Can't you hear Chanticleer heralding his arrival?"

She knew I didn't. I never notice the sun has come up until it's
too late. We kissed again as she led me to a waiting limo. "You gave
me quite a chase," she told me. "Talbot should keep a better eye on
you."

"Who's Talbot?"

"I meant Rachel," she said hurriedly. "I don't know why I said that."

"Okay." We climbed into the limo, and I caught the smell of the
woman whose scent matched Irene's panties from the front of the car
beyond the black partition. Irene kissed me again, and I started unbut-
toning her blouse. "Then who's Rachel?"

"The limo driver, darling," she said. Irene kept talking when I finished opening her blouse, reclining against the seat while arching her
back, thrusting her firm supple breasts outward. "You just don't have a
head for names, do you?"

I didn't answer, but Irene kept whispering sweet nasties in my ear.
I felt like I hadn't seen her in forever. "I've never done it in a limo or in

Paris . . ." I paused, hovering over her left breast. "I don't think I have anyway, not since I was alive. What's the occasion?"

"Eric!" She ran her hand along my chin. "You naughty boy, how can you forget you're on your honeymoon?" She showed me her ring and I checked my hand. I had one too.

"Son of a bitch," I breathed. "How'd you talk me into that?"

"I'll show you"—she winked—"but it will have to wait until we get back to the hotel."

"Why?"

She kissed me again, fiercely, nicking my tongue with her fangs. "Because Rachel's a little busy driving right now, darling, and we'll need her undivided attention." *Yep,* I thought to myself, *that would do it.*

40

TABITHA:
I'M NOT BARBIE

I'm hungry." I sniffed the air. Blood scent blocked out all other odors. If Beatrice was anywhere nearby, I couldn't smell her. "I passed your stupid tests." I paced the unfamiliar room, still in my nightgown. It was lacy and pink and I'd hoped Eric would be able to see it, but apparently that only happened after one final night of testing. "I watched your stupid videos." My feet slapped the cold floor of the room I'd woken up in. "I even wrote an essay and played two hundred billion questions with your version of a psychotherapist."

An antique four-poster bed with decorative fittings lay behind me, comforter askew from where I'd rolled out of it. A French gown covered in a floral pattern with an elaborate green brocade covering the front skirt, bodice, and sleeves had been laid out for me, all Marie Antoinette or Madame de Pompadour, but it wasn't mine and I'd refused to put it on.

"So what is this test about, my willingness to get naked in a strange room and put on uncomfortable clothing? I was a stripper for a year and a half. I think that should get me a free pass."

I jerked on the wooden door, but it was still locked. Could I break it open with my vampire strength? Sure. But did that mean I'd fail their test? Probably.

"Just put on the dress." It was Luc's voice.

"Why?" I slapped the door. "What I wear has nothing to do with my ability to control myself."

"It shows your willingness to change with the times."

"No." I pressed against the door, and his heartbeat came through loud and clear, his warmth like a concealed blaze. "It shows my willingness to play dress-up."

"Why is this so hard, Tabitha?" Luc stepped away from the door. "As you said, you took the tests. You put up with all of that."

"You stole from me."

"Excuse me?"

"You did." I hadn't thought the accusation through before I made it, but I decided to stick to my guns. "How is theft resolved among you guys?"

"We didn't steal from you."

In my head, I could "see" him through the door, a mass of veins with blood inside, a sack of food. That's what this was really about, then, seeing if I could go without blood and keep my cool. "You won't let me have my clothes. They were with me when I went to bed and now they aren't here and you won't let me have them back. By definition, you stole them."

"No." Master Ji spoke, and hearing his voice made me jump. I couldn't hear his heartbeat. I concentrated. No, there it was, muffled and slow, but there. "Your clothes are still in your room. We moved you, not the clothes."

"Kidnapping, then. How do you resolve that?"

"You aren't bound by our Treaty of Secrets yet, Tabitha."

"True, Ji, and I never will be. Not exactly. *La Bête* said we couldn't fully join." I clenched my fists to keep myself from batting down the door. "And he also told you to grant me every courtesy. I'm guessing this test is really about me keeping under control while I'm hungry. I can do that, so let's just keep this test to its basics."

"Fine."

Luc opened the door. "You can't eat until midnight. You can wear whatever you want." He was dressed in court clothes that perfectly matched the green brocade dress.

Ji wore dress silks. "But you have to have one of us nearby at all times so we can be sure you don't cheat."

"That means no biting yourself either, Tabitha," Luc added. "Some vampires do that, hoping it will help the hunger pangs."

"Fine." I walked out the door and successfully managed not to bite either of them. We were in the "hunting lodge," by which I mean "expansive mansion estate," which stood in the northwest corner of the grounds. "Who's going with me to get my clothes?"

Ji held up a hand. "I'll go, but we have to hurry or we'll miss dinner."

"Dinner?"

"Yes," he answered as we walked across the grounds toward the *donjon* proper. "We're having steak tartare."

I must have whimpered at the thought of being near all that bloody beef without being allowed to lick the bowl, because Ji patted my hand. The contact ignited my loins and my fangs rent my gums. I jerked my hand away, my skin so hot in comparison to the rest of me, it burned.

"You don't get to touch me unless I get to bite you."

"Eric didn't make a rule like that for him and Aarika," Luc countered.

"Don't lie to me." My claws came out, but I didn't cut him. Instead, I hoisted Luc up by his fancy cravat. "The only way Eric would screw that Nazi bimbo is if she came on to him while he was feeding. And even then he might not do her."

James, Eric's buddy from World War II, came running out of the *donjon*. He was wearing a black T-shirt with a 1-Up Mushroom from Mario Bros. on the front and a pair of out-of-style stonewashed jeans with combat boots and a long coat. "Ji, declare her graduated."

"At midnight."

"No," he argued. "Now."

Panic. I smelled panic from James. Panicked immortals are not a good sign. Had the big furry decided they'd crossed a line?

"Why would I do that?"

"Because Aarika's back and Eric isn't with her."

Luc hurtled through the air. I saw him fly through the air before I realized I'd thrown him. "I'm going."

"In that?" Ji pointed at my nightie. I transformed into a cat, concentrating on leaving my clothes behind. Once in feline form, I crawled out of the lingerie and resumed my humanoid form. When Eric does it, he gets to keep his clothes, but when I do it, I revert to a single outfit, destroying the old one if I'm not careful.

At first, I'd been stuck with the clothes I'd originally been wearing when I transformed, but with practice, I'd been able to change the outfit, to create a default. I'm still stuck with just the one outfit, but at least it isn't stripper gear . . . or not the same stripper gear anyway.

When I became humanoid again, I wore a pair of Valentino jeans, a black leather corset, matching lace-up boots, and a full-length black duster. A studded leather belt, choker, and silver bracelets completed the ensemble nicely even if the heat from their creation burned my skin. I wrapped myself in the jacket for two seconds, wallowing in the warmth and fighting my hunger.

Creating clothes takes even more of a toll than transforming, and I'd already been famished.

"You can't leave."

I snarled, fangs bared, claws out, eyes ablaze. "But if I don't feed . . . ?"

"You'll never pull it off," Ji said. "Not around all those humans."

I forced the fangs and claws back in, willed the eye glow to fade. "I'm going to look for my husband. My husband you were supposed to be looking after." Luc picked himself up off the ground and dusted off his clothes. "I just want to know if I can do so without having wasted the last two days."

"That's fair, Ji," James insisted. "More than fair."

"You can go." Ji chewed the inside of his cheek. "But his thrall will need to stay here."

"How is she supposed to find him without his thrall?" James rounded on Ji. "We screwed the pooch on this one, Ji."

"You don't know that," Ji said firmly. "There shouldn't have been any vampires out there who could pose a threat to him."

"Not even Lisette?" I stepped between them. "She's an Emperor too."

James looked away, and so did Ji.

"Lisette isn't in Europe," Luc said. "She left for Void City by ship over a week ago."

"Why the hell didn't you say something before now?" I stalked toward Luc, and the other two immortals armored up, but he raised his hands to halt them.

"Because we didn't want her to return to our territory," Luc answered. "Most of the older Emperors have their little areas and they stick to them, but Lisette moved around, tried to keep active in society. Now that she has set foot in the Americas, she'll have to formally petition the Council for reentry into Europe. We plan to deny her. You heard *la Bête* the other night. He doesn't want her here. Neither do we. It simply wasn't worth the effort to force her out."

"This is why Eric hates supernatural politics." The eye glow was back and I didn't fight it. "Could one of the other Emperors—?"

"They aren't active," Luc interrupted. "They are still. Calm. Sated."

Another figure came walking across the bridge. It was Aarika. I moved toward her at top speed, all but teleporting to her side. "What happened?"

"A female Vlad," Aarika began. "We'd finished scouting places he thought you might like to see . . ."

He was scouting for places I might want to see? How sweet!

". . . several other vampires showed up to fight him. It had happened two or three times a night, so I vasn't vorried, but then the other Vlad arrived and he seemed to know her. Eric began acting strangely.

Strangely for him, I mean. Drugged or enspelled perhaps. I sensed a thrall and then there was a large amount of energy pouring along the link between Eric, the other Vlad, and the thrall. The magic was overpowering. It even had an odor."

"What kind of odor?" *Please don't let it be . . .*

"Cinnamon. Eric collapsed and when he got back up, he climbed into a limo with the female Vlad and they drove away. I could not give chase; I was . . . injured. When I recovered they had gone, so I returned here."

"I need my cell phone and I need to be somewhere it will work." I rocketed through the complex, tore my cell phone out of my purse, and came back at top speed. "Well?"

Aarika blinked and then two of us stood in the middle of a tourist attraction version of the castle I'd just been in.

"Try it now."

I dialed Eric first, unsurprised when it went straight to voice mail. Then I tried Talbot.

"Talbot, is that you? Damn phone. Hello?"

"Who is this?" His voice was tired, and hearing it gave me a warm tingle I wouldn't have had if I'd been well-fed.

"Talbot! It's me, Tabitha."

"What are you doing up?" he answered, sounding surprised. "It's what, five-thirty over there?"

"Would you shut the hell up and listen to me!" I shouted. "My cell is broken and it keeps hanging up. Is Rachel there?"

"I haven't seen her since you guys left for Paris. Is Eric there? I need—"

"I don't give a fuck what you need, Talbot. Shut up and listen to me. Lisette is headed for you guys. She may already be there."

"Where's Eric?"

"The fucking immortals lost him. And they made me do a lousy three-day initiation."

"Immortals?" He paused. "Oh. I forgot about that. They don't police Mousers, so—"

"Eric was kidnapped by someone with cinnamon-scented magic and a female Vlad."

"Damn. So you think Rachel—"

"Well, don't you think Rachel?"

"Probably. And Eric would want me to stay here and help Greta with Lisette. Fuck!" I don't think I'd ever heard Talbot say "fuck" before.

"Do you know what the Vlad looked like?"

I handed Aarika the phone. "Describe the other Vlad."

"She was petite. Attractive. She'd been turned in her early twenties. The way she moved was distinct, as if she had trouble moving slower than her maximum vampiric rate. Eric seemed to recognize her."

"Put Tabitha back on," Talbot said, as if I couldn't hear him quite well even when Aarika held the phone to her ear.

"You know who it is?"

"It could be Irene," Talbot said. "She's one of Eric's children. He tried to kill her after El Segundo. She was involved with the demons there. To her it was a game."

"What was? El Segundo?"

"No." Talbot's tone sent a chill down my spine. "The end of the world."

"You can't let him be around her, Tabitha," Talbot continued. "He's different around Irene. He'll kill for the fun of it, just because it turns her on."

"He'd do that for me."

"He lets her bite him."

"That bitch!" Plastic shattered near my ear, splinters gashing through my palm and my fingers. "Ow . . . what the hell?"

I stared at my hand without comprehension during the long seconds it took for me to realize I'd crushed the phone. Plastic hit the ground, and I was moving. "I need to get back to the plane or—Damn it! Where did Eric leave *El Alma Perdida?*"

"*El Alma Perdida?*" Aarika asked.

"His magic gun!" I snarled in her face.

"How will a gun help?"

"Ah. Shit. Never mind. It won't unless he has part of it with him and I have part of it with me."

"Explain."

"The last time I had to find *El Alma Perdida*, Eric had been framed for murdering some werewolves. He found one of the bullets, and a mage named Magbidion told us the bullets and the gun were linked to each other. Talbot and I used the bullet to find the gun."

"Talbot is one of your sire's thralls?"

"No!" The thought of Talbot as anyone's thrall repulsed me. "He's just a friend of . . . the family." The memory, not of his touch but the scent of his blood, rushed over me. "He's a Mouser."

"Mousers." Aarika spat on the ground. "They have no respect for societal rules."

"Well, no offense, but your rules suck."

"Our rules are the only reasons your kind still exists." Her shoulders snapped back, a rigid line, and though she'd let her hair down a little over the last few nights where Eric and I were concerned, I was reminded of the brusque businesslike militant who'd wanted us deported at first sight. "And our rules and *la Bête*'s insistence upon our providing you our assistance are the only reason I tell you this: *La Bête* had some other werewolves return bullets from Eric's gun to him while you were daystruck. If he still has them and if they are linked, as you say, then—"

Her words cut off. "Then I can find them. Now where'd he leave the stupid gun?"

Did he leave it on the plane or take it with him in the bags? I hadn't been paying attention. Beatrice would know.

"Aarika, can you take me back to Beatrice? I need to ask her where Eric left *El Alma Perdida*."

No response. The air was warm, but not warm enough. Creatures moved in the night. Some were bloodless little insects, but many contained precious samples of exactly what I craved.

I tapped my foot. "Aarika? Hellooo?"

She blinked.

"Ji has formally objected to being confronted before a supplicant," Aarika said.

"A supplicant? What? Me?" I asked. *Isn't that what they called me when I agreed to the tests?*

Aarika nodded. "Luc, James, and I are to appear before the Council immediately." Another pause. "As a sign of our trust, you are released on your own recognizance to search for your sire. If you manage not to feed until midnight, your petition will be granted." And then she vanished.

"But what about Beatrice?" I shouted after her. She didn't answer, but I'm pretty sure someone heard me, because someone shouted something in French and I ran for the *donjon*. It was different than in the remembered world of the Vale of Scrythax, but the moat was still there, and for a vampire, it was very leapable. "Eric," I said to myself as I landed on the other side, "you'd better have left your gun on the plane."

41

TABITHA:

GHOST ON A PLANE

I couldn't find the gun anywhere on the plane. I sat there with Lord Phillip's employees hovering over me like frazzled parents who can't make things better. What do you do for a vampire who can't feed? A faint buzz clicked under my seat as the warmers kicked on, but I cried anyway, not that there was any blood to come out. Red crept into the edges of my vision as my hunger grew. I could still discern the facial features of the flight crew, but hints of the veins beneath the surface of the skin became increasingly prominent, tattoos increasing in definition as some phantom inker worked her magic.

"If there wuz anything I could do to help, I'd shore as shootin' do it." A voice, southern in the way that grits and crawfish and clubs of little old ladies honoring the dear departed Confederacy are southern. One twang shy of a caricature. "Dern it. She cain't hear me. If only she'd shot the dang gun once."

"Hello?"

"Yes, Lady Bathory?" one of the stewards asked.

"I wasn't talking to you!" I stood, looking for the speaker.

"Now she's so hungry she's hallucinatin'." I saw him. In the back of the plane. A spectral cowboy in a red and white checkered shirt, bloodstained and bullet-riddled, with trails of smoke wisping up from the holes as he puffed on the stub of a cigar. "She's already been tearing about some"—I assumed his next word was "foreign," but he said it "fur in"—"country in her whorehouse clothes. With her woman parts all hanging out."

"Whorehouse clothes?! Hey!" The family resemblance was unmistakable. I realized I'd seen this guy before, in a mystic image shown to me by Lord Phillip, back during the whole Orchard Lake thing. He'd been younger in that image. Seen as he was now, broken neck forcing his head to wobble slightly, you could tell he was related to Eric. "You do not get to call these whorehouse clothes. I look sexy in this!"

"I ain't never said you didn't look attractive, ma'am." He dropped his cigar, stubbing it out on the ground even as it broke apart, little more than smoke. John Paul Courtney removed his hat and gave me a slight, but careful, nod. "I kin see how a getup like that might get a man's pistol primed, but you ain't never gone convince me that it don't make you look more saloon hall night than Sunday morning church service."

"Times change."

"That they do, ma'am." His smile was Eric's smile, but where Eric's smiles could often be hard to come by, John Paul Courtney seemed more practiced at doling them out. "But the Good Book don't change, and I try not ta either."

"Where's Eric?" I leaned forward, and John Paul's eyes dipped down toward my cleavage then up and away with a whistle.

"Put them young-uns to bed, missy," he said, not looking at me. "Or cover 'em up. They're out past their bedtime and getting inta places they have no business bein'."

"Lady Bathory?"

I shooed the attendants away and they headed to the cabin. Looking back at the ghost, I pulled my coat tight around me and tied the sash. "Better?"

"It is at that, thank ya kindly."

"Where's Eric?"

"Fornicatin'." He shook his head from side to side, then caught it before it could topple over. "But I ain't convinced it's all his fault this time. I appeared to him to ask what he thought he was doin' when he had a pretty little filly at home waitin' fer 'im, but he couldn't even hear me."

Crimson overcame my vision, washing away the other colors. If Rachel was screwing my husband again, I'd kill her. Sister or not. I'd kill her. Particularly if she'd cast some kind of spell on him again.

"But where?"

"I don't rightly know, ma'am. Truth be told, I ain't never been to France afore, not to mention Paris, so I shore didn't recognize the sights outside the window." His cigar appeared again, as if in absent-mindedly reaching for it, he'd re-created it. He puffed on it once, a long deep draw, the smoke obscuring his face as it coursed up from his wounds. "It ain't even clear how it is you came to be able to see me. Usually if someone fires *El Alma Perdida* I feel it. That desire to kill someone rings through clear as a dinner bell. And you ain't a Courtney."

"Shooting the gun means I can see you?"

"No, it means I kin appear to ya."

"Well, that settles it then."

"Settles what?" he asked. The perplexed expression on his weather-beaten features looked out of place.

"I dropped *El Alma Perdida* and it went off, the night I brought it back to Eric . . . on his birthday. Shot him in the butt. And yes"—I held up my hand, flashing him my wedding band and engagement ring—"I most certainly *am* a Courtney. We were married in a real church by a real priest, and Courtney is my real last name now."

"Well I'll be." He smiled again, smoke curling around the edges of his mouth. "I guess you're my great-great-granddaughter-in-law then . . . mehbe one more *great*. Welcome to the family, honey." He held out his hand and I reached out to take it, but found my fingers wrapped around the silver cross—etched grip of *El Alma Perdida* instead. The crosses didn't burn my hand.

"How?"

"I ain't lettin' nobody take my gun in amongst no dern demon worshippers." He pointed to his now empty holster. "Not unless Perdy's bein' shot at 'em. If no one's got a holt of her, I kin always take her back."

"I was talking about the crosses not burning me." I examined my unburned palm, holding the gun by the barrel with my left hand. "But that's good to know too."

"The gun likes Courtneys. The bullets don't pay no never mind. 'Course, they're bullets, so I guess that's all right."

I spun the cylinder and only saw one bullet. "Does Eric still have the other bullets?"

"I reckon." Courtney put his hat back on and drew deep on the cigar before breathing out a ring of smoke. "There's a way to reload the gun even without the bullets, though. If'n you know the right words."

"No!"

"No?"

"Don't reload the gun." I handed it back to him. "I can use it to find Eric."

"Naw." Courtney pursed his lips. "Most of the magic got drained out of 'em. They won't build their power back up unless I reload 'em." He drew the gun and snapped open the cylinder, removing the last bullet. "Hold tight."

Smoke swirled around him and he was gone. Before the smoke had dissipated, he'd returned.

"Lord knows I didn't need to see that." He held out the gun, cylinder clicking as he showed me the five bullets and the empty slot. "Shouldn't be running around with all six chambers loaded anyhow," he explained. "That's how accidents happen. Keep an empty chamber and ya ain't likely to shoot when you don't mean ta shoot."

"He didn't notice the swap?"

"Nope. The bullets was in his pants pocket."

"And?"

"Well, ma'am." He puffed on his cigar and waved the smoke away with his Stetson. "I thought I made it clear. He ain't exactly wearin' his pants raht now."

Images of Eric on top of Rachel, Rachel astride Eric, and some nebulous second bitch feeding on both of them ran through my head. A cry of equal parts rage and frustration escaped my throat, and I wanted to hit something, anything. I clenched and unclenched my fists, ignoring the pain as my claws cut my palms.

"How fast can you move?" I asked the ghost.

"Speed ain't exactly a problem, missy." He floated to one end of the passenger compartment and back at a clip roughly equivalent to top human running speed. "It's the range that does me in. Except for special circumstances, I can't move too far from *El Alma Perdida* or my kinfolk. It's that or the In-between and that ain't mah idear of a home away from home."

"Can you drive?"

JPC shook his head, shouting an annoyed, "Dadburnit," when his head toppled over to one side. "I figgered up a way I think I could do it, but I ain't never had no one to let me practice."

"Then we do this on foot. I can see magic, but only when I'm a cat." I turned into a cat, screeching at the emptiness that yawned in my belly as I made the shift. Normally, as a cat, I feel alive, but hungry as I was, my body wouldn't give up the special effects. My feline heart lay still and dead in my diminutive chest. "You lead the way," I meowed.

"I don't speak critter, miss," John Paul Courtney told me. "But I reckon you want me to head on out."

It took a few minutes to get the attendants to open the door and let me out, largely because I didn't want to risk transforming again and also because my vision had gone completely red except for my ghostly in-law. The skin and hair of the humans on the plane had become translucent, the features hard to discern. Instead, all I saw was the blood.

Outside the plane, I ran, a few paces ahead of JPC, my head cocked at the slight angle required to make out the thin blue line of magic linking *El Alma Perdida* to the single round in Eric's pocket. Shin high and at a dizzying slant was not how I wanted to see Paris at night.

If I stopped to take in the sights, I lost the thread. If I didn't stop, the rapid movement, combined with the angle of my head, made the world spin as if I were riding a roller coaster. Farther into Paris, the other shoe dropped. Webs of energy, close to the same as the line of magic I was following, crisscrossed the landscape, a lattice of magic. . . . I ran into the wheel of a parked car and sat still, waiting for the world to stop moving. "This," I meowed, "is going to be a pain in the ass."

✦ 42 ✦

ERIC:

WHAT HAPPENS IN PARIS . . .

Eating the same woman every night is weird," I said to no one in particular. Rachel, the freaky chick with all the piercings and the butterfly tattoo on her cheek, ran her fingers through my hair as I lifted my mouth from her femoral artery. I kissed the fang marks, watching as they faded, and moved my ministrations up and to the right.

"A little faster," she said, shifting me to the right spot and grinding against my mouth, rhythmically in time to some internal pleasure pulse.

Behind me, Irene chuckled. "There are so many ways a lady could interpret that statement." Fangs out, she stalked to where I knelt at the edge of the bed upon which Rachel was sprawled, her body flickering as she moved there and back again in rapid succession. "Is there room for the bride to cut in or do I have to take a number?"

Freshly showered ladies have always been a turn-on for me. I stood up, watching as Irene surveyed her options. She placed a proprietary hand on Rachel's thigh and Rachel winced. "Too sore for seconds?"

"Not if you give me a few minutes," Rachel said, a little short of breath. "I can't—" Her words vanished, cut off by a cry of surprise as Irene went from standing to kneeling, fangs embedding deep in Rachel's thigh.

"Fuck," Rachel managed, her eyes squinting against the pain. "Fuck. Fuck. Fuck!" Tears gathered at the corners of her eyes, but she gritted her teeth and let Irene finish. When Irene pulled away, a line of crimson trailed from her chin across Rachel's sex.

"I want what I want," Irene said, eyes locked with Rachel's. "But I'll make it up to you." She lowered her head to the same task I'd been performing, and my mind was blown yet again. It seemed wrong to me, to see two girls like that, but to be married to one of them and have permission to sleep with both of them . . . I won't say that made it right, but it was new enough that right wasn't exactly high on my list of priorities.

I want what I want.

I heard the words again in my head, and they sounded familiar. I'd heard them before, but in another place. I remembered being angry. Was it in California? *Damn it, Irene,* I recalled shouting, *you can't act like this. I won't stand for it.*

"Babe?" Irene stared up at me from between Rachel's spread legs. She waggled her behind at me, reaching back and running her fingernails along the wetness of her sex. "You going to join us or are you having fun watching the show?"

"Both." I blinked away the memory, momentarily overcome by the scent of cinnamon. I don't think cinnamon was as popular the last time I was here. Either that or the German occupation had put a crimp on the supply. I succumbed to Irene's beckoning and she resumed her "apology to Rachel" while I mounted Irene from behind.

Warm from the shower and sustained by the feeding, Irene felt hot and welcoming, like a living woman, lacking only the heartbeat. As I moved to completion, so did Rachel, her grunts echoing mine. Even separated as we were, a connection was there, deep and primal, as if she were responding to my thrusts more than Irene.

I came in a series of rapid thrusts, gasping for breath, heart roaring to life in my chest, beating faster than I remembered, a runaway pounding of long-dead circulatory muscle. Sagging against Irene, I frowned when she pushed me away.

"And you say that always happens now?" I asked. "The heartbeat?"

"Uh-huh. My turn," she said, tugging Rachel from the bed and flopping down in the still-warm spot where Rachel had lain.

"I may be done," I said.

Rachel smiled at me. "Oh, I think you've got a little more to give."

Surprised to find that she was right, I waited for my heartbeat to fade, then took up my same role, but with Rachel in the middle. If Irene had felt good, Rachel felt like coming home after a long day to all your favorite things, scalding my skin with the heat of her flesh and gripping me tight, craving me even though her hands and attention seemed to be elsewhere.

When Irene climaxed, Rachel and I kept going, falling to the floor with me still on top as she turned her head back and I leaned down to kiss her. She tasted like cinnamon, really tasted, and as we came again together, I heard her voice in my head, or maybe it was a whisper.

We don't need her, the voice said, *she's cold and dead and I'm alive and yours.*

I bit down on Rachel's neck, and her body was warm and hot—spicy hot, not just heat. My heart pounded to life again and I clutched at her breasts, pulling her up with me as I stood, taking her against the wall, where I continued to thrust.

I just had time to catch my breath as it faded away. Lowering Rachel to the ground, holding her lest she fall, she responded by spinning around, throwing her arms around me and kissing me deep and hard, her tongue noticeably warmer than my already cooling one.

"I sooo love belonging to you," she said. "What do you want me to eat for dinner?"

"We'll order room service at the next hotel," Irene said. "Not to be a party pooper, but you"—she indicated me with an outstretched finger—"promised me a different hotel every night."

"But I like this one," I complained. In all honesty, I didn't even remember the name of the hotel, but it smelled like sex with a live woman and I wanted to bask in the scent, in the warmth, in the moment. "And aren't we already going to have to pay for tonight?"

"I want what I want," she said. "And . . . you promised."

"Well . . ." I looked at Rachel for confirmation. "If I promised."

I showered while the girls packed, and in half an hour we were on our way to a different hotel in some part of Paris I barely noticed. I watched out the window as we drove through the city. The Eiffel Tower looked cool with the lights on it and I wondered when they'd put them up.

"We should have brought Marilyn," I said as we flew down the street.

"No," both women said at once. Rachel drove the limo with the divider down this time, eyeing me occasionally as we drove.

"I know it's the honeymoon and everything," I said, mainly to Irene, but to Rachel, too, "but it's not like we're not having an unconventional one already."

"Marilyn doesn't like me," Irene said.

"Or me," Rachel chimed in.

"She doesn't have to like you. I just meant—"

"And someone had to run the bowling alley."

"What bowling alley?"

"Strip club," Irene interjected. "Someone had to run the Demon Heart, and you know what a pain in the ass Roger is about the club."

"I suppose. I miss her, though."

43

TABITHA:

SIGHTSEEING

Appreciating Paris isn't easy when you're cross-eyed, starving, and running into things. With each monument or cool quirk of history or architecture I passed, my ire grew, and with it, the urge to stop and feast on any of the little heartbeats I passed in the night. The first bad one was Saint-Jacques Tower. I passed it on the left, a big Gothic tower well over a hundred feet tall. So what if I was racing to find Eric? I stopped and stared. Paris had been one of my dream destinations ever since I'd read Anne Rice's Vampire Chronicles. Plus, I'd spent hours researching the city and the history so I could sound smart in front of Eric.

"Damn it," I meowed. "You won't find cool stuff like that in Void City."

"That ole tower?" Courtney asked, seeming genuinely unimpressed. "S'all right I reckon. What language is that yore talkin' anyhow? Cat or some such?"

"You can understand it?" I rubbed the back of a paw against my eyes.

"If'n a Courtney says it, I ken, I suppose." He scratched at his stomach. "Guess it took a little while to kick in is all."

"I'll take that as a yes."

I concentrated and examined the trail to Eric. It was moving again, but not as fast as before. It annoyed me. "Stay still, damn it."

As we started moving along the trail again, Courtney chuckled.

"What's so funny?"

"That reminded me of a joke one them ni—ah . . ." He paused. "Is it colored now or . . ."

"Oh. My. God." I stopped dead and lost the trail. "Are you trying to say 'black person'? How long have you been dead?"

Flustered, Courtney looked down at his feet, barely catching his head in time to keep it from rolling over to one side. "Long enough fer all the names ta change, I reckon. I was just tryin' to say I saw this comedian once, yore husband was watchin' it, and the man . . . he had surprisingly clean language fer a . . . black. And—"

"Stop."

"What now?"

"Just stop. It won't be funny now. Whatever it was, you lost it in the racism."

"Well, the punch line was—"

I headed on. If I could have made the trip full speed and on human legs, I'd have crossed Paris already, but I was, instead, moving at a brisk walk, forced to remain in cat form so I could see the trail. The slowness ached.

When we passed the Louvre, I lay down in the middle of the road and covered my head. "That's the Louvre."

"Why's it got a big glass pyramid?" asked John Paul.

"La Pyramide Inversée," I said. "It's so cool. The visitors' center is right under there." I mewled pitifully. "I'm so fucking close to real culture and I don't even get to go inside!"

"Culture?"

Lit up, the museum all but glowed in the night. "Yes, culture." I padded toward the museum. "*Winged Victory* is in there. The *Mona Lisa*. There's stuff from ancient Egypt in there. And a food court."

What can I say, all the trip research made me a fan.

"A food court? Is that one o' them places where you can git all kinds of differn't food all in one place?"

"Ye-es."

"I've always wanted to see one o' them."

We rounded a corner onto a broad avenue. With billions of tiny white lights twinkling in each tree, I could see why they call Paris the City of Light. It made it hard to see the stupid magic line, though. The cat-vision pathway to Eric had stopped moving again and I continued on, ignoring Paris, ignoring everything but the wavering blue line that linked my dead in-law's magic gun with the bullets he'd slipped into my husband's pocket.

Or, at least, I tried to—but then I saw the Arc de Triomphe. I recognized it from pictures I'd seen of Paris, and I realized where we were.

"I'm on the Champs-Élysées!" I screeched. "I'm on one of the most high-scale streets in the entire world! Do you hear me? The entire world?! Rent here is over a million dollars per thousand square feet!"

John Paul Courtney soared down the street and came back. "What is Abercrombie and Fitch?"

"There is *not* an Abercrombie and Fitch on the Champs-Élysées." I scowled, but John Paul scowled back.

"I kin read jest fine, missy. And the sign said—"

"Oh shut up." I squinted one eye, turned my head, and had the trail again. "Just you shut up!" I couldn't stand running past all those beautiful shops. When we came to a crazy six-street intersection, I hung a left and cut through the park, past the Théâtre de Marigny and into the next park. Wide, well-lit sidewalks led me past countless park benches as the line to Eric bent toward my left and I emerged onto a street corner with more bike racks than I'd ever seen in one place before.

I made the mistake of looking to my right, away from the line to Eric, and saw an enormous traffic circle. Though my view was partially blocked by the backsides of two big statues of enthroned women (were those pedestals or entrances to the metro?), I could see that the road made a big oval around an Egyptian obelisk flanked by two spectacular gold-highlighted fountains. Off to the far right, I could see the Eiffel Tower, though from this perspective, it looked shorter than the obelisk. The whole scene was completely Paris, beautifully lit and totally overwhelming, right down to the enormous Ferris wheel. I recognized it. "The Place de la Concorde." I clawed the concrete. "That means the Tuileries Gardens are just past here someplace . . . and the National Gallery of Modern Art."

"There's also a heap of headless ghosts around here. What'd they do, used ta chop 'em off here?"

"As a matter of fact . . ." The blue trail of light had been slanting upward for some time, and the more I looked at it, the more it rose until I realized it was pointing almost straight to my left, toward an upper floor of a large, ornate, white-stone-columned building that looked kind of like a museum, all lit up in golden lights—the Hôtel Crillon, one of France's oldest luxury hotels.

"Eric!" I ran for the building, unsure of how I was going to get inside. Maybe I wouldn't have to. If I could get within mental range of him, maybe I could snap him out of whatever spell he was under.

At that very moment, my surroundings wavered and were replaced by a similar scene, except all of the tourists were gone and so was the obelisk.

James, Eric's war buddy, stood in front of me, a duffel bag over his shoulder. I smelled blood in the bag. "You did great."

"What?" I meowed furiously, spinning about. Vale of Scrythax. They valed me! "You valed me?!"

"Tabitha?" James knelt down. "I can't understand you. Can you change back to your human form? You made it to midnight. You can feed now." He reached into the duffel. "I brought an assortment. I didn't know if you had a preference."

"You idiot," I yowled, clawing at him angrily. The blood called to me. It damn well sang symphonies of desire to my famished little vampire mind, but I was too close to finding Eric to lose control to the hunger. "Eric is in the Hôtel Crillon! I found him. I can eat after he's safe."

I didn't even see the stake.

"It's okay, Tabitha," James said to my paralyzed body. "You'll be able to change again once you feed. You did it! And as soon as the formalities are over, you can pick right back up with your search for Eric."

He stuffed me into the duffel atop the bags of plasma. A car door opened and I heard John Paul's voice. "I'll keep an eye on him, missy." The engine roared to life, and we were off, back to the Château de Vincennes and away from Eric.

44

TABITHA:
WORD FOR WORD

James poured blood into my mouth, removed the stake enough for me to swallow, then slammed the stake back in as I clawed at his arms with my sharp but tiny cat claws. I thought back to Talbot's method, holding me down and letting me drink blood from a blood bag, back when I first turned, and decided I liked Talbot's way better. The feel of the metal hilt of James's custom combat knife–like stake added insult to the repetitive injury's deep thrust of pain, a cold hard chaser of blunt impact following the puncture wound.

After two bags of blood, James released me and I transformed to human, wheeling on him in a rage.

"You total fucking asshole!" I batted him into the brick wall of the small circular room, buckling the stone with the impact. My hands clutched at the vanishing wound left uncovered by my corset. "I was this close to finding Eric." The wall returned to normal, thrusting James toward me and confirming my suspicion that he'd taken me magic-side again, back to the Château de Vincennes in the Vale of Scrythax, which meant we were likely in one of the turrets of the *donjon*.

He held up a hand and I grabbed it, bending back his fingers and hurling him headfirst into the opposite side of the surrounding circle of stone. Blood trailed from his head as he slid down the wall, but he was immortal, so who cared? He'd get better. Right?

"He's in the Hôtel Crillon. I was right there." I stomped his back, rolled him over, and impaled him with his own custom stake, snatching it up from where it had fallen to the floor. "If I pin you to the ground with your own weapon—"

James's eyes sprang open with a flash, his feet sweeping mine out from under me.

"Wood versus stone." He jerked the stake out of his chest, revealing the blunted point. The 1-Up Mushroom T-shirt he'd been wearing vanished, replaced by his combat gear: all black modern body armor and the same long curve-tipped blade he'd brandished the first time I'd seen him armor up.

"What kind of sword is that anyway?"

"It's a Grossmesser. Sixteenth century. I wound up with it in a soul battle last year." His eyes never left mine, but I didn't try to compel him. I knew what would happen. Telepathy? Yes. Control? No. "Oddvar's previous paladin didn't like me much. It's a good weapon. I also wound up with his encyclopedic knowledge of German beers and beer making."

"His knowledge?"

"In a close battle or a very lopsided one, it can happen. Soul burn." His mouth twisted into half smile, half smirk. "Mild case." Eyes looked away briefly. An opening.

Cold metal beneath my fingers as I grabbed for the blade. Sharp edges against my fingers as he reacted. The blade dissipated and he punched me, a rapid jab to the face, breaking my nose. The pain was bad, but the sound of the cartilage giving way was far worse.

"We don't have time for this," he said, manifesting the sword again. "We're in a guard tower on the wall, but someone may notice this."

"Notice what?" I snarled, claws out. "That you boke by nobe?"

"That you lost control and attacked me when I tried to feed you. . . . Wait. Eric is where?"

"The Hôtel Crillon!" My nose snapped back of its own accord, making my eyes water tears of blood.

"So that's what you were trying to tell me. I'm sorry—I don't speak Cat."

I lunged at him, claws tearing through the combat armor, but hanging in the mesh.

He head-butted me, the hard Kevlar helmet rebreaking my nose, blinding me as my eyes filled with tiny dots of light. Withdrawing my claws to free myself, I rammed both fists into his chest, punching him through the stone and stepping through the hole after him before the power of Scrythax's memory restored it to its former state. And then I was falling after him. Landing on the ground. Only now Luc and Aarika where there, too, and Christian, with his spear.

"We were just sparring," James said. "Just messing around." He brushed himself off. "You know how it is."

"Of course," Aarika said. "Otherwise you would have been winning, yes?"

James rose to his feet. "Sure. Sure."

Luc's expression put me in mind of a constipated hamster. "We don't have time for this. Let's get it done. The ritual takes several hours."

"Several hours?"

"Ji won't waive the reading of the Treaty of Secrets and the concordance of law," Luc answered. "It seems he would have been willing to do so earlier, but we bent the rules before, so now—"

"I'm not going to bend them again." Ji's voice rang out from the courtyard. He stood halfway between us and the main *donjon*, wearing orange sweatpants, a matching hoodie, blue-tinted sunglasses, and those same Onmyodo shoes. Our eyes met, and the telepathic contact was instant. "I'm normally pretty laid-back," he thought at me as he walked, "but you should have worn the dress and let me have my little fun with the steak tartare. You made me lose face, and I'd already lost some to *la Bête*."

An image hit my thoughts, him under the massive black wolf's paw. "That was bearable, because he's *la Bête*, but to lose face to a vampire I'm testing? No. Sorry. I won't."

"I'm sorry," I thought back at him. "But—"

"That's right," Ji thought. "You *are* sorry, or you will be. *La Bête* gave you five *nights*, not five days. You got here at night," a mental picture of a Roman numeral one lit up in my head, "June third. I tested you on June fourth, fifth, and sixth." Three more Roman numerals lit up in my head: II, III, and IV. "That makes tomorrow night night five. *La Bête* will have to concede the point once my messenger has pointed things out. Thus, I regain my honor. Hope you have fun on your final night, *gaijin* . . . assuming you can even find your husband."

"Why are you doing this?" I said aloud. "Because I embarrassed you?"

"Isn't that enough?" He stopped beside Luc.

"Doing what?" Luc asked.

"He's playing on a technicality," I snarled. "The big wolf thing gave us five nights here and everyone knew he meant five *more* nights."

The other immortals, James, Aarika, and Ji, exchanged glances.

"Hold on," James said. "We'll remember."

Taking hands, their eyes lit white-blue from within. "Damn," James said when the glow faded. "Ji's right. That's what was said."

"But won't he hold us to what he meant rather than what he literally said?" I asked.

"Unless he's officially charged to keep his word," Aarika answered.

"My messenger is on his way to *la Bête* even as we speak." Ji crossed his arms over his chest, proud of himself.

"That sucks."

"Indeed it does." The new voice was *la Bête's*. His fur bled out of the air as he arrived magic-side, within the Vale of Scrythax. Our surroundings bent and expanded. Reality had a wolf-shaped hole in it that was the color of its surroundings until the blackness at its core poured into the rest of it and *la Bête* was rendered in full color once again. "Do not do this, Ji." The voice of *la Bête* echoed in our minds.

"No, *la Bête*," Ji said. "I hold you to your words."

"All of them that night?"

"Yes."

Luc, Aarika, and James winced as one.

"Very well." The wolf touched me with its nose. "I apologize, Tabitha. I must keep my word. I find I owe you an apology as well, Ji."

"Why is that?"

"Because I also said that night that I would eat the next person who named me . . . and that person was you."

"Noooooo!" Ji backpedaled, hands outstretched to ward off *la Bête*. He vanished from the Vale and *la Bête* gave chase.

"C'mon." Luc grabbed my arm. "Let's get you through the ritual as quickly as possible. With Ji not around to read the text, maybe we can get through this in time for you to get back to the Hôtel Crillon tonight."

"And if I walk out now, then I default and you have to get all stupid and rules lawyer-y?"

"That's about the size of it," James said.

"Fine." I ran to the *donjon*, the three of them in tow. One night in Paris is better than nothing, and if I got this out of the way, then maybe Eric could work out a return trip sometime. "Let's get out of here so Beatrice and I—"

"She won't be able to leave with you," Aarika told me. "Once you are emancipated, she has nothing to do with you and will be held here safely waiting for the return of her master."

"Whatever."

Luc read the ritual so quickly, I don't think he actually stopped to breathe. The formalities flew by faster and faster until I started to feel like Danny Kaye in that movie Eric had made me watch—*The Court Jester*—when the king has the jester knighted so quickly that he has to be literally carried through parts of the ritual.

Though we sped through things at speeds only three immortals and a vampire could achieve, everything seemed to take too long. The second I was pronounced free, I left at a dead run.

By the time I got back to the Place de la Concorde, sunup was a little less than an hour off. The only way I was staying conscious was by seeming human, and even then the possibility I'd fall over in the street and burn up in the sun weighed more and more on my mind.

JPC stood out front of the Hôtel Crillon, puffing on his cigar.

"Are they?"

"Far as I kin tell, they're still here." His "here" made me giggle, more "h'yar" than "here." "This is about as fur as I kin git without going to the In-between or landing raht next to 'em."

Relief washed over me, and it was not the right emotion. Anger keeps me awake, but relief . . . My eyes slid shut and I couldn't get them open.

"Dadburnit," JPC shouted. "Try to turn inta a cat if yore gonna go and do that."

"Tha-yut," I mumbled, mimicking his accent. As numbness worked its way from my skin inward, I thought catlike thoughts. I hoped I had managed to change into a cat. I couldn't tell. Numbness reached my core, and the lights went out.

Help me, Obi-John Paul Courtney. You're my only hope.

45

ERIC:

NOTHING REALLY MATTERS

I was up before the girls. I only sleep a few hours each day, and the soft predawn is my favorite time of the morning. At home, I was often the only one up. Before I turned Greta, she'd alter her sleep patterns to spend those few hours with me watching videos or cable, even running a reel or two over at the Pollux. I knew we'd worn out more than one UNO deck in our time, even though it had been just the two of us. As a result, UNO or Scrabble with more than one other player wasn't fun anymore, unless the third player was Marilyn.

Speaking of not fun anymore: Irene and Rachel lay sprawled on the bed in a tangle of limbs, neither one wearing more than a tiny hint of clothing. A mediciny taste coated my mouth, which wasn't all bad, because almost any taste is better than none. My limbs were heavy, my eyes drooping, and I would have gone back to bed if not for a nagging feeling of wrongness.

"What are you doing, Eric?" I gazed into the full-length mirror near the door of the hotel room, staring at the reflection that wasn't there. Slipping into my discarded clothes, I crept out of the bedroom and into the adjoining sitting room of the suite, trying to remember the name of the hotel we'd wound up in.

Once there, I picked up the phone and punched numbers until I got the front desk or the concierge and got them to walk me through making an international call. I dialed Marilyn's number first.

Three chimes and a message. "We're sorry," said the voice, "but the number you have dialed has been disconnected or is no longer in service."

I dialed it again. And again. I dialed variations of it. No Marilyn. Directory Assistance didn't have a listing for her either. No one answered at the Pollux and when I dialed the Demon Heart's number, I heard my own voice.

"You've reached the Demon Heart Lanes Bowling Alley." I sounded still and unnatural, like I was reading from a script, "Our hours are 10 a.m. to 2 a.m., with Cosmic Bowling after 8 p.m. on most weeknights." My voice then gave the office number to call for special events, and then there was a pause. "Oh and for all you idiots that keep leaving messages about our former business, I said bowling and I meant bowling, and no, it's not some stupid joke.

"If you're interested in seeing naked girls, get a girlfriend, head down to Melons, buy a DVD, or try the Internet, but don't leave a message for me about it, 'cause you morons are filling up the voice mail with drunk dials so much that I'm gonna start tracking you down if you keep it up. So stop it!" My voice got louder. "I miss the girls too, but they have better things to do than dance for your amusement. And I have better things to do than listen to you whine about it. And I'm not changing this number either, because it took me twenty frickin' years to remember the damn thing and I'm not learning a new one. Have a nice day."

I hung up the phone, stared at it a little longer, dialed the Demon Heart again, wrote down the number for special events, hung up, and dialed that one.

"Hi, ya'll." It was a woman's voice, sultry, southern, and familiar. Her name was there, in my brain, but I couldn't bring it to the forefront. "My name's Cheryl and I'm the special events planner for Demon Heart Lanes Bowling Alley. You just go ahead and leave your name, number, and the kind of event you'd like to schedule and I'll get back to you soon as ever I can. Bye, now."

So familiar. Had Cheryl danced at the club and moved over to the new business? And when the hell had I started the new business? I didn't know.

I couldn't think of Roger's number, couldn't even remember his current last name, so I looked around for the television. A fancy remote on a table next to a big rectangular picture frame with a name and a logo promised me television even though I couldn't see one in the room. I clicked the power button and the black expanse within the frame blinked on, displaying a list of channels and services.

"Holy shit!" I jumped from channel to channel with the remote. Everything looked wrong, futuristic, or . . . .I mean, how the hell did France have cooler TVs than the U.S.? It's fucking France, right? The Frogs would all be Germans without America's help and now they had better TV? And the special effects! What the hell? I'd seen Hollywood movies with special effects worse than that.

I'd thought the cars looked a little different, but I'd honestly assumed they were just different models of cars made only in Europe, and it wasn't as if I'd been paying attention to things outside the car much.

Still . . .

Pushing the channel button sent me through more shows: a newscast, a . . . The date on the screen stopped me cold. June 6th. If you aren't a war buff, that date might not mean anything to you. But to me and folks like me, it's D-Day, when me and a whole lot of less lucky men took a stroll on the beach to set the stage for the eventual end of Hitler and his goose-steppers.

"More than forty years ago . . ." I said, my face tightening at the corners as I gave a grim smile. Strains of "Der Fuehrer's Face" by Spike Jones and His City Slickers ran through my mind and I chuckled without meaning to as the image of Göring on piccolo from the German oom-pah band in Disney's "Donald Duck in Nutzi Land" popped unbidden into my head.

Forty years. But the number on the television screen didn't match my head, nor the year. June 6th, 1944, we agreed on, but according to the news, it had been more than sixty years since D-Day, closer to seventy.

I'll be the first man to admit I have a crappy memory, but to be wrong about the present date by more than two decades?

"Wait right there," I told the too-big, too-flat television. Back in the other room, I found Rachel's purse, sat down in an overstuffed Louis XIV chair, and dug through the purse for a passport or something with the date. The stamp on Rachel's passport confirmed the television's story, and I cursed loudly.

"Master?" Rachel leaned up, bleary-eyed and blinking. "I mean . . . um. Eric? Good morning. What are you doing up?" Her heart jumped when she saw the passport in my hand. "Is everything okay?"

"My brain is screwed up," I said slowly. "I seem to have forgotten the last twenty years, and it's the anniversary of one of the scariest days of my life. Marilyn's number is disconnected." I threw the passport back into Rachel's purse. "I can't remember Roger's current last name or his number, *and* apparently I run a damn bowling alley now."

"Oh, baby." Rachel climbed out of bed and cradled my head against her breasts, putting me eye-level with her piercings. "Not again."

"Again?" I asked.

"I know you can't help it, but you have to get past this. It's not your fault, not really."

"What's not my fault? D-Day? No shit. I blame Hitler." I pushed her out to arm's length. Sad eyes and a pout told me she didn't think that was funny.

"Poor baby," she said again.

"What?"

Her eyes focused on the ceiling as if fighting back tears.

"What?" I repeated.

Rachel breathed in and out, a doctor preparing to deliver bad news. "Are you all the way back to the seventies again?"

"Eighties. And what do you mean 'again'?"

"The eighties?" She hugged me, but I shrugged her off, standing. "Well, that's an improvement." She spoke the words at my chest, but I assumed she meant the memory, not her new vantage point.

"Over what?"

"I'm not supposed to tell you unless I have Irene or Greta handy to stake you if you go off."

"Stake me?!" I sat back down with a resigned thud and the chair gave, dropping me to the floor. "Why would they need to stake me?"

"You have a tendency to black out."

"Did I feed from you last night?" The question, generated by my new view of her exposed thighs and easy access to her femoral artery, surprised both of us.

"You feed from me most nights, silly." Rachel ran her fingers along her inner thigh, tracing the vein. "It's okay, I'm your thrall. I make blood faster than a normal human."

"Thrall." I hated that word, hated the whole concept. "I can't believe I made you my slave."

"I'm not a slave," Rachel reassured me. "True, you could give me commands and I'd have to follow them, but you don't usually, and I get really good sex, agelessness. I don't have to keep down a real job, my muscles stay toned, I heal fast, and my body doesn't gain weight no matter how much I eat." Moving closer, she held her legs apart. Her scent revealed a readiness not just to feed my appetite for blood, but any other carnal appetite I had in mind.

I drank deeply, flavor on my tongue, hot and sugary, more cinnamon than blood. My heart beat as I drank, in a heavy steady rhythm, and I had to stop drinking to breathe. "This has been happening."

"I'm a very talented thrall." She sat on my lap, blood from her wounded thigh coloring my jeans. "I can wake your body up for a little while when you drink me or fuck me."

We kissed, and when she pulled away, her own blood tinted her lips.

"Tell me what you're not supposed to tell me."

"Okay, but let me get ready to calm you down, okay?"

"How?"

"It's called tantric magic," she said. "It's what I do. I get in touch with your chakra, help keep you calm, but I'm not supposed to mess with your moods without permission. Do I have your permission?"

"Fine."

As she touched my chakra, warmth and calm settled over me like a blanket. "Wow," I said softly.

"Nice?" she asked.

"Very."

"Relaxed?" She gently kissed her way down my torso, then back up.

"Uh-huh."

"Not too long ago, you found out Marilyn and Roger had been cheating on you, since back before you died. When you died in Roger's car, it wasn't an accident. It was murder. When you found out—"

"What?" I clutched her arms. "What did I do?"

"You're hurting me," Rachel whispered.

"Sorry." I let go, staring down at the row of wounds my claws had dug into her skin. "Did I hurt them?"

Rachel nodded, her voice so low only a vampire could hear it. "They died."

"I killed Marilyn?" Drops of blood wet my face, my voice catching as I spoke, cracking in the middle of Marilyn's name.

"You didn't mean to," Rachel cooed. "Him, yes, but her . . . that wasn't your fault, you even tried to save her. You made a deal with a demon even, but the demon betrayed you." A grown man sobbed as she spoke. I think it was me. "Don't cry, baby. That's my blood in those tears." She kissed my cheek. "You're wasting it."

I hugged her tight as she continued to coo, to comfort me, and my thoughts flew apart, one thought and one thought only resounding all too coherently in my mind: *I killed Marilyn.*

When Irene woke up that evening, the thought was still rolling through my head. She knew something was up, and she was furious with Rachel, shouting, "You told him he killed Marilyn?" followed by "What the fuck were you thinking?" over and over again until I told her to stop.

I was useless to both of them after that, and Irene decided it was time to get out of the city.

"I have this place near Montpellier, not far from the southern coast," she told me. "A winery. I learned to make blood wine. It's not as refined as Duke Gornsvalt's, but it'll do the trick, and I think that's what you need, to get roaring drunk and look up at the stars. Sound good?"

"Fine," I remember saying. "That's fine." The coolness of being able to possibly drink alcohol was lost on me.

Rachel and Irene exchanged a look I couldn't read as we rode in the limo. Maybe she was mad Rachel had put a damper on the honeymoon. As we left the city, I felt a consciousness brush my thoughts. It was a female Vlad. She was young, beautiful, and newish, but the touch was brief and Rachel was driving fast.

"Eric!" the young vampire shouted in my thoughts.

"Hey," I answered back, but the contact was already gone.

"You want to listen to some music?" Irene asked me.

She interpreted my shrug as a yes and showed me how to work my iPod. I scrolled through the playlists and clicked on "Marilyn." XTC's "All of a Sudden (It's Too Late)" played and I closed my eyes. Andy Partridge's soulful musings drove deep, and the French countryside shot by virtually unnoticed and thoroughly unappreciated. When the song ended, I backed it up with a click of the little back arrow and played it again, then pressed Menu and scrolled through the other songs.

A duet by Ozzy Osbourne and Lita Ford, Meat Loaf's "I Would Do Anything for Love," different covers of "Time after Time"—a whole song list devoted to melancholy and lost love.

I whistled—one long note—hit Play/Pause, and scrolled through the artist menu, clicked on "Queen" and selected "All Songs." Freddie Mercury broke out into "Bohemian Rhapsody," and the smile was hard to fight. The laughter followed.

"Eric?" Irene's smile was wary. "What's so funny?"

No wonder Irene had gotten me to marry her. It wasn't the *ménage à trois*. It was that nothing mattered. Just like Freddie sang at the end of the song. With Marilyn gone, I was one step away from, well . . . anything.

46

TABITHA:

UNHEX MY HUSBAND

He didn't even recognize me," I shouted at John Paul Courtney as I ran full speed in human form down the side of the road in Paris. People were noticing, but the way I looked at it, that was the True Immortals' fault. If they'd just left Eric and me alone to have our honeymoon, none of this would have happened. "He sensed me and he didn't even recognize me. He said, 'Hey.'"

"That little sister of yours done hexed the boy." John Paul Courtney's ghost floated alongside me on a horizontal plane like a bad rear-screen projection effect. While he had saved me from burning up by using the handle of *El Alma Perdida* to shove my unconscious little cat body up under a car, I attributed at least half of my survival to sheer dumb luck. I mean, what if someone had moved the car? I'd assume he had a backup plan, but . . .

"Well, duh!" Zipping along the roadside, I took a swipe at the ghost, averted an unintended plunge into the River Seine with sheer willpower, regained my stride, and shot on after Eric and my sister. It wasn't about spending a night in Paris now, it was about getting my husband back before he had to fight *la Bête du Gévaudan*, the thought of which was terrifying. I'd never seen Eric in a fight he couldn't win, but against *la Bête du Gévaudan*, he'd been powerless.

I caught up to the car again, close enough for Eric to sense me, and kept announcing myself in the hope that he'd hear me or remember me. He didn't, though. It was weird: I got a connection, but it was like a one-way mirror. I could see him hovering in my mind's eye, a semi-transparent hologram. Queen's soundtrack to the movie *Flash Gordon*—the football fight portion—playing on his iPod rang clear as a bell to my ears. The scent of him filled my nostrils, but to him, I was invisible. "It's me, damn it! Eric! Eric!"

Everybody's seen those cop shows where the witness is behind the glass, pointing out the suspect, and an idiot turns on the light in the room so the one-way glass becomes a window. In the mental contact, a light turned on and Eric vanished as if I'd been seeing, feeling, and hearing a reflection, and in its place was Rachel, driving the limo and watching me through the rearview mirror. It was just an image, a mental projection, but my little sister stared at me, eyes in a mirror, eyebrows narrowing, and spoke in a voice filled with derision.

"Hello, slut. Your master is busy at the moment, but luckily for you he has a thrall powerful enough to intercept your attempt at reaching him and tell you to fuck off. Enjoying your honeymoon?"

"I don't have time for this, Rachel. If we don't leave Paris tonight, then Eric is going to have to fight *la Bête du Gévaudan.*"

"So? Eric can kill anything."

"*La Bête* is an immortal werewolf, Rachel. Eric already fought him once and this thing batted down the uber vamp like it was nothing. Whatever you're doing has to stop, and we have to get him out of here."

I dodged a little Citroën Nemo, vaulting over the rear and dashing down the hood. My ankle buckled on the asphalt and I rolled back onto the hood for a fraction of a second, long enough for the driver to see me, and balled myself up, feet flat against the bumper, palms on the hood to launch off again. The driver lost control of the car and swerved into another lane, sideswiping a minibus.

"How athletic," Rachel mocked.

"Rachel, why the hell are you doing this?"

"Because I made a deal." Her eyes softened. "I didn't want to completely screw up your honeymoon, Tab. I would have let you have a couple of nights, but I was going to get killed if Ebon Winter hadn't given me a get out of jail free for a favor card . . ."

"Winter put you up to this?"

"He said if Eric didn't lose in Paris, then he wouldn't win in Void City." Rachel's image flickered as the car sped up, and I increased my pace to match it.

"And you believed him?"

"He said it was a bet." Her eyebrows drew in closer at the center, the outer edges arched high. "Have you ever known Winter to lose a bet?"

No, I hadn't. Winter never lost. Eric had to lose here to win there. Win what? Lisette had headed to Void City. Did Winter mean Eric had to become embroiled in all this Immortal Politics crap to have a chance at Lisette?

"Did he explain anything?"

"Does Winter *ever* explain anything?"

"What exactly are you supposed to do?"

"It's a good thang you don't show up on film," JPC shouted next to me. Several motorists had cell phones out, trying to take pictures or video of me.

"Keep him here a week," Rachel said.

"And to do that you decided to kidnap him and make him cheat on me."

"Oh, please." Rachel flipped me the bird. "Do you know a better way to keep Eric occupied than with liberally applied pussy? Consider it his bachelor party come late and forget about it. It's not like he's going to be faithful anyway. Not unless your name is Marilyn—and neither of us are her."

"Damn it, Rachel!" I poured on the speed, leaving my ghost escort so far behind that he blew away in a puff of smoke and re-formed next to me.

"Don't go doin . . ." He fell behind. Vanished. Re-formed.

". . . that, missy. It ain't . . ." He lost the pace, vanished, and re-formed a third time. ". . . fun a t'all."

"Sorry," I mouthed. "You go wait in the In-between or something, but keep track of me." I slowed up to keep from pulling past his range limit. "And, John Paul."

"Yes?"

"If I fall asleep tonight and I don't have Eric . . ."

"Yes?"

"I'll need you to shoot me with *El Alma Perdida*. Can you do that?"

"Well, a certain number of times and in the raht circumstances, but it'll set you on fahr."

"Only if the bullet lodges in me," I said. "You have to make sure the bullet goes clean through, enough to wake me up, but not set me ablaze."

"Maybe you ain't noticed, missy, but Perdy's bullets don't like ta go straight through."

"Then pull the bullet out, but fast. Promise me?"

"Why do you want me ta shoot you in the first place?"

"To wake me up, so I can keep looking. We're on a timetable here."

"Ah promise." He didn't sound happy. "But it'll count as one of yore times."

"What times?"

"Times I kin fahr Perdy on yore behalf."

"How many do I get?"

"I cain't tell you."

"Fine then. Done."

Courtney's body lost cohesion, drifting apart in a roiling cloud of smoke scattered on the breeze, and I sped back up, the repetitive slap of my boots on the pavement jarring my knees and rubbing raw against my skin the longer I kept it up.

"I'm sorry, Rae," I said when we were in full contact again through her thrall-master bypass. "Winter's going to have to lose this bet."

"I thought you might feel that way." She waggled her eyebrows impishly. "Say hello to my little friend."

Irene appeared before me at the same time I sensed her. She was at least twenty years older than me, vampirically. Pink hair and a slight figure masked a core of strength. She was a Vlad, too. That I hadn't sensed her before, I chalked up to Rachel's mystic shenanigans. She wore capri pants and an open ruffled blouse without a bra. My eyes went to the wedding rings on her finger. I'd only seen them once before, but I recognized them.

Greta had brought them back when she finally got around to cleaning out Marilyn's apartment. They were Marilyn's wedding rings—an engagement ring with a large square radiant-cut diamond flanked by two tapered baguettes, and a matching wedding band of channel-set radiant-cut stones. There was an engraving on the inside, but I couldn't remember what it said. "He's going to kill you."

"Nah," she said, jogging backward as fast or faster than I ran forward. "He's got a soft spot for me." She smirked. "And a hard-on."

"Irene . . ."

"Oh, what's the harm?" She darted from side to side, hard to follow with my eyes, so fast—even for a vampire, unbelievably fast. "It's a few tumbles. You'll get him back in a few days and the sex you guys have will be great. Makeup sex is the best."

"Didn't he try to kill you?"

"Oh please." Irene shook her head. "That was forever ago. A tiff. It's hard to stay mad at Eric. It would be like staying mad at Disney World because Pirates of the Caribbean broke down once. The other rides are still fun."

"Irene . . ."

She stopped, going from high speed to stationary in an instant, arm outstretched, and it clotheslined me. My head and body flew in divergent directions and the traffic went nuts, cars crashing into each other as my blood spurted everywhere—not as much as a decapitated human might have, but impressive nonetheless.

I lay in the dark, unable to move, when John Paul Courtney appeared next to my head.

He let loose an appreciative whistle. "That one's feisty."

"Head back on," I mouthed.

"I'll do my best," he said. "I cain't touch you, but I kin touch Perdy and she kin touch ya. Got you under the car at the hotel, didn't I?"

The indignity of having one's head rolled across the highway to be reattached to one's body cannot be underestimated. Particularly when the ghost of an ignorant hick who's doing the job misjudges a car trying to drive past the accident and gets you hit again in the middle of the road. Yes, JPC had rolled my cat-body up under a nearby car just before dawn on the same day, but it hadn't been nearly so far, and I hadn't been awake for it.

In mid-roll, our surroundings shifted and I found myself in a Vale of Scrythax a few feet from my body with no JPC to roll me the rest of the way.

"You are a very determined vampire," a German-accented voice said. Aarika stepped into view, armored up and ready for a fight. "And an even more determined wife. I've convinced the Council that if I don't provide you my assistance, our furry itinerant dinosaur will hold it as a breach of trust."

She rolled my head back to my neck and when the flesh touched, my body reawakened and the healing process screeched to life.

"Do you have a car?" I asked.

She helped me stand.

"I do."

"I can track Eric, but only as a cat. It's hard to explain." My outfit was ruined. "Can you understand Cat?"

"I can link us temporarily." She touched my forehead, and a telepathic link opened between us.

"Say something."

"This feels different, more . . . organized than when I talked with James."

"Of course," she said with pride. "I am German. Now transform."

I did, reassured by the familiar feel of my feline form, a welcome change from sore ankles, wrecked clothes, and dirt.

"Can you still understand me?" I thought.

"Of course."

We walked to where she said we'd be out of the road and we left the Vale, appearing in the real world next to a silver sports car with futuristic lines and a front grill reminiscent of a guitar pick. The doors rotated up like the wings of some stylish insect.

"Wow."

"You like it?" she asked.

"Yes."

"It's a Wiesmann GT MF5. A good German car. Don't claw up the seats or I will be forced to kill you."

I climbed into the seat.

"Shedding is to be kept to a minimum."

She pressed the silver Start button and the car roared to life. As we pulled onto the road, JPC appeared in the passenger's seat, overlapping me.

"I like this un," he said. "I put Perdy in the trunk."

"Thanks, John Paul," I meowed.

"Think it," Aarika corrected. "Don't speak it. I can understand your thoughts, not your words."

She pulled back into traffic, ignoring the emergency vehicles behind us.

"Did anyone get hurt?" I asked.

"Of course," she snapped. "Vampires played among humans."

"Keep going straight," I thought at her. "I may not have a whole lot of notice on turns." I switched to meows for talking to John Paul. "John Paul, you go ride with Eric. Come back and tell me when they turn."

◆ 47 ◆

ERIC:
BLIGNORANCE IS HISS

Two hours later, I finished watching *Casablanca* and started on *Singin' in the Rain*. Gene Kelly had just escaped his fans and was jumping off the roof of a streetcar and into the passenger's seat of Debbie Reynolds's car when I hit Pause.

"Debbie Reynolds was Carrie Fisher's mom, wasn't she?"

"What the hell are you talking about, babe?" Rachel asked. She was driving too fast, had been the whole trip, not that I mind fast cars, but I'd noticed.

"She married Eddie Fisher and he dumped her for Elizabeth Taylor when Mike Todd died in that plane crash," Irene said.

"Oh, yeah." I remembered. "*The Lucky Liz*. Lucky for Liz she wasn't on that plane, I guess. Not too lucky for folks on board."

Irene elbowed me. "Be nice."

"I am nice."

She took another look out of the rear window and tried to hide it. A human might not have noticed it, but I did. "Why do you keep looking out the back window?" I looked out into the night. Maybe you could see the Alps in the distance, maybe not. By day it would have looked special, but not at night, not to me. It was a long drive to Montpellier . . . I hadn't thought France was so big.

"It's pretty," she answered. "Just watch your movies. Don't you have *Casablanca* on that thing? You love that movie."

"I just watched it." I settled back in. "You'd have noticed if you weren't so busy *looking* out the window for bad guys."

"I wasn't—"

"Hey." I warded off the explanation with upraised palms. "I'm a no-questions-asked kind of guy. I don't need to know and generally I don't want to. You know that, but if there's a problem and you need help, well, we're married and I probably take that a little more seriously than you."

A combative response lingered on Irene's tongue and teetered on her lips before sliding back down her throat in an uncomfortable swallow. "You do, don't you?"

"Yep." I looked out the back. Vamp vision made things look clearer than I let on. Beautiful countryside at night, speckled with quaint, crowded, beautiful towns and cities, the modern meeting the historic and, even an hour away, I fancied that I could smell the sea. "On the other hand, if you're trying to keep secrets from me, then do a better job."

"Why, what did you hear?"

"Well . . ."

If you want an insight into the way my head works, here it is: I could have told my new bride I'd heard her telling a gorgeous little Vlad that she could have me back in a few days, describe the telltale sound of neck muscles giving way, and stop pretending I'd been so wound up in the movie that I hadn't noticed the accidents behind us or the sirens . . . or the blast of wind when Irene had opened the door and jumped out of the moving car, the second blast when she'd come back in, the blood under her fingernails and down the back of her capris. . . . I could demand to know what the hell was going on.

Or . . . I could paint my brain with Liquid Paper and enjoy the ride while it lasted, have one or two more three-ways while I didn't know what they were costing me and I could still enjoy the sex without focusing on the bill.

Guess which one I chose.

"Well, I heard a whole lot of sirens . . . and then you said something about my hard-on. I only heard that much because when you went walkabout, I had to scramble to keep my headphones in.

"But what's annoying me is all the backward glances." I touched her chin and drew her into a soft kiss. "You can either tell me what's up and let me help or keep me in the dark. But if you choose option two, then, like I said, you need to do better, because I can only ignore so much. Okay?"

"What if I'm trying to kill you?" Irene started undoing my belt buckle, nipping my lower lip with her fangs as she kissed me.

"Then you'll die disappointed and a failure."

Irene's gaze flickered to Rachel and back . . . and I smelled cinnamon.

"Oh for fuck's sake!" I pushed Irene away less gently than I should have and she slapped against the door. "We're nowhere near a *pâtisserie* and there isn't a Cindy's Cinnamon Rolls in this whole damn country . . . so don't start doing whatever magic you ladies are doing, and—"

"I was just trying to calm you down," Rachel said. "You're right, it was me, and it was magic, but only because I'm not supposed to let you get too angry. You remember? I'm supposed to keep you calm?" She flicked on the emergency lights and slowed down. "Remember?"

Nice save, I thought. *It might even be true. Partially.*

Rachel stopped the car, got out, and opened Irene's door. "You drive," she said. "He needs me and you know the way."

Irene's look shot daggers at Rachel, "I want what I want" so close to being said that my ears were picking up on the initial inhalation of air. "Fine."

Rachel and I partied in the back while Irene drove (partition up and radio blaring). Live women are more fun anyway, and Rachel's affections were desperate, her lovemaking urgent, as if she knew it couldn't last.

"Why don't you tell me what's going on and get it over with?" I whispered in her ear.

"You don't want to know," she said, and it was the truth.

"That bad?"

Her tongue traced the lobe of my ear, the heat as intoxicating as her breath, coming in shorter gasps against the side of my face. "Uh-huh."

Our clothes came off and we moved together. No foreplay this time. She didn't want it.

"Wherever you'd kiss me," she hissed as she thrust against me, "I want you to bite."

"These aren't toys," I said needlessly. "It'll hurt like hell. Mine heal fast, but—"

"I want it to hurt," she said. "Everything's fucked up. Unrecoverable. And I want to feel it as much as I can."

"Just tell me what's going on and then tell me you're sorry—"

"I did that once." She increased her rhythm as she spoke, breath shorter, our flesh meeting and separating in hard angry slaps. "You won't be so forgiving next time."

I sank my teeth into her wrist following a kiss, kissed my way up her arm and across her shoulder, leaving wounds in my wake, smeared with blood, mine and hers. Scraping the skin of her cheek with my fangs when I couldn't bring myself to bite, I left red lines on her body, down her jaw, her throat, the underside of her breast, where I bit hard and she lurched, resisting the natural urge to pull away from the injury, leaning into it as I pressed my fangs deeper into her breast.

"Should I turn you?" I asked her. Her laugh caught me off guard.

"No, baby." Rachel's nails dug into my shoulders, her thrusts constant. "I've got a way out. I don't want to take it, but I have one."

"Yeah?"

"Yeah."

My heart woke. My lungs drew air, and blood ran through my veins. I lost track of the time, one sexual act leading into the next, each climax spurring the next one on until the scent of her sex and her cinnamon magic ran together and I tasted not just the cinnamon or the spice of her blood, but the sweat on her skin and her skin itself.

"I want you to do everything and I want you everywhere," she told me. "Parting gift. Okay?"

I responded wordlessly, ignoring the fact that I'd climaxed multiple times with no sign of an abatement of my ardor. At some point, we reached Irene's villa and when the car stopped, I carried Rachel out and onto the hood, the engine-heated metal shy of scalding, but uncomfortably hot. She smiled into the metal as I pulled at her hair, fangs buried in the nape of her neck.

"Hit me," she said, and I couldn't.

"No."

"Scratch me then. I want to feel your claws on my skin."

I raked her back, not as hard as she wanted, because she wanted blood, her own, wanted it running down her back and dripping off my claws, but I couldn't do that either.

"Now change."

"What?"

"It's the only way you can get deeper," she said. "I'll help."

I smelled cinnamon and the skin on my arm blackened in the night and I grew. The skin on my back broke open and I looked sideways at the tenebrous wings that sprung forth. *What the hell?* Purple light from my eyes tinted her skin an alien tinge, her blood darker in that light, close to black, and Irene cursed. The weird part was, I wasn't surprised. I couldn't remember changing before, but it felt natural.

"You're doing the uber vamp?" Irene asked.

"The what?" I asked the question, but Irene didn't answer.

Rachel hissed. "Eyes on me, Eric."

We built toward a final climax, her cries filling the night, and when I pulled away from her, I was slick with sweat and the normal secretions of sex, not blood.

"What the hell?" My voice was deep, rumbling.

"Now *that*," Rachel said with a leer, "is unsafe sex."

"Can he get you pregnant like that?" Irene asked.

"Blood," I gasped. My heart sped up instead of slowing down. "I . . ." Knees buckling, I collapsed onto the front of the car, grasping at my chest. ". . . need blood."

With my throat drying, it became hard to speak. My tongue was thick in my mouth. My stomach clenched. My intestines writhed like snakes.

"Cecile," Irene bellowed, "bring blood wine!"

We were parked in the driveway of Irene's villa. Lights sprang on and servants came running. When I saw them, Irene's face masked theirs the instant I saw each of them.

Gunpowder odors wafted past my nostrils, and my skull ached, flashes of white hot searing it, seemingly from within.

"What did you do?" Irene asked.

"Get some blood in him," Rachel shouted. Exhausted herself, trembling as she tried to rise. "I used up too much of my power and he's fighting it."

"Fighting what?" I murmured.

"Maybe if I tweak his hunger . . ."

I remembered El Segundo. Remembered Irene's betrayal. And someone was calling my name. Someone important, but very far away.

"What . . . ?" I turned my head, and blood was pouring into my throat, but not just blood—there was a fruitiness to it, an alcohol taste. Blood wine.

A hockey game. I remembered tasting blood wine for the first time at a hockey game with Rachel and Roger . . . Roger who had betrayed me.

I roared, blood wine spattering my lips as the person trying to pour it in could no longer reach. More blood. More wine. It was nearby, I could smell it.

"More."

"The cellar," said a woman near me. She was short and plump. I batted her away, stepping on another human in my way, biting another and draining them as I passed, pulling the hapless stranger along as I went, dropping him at a wooden door behind which I smelled blood. Beneath the house I found tunnels full of bottled blood in bottom-up bottles, racked like wine. A young vampire was there turning the bottles, and I drained him too.

Aboveground, Rachel screamed in pain, shrill and high, chased with the guttural wrench of betrayal.

More blood wine, some ready and tasting of alcohol, other bottles unfinished and familiar in their coppery flavor.

I think I downed a dozen bottles before I blacked out completely and the world went away. When it came back, I lay in, or rather next to, a bed. Irene was cold and still beneath the covers and Rachel dozed in an armchair against the wall, a crossbow cradled in her lap. A bushy-eyebrowed servant with a stake stood over me—he'd almost staked me before I noticed him.

Humans are easy kills. So easy, in fact, that you can tear a human heart out with your bare hands and, only as you're holding the gore-covered pump box, realize you probably should have asked its previous owner a few questions first. Rachel, stirred by the man's death throes, opened her eyes, taking one look at me and another at the second human coming at me, and fired her crossbow at the human. *Nice save,* I thought.

I recognized a few of the faces as more crossbow bolts hurtled through the door and toward my chest.

"Hard to find good help these days?" I asked.

"Sorry," Rachel said. "I must have fallen asleep. Irene's thralls are . . ."

I shook my head. "Nah. I'm not buying that one."

"It's a spell, Eric . . ."

"Maybe if you'd opened with that . . ."

"Back off," Rachel shouted, and the attack ceased, leaving me with a few arrows sticking out of me, but none in very important places.

Then I sensed Tabitha and I half-remembered her.

"Eric," she said in my head. "You better listen to me this time. Rachel is using magic on you. I know you might not believe me, but she is."

"I believe you," I answered.

"You do?"

"Something is damn sure rotten in the state of Denmark."

"Huh?"

"Never mind."

Gunpowder, mint, and cinnamon assailed my nostrils.

"Quit," I told Rachel.

"I'm in a cellar," I said to Tabitha.

"Great! Just please stay there and don't trust my sister."

"Your sister?" I said mentally and aloud.

"Rachel," Tabitha answered. "We've been trying to find you all night, but I couldn't sense you until now. Not even John Paul could find you."

"Does this room have some kind of cloaking device?" I asked Rachel.

"Yes," she nodded. "We should have taken you here first, but Paris was too much fun. Is my sister here?"

"Yep."

"Fuck." Rachel stood, rubbing sleep out of her eyes, not even bothering with the crossbow. Since the last time I'd seen her, she'd changed into silk pajama bottoms and a keyhole top. "I wish I knew how your power spiked. It's like your *memento mori* suddenly became more powerful or something." Stretching her arms up, I saw her belly piercing and scoffed. It was a diamond stud. "I should have had you for a few more days easy. Do you remember yet?"

"No." I walked over to her.

"You will." She cocked her head to the side, offering me her neck. "Last drink?"

"Sure."

She didn't give me the bells and whistles. It was just blood, but blood was what I needed and I'm not much of a complainer.

Tabitha, bleary-eyed and dressed in what struck me as very high-class hooker gear, walked in the door. A German woman stood next to her, wielding a Walther PPK like she'd used it before.

"Don't let her touch you," Tabitha said to the woman, shaking herself more firmly awake. She felt real, alive—even from across the room I could hear her heartbeat.

"Hiya, slut," Rachel said affably. "I don't suppose there's any chance you'll let this count as the bachelor's party he didn't get to have?"

"If she talks again and it sounds unreasonable, shoot her," Tabitha said to the blond with her.

"How are you doing that?" I asked.

"Doing what?"

"You read as a vampire, but your heart is beating, you're radiating warmth. How?"

"It's my special ability, Eric. I can seem human. It's one of the reasons you married me."

"I thought I married *her*." I indicated Irene.

"No." Tabitha held up her wedding ring. It couldn't have looked less like Marilyn's, but it seemed familiar. A monetary figure appeared in my head, a remembered receipt. "She's in league with Rachel."

I uncovered Irene's naked sleeping body and pulled the ring off her finger. If I was wrong, she could have it back, but no one gets to wear Marilyn's ring under false pretenses. Warm in my hand, the ring made me think of Marilyn, and I slipped it into my pocket.

"Star Dust" started playing on my iPod when I dropped the ring in. Hoagy Carmichael sang it and I remembered pain, gold melting and burning my skin. I took off the wedding ring I was wearing and inside there was an inscription: Eric & Marilyn 1965.

The memory hurt.

Someone said my name again, far off, but louder. Before the cry had been plaintive, but now it was tinged with fear, the voice of a child watching a scary movie and calling for a parent who's stepped away for more popcorn. "Daddy?"

"Greta?" I whispered.

"No!" Tabitha grabbed both sides of my face. "It's me, Tabitha. Your wife!"

My memories rushed back, a Slinky resuming its natural shape after going down stairs. Greta's fear became terror and my essence reached out for hers, but she was too far away. I could feel her, but she didn't feel me. I could hear her, but it was one-way.

"Greta." I started for the door. "I'm coming!"

"Eric, what the hell?" Tabitha grabbed my T-shirt, and I took her hand as gently as I could.

"I'm back," I said. "I know it's you, but I have to go. Greta is in danger."

As I said "danger," a wolf the size of Texas padded down the stairs from the house to the cellar. The cellar had a door on both ends providing access from both the house and the courtyard of the villa, and, had I not been able to see the first few rays of sun peeking in under the courtyard door, I might have walked out on him. That gave me an idea . . .

"I had intended for you to have more time, and I know circumstances went beyond your control," he said smoothly in my head, "but I am being held to the letter of my words by the Council, and I am a creature of my word."

"Yeah," I said. "Sorry. Wish I could chat, but my daughter needs me."

"You don't understand, vampire." His paw touched my chest, and unlike before, the shock only tickled, it didn't knock me down.

"You're stronger?!"

"So what?" I pushed the paw away. "Here's the deal. I'm going to walk out into the sunlight and you're going to let me."

"Of your own volition?"

"What part of 'my daughter needs me' do you not understand? If my body is destroyed, then I re-form at my *memento mori*, right?"

"Eventually, but it could take months."

"I don't have months. So, here's what we're going to do. Rachel." I locked eyes with her and sent a command: *I order you to help your sister face la Bête and make it safely home. If convenient, you are to get yourself killed in the process. If not, come straight home afterwards and wait for me to talk to you about this little bachelor's party. Oh, and no using your powers or magic on anyone but la Bête.*

"Bastard," Rachel spat.

"Tabitha," I said. "You're going to have to fight *la Bête* on your own." With that, I shoved past a surprised *la Bête* to find John Paul Courtney staring at me.

"You making the right call, son?"

"Greta's my little girl. And Tabitha can handle herself . . . she'll be fine." Without breaking stride, I walked into the sun and I didn't flinch away. Flames caught more slowly than usual, but then sank deep, burning away my skin and clothes, then slowing to a smolder when they hit the muscle underneath. A spark and a hiss and my muscles caught too. Long after I would have normally run, I fought my instincts and stayed put, turning to burn evenly. Fire caressed my bones. My ashes began to scatter on the wind, but I held them in place too, a mass of human-shaped ash, until all that was left was that which was shielded by the grass. I strained upward into the light, rising like a small gasp of dust that popped and hissed in the sunlight to make sure every last bit of me burned until there was nothing left.

Floating through nothingness as my body vanished, I reached for Fang, trying to feel his wheel beneath my hands. As I was reaching, I felt another scream from Greta punctuated by sadness—loss.

"Don't you give up, Greta!" I screamed. "I'm coming."

"This is like that movie *Groundhog Day*," a demon's voice said in my head, "when Bill Murray tries to save the old man. It's never going to work."

"Shut up, Scrythax," I thought.

Concentration broken, my stomach dropped out like I was free-falling and a tether I'd never noticed before snapped taut between my spirit and Fang. I landed in the car, soaked with blood sweat, hands on the wheel and staring at the Highland Towers.

Then I felt it happen: Greta letting go.

Too late.

48

TABITHA:

TAKING OUT THE TRASH

When I married Eric, I thought there might be a little housework involved. He doesn't like clothes to be left around on the floor. He likes the bathroom to be nice and tidy. In the back of my head, I probably even assumed I might need to help dispose of a body or two. Never once, however, did I expect it to include taking care of the bad guy for him all by myself while he fled to another country . . . in the middle of our honeymoon.

"Well," said *la Bête*, "this is awkward."

Sunlight turned the boards an inch from the toe of my boots a warmer brown than the dark wood under fluorescent lights. Heart pounding in my chest, I took two steps back from the giant werewolf. "Okay. Wait. Does this really have to happen?"

"I gave you a time limit. You exceeded the time limit." His chest moved in and out with a sound like bellows. There was spiced meat on his breath. "And so, I have to carry through with the punishment I promised to deliver." He sounded remorseful. "Had I realized how much interference you'd experience, I would have left more room for leniency."

"My apologies then." I looked away as I spoke, searching the area for John Paul Courtney. He was hanging back among the wine bottles in Irene's wine cellar (or do you call the tunnel where they let the wine sit a cellary?). He gave me a nod and flashed me *El Alma Perdida*, the gun that might give me a chance.

"He's a strong 'un, Tabby," John Paul said through teeth set in a grimace. "Best not stop at one bullet."

La Bête said something while I was listening to JPC, and I missed it.

"Excuse me?" I asked, adding a hint of attitude and confidence I didn't feel. I don't think it showed, though. You get used to hiding that sort of thing once you've danced on a pole a few times. You learn to exude confidence whether it's real or not.

"Perhaps it is obvious to you," *la Bête* said, "but I'm uncertain why you feel you owe me an apology."

"Oh, that." I met his gaze. "I apologized because I'm going to kill you."

His eyes widened in surprise.

"It's true," I continued. "You're going to underestimate me. Don't worry, though. I'm not offended. Everybody does it."

"Only another immortal can kill an immortal." He was saddened as he said it. "Our souls must battle. One soul defeats the other and the power is sublimated and absorbed. Each time we do it, we become stronger, and I am one of the oldest, the most powerful. The best you could hope for is to pin me to the ground with my own weapon, but I tend not to draw weapons."

"Aarika?" I asked, hoping for help from the German immortal.

She shook her head. "I'm not allowed to fight him. I'm sorry."

"That's not fair," Rachel chimed in.

"It's not about fairness," *la Bête* intoned. "It's about punishment." His fur seemed to slide beneath his skin, the skin stretching to enfold it. Claws withdrew into skin that bulged to cover them, and the horrid cracking and breaking of bones that I'd heard before when he changed to human sounded once more. His clothing appeared last, this time a plain white *gi*. "But out of fairness, I can agree to fight you like this."

Aarika winced when she saw the *gi*. "Then, Master Ji . . . ?"

"Is gone. Devoured. Consumed for his impudence and the price of his pride," the ancient immortal answered.

"Last chance, then." I put my hands on my hips in the basic heroic Wonder Woman pose. "You never clearly defined what you were going to do to us. You just said you'd make us regret it. Well, I do regret it. You were nice to us, you extended your hospitality, accepted us in your territory, and we unintentionally overstayed our welcome and offended you. I feel I was ill-used by the Immortal Council, who deliberately worked against my efforts to meet your terms—when you'd instructed them to grant us every courtesy. Despite that, I'm upset that we failed to keep our end of the bargain. I'd hoped we might be able to visit again."

"I will deal with the Council of Immortals," *la Bête* snarled, "and I appreciate your candor, but an example must be made, and my word is at stake. I would have preferred to make such an example of your husband or even your sister. He would have survived, and she is more deserving. Even Irene cannot be held completely accountable, as she is a member of the Treaty of Secrets. It must, therefore, be you."

I opened my mouth to interrupt, but Rachel was a step ahead of me. "More deserving?!" Rachel sneered. "What the fuck are you talking about?" She marched closer, gesturing with her forefinger as if it were a weapon. "I'm Eric's thrall, not my sister's, and a big part of my job is making eternity fun for him, giving him what he needs. What he needed was a fun honeymoon with lots of sex and blood and all the sights. If I'd known about your stupid deadline, I'd have—" Rachel thrust her finger at *la Bete*'s chest, but he caught it, bending it all the way back against her hand.

She screamed, grabbing at her right hand, trying to break his grip.

"You will not ensorcel me, witch!" *la Bête* spat in her face, leaning close.

Rachel responded with a self-satisfied sneer and a palm to his forehead. He hurled her away, and she landed with a crash and the sound of breaking glass atop a stack of wine bottles, bottoms angled up and out for turning. The pungent odor of fermented grapes, which had been strong before, grew stronger still, and *la Bête*'s howls were not quite as loud as Rachel's laughter.

"I learned my trade in hell, asshole!" she shouted at *la Bête*. "Do you really think a little pain will keep me from using it?"

"Fine," *la Bête* snarled. He seized my shoulder and pulled me close, blinking his eyes and rubbing at his head while he spoke. "If you agree to it, I will punish your sister instead of you. The delay in your departure appears to have been, as you say, completely her fault."

"Kill him, sis." Rachel choked. "I shut down *Ajna*, his third eye. I can't hold him long, but—"

"Done," I said. "But I want to be able to come back next year, to spend a week here with the family, and I want to bring my husband."

"You cunt!" Rachel bellowed, still trying to extract herself from the bottles. "I'll fucking kill you. I—"

"Agreed." *La Bête* turned to face her, drawing a well-worn but expertly maintained hunting knife from what seemed like thin air. "Look at it this way, witch. All I'm going to do is skin you alive. As powerful as your master is, you might even survive."

Rachel's skin turned black, purple glow shining from her eyes as she drew on power stolen from Eric. "I won't go down easily, motherfucker!"

I held my hand out toward John Paul Courtney, and he pressed *El Alma Perdida* into it.

"One shot, maybe two before he reacts," John Paul whispered. "It might not be enough."

"Good. It's more sporting if you have a chance, however remote." *La Bête* raised the knife and I focused on the blade, on the idea of my sister being skinned alive, on what she'd done to my honeymoon, on Eric leaving me here, abandoning me to go save Greta, and, though dawn was now long past, the anger turned my powers back on. My eyes flickered red, casting hints of crimson on *El Alma Perdida*, and that was my cue. Six shots rang out, so close together it sounded like a short burst of machine-gun fire.

The werewolf seemed to teleport. He'd been standing over Rachel, but when my final shot rang out and he stopped, he was in front of me on his knees. I dodged the knife as he flailed at me like a drunken man, blood covering his chest. *El Alma Perdida* tumbled from my hands as I tore the knife from his. Kicking *la Bête* backward with my booted heel, I drove the blade of his own knife through his stomach and out his back, where it bit into the stone.

He laughed—a wheezing gasping sound. Blue beams shone from his bullet wounds. *El Alma Perdida* singed my palm when I stooped to scoop it up.

"John Paul?" I prompted.

JPC knelt over the gun and tried to pick it up as well, drawing back sharply as if it burned him, too. He took off his coat and wrapped it around the Colt.

"Git yore sister if'n you want her, and let's skedaddle!" the ghost shouted. "I ain't never seen *Perdy* do this afore. I ain't shore whut's goin' ter happen, but it might not be pretty."

I lifted Rachel off the pile of broken bottles and she winced, shards of glass poking out of her back. She sagged back to human as if she'd barely managed the uber vamp energy she'd used.

"Can you walk?" I asked.

"I'll walk away from him," Rachel answered. She tried to stand and leaned against me hard. "My healing's not as spiffy when Eric's this far away. Shit. Transforming saved my life, but it used up all my uber juice."

La Bête's laughter grew, and so did the light show. When I looked back, it reminded me of the scene in *Predator* (one of the many sci-fi movies I'd sat through just to spend time with my dad) where the Governator realizes the alien is going to nuke itself.

"Run! Dang it all! Run!" John Paul shouted, clutching the smoldering bundle he'd made from *El Alma Perdida* to his chest. "He may be dying. He may not be, but whatever he's doing, I think it's going be about as fun for onlookers as a front row seat at a volcanic eruption."

"But it's sunlight outside!"

"Turn into something portable," Rachel said. "But not a cat."

"I'll probably pass out when I do."

"I'll get you out of here, Tabitha."

"You need to go to Orly," I told her. "It's where Phillip's private plane is waiting for us. Can you find it?"

"I'll find it."

"Can I trust you?" I asked.

"You don't have to trust me," Rachel said, venom creeping into her voice. "Eric ordered me to help you. It's a command and he's my master. I can't go against him when he's made it an order. Trying to defy orders will just make me age."

"I can do a sparrow," I offered.

"Take off your coat first," Rachel instructed.

"Why?"

"Because blood-covered women attract the wrong sort of attention!"

I gave her the coat and transformed into a bird. She stuffed me into a coat pocket and ran. As we took the elevator up and the doors opened, I heard the crash of thunder under a cloudless sky. The ground shook. I had just enough time to wonder if John Paul Courtney was okay—if a ghost could even be hurt—before the sleep of the dead claimed me. Whether la Bête was coming after us or I'd heard the sound of his explosive demise, I wouldn't know till nightfall. By then, we'd either have made it or not.

✦ 49 ✦

ERIC:
DESTROY ALL MONSTERS

You're too late. Words. That's all they were: words in my head. And whether they were mine or Scrythax's or even Rachel's, I'll never know. *Too late.* A litany of failure hammered nails in through my skull.

Too late.

Too slow.

Too stupid.

And you deserve it. So did she. That one was definitely not mine.

"I'm not done yet." My voice echoed, a stereophonic halo of sound leaving my lips and Fang's speakers. I climbed out from behind the wheel and stepped over the windshield and out onto the hood. Akira Ifukube music blared, *Godzilla vs. Mothra*, and we rolled back from the front doors of the Highland Towers.

A scream of rage. The roar of a V-8 engine. Two bodies—one metal and one organic—charged forward as one. All of the magic in the area winked into view, revealing the soul-spangled web of protection surrounding the building: werewolf souls and a tiny piece of Scrythax all tied together and put to ill use. We clashed against it, Fang and I. There was no need for the uber vamp, not yet. My eyes burned violet, infecting the shield with incandescent fury.

Phillip popped into my mind, clinging to the legs of another vampire, Percy, the one I'd always seen in the glass case.

"Help me," Phillip begged Percy.

"*Nomen est omen,*" Percy whispered. "Names are destiny. Yours means 'lover of horses,' and his"—the bespectacled vampire looked at me—"his means 'all powerful.'"

A sense of Percy bounced against the wave of my psyche. He was powerful, an Emperor like me, and old—from an age of chamber music I didn't recognize. Percy'd been around for centuries . . . at least. One more Emperor to add to my hit parade.

"Sorry about all this," Percy thought at me. "He's controlling the wards, and I fear he's gone and activated his failsafe. No one can get in or out." He faded before I got out a reply.

The wards will tear you apart! That time it was definitely Scrythax.

"So what?" Fang and I rolled backward once more, the magic shield sliding with us, drawn by the purple fire in my eyes. "It doesn't take all that much to put my dead ass back together again."

On our next charge, the shield cracked and so did my jaw. Shards of magic sliced me to ribbons like paper through a shredder, but Fang kept rolling until his front end knocked the front doors down. I slid off the hood in a mass, re-forming legs first as he stopped. Almost formless, I kept moving, a mass of writhing reincorporating flesh, all sliding back together into the shape of one very angry vampire.

Thralls, some belonging to Phillip, others not, rushed out to meet me, weapons in hand. A man thrust a stake into my chest and the stake exploded, taking his hand off and splintering him with slivers. Spirals of blue protective magic formed around me as the wards thrust me back out into the street, still crackling with bursts of electricity.

Wings of tenebrous leather tore through my T-shirt, and my fangs and claws became disproportionate to my size as I turned into the uber vamp. My claws, normally black like my uber-vamp skin, were edged in gold, my body larger than before, a good eleven feet, maybe twelve.

"Little pig, little pig," I roared.

"We defend the masters," a young man with dark hair shouted. The flamethrower in his hand shook, the fear-tremble uncontrollable.

He cut loose with the flames, but I didn't move. Fire lit my skin, tracing my muscles like red orange highlighter, and didn't burn me so much as illuminate me—more Balrog in appearance than vampire.

"Let me in!"

The thralls faltered as one. Retreated. Bats covered the moon. Rats poured out of the sewers. But when they touched the protective ward, they burned.

Or I'll huff and I'll puff and I'll blow your house in . . .

"Hmmm."

Buildings like the Highland Towers, built between the turn of the century and the start of World War II, were already using steel construction. Before steel they'd been using massive iron columns with load-bearing walls. The Highland Towers' more modern construction was problematic. Modern buildings are sturdier, the weight well distributed . . . but maybe . . .

Anticipating my command, Fang zoomed off, looped the block, and came back at top speed, plowing into the northeast corner at more than a hundred miles an hour. Shards of stone facing filled the air, and when the wards bounced him back, Fang was already regenerating. I'd seen him do it before, but he did it faster now, healing as quickly as me.

The exterior facing broke free, but the concrete underneath it was only cracked. Fang revved his engine and began to make another pass, but I shook my head. I needed something bigger than my car to break these wards, something so epic that they couldn't just hurl it back out . . .

"Something"—my eyes raked the building—"really"—I looked at a manhole cover in the middle of the street—"massive."

I wonder . . .

What are you doing, Eric? Scrythax asked, his voice high-pitched and singsongy.

Tearing the cover off a manhole is easy. Fitting an uber vamp–sized body down one isn't. Void City's sewer system is huge—not Paris huge, but still big. Punching an uber vamp–sized hole through the street isn't easy, but if you have a sturdy metal tool, say a manhole cover, and you have a tremendous amount of supernatural brawn, you can get the job done.

I kept waiting to hear sirens, to have Captain Stacey and his goons from the VCPD show up to mess with my day, but they didn't. Hacking and chopping, I broke through the road, turning the sewage tunnel into an open trench. Once inside the trench, the going wasn't any easier, but determination, rage, and the need to kill kept me focused. Pain from the bones of my hands breaking and reknitting with each blow gave me something to keep me company while I worked and waited.

Eric? What are you doing, Eric?

Character, I quoted, *is like the foundation of a house—it's below the surface. Excuse me?*

"You're being dense, Horn Head." I stopped working and closed my eyes, trying to reach for the power I needed. "Try this one by Yeats: 'Things fall apart; the center cannot hold; mere anarchy is loosed upon the world, the blood-dimmed tide is loosed, and . . .'" I couldn't think of the rest of the quote. "And I am going to knock this goddamn building down and see what Phil's motherfucking wards have to say about it!"

The speed came. It came in a steady flood from Fang to me and, through me, to all the creepy-crawly things I could hurl at the ground and at the concrete, at the brick, and at the stone. The power came too. Power like I'd felt a week ago when I played "Star Dust" and almost lost my mind.

The story of John Henry battling the steam engine flashed through my thoughts and I felt I understood what that was like, just a little, but the machines I fought were political and magical. Despite my abilities, I could never take them all on. Success was flat-out impossible to achieve, but I was going to do it anyway.

Even if I had to work through the night into the day with fire leaping up from my back, even if I was reduced to ash and re-formed again, I was going to do it anyway, because Greta had called my name, had screamed for her daddy, and nothing was going to keep me from her, too late or not too late, even if it was just to stand over her body and hold the head of her killer next to her still, unmoving corpse and say, "I got him for you, Greta. I killed him."

I didn't notice when the building began to tilt, its foundation utterly destroyed. I was trapped in a loop of pity, hate, loss, and vengeance, because I hadn't just lost Greta, I'd lost Marilyn all over again, and now possibly Tabitha, too, and a man like me doesn't know what to do with those emotions except to lash out at something.

A car horn—Fang's horn—cut through my reverie.

"Who the hell is honking my horn?" The words passed my lips and then I heard it, a steadily increasing groan of shifting concrete and steel. It didn't happen fast, but once it started, there was no stopping it. My animals, the survivors, scattered—fully aware, as animals often are, that it was time to get the hell out of Dodge.

The wards held for an hour. Fang played "Toy Soldiers" by Martika as the two of us watched from the top of the neighboring parking deck. Sparks of prismatic energy arced between the sagging frame of the Highland Towers and the concrete around us as the wards lost their game of inches. And when they failed, it was with a whimper, not a bang. The wards winked out. All went still. Then the walls of Jericho came tumbling down, straight for us. Fang kicked into reverse and hauled ass through the far wall of the deck, off and over.

Concrete crumbled as the Highland Towers broke and twisted near the middle, a jagged crack spreading out along the points of structural failure. The fifteen-story building struck the eight-level parking deck we'd just vacated and continued through the deck, crushing it almost to ground level. Joined together in catastrophic architectural union, the two buildings became one, the Highland Towers semi-intact and at a steep angle, supported by the collapsed bulk of the parking deck and the overpriced cars within.

I became the revenant and ghosted through the wreckage—an angry, vengeance-seeking ghost with hell in my step and damnation in my gaze.

50

ERIC:

DEATH TO MING

There was no need for words. Not for me. No explanation, no story could have averted my wrath, but that didn't stop Phillip from trying. At the new intersection between the parking deck and Phil's penthouse, I was met by a wavering blue ward, Phillip's secondary backup. It wasn't nearly as powerful as the main system. Overtaxed by holding the room together as best it could, the ward granted me a view of Phillip's ruined lair.

With the floor at an angle of over forty-five degrees, all the knick-knacks had fallen from their shelves and many of them lay broken on the floor, collecting at the lowest point of the room, past curtains askew and partially detached from the rods upon which they'd once regally hung. Roger's soul spiraled up from the broken soul warden—the overgrown marble that had imprisoned him. He passed through the barrier, recognizing me too late.

"Eric, enough—"

I had no words for him either, only death more final than he might have deserved. He sank into my ghostly body and if he screamed, I didn't notice because my eyes were on the corpse of a fortysomething woman with blond hair, lying on the ground. When most Vlads die, those few whose kill requirements don't result in a destruction of the body, they rapidly age toward their true span of years upon the earth. I'd turned Greta when she was twenty-one. I'd often wondered what she might have looked like as she aged. Now I knew.

"Eric." Phillip scrambled about the wreckage, fumbling for something amid the debris. "Look." He gestured toward a vampire who was staked and bound. I recognized her from a distantly remembered dream—Lisette. "We found Lisette for you. See? You went to Paris to find her and she came here."

He'd killed her. He'd killed Greta. No one had to tell me. I knew.

Percy sat in the remains of an easy chair.

"Percy." Phillip's voice cracked, panic reined in but not conquered as he continued to search. "Tell him, Percy. You saw everything."

"Yes," Percy agreed. "I saw everything. I'm seeing everything now. It's what I do."

Phillip sobbed, eyes lighting from within as he found what he'd been searching for and attempted to conceal it within the sleeve of his Victorian jacket.

I flicked the ward with my thumb and middle finger. Bright blue sparks flew like mutant fireflies as the energy field collapsed. A groan announced the absence of the structural reinforcement it had been providing, and dust fell from the ceiling as everything shifted a bit more.

Methane rose from the gas fireplace in a steady stream, tainting the air. Lord Phillip gestured at me with a piece of copper in the shape of a rod, and lightning rushed along its length, striking me and igniting the methane in one big kaboom. I ghosted as it happened and when the smoke cleared, Phillip gasped at the sight of me, standing exactly where I had been before the explosion.

A single step brought me inside his lair. When the second lightning strike came, I mistimed my shift to revenant form and took the full brunt of the blast. It cooked my clothes and fried my synapses, but it couldn't kill me. It was only lightning. My foot struck the frame of an ornate mirror wrought with dragons and I picked it up. My reflection looked up at me, out of synch with reality, and I gave it a head butt, shattering the glass. A small demon trilled its freedom to the universe as the fly-sized being rose from the mirror, but I caught it in my fist and crushed it until it popped, a tiny jelly-bean of ichor.

Then, I threw the mirror at Phillip. It shattered all over the floor and the wall behind him. He'd turned to mist.

"Come now, Eric," he said. "I'm sure we can . . ."

But I wasn't hearing Phillip any longer, I was hearing the voice of Sydney Greenstreet in the movies behind my eyes, the good ones in black and white where this kind of thing turns out right at the end and the bad guys go to jail and the hero . . . the hero . . .

But I'm not a hero.

If I was, he wouldn't have beaten me. If I was, I wouldn't have been having three-ways in Paris while my daughter was being captured and tortured to death in Void City. If I was a hero, none of this would have happened.

But monsters can win too. Just watch a slasher film or, worse yet, pick up a newspaper.

Phillip's words went by unnoticed. It was a grand speech, peppered with quotes from famous men in languages long dead or rarely used. It was witty and irreverent, clever and charming. I probably would have laughed if I'd been paying any attention to it. Perhaps I did laugh. I don't remember.

I inhaled, my mouth gaping open in defiance of its natural boundaries. Percy drew a small golden ankh from beneath his shirt, but remained otherwise motionless. His ankh blazed brightly, a flickering candle against the hurricane, but a candle that did not go out.

"Eric! No!" Phillip screamed. "Please. We'll—"

Light, all of it save the light from Percy's ankh, bent as if my inhalation was sucking it in. Phillip came with it, his spirit torn free of a long dead body, transmuted to water vapor, which, absent his spirit to bind it together, fell apart and rained down upon the rubble like a brief summer storm.

I devoured Lisette next, ignoring the few French words her spirit muttered as her body turned to dust and even the dust was drawn into my vortex of anger, hate, sorrow, and desire. It was a desire for a better time, a wish for things to work like they did in the movies, a crushed hope that just once, just this one time . . .

Unlike Phillip, she tried to fight me. We merged together with the same unholy intimacy I'd shared with the girl whose name I no longer remembered, the one from my honeymoon night, the one who'd wanted to see the Eiffel Tower.

"This can't happen," Lisette screeched as she tried to push free of me, arm against my shoulders, only to scream again as her spirit sank back within mine. And it was done. I killed Lisette and I killed Phil.

"I got them for you, Greta." I reached for her corpse. "I'm sorry I was late, but—"

"You can get her back." Percy spoke the words, and they knocked me down as surely as *la Bête*'s mighty paws had done in our first encounter.

"Don't fuck with me, Percy."

"Like you, I am an Emperor." Percy stood, and as he did the room seemed to right itself, the walls changing to sandstone, like you'd see in an old mummy movie. "Like you, I am two different types of undead. And like my offspring, Lisette, and my would-be captor, Phillip, I arrived at my state by magical means."

"Get to the part where I can get Greta back."

"Lisette was an experiment in creating an Emperor purposefully. It worked, though perhaps making her a zombie and a vampire was a bit cruel, but I certainly couldn't have her awaken to be as powerful as I am, now could I?"

Sirens blared in the distance.

"Look, I—"

"Without a brief explanation, you will not understand my offer." He interrupted. "I—unlike Phillip, who fancied himself a worker of magic—am an extremely talented practitioner, which opened a unique pathway to me. I discovered two paths to immortality with which I became enamored. The first was vampirism; the second, the rituals of ancient Egypt."

"What, you're a fucking mummy?"

Percy removed his glasses and cleaned them.

This isn't a good idea, Scrythax said in my brain.

"I am a mummy and a vampire and like yourself. I am indeed fully functional, though my interests tend toward voyeurism rather than actual participatory bliss."

"So . . . you're a mummy. So what?"

He handed me his glasses. "An Emperor forged of the unique combination of mummy and vampire. You now hold my *memento mori*. Use your *memento mori* to destroy it, and you will halve my power."

"What?" I looked at the glasses. They seemed normal, but . . . "Why?"

"I want to make amends. I feel responsible, and I have no desire to go to war with you. I'd prefer to watch you from afar or via my thralls." He rolled up his sleeves and aimed his ankh at the wall, where cuneiform images manifested in eerie silver hues. "With that in mind, I'm willing to open a gateway to the Paths of the Dead. As a revenant, an angry ghost, you can set foot on them and go after your daughter." Greta's body lifted up into the air, surrounded by matching silver light.

"Find her spirit before it reaches a final destination and bring her back. While her body exists, it's still possible she could be reunited with it."

"Would she be human or vampire?" I asked.

"Does it matter?" Percy asked, his expression curious.

"It should." I eyed the gateway.

"But does it?"

"No." I hung my head.

"Either is possible." He clucked his tongue. "The choice will ultimately be made by chance, but may be influenced by her wishes."

He said words in a language I guessed was Egyptian, and a dark doorway opened in the wall, sending sand to swirl about my feet.

"What's the catch?"

"It's never been done before," Percy quipped. "Not by one such as you. In theory, it should work, but in practice either one of you could be changed substantially, particularly now that you have undone Lisette, effectively ending the Courtney curse."

"That's all I had to do to end the curse?"

"You act like it was easy, and I suppose it was, given that Greta did all the heavy lifting for you, but you struck the final blow and destroyed her. Now, the Courtneys are free and—"

"So why am I still a vampire?"

"Because you haven't cured yourself, but if you were to find such a cure, the curse would no longer undo it."

I stared at the doorway. Hard.

Eric, Scrythax said to me, *don't risk it. She's not—*

I poked my right hand through the doorway and offered Percy's glasses back to him with my left.

"Take them with you," Percy said. "I want to see what happens if you go. Will you?"

Greta was probably better off dead. She was a monster, in so many ways worse than I was. She killed recklessly, and her appetite for slaughter could be endless. Going could destroy me. Coming back could make her worse. What if she came back human and wanted me to turn her again? What if she was stuck in the body of a fortysomething woman, forever unhappy at the youthful appearance she'd lost?

Would I go? Good damn question.

✦ 51 ✦

ERIC:
POWERSLAVE

I went. What else was there to do? She was my little girl. Greta had headed to a place where only spirits (and the beings, be they demons or angels, that herd them) can travel—along the paths of the truly dead. The light from Percy's ankh showed the way and a path, hard to see and even harder to fathom, came into crystal clarity. The wall vanished completely, widening the gate, leaving a yawning gulf of mist and light in its wake.

A golden path, the same shade as the light from the ankh, wound its way through the mist and, far off in the distance, I saw Greta. She wasn't alone. Other souls in various states of coherence traveled the same path she did, or paths of their own that I couldn't quite make out. My daughter ran as if the devil himself was behind her.

I spared a last glance at Lord Phillip's lair and supposed the analogy wasn't far wrong. I steeled myself against the cold that being dead brings. It wasn't hesitation, but Percy thought it was.

"You don't have to go after her." Percy's voice came from the glasses I still carried in my hand. "You could try—"

"Mommy!" Greta's cry cut through the low-level thrum of the other souls, and I didn't spare Percy a word of explanation. She needed me. What else was there to know? I tucked Percy's glasses into the neck of my shirt, the metal cold against the hollow of my throat, and I ran, watching the spot where the floor of Phillip's suite faded away into the chaotic ramble of paths, mist, and souls beyond. A sound like ripping fabric broke the silence as my feet hit the semitranslucent path, and I was frozen.

"Where *are* you going?" It was Scrythax, his voice, in my ears now rather than my head. Ignoring him, I pushed forward, pain blossoming in my chest—my heart. I looked back and saw a red thread similar to the one I'd seen in Vincennes stretching back into Phillip's suite at the Highland Towers and beyond. Percy was still visible in the room, ankh aloft. He stood out against the normal watercolor brushstrokes to which my world was normally reduced when I was in ghost mode.

I pulled, and it felt like there was a hook in my chest. The Stone of Aeternum. The Eye of Scrythax. One and the same.

"She's not human, Eric." The voice of Scrythax rang not in my ears but in my chest, reverberating as if I were a bell.

"Neither am I."

"Yes, you are." Pain increased. I pulled against the pain like a fish on a hook—straining, hoping that the line would snap, that something would give. "I'll show you."

"What happened to the Prime Directive?" My mouth didn't move, but the sound echoed forth.

"What?"

"Non-interference," I translated for the apparently *Star Trek*–deprived demon. "You said you wouldn't get involved, wouldn't dream of giving me orders."

"That was before you decided to leave the material plane," Scrythax said. Pressure in my chest increased, pain intensifying. "Turn back and I'll be hands-off once more. You can't go there, Eric. If you do, they'll see."

"See what?"

"You. Your purpose. Then, your destiny will change again. My daughter, Scrytha, will see to it."

"I. Will." My body began to re-form, became solid again, and slid back to the gate, but I fought the sensation. "Save. My." I turned away from Percy, legs straining forward against the path, eyes locked on Greta. "Little girl!"

Anger has always been a part of me, a force so real, so tangible I could drown in it. I've learned to fight the anger. I've even had magical help, but in that moment, it burst the bonds, roaring free, washing over me. I heard a snap, a clink, and behind me, even though I knew I couldn't see it, a chunk of the Eye of Scrythax hit the ground in Phillip's room.

"It's broken." Percy's words fell on deaf ears. Nothing more restrained me, and the sudden freedom sent me stumbling, but I did not fall on the path, I flew. A heartbeat thumped in my ears. The sounds of breaths drawn in hard and deep like a bellows surrounded me, but I flew on.

"You fool!" Scrythax shouted, his voice fading the further I flew.

Flight without wings made me sick inside, or maybe it was whatever Scrythax had tried to do. I was used to wingbeat cycles, not Superman-style antics. Bile filled my mouth, the sick acidic twang carrying into my nostrils as well. How long had it been since I'd last had that taste in my mouth?

Summoned by the taste, memories of a night with Roger at a bar, back when we were both alive, filled my head. Images of the bar, Roger, the drinks, appeared before me like phantoms obscuring my way. I tasted pretzels, too. The salt lingered on my tongue. Marilyn. Kissing her afterward as we laughed. Her smile. A distraction.

"Mommy!"

Greta was looking for Mommy because as far as she knew, when she'd screamed for Dad, for me, I hadn't come. I hadn't been there. She didn't know I'd been on my way as soon as I felt her, had been seconds away when she died. If she had, she might have hung on a little longer.

My speed increased and the souls I passed began to shrink away from me, moaning loudly. I reached out to one of them, intending to use it for fuel, but nothing happened. They weren't afraid I was going to eat them, they must have feared my emotions. They parted for Greta, too.

"Greta!" I called her name over and over again, but as fast as I flew I couldn't seem to overtake her. After a while it felt like we'd begun to descend rather than proceed along a horizontal plane and the path turned and twisted, a knot of pathways like a rubber band ball, the interior parts packed so tight together for so long that they were indistinguishable from one another. I lost sight of Greta, was forced to listen for her cries.

Then I was no longer flying. My body crashed down onto the path and tumbled to a stop. Watercolor images faded, darkened, then sprang back to life, no longer in watercolor hues, but vivid high definition, crisp and clear, but tinged with blue like retouched force ghosts in the *Star Wars* Special Edition movies with a techno dash of *Tron's* digitally rendered world. My heart beat. My lungs drew in air, and the spiritual energy around me . . . I could sense it, touch it.

"I wish the universe would make up its mind."

I was in a long dark hall, made of the same sandstone walls I'd seen before. Decorative columns held up the ceiling, but it was all dark, the only light, a faint one, seeming to come from the illuminated lines of each object. A line of dead people, each holding a heart in his or her hands, extended before me, and I went past them. Jogging by on the left, I saw a dais upon which there were a set of scales and dudes in Egyptian apparel. A feather was on one scale and on the other, a man with a jackal head took the heart and weighed it. Sitting hungrily nearby, a being with the head of a crocodile and the body of a lion sat waiting.

"Halt!" Bare-chested guards with too much eyeliner and deadly-looking spears appeared from nowhere, thrusting their spears in my face. "You came through one of our gates, your heart must be weighed."

"You're not ripping my heart out, pal." I shoved one of them, but the vampire strength wasn't there. My heart appeared in my hands, and more guards appeared.

"I'm trying to catch my daughter, asshole. I'm not even properly dead . . . I . . ."

"Come," Dog Face said from the pillar. "Compliance will be faster than resistance." Dog face. Shit! I flashed back to memories of *Raiders of the Lost Ark* and the statues of Anubis that guarded the Ark.

"So . . . you're supposed to be Anubis?" I asked.

"I prefer Inpu, but Anubis will do."

I stepped to the front of the line and handed him my heart. He took it gingerly, surprised by some aspect, either its weight or its color. Smell? Hell if I knew.

"Don't fuck that up, Inpu," I said. "I need that back."

The crocodile thing snapped at me, but Inpu shushed it. "Ammut, I suspect this one is not for you." He looked at me. "Do you know the affirmations?"

"The what?"

"It's customary to declare your nobility, your . . ." He searched for a word. ". . . sinlessness."

"Screw that. I've done all kinds of bad things, killed people—you name it and I've done a lot of it. Of course, most of that was to survive, but still . . . I did it, and most of it I'm not sorry about."

The souls behind me gasped.

"Is that bad?"

"It isn't good," Anubis said, his tall canine ears twitching. "Have you done nothing good?"

"I don't hurt kids. I take care of my family . . . and one time . . . well, I don't remember all of it, but people tell me I saved the world." The crocodile thing, Ammut, tossed its head to one side and I realized it was wearing a headdress. "Do I fight that thing now?"

Anubis set my heart on the empty scale opposite me, nostrils flaring in surprise when the scale with the fluffy white feather on it dropped to the floor.

"No," Anubis said, his voice unsure, "now you move on to Osiris, where you may leave Duat and enter Aaru."

"Aaru?"

"Paradise."

"Screw paradise. I told you, I'm looking for my daughter."

"I'll take him," a voice, soft and feminine, spoke from ankle level. A housecat with fur the color of blood, wearing a golden collar with an ankh hanging from it, sat next to my foot.

"Sekhmet?" Anubis was confused.

"He's friends with my son." The cat rubbed against my legs, darting in and out of them as she spoke. "And he doesn't belong here."

"Do you wish to go with her?"

"Can you take me to Greta?" I asked.

"I can put you back on the right path to her. She came through a different gate, thus her path does not lead to Aaru."

"Just get me as close to her as you can."

She didn't move.

"Please," I added.

With a nod I was gone from Egypt Land and deposited on a country road. A split-rail fence ran along one side of the road, and on my right, scrubland stretched into infinity. "This is like a damn *Twilight Zone* episode."

Sekhmet sat atop a fence post, preening.

"If I see Rod Serling, I may—"

"Mommy!" Greta's voice came from farther along the path, and I took off running, barely pausing long enough to shout a thanks to Sekhmet.

Though more infrequent, her shouts sounded less strained and more expectant. Greta thought she was getting close. Running as fast as I could, plagued by a stitch in my side and the beginning twinges of a charley horse, boots and jeans (where had those come from?) covered in a patina of red dirt, I came to the top of a rise and looked down upon what I can only describe as Hell. Greta stood in front of it.

"Greta!" I bellowed, stumbling down the hill. "Stop! Don't you fucking take another step! Goddamn it, Greta! Do you hear me? Don't you fucking move!"

Wreathed in flames, soot, and smoke, the boundary of Hell carved an even delineation between the road and the pit. The rising heat waves made it hard to focus on exactly what was happening within the inferno, but from the sound of it, folks weren't having a good time.

"Stay right there," I shouted. "Right. There."

Greta stopped, but didn't turn. Limping, I made my way toward her, admonishing her to stay put with every step. Up close, the flames faded. Hell's gates were golden and inviting and the shouts of despair and pain twisted in the ear, sounding more like cries of joy and laughter. Next to the wall, Greta stood still. Watching.

"Greta."

"Dad." She reached back and touched my shoulder.

"Come away from there," I said. "I came to get you. I'm sorry I was late, but there's still time. Come on." I pulled at her arm, but couldn't budge her.

"But, Dad," she said, pointing past the gate. "Look. It's Mom."

"I don't want to s—" And then I saw Marilyn.

She wore the same clothes and the same form in which I'd last seen her: fiery red hair, leather jacket, ready to ride Roger's Duo-Glide. And in that instant, I wished I hadn't come after Greta at all.

Movie moments work like this: Two lost lovers stand on either side of a crowded room at a party filled with people in fancy clothes dancing and having fun. The lost lovers might as well be rendered in black and white or shades of blue, but music swells. Their eyes meet. Cue close-up as their eyes light up with tearful joy at the sight of one another. They run for one another. The crowd vanishes or maybe they have to fight their way to one another, but when they meet, they grasp each other tightly, clinging to one another as if only their love can hold them up. Without each other, without their love, they might literally fall apart.

It worked exactly like that for Marilyn and me, except that she was in Hell and I wasn't, and when we reached for each other there was a gate between us and beyond the gate a clear barrier, like the surface of a snow globe surrounding Hell. We couldn't even touch. Love left impotent by reality. My hand hovered over hers and I felt like Kirk in *Star Trek II: The Wrath of Khan*, watching Spock die, with nothing left to do but say good-bye.

"Ship out of danger?" she quoted, proving she was my Marilyn and demonstrating with four simple words how well she knew me.

"Have they? I mean . . ."

"They haven't done anything to me yet." She looked away. "She's been saving me for something."

I punched the barrier and it bloodied my knuckles. I hit it again and again, and something gave in my fingers, one of the small bones. I winced, then cursed when the bones popped back into place and healed in less than a second.

"For what?"

"I don't know."

"How touching." A demon with asymmetrical ram's horns and long white robes stood at Marilyn's side. Though her face was more human than her father's, more pleasing to human eyes, her teeth were in multiple rows, not keeping time with each other as she spoke. Jewels encrusted her horns and painted colors on her skin, making it impossible to tell what color the skin actually was. Unlike her father's, the demon's eyes were intact, blazing like flame-lit diamonds, obscured on the left by bangs of white hair curling slightly, as did the long strands of hair cascading down to her mid-back.

"You're prettier than your dad," I told her.

"You should have seen him in his prime," she countered, her voice devilish and pleasant. "He was a marvel to behold. His phallus alone—"

"Whoa!" I blinked away the image. "TMI."

"So *you* are Eric Courtney." She appraised me with a long slow look.

"And you're the daughter of Scrythax."

"My name is Scrytha," she corrected. "Lady Scrytha—"

"Geez," said Greta, "somebody would have rather had a boy. Scrytha, huh? Ouch."

Scrytha didn't bat an eyelash, didn't even appear to have them, now that I was looking more closely. "Also the mother of J'iliol'lth and J'hon'byg'butte," Scrytha continued. "You may remember them?"

"I fed them both to Talbot." There was no point in lying. "One in Void City and the other in El Segundo."

"Yes, you did."

"Still, I mean, no offense, but they were pretty ugly little spuds when it came down to it."

Greta laughed and so did Marilyn. Scrytha's expression remained icy.

"Sorry," I said with a shrug, "I can't help myself."

"No." Scrytha put a hand on Marilyn's shoulder. "You can help yourself. You can't help her."

I ground my teeth together.

"Did you know he attempted to replace you," Scrytha asked Marilyn, "with that dark-haired stripper, Tabitha? The night after, his wedding ring melted off his finger. The power of Love." Mocking laughter rose in her throat and assaulted us.

Marilyn looked away.

"The only way they could get it to stay on his finger was to replace it with the wedding ring you bought for him." More laughter. She was enjoying this. I reached into my pocket and closed my hand around Marilyn's engagement ring and wedding band. I would have given anything to put the rings on Marilyn's fingers, to travel back in time to 1965 and live it all over again. To stake vampire Roger and stay human, fuck the Courtney curse, and be a normal dysfunctional married couple. I'd have been suspicious of Marilyn because she'd cheated on me with Roger, and it would have driven a wedge between us.

We'd have gotten divorced or maybe we'd have learned to deal with it and opened a biker bar. I couldn't have cared less. I just wanted a do-over. Though I'd be in my sixties, I'd still break down the door of Greta's foster parents' beach house and rescue her, too, or maybe we'd even manage to adopt her early on and save her the mental trauma altogether. If I lived long enough, I'd even show up on Tabitha's doorstep and give them an early warning about Rachel's leukemia . . . they'd have plenty of time to do something about it. And if the world ended in El Segundo because I wasn't there to stop it? So what, then?

"Oh, I smell wishes," Scrytha said with gusto. "How cute. How human."

"I'm not wishing anything." And then I was the uber vamp, Marilyn's rings still gripped in my massive fist. Behind me, I heard the roar of an engine and Fang careened down the red dirt road, kicking into a slide and coming to a halt against the fence surrounding Hell. How the fuck? I would have asked Fang how he got down here, but it's not like he could answer. My heart stopped beating, skin cooling, breath still. "You can want a thing without wishing. It's kind of a hopeless hope."

"Hope is abandoned here, Eric." Scrytha leaned forward, eye to eye with me. "Haven't you read our sign?"

She removed Marilyn's jacket. "Would you like a demonstration?" Marilyn fought her, but human strength versus a demon's is useless. "Shall I have her raped before your eyes?"

"Do it," I said. "Harm her in any way and I will storm the gates of Hell. I will bring them crashing down and I will kill you. It's a promise." I don't make promises, but my ire was up. "I will spend the rest of my existence destroying you and your kind. You will die by tooth, by claw, by soul sucking, by maw of Mouser, or screaming underneath my car as the flesh is ripped from whatever you have in place of bones. I'll even break out the magic sword I have in the freezer back home and cleave you if I have to. I will not stop. Do you"—I hit the barrier—"under"—Fang's engine revved high, wheels spinning in place—"fucking"—smoke escaped my fist as the rings seared my skin—"stand me?"

Crack.

Shards of Hell glass tumbled to the hardened lava floor where Marilyn and Scrytha stood, and my fist rested cleanly against Scrytha's ample bosom. I hadn't expected Scrytha to grin in response, but grin she did, and her grin, like her father's, overstretched the natural boundaries of her face, exposing muscle, bone, and ligament.

"So that's why he covets you," Scrytha said gleefully, eyes spar-kling. "Satan's beard! How remarkable. I won't harm her or allow her to be harmed. Hell is where she belongs, but perhaps being away from you, perhaps loneliness is punishment enough. No, not quite. I wouldn't get past Fair Standards and Equitability with that one, but perhaps . . . Yes . . . Yes, that would do it."

"What?"

"I'll put her in a house, a replica of the one the two of you had purchased. She will have groceries delivered to her and have to cook her own meals. She'll have books and CDs, music, but in every room there will be a screen encompassing an entire wall upon which the volume may be turned down, but never off, and on that screen will be you, whatever or whomever you're doing—you. It echoes more to the Machiavellian and the ironic, but I can sell it."

"Why so helpful?" I asked, not moving. "Because I broke the glass?"

"In exchange for your promise not to enter Hell. We can war in the physical world, but you do not get to chase us here."

"Really?"

"Oh, we would win, that is certain, but if you set foot in Hell, well . . . your heart weighed less than a feather for a reason. You've been rewarded. No hell may hold you or even accept you. If you came here, it would cause . . . problems. I'll deal with the paperwork if I must, but it would be an exceedingly large amount, so I'd rather you considered my offer."

Paperwork, huh?

"Can you put up with that?" The question was to Marilyn.

"Of course I can, but Eric—"

"Done then." A crowd was gathering on the other side of the bar-rier, demons of all shapes and sizes, and the most frightening of all a human-looking demon with empty eyes and a bound journal in which he wrote with a bone quill in blood he drew by stabbing the nib into his forearm as he wrote. "And Marilyn gets to step outside and give me a hug good-bye."

Scrytha looked at the wizened little man with his quill and bushy eyebrows. "Does Fair Standards and Equitability find it acceptable?"

The little man nodded, bone quill scratching red lines in his note-book.

"Done."

"Promise to adhere to the agreement," Scrytha said.

"I promise."

Marilyn stepped beyond the gates of Hell through an open arch-way in the wall as if it had always been there. I fought the urge to grab her and run away with her. It wouldn't have worked, but not to even try . . .

I turned human as I hugged her, and it felt natural again to be in that form. She was warm and I was cold. I held her hand in mine and slipped the rings on her finger, wedding band first, then engagement ring.

"I'll find a way to get you back," I whispered.

"Damn it, Eric." She wiped away a tear. "Don't do anything stupid."

"I'll find a way," I said as she was drawn back through the archway, before I could kiss her or do anything else. "I promise."

As I said the words, a Klaxon called, alarm bells rang, and other noises like elephants farting to death through didgeridoos, growling mice, and trampled zebra split the air.

Scrytha spat on the ground. "Bastard."

"What'd I break?"

Greta covered her ears. "Too loud!"

"There's a hope in Hell." Scrytha took Marilyn by the wrist and held her hand up for inspection. "It's none of your concern. Depart as promised."

Greta and I climbed into Fang, and before I could ask if anyone knew how to get out of here, we pulled away. Fang knew. I tucked Percy's glasses in the glove box and closed my eyes, in case I wasn't supposed to look back, and held Greta's hand to make sure she didn't go anywhere.

"How are you going to rescue Old Mom?"

I didn't answer. I couldn't. I had no idea. But maybe Percy would . . . or Magbidion.

"When we get you back to your body, I want you to do me a favor. Okay?"

"Anything, Dad."

I explained the favor and, as I suspected, Greta was happy to comply.

52

GRETA:

STUPID PET TRICKS

New Mom, Beatrice, and Auntie Shenanigans got home from Gay Paree the next night, but they didn't look too happy. Dad and I met them at the airport, and Daddy left me in charge of Auntie while he, New Mom, and Beatrice went off in a taxi to screw or unpack or whatever they do when I'm not around. Auntie Rachel's eyes had bags under them.

"Are you resisting Dad?" I asked.

"Fuck you, cunt rag," Rachel snapped.

"Be nice," I ordered.

"Yes." She kicked the concrete wall of the airport parking deck. "Ma'am."

"Aw." I pinched her cheeks. "You don't have to call me ma'am. Magical Pretty Lady Greta will do."

"What?"

"Magical"—I stepped over to her in a wink of speed—"Pretty"—spread her legs into a split—"Lady"—dug my claws into her thighs and buttocks for balance and lifted her over my head, banging her head against the ceiling of the deck—"Greta"—and bit into her femoral artery. She screamed and it surprised me when the security guard, doing his rounds, opened fire. I dropped Rachel as the shots pelted my arms and torso. I turned to face him, blood dripping from my fangs and the scent of Rachel's private parts on my cheek.

"Holy shit," he babbled into his walkie-talkie. "I've got a fucking vampire up here . . . a real one!"

"So you make me pay a fang fee," I shouted. "You don't get to shoot me."

Fang clipped the guard from behind, slurped him up, and rolled back into the parking spot in which Dad had left him.

"Did you see that, Auntie Shenanigans?"

"Yes, Magical Pretty Lady Greta."

"What do you think happened?"

"Eric said he knocked down the Highland Towers and killed Lord Phillip?"

"Uh-huh."

"The Veil of Scrythax was underneath it in a vault. My guess is, Eric broke the veil. And when he killed Lord Phillip, all the spells Phillip used to control the police and city security personnel . . . went away."

"Cool!"

I grabbed her leg and dragged her across the deck to Fang, leaving road rash on her butt and part of her left arm. "Will you please stop?" Her eyes ran with tears. "Eric won't let me use any magic, so you might be enjoying this, but it hurts."

"I'm the boss, applesauce." I broke her left tibia and fibula with a twist of the wrist and she howled in pain. Then I snapped her femur over my knee, gouging my claws into her belly button to shock her awake when she passed out.

"Daddy told me what happened to me was your fault," I hissed at her. "He said you made a deal with Winter and then fucked over all of us."

"Be mad at Winter then." Rachel grabbed at her leg, trying to do something to help the pain as the break began to heal crooked. "He—"

"Winter's a vampire." I pulled her femur straight, let it set a second, then did my best with the lower bones. "Vampires do that kind of thing. Besides, he sang my favorite songs to apologize. In advance. And he's prettier than you are."

"I'm sorry," she said. "What can I do to make it better?"

I removed her piercings one by one, the quick way, and I think I know which hurt the most. Did touching her there to get at it make me a lesbian?

Nah.

She shook at my feet and another guard stepped off the elevator. "She's hurt," I shouted. "That other guard shot her and ran off." His confusion lasted a few seconds, more than enough time for me to make it across the deck and tear his legs off. Blood dripped from my hands and down my chest as I walked casually back across the deck.

"Is that enough?" she asked. "Will Eric be happy now?"

"Oh." I kissed her on the forehead, leaving security guard juice there when I pulled away. "Poor Auntie Shenanigans. Daddy didn't say to punish you; he said to kill you. I think he was afraid you'd talk him out of it." Her little finger came off easily at the joint and I stuck it in the side of my mouth like a cigar. "He didn't say how fast, though."

"Please, no, Greta." Rachel tucked herself into a fetal position. "Let me go. I'll do anything." Her butterfly tattoo glowed and she didn't wince as it burned her face. "I'm stronger than him. I . . . I . . ."

She had trouble talking once I started kicking her in the stomach. I guess there's important stuff in there for humans. I heard sirens in the distance. Would Daddy mind if I killed all the police? Probably. With a deep sigh, I held Rachel up by the throat.

"Daddy gave you three options. You 'member? Option one was to go away, which you didn't. Option two was to stay and be good, which you didn't. And option three . . ." I turned her around to face Fang.

"Lady Scrytha," she choked. "I accept."

"Fang," I ordered. "Sit."

Fang's rear wheels clung to the ground and while he slowly rotated them, he lifted his front end up into the air, headlights an inch from the roof.

"Good boy." I tossed Rachel against his undercarriage and she stuck there.

"Please," Rachel bawled. "Lady Scrytha, I accept!"

Rip. Crack. Slurp. And her bones landed in the trunk. I have to say, her lungs weren't nearly so pretty as Telly's.

"Fang, down."

His front wheels touched the ground again and I plopped into the driver's seat. "I'm still hungry," I said wistfully. "I wish she'd been twins."

Fang replied with "Evil Woman" by Electric Light Orchestra.

"I suppose," I said. "Let's go."

We drove past the police and I rubbed the blood into my skin, surprised at how much it would absorb. With Auntie Shenanigans taken care of, that just left Kitty. Kitty Talbot was still MIA, but I knew he'd be back. Daddy was home and Talbot wouldn't stay away for long. I had a message for Kitty, a personal matter between me and him. Private.

I flexed my claws, frowning at the chipped nail polish. Uneven nails are trashy. Maybe I should have had Rachel do them for me before I killed her.

"Hindsight," I murmured. "Hey, what do lungs taste like?"

Fang played "The Chicken Dance" and if my bladder still worked, I'd have peed myself laughing.

Three blocks from the Demon Heart, Talbot conveniently

appeared. He opened the passenger door and stepped in while Fang was stopped at a light.

"It would have been cooler if you'd jumped into the car." Fang rolled forward when the light turned green. "Opening the door was kinda pansy."

"I'll do better next time."

"If I don't kill you before next time, Kitty Cat." At the thought of killing Talbot, knowledge queued up in my brain the same way it did when I was hunting Vlads. Just as the data on their kill conditions came to me on the third night of the hunt, I now knew how to kill Talbot. You had to skin him alive first. How funny!

"It takes a lot to kill a Mouser, Greta."

"Oh, I know. First, I'd have to skin you alive, which would be cool because there's more than one way to do that, so you wouldn't know exactly how I was going to do it."

Talbot froze.

"And then I'd have to tie your neck, hands, and feet with your own intestines, tear out your organs and fill your chest cavity with sand, salt, or sawdust." We turned the corner and stopped in front of the De-mon Heart. "It's amazing how creative you can get when killing a Mouser. Nowhere near as specific as killing a Vlad."

"Greta, who told you that?"

"I died of my own accord, walked the Paths of the Dead to the edge of Hell, and then came back again." I tried to make my voice sound spooky and mysterious. "I know how to kill all sorts of things now. But we don't have to worry about that, do we, Kitty Cat?"

"We don't?"

"No, because you're never going to leave me when I need you, not ever again, and also you're going to say you're sorry and paint my claws and toenails Candy Apple Red. And you're going to tell me all about cat sex even though Dad told you not to tell me. Aren't you?"

"Sure, Greta." Tension. Edge of combat tension eased out of his muscles. He'd coiled to pounce, but so had I. "I'm sorry, where's the nail polish?"

Fang dropped open the glove box and Talbot fetched the bottle and a small round tub of nail polish remover.

"You want to do this here?" he asked. "It might mess up the uphol-stery."

"Fang would just regenerate it." I kicked off my shoes and put my foot in Talbot's lap. "Now, tell me all about what happened while you were gone."

53

ERIC:

SHAKING HANDS

Tabitha suddenly turned and slapped me, which answered my question about Rachel's death undoing the magic memory whammy I'd had done to her.

"You had a three-way with me and my sister on our wedding night and then you had my sister erase it?" She slapped me again. "You let Magbidion show Rachel . . . *Rachel* . . . how to alter a vampire's memory?"

"Technically, it was a four-way because of the Asian girl."

Claws sank into my shoulder and Tabitha hurled me at the wall of my bedroom at the Pollux. I spread my arms and legs, letting my impact hit in as wide an area as possible. It hurt like a bitch, but at least I didn't go through the wall.

"If you hadn't had her learn—"

"I know."

Her hands were in my hair and suddenly she was using my noggin for a battering ram.

"What happened in Paris. What happened here. It was all your fault." Each word acted as some strange punctuation, spacing out each new meeting of my head and my bedroom wall.

"Right again," I managed to choke out.

"Damn it!" She climbed off my back and I rolled over. She sat on the edge of the bed, crying real tears.

"I'm sorry."

"I know you're sorry, you dumbass." She wiped at her eyes, makeup smearing. "Of course you're sorry. If you weren't sorry, I'd know what to do. It would be the last straw, but this . . . What am I supposed to do with you apologizing? And meaning it?!"

I sighed. "Maybe this will help." I slid to a sitting position. "I'm go-ing after Marilyn. I saw her down there and . . . I can't let her stay down there, even if I have to destroy her soul. I bought her some time, but it's just another kind of torture . . . and I can't just charge in after her—there's that whole deal with Scrytha."

"Well obviously." Tabitha threw her arms up. "It's you. The rules don't apply to you. You just do whatever the hell you want and—"

"I'll understand if you want a divorce," I said softly. "I mean, I don't know if Rachel was already controlling you or not, but if you want one, I—"

Tabitha got up, and I winced despite myself because letting your wife beat the shit out of you without taking a swing back at her is harder than you might think—even if you have it coming and know it. "You can have pretty much whatever you want, but . . ."

She put a finger to my lips.

"Wait here." Tabitha pulled me to my feet.

"Why?"

"Because I'm not going to Hell in these shoes." She kissed my cheek and turned to go.

"Like I said, I can't go down there again, not to fight," I said, "but it's nice to know you're in." It's official. I will never understand women. "Let me go run it by Magbidion."

"Don't get kidnapped," Tabitha called after me as the door shut.

"You don't deserve that one," said a ghost with a familiar southern drawl. "She went to Hell and back for—"

"No." I scanned the hallway and saw a figure by the rail at the top of the stairs. "That's what I did for Greta." It could have been John Paul, but his clothes were untorn, and his neck was all in one piece. Clean-shaven except for his mustache, the cowboy wore a blue button-up shirt with clean pants. Even his coat was clean and whole. The hat and cigar were the same, though.

"John Paul." I gaped. "How the hell?"

"That's fer me to know, son." He smiled and took a puff off his ci-gar, the last puff, and this time the cigar burned down. His eyes closed as he let the smoke out through his nostrils, the vapor pooling around his body. "I ain't one to tell tales what ain't mine to tell. Let's jest say you ain't likely to be borrowin' that gun o' mine agin fer quite some time. She ain't likely to do ya much good, the shape she wound up in, anyhow."

"So you're free?" I laughed. "That's great!"

John Paul looked at the cigar before setting it on the rail as if he hadn't heard me. "That was one fine cigar."

"So—"

"Nope," he cut me off. "That ain't the word I want to hear. I want to hear the one you interrupted me with a moment ago."

"No?"

"That's the one." He nodded, touching his neck self-consciously out of years of habit. "But it ain't a question. Say it like you mean it."

"No," I said halfheartedly.

"Like you mean it, I said," Courtney barked. "Like Greta is asking you if she can come along on the little vacation to the underworld that you're plannin'."

"No!"

"Fine." His eyes lit from within, and the light was warm and pleasant like sunshine and fresh-cut grass. "That's jest fine. You remember that word, them two important letters, and you jest keep sayin' them when you talk ta the lady waitin' for you downstairs."

"Lady?" I looked over the rail, saw no one, and glanced back, but he was gone, leaving nothing but his still-smoldering cigar on the railing.

I smelled brimstone and started down. Faint at first, the odor grew as I neared the doors to the theater. Pushing the doors open, I saw a woman in a white dress and started toward the stage.

"Hello, Mr. Courtney." Lady Scrytha stood center stage, lit by a single spotlight, the jewels studding her twin ram's horns sending sparkling sprays of color out from her face. Her gown was low cut and she wore it well, like a movie star. Lauren Bacall in *To Have and Have Not* maybe . . . except when Bacall wore high heels, they weren't cloven.

"No."

"You can't say no to a hello." Her tail twitched, peeking out below the hemline of the dress. "We got off to a bad start earlier, and I'd like to make amends."

"No." I turned on my heel, heading up the aisle.

"You and I both know that you'll be coming for Marilyn."

I stopped.

"You'll find a way, but while you're down below, I'll wreak havoc above, and when you come back they might all be gone."

"You don't want to go there." I turned back to her, hands clenched into tight fists.

"No, I don't," Lady Scrytha agreed. "It's a waste of effort on both our parts. You see, Mr. Courtney, I finally understand what my father and certain other supernatural beings see in you."

No. I tried to say it, but the word didn't come. My mouth was dry, even of blood.

"Do you have any idea how many prophesies you've invalidated, without even meaning to, over the last few decades?"

"No." See, there it was, I could still say it. It's an easy word. Two letters.

N + O = NO.

Simple.

"It's a large number." She walked off the stage, down an unseen stairway, shocks of fire sparking from her hooves at each step. "You see, I thought you were completely unimportant, because none of the prophesies are about you. You aren't pivotal in any great battle. You don't lead an army of light or an army of darkness. But what you do is even more astonishing."

"I'm good in bed," I told her, "but I wouldn't say it was world-altering."

"Never underestimate the importance of those talents, Mr. Courtney, but those are far from your greatest assets." She set foot on the aisle, and I winced, but there was no fire; my carpet was safe. "You can change the game. Bend the rules. You can affect the whole."

"Now, there you're wrong." I shook my head. "I've never been a very good masseuse. I do okay, but—"

"Heroes are a dime a dozen, Mr. Courtney," she said impatiently. I noticed the spotlight had continued to follow her under the mezzanine, at an impossible angle, and I searched for the source but couldn't find it. Magic. "Villains are a penny a pound, but those who can alter the status quo on a fundamental level, redraw the board as it were. Well, those—"

"A whole quarter?"

She gave an exasperated laugh, a sharp exhalation of air. "Far more than that."

"Well, I ain't for sale."

"Obviously, but perhaps." Her voice went low and husky, and she reminded me of Bacall all over again when she asked Bogie if he knew how to whistle. "Perhaps you are for rent?"

"No." I began to relax. Maybe John Paul had been worrying about nothing. Maybe.

"Not even if I gave her back to you."

My heart beat twice and Rachel was dead, so I knew it wasn't her doing.

"Her who?" Like I didn't know exactly who.

"Marilyn. Your Marilyn. Maiden name Robinson." She stepped closer, her voice dropping in volume, her body leaning close to mine, her cheek touching mine as she whispered in my ear. "You proposed to her once and you died two weeks before the wedding day. She cheated on you with your best friend and regretted it for the rest of her life. The woman whose soul my offspring used to try to trick you into losing your own. That 'her.'"

"She'd have to be young again." I reached into my wallet and pulled out the picture of Marilyn on the Duo-Glide. "This young."

"Easily done."

"And she'd have to be healthy again and stay healthy."

"I can make a true immortal of her if you wish, like your dear old war buddy James."

"And she can't be mind-controlled or hypnotized or under some sort of geas. She'd have to be her own person."

"Of course."

"What do you want me for?"

"What does it matter?" Scrytha laughed. "This is Marilyn. I won't pit you against Greta or any of your creations, but I will use you for what you're good for: to break prophesies. Those 'best laid schemes o' mice and men' of which Robert Burns spoke. You will help ensure they go awry. Does it matter how?"

"When do I get her back?"

"If you say yes now, I can have her here tomorrow."

My heart beat two more times, stuttered, and kept right on beating. I heard the sound of feet pounding down the stairs, then Tabitha threw open the lobby doors.

"Eric," she said, chest heaving. "Don't you dare."

I looked away from Tabitha, unable to meet her eyes, so when I spoke, my words were directed at the floor. When it comes to vampires across the years in books, in movies, or on television, there are certain rules:

Buffy loves Angel.

Louis loves Lestat.

Bella loves Edward.

And Eric . . . Eric loves Marilyn.

"I'll do it," I said. "Whatever it is." I put my hand in Lady Scrytha's and shook it firmly. "I'll do it."

EPILOGUE
AS TOLD BY EBON WINTER

WINTER:

I WIN AGAIN

They came into the Artiste Unknown like rats fleeing a storm. Confused. Lost. Panic in their eyes and shrillness in their whispers. Panic. Marvelous! Marvelous! MAR-velous panic!

One by one I sensed them, giving Andre telepathic instructions from my bed in the ductwork, above the sprinklers. Hidden. With a friend. We watched, my friend and I, as Andre shifted the vermin from one portion of the club to another, quietly sorting out the Vlads and Masters from the general populace, sending them to the Velvet down below where quarters were more intimate.

"Mother Goose," I said into my microphone. "This is Rock-star." Melvin does so love code names.

"I copy you, Rockstar."

"How are the preparations?"

"Everything's okay on this end, Rockstar." Static and the sound of a van engine filled a long pause. "You're sure you're well above the red line?"

"Why, aren't you the overprotective hen, darling? I had Andre draw a blue line two feet above the red line and I'm half a foot above that one."

Most vampires don't sleep in coffins, but I do. Concealed in what many would presume to be a central portion of the exposed ventilation system, I rest snugly in a soundproof steel box complete with a Sealy Posturepedic mattress (custom fitted, of course), a high-tech surveillance system Melvin made for me (it even picks up vampires), room for a second occupant, and a six-hour supply of oxygen . . . for those who need that sort of thing.

Father Ike, my friend, watched the monitors, light from the black-and-white displays moving like shadows on his stern priestly visage.

"And this is half the vampires in the city?" he asked.

"Closer to sixty percent," I crowed, "but the best part is, it represents ninety percent of the Masters, eighty percent of the Vlads, and the most powerful of the Soldiers. Almost no Drones, but who can bear to be around them in the first place?"

"And it will work?"

"How dare you, Ike?" I swatted his shoulder, giddy at the tinge of flame that warmed my fingers upon contact, however brief. "It's an open secret that Melvin works for me, and when I told a few discreet friends (all the most incorrigible gossips) I'd warded the establishment and had a plan for dealing with the failure of the Veil of Scrythax . . . well, it guaranteed they'd come, didn't it?"

"This is why you had me agree to marry Eric and Tabitha?" Father Ike sniffed at the burned smell of my fingers.

"No, Ike." I clicked the walkie-talkie button. "Rockstar to Mother Goose. Phase one of Operation Dorothy Gale is complete. Prepare to begin phase two."

"Dorothy Gale?" Ike asked.

"Of course. We dropped a house on the Wicked Witch of the East."

"The Highland Towers on Lord Phillip?"

"While displacing the other most politically important vermin in the city." I nodded, hands clasped beneath my chin. "And now, we deal with the metaphorical Wicked Witch of the West."

"Is Pretty Boy clear?" Melvin asked.

"Just a moment." I watched my best thrall, Andre, conversing with Lady Gabriella.

"Winter," Andre thought at me, "she suspects something."

"Let her go, then," I whispered telepathically. "In fact, see her out and offer to drive her to Sable Oaks."

"Of course, Master."

She seemed agreeable to that, the greedy little rat. I watched Andre lead her out. I focused on the door as it shut, the click of the lock.

"He's clear, Mother Goose."

"Spikes and sunlamps are set for the Velvet, Rockstar."

"How does that fit into the Wizard of Oz?" Father Ike asked.

"It doesn't." I watched my waiters and servants exiting the building, none at the same time, all through different exits. I observed closely as the exits shut. "The Velvet is more along the lines of Indiana Jones, a riff on the temple sequence at the beginning of *Raiders of the*

Lost Ark. Everyone knows that Dorothy threw a bucket of water on the Wicked Witch of the West."

"That would take holy water, Winter, and I haven't—"

"Of course not, Ike," I purred. "You're far too squeamish. I had the Lycan Diocese send some down. They were quite amenable."

"Mother Goose." I blinked my eyes rapidly to ensure I wouldn't need to blink again during the show. "Shields up."

A thin red glow spread out from along a red line two and a half feet below our hiding space in the ductwork. Unseen by those without particularly acute mystic sight, the ward rolled down and trapped them all.

"Shields up, Rockstar," Melvin said.

"Make them dance for me, Melvin." My words rushed together, excitement rippling through me, heightening my senses. "Start the double feature."

Screams can make a kind of music, a terrible symphony of pain. Mine was writ in treachery and surprise, in sizzling skin and wood-pierced hearts and bubbling blood. It's saddening to admit Father Ike seemed to lack the refined ear I have.

"I know you hate them, Winter, after what they did to you and to John," he said finally, "but this—"

"Is just the beginning," I crowed. "I know. We're going to kill them all, Father. And then, Eric Courtney is going to help us whether he wants to or not."

"Us?" Father Ike pulled away from me as far as the close quarters would allow. "I'm helping *John* through this, Winter. I cannot be a party to this kind of slaughter. Not all vampires are evil. Some, like you, who have never given in to the urge to feed on human blood . . ."

"Not you, Father, I know that."

I held up my treasured possession, a small crystallized orb. "The immortals may have seized his head from the Knights Templar, but they did not escape with all of him."

"All of who, Winter?"

"Scrythax," I answered smoothly. "I have his eye, and with it . . . oh, the futures I can see."

BURNED

To the readers:

For buying my books, reading the words,
getting the jokes, and enjoying the ride.

ACKNOWLEDGMENTS

This book, like all of the others, had a lot of help. To everyone who pitched in, cheered me on, caught typos, misspellings, and made me rewrite until I'd written what I meant to say instead of something else . . . Thanks!

1

ERIC

ALL A PART OF THE PLAN

Vampires burn.

It's a rule.

A blanket hit me from behind, smothering the flames, and I felt strong arms around me, patting out the more stubborn patches around my neck and shoulders. I pushed Talbot away and rubbed at the smoldering remnants of the sun's wrath the same way a mortal man might dry himself after a shower.

"You could have just turned into a mouse," Talbot said. "I would have carried you in from the car."

Talbot's a mouser. He'd probably tell you that I'm his vampire. A pet of sorts. Mousers are basically cats that can be humans when they feel like it. Talbot has been with me since El Segundo, when the world went crazy and I had to play the hero. He believes I have hidden depths. I think he's deluded.

I tossed the blanket on the floor and stared up at him. Talbot is bigger than me, over six feet tall, and he has better taste in clothes. He's almost always wearing a bespoke suit, with well-tailored silks and satins setting off the dark color of his skin, the bright green of his eyes, and his bald head. I, on the other hand, have all my hair and prefer jeans and a T-shirt.

Smoke rose off my T-shirt as I seated myself calmly in a metal folding chair, waiting for my burns to heal.

"I forgot the sun was out," I said with a shrug.

I've never been too good at keeping track of whether it's day or night outside . . . which may sound funny coming from a person who catches fire if he gets it wrong, but it's the way I am. When I died (okay, if we're being picky, I was murdered), it was daytime when I rose as a vampire, so at least it's not a new development or anything.

I needed to keep it together. This was going to be The Big Day.

With an exasperated sigh, I stopped worrying about having forgotten the sun and decided to blame it on the sunproof glass they have in the back of the squad cars in Void City. One of the perks I get is cop-chauffeur service; I'll explain why later. If I ride around in a squad car too long, though, I forget why it's so bright outside.

Bright.

It was bright inside the warehouse, too. The place was old, but the lights worked well. I closed my eyes, waiting for the last trace of pain to vanish with the burns. My mind doesn't always work properly. It works better at night, but I still have good days and bad days. I needed today to be a good one. This was it. Day number one of my Big Plan.

When I closed my eyes, my other senses kicked into overdrive on instinct. The sound of heartbeats came first. I'm always aware of them on some level, the heartbeats of those who have them. It's worse when I'm hungry. I hadn't fed yet, and there were a lot of heartbeats to hear. Talbot's heart—a strong steady thumping; Magbidion's—a fluttering weak sound; and all the cops who were in on at least this portion of my Big Plan . . . their hearts beat in different ways: harder, softer, faster, slower . . . as unique to me as a face or a voice.

After the heartbeats, other sounds came into play. Outside the warehouse, I knew Sal was still sitting in the front seat of the squad car that had driven me here, wearing a portable radio, with one earbud tucked into the collar of his uniform and the other snaked up into his right ear. He and Little Carl have never been able to agree on a station, so he listens to an earbud and Carl listens to silence. Vampire hearing is good enough that I heard Sal's favorite station as well as he could. Better, even.

I don't know how the station does it yet, but when the Veil of Scrythax, the mystical artifact that used to prevent mundane citizens from seeing or remembering encounters with the supernatural, got ripped to shreds last year, 100.6 FM (WVCT—Void City Talk Radio) kept broadcasting the same as it always has. Mundane listeners seem to hear Christian or sports talk programming, but the rest of us hear the never-ending jabber of Sly Imp: Void City's demonic voice of the airwaves. The damned shock jock is distracting enough to make me forget about the sun, although apparently, that doesn't take much. I'd been thinking about something he said, kind of a tagline of sorts: "In Void City, the vampires run the town, the cops are on the take, and the werewolves have found religion."

Sly Imp's voice caught my attention, and I focused in for a moment. If I recognized the background music, Denis Leary's "Asshole," correctly, Sly was about to discuss me.

"And what do we think of our new Lord and Master, the great and powerful raging erection that is Eric Courtney?"

"Cue laugh track," I mumbled. And as if on my cue, the laugh track sounded. *Who the hell still uses a laugh track?*

"I mean, is it just me, or if our fearless leader is going to fly around in his combat form killing things left, right, and sideways, does he really have to do it with his 'staff of office' swinging in the breeze? We know it's big, pal. You don't have to wave it around out in the open like that. Save that thrill for the little woman back home. Am I right? Oh, oh, and speaking of the little woman . . ."

I really need to put some pants on the über vamp. A pair of shorts. Something. The über vamp is my "big bad combat" mode: all leather wings and ebony claws. Real balls-out vampire badass mojo. Quite literally balls out in my case. I don't know why I can shape-change into a mouse and back while keeping my clothes, but I always wind up naked when I'm the über vamp.

I tuned out Sly's ongoing roast and concentrated on the task at hand. Lord Phillip, the former vampiric ruler of Void City, never had the kind of trouble I was having. Killing him had set loose such a world of shit that I was still dealing with it almost a year later. In my own defense, I hadn't intended to take over.

Lord Phillip had been a twisted freak, which was fine with me—or would have been, provided he kept out of my way. I'm not the sort of guy who runs around righting wrongs and slaying dragons. But Phil messed with Greta, my daughter. She's adopted, one hell of a vampire, and can generally take care of herself, but if you mess with her, I'll kill you, knock your ivory tower down, set it on fire, and slaughter all your friends. It's a rule.

Unfortunately, the act of following said rule put me in charge.

I don't like responsibility, but it's not something I shirk, which is why my singed sorry ass was seated on but not sticking to (thanks to my blue jeans) the aforementioned folding chair, watching Captain Stacey in his office on the other side of town, through the eyes of one of my thralls.

It had been almost a year since I'd knocked down Lord Phil's Highland Towers and taken over, and this was a part of The Plan I couldn't put off any longer. Like I said before, I had a plan. If you know me, you know the idea of me with a plan should scare the hell out of you.

Maybe sometimes in the past I've been willfully ignorant, but I'm not stupid. Remember that bit about not shirking my duty? Keep it in mind. Step one of The Big Plan involved just that: doing my duty. It also involved Captain Stacey of the VCPD.

Captain Stacey had been in charge of the VCPD since the late sixties. Well, mid- to late sixties. Shortly after my death, let's say. He surely must have felt safe, protected, sitting there in his office. No mortal man would be a threat to him. His door wasn't locked. His gun wasn't even on his desk or at his side. I'm sure a being like him doesn't feel the need for such things the way a mortal might. As a mouser, like Talbot, Stacey was nigh immortal, incredibly hard to kill, and his morals were, to say the least, mutable and open to negotiation. I mean, mousers basically have the same morals a cat has. Even so, there are good cats and bad cats.

Stacey was a bad cat. The VCPD badge with his name on it meant he was part of the biggest gang in Void City. Every last cop was either crooked or kept under his mystic control by an ages-old deal with the Mages Guild. A thing like Stacey made the perfect public servant for Vampire High Society. For years I had no interest in him at all, even when he was hired to help capture me a few years ago. I've been historically willing to ignore all kinds of heinous crap as long as the other denizens of Void City stayed out of my way or were willing to offer a simple apology.

That changed when I walked the Paths of the Dead to get my daughter back. Ever since, I'd been remembering some things. Things I was finding it harder and harder to ignore. Too many things, maybe. As a result, I'd been making plans and recruiting allies.

Through the eyes of one of my newest allies, I watched Captain Stacey sitting at that desk. And I remembered it. It was a classic steel tanker desk. It brought with it flashes of memory: eating lunch with Marilyn, being intimate with her, looking at crime scene photos, drinking with Sal and Little Carl . . . Stacey couldn't see me, of course, because I was in a warehouse all the way across town.

How could I see him?

Interesting question.

Vampires can create a bond with humans, share a little of their power. The human generally does the vampire's bidding and, in exchange, gets increased longevity and some measure of vampiric resilience and strength. They're called thralls. As a rule, I don't like having any because the whole "master" thing makes me uncomfortable.

Now that I have a bunch of them, I've been trying to think of them as little helpers. *Not just for Santa anymore. Heh.* Like it or not, I needed them for the plan to work. And at least they'd all been willing volunteers. While it is possible for a vampire to enslave a human, make a living person into an unwilling thrall, I've never done it, nor will I. My ex-buddy Roger did that to Marilyn (the love of my mortal life), and for that reason alone, I'm glad I killed him. And speaking of killing . . .

Refocusing on my own surroundings, I glanced around the warehouse. It was basically empty except for an abandoned set of old metal folding chairs. Magbidion—I guess you could call him my personal mage, another of my little helpers—was leaning against the wall. Talbot took a seat next to me in one of the empty chairs. A two-way radio indicated in glowing red numbers that it was on the right channel.

Talbot coughed. "Well?"

I closed my eyes and checked in with each of my little helpers. "Everything's ready. Do a quick look around to see if you spot anything?"

"Sure." Talbot stood, smoothing out his slacks. The sunlight outside made him seem bigger, more imposing, than he actually is. Maybe it was the way it reflected off the ebony skin of his bald head or the way he filled up the space. Could just be that he's that much bigger than I am.

Magbidion slumped into the vacant chair. His hands were shaky, his long greasy black hair swept back out of his face. He'd been overdoing it for almost a year. It's hard to keep spells running for long stretches of time, and Mags had been hiding so many of my dirty little secrets for so long, it was no surprise the strain was showing.

At night, I'm not what I used to be . . . and thanks to Magbidion, the number of people who know that can be counted on one hand. He's hiding my thralls, too. Normally, other vampires can sense them, can tell who's a thrall and who isn't. For the time being, all my new thralls are secret. That takes a lot of magic mojo.

"You sure you're up to this?" I asked him.

"When the demon who owns my soul comes for it, will you really feed him to Talbot?" Eating demons is one of Talbot's talents. I don't know how he fits the whole thing inside, but I've seen him slurp up a demon twice his size without so much as an untamed burp or excess bowel movement. That's not a typical mouser trick, though. It seems to be unique to Talbot. Maybe he got it from his mom. I met her in the underworld, a cute little bloodred kitty cat that could probably tear me and a whole army of me's to shreds. Name's Sekhmet.

I realized Magbidion was still waiting for my answer. "Yeah. Of course. Demons are assholes."

"Then I'll manage," he said. The tired smile on his face was born of a long time without hope followed by a sudden change that might make everything right again. I was familiar with that feeling. I had it then. I still do. When I'd gone to the underworld, I'd gotten back more than just my daughter. I'd found hope, too.

Talbot leaned back in through the warehouse door. "I'd have the SWAT team and the uniforms pull back another fifty yards, but other than that, you're good."

"Even the squad car?"

"Yeah. Stacey knows you've been using it, and he'll wonder why they didn't call this in."

I gave those mental orders, listened as the extra yardage piped Sly Imp's yammering down low enough that I couldn't really make out the words anymore, then pulled my smartphone out of my jeans pocket. I dialed in Stacey's desk number and, through the eyes of his deputy, watched him watch it ring. He took a sip of coffee, swallowed slowly, then answered the call on speaker. I hate being on speaker.

"Stacey."

"This is Eric." I looked at Talbot while I spoke, wanting him to give me a look or something if things sounded off. "I need a favor."

"Been a while since I heard from you, Mr. Courtney."

I laughed at that. He almost sounded respectful. I guess killing Lord Phil had bought me a little bonus respect in Stacey's eyes.

"Yeah, well, I haven't been sloppy lately, but I need you now."

"I'll send a few—"

"No. I need *you* out here," I cut him off, "and I need it kept quiet. Not a word in any log or a call ahead to the Mages Guild. I can't even write you a check for it. Everything has to be off the books and under the table." The Mages Guild had worked hard to fill in the gaps that the Veil of Scrythax didn't cover or didn't handle well enough. Now they were handling the whole ball of wax, and the strain on their resources was showing.

"You've never asked that before . . ." There was an implied question there.

"Can you do it or not, Stacey?" I grabbed one of the metal folding chairs next to me and hurled it straight down at the concrete floor. It came apart, scarring the concrete, the pieces clattering to the floor.

"Of course I can, Mr. Courtney." I watched him smile at what he took to be my little display of anger. "With Lord Phillip gone, you're the boss."

"Good." I gave him directions. "Get your ass out here. I already have Magbidion here to help with the cleanup, but I need to walk you through what happened, and then I need some advice."

"What the hell did you do, Courtney?"

"Get out here and you'll know," I said, thumbing the call to an end.

Talbot whistled. "What's he doing?"

"Disregarding my instructions and heading this way." Through borrowed eyes, I watched Stacey tell his deputy, one of my newest thralls, that the Mages Guild should be called if he didn't check back in about half an hour. Stacey walked out into the sunlight, and I watched until he was out of sight.

I clicked on the radio. "Melvin?"

"There's no Melvin here," Melvin said testily.

"Half-n-half calling Mother Goose," I said with a sigh. "Come in, Mother Goose."

"Half-n-half, this is Mother Goose. Come in."

"How's our kitty kat? Over."

"I'm watching his GPS now. He looks to be heading straight your way. He also called the on-duty mage and reported himself en route to a vampire call. Over."

"And, just to clarify, you are the on-duty mage, Mother Goose? Over."

"That I am, Half-n-half. Over."

"Rockstar asks that you remember the favor. Over."

"Will do, Half-n-half. Mother Goose over and out."

"Half-n-half?" Talbot asked with a low, velvety chuckle.

"Ebon Winter's way of keeping me in my place. Or something."

"I don't like that vampire," Talbot said, more to himself than to me.

"Me, either." I stood and started stripping down to my jeans and belt. Then I called in the next part of the plan. The large loading doors of the warehouse opened, and thirty men and women dressed in casual clothes entered. The afternoon sun cast additional illumination across a swath of empty warehouse. It had been abandoned for years, and graffiti covered parts of the floor as well as the walls.

"You're all volunteers," I said as my claws slid out with a familiar creepy nail-bed crawling sensation. Twinges of pain sprouted in my gums as my fangs came out to play, too. "If you want to back out, do it now. I won't hold it against any of you. This is dangerous as hell and there's every chance some of you—maybe all of you—could die. I'll do my best to make sure that doesn't happen, but once we get going, it won't be up to me anymore. Talbot will not step in to stop me."

Some of them said no. Others simply shook their heads.

"Then let's make this look good, shall we?"

I charged into their midst, and the blood that flowed was as real as it gets. So was the pain.

By the time Captain Stacey walked in, the sun outside filled the warehouse to the midway point, picking out the mangled bodies strewn from one end of the warehouse to the other, highlighting the remains of a slaughter that caked the concrete with blood, urine, excrement, and fear. Magbidion and Talbot stood off to one side, letting Stacey see the whole thing in one glance. His gaze lingered longest on a body near the west side of the warehouse: a woman named Katherine Marx—Officer Katherine Marx.

Stacey had always been able to control the good cops and compel them to do things they wouldn't normally do, make them forget what he wanted them to forget. I wasn't supposed to know it, no one was supposed to know it, but Stacey had been using the same ability that he used to wipe the minds of his subordinates to have his way with Katherine and a few of the other lady cops.

Katherine had been his favorite recently, and she was the granddaughter of a friend of mine, a friend who'd been a cop back when I was alive . . . Thanks to Magbidion's assistance and the peculiarities of my new nighttime circumstances, I was remembering all kinds of things from those days . . . back when . . . when I'd come home from Korea and Marilyn had convinced me to apply for captain of the VCPD. Katherine wasn't the only cop in the pile; in fact, they'd all been cops at one time or another, but she was the one who would distract him. You can't look at a dead lover and feel nothing. Not unless you're dead inside.

"Some of them are cops," I said.

Stacey looked up at me blankly, his eyes taking a few seconds to focus. Where Talbot was impressive and smooth, Stacey seemed a petty creature, his belly showing signs of trained muscle going to fat. His eyes, normally cold and emotionless—mercenary—now showed a broken warmth, a wet edge.

"What the fuck happened?" Stacey shouted, discarding the grief and giving in to rage. It was a move I'd made myself many times. It feels good, but it makes you stupid. Stupid was not a part of The Plan. Stacey saw the blood on my hands, coating my bare chest, my jeans, slicking my face like a gruesome moisturizer mask, and then he was in my face, shoving me back. "What the fuck did you do to my cops?"

"Curiosity," I said. *Killed the cat.*

"What?" He shoved me again. Hard. Hard enough to knock me back against a row of folding chairs. "What?"

Of course, the word wasn't meant for him. It was The Signal, a part of The Plan. With Stacey focused on me, Magbidion dropped one of the spells he'd been maintaining, the subtle one that kept the thirty men and women I'd fought (every last one of them another new thrall) from regenerating. He kept the other spells, including the massive one concealing their thralldom, up and running.

"Nobody preys on my cops, asshole!" Stacey transformed. I have to admit that I dig the way mousers change. They get to skip the snap, crackle, and ouch of a werewolf transformation and the aching discomfort of a vampiric one. A slow glow of golden light suffused his skin, flowing over him. As it faded, the man with the paunch was replaced by a seven-foot-tall, massively muscled feline beast with metallic gold claws and fangs, fur in patches of white and orange, and glowing star-sapphire eyes: the all-cat version of a well-done werewolf special effect.

Stacey yowled, swatting me to the ground with one massive paw. My chest sizzled where his claws punctured my skin, but the pain felt nice. The truth is, I deserve to hurt. I've killed thousands of humans over the years. I can't bring myself to feel bad about it, because becoming a vampire was never my decision—Scrythax, the demon with a wacky sense of redemption who created the Courtney Family Curse, is to blame for that. For years I tried to minimize the number of people I killed by running a club and feeding off my employees as much as possible. If animal blood worked for me, that would have been great, but it doesn't.

"Don't make me go über vamp on you, Stacey," I spat through gritted teeth.

He responded by disemboweling me and hurling me up into the rafters, where I clanged against the ceiling. When I came back down, he was even bigger and more muscular, standing about ten feet tall. His fangs and claws glowed to match his eyes, and I fought to hide my grin. Mousers are different from other supernatural creatures in a whole lot of ways, but one of those differences is stranger than the rest. They exist on more than one plane of existence at once (the physical world, the world of dreams, and something Talbot calls the Akasha), so . . . to kill one, you have to get him all on the same plane with you or be able to affect him on those other planes of reality, too. I glanced over at Talbot. Yep. The way Stacey looked now was his whole being all in one place.

I think he expected me to transform, to become the über vamp, but this wasn't my fight. It wasn't Talbot's, either. I boxed Stacey's pointy cat ears as he seized me in his paws, but if I hadn't started his ears ringing, the gunfire surely would have. The VCPD SWAT team rolled in wearing full supernatural suppression gear and carrying weapons made for taking down monsters. Holy symbols, Elder Signs, and other marks of magical protection bedecked their body armor. Not one of them looked the least bit friendly. And every single one of them was one of my thralls.

The opening volley, twelve shotguns loaded with the VCPD's specialized flechette rounds (twenty tiny flechettes in one cartridge—fourteen steel, four silver, one hardened wood, and a single gold one), blasted Stacey mercilessly, followed almost immediately by two cops with flamethrowers lighting the dirty bastard up as he turned. The VCPD was usually more concerned with protecting society from knowledge of the supernatural than taking the supernatural on head-to-head, but the previous management had equipped them for any eventuality, and this was their fight. Stacey had made them do unspeakable things, had corrupted everything that police were supposed to be, had raped their minds and some of their bodies . . . and now they all knew it.

"Hard to shift part of yourself elsewhere when you're pumped full of metal, isn't it?" I asked as I rose to my feet. Stacey didn't answer. He'd gone straight into that wounded-animal place mammals go when they're scared, confused, angry, and in pain.

Mousers are not easy to kill. It's a messy business. I wasn't staying for all of it. I had to get cleaned up anyway, because for once I had a bigger plan . . . and if somebody was going to screw it up by letting the cat out of the bag (okay, bad pun), it was not going to be me.

I walked over to where Talbot stood, grimly watching the men and women of the VCPD as they worked with hunting knives and machetes, skinning Stacey alive while others struggled to hold him down. Two officers with spears took turns jabbing him in the spine to keep him mostly paralyzed despite his mystical regenerative properties. Katherine was one of them. She had the slightest twist of a smile on her lips, though her cheeks were wet with tears. Other officers carried in twenty-pound bags of sand and huge bags of salt they must have gotten from a pool supply store. I hoped it would be enough.

"You going to get in trouble over this?" I asked Talbot.

"I didn't tell you anything Greta hadn't already figured out, so no." He frowned. "I can't share any information gleaned strictly from the Akasha, Eric, but as long as I can demonstrate that you could have reasonably had access to the knowledge yourself, the other mousers won't be adding any additional time to my exile. That and I hate this son of a bitch." His frown became a grin as he said the last few words. Talbot doesn't curse often, and I was willing to bet that "SOB" was a much stronger insult for mousers. "But it's flattering that you care."

"You mind taking me to the car?" I turned into a mouse. Talbot tucked me in his breast pocket to protect me from the sun, and off we went. He walked us over to the squad car in which I had arrived and dropped me off in back, then, after a pause for me to change back to normal, Talbot climbed in as well.

"He dead?" Sal asked.

"Yep, or will be soon enough."

"Wish I could have been in on that."

"Yeah," I said. "Sorry. Only room enough for so many."

"Don't apologize, boss," Sal said, the gratitude in his voice making me uncomfortable. "I'm just glad you're back."

The gratitude . . . I didn't know what to do with that or how to react, so I patted the back of his seat and ignored the rest, giving my attention to Talbot.

"You really coming with?" I asked.

"Yes. I want to watch you get haunted. I haven't seen that yet." Talbot folded his arms. "Are they here? When will they get here?"

I shook my head. "Sometimes it takes a while. Don't worry, Talbot, you'll get to see me tortured soon enough."

"That's why I hang around," Talbot said. "You're better than a ball of yarn."

2

ERIC

VAMPIRES NEVER LIVE ANYTHING DOWN

I woke with a start to the familiar sound of crying. A quick glance at my watch revealed that I wasn't wearing one. The sun was still up, but the car had moved. The Artiste Unknown, or rather, the burned-out remains of the Artiste Unknown, which had once been one of Void City's premier vampire hangouts, loomed outside the driver's-side window. Yellow police tape still marked the entrances, and the front windows had been boarded up.

I couldn't remember why I was here. Obviously, I'd been driven, but hadn't Talbot been with me?

"How long have I been asleep?"

"You could try your cell phone, jackass." I knew the voice, had known it since I was nine. Talbot had left me alone in the backseat of the squad car, and now he was going to miss the haunting. Served him right.

My cell phone wasn't in my pocket, but I found it in the floorboard, pressed up against my combat boots. The network claimed it was 3:16 P.M., which meant I'd been asleep for at least an hour. As a vampire, I've always slept in tiny little slices. Usually no more than four hours, often closer to one or two, but in the past I could always feel it coming on. Now sometimes it just happens, as if I'm narcoleptic.

"What, no thank you from the goddamn king of the vampires?" the voice snarked. I still couldn't see him. "Is the golden boy too lofty to pass the time with an old murdered friend?"

"Fuck you very much, Roger." Roger used to be my bestestever pal, until he started sleeping with my fiancée, had me killed, and found someone to turn him into a vampire. Not necessarily in that order. When I surprised him by coming back as a vampire, and a more powerful one than he was, he pretended to still be my friend. The whole thing got all melodramatic and shit. He forcibly enthralled my fiancée and used her soul as a bargaining chip to come back from the dead. Then he even tried to steal my soul. I prefer to simply think of him as an asshole who didn't stay dead properly. I waited for him to talk again, listening for directionality.

He stayed quiet, but I knew he was there, and he wasn't alone. The other three had to be somewhere nearby. When the knock on the window came, I was surprised that it wasn't one of my ghosts. It was somebody else's. John Hawkes knocked on my window, peering through his glasses at me with eyes such a startling shade of blue that it always takes me a moment to process them. Some people think they're contacts, but they aren't. He wore a LET THEM EAT SOYLENT GREEN T-shirt underneath a rainbow-tie-dyed Hawaiian shirt. Tan cargo shorts and a pair of multicolored Crocs, the summery kind with holes in them, completed his ensemble. Picture the most handsome guy in the world, with golden-blond hair and a David Bowie–like elfishness, and you'll be picturing John Hawkes.

"We're across the street." He pointed at a trendy little coffee shop that bore the name Hawkes Coffee Jam. Talbot and the two officers who belonged with the squad car were having beignets and café au lait. Now that I saw it, I registered the smell, and the odor brought my fangs out. Though vampires can't eat, we crave food. Most of us try to make our thralls or friends eat food we crave so we can watch them. Polite vampires call it voyeuristic eating. I call it food porn.

Talbot waved at me. "You being haunted yet?"

"Yes, but I don't see them."

Talbot dropped his beignet, sending out a tiny cloud of powdered sugar that would have hit his suit if he hadn't used his catlike reflexes to vault backward out of the chair. His eyes glowed green as they transformed from human to slit pupils and on to luminescent star emeralds. I didn't like the frown I saw on his face. It was two parts "damn" and one part "I don't like the look of this."

"*Mauvais le chat,*" came a woman's voice.

"Bad kitty?" I said aloud.

"What?" Talbot raised an eyebrow.

"The French chick just called you *mauvais le chat.* That's 'bad kitty,' right?"

"Close," Talbot answered. "Since when do you speak French, though?"

"Just shout right past me," John said with no sign of the slight having impacted his good mood, "it doesn't bother me at all."

"Sorry, John."

"Scoot back?"

I did and he opened the car door, offering a cardboard pastry box as my chariot for crossing the street unbarbecued. Taking the hint, I went all mousy, trying to ignore the weirdo balls-receding-from-the-cold sensation that comes with turning into something way smaller than I actually am.

Cars passed by on the street outside my box, and after waiting a few minutes for a lull, John hurried across the street and took me inside his coffee shop. Which is kind of like hell. For all that it's a coffee shop first, John always has the best pastries, confections, and chocolate-dipped anything (ranging from pretzels to strawberries to dried apricots). To put it mildly, the scents, though pleasant, make one hungry for the taste.

"My windows are sun-safe," he said, tossing me onto a small two-top inside. He opened the box and I crawled out, hopping off the table and transforming back to my more human shape. At least that came with the bonus of a little warmth. Vampires don't hold body temperature well, so we're almost always cold. For those of us who can bring our clothes with us when we transform, the transformation leaves our clothes clean, repaired, and fresh-out-of-the-dryer hot. If I concentrate, I can keep whatever outfit I'm wearing, but if I don't actively think about it, I wind up in combat boots, black socks, tightiewhities, jeans, my favorite brown belt, and a black WELCOME TO THE VOID T-shirt. It saves a lot on clothing costs, but the process doesn't come free. It tends to deplete my blood supply, especially when I do it more than once or twice in a day . . . unless, of course, I've eaten thirty police officers' worth of blood first.

I didn't ask John why he had sun-safe windows, and he didn't offer an explanation, but I had a pretty good idea.

"Winter," John said, "wants you to know that she will come tonight to give you the first task." Winter would have been most High Society vamps' first choice to replace Lord Phillip, if I hadn't come along. Since my rise to power, Winter had gone from master manipulator to terrorist. He revealed himself as a total anti-vampire activist and killed half the city's vampires in one glorious death trap of an extravaganza last year. Winter is the most attractive man I've ever met, and he's got more musical talent than your average high-end orchestra shoved together in a bathroom with Elvis. When he isn't singing or playing, he's gambling, but not at cards or in a casino; he bets on outcomes, social interactions, weird stuff—and he always wins. He and John Hawkes bear a striking resemblance to each other, and I've never seen the two of them in the same room together, which doesn't exactly mean Clark Kent is Superman, but I have my suspicions.

"She?" I said. "She as in Lady Scrytha, she?"

The young woman behind the register giggled at that. She was cute. Early twenties. Brunette. Eyes the color of milk chocolate. She had at least three cats at home, one gerbil, and some sort of bird. She didn't smoke anymore, but I could smell the nicotine in her system. Her name tag dubbed her April. I guessed she was trying the gum route to quitting. I wanted to rip out her throat and drink her dry. Not because I disliked her, but because that's how I feel about most humans when I'm hungry.

What?

Vampire, remember?

John put his hand on my arm. "April, why don't you fix Mr. Court-ney a whole-fat nukeless venti red blend?"

"I wasn't going to eat her," I said churlishly.

He ignored that with a charming smile and didn't let go of my arm. "Not Lady Scrytha," he said, jumping back to the other conversa-tion.

I blinked, trying to remember what we'd been talking about. "Oh. Right. My first task. So, does he know who it's going to be? Am I right?"

"Winter thinks you are." He steered me to the window, where I could see Talbot gathering his small plate of beignets and coffee, pre-paring to carry them inside to join us.

"Anything else?"

"He says 'The War' will start tonight when you go to accomplish the task. So be ready for that. He says that I'm to say if your task is what you both suspect it will be, he won't allow it to happen, not the way Scrytha will want it to happen."

"So I'm right about that, too." April handed me a fancy coffee cup with the special sip cap on top, just like everyone else's. The blood in the cup was warm, just a hair under ninety-eight degrees. I hesitated, but given that I was already being haunted, feeding probably wasn't go-ing to bring on anything new. I gave it a tentative sip. It was a mixture of blood types, I guessed from the name, but it isn't like they taste dif-ferent. I drank it down and felt more civilized and less civilized at the same time. "Damn."

"What?" Talbot asked as he came in.

"I don't like being right," I said, smiling despite myself. "If I'm right too often, it's a sign of the apocalypse."

Everyone laughed. Even April. My own laughter died down when I heard three voices join in from throats I couldn't see. Somewhere off in the distance, a fourth voice I recognized was crying. I hate ghosts. I used to be haunted by an ancestor of mine: John Paul Courtney.

I hated that at the time, but given the chance, I'd take him over my four new ghosts any day. These were the ghosts of souls I'd effectively eaten when I was a revenant.

Clearing my throat, I asked Talbot to finish his food so we could head back to my place. If I was lucky, I'd have time to get in some sword practice and a shower before I had any visitors. If I was even more lucky, my ghosts would let me do it in peace.

3

ERIC

HAPPY IN HELL

The infernal deliverer of my presumably never-ending demonic honey-do list stood in a rapidly dissipating puff of red smoke, filling my bedroom with her signature scent. A sulfurous stench would have made sense, would have matched the tiny twin black horns peeking out between her triple-toned blond hair and gone well with the black leather dominatrix dress, nine-inch spike heels, and choker she wore. But the odor wasn't sulfur. Instead, as in life, Rachel had a very distinct aroma: cinnamon.

I looked up from my seat on the edge of my bed and smirked. Rachel. Of course she would be the one they would send to be my boss. How original. I'd been right. I put down the washcloth I'd been using to wipe down my sword, not caring if it got the bedsheets a little wet. "I thought the devil wore a blue dress."

"Get up. You've got a job to do." Rachel eyed the steel long sword in my hand. As she watched, a coat of ice surrounded the metal. It's a great sword, magic and everything, though I think in the long run, a fiery sword would be more useful than an icy one. I'd taken it away from a demon some time ago and pretty much left it in the refrigerator. Now, given the limitations of my powers at night, I was taking time to learn how to use the damn thing. There's more to it than meets the eye, kind of like with Transformers, and well . . . me. What can I say? Boys love their toys.

"Well?" Hands on her hips. Rachel's body language spoke volumes. She was perturbed by my lack of reaction. I'm not sure what she expected. A hug? A curse? A death threat? Before I'd had Greta kill her, she'd been a human, one of my thralls, and my sister-in-law . . . and my lover . . . and things had gotten messy.

"Well what?" I asked.

"Aren't you glad to see me?" She winked. "Or surprised?"

"Nope."

I got up and walked across the bedroom, sword still in hand. Back in my bachelor days, I'd made do with little more than a bed and a sink, but when I got married to Tabitha (Rachel's older sister), Ebon Winter repaired, refurbished, and redesigned the Pollux, the old-school movie palace I call home, as a wedding present.

In my bedroom, he'd knocked out a wall and extended the space. The old queen-size bed had been replaced with a California king. A proper bathroom had been installed. I had a fifty-two-inch widescreen LCD on one wall and a fridge with a specialized holder for my ice sword. Winter is one helluva interior decorator, even though he's also one of the scariest vampires I know. And that's saying a lot, given that when most folks in Void City think Scary Vampire, they picture me. Or my daughter, Greta.

I opened the chrome door of the refrigerator and put the sword away, which isn't to say that I put it in the fridge, necessarily, but that's what I meant it to look like. I assumed I'd have more time to practice with it later. *Too many secrets.*

"Not even a little surprised?" Rachel pouted. "A little glad?"

"I figured it was going to be you," I said over my shoulder, perusing the contents of the fridge. It made sense, particularly the cruelly ironic sort of sense that demons prefer. I'd once been Rachel's boss, and now she was mine. With that said, take a little advice from a being who knows: When dealing with demons (whatever the breed), never use the phrase "Whatever it is, I'll do it." No matter what they offer, no matter how great the need, a smart person—a rational person—will pull a Nancy Reagan and "just say no." I guess that makes me a romantic, because in order to get Marilyn back from hell, I took that deal, and now there was quite literally hell to pay.

Hell isn't what I'd call a nonprofit organization, either. Demons don't take Visa or American Express (I haven't tried MasterCard or Discover, but I'm guessing they're out, too). Not that I'd expected Marilyn's resurrection to come cheaply. Quite the opposite. But what I'd found out since then was that I'd made a deal (an obnoxiously open-ended deal, I might add) with an Infernatti. Infernatti are the demonic elite (a capo, in mobster terms), and I'd made my deal with Lady Scrytha, one of the Infernattiest of them all. She expects a lot of bang for her spiritual buck. And she does love irony.

"When Magbidion gave me the appointment time and location"—I kept my eyes on the fridge—"well, who else but Scrytha's new cathouse hall monitor would want to have the meeting in my bedroom?" In the fridge, a six-pack of Coke (one missing) in real glass bottles (bottled in Mexico with real sugar, not corn syrup) stood side by side with the remains of a BBQ pizza from Carl's down the street. Atop the white cardboard pizza box was a bowl of ranch dip and a plate of curled daikon chips, both covered in plastic wrap. Stacked next to all of that, up against the wall of the fridge, were six full blood bags, each tagged with a sticky note bearing my name: Eric Courtney. "Do you want a Coke?"

"Do I want a Coke?" Rachel scoffed.

"If you're hungry, I have some cold pizza." I smirked again when I said it, but I don't think Rachel noticed.

"Do you want to watch me eat something for you, baby?" Rachel sidled up next to me, her expression tipping toward the lascivious. Rachel knew all about food porn. "For old times?" She licked her lips.

Rachel had been the best and worst thrall I ever had. She'd been an enabler, pushing me to be more and more monstrous, to kill anyone I wanted when I wanted, and to use my powers to their fullest. She'd screwed up in the end, not by doing bad things so much as by letting me find out about them.

I'm the poster boy for blissful ignorance, but once I know something, once I can't ignore it, I have to act. Hoping my brief reverie had been convincingly long, I closed the fridge, wondering if Rachel had gotten a good look inside. Hoping she hadn't.

"No." I snagged a small wooden box from the top of the fridge, opened it, and drew out the steel chain necklace within. A large pendant hung from one end, an unpolished black stone set in its center.

Dropping the empty box, I slid past Rachel, our bodies brushing against each other. Back when she'd been alive and my thrall, our bodies had done more than that. The last time I'd touched her, it had been one last orgiastic good-bye fuck. The sex had been followed almost immediately—once I found out everything Rachel had done (which amounted to mindwiping me so that I forgot about my marriage to her sister, Tabitha)—by me asking Greta to kill her. I wasn't sure I actually would have killed her, but I knew Greta sure as hell had. Rachel seemed to have taken it all pretty well. Better to rule in hell and all that jazz, I suppose. *You think you won,* I thought. *Your boss thinks she won, too. But you're wrong. I saved Marilyn. I won.*

And I'm going to keep on winning.

"Somebody just fed." Rachel puffed up her chest, and I let my eyes go where she wanted them to go, straight to her breasts. "You're all warm on the outside." She'd been a beautiful woman, and despite her newfound demonhood, her blond hair was still perfect. Her body was perfect, too, frozen at approximately nineteen forever.

I missed the butterfly tattoo she used to have on her cheek, but its absence aside, she'd always be gorgeous. I missed being with her in a remember-how-fun-it-was-that-time-when-we-jumped-out-of-an-airplane-without-parachutes-and-were-saved-by-a-freak-tornadic-microburst-only-to-be-caught-naked-together-in-our-hotel-room-later-and-have-our-lives-destroyed-by-the-relationship-fallout-but-what-a-rush-that-was sort of way.

"Everybody does," I said.

"Does what?" she asked.

"Feeds. So . . . what's my first Herculean task? Are there some stables in hell that need cleaning? Want me to blow up an orphanage?"

Rachel sighed. "All business, huh?"

I took a long deep breath and let it out. "Pretty much."

"Okay. Fine." Rachel clapped her hands together. "But this could be fun for us, Eric. Lady Scrytha sends me to you with your assignment . . . we screw each other's brains out. You feed on me, complete your assignment, and report back. Then we—"

"What's the job?" I wrapped the chain of the necklace around my finger. Cold metal on warm skin. Light not catching on the stone's reflective surface. I caught sight of my warped reflection in the chrome of the refrigerator, and my smile broadened. If people were going to keep meeting me in my bedroom at night, I was going to have to do something about that shiny surface. But the truth was, I liked it despite the risk of someone noticing.

"Would you stop smiling?" She stomped her foot, and a brief flash of flame punctuated the motion.

"I don't think so." I made a deal with a demon and I got screwed . . . those are the rules, right? I thought I was agreeing to do any one single thing, and then that "one thing," from Scrytha's point of view, was apparently "be my bitch for all eternity." Typical demon screw job.

So how come I felt like I won? It's a fair question, but I won't answer it yet. Even when I found out who was going to be giving me orders, the smile on my face just wouldn't go away. It was like being the Joker or something. The grin wouldn't fade. I was the only one who got the joke, and my joy wouldn't die. Even though Marilyn still wouldn't have anything to do with me, not romantically, even though Tabitha (who still thought of herself as my vampiric bride) was furious . . . none of it mattered, because Marilyn, the woman I'd loved most of my adult life and all of my undeath, was alive. As the cliché goes, where there's life, there's hope. And it had been a long, long time since I'd had a strong dose of hope, going way back to before I died and came back as a mass murderer.

I still remember the moment I got hope back. Scrytha was standing onstage at the Pollux, and she offered to give Marilyn back, new and improved—a true immortal. My answer? The insanely stupid one I warned you about. "Whatever it is, I'll do it." Yeah, I know. Not so smart. But since Marilyn was alive, okay, nearby, and even young again . . . Why should I care about the bad things that happen in the world as long as they don't happen to her? I'd seen her die with my own eyes, watched her soul get sucked into hell, and then . . . in spite of everything . . . I got her back.

I won. I won. I fucking won! I still wanted to shout it from the rooftops.

"What if I told you that you had to kill someone?" Rachel's voice snapped me out of my literal reverie. What can I say? I have a tendency to wander off mentally. Maybe I need Ritalin?

"Unless the target is a member of what I consider my family," I answered, "I'll do it."

"It's an old friend."

"Talbot counts as part of my family," I reminded her.

"Older than that."

"Roger's already dead." *And haunting my happy ass every time I feed,* I added silently. Not that I understand exactly what the link between the feeding and the haunting is . . . or if I'd figured it out, I couldn't remember. Hell, I couldn't remember exactly how Roger died the last time, either, but I knew I was responsible. My memory is better at night now, but it's far from perfect and very hit or miss. Then again, I guess expecting my Alzheimer's to act up only when it's convenient is a little unrealistic. I used to think the memory problems had something to do with being embalmed before I rose as a vampire. Now I knew better. "Isn't he?"

"You ate his soul, Eric." Rachel rolled her eyes. "This time he's dead."

Soul eating. I shuddered. *Right. I remember now. That ability, I don't miss.* "Then I don't see a proble—"

"It's Father Ike." Rachel's gaze went to the hardwood floor. "Lady Scrytha wants you to kill him as proof that you'll keep your part of the bargain."

Bingo! Of course it was Ike.

"No."

"I knew it." She snapped her fingers and pointed at me as she spoke. "You're going to break the deal. Marilyn is going straight back to—"

I donned the necklace and crossed to Rachel in one smooth motion. My right hand closed around Rachel's throat. Her eyes went wide, confused.

"Nothing happens to Marilyn, even if I break the deal." Rachel winced away from my shout. She squinted, trying to see me, but thanks to my nice new necklace, her demonic upgrade prevented it. "That is the rule I do remember. If I break the deal, I get punished. Other people get punished. But not her. Besides"—I stroked Rachel's hair with my left hand, and she leaned into it—"I didn't say I was breaking the deal."

"Why can't I see you?" she choked out. "What is that necklace?"

"I call it the Blind Eye."

Rachel turned her head, brushing my hand with her cheek as I let her go. Good Lord, we have a strange relationship. I went on, "One half of the Eye of Scrythax. It broke when I went to hell to get Greta back. It's blind now. Magbidion rigged up the necklace for me. When I wear it . . ."

"Demons can't see you." She chewed her lip. "Give it to me."

"Sure," I said.

I'd had help planning for this ever since we'd figured out who my handler was going to be. One great thing about having Magbidion—a thrall who has actually signed a demonic contract before, sold his soul, and had years to sweat about the details—is that guy knows the rules inside and out; information gleaned from hours and hours spent searching for loopholes. I unfolded a little sheet of paper from my pocket and read the words Magbidion had scrawled on a Post-it note for me: "'As long as that is Lady Scrytha's request and she understands that it changes the nature of our transaction.'"

"You have to do anything she wants." Rachel spoke to the room, doing her best to approximate my location. "If she says hand me the necklace—"

"Then it's an exchange of goods, not services," I said, moving closer to her. She tried not to flinch when my breath hit her cheek. "I agreed to *do* anything, not *give* anything. She could make me buy her a hot dog. She could order me to steal something for her but not to give her what's mine. Apparently, in demonic contract law, there is a distinct difference. You said she wanted me to kill him as proof." I shook my head. "The deal doesn't require me to prove anything. If, on the other hand, killing Father Ike is an order made in accordance with the terms of our pact . . ."

"Semantics." Rachel laughed. "You have to do whatever I say."

"And I will as long as you, as her duly authorized agent, say the orders are from Lady Scrytha and you make it a command."

"Fine." Rachel ran a hand through her hair. "Lady Scrytha orders you to kill Father Ike."

My gut tightened as I felt the compulsion of my oath: an itch between my eyes, fleeting but unmistakable. "When?"

"Tonight."

"Kill Ike." The sensation grew from itch to phantom pain, as if a talon hung just above my forehead. "Got it."

I served with Ike in Korea, before I left the military and took the job as captain of the VCPD. He was the company priest. He knew about my troubles when I'd been alive, the problems I had after World War II. Ike knew me inside and out. Even after my decades as a vampire, all the people I'd killed, the stupid things I'd done, Ike still had faith in me. I picked up my iPhone from the nightstand and sent a quick text, then looked up Ike's name in the contact list and made the call.

Rachel saw the iPhone move, then vanish, and started. "Will you take that stupid necklace off?" she growled.

"Is that an order from Lady Scrytha?" I mocked.

She stomped her foot again and made an exasperated noise, but I wasn't paying much attention. The iPhone had my full focus. It stopped ringing.

"Eric," said a sleepy voice on the other end, "when will you remember that not all of God's creatures are nocturnal?"

"Hey, Father." I spoke into the phone, watching Rachel's confusion play across her face. "I made a deal to get Marilyn back."

"Get her back?" He paused. "How? When?" Another pause. "What did you have to do, Eric?"

"About a year ago. And I agreed to do whatever Lady Scrytha asked."

"Eric!" He was wide awake, with shock and outrage clear in his voice. That one word rang like the slap Marilyn had given me the minute Scrytha brought her back. Idiot, she'd called me. Father Ike was too polite to say it, but he was thinking the same thing. "Surely you understand—"

"They want me to kill you," I said matter-of-factly. "But due to recent . . . political changes . . . if you leave town, they probably won't want me to follow you."

"I'm not going anywhere, my friend."

"Up to you, Ike," I said after a pause. "But I'm taking a five-minute shower, putting on a change of clothes, and then I'm heading over there to wrap my hands around your neck and choke the life out of you. Afterward, to finish the job, I'm going to burn down your church, because let's face it, that building is a part of you."

"So be it," Ike said softly, "and may God forgive you."

As he hung up, I got a text reply to the one I'd sent. Three words: *I win again.*

I laughed and thumbed off the phone. Believe it or not, everything was going according to The Plan.

"You warned him," Rachel spat.

"Was I not supposed to?" I stripped out of my clothes (except for the necklace), went into the bathroom, and started up the shower. "You should have clarified."

"Want a little company?" Rachel asked.

"Why?" I stepped into the shower, even though the water was still a little cold, and put my head under the torrent of water. "Do you think Marilyn would join me?"

Rachel vanished in a puff of cinnamon and I whistled, letting the warm water rush over me. *You can do this,* I told myself. *It's for Marilyn. You can do anything for Marilyn.* I hoped I was right. I had a very big secret, one I'd been hiding almost a year, and I would have to keep it as long as I could. My heart pounded in my chest, but it made no sound. One of Magbidion's enchantments was busy making sure of that.

Yeah. Yeah.

I know.

Sneaky. Sneaky.

4

ERIC
I LIKE IKE

A 1964½ Mustang convertible pulled up in front of the Pollux. Light from the marquee reflected in the red paint of the car's long blunt hood. If I hadn't been smiling already, the rumble of the 271-horsepower V8 engine would have brought a grin to my lips as I pushed open the glass double doors and stepped out onto the sidewalk. Beatrice, her storm-cloud-colored eyes sparking and long fiery tresses windblown but beautiful, waved at me from the driver's seat, having obviously enjoyed her turn as Fang's human "cover."

There's a long story behind Fang, but the short version is this: He's around 3,100 pounds of all-American Ford automobile. He's undead and we're linked. To destroy me, you have to destroy Fang. In Emperor vampire terms, that makes him my memento mori, which, for vampiric purposes, is Latin for "remember that you are mortal." He has a mind of his own, but it's based on mine. Oh, and he eats people.

An Emperor has to store a portion of his might in an object, a memento mori, and mine is in Fang. Through his memento mori, an Emperor also becomes vulnerable to true destruction.

My sire, Lisette, had been an Emperor. She'd risen as a zombie and a vampire at the same time. To end an Emperor, you have to destroy her memento mori, kill her vampire self, and then destroy her other undead form (or vice versa). Fang ate Lisette's memento mori. My daughter, Greta, destroyed her zombie nature, and me . . . I ate her soul. Soul sucking is what revenants do. Once upon a time I rose as the ghost of a murdered man and a vampire simultaneously, courtesy of the now-defunct Courtney Family Curse. You won't see me sucking any more souls, though. And whether I still count as an Emperor is an open question. With Marilyn back, I'm a new man.

Yay, me.

Ever since the Veil of Scrythax was destroyed, the mages had been working like crazy to keep the genie in the bottle. It was running them, and me, a little ragged . . . and don't get me started on the price tag. Fang has been able to do a little influencing on his own ever since he ate my sire's memento mori, but doing it drains him and makes him hungry, so it's best to let one of my thralls cruise around with him when he's out and about without me or Greta. I think Beatrice enjoys it more than the others.

"Hungry?" Beatrice asked me as she climbed out of the car. She was wearing a forest-green V-neck swoop top and a leather miniskirt that had risen to scandalous heights from her time behind the wheel. She patted her inner thigh, the flesh exposed by her miniskirt. The femoral artery used to be my favorite feeding spot. In previous years, my fangs would have come out at the suggestion, but given everything that was going on . . . it was the wrong time. Of all my thralls, Beatrice was the only one who used to serve another vampire. She was the most knowledgeable, and to be honest, she was the one most likely to suddenly figure out the whole "vampire by day, true immortal by night" thing that I was trying to keep under wraps. Maybe if the Eye of Scrythax hadn't split, I'd have ended up a true immortal all the time, but that's not the way it happened.

"No." I shook my head. "I'm fine."

Beatrice put a hand on my chest. "You're still warm. They can't have gotten too far." She scanned our surroundings and saw no one special. "Who is it?"

"Who is what?"

"Who are you feeding on, Eric? You haven't fed on me in a month." A gust of wind caught her red hair and tossed it about her shoulders. "Or on any of the other girls, as far as I can tell."

"Tomorrow," I said. "Or maybe later tonight, but definitely tomorrow morning . . . or afternoon."

"Really?" She perked up. "It won't make her mad, will it?"

"Who?"

"Marilyn." She leaned in close, breath warming my skin. "We all think you've been feeding on her when—"

"No." It came out harsh—angry—my smile faltering. "I don't feed on Marilyn. I never feed on Marilyn." My voice got louder, adrenaline pumping. "No one does! Ever!"

I stopped shouting. Stupidity had no place in The Plan.

"Sorry." I maneuvered past Beatrice and sank down into the still-warm driver's seat. "We'll talk about it later. I have to go kill an old friend."

Fang pulled away, leaving Beatrice yelling questions after us, but I couldn't make out what she was saying.

"Kill Father Ike." I covered my eyes with my hands. "Right."

Being a monster makes killing easier. Having had to do it for so long to survive had taken the edge off of the guilt, formed a scar where that portion of my conscience was. Ike had been warned. Fang went for a semi-oldie and played Alien Ant Farm's cover of "Smooth Criminal."

"No, Fang, I'm not okay, and my name's not Annie." We drove down back streets, cutting across town to Ike's church. I parked in front of the brick rectory and stepped out of the car. The old brown church loomed over me, a potential avalanche of guilt, and I fancied I could hear the church bell tolling out midnight even though it was only a quarter past eleven. The doors had been propped open, candles lit, all the lights ablaze. The welcome mat was out. Literally.

"Damn." I almost forgot to take off the necklace, but I leaned back in and hung it from Fang's rearview mirror.

"What do you think you're playing at?" The voice was Ebon Winter's, and the vampire himself swirled, an angry mist in the shape of a man in leather rock-star pants.

"I don't have time for this, Winter."

"You're here for Isaac?" he snarled, fangs out, blocking my path. "He performed your marriage ceremony in this church. I played the organ. And I sang!"

I caught sight of Rachel out of the corner of my eye, watching the exchange from the shadows of the alley across the street. She'd turned up to keep an eye on me. Good. That was part of The Plan, too.

"It was a lovely service." I stepped through his mist form. Winter looked like he'd run halfway across town after having jumped directly offstage mid-performance to intercept me. "But I have a job to do."

A line of pain scratched across my back from an inch or so below my right shoulder to high on my left.

"Ow. Fuck." I wasn't used to having pain last. Before the Eye of Scrythax split while it was lodged in my heart, I had felt pain like most vampires—the initial sensation and then nothing else unless the wound got worse or I moved wrong and aggravated it. Now—at night, anyway, when I was a true immortal—pain lasted until the wound healed, though that wasn't long. By the time I turned to face Winter, the wound was nothing more than a thin line of blood at my back and a tear in my WELCOME TO THE VOID T-shirt.

I took a swing at Winter, and he dodged it easily.

"Powers acting up?" He smirked. "No vampire speed?"

He sliced me again, his silver razor gleaming in the moonlight, opening a slash on my cheek, another on my chest, and a third one across my forehead. *Huh. I'd never noticed that Winter had no claws. Fighting with a razor. How very Jack the Ripper.*

"I don't need powers to take care of you, queer boy."

Winter's eyes sparkled. "I hope you mean *strange*, darling, because I find the implication that I even possess sexuality, regardless of gender specificity, grossly insulting."

My next punch went straight through Winter's chest, his body misting before I made contact, curls of vapor trailing after my knuckles.

"Coward." I dashed through him, trying to make my way through the open doors of the Gothic church. A kung-fu-movie *swoosh* broke the air as Winter hamstrung me. My Achilles tendons rolled up to the back of my knees, splitting the skin and etching twin lines of agony along my legs. I cursed, nearly blacking out, the edges of my vision blurring. Another slash opened my throat, severing the jugular and sending a gout of crimson across the steps.

"Fang!" I tried to gasp the word, managing nothing more than a gurgle, but Fang understood. His engine roared, and my undead Mustang came into play, grille angling for Winter, mist or no mist. Winter did as expected, and the bumper never touched him, but Fang didn't slow. Winter had never been the real target.

Fang's grille cut into my back; the kinetic force of the impact sent me toward the church doors. Back broken, legs useless, I lay flat on my face and let the wounds knit. The healing of my Achilles tendons hurt more than the initial injury; the sound of my vertebrae realigning was like a bone xylophone to my ears.

Winter shouted, "No!" as I rose to my knees, head still spinning, eyes unfocused, and Fang slid into reverse, seeming to catch him by surprise, rolling over him and giving him the old chomperoo. Winter's skin came off with the sound of shucking corn, but he didn't stop talking.

"This will be war, Eric, not just with me—" The rest of his sentence vanished as Fang stripped the muscle layer and Winter's bones landed in the trunk. A little blood and he'd be good as new. Angry as hell but okay. After all, Winter's a Vlad. Practically top-tier vampire stock.

If you're new to Void City, you may not know that vampires come in four basic levels: Drones, Soldiers, Masters, and Vlads. In cinematic terms, Drones might be instructional videos you watched in high school (better than nothing but not much entertainment value); Soldiers would be the cartoon before the movie (fun but not really worth the price of admission, if it's all you're going to get); Masters would be black-and-white movies (some real classics, but most don't stand the test of time); and Vlads . . . would be modern classics or remastered greats (they might go out of fashion, but they're impressive as hell and keep coming to theaters again and again).

There's another tier, kind of a best of the worst, in which two kinds of undeath happen to someone at the same time. Most people would still count me as one of those—a damn near unkillable Emperor-level vampire. In movie terms, an Emperor would be like the hybrids you see at high-end theme parks where the special effects encompass 3-D, physical effects, live actors, and damn roller-coaster motion, updated with all the new gadgets. The kind of movie you never forget. An Emperor is the kind of vampire who can walk into a church . . . if he has to.

Father Ike was waiting for me in front of the altar, a short, fat, wonderful man with a heart so pure, I don't think he needed Clorox to keep his whites white. He wore a priest's alb and preaching scarf over a single-breasted cassock, and he clutched his Bible in both hands.

"Vampire hunters are already making their way into Void City now that Lord Phillip has been dethroned," Ike said softly. "Kill me, and the last barrier between them and you will be gone."

"You sure know how to brighten a murderer's day, Padre."

"If you do this, Eric," Ike began—his voice, not pleading, sounded more concerned for me than for himself—"where will it stop? How many tasks will you have to perform before you are free? Have you thought of that, my friend?"

I had, actually. It was all part of The Plan, but I couldn't share that information with Ike or nearly anyone else, even the folks who knew part of it: Talbot, Magbidion . . . every new person was a risk. Hell, I hadn't even told Greta.

Fang crashed through the doors of the church behind me, and Ike winced as the pews pulled out of the floor.

"I have a plan," I said.

Ike laughed bitterly.

"I'm not stupid, Ike," I told him. "I may have early-onset Alzheimer's, and I may have spent a lot of years trying to ignore what was happening around me, trying to let the world spin by until Marilyn died and I went crazy, but that's not what's happening now. I got her back. She's immortal. If I'm lucky, she might even learn to love me again. I just have to show her I'm worthy and that she's worthy, too."

"And killing me is step number one?" He spread his arms wide and knelt before me. "I can't understand your logic, my friend. Not a bit. But I won't fight you."

"Think of it this way, Father . . ." I put my hands around his throat and began to squeeze.

Ike's flesh didn't burn me. I'd thought that it would have, even with the whole immortal-by-night thing going on. I tightened my grip and waited for his breathing to stop. When it did, I dashed out to Fang, grabbed the Blind Eye necklace, and returned to wrap it around the dead priest's neck, arranging him neatly so that he stared up at the ceiling, his head tilted back to show the bruises still forming around his neck.

"Kill Father Ike," I said aloud. "Done."

"Good job, baby," Rachel called from the broken church entrance. "I know it was hard." She held her arms out to me. "But if there's anything I can do to make you feel better . . ."

"Get away from me," I snarled. "It's done, and so is your job, so fuck off to wherever you fuck off to or I swear to God I'll kill you and lay you out right next to him."

"You're so cute when you're tough," she said, but before I could charge, *poof,* she was gone. The compulsion to complete my task faded, and I went on with the next step of The Plan.

◆ 5 ◆

GRETA

MY TWO MOMS

Marilyn . . . No, that wasn't right . . . And neither was "Old Mom," now that she was back from the dead, young again, and apparently immortal. Mommortal?
No.
Mom.

Mom looked lost behind the counter at the Demon Heart. She'd been used to serving drinks and tending bar, not spraying disinfectant into used shoes and selling lane time. Her fingers twitched, eager for a cigarette, something to do with her hands, but the Demon Heart is nonsmoking. It smells better that way. I don't really care about people's health, but to a vampire's nose, cigarettes smell extra bad. Cigars are nice, though, cigarillos, too. The aroma wakes up a really old memory in my head of some old guy who was very nice to me. *I think I'll eat a cigar smoker tonight.*

Despite Mom's discomfort, I was glad to see her. She was younger than when I'd first met her (and I'd known her since I was nine) and as pretty as the picture of her that Dad keeps in his wallet. The red and black of the Demon Heart Lanes bowling shirt suited her, even though she wore it unbuttoned like a jacket, the white T-shirt and tight jeans underneath showing her hourglass figure in a way that would have driven Dad crazy if he wasn't out doing . . . stuff. Secret stuff. My problem with that was I didn't know if it was supposed to be a secret from me, too, or if it only seemed secret because I was supposed to have figured it out on my own.

I sat on the burgundy felt of my favorite pool table in the Demon Heart, idly rolling a cue ball around and around. Blood dripped off my fingernails, marking the off-white of the ball with bright unclotted red.

A troll wearing a big gray hoodie bowled on lane twelve, keeping to himself. He was small for a troll, only about seven feet, but his mottled green skin and gnarled knuckles would have thrown up a big warning flare to anyone paying close attention. Or it would have if he hadn't been paying some guild mage to cover the entire bowling alley with a spell to keep norms ignorant. His presence gave Magbidion time to go running off with Mags's new friend, the midget bitch, to talk bad about me.

"Hey, uh, Greta," one of Dad's thralls—a mousy little blonde—said to me as she walked past with a big order of fried mushrooms for the troll. I smelled fear on her skin, beneath the smell of grease, hair spray, and deep-fried veggies. Then her name came to me.

"Hey, uh, Erin," I said back. "Does my hair smell like smoke?"

She leaned forward instantly to sniff it. "No," she answered. "Should it?"

I didn't answer, and she hurried on her way with the tray. I like Daddy's thralls. On the other hand, I've seen the way they watch Mom when they think she isn't looking, like she's a threat to them. No one was rude, but I could hear it in their breath, their heartbeats.

Dad would do a lot for any one of them, protect them, feed them, take care of them, even; but he wouldn't go to hell for them like he had for me and for Marilyn.

I sensed New Mom's . . . Tabitha's . . . no, *Stepmom's* approach and compared her style of dress. She was still outfitting herself like she worked in a strip club or burlesque. Tonight's over-the-top-sexy attire resembled the collision of a Victoria's Secret and a Calvin Klein catalog. I could dress that way, too, if I wanted, and be more impressive than she was. I'm taller than her, just over six feet, my breasts are bigger (and perkier), and I was in better shape when Dad turned me at twenty-one. My long blond hair stood out in contrast to the short cropped look she was sporting again. But I prefer to wear jeans and a T-shirt when I'm hunting, like Dad.

Stepmom saw Mom and stifled a sneer, walking in a wide arc to avoid her yet still approach my perch. I shifted my view from Mom to Stepmom slowly, rolling balls around the table with my hands.

"Where is he?" Stepmom asked.

"Beatrice said he took off in Fang an hour or so ago." I picked up the eight ball and fought the urge to throw it, not because I felt like I shouldn't but more because I couldn't decide whom I wanted to hit with it. Who was married to Dad? Who was going to be married to Dad? And could I eat the other one to cut down on confusion?

"That's just great." Tabitha adjusted her bustier. "We were supposed to talk over . . . dinner."

"He probably forgot." I rolled the eight ball into the corner pocket and settled on the fourteen ball, spinning it on the table as if it were a top.

"He didn't forget." Stepmom looked at the clock.

"Maybe"—I stood up, my nail beds crawling with sensation as my claws slid out—"he *did* forget." My eyes went red. "Or maybe *you* got the time wrong!" My jaw popped as my fangs tore through my gums and locked into place.

Or maybe—Dad popped into both of our heads as he got close enough for us to sense his presence—*he got sent on his first little demonic errand and had to kill an old friend.*

Who? Stepmom thought at him.

Ike, Dad thought back. *And now there are representatives from Sable Oaks, the Shifters, and the Mages Guild to talk to me about more City Council shit. Can I get a rain check on our chat?*

Oh, baby, Tabitha thought, *they made you kill Father Ike?*

But Dad had already cut her off.

Oh, get down, Stepmom said to me irritably. *Eric wouldn't let us kill each other anyway.*

Not that you even know how to end me, I thought to myself. *While I keep what it takes to end you in Fang's trunk—and a duplicate set in my room in the panel hidden under my recliner.* I jumped off the pool table just the same.

"I don't see what the big deal is," I said. My claws retracted, fangs receded. "I took my shoes off first."

"Sorry." Stepmom rubbed her eyes, glancing over at the troll and his mage. "You know what? You're right. Sit on the pool table all night. It's fine."

"Thanks," I said. *Not that I need your permission.* Unless she was really going to be Mom instead of Stepmom. Then maybe I did need her permission.

"Will you tell your father I went to my apartment?" Stepmom asked.

"Why don't you just stay with Dad?" I slid my sneakers on without bothering to untie them. "You could stay in my room until he's done with his meeting," I added hopefully. "I cleaned it up."

"Not yet," Stepmom said. "Your dad and I need a little time apart."

I'd heard that before. It wasn't as though Dad hadn't had plenty of girlfriends before; he just hadn't married any of them before Tabitha.

"Okay."

She turned to walk away, then stopped, turned back around, and lightly touched my arm. "You know this has nothing to do with you, right?"

"Yeah," I answered. I'd heard that before, too. It came before bad times and foster homes. Her fingers tightened around my arm incrementally—a gentle squeeze—and then she left. Mom watched her go without a word.

Mom came up to me next. She still smelled like smoke, but not like sickness or old age. A slight tang of disinfectant and sweaty feet hovered around her forearms, but her heartbeat . . .

"Can I?" I asked.

Mom let out a single braying "ha," following it up with "Knock yourself out, kiddo."

I rested my head against her chest, feeling the drive of her healthy circulatory system, blood coursing through her veins without the slow buildup of plaque she'd had when she'd been old. Her lifeblood flowed smoothly, the rhythm of her heart: pristine and good.

"You're so healthy." I hugged her around the waist and lifted her into the air. "Dad did good."

"I wasn't worth it." It was a lie; her heartbeat betrayed her.

"Fibber." I put her down again. "You're glad to be back."

"I'm glad to be back," she admitted. "But it wasn't worth the cost. I know he hasn't had to do anything yet—"

"Sure he has." I pointed to the television in the game room. "We were just talking about it." Above the caption BREAKING NEWS, a blond newscaster blabbed on about the scene behind her. Father Ike's church was in flames.

"My God." Marilyn gripped the edge of the pool table. "He had to burn down the church? Why?"

"No, silly. He had to kill Father Ike, and then he burned the church down for free. Nothing big or horrible. The fire smelled nice. It must have been the incense or something . . ."

I was surprised when she threw up. *I hope she's not catching that stomach bug that's been going around.*

6

ERIC

PUTTING OUT OLD FLAMES

A vampire, an Alpha werewolf, and two mages were waiting for me in the Pollux lobby. Sounds like the beginning of a joke, but it wasn't. The vampire, Lady Gabriella, represented the Sable Oaks contingent, the surviving group of High Society vamps who'd escaped my attack on the Highland Towers and the subsequent attack by "unknown individuals" on Winter's club, the Artiste Unknown.

I sensed Gabby on the way in. Her recently dyed black hair hung loose and long, as unfamiliar as her modern apparel. She was one of those vamps who preferred old-style clothes, real Renaissance stuff, fancy brocade gowns and the like, but given recent developments, she—like most of the remaining supernatural citizens—was finally having to learn how to blend in. For her, that meant designer slacks and a matching silk blouse. She looked uncomfortable wearing pants in mixed company.

"Lord Eric." She inclined her head, offering her neck.

"Don't start with that shit, Gabby." I waved off the formality.

The Alpha was William, the occasionally overzealous leader and reverend of the local werewolf pack that claimed the Orchard Lake area. His hair had begun to go a little gray around the edges, but he was a big guy, a good half a foot taller than my five-ten. He held a Bible in his hand, and every time he shifted his grip on the book, Gabby surreptitiously checked its potential trajectory.

William nodded. "Good evening, Eric."

"Hey, Bill."

One of the mages belonged to me: Magbidion, one of my thralls.

His immediately apparent nervousness bothered me more than the presence of the other mage.

"This is Paula Mallory?" Magbidion indicated the four-foot-tall woman next to him, making it a question, like he wasn't sure.

"She's a fuck'n midget," I said. "Sorry. Shit. What's the term now? Little person."

The young dark-haired woman raised an eyebrow. "Aw. How sweet. Someone's been watching *Little People, Big World*."

"No. I just got the last season of *Boston Legal*. You look like . . . what's her face? She played the short lawyer . . ."

"Candice Bergen?" Paula smiled sweetly, batting her eyelashes.

"Candice Bergen's not a midget." I let myself wince slightly after the fact. I wasn't trying to offend her, but people have to remember, I'm effectively in my eighties, and the "correct" words have changed a lot over the years.

She laughed. "Meredith Eaton, then?"

"I guess."

"I'll take that as a compliment," Paula said. "She's hot."

So was Paula. She wore a red pantsuit that must have been altered to show as much cleavage as it did. A single ruby on a platinum chain hung around her neck. Long dark hair with subtle red highlights framed her face, and her makeup was warmer than I expected from a gal wearing that type of business suit. A golden rune was etched into each painted red fingernail, and a single gold piercing glittered between her chin and lower lip. She felt like magic all over, exuded it. Warmth, too . . . more than a fever. Like she was her own little space heater.

"So are you." My face twitched. "That's not a hit, by the way," I added quickly, "observation only. No flirting intended." Then it struck. "Wait. Paula? Shouldn't you have an M name?" *Don't all mages have M names?*

"Shouldn't you be named Varney or Vladimir or something?"

"I didn't know we were actually *trying* to be rude." I winked. "Do I get to break out the C word now, or do I have to start with the B word and work up to it?"

"Okay." She chuckled. "Okay. A mage traditionally picks a working name that matches the first letter of her specialty. A garden-variety multipurpose mage gets an M name. A specialist can go with an M or with the letter signifying her area of expertise."

"P." I added it up. "Pyromancer?"

Her runes flared. The inside of her mouth glowed a fiery orange—a jack-o'-lantern effect I could see right through her skin as well as through her open smile—and her irises lit up in a matching shade. "That's me."

"Burn down my building, and I'm killing every mage in the city except for Melvin and Magbidion."

She laughed again, a single brightly accented squeal. "Oh, please, I think we both know I'd toast you."

"Try it and I'll sic my car on you."

"Steel frame?" Paula narrowed one eye, bobbing her head slightly from side to side as she weighed the options, her hands mimicking the movements of a scale. "Steel vaporizes at about fifty-five hundred degrees Fahrenheit . . . I can get that hot, but it's a pain in the butt, and it does horrible things to my hair. Wouldn't have to vaporize it, though. Steel melts at what? Twenty-five hundred degrees Fahrenheit? I think it's a safe bet you'd both be nice and melty before you ever laid a hand on me. You might come back, of course, but if there's one thing I'm not short on, it's BTUs."

"That wasn't some sort of weird come-on, was it?" I asked.

They all stared at me. I stared back. Paula shook her head, a definite no. *Whew.*

"So . . ." I let the vowel sound linger on until it became an inquiry. "You guys are all cluttering up my movie theater because . . . ?"

"I believe we're still waiting on Captain Stacey?" Gabby said.

I'd opened my mouth to make his excuses when Katherine Marx walked in. I'm sure it looked like I was checking her out when I glanced down at her chest, but I was really just making sure Magbidion's spell was still in place. When a vampire makes a thrall, the thrall gets a blood tattoo. To a vampire who has made a thrall, that tattoo can show up even through clothing. Katherine asked me to put hers right over her heart. I couldn't sense her thralldom, and since that was a power I had all the time—even at night—probably because of Fang, I hoped the others wouldn't be able to sense it, either.

Katherine had cleaned up so well that I didn't think anyone present would smell Stacey's blood on her. I couldn't, but that wasn't a sure sign, given how different my daytime vampire powers are from my nighttime true immortal powers.

Katherine wore the dark blue uniform of a VCPD police officer; the only sign of her different status was the SWAT patch on her shoulder. She was model-pretty when you got past the cop aura, though most people wouldn't. I thought the shotgun she was carrying might be a little over-the-top, but she was a human among the supernatural, and if it made her feel safer, who was I to object to a tiny equalizer?

"Sorry I'm late," she said to all of us, then directed the last to me as if mine were the only opinion that mattered. "Mr. Courtney."

"Is Captain Stacey okay?" William asked.

"He was a pussy, and I fired him," I said curtly. "Marx is handling things now, and she's better than Stacey because she has a pussy but isn't one." Gabby looked offended. Paula cracked a smile. Marx was cold as ice and twice as frosty. "So what the hell are we here to talk about?"

"Eric," William began, "you know what this is about."

"You promised to consider it," Gabby added. "And we've brought in the Mages Guild, as requested."

My heart sank as I realized what it was about. "Greta again?"

They nodded. Paula spoke up. "Without the Veil of Scrythax, we simply don't have the mage-power to cover every supernatural citizen. The . . . culling . . . of the vampire population has certainly helped, but the Supernatural Citizens—the SCs—absolutely have to help us help them. Most understand this. But your daughter is still hunting as if it's the good old days. Her actions alone require up to six interventions a night—she's a staffing nightmare!"

"I'll talk to her again."

"That's not enough, Eric." Gabriella was faking a light French accent. "As we have told you before, you need to stake her until the new Veil or a sufficient substitute is in place, or—"

"Like that's gonna happen," Paula cut in. "You stake his daughter, or try to make him stake his daughter, and he'll respond by killing or staking whatever number of other vampires is required to bring the feeding requirements down to acceptable levels so that we can cover Greta."

I like Paula. She's smart.

"We all know that, don't we?" Paula continued.

"If we kill all the Drones and Soldiers . . ." I let that sentence hang there.

William nodded. "Obviously the therianthrope community is okay with the destruction of as many vampires as Eric *and* the Sable Oaks contingent"—he gave a brief nod to Gabriella—"will agree to, but there is still the problem of the demons."

"Triple-T Waste Disposal," Paula joined in. "Tiko, Timbo, and Tombo are Oni. As Japanese Ogres, they've helped the SCs in Void City with body disposal for years, but they're also big monsters with a nonstandard number of eyes or horns and an obviously avant-garde skin color. It's taking twenty-four-hour magical coverage because Triple-T is also a legitimate waste disposal service with mundane clients and without the Veil—"

I held up a finger. "Did I or did I not bequeath half of Phil's surviving assets—a sum with more zeroes than I like to count—to the Mages Guild in exchange for you guys taking care of this shit for me?"

"Money can only do so much, Eric," Paula said. "I'm not asking for more money. What we need is more time, more mage-power, and more cooperation from the SCs. Yes, Greta, but not only her. The Fae largely police themselves, and the mouser population isn't an issue, but the more outré SCs have to take up some of the slack."

"Then it's a rotating curfew." They all stared at me like I'd grown an extra head. All of them were used to cursing, enchanted, drunk, or fatalistic Eric. I'm not unintelligent or uneducated, though it's true I've had a penchant for taking the easy way or letting things go on too long. It's simple and thoughtless and . . . fun. But it wouldn't get me out of this contract, and it wasn't going to win Marilyn back.

"No more than one problem population out past sundown on a given night. Vampires get Mondays, Wednesdays, and Fridays. Demons get Tuesdays, Thursdays, and Saturdays."

"What about Sundays?" Gabriella asked.

"The Mages Guild gets to work a skeleton crew on Sundays." Paula brightened, literally, when I said that, letting me know that at least one person in the room liked the idea.

"And therianthropes?" William asked.

"Don't get seen," I said. "If you do, you pay a double-sized Fang fee and wind up on my shit list."

"What happens to curfew breakers?" Magbidion asked.

"I happen." I snapped my fingers and grinned.

"That's nice, Eric," Paula cut in, "but most of the infractions will take place at night."

Did she know? I tried to cover my concern with bravado. "I suppose you have a better suggestion?"

"Than you?" Paula chirped. "Almost always." She held out a small sachet of leather, a medicine bag. It smelled like ashes, demon, and magic. "The council and I got together and whipped this up using the remaining ashes of the Veil of Scrythax. It basically does what the Veil did, but for the bearer and his—or her—immediate vicinity only."

"And I don't get it because?"

"Oh, you can have it." Paula's smile widened, and her eyes flickered from within. "But why don't we kill two birds with one stone? We'll give it to Greta—"

"I object," Lady Gabriella spoke up. "As the senior vampire—"

Marx casually shifted her shotgun so that it was aimed (and yet somehow not quite aimed) at Gabby's chest. It was the first time she'd done more than breathe since entering the room and being introduced.

"And," Paula continued, "we'll let her play sheriff. If the SCs won't play nice, then she gets to eat them. She'll love it!" She waggled the sachet, then tossed it to me. "What do you say, Tall-dark-and-scary? Based on what Greta did to Lisette when she came to Void City, there's a sizable portion of the population who's a hell of a lot more terrified of *her* coming for them than they are of you."

"With me, they could probably talk their way out of it." I sighed. I'd followed similar logic when sending Greta to kill Rachel. "Can the VCPD work with her?" I asked Marx.

"As long as you make it very clear to her that she's not allowed to hurt us," Marx said, shifting her shotgun back to a more neutral position.

"Can do," I said. "Gabby?"

Gabriella nodded, not even bothering to disguise her displeasure. "As much as I'd like to make an argument for the sachet coming to me, Paula's right. Eric, you're a threat with whom one can reason, but Greta . . ."

I held the sachet in my hand and frowned. It was a good plan. I didn't like it, but the little mage had it right. Greta would be happy to play sheriff, and it would keep her out of trouble—or at least out of trouble she wasn't supposed to be in.

"Is everyone agreed?" I asked after a few seconds. They were. "Then look out, Void City, there's a new sheriff in town."

As we broke up, Gabriella pulled me off to the side with a subtle nod. Hoping this wasn't some weird try-to-bang-the-new-top-dog thing, I dismissed Marx and joined Gabriella on the mezzanine. "You come-hithered me?" I said.

"I didn't want to bring it up in front of the others, because I'm not entirely sure how much they understand about how the city really works . . ."

"Uh-huh," I prompted.

"But I'm surprised that you haven't made a move toward vampire repopulation. Our numbers were cut by more than half in Winter's strike against us, artistic though it may have been, and . . ."

"And?"

She looked me straight in the eye. "And are you sure Population Control can handle all this?"

"Population Control?" I had no fucking clue what she was talking about.

"Yes," she said. "You've spoken with him?"

"It's covered," I said abruptly. What the hell was she talking about?

"Oh, good." She breathed a sigh of relief that was more for effect than anything else and kissed me on the cheek before taking her leave. "I was afraid you didn't know. I wouldn't want him to start bringing in more chupacabras."

I watched her go, then called Talbot's cell. "You ever heard of some guy with Population Control?"

"No." He sounded genuinely confused. "Why?"

"No reason, " I said after a moment. *Chupacabras aren't real. That's UFO-nut bullshit.* I was this close to asking Talbot about it, but I couldn't do it. I shook my head, still holding the phone. *I mean, if chupacabras were real, I'd know about it, right? Gabby was just having you on, dude. Got to be.* I hung up and stared at the phone for a minute before heading off to explain Greta's new job to her.

"Chupacabras, my ass."

7

GRETA

HAVE FANGS, WILL TRAVEL

Do I get a badge?"

Daddy stared at me without comprehension from his spot at the doorway to my room in the Pollux. He didn't come in because it's pretty small for two people, even with everything unboxed and half of it thrown away or put into storage. I used to sleep on top of all my stuff before I got used to bunking in Fang's trunk. Now that I'd converted the space into what basically amounted to a huge live-in closet, there was room to stand in. The space had hanging racks on either side of the room, the comfy recliner from my old apartment, a wall-mounted smartboard (which doubled as a TV), and my skull collection (each skull mounted to the cornice-work and wearing a different hat). I took the black Stetson off of Telly's skull and donned it, adjusting the brim to a rakish angle.

"A star," I tried again. "You know, like a badge, but an Old Westy one?" I tipped my hat.

He smiled, which was good, because I'd come close to saying "badge" again instead of "star," but I thought a sheriff's star would be more endearing. I know I'm his number one and only daughter, but Daddy's fickle, or he can be, or it seems like he is sometimes. A frown thinned my lips and pulled at the corners of my mouth. Being critical of Dad is bad unless it's with my out-loud voice and I'm teasing. *Bad, Greta!*

"What are you frowning about?" Eric's brow furrowed. "I haven't said no yet. Of course you can have a star. I'm sure we can order—"

"Thanks, Dad!" I wanted to hug him but settled for a kiss on the cheek instead. Dad wasn't smiling, and I needed him to smile, needed to see it, to know he was okay. "So . . . I can eat anybody I want as long as I can make them break curfew first?"

"No. They have to break curfew all on their own." As he spoke, I got my smile. "If you have any questions about whether somebody broke curfew or not, you need to ask me, Paula, or Talbot."

"Okay." Now for my real question. "What about Mom?"

"Marilyn?" He crossed his arms. "Yeah. Yeah. Okay, but try not to bother her too much about it—"

"Marilyn, right?" My teeth clamped together, cutting my sentences short, jaw tensing as I spoke, stomach churning. "Marilyn is Mom. Not Tabitha. Right?"

"That's your thing, Greta, I—"

"No!" The shout surprised us both, even though I was the one shouting. "You have to say who Mom is, because you're Dad." Unconsciously balled into a fist, my hand tapped his chest. "Who is more important? It's Mom . . . Marilyn Mom, not Tabitha Mom, right? Marilyn is . . ." I looked around for words and found skulls instead. Telly's skull couldn't tell me anything. He was just a skull with a bullet hole. Unless the answer was zero, circle, or the letter O, he was useless.

"It's Marilyn," Dad said finally, his tone soft. He hugged me and I felt his warmth, ignoring what he seemed not to want me to know. He kissed me on the forehead. "Always Marilyn."

"So Tabitha is just—"

"I don't know what Tabitha is, sweetheart. Why don't you go ahead and end her just to keep things simple?"

Or . . . that's what I wanted to ask, what I wanted him to answer. Instead, Dad said it was my thing, and that was the end of it. Instead of challenging him, like I was dying to do, I said one meek little word, "Okay," and smiled sweetly as Dad kissed me on the forehead.

"Oh, and Dad?"

"Yes?"

"If I'm going to be sheriff, are there any things, you know, that I should know about?"

"Know about?" He played it cool, but my line of questioning clearly worried him.

"Secret stuff," I said. "Because I know there is some strange . . . stuff going on, and I don't know if it's okay to investigate it or not. I want to check it out, but . . ."

"Just use your best judgment," Dad told me, and walked out like everything was settled.

But that doesn't answer my question, Dad! If I'm sheriff, what does that mean? Am I really just a big bogeyman scaring everyone into line like John Paul Courtney did when he was alive? Do I arrest people if I don't want to kill them? I mean, I'll probably want to kill them, but what if I think you don't want me to kill them? Are there crimes for which I don't kill? Do I hand out Fang fees for those? If so, is there a chart? Is this a real job? Do I get paid?

I came back to the mom question again just then, grabbed one of my pet skulls, and smashed it on the floor. I realized too late that I'd grabbed Telly's skull, so I sent another down to join him in a shattered pile of splintered bone.

Dad's just really stressed right now, I told myself. *I need to be more understanding. I can work this out. I can.*

"Maybe if I killed both of them . . ."

Public Safety Tip #1: Perpetrators will be eaten.

8

ERIC
HOME TO ROOST

Used to be there was a time when dawn surprised me. Not anymore. I know it's coming. It starts with a burning in my gums, nagging and insistent. More painful than having popcorn stuck between my teeth but just shy of the ripping sensation I get when I pop my fangs. Greta wanted to talk more. I knew she did, even an hour from dawn, I felt it. The pain spread to my throat, like acid reflux or heartburn, then down to my belly, which churned and roiled like a cauldron of witches' brew or battery acid.

My nail beds started to crawl (toes and fingers). I tore down the hallway to my room as fast as I could. Mags stood in the center of the room, runes set up and glowing. Waiting.

"A little early, aren't you?" he asked, but I couldn't answer—my fangs extended, painfully so, to their maximum über vamp size and length, but in a human-sized mouth, uppers and lowers gouging holes in the roof of my mouth and piercing my lower jaw. My eyes quivered, vision blurring. Etched in red, like blood poisoning chased with lava, my veins stood out raw and angry.

I blame Scrythax.

The door to the hallway closed behind me. I felt the ear-popping *Zot!* of Mags's ward going live, then I dashed into the bathroom and got it over with. No one heard me scream. Mags warded up the bathroom door, too, a second layer of protection for my secret. Maybe it was getting worse. Maybe it wasn't. I wondered what would have happened if I hadn't broken the Eye of Scrythax—or if the other half had broken. Would it have mattered? Would I be a vampire by night and a true immortal by day instead of the other way around? Would the sun and I have been on friendly terms again? I like to pretend it wouldn't have made any difference, but deep down, I suspect it would have made all the difference in the world.

An hour later, the sun outside was bright and shining in the sky. Not that I could go out and take a look without bursting into flames, but she was there. I could feel her laughing at me. Sitting on the bed in a pair of tan slacks, a white undershirt, and a button-down blue dress shirt, I slipped on my new brown belt, dress socks, and the loafers I'd had Talbot pick up for me, while forcing myself to keep taking hits off a blood bag fresh from the fridge.

The first blood bag always goes down easy, no matter what, but tonight the second one was tough to stomach. My brain was playing games with me, more than usual. I didn't want blood. If I had to drink something hot and red, I preferred a Bloody Mary. So far none of my thralls had figured out the whole taste-enhancement side of what Rachel used to do when I fed on her.

I finished the second bag anyway and headed down to the garage to check on Greta. Fang's trunk popped open as I approached. My little girl slept amid the bones of Fang's victims and her own. She'd started taking a skull to bed with her a few months ago; her favorite one had a large bullet hole in the forehead. She'd apparently forgotten it today. About the same time she started cuddling up with a skull, I stopped having to do as much when I tucked her in. She still needs a little cleanup now and again, but mainly, I lay out new clothes for her and clear away any random bone fragments she's fallen asleep on.

Talbot walked into the parking deck from the street, his footsteps as recognizable as his breath, his heartbeat, his smell, or his laugh.

"So this is what you used to dress like, huh?"

I looked up at him and smiled. Wearing a custom suit, as usual, he looked better than I did. Ladies really go for the whole big, black, and confident thing he has going on. Even being bald works for him.

"I'm not the one in the suit," I muttered, closing Fang's trunk. "Where'd Tabitha sleep?"

"Back at her apartment," Talbot said. "She said to tell you to drive over and force her awake if you want to talk or hang out."

I shook my head. "That's not happening."

"Eric—"

"Follow The Plan, Talbot." I looked at him. Did he seem a little older now? A touch softer around the middle than he had when I met him? A few more laugh lines? "Can you do that?"

"Sure." He broke into a wide grin. "Mom says you should come around more often. She liked chatting with you."

"She could always visit," I offered. Talbot's mom had helped me through the afterlife when I chased after Greta. She was nice, as far as ancient Egyptian deities in whom I don't want to believe go.

"No," Talbot answered. "She's too mythic for the real world now. She can affect things here, but showing up in person takes a lot of power and leaves beings like her too exposed."

"Where's Marilyn?"

"Over at the bowling alley."

"Did you talk things over with the Iversonian?" Talbot winced when I said the name. The Iversonian is Void City's senior true immortal, not that we have many. He and Talbot have some kind of history I don't want to know too much about.

"I did, and he'll do it, but I think you'd be better off sending her to Europe to study with . . . what was it you called him?"

"Fuckup Courtney?" I spat on the concrete deck, leaving a splatter of blood on the ground. "Dumbass the First?" Jean-Paul was my oh-so-bright ancestor who got the family cursed in the first place. He was turned into a vampire when Scrythax decided to impersonate a god, respond to his plight, and turn him into a true immortal rather than a vampire. Instead of killing Lisette (the vampire who'd turned him) and ending the curse before things got weird, Dumbass the First ignored her completely and let generation after generation of Courtney take it up the rear for his stupidity. Let that idiot teach Marilyn how to use her powers? I spat again. "No. Maybe the German chick, but she's probably busy. Anyone else would just screw Marilyn up. The Iversonian, I can keep an eye on."

"You're the boss." Talbot spread his arms and dipped his head in a mock bow.

I shrank into mouse form, feeling like too much person in too small a package, and let Talbot pick me up by the tail.

"Take me over to the bowling alley and quit screwing around," I squeaked as he dangled me over his open smile. "If you eat me, I'll turn into an über vamp in your stomach."

"If I ate you"—his fangs slid out, his eyes shining a brilliant emerald green—"you'd be dead. Mine is the power to devour. Remember."

"You want to give it a shot, T?" I squeaked at him. "You wanna take the old man out? Bring it."

He laughed a rich velvety laugh and slipped me into the front pocket of his suit coat. "I'll pass."

"Coward," I squeaked.

Waiting in Talbot's pocket for a safe second to cross the road, I panicked. It's one thing to make a plan and another to pull it off. I had no doubt Marilyn would have stayed with me, working in the bowling alley until the end of time, watching me sleep with other women and refusing to have anything to do with me, just like she had when the Demon Heart was a strip club. But the status quo wasn't good enough. At least the Stacey thing was over. Marx could handle herself, and she was on my team.

"Don't have a little mousy heart attack in there," Talbot purred.

"Fuck you, cat."

"Hey!" Talbot darted out between cars, and I shifted around in his pocket. "No need to be insulting."

"Fuck you, mouser, then."

A horn beeped at us, blurred by the Doppler effect. "Much better," Talbot answered with a chuckle. "None of that cat stuff. Not from you. You know better."

He lifted me out of his pocket, and I concentrated on reforming with my new clothes intact. This early in the morning, Marilyn and Erin were the only two up and about. Erin looked down when she saw my clothes, blond bangs falling over her eyes. "I'll go check . . ." She headed down to the lane without clarifying what, exactly, she meant to check.

"I'll go check, too," Talbot said wryly, heading back out the front door.

"Hey," I said, walking toward Marilyn. She was behind the counter next to the register, double-counting the till. She used to do the same thing at the original Demon Heart, twice when she counted down the drawer before running the deposit and twice more in the morning checking for payouts from me or what's-his-face (Edgar, maybe? some vampire I used to run the club with) in case she needed to run to the bank for more cash or change.

"Greta's stealing money out of the till again." Marilyn set her jaw. "You need to speak with her."

"How do you know Greta took it?" I put my hand on the counter, resisting the urge to pull myself up on it, slide across the intervening space, and pull Marilyn into my arms.

"Well, gee, Eric," Marilyn snapped. "Who else do you know who would steal all the quarters, spend them on bouncy balls and capsule toys from the vending machines, and then leave all the plastic capsules sitting on the floor around the machines?"

Heh. I smirked. "She can have it." I waved the crime away. "I—"

"I know she can have the money." Marilyn slammed the drawer closed, still holding a red Void City Metro Bank bag in her hand. She'd written out her change order on a purple Post-it and had it stuck to a fifty-dollar bill. She slid the bill into the bag. "But you have to get her to do the paid-outs right so I don't have to recount the drawer and figure out how much she took."

"Fine." God, she looked beautiful. The smell of her, and not just the low-down feminine scent but her hair, the toothpaste on her breath, her detergent . . . her youth . . . it was so much worse during the day, so much harder to ignore. "Listen—"

"It's not fine, Eric!"

I blinked, recoiling instinctively. Why was she yelling?

"Greta only does this kind of thing when she's seriously upset." Marilyn dropped the bank bag on the counter.

"I'll talk to her about it." I leaned against the counter, trying to ignore the furnace-like glow of her body heat. Feeding on cold blood lowers a vampire's internal thermostat below room temperature, and despite the warmth of my newly re-formed clothing, my skin was hypersensitive. My fingers unconsciously tapped out her heartbeat on the countertop before I noticed and forced my hand to be still.

Marilyn didn't seem convinced.

"I will," I insisted. "But she's down for the day and we need to talk about something else."

"Where's your wife?"

"Technically, I don't have one," I said. "Tab's and my vows were—quote—until one of us departed this world—end quote—and I did. I ran through the Paths of the Dead. I was judged—"

"You came back."

"True, but it still counts, *and* she was brain-whammied by Rachel when we made our vows, so the ceremony was bullshit to start with—"

"Tabitha doesn't feel that way about it." Marilyn's tone was measured and sure. She'd been waiting for this talk; she'd had time to think it all through. "I asked her the week I came back from the dead. She loves you, and you married her."

Oh . . . gut shot! But one I'd expected all along.

"But I love you," I said.

Marilyn smiled, a tear in the corner of her eye. "Of course you think that, Eric." She touched my hand. "I love you, too—I always have—but that doesn't make it right."

"What do I need to do to make it right?" I knew the answer to that one, too, or thought I did. I couldn't make it right. Not really. Even if Tabitha stepped aside, Marilyn would suspect I'd used my Sire abilities to force Tabitha to be a good little offspring and get out of my libido's way. Which I'd never do, of course, but the doubt would be there, and it would poison everything. So I had to eradicate the doubt.

She laughed that single braying "ha" with which I was so familiar.

"Eric, even if you could make it right, if we got married right now . . . would it really change anything?"

"Yes."

"And you'd still want me after I cheated on you?"

"With whom?" I asked. "When?" There are things I decide to forget. Marilyn's infidelity was one of them. I didn't care, and I didn't want to know, and if I don't think about something for long enough, whatever's wrong with my brain, whether it really is early-onset Alzheimer's or something else, it takes the memory and eats it. When it comes back to haunt me, then I ignore it, and if I pretend long enough, eventually, I forget for real. I remembered that she'd cheated, but in my head, there were extenuating circumstances, and it had happened after I was a vampire. That wasn't quite true, but I wanted it to be, so I had every intention of acting like it was.

My memory was working . . . and I knew Marilyn had slept with Roger. I killed and ate Roger. If it was a question of revenge, I think that counts as handled.

She searched my eyes with her gaze. "You really don't remember?"

"I know some bad stuff happened, and the guy who did it is dead now," I answered. "Anything that happened between you two, I don't hold against you."

A tear ran down her cheek. "If we walked down the aisle right now, what song would you pick for the first dance after?" she asked.

" 'We've Only Just Begun' by the Carpenters."

"Why that instead of 'Stardust'?"

"Because we have forever now, or we can have it." *And weird things happen when I play and sing "Stardust."*

"Damn."

A car pulled up and parked in the back. V8 engine but not Fang's. Two more parked next to it. Car doors opened.

"What?" I asked, trying not to notice the sound of booted feet on concrete and asphalt.

"That's a good answer."

"I guess that's love, then." I smelled gun oil, too, and kerosene. I listened for heartbeats. Talbot was no longer within hearing distance, but there were a dozen humans behind the club. I also heard a mechanical whine cutting through things. A winch? I started rounding the counter, not to get closer to her but to make sure I was between her and the back door.

Fang, I thought as loudly as I could. There was half a reply, a disembodied engine rev, and then—

"Eric, we never really loved each other."

"Bullshit." A stabbing pain punched through my chest. I balled my hands into fists, trying to cover up the pain and hold in a yelp. Somebody had just staked Fang. I could sense it, but I was finally having The Talk with Marilyn, and . . .

"Don't be mad, I—"

"Oh, I'm not mad, I just recognize bullshit when I hear it." I clutched my chest over my heart, the sensation of sharp, intense agony still clear and present. "If we weren't in love with each other, or . . . if I wasn't in love with you . . . then it's like that poem I learned for our wedding."

"What poem?"

"Shakespeare's." In my mind's eye, I could almost see the group of men around Fang. One of them reached for the trunk release, but another man stopped him. "Sonnet 116."

We'll count the bones of the victims later, the man seemed to say.

"You were going to recite a poem?"

I nodded. Gun oil filled my nostrils. *Maybe I have enough time,* I thought. As they formed up at the rear door, the whining stopped, and I heard what sounded like rubber wheels on the concrete—a wheelchair?

"I thought it would be romantic. It goes like this: 'Let me not to the marriage of true minds / Admit impediments.'" I felt for the power of the über vamp and couldn't touch it. "'Love is not love / Which alters when it alteration finds,'" I closed with Marilyn as I recited the verses, and she didn't fight me when I put my hand on her arm. "'Or bends with the remover to remove: / O no! it is an ever-fixed mark.'"

More heartbeats approached the front of the building, but I didn't stop reciting. "'That looks on tempests and is never shaken; / It is the star to every wandering bark, / Whose worth's unknown.'" My eyes locked with hers and I felt her soften. The key to Marilyn's heart was and always would be in revealing within myself the man she once loved, the man who went to war and came back broken. A man she fixed and sent off to war again. "'Although his height be taken. / Love's not Time's fool . . .'" But I was Time's fool. There's a sound of metal on metal when a lock is being picked. I heard that sound. ". . . 'though rosy lips and cheeks / Within his bending sickle's compass come . . .'"

Walkie-talkies beeped from the front and back of the Demon Heart, audible only to me. The attack was coming, but I was almost through. My chest tightened. If I'd been human, I wouldn't have been able to breathe, but I was almost through. If I could only kiss her . . .

"'Love alters not with his brief hours and weeks, / But bears it out even to the edge of doom.'" I pulled her tightly to me, crushing her against

my chest, her breasts against me. Even through our clothes, the sensation brought out my fangs, but I forced them back in. "'If this be error
and upon me proved, / I never writ, nor no man ever loved.'"

I leaned in to kiss her, and her eyes closed. Maybe I hadn't won her
back, but it was going to happen . . . she would allow something that
had been off limits to me for almost fifty years: a simple kiss. Our lips
almost touched . . . and of course that's when they opened fire.

9

ERIC

IT'S ALL ABOUT TIMING WITH SOME PEOPLE

I hate bullets, especially when some jackass has blessed the damn things and started shooting me with them. Why can't all vampire hunters be like that dumbass in El Segundo who tried etching crosses onto the shell casings—you know, the part that doesn't actually hit the vampire? Heh. That was classic.

All sounds except for a high-pitched whine went away as I shoved Marilyn to the ground. These guys couldn't kill her, but bullets hurt. They lit me up from both sides, the rapid jerk of automatic-weapons fire making me dance like a squirrel under high voltage. I counted a dozen assailants, including one in a wheelchair. At night, the wounds would've kept burning, but not during the day. During the day, my powers work close to normal, which should be taken as a sign of how screwed up they've gotten.

Spirals of smoke wafted up from my wounds and in my best Southern drawl, I said, "That ain't the way my momma taught *me* to say hello." No claws. No snarls. Not glowing eyes. Not yet. This was all part of The Plan, too, not the Win Back Marilyn Plan but the other one . . . or maybe it's a subsection of the Marilyn Plan. I'm calling it Operation Let's All Get Drunk and Screw, but that's mainly because I want to confuse anybody who can read my mind. I may have already said that. Very prone to the fuzzy is my brain.

"I don't want to fight any of you guys."

They continued to fire, so I closed my eyes and concentrated. Turning to mist is like walking out into a freezing winter rain. You feel cold, soaked to the bone. Everything goes hazy, like there's gauze over the camera lens, or there would be if I opened my eyes. Misting makes me motion sick if I move too quickly or look around too much. I don't know how Winter does it without throwing up all over the place.

Once I felt soaked to the core, I opened my eyes. The weapons fire had stopped, but the vampire hunters were still there. I closed my eyes again and focused on pulling myself back together, becoming whole. The bullets made it harder. I wanted to be whole and healthy when I rematerialized, but the bullets wanted to be inside me, burning my undead flesh and generally showing their disapproval.

Being water vapor sucks. Resuming my physical form felt great, almost as good as jumping into a swimming pool on a warm summer day. Even though I lost my courting clothes, reverting to a WELCOME TO THE VOID T-shirt, jeans, belt, and combat boots, it seemed to have done the trick.

"That was mist," said the man in the wheelchair.

"Yes, it was." I turned to face him slowly, palms up, hands at shoulder level. "I don't want to fight you guys."

"My research says you turn into a ghost."

"I used to," I agreed. "You're about one version behind in my development cycle."

"How?" he asked. His crew smelled of fear, hate, and resolve, but not him; his scent was neutral.

"I close my eyes really, really tightly and try to turn to mist. It feels similar to the way turning into a ghost did, but I don't glow blue, and the world doesn't go all screwy watercolor-painting."

"No." He met my eyes without fear. "How did they change? A vampire's powers, even an Emperor's, don't usually change so abruptly."

"My powers change more often than a stripper swaps outfits on a Saturday night," I said. "It's from all the powerful muckety-mucks who keep messing with me. Now here's the deal. I . . ." And then I forgot the deal. It went right out of my head. Told you I was addled. Fortunately, I had an app for that. "Crap. Hold on."

I pulled out my cell and pressed the question-mark symbol I'm supposed to use if I utterly blank.

My screen displayed a tiny rolling smiley face and:

CONNECTING . . .

DAYTIME SUPPORT: *What happened?*

ME: *Vampire hunters just shot me up in the Demon Heart.*

DAYTIME SUPPORT: *Did you kiss her first?*

ME: *No time. They were too fast.*

DAYTIME SUPPORT: *No worries. That will work out sooner or later.*

ME: *I think I'm not supposed to fight the vampire hunters. Right?*

One of the vampire hunters cleared his throat. Marilyn brushed herself off and got to her feet. "What are you doing, Eric?" she asked.

"Sorry. Just a second."

I looked back at the phone and frowned. I understood what I read, but even seeing it didn't make it ring a bell.

ME: *I don't remember that part.*

DAYTIME SUPPORT: *N_CASE_OF_HUNTERS1.*

ME: *Seriously?*

DAYTIME SUPPORT: *Do it or don't, but it's the next step in The Plan, and you do want The Plan to succeed, right?*

ME: *I'm doing it now.*

I thumbed through the contact list, and sure enough, there it was, just like Daytime Support had typed: N_CASE_OF_ HUNTERS1. I thumbed the contact and let the call connect. The voice on the other end of the phone was one that always made me smile, even if it did sound a bit more hoarse than usual.

"I got vampire hunters, and they staked my car," I said. I could only imagine how strange it must have looked to the people in the bowling alley. This is not how fights with me work. I'm usually all bull and no china shop, but that was back when I had little to lose and nothing to gain.

"Mr. Courtney," said the man in the wheelchair, "if you're calling in mage support—"

"I swear on Marilyn's life that I'm not calling in any kind of air strike or hit squad."

The man swallowed hard, looked more confused, and nodded. His unease was hard to miss.

"Do I send her in yet?" one of his men called in on the walkie-talkie.

"Give us another minute or two," wheelchair boy said calmly.

"She won't wait much longer," the voice on the walkie said.

"Understood, but the situation is not as expected."

"What's your name?" I asked, interrupting.

"Um . . . Pythagoras."

"Here." I thrust my cell at him. "He wants to talk to you."

"Who wants—"

When he didn't take the phone immediately, I held it up to his ear. Vampire hearing let me get both sides of the conversation just fine, but I'm keeping one side of it to myself 'cause I'm all sneaky and shit.

"Eric?" Marilyn tried to catch my eye, but I was too busy watching Pythagoras. He had the look of a guy who wasn't often surprised, was unsure how to react when he was, and definitely was now.

"Even if I did believe that I—" Pythagoras found himself cut off by the person on the other end. His eyes widened. "But surely. Ah. Yes. Are you certain? Can— No, that's true." An exasperated sigh. "No. Yes. Well, obviously, that's accurate, but . . . No. No. I agree that he would be quite valuable in that role." One last long look at me. "But . . . he's a vampire! What? No. I was unaware of that. Very well. Out of respect for you, then. Seventy-two hours. Yes, you have my word."

He pulled his head away from the phone, and I put it up to my ear, but the call had already been terminated. I said "Thanks" to the empty air and clicked back over to the app represented by the smiley-face icon.

DAYTIME SUPPORT: *Do you remember step seven of the M protocol?*

My heart sank. How could I ever forget step seven of the M protocol? I had nightmares about it, even though I'm the one who came up with that part.

ME: *Yes.*

DAYTIME SUPPORT: *Do it after the fight.*

ME: *What fight?*

CONNECTION TERMINATED.

It kicked me back out to the main menu, and I frowned. Pythagoras and his men were arguing, but I could tell they were going to comply. There was a halfheartedness to the objections. Deep down they trusted him, and he trusted N_CASE_OF_HUNTERS1.

Pythogoras held out a hand, and I shook it.

"I can't believe I'm saying this, Mr. Courtney, but I wish you the best of luck." He spoke into the walkie-talkie. "We're pulling out. Password: Golden Triangle." He took his finger off the button and said, "This may not go well with one of our allies, but my men will all follow orders."

"Which ally?" I asked. If I'd waited a few seconds, I could have spared myself the breath, because my front door slammed open so hard, it came off of its hinges. Standing in the doorway was a woman who looked vaguely familiar. She stood out on the sidewalk, blond hair illuminated by the sun, eyes awash with glowing red fury, nails extended into claws, fangs bared. She wore a pair of tight blue jeans with decorative lacing up the sides, brown boots, a red leather belt, and a cream-colored silk blouse. A red scarf around her neck and the matching pair of fingerless gloves completed the odd ensemble.

"There is no way in hell we're calling off this attack!"

Normally, vampires can sense each other at a distance. Vamps we're used to sensing barely register if we're busy. Greta and Tabitha, for example. I sense them all the time, so if I'm distracted, I won't get a full contact; I kind of dismiss it instinctively without paying attention, like hitting the snooze button on an alarm clock. But this woman— why I didn't sense her until we locked eyes, I can't say.

Now that I sensed her, she felt like a Motörhead album, one of the newer ones. Her name was Evelyn Courtney-Barnes. I guessed she'd been made a vampire no more than three to five years ago, and where I'd normally get a sense of a vampire's power level, from her all I sensed was: KILL ERIC COURTNEY.

Never a good sign. I had time to ask, "Do I know you from somewhere?" and then she was heading toward me at top vampire speed, and the fight was under way.

10

ERIC

WHY *NUKEKUBI* SHOULDN'T FIGHT IN BOWLING ALLEYS

She wasn't expecting me to block. It's not something I do, but one can't start learning more about fighting smart without having some of it stick, even with a memory like mine. Evelyn aimed two claw rakes at my neck. I batted them both aside and tried to sweep her legs. The fight would have gone faster, but thanks to my newest batch of power issues, I can't go über vamp without help from Fang, and with Fang staked . . . Is it still staking if it involves a tire iron and an engine instead of a piece of wood and an undead heart?

I was wondering that when a knee to the crotch filled my world with pain and nausea. It was only luck that I saw the stake and misted right before it would have struck home. Misting made the nausea worse, and I vomited, a cloud of pinkish mist puffing off my main "cloud," which turned solid (or, well, liquid) and splattered the floor once it was clear of me and the magic keeping it mist. One good thing about having all your bodily fluids replaced with blood is that when you hurl, at least it doesn't stink. True, there's blood everywhere, but . . .

It's not always easy for me to stay mist. If I get distracted, I can go physical again without meaning to do so. The rush of transformation is unmistakable, though, so the moment I was solid again, I knew I was. Score one for Team Alzheimer's.

"Look. I've pissed off a lot of women, but—" I ducked another angry volley of claws, rolling backward, then leaping over the seats bracketing lane six. I landed with the squeal of rubber soles on wood, wincing as they left skid marks near the approach, the cool solidity of the ball return against my calves. Momentum sucks.

"Bastard!" Evelyn snarled.

"My parents were married, but if you want to try 'asshole' or 'motherfucker'—"

We clashed, hands locked in more of a push-and-pull than a fight. She was strong, if not as strong as me, then close.

"You murdered me!"

"It obviously didn't take, so that's a bonus."

To the left of the angry woman with the claws and accusations, I saw Marilyn heading toward the door. Being a true immortal doesn't exactly come with superstrength, as far as I can tell. There are ways to make yourself stronger and faster, but most of them are visible to other supernatural types, and I didn't think Marilyn had taken the time to learn anything about them yet. All the same, I knew she was headed to get the tire iron out of Fang.

Marilyn Amanda Robinson, I love you so much, I can't stand it.

Full names.

Evelyn Courtney-Barnes.

I'd heard it as Evelyn Courtney Barnes in my head, but when I'd seen it, it'd had a hyphen like a bra burner's last name. My family name is Courtney. Another knee to the crotch nearly broke my train of thought, but I found it again pretty damn quick. When I was murdered, it was the Courtney Family Curse that brought me back as a vampire. The curse turned any Courtney who died while not following the usual family path of religion into a vampire or something else it thought suitable. John Paul Courtney, my great-great-(great?)-grandfather, had been turned into a ghost and attached to his magic revolver, El Alma Perdida. I'd broken the curse and lost the revolver a year ago, but unlike in the fairy tales, breaking the curse hadn't suddenly made me human again.

"Wait!" I shoved her away. Regardless of our almost equal strength, I had at least fifty pounds on her. "Your maiden name was Courtney? As in related to me?"

She growled, charged, and went for a tackle. We tumbled together out onto the approach and slid halfway down the lane, the mixture of mineral oils on the polished wood letting us slide farther than normal. She rode atop me, growling and lunging. Typical vampire move to go for a bite when in close. She snapped once, twice, then smiled. "You think you're so damn smart." Her fangs grew a little longer and turned up, more tusklike. "Can you mist while I have a grip on you? Can you do it, asshole?"

I tried, but "no" seemed to be the answer. "Look, if you're my relative, I understand why you might be mad at me. Maybe you wish I'd broken the Courtney Family Curse earlier on, and then you wouldn't be a vampire, but—"

"Screw the curse!" Evelyn snarled. "You think I give a shit about some damn curse? You murdered me, asshole! I was heading to my goddamn bachelorette party, and you swooped down out of nowhere, snatched me away to a rooftop, and beat the hell out of me before tearing off my clothes like I was some damn Christmas present."

"I—I don't rememb—" But then I did remember . . . maybe. I've killed a lot of people, well over ten thousand, but I've never done much dragging off to rooftops. I don't know why, but there's usually a more convenient place, and—"Wait. Rooftop?"

"I parked my Jag across from Starbucks and ran in to load up on coffee, because I hadn't been sleeping much and I wanted to be awake enough to enjoy the party, but I never made it there. You killed me, ripped off my fucking head, dropped it down a sewer drain, and left my body on the roof." She hissed, then let loose with a catlike yowl, a frustrated mixture of rage and regret. "You probably don't even remember it, you useless—"

I did remember. It all came back: the smell of her expensive perfume, the smoothness of her newly shaved legs . . ." You were wearing purple lingerie, right?"

"How sweet," she said sarcastically. "You remember."

"If I ripped your head off, then how?"

"How did I come back?" She grinned a wicked self-satisfied grin. "Oh, the Courtney Family Curse was one insistent bit of magic, I'll give it that. It always found a way. Have you ever heard of a *nukekubi?*"

"A what?"

I felt her claws dig deep and lock; her legs were rigid, gripping mine. Her grin broadened, and then her head came off, letting the scarf fall loose to reveal a line of glowing red *kanji*-like symbols. They looked Japanese, but they could have been any Asian language. My vampire sense tingled again, and KILL ERIC COURTNEY was replaced with a feeling of power levels and might. It felt strange and ephemeral, not like normal, but she was definitely Vlad-level, at least. Was she an Emperor? I had no clue. She was a vampire whose fucking head could pop off and fly around. How the hell was I supposed to know? That never happened to me when my head got ripped off.

"That's convenient." I struggled against her grip, but locked in one place, her strength seemed to have increased. "An undead chick with a detachable head: the blow-job potential alone . . ."

Never underestimate the capacity unrestrained lewdness has when it comes to deliberately pissing off a female opponent. Just ask my almost-hopefully-soon-to-be-ex-wife, Tabitha. Free of her body, Evelyn's head was transfigured. Long blond hair floated about her as if only tangentially affected by gravity, as if she were floating on her back in a pool. Her skin took on a porcelain pallor, and the fangs receded to a more normal length. I watched the whites of her eyes go crimson, as if they'd been injected with red food coloring. When she spoke, her voice, though clear and comprehensible, sounded like it came not from her mouth but from all directions at once.

"Pig." She spat the word, then buried her fangs in my throat.

I don't like to get bitten. It's a whole thing. But there are few times a vampire is more vulnerable or more distracted than when he's feeding. I felt my strength begin to fade, my hunger grow. My thoughts went cloudy, and then . . . then I felt an engine turn over, felt it deep in my chest, in the very core of me. Fang revved his engine, pegging out the RPMs while staying in one spot, tires squealing and throwing up smoke. And I I . . . well, I went über vamp.

I halfway expected Evelyn's legs and arms to snap, but they gave way instead, like the spring-loaded arms of a life-size doll. Evelyn tried to disengage her fangs from my rapidly expanding throat, but my hand was already there, locking her into place. A gruesome *crack-snap* made me wince as one of her fangs broke, snapping midway down the tooth. My skin flushed black, a wave of jet staining me obsidian. Leathery bat wings erupted from my back with a sound like sailcloth catching the wind.

"Okay." My claws sank into the approach, and I winced again, wondering how much it would cost to fix it or if I'd have to replace the flooring. "Nobody bites me." I pulled her free, my long black claws glistening against her blond hair. "It's a whole thing—a rule—don't fucking do it."

"I'll kill you!"

"Already dead, cousin. It is 'cousin,' isn't it?" I held up her head so I could see her expression, careful not meet her gaze, because I didn't want to get into some weird mental battle and find out the hard way that she had more going on upstairs than me. Most people do. "Are we like first cousins? Second cousins? Once removed? I'm guessing at least once or twice removed, no matter what, because of that whole generational thing, yeah?"

Beatrice caught my attention from behind the computer controlling the lanes. She held up a crossbow, and I gave a slight shake of my head. Marilyn could have made the shot, but I doubted Beatrice could. With my off hand, I made a little circle in the air with my forefinger. Bea smiled and shook her head, not a "no" but more of an "I can't believe he's going to do this."

Evelyn had answered my question while my mind was on Beatrice, so I had no idea what she'd said, but frankly, I didn't care. I knew I'd been an asshole. Even with the new plan, that wasn't going to change. It's how I am. It's in my DNA or something. I try to play nice, give folks a chance to back down, but it never works out. When it doesn't, I wind up looking like even more of an asshole after I take drastic actions, like I had with . . . cat guy . . . orange and white fur . . . evil police dude . . . Whatever his name was. Stacey.

The fog effect from Cosmic Bowling kicked in along with disco lights and the Scissor Sisters' cover of "Dancing Queen." Behind me, I heard the lane resetting. Pins setting up.

"Can you drink animal blood?" I asked over the music.

"Of course," she spat. "Unlike you, I make it a habit never to feed on humans. I—"

"Yeah?"

I'm a monster. I'm trying to be a kinder gentler monster, but like the asshole thing, that will always be there. And the monster doesn't like it when people who have it easier than me piss and moan. The monster doesn't even like it when I piss and moan.

"Well, fuck you, then." I held her head up closer and snarled. "Animal blood makes me hungrier instead of nourishing me, and trust me, I've fucking tried it all. Bats. Cats. Mice. Rats. Cow blood. Pig blood. Mouse blood. Snake. Birds. Fish." The light from my eyes turned purple, and where it struck her face, it canceled out the disco lights. "I even tried this really damn complicated mosquito idea once, and all it proved was that I have to drink the blood of sentient beings to feel full. When it's real bad, I can't control it, and I know that if I feed, I'm going to kill, so I hunt far away from my friends and my business to try and make certain I only kill people I don't know."

"You murdered me! I'm not going to feel sorry for you. You should have just committed suicide, greeted the sun, or—"

I gave her a head butt to cut her off. "I'm not complaining. I just want you to understand why I think you're a spoiled little bitch. I could have saved myself a whole lot of aggravation by staying in the seminary and never going to World War Two, but I didn't. As a result, I died on the wrong side of the holy whoever, and you know what? So did you, or the family curse wouldn't have done shit to you when you kicked it."

She flinched at that.

"As for the sun thing? Been there. Done that. Early on. Add a little blood to my ashes, and presto change-o: instant vampire." We locked eyes for a moment, the idea of avoiding mental contact having flown out of my head. "I've been staked, beheaded, blown to smithereens, and had a demon try to steal my soul. Shit. I even walked the Paths of the Dead and let Osiris judge my soul, and do you know what he told me?"

The look on her face said she didn't want to believe me but did. "I saved the world once back in the eighties, so it's all good. Water under the fucking bridge. I guess if you save a few billion people, the Powers That Be are willing to overlook it if you have to murder a few thousand of them to survive." I waited until she opened her mouth to respond, and then I turned and bowled her at the waiting pins.

She made a piss-poor bowling ball.

No proper spin, and she left me with a terrible split. The seven and ten pins sat there mocking me as the lane reset. The seven pin wobbled, but it wasn't going to fall. I eyed the ball return, wondering if Evelyn would make it through, like on that episode of *CSI*, or get stuck under the lane. She did have kind of a roundish head, and it was on the smallish side. Who the hell do you call to get a decapitated head out of the ball return? Surely someone at the Mages Guild would have an idea. Maybe Melvin . . .

A cacophony of thudding, screeching, and cursing came from the ball return. Leaning over, I shouted down the hole, "Try to roll with it."

Leaving that be, I walked back to her headless body and yelled, "Stake!"

Bea slid across the counter, crossbow bolt in hand, which she tossed to me when she thought she was close enough. I caught the bolt and rammed it through the heart of Evelyn's headless Barbie-doll-stiff body. No whooshy dusty end of undead existence, but then again, I hadn't expected it to kill her. A stake through the heart usually only does that for Masters and below. Hmmm . . ."See if you can Google 'nuk' . . . 'knuck' . . . 'headless vampires,' and see how I kill one," I shouted.

"Bastard!" Cousin Evie's head shot out of the ball return. "You don't even have the decency to feel guilty."

"Oh." I stood between the head and the body. "I'm guilty as a motherfucker, and it tears me up inside sometimes, but you won't hear me whining about it, and I'm not sorry."

"There's a difference?" She circled me, trying to get an opening to reconnect with her body.

"Between guilt and regret?" I laughed. "A big one. I'm guilty because I know a lot of what I've done is wrong, but to be sorry, I'd have to regret doing it, and the only thing I'm really sorry about"—her head darted in, thinking she had me, but I was too fast and caught her by the hair, slinging her around and letting go as she rocketed back toward my lane—"is that horrible first frame split."

"You son of a—" The ball return cut her off again.

"Hey," I yelled, "here's an idea. If your head comes off, don't start a fight in a goddamn bowling alley."

By the time she came back up a second time, Bea had Googled *nukekubi*, and I had ripped the metal plate off Evelyn's headless neck and jammed two pens and a pencil in its place, like ungainly spikes. There was nothing on the net about the metal plate; then again, the net is not the end-all, be-all of human knowledge. The copper plate was shaped exactly to the dimensions of her neck and about a centimeter thick, with a hole matching the dimension of her throat and inch-long spikes countersunk to help keep the thing in place. Where her neck had a simple line of *kanji*, the plate was covered in finely engraved patterns of the stuff.

"No!" Evie's head flew straight for her body, and I let her past me. "I can't stay detached from my body for long without the copper plate. Not during the day." She bit down on one of the pencils and started working it loose, ignoring the way the pen gouged at her cheek when she did so. Blood ran down her cheek, and all at once, the memory of feeding on her rushed back at me hard. Her blood hadn't tasted special, but all blood is best straight from the vein. Feeding thoughts can also get all wrapped up in other urges—lower ones, sexy ones.

The über vamp's arousal was obvious. The urge to feed . . . and do that other thing . . . was almost overwhelming. I had to do one or the other or I was going to do both. And I was certainly not going to rape my cousin or anyone else.

"Beatrice," I said. "I—"

I didn't even need to finish the sentence. She knew from the sound of my voice—the twinge of desperation—that I needed blood. I've been trying to avoid feeding on live humans, even my thralls, because while feeding in general brings out the souls that are haunting me, live feeding tends to make the haunting worse. It had to happen eventually; I'd be nuts to believe I could get away with it forever. Maybe it was less nuts to think I could go a whole day, but . . . this is me.

"Whatever you need, Eric." Beatrice bared her neck, but I lifted her into the air, sinking my fangs straight through her jeans to get at her femoral artery. That was a mistake, too. I've always thought of Beatrice as safe, since she didn't become a thrall because she was some vampire groupie; she did it because she wants to live forever and thinks getting bitten whenever her "Master" needs to feed is a small price to pay. It's not like vampire bites feel good or anything. They hurt like crazy, but based on the scent of arousal that filled my nostrils, it's a pain some begin to enjoy.

Blood and warmth flowed through me. No matter how warm I stay, there's nothing like that feeling—not warm clothes, not a sauna. Nothing. It was only the third time I'd fed live since I got Marilyn back, and I wasn't ready. The world beyond Beatrice and me fell away.

"Oh. Master. Don't. Stop." Beatrice pulled my head to the right. "Just let me get these—"

Thank goodness she said "Master." Vampires subconsciously emit a signal to their thralls. I don't know if it's a pheromone or magic or what, but if we concentrate, we can negate the effect. Most vampires don't give a shit and treat their thralls like little fuck-bunny slaves. Not me. I don't like having thralls at all. The reason I have Erin, Gladys, and Cheryl is because I'd rescued them from their Masters on Sweet Heart Row, who had them working as blood whores. I'd have let them go, except that Gladys was so old that resuming her natural age would mean nigh-instant death; Erin needed protecting and didn't want to leave; and Cheryl . . . she didn't want to go any more than Beatrice did. My mage Magbidion is with me because he sold his soul to a demon to gain magical powers and because his term is coming up and he wants my protection from the demon coming to call in his marker and drag him to hell.

The short version is: They all know not to call me "Master." So when they do, it's a sure sign that I'm influencing them accidentally. I concentrated on making Beatrice not want me, but that didn't work either, though from the look on my face, she seemed to understand what I was doing.

"It's not that," Beatrice said. "I . . . I can't describe it. You haven't bitten me in months, but it wasn't like this before. Your bite hurt at first, but then . . . I . . . I felt this rush of warmth and safety, like there was no place on earth I'd rather be than wherever you are and with your fangs inside me. I was . . . I felt so . . . grateful that when I saw how excited you were, I thought, *What the hell, let's do this. Whatever he wants.*"

"Oh, fuck you, you goddamn asshole piece of shit," came a familiar voice. Told you the haunting comes on fast when I drink live. "That's my fucking special ability! Some best friend you are."

I flinched, ignoring the voice and knowing damn well I was the only one who could hear it.

Evelyn had gotten the first pencil out of her neck and was working on the second one, but I'd jammed them in well.

Beatrice gestured at my groin. "I'm feeling normal again, but if you do need to take care of that, I could manage something . . . um . . . it's a little large for . . . um, traditional—"

I looked down. I'd forgotten I was the über vamp. The more I purposefully change into it, the more comfortable it feels. In the back of my head, I worry that one day I might be the über vamp all day, looking human only at night, when I'm a true immortal. "I think I need to put some pants on the über vamp," I interrupted. "Go steal some of Talbot's workout shorts. The black ones. That shouldn't look too stupid."

"Sure!" said the voice in my head again. "Steal my special gift. Steal the fucking cat's pants. Why not? Now, while she's gone, why don't you go for the triptych and ass-rape your cousin over there? She's in the right position for it."

"Shut up, Roger." I looked around and found him leaning against the ball return, smoking a cigarette. I didn't smell the cigarette smoke until I saw it. In Talbot's absence, my ghosts were happy to come out and play. Nice. I wondered what they were hiding from him.

"Come now, my boy," another voice began. "Though I admit the language is certainly of the low quality one might expect from a person whose name means 'famous with the spear' and has become slang for 'having sex.'" I looked at the new speaker and found a short, fat, balding man with an evil smile, standing, arms crossed, near the register. He wore the same open robe he'd had on when I ate his soul. "Still." He crossed the room to eye Evelyn's rump appraisingly. "I must admit that I see little reason why you should deny yourself."

"Because it would be rape, Phil. Um . . . I know I kill people, but that's 'cause I have to eat." I grasped for a comparison with my left hand, as if I might be able to snatch the perfect analogy out of the air. "Hunting just to kill things is evil. Rape is evil. And evil is something I try not to be."

"'Pleasure *is* the greatest incentive to evil,' or that's what Plato claimed." Phillip moved closer, and I caught the hint of blood and sex on his breath. "Of course, I prefer to side with Oscar Wilde in that regard. 'An inordinate passion for pleasure is the secret of remaining young.'"

"Wow, are you ever a pompous jackass," Roger quipped. "You almost make me forget how much I hate this asshole." He gestured at me with his cigarette.

Lisette didn't say anything when she appeared, but she was dressed in the freaky Victorian bordello outfit she'd been wearing when I ate her soul. The worst was the crying. It came last, though it was fainter now. I spotted Suzie in the corner of the Demon Heart, hugging her knees to her chest and rocking. Hers was the first soul out of four that I'd ever eaten on purpose. When I'd been a revenant *and* a vampire, before the whole breaking of the Eye of Scrythax thing that made me undead part of the time and ever-living the other half, I could do stuff like that, eat souls, but apparently, when I lost that side of my super-natural self, it stopped the digestive process. Or that was my theory at the time. I was wrong, but it was a good theory.

Beatrice came back with the shorts, and I slid them on the über vamp before transforming back into my more human size and shape.

"Are you all right, Eric?" Beatrice held up her hand so I could see the purple light hitting it. "Your eyes are glowing purple."

I held on to the sensation of warmth, from both her blood and my newly re-created clothes, before I answered. "They'll fade after a while." I was looking at my mind-fucked menagerie of the mostly-but-still-annoyingly-not-quite-totally-dead assholes. "They always do."

"C'mon, Eric, that's cold. Even for you."

Evelyn had gotten the second pencil out by then and was working on the pen when I walked over, pulled the pen out, and tapped the small metal plate back down where it had been.

"What are you doing?" Evelyn snapped.

"I just wanted you to know that I can kill you." I put one knee on her back and yanked the crossbow bolt out of her heart. "I know how to do it, and I can do it anytime I want."

"Oh." Phillip closed his eyes rapturously. "Oh, I see. How marvel-ous. This might be equally entertaining. I never thought you had it in you, my boy. The luscious thirst for adequate enemies. Humiliate her. Show her how powerless she is and then . . ."

"This isn't about you." I aimed the comment at both of them, a skill I learned when I was haunted by my great-great-great-grandfather John Paul Courtney.

She and Phillip responded at the same time. "No?" Evelyn sneered. "Then who do you think it's about? You?"

"Come now, Eric. *Fas est et ab hoste doceri!*"

I translated what Phillip had said and used it as my answer to Eve-lyn, ignoring Phil completely. I even remembered where the quote came from. "There was this guy, Ovid, from back in the day, and he said, 'It's proper to learn even from an enemy.' He also said . . ." I paused, looking directly at Phillip.

"You expect me to give you the quote?"

I kept staring.

"Did you forget it?" Evelyn tried to slip past me to reattach her head, and I let her by.

I didn't answer, but suddenly the answer came to me, like Phillip was thinking it, and purposefully not saying it, but I could hear his thoughts. Interesting.

"The Latin is *Perfer et obdura; dolor hic tibi proderit olim.* It means 'Be patient and tough, someday this pain will be useful to you.' He wrote this story about a mom who kills her own children to get back at their dad. An asshole I used to know would quote shit like that at me all the time. Usually right before he did something nasty."

"You!" Phillip jabbed his finger at me. "You stole that out of my mind!" When his finger touched me, we both blinked in surprise. Phillip took two steps back, his mouth opening and shutting like a fish's, before he vanished. *If they can touch me,* I thought, *then I . . .*

I glanced at Roger, but he and Lisette had already fled, and though Suzie was still in the corner, I wasn't interested in messing with her. I felt bad for her. *Phil seemed as shocked as I was. Hmmm . . .*

"Sounds like a real bastard." Evelyn stood, adjusting her scarf so that it covered the thin line of copper separating her head and her neck.

"He was. He killed my daughter, so I ate his soul and knocked his building down before charging into hell after her."

"Bullshit!"

"It happened." We turned to look at Marilyn, who'd come walking in the front door. She held a crossbow and had a cigarette sticking out of the corner of her mouth. "Because I was down there, too, and then this moron cut a deal to get me back. A deal with a demon."

"You were in hell?" Disbelief sounded loud and clear in Evelyn's voice.

"It wasn't all that bad," Marilyn said. "They were too afraid of him"—she gestured at me with her chin but kept the crossbow trained on Evelyn—"to actually torture me. But it's not a place you'd want to visit."

"Why does he get to be so special?" Evie's voice was angry and tinged with something else. Envy, maybe. I saw the welling of bloodred tears at the corners of her eyes. "Do you know how hard it was to convince those vampire hunters to trust me? And he . . . he puts them on the phone with someone with a raspy voice and . . . and they just call everything off!"

"You want to kill me?" I asked matter-of-factly. "Then come work for me. I'll let you try a new method once a year, starting with today. I'll even cooperate, but in the intervening time, you work with me and with my daughter to keep the vampires and other supernaturals of this city in line."

"What?" she scoffed. "Like if I said, 'I want to stake you and leave you in the sun,' you'd say okay."

"On your one day a year, if that was your one attempt, sure."

"Eric, no!" That one came from Beatrice.

Marilyn just let loose one braying "ha!" and lowered her crossbow.

"And if it doesn't work and I break my word?" Evelyn asked.

I gave her my most charming smile and bared my fangs. "Then I'll drag you back here and bowl ten frames with that detachable head of yours. Or worse: I'll sic my daughter on you."

Well, I thought as I let Evelyn stake me and drag me out into the sun, *that's one way to avoid killing your cousin.*

I'm not sure I can recommend it.

✦ 11 ✦

ERIC

NIGHTTIME IS THE RIGHT TIME

Sunset brought me back like a bad penny or gum on the shoe sole of the world. One moment I'd felt the fire raging over my body as that big old Southern sun wiped me off the face of her favorite planet, and then snap, crackle, pop, the setting of the sun brought me back. No blood required. I arrived without clothes, which might have been a clue to someone who knew me well, but Cousin Evie was not that person. I drew in two sweet draughts of night air before opening my eyes.

Evelyn stared at me with a slack jaw and furious eyes.

"Okay," I said as I stood up, wiping parking-deck grit off my butt, "so obviously, that didn't work." A quick look around told me we were on the top of the parking deck adjoining the Pollux. Convenient.

"You . . . you just re-formed." Evelyn poked me with a foreclaw. "You're even warm!"

"That's how it works." I glanced toward the stairs, trying to resist the urge to bolt to my bathroom and let Magbidion do his daily maintenance to hide all the things he's hiding for me: the true immortality at night, all the new thralls . . . I have to admit that in some ways, being burned to ash was less painful than what's been happening to me each morning since my trip to the Paths of the Dead.

Making the transition from ever-living true immortal to undead vampire feels like going through the transition from human to vampire every morning, like dying over and over again: body emptying of all fluids but blood, purging itself of any human waste, heart growing still, warmth draining away. Burning is less complicated. I'm not saying it's a good alternative, but it's a more familiar pain. Hmmm. Note to self: *Eric Courtney, you have spent way too much time on fire.*

Sunset is way better. Going from undead back to everliving—anything I could say to describe it seems inadequate. It's like waking up after a car crash to find out you're Captain America. I just wish I were as powerful an immortal as I am a vampire. A vampire's power is tied to the strength of personality, willpower, drive, creativity, and force of character. No problem. A true immortal's power comes from age and the number of other immortals who owe fealty to you. As a true immortal, I come up short in both areas.

"Your heart is even beating."

"Look." I headed for the stairs. "I have some things to take care of real quick. You wait here. Greta's not supposed to be up for an hour or so, but she can be erratic when she feels me in pain. Talbot should have been standing by to inform Greta about our arrangement, but she's likely to be a little . . . put out with you for wanting me dead, much less having a go at it. Whether I was willing to allow it probably won't enter into the equation for her."

"I can hold my own." Evelyn crossed her arms over her chest.

"Not against—" I began.

A shadow passed between Evelyn and me, and then her body was falling backward, headless, to the concrete. A sound like a steam whistle was all I heard of Evelyn's scream before I saw Greta's silhouette on the edge of the concrete wall of the parking deck. She held Evelyn's head firmly in her hands, her own eyes bright with crimson sparks. "Me," she whispered. She was far enough away that I couldn't hear her words, not without my vampiric hearing, but I knew what she'd said.

"Let me go!"

"Your head really does come off," Greta continued, oblivious to Evelyn's objections, "kind of like LEGO."

Talbot arrived via the stairs moments later. "Greta! I told you. Your dad said—"

"Don't hurt her, Greta." I spoke softly, trying not to sound proud of her overprotectiveness. "She's your new deputy, and I'm fine."

"Okay, Dad." Greta shifted Evelyn's head to one side and cradled it under her right arm like a football helmet. "We'll just . . . talk . . . a little."

"Promise?" I asked.

"Pinkie swear," Greta said with a nod. She was wearing pajamas (pink bottoms with a Void City Howlers hockey jersey as the top), and someone had put her hair in pigtails. When she nodded, they flounced in a way that was far too cutesy.

"Fine." I headed down the stairwell, ignoring my cousin's muffled protests as the door cut them off. On the way into the Pollux, Gladys greeted me with a leer and a whistle. Her hair was purple, though she'd been playing around with hairstyles. She currently had it done in sort of an updo held in place with a black lacquered chopstick. Two long, purposefully errant strands framed her face, and her makeup had been done in smoky bluish-purple. She wore a tight white baby-doll T-shirt under an unbuttoned Demon Heart Lanes bowling shirt, the thinness of the material making it clear to everyone that she was wearing a very lacy purple bra. Daisy Dukes and high heels finished off the ensemble.

Without the benefits of my thralldom, Gladys is older than me by at least a decade or two, but her spirit has to be mid-twenties, tops. Back in my day, women would have called her a "bad girl" or a "whore," while men would have used terms like a "real sport" or a "good-time girl."

"I think I have the taste thing Rachel used to do figured out," she said as I walked past her toward the stairwell that led up to the mezzanine and back around to my office and bedroom if one took a left at the top. "Want to give it a try?"

"Not tonight." I stopped at the bottom of the stairs. "Maybe tomorrow morning. I appreciate it, though."

"Magbidion's already up there," she offered, taking my refusal in stride.

"Good." I started up the stairs.

"So's your wife."

"Fuck!" I slammed my fist down on the wooden railing and was surprised when it hurt.

"Beatrice said I should give you a heads-up."

"She was right." I rubbed the heel of my hand. "Thanks again."

She whistled again. "You're thanking me enough just by walkin' up those stairs in the altogether, darlin'."

I laughed, which I think was all Gladys really wanted out of the exchange, and continued up the stairs. When I hit the top, I felt the familiar tingle of Magbidion's magic and spotted a hastily drawn mage circle scribed in chalk on the hardwood. *Clever boy, Magbidion,* I thought, *you deserve a raise.*

Standing in the portal, I suppressed the nausea that usually accompanies this particular set of spells and shivered as magic, like a cold washcloth, slid across and then within my chest. My skin lightened, and I fought the urge to scratch as my skin went dry. My lips felt chapped and rough when it was over, and my entire body felt as if it were raw with razor burn. Hunger bit deep in my belly, but I ignored it. First things first.

Tabitha was sitting on my California king, reading something on her e-reader, when I opened my bedroom door. I have to admit that she's a beautiful woman. She wore an Asian-style floral halter dress that came down to about three inches above her knees. Long black ties cinched it tight around the waist, going up over her shoulders to hold it up. The dress accentuated her wasplike figure. She'd left her long raven-black hair down (the way I like it). Hadn't it been short yesterday? I didn't remember. I didn't see her shoes, either, which was unusual, because Tabitha is the kind of gal who tends to leave whatever clothes she takes off wherever they happen to land, often putting shoes right out in the middle of the floor.

"Hi." She lowered the e-reader and gave me a smile meant to convey a message somewhere between "Hello, stranger" and "What the hell have you been up to?" I couldn't decide which one.

"Nice dress," I said, looking around for Magbidion. "You look pretty."

"Thanks." Her eyes brightened. "I asked him to give us some privacy," Tabitha offered when she realized I was looking for Mags. "He said he had some rituals to perform for you in the bathroom anyway. Do I even want to know what that's about?"

"No." I headed for the bathroom door, but she beat me to it with vampire speed.

"What? You're just going to walk past me?" She put a hand on my chest and shuddered at the bit of warmth the magic hadn't washed away. "You already fed."

"Something like that." I gently pushed her hand back. "Look, I have parking-deck grit all over my butt. I want a shower and some clean clothes."

"Why don't you just turn into a bat and change back?" She tried to make it seem like a casual question, but there was venom, too.

"When I do that, it wastes blood."

"You used to do it all the time."

"I was showing off." I looked past her impatiently. "Look, can I please go take my shower now? I was staked through the heart and burned to ash in the sun. It was not the best start to my evening."

"Fine," she said, meaning it wasn't. She did step out of the way, though. "Do you want some company?"

I fought off the sigh. I may be a murderer, but I'm an honorable man. I truly love Marilyn, but I guess I might be actually married to Tabitha, even though I think I shouldn't be. As long as Tabitha insists we're married . . . gah. When I married her, I didn't think there was any way to get Marilyn back, and I still left myself all kinds of loopholes in the ceremony. I told Tabitha I'd cheat on her. I told her I was marrying her only because I wanted to keep fucking her. Instead of saying "I do," I'd said "I'll do what I can." Our vows had definitely ended when I left this world and came back, but I couldn't just ditch her because Marilyn wouldn't like it. Sometimes being a man of my word sucks.

"If you really want to join me," I said after a minute. "But I'll warn you, I'm tired and—"

"Do you want me to seem human for you, baby?" Tabitha's green eyes sparkled. Seeming human is her special gift. All Vlads seem to have one, and some lesser vampires do as well. When Tabitha used her gift, her heart beat, she breathed instinctively (and quite convincingly), she could even eat and drink (though apparently, her taste buds didn't work). It's a rare gift. Vampires who possess it are called Living Dolls. It even gets their bodily fluids going again. Normal vampires have all their bodily fluids replaced with blood: saliva, tears, other things. But Living Dolls can turn that stuff back on. Which meant if Tabitha did that, she would almost certainly notice that where I was supposed to get bloody, I wouldn't. At night, I sweat real sweat and have real saliva, and all the downstairs plumbing works, too.

Damn.

"Whichever you want, Tabitha." I let my forehead rest against the door frame. "I feel like a heel asking you to jump through hoops for me. I don't deserve it."

"Oh, Eric."

Well, that was the wrong fucking thing to say. I felt her breasts against my back, cold at first but warming as she concentrated on bringing her body to a deceptive semblance of life. On the other hand, since doing so dulled her vampirically enhanced senses and totally killed her taste buds, maybe I could pull it off.

Sometimes I do the wrong thing. Have I mentioned that?

Case in point: Tabitha joined me in the shower. She slid out of her dress and followed me in, handing the garment to Magbidion as she walked past him. Mags looked more drained than normal, his eyes half open and underscored with purple bruising. He tried to hide the two empty, unused blood bags he had with him, but he needn't have bothered. Tabitha wasn't paying attention.

"Should I . . . ?" Magbidion looked toward the door.

Neither of us answered him. He sank down onto the toilet seat (lid down) and let his head rest on the counter. My new shower is impressive. Winter went all out when he put it in. I'm not a big sauna guy, but the ceiling shower system (with central and outer ring rain), combined with three wall sprays, rubbed brass fittings, heated shower bench . . .

even at night I was a true believer. Hot water rained down, steam rising up around us. I'd wondered if I'd need to use a blindfold for Tabitha to hide the lack of the blood that usually accompanies vampire sex, but I didn't.

Tabitha rubbed the grime from my back, soaped up the loofah, and slowly scrubbed all traces of parking-deck grit and grime from my back.

"Want me to wash your hair?" Tabitha wrapped her arms around me from behind again, breasts pressing against my back. I love that feeling. She kissed the nape of my neck and let the tip of her tongue touch my skin following each kiss. Where she got that from, I don't know, but it gets to me.

"Tabitha," I protested softly.

"We're married, Eric. It's okay for me to turn you on."

"Maybe."

She reached past me to grab my shampoo, and a little squeal of a laugh escaped her lips. "When did you start using Garnier?"

"Paris."

Tabitha guided me to the shower seat and poured a small amount of shampoo into her palm before rubbing it in my hair, leaning my head forward to rest below her breasts as she worked the shampoo into a lather, the fruity smell mixing with her clean odor. *What is it with me and showers?*

I remembered a time before I died when Marilyn briefly considered a change from tending bar to beauty school. A warm towel on my face as her fingernails worked across my scalp, waking it up, making my skin tingle and my senses flare to life. The smell of her cigarettes banished by the fragrance of the shampoo. She used to love to shave me, too. Her hands soft and loving on my skin just before she brushed on the lather and starting shaving with careful strokes of the straight razor against the grain for a closer shave.

As the warm false rain washed the shampoo from my hair, I felt Tabitha's hand questing low, between my legs. "There you are," she said as that part of me decided it was ready for more than just a shower. Our lips met, and there was no turning back. She kissed her way down my chest, and I pulled her head back up, not wanting to risk her noticing the lack of blood down there if things went on too long and I climaxed.

Instead, I kissed her again, hungrily. Call it lust or whatever you want, but I do care for Tabitha; it's just not the same emotion I have for Marilyn.

"Do you want—" she started as I stood, pushing her against the wall and reaching down to grasp her sex, finding purchase there, warmth and access, first with one finger and then a second. We knew each other's bodies well, even if I sometimes felt like we were strangers as people. What is there to know about a person as young as she is? Which isn't fair, but it felt true. There's a rhythm she likes, a pattern of thumb, index finger, and forefinger, a rocking that's all in the wrist.

She cried out, not my name, but a nonsense noise of passion, and my lips found one breast as my left hand found the other. Her climax built, harder to detect with my senses dulled down to almost human, but unmistakable. A twitch at the corner of her lips, sharp animal breaths, and the sense of tightening centered in an area ranging between her knees and belly button.

"You're so beautiful," I said.

She didn't answer with words but with the rapid movement of her hand, a series of milking strokes followed by an urgent pull at my thigh.

"Now," she said, and then the slick tile squeaked as I moved her up, then let her drop, joining us at the groin. "I love you," she said, and I didn't return it, not with the same words.

"You're beautiful," I said again. I guess it was enough, because she smiled, biting her bottom lip as I moved inside her, my hands gripping her breasts for purchase. When she climaxed once more, I pulled her toward the shower seat and sat down, pulling her onto my lap, my chest against hers. I missed the mark and she reached back, guiding me into position, her gasp matching mine as we were joined again. When I finally found completion, she did as well, our peaks overlapping, close enough to simultaneous that it may have been.

Panting, she let her full weight rest on my thighs and leaned back as I cupped her breasts, rubbing her nipples between my fingers the way she likes right after sex. Sighing, she touched my hands after a minute or so had passed, and I ceased my digital manipulations. "I needed that," she said.

I opened my mouth to reply in kind, but instead, I said, "I want a divorce."

Yeah . . . I could have picked a better time.

12

GRETA
DEPUTIZED

W e should have special cop names," I said to my new
deputy. She'd finally stopped struggling under my arm,
but I didn't think she was happy about her positioning,
like maybe she wanted me to reattach her head to her
body, which was fine and dandy, really, but it's important to make sure
that your subordinates understand who's in charge.

"What," she asked, "like Holmes and Watson?"

"You're very good at conveying incredulousness." I let go of her
head so I could watch it not fall. This time she didn't try to float back
to her body, simply spinning in place to face me. "No, I meant more
like Batman and Robin."

"Pinky and the Brain is more like it," she grumbled, letting her
head drift higher so we were almost looking each other in the eye.

"Hmmm." I thought that over. "I don't know that it fits." I narrowed
my eyes at her, flashing them red for a brief moment. "Try saying 'Narf.'"

"Narf," she said without enthusiasm.

"Nah." I waved my hand under the clean smooth base of her neck.
"It's so cool that there are no bits of spine or anything dangling down."

"I agree."

"Does it hurt?"

"You already asked that."

My eyes flashed red. "I'm checking again."

"No. It doesn't hurt."

"And you can walk around in the daytime?"

"Yes."

"Do your powers work any differently then? During the day, I
mean."

"Not especially, but apparently I'm a very powerful *nukekubi*. The equivalent of a Vlad or something."

I nodded to her body. She paused, waiting to see if I was going to play more Charlie Brown and Lucy games with her, then floated back over and reattached herself. When she was all together, the glowing red symbols on her neck faded quickly, first to a dark black, giving them the appearance of tattoos, and then to a light pinkish-white, like faint scars.

"And you're Dad's cousin?" I asked.

"Yes. Second cousin twice removed."

"Interesting. So . . . technically, you could get married."

"No chance."

"Your loss." Dad's soundproofing has been improved by Magbidion, but I heard something loud from the Pollux and cocked my head in that direction like Superman or Lassie. "I wonder how many of Dad's other relatives are running around as weird funky undead things."

"Not many, I'd guess." Evie stood, rubbing at the thin line of copper separating her head from her body by the width of a penny. She wrapped a scarf around it. "At the last family reunion, the hyperreligiousness almost made me vomit. Then again, I guess they're all right. If I'd been going to church and saying my prayers at night, I'd probably be in heaven now instead of being undead."

"I went to hell once," I said in as chipper a tone as I could manage. "Well, to the gates. Dad wouldn't let me go inside."

There was another loud noise from the Pollux: sort of a *thoom*. Was that Dad's *oof* I heard?

"Do you hear that?" I asked.

Evie shook her head, and it didn't come off. "My senses evidently aren't as keen as they are in other types of vampires." I was already walking for the stairs. At the last second, I changed my mind and hopped off the roof of the parking deck.

". . . son of a bitch!" I heard Tabitha shouting as I got closer. Hitting the street would have hurt if I let myself feel it, but for vampires who know, who understand what they really are, the body is just an interface, a tool, and if I'm expecting the pain, I can prepare myself not to feel it. I hit the sidewalk feet-first, knees loose to ablate some of the damage from the fall. Things broke and fractured in my legs and, as I fell backward and caught myself, my hands and arms. Rolling backward with the fall, I came up, claws out and fangs down, already healing.

"I should have just moved to Hawaii," Evie said as she stared down at me from the top of the parking deck. "What the hell are you doing?"

"Sheriff," I corrected. Flexing my arms and legs as the bones snapped, crackled, and popped back into place, I twisted my neck and my back to loosen up. "I'm pretty sure you should call me Sheriff. Or Sheriff Courtney." My back gave another deep pop, and I was all done healing. There was barely any blood on the sidewalk.

"Fine! What the hell are you doing, Sheriff?"

"I think I'm about to kill someone." I looked at the doors and decided outside would be fine. Dad was doing another summer series, and the movie poster from *Mr. Blandings Builds His Dream House* was illuminated brightly in the window of the box office, with Cary Grant looking angry, Myrna Loy looking wry, and Melvyn Douglas in a state of disapproving bemusement. I wanted to watch *The Shining* instead (I like the cute little girls), but Dad's not into horror movies.

"Tabitha." I heard Dad's voice more clearly from down on the street than I had eight levels up. "Would you fucking stop? I don't want to fi—" There was another *thoom*, and Dad came right out through the wall of the building, brick and insulation raining down around him. I would have caught him if I'd thought he needed me to, but he's tough, and I don't want to insult him. Instead, when Tabitha poked her head out of the hole, I shouted, "Fang, it's time!" and leaped.

Tabitha swore, ducking back inside. Like Dad, she wore no proper clothing but was covered in his blood. It wet her fangs and gloved her claws and fingers. It left a trail from the broken exterior wall of the building, through the hall, into the bedroom, and back to the shower, where Magbidion lay unconscious on the tile. Where Tabitha ran out of room to run.

"What did I tell you I'd do?" I shouted.

"What are you talking about, Greta?" Tabitha did a quick change from humanoid to sparrow and back. When she reformed, her default outfit came with her, though the blood was still there. "You ought to be on my side. Do you know what he said to me?"

"I don't care, Tabitha."

"He—"

"I! DON'T! CARE! what he said or did, Tabitha." I took her hand and turned it back and forth, examining the blood. "That's not your blood, Tabitha. I didn't see any of your blood on Dad either, Tabitha. Why is that, Tabitha?"

She tried to jerk her hand away, but I didn't let her.

"Why do you keep saying my name?"

"Because you need to understand something." I released her and sniffed the air. Scent reveals so much. Chalk loomed underneath the blood, which meant magic. Filtered water. Tabitha's sexual excretions. Dad's semen. I hadn't smelled that since the wedding. The very faint odor of cinnamon (which kind of explained the semen to me, though to be honest, I was not that interested in how Rachel had or had not been involved with what Dad and Tabitha had been doing in the bedroom). Magbidion's cigarettes. Urine from where Magbidion had fouled himself. Adrenaline. Anger. Dad's sweat. "You are not my mom. And no matter what happened, this is your fault. Dad is never at fault."

"Bullshit!" Tabitha's eyes flared as red as mine. "He said he wanted a—"

"Never." My slap sent her backward into the bedroom, where she clipped the wall and came to a stop. "At." Tabitha rolled back to a ready position, but I was already behind her. "Fault." Her skull cracked as I rammed her into the doorpost, increasing the damage she'd already done to it with Dad. Not that anyone would be able to tell. They'd wrecked the room and torn both the bathroom and bedroom doors off their hinges. Holes dotted the walls, and it looked like Tabitha had purposefully put Dad's head through his television.

"You bitch!" Her claws caught the meat of my thigh, but who cared? There wasn't any blood. I refused to bleed for her.

"If Daddy confuses us, it's because we're supposed to be confused, or we've been too stupid and have failed him by not understanding." Tackling her was easy. She clawed great rents in my face and stomach as I wrestled her into position. "If he makes us sad, then we're supposed to be sad, or we've failed him by reacting inappropriately to his actions."

Ripping off an arm isn't easy. The required strength isn't the problem. It's the leverage. But I've practiced. Ripping off a hand or a forearm isn't so hard, but getting the whole thing off cleanly requires a special two-part twist and tug. You have to dislocate the shoulder, then tear the muscles without losing any of the arm. It seems to hurt a lot, too. Tabitha screamed a wounded-animal scream and went from fighting to trying to get away. Typical. It's astonishing how much other vampires whine about pain.

"Greta!" Dad yelled my name, but I didn't answer.

"I told you," I hissed in her ear. "Do you remember?" I grabbed her cheeks with my left hand and forced her to look me in the eye, then I made contact and brought her into my head. With vampire telepathy, someone always has the upper hand. Whoever has the strongest will, the most agile mind, usually wins. I'm quite insane, so that gives me an edge. I took her to my special place of remembering, front row, center stage, at the Pollux. I wasn't in my pajamas anymore, having clothed the mental me in jeans, a pink baby-doll WELCOME TO THE VOID shirt, and Skechers.

I kept Tabitha the way she was in the real world and pointed at the movie screen with her dismembered limb. "Right there!"

Public Safety Tip #2: Ignorance of the law may be a reasonable excuse, so I will educate you immediately before your sentence is carried out.

Darkness fell as the theater lights went down and my memory lit up the screen like a film.

We were in the hallway of the Pollux, right outside my room. It was shortly after we (by which I mean all Dad's allies except Tabitha) found a way to regenerate Dad's body after he'd been blown up in the first Demon Heart, back when it was a strip club. Tabitha had been nosing around the dressing rooms while drying off after a shower.

My hands slid across the surface of my door, making sure I'd closed it properly by giving it a gentle nudge.

"This is my room and my stuff," I said, baring my fangs.

"I don't want any of your junk."

"You want my dad."

"Maybe," Tabitha said, rubbing her privates with the towel as she spoke. "I guess I do. I'm really not sure."

"Cut off your head, stuff your mouth with garlic, stake you through the heart with any kind of hard wood"—I narrowed my eyes—"then bury your head and your body in two different plots on consecrated ground. That's all it would take."

"What?" Tabitha pulled her hands away from the towel as if that could conceal that she was so hot for my dad, she'd started touching herself at the mere mention of him.

"You're so unimaginative." I watched her hands, making sure she wouldn't try to go for a claw. I hadn't had the chance to fight her, so I couldn't be sure how fast or slow she might be. "I know vampire hunters who would try that method first thing, and then you'd be gone forever."

Her fingernails stretched into claws, but too slowly to be a real threat. Either that or she was trying to undersell her abilities. "Is that a threat?"

"No." I poured on the speed, sliding around behind her and shoving her head at the floor. I sort of thought she'd catch herself, but she was so darn slow. She hit the floor face-first, breaking her nose, and started crying. It was hard not to feed on her then and there. Any vampires displaying that much weakness make me want to end them. By the time I realized what I was doing, I'd twisted her arms behind her back and broken them, and my fangs were at her neck. I almost forgot the rest of my sentence, what we'd been talking about . . . So I decided to make sure she understood how serious I am about protecting Dad. "This is."

I zoomed around in front of her, and I could see a trace of a reflection in her blood on the floor. When I knelt on the ground to get a better look at it, the reflection was gone. Then I gave her my warning. She looked so pitiful that I had to fight not to pop her chest and tear out her heart. I mean, come on. She was crying! "Hurt my daddy," I said, "and I'll kill you."

Tabitha, the one with me in her head, not the one on the screen, winced as the memory faded and the lights came back up. I blinked and broke the telepathic contact. "Do you remember now?"

"I never forgot." Tabitha stared at me coolly, the pain in her shoulder obviously having subsided. "Eric wouldn't, either. If you killed me, he'd remember it forever, and you'd see it in the way he—"

My laughter cut her off. "This is Dad we're talking about, you moron. He forgets *everything* eventually!" I blinked away tears of blood, uncertain why I was shedding them. "Given long enough, he'd forget you, me, everyone. Everyone except her!"

Out in the street, Dad was trying to get to the front door. He'd had no way of knowing Fang was going to stop him. Fang and I had already talked this through. Fang knew what to do. It wouldn't hurt Dad to land in the trunk with the bones. He'd be angry, but it was for his own good.

Tabitha took that moment to try to surprise me with her remaining arm, so I tore it off at the elbow. It wasn't as elegant as taking off the whole arm, but she screamed. I growled.

"I keep what it takes to kill you in my bedroom, Tabitha, all the time . . . just in case." I grabbed her by the neck, hauling her along behind me like a struggling cat. "Let's go give Daddy the divorce he wants."

"Hiya, slut." I smelled the cinnamon and heard the voice in unison. Then I was on fire. "How ya been?"

I hate Auntie Rachel.

13

ERIC

MY CAR HAS A MIND OF ITS OWN

Only in Void City can a man wind up naked in the street, cornered by his undead car while trying to stop his daughter from murdering the wife he wants to divorce. Fang's engine revved, and "Tubthumping" started playing over his stereo.

"Chumbawamba?" I shook my head. "Really?"

Fang revved his engine again.

"Really?" I said again. A plume of fire spat out the hole in the side of the Pollux, and I tried to use the distraction to go up and over Fang's hood, but he was too fast, rocketing into reverse with such alacrity that I wound up on my ass. Fang took the opening and rolled over me. Whatever magic he uses to pull things against his undercarriage and eat them slammed me against him. To be honest, it looked sort of like a mass of purple glowing tentacles, but even with my true immortal nighttime powers, I could only see the energy in a very out-of-focus way.

"Dammit, Fang!"

Greta screamed, and Fang let go of me at once, rolling off as quickly as he could, replacing Chumbawamba with Sam & Dave's "Hold On, I'm Coming." I jumped to my feet and ran for the building, letting myself tap in to a little speed. It felt different than vampire speed, and doing it ran the risk of lighting me up spiritually, tipping my hand.

Greta is my little girl, and if saving her fucks up The Plan, then I'll just get a new plan. I tapped in to the strength for a split second as I hit the sidewalk and jumped for the hole. My heart pounded in my chest, not the too-fast pounding of an out-of-shape human but a steady and efficient thump. Small strands of blue sparked between me and surrounding objects, then faded as I was airborne and released the strength.

"Greta?" I yelled. "Tabitha?"

Greta rolled on the floor in my bedroom, singed and yowling. Tabitha didn't have pyrokinetic powers, which meant . . . I spotted Rachel, arms folded across her chest, in the bathroom doorway. She was wearing a blue dress this time, and if Greta hadn't been hurt, I might have laughed. Tabitha stood behind her sister, feeding on Magbidion as her arms grew back. One arm seemed to be making more progress than the other.

"Hellfire doesn't just burn the flesh, Greta." Rachel's voice was edged with menace. "I don't want to burn you again . . . okay, well, I actually do, because you killed me in a very unpleasant fashion the last time I was alive, but your dad would be really pissed at me if I did, so please stay back."

Greta wasn't healing.

I opened the fridge and pulled out two of the bags labeled ERIC COURTNEY (only two more left, I noted) and handed them to Greta as I walked past. "Demon fire can be as slow to heal as holy wounds for vamps with that problem." Greta snatched the first bag and bit into it.

"This is yours," she said with her mouth full of blood, wounds healing readily now.

"Yup." I stood between her and Rachel. "That's enough, Tabitha."

She reluctantly pulled her mouth from Magbidion's throat. "I didn't take too much," she said defensively, "and your psycho bitch of a daughter tore my freakin' arms off."

"Oh, shut up," Greta snarled, my blood dripping from her lips. "I didn't even have enough time to end you."

"You." I pointed at Greta. "Are you okay?"

"I'll be fine now, Dad." Her wounds were already fading.

"Good. Go get dressed and patrol with Evelyn."

"But I have to kill Tabitha!" Greta was on her feet in a blink. "She created a disturbance that could have drawn attention to everything, and I get to kill people who—"

I cut her off. "I'll handle the matter, Sheriff. Go." She stood up to leave. "And be careful out there. You're my girl."

Greta smiled a smile designed to let me know I'd set the world to rights, but I suspected she was angry underneath. I watched her go, then walked over to my wardrobe and pulled out clean socks and underwear before crossing to my closet to dress.

Rachel whistled at me, and I blushed. "You shut up." I pulled on my undies and jeans. "Why are you here, anyway?"

"I have a new task for you from Lady Scrytha."

"Lovely." I shrugged into a clean WELCOME TO THE VOID T-shirt and sat down on the edge of the bed to put on a pair of thick black socks. "Tabitha, are you rearmed over there?"

"Yes." Her voice was sulky. "I'm still hungry, though."

"I told you, you should have stuck them back on and healed that way." Rachel crossed the room and pointed to what I assumed were Tabitha's dismembered limbs. "It would have been a lot less draining."

"That's stupid." Tabitha stalked out of the bathroom.

"No," I corrected as I pulled on my combat boots, "it *sounds* stupid, but it's pretty good advice. I've tried it both ways, and putting the severed limb back on feels weird but works better."

"Well, pardon me." Tabitha looked away. "It's my first time having parts ripped off."

I gave a noncommittal grunt and tied my shoes. "So, here's the thing." I grabbed a new black leather belt from my top drawer and slid it on, missed a loop, and got it right the second time. "I get that you're mad at me."

Tabitha scoffed. "You GET it, huh?"

"Yes," I said calmly, "I do, but I can't have you causing shit like this to happen in my home."

"I didn't cause anything, you fucking prick!" Tabitha's eyes blazed red. "You wait until after we have some of the most tender, romantic sex we've ever had, and in the afterglow, you tell me you want a divorce . . . and I caused it?"

"I gave the most unromantically truthful and pessimistic warning to you during our wedding. I promised I would fail you eventually and that I'd try to be faithful but would not succeed. I wouldn't even say 'I do' to the vows. I said, 'I'll do what I can,' and you married me anyway."

"I was being mind-controlled!" Tabitha spat.

"Exactly my point."

"Not controlled," Rachel corrected. "Heavily influenced but not strictly controlled."

We both glared at Rachel.

"In demonic terms, it's a very important technicality," Rachel said with a shrug.

"I don't think our ceremony counts. And if it did, the vows would have ended when I went to the underworld. But obviously, you think differently, so I offered to let you out of the marriage. You said no." I walked back over to the fridge and pulled out the last two bags of my blood. "Look, I'm not going to argue with you while you're still hungry. Here." I handed her the bags, and she smirked.

"I didn't know you'd taken to labeling them."

"Ever since someone spiked them and no one noticed." I pulled off the label, and the writing faded. "Magbidion made them for me. They identify the donor and detect most major contaminants or spells that affect vampires. I have twelve hundred of the things."

"That's clever," Rachel said, squinting at the Post-it. "Simple but very hard to fool. Elegant, even." She looked at Magbidion lying unconscious on the bathroom tiles. "You got a good deal when you enthralled him. Diaxicrotioush'nar has been scared shitless to come to collect on his debt because he saw what you did to the last demon you took down. Magbidion has a real flair for the sort of work you want him to do." She smiled. "He uses magic so efficiently, too. His enchantments are nigh invisible, not a speck of magic wasted."

Tabitha cleared her throat. "If you guys start making out in front of me, I'm attacking you both." She'd downed the first bag of blood and was sipping on the next.

"So . . ." We waited in uncomfortable silence for Tabitha to finish the second bag.

"Okay." Tabitha sat the empty bags in the sink. "That's better."

"Good," I said. "Now fuck off."

"What?" Tabitha snarled, and Rachel laughed.

"You're a beautiful and intelligent woman, Tabitha," I said softly. "You deserve someone who will love you. You won't get him, 'cause your taste in men is shit, but I want you to be happy. You'll never be happy with me. You need to figure out what you want to do with the rest of eternity and do it. The reason I insisted all the strippers who worked at the Demon Heart go to college was because you need that scrap of paper in this world for people to take you seriously. You've traded on your looks and men's desire to get in your pants for so long that you think about that first and foremost: finding the right man and keeping him."

I touched her cheek gently, almost afraid she'd bite me. "The right man won't need to be kept, Tabitha. He'll be too damn busy trying to keep *you.* I'm not that guy."

"So . . ." Tabitha took a deep breath. "So what? You're going to go back to screwing Rachel?"

"Been there." I held up my hands as if warding off the thought. "Done that. It was a blast, but I wouldn't go back in with a borrowed dick."

"Oh, sure," Rachel said, "you say that *now,* but—"

Tabitha and I both shushed her.

"Marilyn, then?" Tabitha asked.

"Probably not." That seemed to take them by surprise. "Oh, I love her more than any woman I've ever known or ever will know. But unless something changes, that ship has sailed. Roger sabotaged it beyond all reasonable hope of repair."

"Do I have to leave Void City?" Tabitha's voice sounded distant, like it was just clicking that things were really over.

"Of course not." I sighed. "You know, I think the worst thing about us as a couple is that maybe we were never meant to be more than friends. If I'd been my right age when I first met you, I'd have been too old for you. I could have been the dirty old man who steered you clear of the wrong guys and set you on the path to a great career in classical dance or psychology or some shit. We're too much alike to make it as a couple."

"You're really not that much alike," Rachel butted in.

"Really?" I asked, enumerating points on my fingers. "We're both smarter than we look. We both have serious anger issues." I grinned. "True, I've never learned to tie a cherry stem into a knot with my tongue, but . . ." I looked to Tabitha, hoping for something like a laugh.

"You're giving me the 'Let's be friends' speech?" Tabitha frowned, her eyes rimmed with anger. At least she wasn't crying. "Fuck that!"

"I don't want to have some ongoing war with you, Tabitha. I'll give you a nice and official divorce settlement. Money. Your apartment. I'll make sure Greta knows she doesn't get to kill you."

"Fine." Tabitha's face was torn between resentment, hatred, and maybe a glimmer of some positive emotion. "You're right. My life can't be about you."

"Friends?" I held out my arms, offering a hug but fully expecting Tabitha to attack me again. Instead, she gave me the briefest of hugs.

"Go fuck yourself." She pulled away. Her claws extended, but she didn't seem to realize it. She wiped at her eyes, blinked, sniffed, and gave an irritated grunt, throwing her arms down by her sides. "Send my money and my shit to my apartment, asshole."

Brushing past me, she transformed into a cat (probably to mess with her sister, who was always afraid of them) and sauntered off. She didn't look back, and despite myself, I almost went after her. That was not part of any plan, though, so I stuck by my guns and stared out the hole in the Pollux. *What a mess.*

"I could have sworn she was going to attack you." Rachel put an arm around my waist.

"Me, too." I smelled cinnamon, but I let it pass without comment. She really is God's gift to cock, but the baggage is too extreme to mention, and I have my Plan. A Plan she's not in . . . at least not in a knocking-boots way. I extricated myself from her grasp and asked a question. "Why did you save her?"

"She's my sister." Rachel gestured, and a reflective surface wavered into existence, hovering in the air. She touched up her lipstick and her eye shadow with a touch of her fingertips, then straightened out her low-cut blue dress. She looked over her shoulder at me and wrinkled her nose mischievously. "No one gets to murder her but me."

14

ERIC

DO I OR DON'T I ACTUALLY HAVE TO DO WHAT I DONE DID?

After that, we had work to do. As commands go, my second one, helping to install an artificial locus point in the middle of the street between the Pollux and the Demon Heart, wasn't a hardship. Certainly not compared to strangling Father Ike. Demons have to use locus points if they want to travel quickly from the Pit (some kind of staging area for hell) and the material world. Talbot and I had been forced to chase a demon all over Void City a few years back, trying to kill him and succeeding before he made it to one of the locus points around town to make good his escape.

My deal with Scrytha apparently allowed her "rightful representative" to appear in my vicinity or near my places of power without one (which was how Rachel got to *bamf* back and forth so darn easy), but that wasn't enough for Scrytha. The whole locus-point thing can only be installed by powerful supernatural beings . . . I couldn't decide whether I should be flattered, but I didn't much care.

VCPD officers manned roadblocks at either end of the street with flashing squad car lights, Mages Guild representatives, and the whole spiel. It was a lot more impressive than the job Melvin had done back when I was obliterated and reduced to a ghost, but strangely, it cost about the same in man-hours and overtime. Maybe that was because my new "man" in charge of the VCPD side of such things, Katherine Marx, was an evil mercenary bastard like the old one.

Melvin, the member of the Void City Mages Guild most likely to be mistaken for one of the Blues Brothers, was overseeing the operation on behalf of the city and the Mages Guild, but the magic was being done by Rachel and me. Yeah, I'm so multitalented. Watch me pull a rabbit out of my ass.

So far, my involvement had involved ripping a goat into thirds and waving the pieces about in whatever direction I was told.

"So is this thing safe to leave out here in the middle of the street?" I asked.

"Yes," Rachel instructed. "No demon would mess with it, because breaking an artificial locus point would blow all the natural ones for most of a day and piss off every last Infernatti something fierce. Now hold out your hand and agree to allow this area within your power to be used as a locus point."

"Say it," I said.

"Say what?"

"Say it's a command from Lady Scrytha."

Rachel narrowed her eyes at me. "On Lady Scrytha's behalf, I command you to hold out your hand and agree to allow this area within your power to be used as a locus point."

"How do I do that?" I asked while waving a goat head in a small spiral with my left hand. I waited for a painful twinge like the one I'd gotten when I'd been ordered to kill Father Ike, but as I suspected, it wasn't there. I kept my face frozen. No sign of expression.

"You just say it."

"It," I said with a smirk. Melvin chuckled but didn't lose his concentration. He stared between a frame composed of his right and left hands, like a director trying to frame a movie in his head, his attention on Rachel.

"Dammit, Eric!" Rachel flared her nostrils at me.

I frowned because I was supposed to, and asked the question that interested me. "So what are these locus points for again?"

"We already went over this."

"Go over it again," I said calmly. "Maybe I'm finally getting curious about magic."

"Why?" Rachel asked with a wink. "Thinking of taking it up? I might be available to tutor you. We could take it out in trade."

"I want to know."

Rachel reached down and lifted a golden pentacle roughly the size and heft of a manhole cover out of the now-shimmering air. She lowered it over the two thirds of the goat I'd already spent time rotating in little circles. "Time really is of the essence here."

"Then talk fast," I said, not budging. Still no ache.

"It focuses power. So Magbidion and any other mages you have around will get a boost out of it, too, and any true immortal in the area could more easily draw soul energy, but Scrytha wants it here because there aren't any convenient ones on your side of town, and it makes scrying easier."

"Soul energy?"

"That's what they call it. They get most of theirs from each other, humans, or in duels or other crap, but it's basically spiritual power. It flows through most living things. Plants. Even the planet."

"Fine." I swung the goat and gave my mental permission for the locus point to be installed. I knew this was part of The Plan without having to check in with my app, which I considered a bonus. "But do I need to post a guard or . . . ?" I asked.

"Nah," Rachel said, as if the reason for my questions suddenly made sense to her. "No extra work for you. Mundanes couldn't hurt it with anything less than a nuclear bomb. It takes a powerful supernatural force. Something like you or another Emperor. One of the Infernatti. No need to babysit it."

"Good." I let the questions drop after that.

An hour later, I was showering again despite the large plastic sheets billowing in the wind that blocked the large hole Tabitha had made in my building. Talbot stood guard while playing the part of goat-stench detector.

"Well?" I asked.

Talbot leaned into the bathroom and sniffed the air. "Yes"—he sounded relieved—"that's got it. You don't smell a thing like goat now. Or, well, I think it's mainly the shower now, not you."

"How's Magbidion?"

"Weak." Talbot leaned back out. "You've been overtaxing him."

"He'll be okay, though. Right?" I turned off the shower and grabbed for my towel. "The locus point will help?"

"I think so."

Yeah, I told myself. *Let's hope so.*

Showered and dressed, I left Talbot milling about and walked back over to the Demon Heart. We'd had to "officially" close for the evening, what with the work Rachel wanted done in the street out front, but Marilyn had thoughtfully arranged to offer discounted lane time to the Mages Guild as a thankyou for all the good work, so the place was crawling with magic freaks who didn't go by their real first name. A couple of mages were being difficult with Erin about the discount, wanting a better one. Still, it looked like most of the bowlers were drinking pretty heavily, and Cheryl, over at the concession stand, was doing brisk business in pizza, burgers, and popcorn. The smell of burnt popcorn was there, too . . . I think.

I've always loved bowling.

I walked up to the counter and said hi to Gracie, the cute little brunette behind the counter. I don't know why, but it felt like forever since I'd seen her. Which was weird, because she was almost always behind the counter when it was League Night. Glancing around the place, I didn't see my bag. My car was back at the station, so the bag couldn't have been there. I remembered walking over, the cool night air blowing away the smell of popcorn burning on a stove. It had to be all in my head, but the odor clung.

"Gracie," I said, feeling a little embarrassed, "I must have left my bag back at the station. Could I get some size tens?"

"Are you feeling okay, Eric?" Gracie had done something with her hair. It looked different in some way I couldn't put my finger on. She had it pulled back into a simple brown ponytail. Hmmm . . .

"Yeah. Sure." I gave her a friendly smile. "Maybe I'm coming down with something. Nothing to worry your pretty little head about, though. It's just a bowling bag. I'm sure it's back at the station."

"Ummm . . ." Gracie chewed her lip. "If you're sure."

"Yeah," I said, staying friendly but getting a bit impatient. "You got those size tens?"

She got the shoes and came back with them, skirt swishing as she walked. "Here you go, Eric."

"How much do I owe you?" I asked. I'd had my own bowling shoes for years and couldn't remember how much the rental was.

"Don't worry about it."

"Hey." I smiled. "Thanks. You're a pip. You seen Marilyn? Usually she beats me here."

"I'll go check." Gracie ran off like a cat with her tail on fire. If I didn't have Marilyn, I might have to . . . No, best to put that thought out of my head. I walked down to lane three and sat down next to the guys to put on my shoes.

"Hey, boys. I feel like a real heel. I must have left my bag, ball, league shirt, and everything back at the station. I hope you don't mind having an unmatched sock bowling with you tonight."

Steve, Little Carl, Jones, and Bill all stared at me like I was a raving lunatic or some drunk they'd hauled back into the station to sleep off the one too many he'd had after work. Sal took a different approach. "What the fuck are you talking about, man?"

"Hey." I looked around warily, my voice hushed. "Sal, watch the colorful commentary, buddy. You want Carol or Marilyn to hear you swearing like a sailor? They'll think you flipped. Is it about the Murcheson case? I know how tough it is to respond to a crime scene like that one. Anytime a kid gets . . ."

The scene flooded back to me. Those two little girls. Standing over their remains. It came in snapshots. Blood. Two little bodies. Blood-soaked clothes torn to tatters. Sal staring at me. "I can't find the heads, Cap. I looked everywhere, and I just can't find them." The sound of vomit hitting linoleum in the kitchen as Little Carl found the heads. The popcorn burning on the stove. Taking it off before it started a fire. The thing that charged out at us. My brain telling me that it was only a wolf, but . . . but . . .

"I didn't do this," the wolf had yelled. "That fat bastard wants us out of the city! He did this! Can you even hear me? He did this!"

Opening fire to stop the thing from howling. Me, Sal, but not Little Carl. Little Carl just stood there in the kitchen, screaming and vomiting and . . . that weird stray thought. How much must it cost for us to be packing these silver bullets? What is it with the VCPD; are we each supposed to be the Lone Ranger? I've always—

"Eric?" Marilyn stood over me, flanked by Gracie and another girl I didn't recognize. "What's going on?"

"I left my bag at the station," I said numbly. "It's nothing big, angel."

"What kind of bag, Eric?" Marilyn seemed genuinely perplexed.

"What do you mean what bag? My bowling bag."

"Guy's freaking out," Sal said derisively.

"You watch it, Sal." I raised my voice. "You aren't the only one who had a rough day today. I'll cut you some slack. Sure. Yards of it, but don't forget, I'm still your captain."

"Oh, fuck." Marilyn barely breathed the words, but they hit me like ice water. She wasn't one to curse, not out in public. Not until . . . not . . .

I went limp, sliding out of the chair like a sack of potatoes. Marilyn and the strange woman grabbed me to keep me from hitting the floor.

"What the hell?" said the mage with the dagger tattoos on his face. One minute I'd been sure Sal was standing there, and the next some guy with so much metal in his face I could mine him for gold was staring at me. Marilyn, Beatrice, and Erin stood over me.

"Eric," Talbot said as he burst through the doors of the Demon Heart, "I was standing out front when I smelled them. I tried to call Greta, but . . ."

"Smelled what?" I said weakly.

"For lack of a better word: a chupacabra hit squad. I've heard of them taking over towns near Texas, but . . ."

"You're shitting me." I watched closely for any crack of a smile that might tell me it was a joke. "Chupacabras are real?"

I looked around me at the assembled mages. They seemed to believe him, too. *Damn*, I thought, *here it is*. I always screw up over something dumb, and here's what it is this time: lame-ass Scooby-Doo monsters that— Suddenly, I knew what to do. "I'll pay fifty grand per dead chupacabra, but only for the next two hours."

Half the mages dropped their shit and ran for the front door as if someone outside had shouted, "Free beer!"

Talbot opened his mouth and started saying something else, but I couldn't hear him because my world was going fuzzy and dropping away. For the record, I'm fairly certain that hallucinating and then passing out was not part of The Plan.

15

GRETA
CLUE CLUB

W hat are you hiding, Dad?" I mouthed the words from under the bed as soon as Marilyn left him. When the Demon Heart had been redone as a bowling alley, Dad had them put in a bedroom, like the one he'd had at the original Demon Heart. I think it was there in case the Pollux got messed up (which had just happened, so good planning, Dad) or in case someone needed a place to crash or canoodle. It was small, but it had a king-size bed, even if the shower/bathroom area was tiny and utilitarian. Marilyn left the television playing reruns of some old black-and-white show.

"Does this mean she's Mom again?" I asked, but Dad didn't answer. Marilyn's footsteps clicked down the hall, and I heard her talking to Talbot, their voices hushed, urgent.

"I don't want them near him, Talbot."

"Someone has to check him out, Marilyn."

"Magbidion can do it as soon as he's well, but I don't trust those guild mages any farther than I can pee standing up."

They went on arguing, and I locked the door, sneaking back to Dad's bed. He was warm to the touch, and not just warm: fed-hot or alive-hot. Fever-hot! Marilyn had stripped him down and rubbed cold washcloths across his skin. I can't see magic or ghosts, but this seemed like it to me. Laying my head on his chest, I listened but could neither hear nor feel a heartbeat. His smell, though—it was muted but different—

Jumping clear of him, I retreated to the bathroom and hid behind the door, staring through the crack at his chest. It rose and fell, though there was no sound.

"Sneaky Daddy," I mouthed, not wanting to make actual words lest Talbot hear them. They'd told me to stay outside, to patrol, but they aren't the boss of me. Only Dad and Mom get to tell me what to do. Right now Mom's identity was vague and mysterious, scary even. Who was Mom? Only Daddy could know, and until he gave me enough information, I couldn't deduce it on my own. Still, Marilyn seemed to be in the running again. Which is a good thing. I love Marilyn. When Dad wasn't raising me, growing up, she was. The back-and-forth of who was my mom confused me, but not as much as Daddy's chest. I watched it rise and fall and got an idea.

Approaching him carefully, like a bomb that might go off or a frightened child I wanted to grab before he could scream, I laid my head on Dad's chest and thumped him with my finger, softly once, then harder when I heard no sound. Oh, I heard the sound of flesh on flesh, but no resounding noise from within. With no sound to go on, I watched the vein at his neck. My mouth made an O as I discovered part of Daddy's secret in that gently moving vein.

Thump-thump.

Thump-thump.

Thump-thump.

Under everyone's nose, Dad's heart was beating. I straddled him in the bed, eyeing him for more signs, rubbing one finger across his lips, then daring to explore his mouth with it, to touch his tongue. My finger came away wet but not bloody. Extending the nail of my forefinger into a claw, I carefully opened a line on his side, watching blood well up and run, catching it with my tongue, feeling the strange sensation of the wound closing as I licked it.

"Seeming human, Daddy?" I said, licking his blood from my claw. "Is that what you're doing? Why you don't want Tabitha anymore? And you don't want me to kill her because it's something she taught you and you're grateful?"

I rolled off the bed, smiling when Dad's manhood responded to the motion. *Silly penis,* I thought, *I'm not Mom.*

Unlocking the door, I slid back under the bed to smell Dad's shoes. *Where has he been?* An odor clung to them. A hospital smell but not quite. Slipping out from under the bed, I rearranged Dad's covers and kissed him lightly on the cheek before vanishing down the hall past Marilyn and Talbot.

"Greta," Talbot called, but I didn't listen. A law unto myself, I slammed the door behind me and rejoined Fang and my deputy one block over.

"Dust-bunny central," Evelyn said when she saw me.

"Oh." I looked down at my shirt and touched my hair. "Sorry, I had to hide under the bed. Can you?" I turned around, and Evelyn brushed the dust bunnies off as best she could.

"Why did you hide under a bed?"

"Because they would have thought to check the ceiling."

That gave her pause. "You know you're screwed in the head, right?"

"You're the one who wants to kill my dad." I vaulted into the driver's seat, and Fang started up without giving me time to touch the keys.

"He killed me first." She stressed the words in the same way a child might complain that the other kid started it.

"Look!" I snapped. "Dad says it's okay for you to try and kill him once a year, so I'll go along with it because he says I have to and because it is officially impossible to kill him." Fang revved his engine, and I swatted the steering wheel. "Start taking me places that Dad drove to over the last few days, Fang. Do I have to spell out everything?"

"What do you mean, impossible to kill?"

"I arranged it." Fang drove around the block twice, as if deciding where he wanted to go, almost as if he had instructions not to take me someplace. On the third loop, he took a right, taking us farther into the east side.

"You arranged for Eric to be unkillable?"

"Yup." A burned-out warehouse loomed on our right across from the worn redbrick of the Alexander Greyson Mission. I sniffed the air, trying to capture familiar scents and traces of Dad. A homeless man lay on the sidewalk at the mouth of an alley, so Fang and I detoured, not even slowing as the man vanished underneath the Mustang's front bumper and was consumed with a brief scream silenced by a wet ripping and the tinkle of bones landing in the trunk.

"Motherfucker!" Evelyn shouted, her hands gripping the door and the dash. "What the hell?" She glanced back as if Fang might be messy enough to leave a scrap behind. "You just—"

"He was sick and homeless." I looked askance at my deputy. "Some sort of cancer, it smelled like. He wasn't going to last long."

"But—"

"But what?" I reached for the glove box, and it fell open before I touched the latch. Inside, I grabbed the gold-rimmed glasses that Uncle Percy had given Dad. I put them on and glared at Evelyn as the lenses tinted. I wanted Uncle to get a good look at her. Uncle Percy used to live in a glass box with a plaque on it, back when Uncle Phil was still around. Everyone thought he was Phil's prisoner until he revealed himself to be an Emperor whose special ability was immunity

to the effects of being staked. Instead of hurting him, staking him
made him not need to feed and concealed his mind from the sort of
mental detection experienced between Masters, Vlads, and Emperors.

He's a creepy-kinky voyeur, but he helped Dad onto the Paths of
the Dead to come find me, and he agreed to live in a glass case in my
old apartment to make it up to me. Plus, he's fun to talk to.

She's going to try and kill me, isn't she, Uncle? I thought.

Oh, you dear thing. The words formed before my eyes so that only I
could see or read them. *You knew I'd want to get a good look at her.* I knew
Uncle Percy could have spoken to me directly, mind to mind, but after
what has happened to others who mess with me telepathically, I think
he's too chicken to risk it himself. Silly Uncle. Just because I might
decide to play with him a little . . . It's not like I'd do much permanent
damage. Not much. He could hear me think, though, when I wore the
glasses.

*Answer me or I'll feed your memento mori to Fang, and you can just be a dried-
up old mummy.*

*Yes, I think she will, but she may surprise you. Where are you going? May I
please watch?* The words appeared on the lenses.

Why don't you put one of your little spies on me, like that so-called bum?

You keep eating them yourself or feeding them to Fang.

So?

*Please, Greta, I thought Phillip was a monster, but you, you're so . . . fresh, so
unique. I just want to—*

Evelyn was saying something plaintive, but I'd tuned her out while
reading what Uncle had to say, so I answered them both aloud. "Some
vampires you are."

"You killed him without even blinking or thinking about it. I'm
surprised you didn't giggle."

"So?" I knocked her head off and floored the gas pedal. Fang ac-
celerated so fast that Evelyn's head couldn't keep up with the car. She
cursed almost as well as Dad, though. A familiar mediciney odor hit
my nostrils, and I stomped on the brakes to make Fang slow down.

Okay, you can watch for a bit, Uncle, I thought. *But if you notice something
and don't tell me, I'll leave your glasses in the glove compartment for a month. A very
interesting month.*

As you wish, my dear.

"Did you take him somewhere near here, Fang?" I demanded.
"Where? Which building?"

We slammed to a halt in front of a series of shotgun houses that
looked older than Void City. I scanned the area, sniffing. A glass-
strewn parking lot held a general store with a busted neon sign and

one gas pump. There was a pharmacy next to it that looked clean even though the burglar bars and the partially lowered steel shutter over the front door made it look more like a fortress than a pharmacy. Fang crept forward reluctantly and turned in to the driveway of a small apartment building. He stopped in the driveway and turned off his engine as Evelyn's head caught up with us.

"Will you stop goofing around?" I said absently. "Help me figure out why Dad would come here."

"Please stop knocking my head off," Evelyn said as she reattached herself.

"Why does it pop off and on if I'm not supposed to play with it?" I asked. "What is this place?"

There was magic here, but of a very subtle sort. I can't tell whose, but I'd guess Magbidion's, Percy spelled in my glasses. *That mage hoards his magic like a miser. I guess it comes from feeling its cost more and more dearly with each moment past his contract's collection date.*

Evelyn opened and closed her mouth like a fish a few times before she could answer. "Agh. This place smells like an old folks' home. Just like the one Nana went to before I got bumped up to anchor and moved her to Westside."

"It smells like death, pee, Clorox, and licorice." I walked up the gravel drive, expecting to see a few old geezers sitting around in folding chairs or nurses carrying bedpans. A small tarnished plaque at the front walkway read: VOID CITY MUNICIPAL RETIREMENT COMPLEX FOR LAW ENFORCEMENT OFFICERS.

"Void City has a retirement home strictly for police officers?" Evelyn asked. "You'd think I would have heard of that before."

Inside, the place was abandoned. "I don't hear any heartbeats," I said. "You check that side, and I'll check this one."

"It's locked," Evelyn said, trying the knob.

I kicked mine in, looking back at her to make sure she got the idea, but she was already kicking in hers. Each small living area told the same story: bed, bathroom, sitting area, and kitchenette. The appliances were old but well maintained, and each unit was spotlessly clean. Some units had a copy of the Void City *Echo*, our local paper, folded up on the bar or on the table in the sitting area. The papers were only about a week old. When I met Evelyn back out front, she'd found the same thing. One thing that concerned me was the scent of blood. Dad's blood. It would have been too faint for most to catch it or identify, but I know Dad's smells by heart, and the scent of his blood was in each apartment. Sometimes in the kitchen or the bedroom, but in all thirty units of the three-story complex, it was there.

"Did he kill them all?" Evelyn asked as we walked back to the car.

"I don't think so." I watched Evelyn walk a wide arc around Fang's hood. I think if I'd told her that his simulated knockoff hubs could become spinning blades of death, she'd have believed me (I wonder if they can). "The blood I smelled was from Dad, not a bunch of old police officers."

Evelyn jumped into Fang the same way I'd seen children do when I looked in their windows at night, leaping into bed from a distance to make sure nothing underneath could reach out and snag them, dragging them under to be eaten or worse.

"Then what?" Evelyn asked.

"Not sure." I scanned the street. "Did you see an office building or anything?"

We looked past it twice before noticing the square of newer gravel. Kicking at it with my shoes, I found a concrete slab. Evelyn located two shorn connections: one for power and the other for phones or something with similar cables.

"They tore down the whole building?" Evelyn squatted next to the wires, a vampiric Nancy Drew.

"Dad did it." Closing my eyes, I sniffed slowly, mouth open so I could breathe out that way. I don't know why, but it helps. Faintly, under the smell of shifted dirt, the raw primal odor of the über vamp clung to the slab. "And . . ." I knelt low, gravel digging into my jeans and my palms. "Something . . . else."

"What are you? A drug dog?"

"I'm better." Waving a claw in her direction, I worked my way from one corner of the slab to the other. Then I got it. Fire was the missing element. "He was here during the day," I muttered. "The über vamp was sizzling. Come on." I hopped up. On the way back to the car, Evelyn touched my shoulder, and I realized that I really must like having Deputy LEGO-Noggin, because I hadn't clawed out her heart or even growled.

"If we're going to work together, Greta—"

"Sheriff," I corrected.

"Sheriff," Evelyn conceded, "then you're going to have to stop killing people in front of me."

"Where would you prefer I kill them?"

She sighed and started saying something else, but I didn't care what it was. My thoughts were all on Dad. Maybe if I tried repeating his experiment from yesterday, it would all make sense. *I will know your secret, Dad, and then you'll be proud of me for figuring it out all on my own, and as a reward, you'll tell me who Mom is.*

"Uh-huh," I said, because I had to say something to cut Evelyn off. "Let's go down to the old Bitemore Hotel and check for curfew breakers. We can eat them while I think this over. Then I need to go to church."

We climbed back inside, and Fang's engine purred to life. Strains of Jan Hammer's *"Miami Vice* Theme" filled the air. "Why church?" Evelyn asked, but I was already on to my next train of thought.

"Maybe we should buy an alligator."

16

GRETA

NATURE ABHORS A VACUUM

They aren't vampires." Evelyn sat next to me on the edge of the fire escape, overlooking what used to be called Sweet Heart Row. "What are they?"

Chupacabra, Percy spelled in my glasses. I think he would have written more, but he knows I don't like lectures. I wasn't thinking about other monsters anyway; I was remembering the three children I'd rescued, turned, and let loose here: Petey, Darla, and Spanky. I couldn't remember their real names, only the ones I'd given them because they reminded me of the Little Rascals. I considered the memory of their rescue and decided it might be fun to throw at Evelyn when she eventually tried to mess with me. A dark basement. Pain. Tears. Blood. And then me. Dark. Furious. And vengeful. The hero. I shook off the thought and focused on the new monsters.

Seven curious creatures sniffed around the edge of the hotel, yipping to one another in a series of hisses and barks that might have been a language. Cracked gray skin hung from their muscular forms, with patches of fur turned greenish-gray by the presence of what smelled like moss or lichen. A ridge of giant porcupine-like spines ran down each one's back, growing longer and sharper at the end of their kangaroo-like tails. Broad boarlike muzzles ruined the puppy-dog look of their faces, and forked black tongues tasted the air. Claws tipped the fingers of their obviously functional hands, but even bigger talons curved raptor-like at the ends of each massively splayed five-digited hind paw.

Their scent, equal parts sulfur, iguana, and dog, with just a hint of lime, rolled about my nostrils and was cataloged, not to be forgotten. The stink of human fear coated the air, too, but not in equal measure.

"Look how they herd that hooker and her john." I elbowed Evelyn. "They're good. Watch how the big one is deliberately leaving an opening for one of the food to bolt."

"That's on purpose?"

"Sure." I stood. "They could tear the two of them to pieces, but they're careful. I think I like."

The hooker, a bedraggled blonde in hot pants, opened her mouth to scream, but when she did, the creatures hissed, tongues vibrating and extended. Her face twisted in confusion, and she tried to scream louder, but nothing made it to my ears except the hissing. "Noise cancellation." I stepped up onto the steel rail and leaned out for a better vantage. "How cool is that? I didn't know chupacabras could do that."

"Chupacabras?" Evelyn wrinkled her nose. "I thought those weren't real. Didn't they prove those were all just diseased hyenas or weird dog hybrids spotted by drunken hunters, farmers off their nut, and UFO wackos?"

"What else could they be?" I grinned. "I've heard about them, but I've never gotten to eat one."

"You want to feed on them?"

"I want to feed on everything." I licked my lips. "What do you taste like?"

"Ugh." Evelyn shook her head. "Can we at least save the humans first—"

I frowned. "I want to see what their bite marks look like."

"Please," Evelyn touched my shoulder gently, "Sheriff?"

"Oh." I grinned again, "That's either assault or sexual harassment. Thank goodness you weren't fat when you died, or I'd be offended." I rocketed down the fire escape at top speed, halting only when I reached the bottom. Knowing Evelyn was sitting where I left her, I waved up at her with impatience. "Move your ass, Deputy!"

Evelyn stepped off the ledge. Instead of plummeting to the ground, she glided to the pavement with all the grace of a wire-fu martial artist. "I thought chupacabras fed on livestock."

"Humans count as livestock, don't they?" I asked rhetorically.

Evelyn rolled her eyes.

"I wonder how easily they die." Darting into their midst brought me a wall of near noiselessness, nothing making it through to my ears except the hissing. The seven chupacabras swapped off hissing, rotating their noise cancellation, keeping out all sound. I struck at the one closest to me, avoiding his spines and going for the throat, only to find my hand full of quills from its tail. I sat there staring at my palm, trying to fathom how it had been fast enough to swat me, when I realized it hadn't. The one I'd struck at hadn't even moved. The attack had come from the one next to it.

I tried to block out the pain, shut it down, but it grew brighter, more insistent. Just because I couldn't block it out didn't mean I couldn't take it. Attempting to yell a warning to Deputy LEGO-Head, I smirked when hissing from the chupacabra nearest me swallowed the sound. We fought in silence broken only by that hiss. It caught up everything: the sounds of claws on pavement, screams from the humans, and grunts from me. None of it escaped.

Greta, Percy thought at me concisely, so as not to obscure my vision with words, clearly trusting I wouldn't leave myself open to attack to thwack him with my brain, *maybe you should withdraw.*

Why don't you shut the fuck up and watch? I sent back. *It's what you're good at.*

As you wish.

On my right, a chupacabra struck out with its tail. I rolled left to avoid it, only to discover that was a feint and catch a savage hindclaw from the chupacabra to my left side, opening up four long gashes from the back of my neck down to my mid-back, ripping my shirt and cutting my bra strap. Hissing noiselessly against the pain, I leaped up and back as hard and high as I could, reaching for the gun in my thigh holster. Red and hungry, the tearing pain from my wounds hit a crescendo and leveled out, intense, unbearable for a human, but I haven't been human since the eighties. I hate wounds that cheat. Holy ones. Demonic fire. And now whatever was up with chupacabra-inflicted injuries.

Normally, I carry my 9mm (it's a Glock 17) when I hunt vampires, to inflict pain at range (most vampires aren't as good as shutting out pain as I am), but there was no rule that said I had to use it only to kneecap vamps or shoot them in the eye. Speaking of eyes, I shot the chupacabra that had slashed my back in the eye, following it up with a potshot at the one who'd feinted me into the attack. Two shots. My clips hold seventeen, but I couldn't remember if I'd reloaded after I went hunting the other night. I thought I'd fired three shots then. Three is my average: eye shot, knee shot, crotch shot. So, possibly only twelve shots left . . .

At top speed, I got ahead of wound perception, and was forced to wait several beats to see the impact of ranged attacks. Counting off beats in my head to keep from pulling the trigger too fast, I got to three before firing at the next monster in my sights. Turns out their sights were on me, too.

A barrage of quills struck my gun hand, one quill penetrating the chamber of the gun itself, the other pinning my hand to the pistol grip. But the ones I'd shot went down. Laughing soundlessly, I rolled as I landed, dodging another group of quills. That time I saw how they shot, snapping the tips of their tails like whips, hurling the quills free like wicked slingshots from hell. I tried shouting for Fang, but the hisses caught that, too, and he can't hear my thoughts like he can hear Dad's.

Where the hell was—?

Evelyn's head came shooting past me. Fangs curled like tusks at the corners of her mouth. I didn't see how she could bite anything, but as it turned out, she didn't have to. Droplets of blood poured out of the mouth and eyes of one of the chupacabra, flowing into Evelyn's open mouth. The chupacabra sank to its forepaws, struggling in a battle that it had already lost. My "How cool is that?" didn't make it past the hissing, but another volley of quills lit up my side in pinpoint spots of ragged agony.

I cursed, pulling quills from my hand, and hurled my Glock at the nearest chupacabra. The gun struck it in the forehead, caving in its skull. I guess maybe guns do kill if you throw them hard enough. The fight turned for me when I flinched. The three remaining beasts honed in on me, moving wide and trying to herd me, letting the humans, their former prey, escape in the process. My left hand snagged the man as he tried to shoot past me out of the alley. I snatched him off his feet, pulling him upside down so I could get at his femoral artery. His neck snapped as I rammed it into the ground, dropping to a crouch. As it turns out, the other way is better: grabbing a human by the throat and sinking my fangs into his neck while using him as a shield. I'd wondered if a leg over each of my shoulders might work out, but no. Too awkward.

The chupacabra on the left flexed its tail at me, and I flinched. I never flinch! My rage isn't like Dad's, there's no über vamp, no massive swinging phallus (he really does need to put some pants on that thing), but it's berserkery enough. Tearing my human into two unequal pieces, I roared silently, hurling the part of a leg that came loose in my left hand at the chupacabra on the right and the bulk of the corpse at the creature on the left. I'd like to say I was smart, using the larger portion of corpse as a shield, chasing it to that chupacabra. Instead, I charged right down the middle. They lit me up with quills. Magnificent plumes of pain, like barbed holy arrows, pincushioned me, but I would not surrender to it.

My target stayed in place, waiting for its companions to intervene: a neat tactic, but they needed bigger numbers for it to work on me. Plunging my claws through its chest, I grabbed the spine and pulled out a chunk of it, my hand covered in foul-smelling blood as I hurled the vertebrae at the chupacabra to my right.

"Kill you!" My voice rang out in my ears. "Kill you! Kill you!" I hadn't even realized I'd been shouting. My ears had become so accustomed to the hissing and the absence of other sound that the sudden return of my own voice made me dizzy. Then sound went away again as I saw the others. Not just seven—three times as many, filling the street from the east end. They approached slowly. Hissing.

"You can't kill me," I screamed without sound, "only I can kill me!" My right hand wouldn't unclench, for some reason, and my neck tensed and relaxed with a pulse not unlike a heartbeat, but I didn't stop. I didn't care what they thought they could do to me. So they could make me feel pain. So what? I fell onto my left side, my leg unresponsive, and then the human blood I'd gulped down from my temporary hostage came violently back up, splattering the road. It smelled sour and sick.

Vampires don't get sick.

"Vampires don't get sick!"

I don't change shape often, because I can't bring my clothes with me and I only have two forms. When I do change, I usually use my nonsecret form, my favorite bat—a golden flying fox—but I have another one. A better one.

The way I figure it, most vampires who aren't Dad have a certain number of slots, and each time they transform into a type of animal, that animal gets programmed into a slot. The more specific or unique the animal, the more slots it takes up. Vlads get a lot of slots, and my secret form used up all the rest of mine, every last one. My arms began to lengthen, as did my fingers and claws. My jaw unhinged and elongated as my teeth stretched and additional ones thrust up out of my expanding jawbone.

My flesh burned and bubbled as I grew, like I was a skin balloon being pumped full of acid. I felt stretched and overfull, painfully so, until the pain of the transformation overran the pain of the chupacabra wounds. A tail burst out at my butt, and it felt somehow like I was defecating the massive muscular thing. Skin thickened and turned reptilian. *You think you're the monsters,* I thought at them. *I'm the motherfucking monster here. Nobody but Dad is allowed to be scarier than me! NO ONE!*

The frames of Percy's glasses stretched, and as they were dragged away from my eyes by my expanding muzzle (or is it "snout"?), I saw *Bravo, my girl* appear in gold script on the lenses. Best of all, my transformation forced the quills out of my body. I still felt sick and trembly, but it was nowhere near as bad. Then I roared. Crimson light from my glowing massive eyes filled the street like twin spotlights in some crazily lit zombie movie. All twenty-three chupacabras pulled back and bolted as if they'd heard their master's voice and had to run home. I'm embarrassed to say it, but I let them go. I didn't even swipe at the two closest to me when they ran past.

Sound came back, and it was nice to hear the background noises of my city. LEGO-Head reattached herself, but I stood there roaring over and over again until Fang pulled into the alley. I lumbered in a circle, the red light of my anger reflecting off of windows, daring something to jump out at me so I could chew it up in my fanged maw and spit out the pulped flesh and bone, the unneeded solids. No challengers arose.

Changing back felt like being a blimp punctured by a giant spear. All my mass collapsed in around me, and I deflated and plummeted toward the ground. With the impact, the pain from my wounds returned, though the quills were long gone.

Evelyn caught my arm as I sagged, though I did manage a weak smile when I noticed Fang was playing Blue Öyster Cult's "Godzilla."

"Holy shit!" Evelyn said breathlessly. "You turn into a goddamn T. rex?"

"Don't be stupid." I swung, trying to knock off her head but failing. "T. rexes are scavengers, and they had tiny little arms. No way I'd turn into one of those pussy dinosaurs. Appalachiosaurus is way cooler. It was a predator. It would have eaten"—I slumped to my knees as Evelyn failed to completely hold me up—"T. rex for lunch and shat on the corpse."

"But . . . a dinosaur?"

"Nobody said I couldn't try something extinct."

"But . . ."

I growled, and that shut her up. Naked, cold, and shivering, I made it back to Fang, where I had a set of clean warm clothes in the trunk. I always let him eat a few changes of clothing, just in case I need them, since Dad says he doesn't want me walking down the street naked and covered in gore unless it's absolutely necessary.

"So the only clothes you keep when you transform are your sunglasses and your . . . what is that hanging around your neck? A grisgris bag?"

"No, it's . . ." I started to explain about the whole Veil of Scrythax getting pulped by Dad and then turned into a personal veil for me by the Mages Guild, but I let my sentence trail off. Let her figure it out herself.

Once I was dressed and leaning up against the car, I noticed the weirdness. I wasn't hungry. In its place was nausea. I knew I needed to feed, but the thought of it made the sick feeling worse.

The queasiness didn't keep me from sensing the cloaked figure that entered the alleyway. Evelyn saw him, too. He moved with a limp, and there was something wrong with his face: It was diseased, and though covered in flesh, it was skeletal, with sunken eyes and a gaping cavity where his nose should have been. What skin there was seemed scabrous and discolored.

"We need to talk, Sheriff," he said in a voice that sounded all business despite the slight lisp and the accent I couldn't place.

"Who the hell are you?" I snapped.

"Most people refer to me simply as Pop C or Poppa C. It's more of a title than a name, though it's close to the same with me."

"Popsie, huh?"

He moved closer, so that Fang's brights (which snapped on as if on cue) lit him up. The cloak was a very expensive-looking black number, and his suit was an Italian bespoke custom job that I bet would have impressed even Talbot, if the damn cat had been here to see this. Two fingers were missing from Popsie's left hand, and the others curled uselessly.

"It's short for Population Control." His voice was hoarse, as if speaking was an effort. "Or did you think that a city in which vampires kill, on average, 4,239.7 humans per year maintains a steady population rate and a burgeoning economy without someone at the reins?"

"No?"

"No," he agreed. "Phillipus and I had an understanding, but your father has not yet met with me, and his current goals are a mystery to me. Mr. Courtney cannot simply allow the vampire population to dwindle as it has. The machinations that support the harvesting of humans cannot be turned on a dime. I plan decades in advance. He cannot curtail the killing so extremely and expect me to be able to readily adjust without substantial advance warning."

"He can do whatever he wants," I barked.

"To a degree, I concede," Popsie purred, "but I must cull the humans somehow while Mr. Courtney makes up his mind. From what I've seen, you appear to object to chupacabra. So I'm here to ask you, Ms. Courtney, as his sheriff . . . how would you prefer that I proceed?"

17

GRETA

POPSIE

S o if I kill four people every night, that puts us at . . ." My wounds still burned and had yet to heal, but I had sheriff work to do; I wanted to make Dad proud. I'd just sneak in and steal some of his blood before bed. Surely that would make me feel better.

"Fourteen hundred and sixty." Pop C sat across the desk from my deputy and me in a well-worn office chair that might have been quite expensive once. We had folding chairs, though he had offered to clear a chaise longue for us. His office was on the top floor of the Lovett Building, which made perfect sense. Demons tended to keep offices there, as did many of the larger supernatural movers and shakers. Now that the Highland Towers were no more, plenty of vamps had moved into the place. What didn't make sense was the decor.

I'd expected something well outfitted and impressive. Instead, his desk was a plain wooden affair with a central strut held up by a box of printer paper. Boxes of paper covered the place. And where there wasn't paper, I saw tech. A row of laptops, tablet computers, and smartphones were plugged in to a bank of chargers and lined up on an old folding table. Other workers moved swiftly and efficiently through other similarly outfitted offices, and I don't think I passed a room that didn't hold at least three doggie beds with snoozing mange-ridden mongrels.

"You have the entire floor?" I asked, distracted by a rumbling in my belly.

"Indeed," he answered casually, as if the topic change didn't frustrate him.

"How many people work up here?"

"Several hundred."

"Are they all——?" I chewed over the word. "Do they all wear the weird cloaks and stuff?"

"Most of them choose to, yes, but I don't enforce a strict dress code unless they are in a customer-facing role."

"So why are you so fucked-up-looking?"

"Greta!" Evelyn objected.

"What?" I had no clue what she was pissy about. The dude had almost no face. He was alive, and he didn't have that weird spicy smell Uncle Percy has, so I assumed he and his crew weren't mummies. Zombies look even worse, and the scent of rot is hard to hide, so these guys couldn't be zombies, either. I was curious. Besides, it wasn't as if I'd asked him whether his dick was as scabbed up and grody as his face. Probably was, though.

"Leprosy is unkind," Popsie answered.

Evelyn wrinkled her nose. I don't know why. It's not like either of us could catch it. "Don't they have a cure for that?" I asked.

"Let us say simply that they didn't when I contracted it, and now my condition is beyond what mortal science can arrest or repair."

"Sucks to be you, then, Mr. Scaly Pants." I fought the urge to claw at my hand, where the quill wounds laid my flesh open to the world. The world didn't have any business seeing it, but what could I do? Wear gloves? That certainly wouldn't take care of the wounds to my face, back, neck, and side. Popsie didn't seem to mind. I guess from his point of view, I was pretty hot. "So . . . wait. Can't the Mages Guild help?"

"They help keep the supernatural a secret and adjust the memories of survivors when absolutely necessary, and they work with me in other ways, though I doubt they're cognizant of that fact. My plans are far-reaching, dipping into many different realms: the mundane, the supernatural, the legal, the economical, and the political."

"Sounds boring as hell to me." I stood up, wincing against the pain I'd known would be coming when I stood. *That's not a good sign.* "I'll talk to Dad about it. I don't see why he'd have a problem. We'll just have to set up some sort of hunting trips to cull the humans like they do deer. And you can get rid of the chupacabra or whatever."

He started to say something else, then thought better of it.

Evelyn cleared her throat. "Actually, I have a few questions, too." She looked at me. "Sheriff. If that's all right?"

"Fine." I leaned against the doorway. Percy started to write something on my glasses, so I took them off and put them in my pocket.

"You implied that you're older than you look, Mr. C. Do you mind if I ask how old?" Evelyn asked.

"I'm afraid it's none of your concern, Miss . . . ?"

"LEGO-Head," I blurted. "She's my deputy. Deputy LEGO-Head—or Bobblehead." I blinked, fighting off the urge to vomit. I wanted to lie down. To go home or . . .

"I'm Evelyn," she said, correcting me, and offered Popsie her hand. He shook it, firm but brief. Power lurked behind it, not only political power but physical strength beyond his outward appearance. It didn't take Evie by surprise, either. She'd expected it, and maybe I should have.

"Evelyn . . . ?" Popsie drew out the word, turning it into a question.

"Courtney-Barnes," she added. She didn't like giving up that information. I don't know why, but it seemed to give Popsie the upper hand in a way that didn't tend to work with me. It's hard to bargain with someone who might eat you at any second. That's why, or I think that's why, Dad chooses to be so unpredictable. There is power in madness. Makes people fear you and respect you. Let them believe they can placate you. Barely. Makes placating you hard but the cost for not doing so even harder. No, that's not what Dad does. I . . . couldn't think about it properly. My head hurt and my wounds hurt and I . . .

Someone was growling. That someone was me.

"Sheriff?" Evie said my name like it was a wuh-wuh word: a question. Who, what, where, when, or why.

I growled louder.

"I think your sheriff is succumbing to her injuries, Ms. Courtney-Barnes," Popsie commented. "Or do you truly prefer to be called Deputy LEGO-Head?"

"What?" Evie was thinking about Dad. She liked me and wanted another shot at killing him. I confused her. Dad confused her more. Popsie confused her, and she wasn't the sort who liked being confused. "Can we help her?"

"I can, but only if you're willing to—"

"No!" I wasn't sure about anything else, but I was sure Dad wouldn't have let Scaly Pants dictate how things worked. I yowled again, spines, new ones, growing, poking out of my skin. "I'm the boss, applesauce."

Evelyn opened her mouth to say something, and I hissed, my tongue splitting into twin vibrating tines. Like a tuning fork, my mouth shook, vibrations blurring my vision as my hiss blocked out her sound. Popsie's sound.

Popsie smiled. His mind pressed in on mine, even without eye contact, as if he slid in through my wounds. My mind was breached. Laid open. He walked inside. Then he stopped smiling. In my own mind, I fear no one. *Big mistake*, I thought at him. *You're in my house now.*

"What issss thissss, Popsssie?" The forked tongue made it hard to speak, even in my own head. The pain was there, too. My skin split open, spines bursting through the open gashes. My mouth stretched into a muzzle.

"But you're infected." Popsie took a step back. We were in the desert, somewhere like Mexico, and I didn't like it there, so I dug down deep and willed us into a memory, the one I'd prepped for Evie. I'd let Popsie have it. My deputy wouldn't mind. I'd find her another one. I have plenty.

The ground split open, sand blowing away, drowning the sun until the day became night as the sand-choked sun surrendered, becoming the moon. Popsie stepped away from me, but I didn't care. Where could he run inside my head where I couldn't find him? It was like swimming farther into the ocean to hide from the sea. You're in it. There's no place to go.

Lightpoles erupted from the street revealed by the sand's absence, and buildings, too. It was a bad part of town. Not sort of bad, like the area around the original Demon Heart, but really bad. The part of the city where piss stained the streets and lay beaded like dew on the walls of unused car parks. I didn't remember the address. I always found the place by smell. Despair has its own odor, and that's what this place was.

I'd been here before. Watched three children. Listened to their fears and the evil of their foster parents. Watched and waited. This memory was of the night I needed to wait no longer. Intercession time. Rescue time . . . hero time . . . Greta time was at hand.

Still changing, I leaped onto a skyward-rocketing fire escape, rusted red and creaking where I touched it.

Inside, Petey, small and fightless, crouched in the corner while men took turns with Darla. She was younger than I was when I had my first time, and this wasn't her first. She made more noise than I had, but then again, there was more than one of the men. Bad men. It was the work of an instant to break their arms and legs so they'd be more manageable. They weren't like Dad. None of them were good men, like him.

Dad doesn't hurt children. He rescued me from my foster dad at the age of nine. I'm always trying to understand why. The window was open, so I stepped inside. I don't know how many men there were, but it felt like seven or so. I didn't count the bodies, and there was no need to count them before the fight. Humans are no threat to me. They die too easily. Not that I killed them. I just hurt them. One of them, the biggest, fell to his knees before Petey and I tore open the man's chest; I pulled out his sternum to show Petey how to find the heart. Petey didn't smile and lap at the blood or bite the heart. He hadn't been turned yet. He screamed and screamed.

"Why did he scream?" I shouted at Popsie.

Daddy made me strong, so I tried to do the same for them. I thought Petey was defective, so I took a different approach. They'd hurt Darla more directly, more intimately, than Petey, so I tried to help her hurt them back. She was so weak and small. Her black hair lay matted with sweat and baser excretions, so I lifted her like a doll and held her to the neck of the man who'd sold her body. Darla didn't want to bite through his veins at first. Maybe it was because I hadn't turned her yet, but I wanted her to be prepared, to know what to do.

Finally, with help, she managed it. I don't know why she cried.

"Why did she cry?" I screamed at Popsie. He trembled as if he didn't know how to react. He tried to block the noise. His tongue split and began to vibrate, so I tore it out. "This is something special I'm sharing with you," I growled. "It is knowledge and insight and—" He covered his ears, so I dragged him into the next room. There was still the fat boy, Spanky, left to go.

I found the boy playing video games in another part of the rambling squatter's hovel. Ozzy Osbourne's "Mr. Crowley" played from the speakers of the entertainment center. He cried worse than Darla. "I'm making you strong now!" I shouted at him as I showed him how to use claws to get to veins blocked by fat or muscle. "Don't you understand? Strong!"

He didn't.

None of them did.

I dragged them out kicking and screaming under the stars to the rooftop so they could be free. The moon shone brightly for them, but they failed me. Still, I wasn't angry. They cried and mewled when I drained them. They turned away from the blood when I offered them mine, tried not to drink it, but I forced them to be saved. I took their little bodies, dragging them behind me to Sweet Heart Row, and hid them in the sewer access so they'd be safe from the sun. Popsie wanted to run away, but no matter where he ran, I was in front of him with Petey, Darla, and Spanky.

"I don't understand what I did differently," I shouted at Popsie. "If you're so fucking old, explain it to me!"

He withered before me. "I can't. You're insane. You—"

"Then make me feel better." I leaned in close. We were back in the desert. "Make me feel better, or you can see it again and again until we both understand why they didn't turn out like me."

I took us to another night. Popsie and I watched as the me from only a few years ago wandered Sweet Heart Row, trying to catch a glimpse of my children. We watched the remembrance of me torturing the vampires I discovered until I found one who knew what had happened.

"The Big Guy killed them. The Eric guy. Him and that car of his."

The other me tore the vampire into little pieces while I stared at Popsie, watching his expression. He'd considered himself scary. He'd considered himself better than me, superior. Now he knew. He was never going to make it out of my head unless I let him go.

"I can cure you," Popsie whispered. "I can undo the chupacabra infection. We can work together. Population Control and the Courtneys. I—"

I let him go.

He fell backward out of my head, and I stared across the room at him. Evelyn was surround by chupacabras, but they withdrew at a gesture from Popsie. "No. No. We have an accord. They are the new masters of Void City." The chupacabra transformed, some becoming leprous humans in their tatty robes and others mangy dogs scampering back to their warm doggie beds. *So that's how that works*, I thought. *Sneaky. Sneaky.*

"Drink." Popsie held out his wrist. "The blood will taste foul, but I'm the Prime Contagion. My blood can cure you."

I drank and grinned. I hadn't even needed to bother Dad.

I'm a good sheriff. Look how scared my citizens are!

18

ERIC
WAKEY-WAKEY

At dawn, my eyes snapped open. If I'd been a rooster, I would have crowed. Farmers would have shouted at me to shut the hell up, which would've done as much good as the voices of those around me. Words filled my ears, but they had no meaning. Crimson tinted my sight, lending reality an ink wash of blood. Heartbeats throbbed about me, blood coursing through veins so loudly that it hurt all the way to my hair. Sounds I knew well. Figures leaned over me, their features obscured by my need; a desire for blood screamed in my mind, blocking out other thoughts with near-complete success.

What the hell? I don't usually let the hunger get this bad.

A vampire's thirst is never weak, but this was different. It was the thirst that comes on after several nights of not feeding: a killing thirst. The kind where one drop of blood can send me over the edge and I'll kill anybody . . . well, almost anybody. I heard Marilyn's heartbeat and howled. I didn't want her blood, have never had the slightest desire to drink from her, not even when I first rose. But there were other things I did want to do, and I didn't have permission to do them.

Hands touched me, bringing with them the scent of jungle cats and sacred waters. Talbot. Blood filled my mouth, cold, from a bag. It was human blood, but my body didn't want it cold; it wanted fresh blood. Strong blood. The blood in my mouth was straight human, and I swallowed, but my body rejected it, violent heaves sending it all back up, like the first time I tried to drink animal blood. I don't know why animal blood doesn't work for me, but it never has. Human blood, though—unless some idiot had microwaved it—had always done the job, warm or cold.

"Not working," I panted.

Other voices were trying to make themselves heard, but they made no sense, as if the part of my brain that spent time decoding such things didn't consider that function important until after I fed. Out. My wings flapped involuntarily, sending two sources of blood with heartbeats against the wall, my first sign that I'd gone über vamp as I woke. I wanted—no—needed out of the room to hunt, needed to hunt far away from the people I knew. I couldn't remember all their names, but I could feel them near me, willing to be drunk from, marked with my blood and my essence, but not perhaps as deeply as I feared I would drink.

Why does all the really fucked-up shit keep happening to me?

"At least you still have a body," said a weak female voice from nearby. The soul of Suzie Hu, caught in a state of undress from being eaten on my vampiric wedding night, sat on the ground next to me, rocking back and forth as she hugged her knees. No, not next to me. Her form intermingled with the über vamp's, her rear end overlapping with my taloned foot. At least the über vamp was wearing pants.

The inner part of me that senses prey assessed her and, discounting her as a source of blood or a potential threat, howled again. I felt Talbot's claws sink into my skin, and he yowled, releasing me. Singed cat filled my nostrils. For the second time ever, the nature of the über vamp overwhelmed Talbot's holy blood, burning him where his claws normally burned the undead or demonic creatures of the world. Beneath my talons, something trembled, not the ground, not even a physical thing, an undercurrent of magic, the turning of the world. At the edge of perception, I sensed Fang, not heading for me but coiled steel, ready to pounce if I summoned him.

Next to him, distant but not far removed, I felt my thralls, my army of little helpers. The über vamp howled one long note, and they all responded, some nearby . . . mine for years . . . familiar, others new and yet in some ways older, but all answering my call with one of their own. Farther still, beneath the wave of contact, I sensed animals gathering to act. A single thought could call down a plague of rats, a horde of bats, and other creatures. Above it all, I felt my offspring in their various states of wakefulness or slumber. All of them said "Master" except one:

I love you, Dad. Greta rolled over in her sleep and smiled. *I took care of the chupacabra and Mr. Scaly Pants.*

I had no idea what she was talking about, but I was proud of her all the same. *Good girl,* I sent.

My oldest, Lisa, squirmed in her sleep, long blond hair cascading over her breasts. She'd fallen asleep with her jeans on, as usual. She was staying as Lady Gabriella's guest out in Sable Oaks. This close, my presence forced her awake. "Master?" It was a question.

Not yet, I sent.

She waved a hand in the darkness, and a human, not the one I'd sensed a few years ago, a new one—a girl—began playing the cello. Lisa drifted back into death's temporary embrace.

Not in the same house but in the same neighborhood, Nancy, my second offspring, slept in a coffin with dirt in the bottom, the interior lit with black lightbulbs. She'd always been superstitious. Nancy wore a red silk nightie, her supple chestnut-colored skin standing out in sensuous contrast, as it always seemed to do. We shared the same exchange I'd shared with Lisa, and she hit play on her iPod, sounds of a podcast starting up. *Drunken Roundtable* scrolled past before the backlight winked out. The host, Kate, sounded like she might be a fun person to know.

Irene twitched in her sleep. Of the first three girlfriends I'd turned into monsters, she was physically the closest, safely ensconced in the uppermost suite of the Void City Hilton. Her eyes snapped open, closed, then open again. In my mind's eye, she slept naked with two anemic or soon to be anemic young human men sharing the bed to keep her warm. "Master?" she asked, anger flashing across her face, replaced quickly by fear, then neutrality.

Not yet, I assured her.

She bit the bicep of the sleeping man on her right, playfully but penetrating, and fell asleep once more as the human yelped in pain and surprise. Being bitten doesn't feel good.

"Master?" Tabitha woke fully, grimacing against the word. "Fuck off!" she said, rolling out of bed in her apartment. "I'm tired of your shit." She faded from view, still angry. She wasn't in on The Plan.

I can't count the times I've stood on the edge of, well, not the edge of becoming a monster, because I am one, but on the edge of losing who I am to the monster I've become. Giving in, letting myself . . . A quote came to mind, one I hadn't thought about in years, and then Phillip, or the apparition of Lord Phillip, coalesced next to me, a wry expression on his face as he gave voice to the quote: "'Be sober, be vigilant.'" He said it mockingly, phrasing it as a question. "'Because your adversary the devil, as a roaring lion, walketh about, seeking whom he may devour.'" He laughed. "You aren't the devil, my boy."

"Then you haven't heard 'Devil Inside' by INXS." I thought I said it, but I didn't. The über vamp was quiet. On the precipice of power, my form was frozen, my might summoned. I could use it or not. Part of me wanted to, but not the part with The Plan. The hungry part that didn't care.

Phil's form quivered as the über vamp roared again. It wanted to rage, like some werewolf without an Alpha to rein it in come full moon. Heartbeats retreated from me, all except for Marilyn's. I couldn't see her, but I didn't have to see her to know her. A succubus made that mistake once in El Segundo, back when I first met Talbot. She took Marilyn's shape, trying to seduce me. I didn't even notice the resemblance. Like I said, I always know Marilyn.

And she knows me.

"Looks like she's sending the children to bed, hoss." Roger bloomed into being at my back. "When you feed, she'll really want it. You won't have to try any poetry or flower nonsense. Just take her." Roger cut his eyes to Phillip, and the fat little bastard gave the barest of nods. "Try her ass," Roger continued. "I did. She makes the weirdest little faces."

Roger wanted to make me angry. I don't know why. It worked, though. My sense of connection snapped off like a light, and all my attention rested on the oily little man who'd been my best friend—or played the part.

My hand closed around Phillip's neck, and he felt solid to my touch. He choked, gargling as I broke his neck, but I couldn't kill him. Not now. Phillip laughed as if that were all he'd wanted to determine. Roger flailed at my forearm, but his hands passed right through me. I could touch him, but he couldn't touch me.

"Joke," he choked. "It was a joke."

I sank my fangs into his arm, but those veins held nothing for me, nothing I could drink.

"What happened to you?" he asked as I pummeled him with my free fist. "Why don't you just digest our souls? Why keep us like this?" His eyes widened as he reached the same conclusion Phil had reached moments before. "You can't."

I opened my mouth to answer and felt soft skin at my lips. I forced my mouth wide to avoid the bite, but then Marilyn pressed her flesh against my fangs, literally impaling herself on them. Her blood was in my mouth, and all other thoughts fell away.

Blood doesn't have much of a taste—I've described it as sucking on a copper penny—but this wasn't about taste. It was about longing and proximity, about physical contact and warmth and the woman I love. Memories flooded back to me on a tide of sense memory as she wrapped her arms around me and her blood drove the red from my vision and filled in the gaps, draping veins in flesh once more, lending meaning to words that had been meaningless noise.

"I've got you, Eric," she said.

I collapsed to my knees, shrinking back to human size, but there was no pain or discomfort. For the first time in a long while, I felt at home in my own skin. This was the Marilyn who'd held me when I came back from World War II, who'd held me when I was drunk on both alcohol and the horrors of war, who'd held me but stopped me from going too far that night, and the Marilyn whom I didn't stop from going too far the next night in Fang's backseat, before I was an undead monster.

It was the same Marilyn who'd disagreed with my decision to re-enlist for Korea and who'd talked me into changing careers after that war, convinced me to do something good or try it. If we hadn't lived in Void City, I think she would have fixed me, and I would have died an old man after church one Sunday. Maybe I would have tried preaching again eventually. But in Void City those things don't work out. Neither one of us had any idea vampires were real back then and that the cops, even the good ones or the ones who were trying to be good, all worked for Lord Phillip, whether of their own free will or with a little magical coercion to ensure acquiescence and memory adjustment to avoid any troublesome issues of conscience. Some might call it destiny, but it wasn't. It was just bad luck.

Until my Plan, it had been decades since I'd thought about my time as Captain Courtney of the VCPD. It had been Halloween, when Magbidion shot a mage with my service revolver, that had brought it back to mind. Until things started coming back to me recently, I didn't have many memories of my time as a cop at all. In this town, I guess, more than anything, that's a sign that I was an honest cop. I've always been honest.

I was about to be honest again, but in a very bad way. It was part of The Plan, but I'd been having trouble managing it, because I can't fool Marilyn. It had to happen naturally. She had to give me a reason first, any reason.

I pulled away from her and realized we were already on the bed, my shirt was off, my belt undone, and for reasons unbeknownst to me, the pair of jeans I'd come back wearing were old-school button-flys. My hands cupped her breasts, one over the bra, the other underneath. Our mouths were rimmed with Marilyn's blood, like strawberry jam on children's faces. She undid the first button and I stopped her, calling myself an idiot the entire time. I could have had her again, but I didn't want an easy tumble with my girl. Something she and I could both question. Even if that meant she was never mine again. When we were together, at the end of The Plan, it would not be like this.

"You stupid jackass." Marilyn laughed. "After all this time, I finally—"

I rolled off the bed, buckling my belt. "You're fired."

"Ha!" Marilyn let loose one of her trademark braying laughs. "Okay, let me hear it."

"Hear what?"

"Whatever this is." The line between angry and amused with Marilyn is like oil on water. You can see them both together, but the only way to separate them is to burn off the film and see which one there's more of. Her shirt was going back on, too. Wounds at her neck, thigh, and wrists where I had apparently fed sealed as I watched. True immortals heal with impressive alacrity. Marilyn was no exception.

"I'm not sleeping with you like this." I wiped at the blood on my lips and held it out, tacky on my fingertips. "Not in some vamp feeding-frenzy afterglow."

"But you would have screwed my brains out if the vampire hunters hadn't interrupted us yesterday at the bowling alley?"

As her clothes went on, it got easier.

"I told you and everyone else to let me go so I could fly off and feed somewhere."

"You would have rather murdered some stranger than drink my blood?" She gestured wildly with her hands. "That doesn't even make sense!"

"I don't drink from you, Marilyn. It's a rule."

"Eric." She slapped her sides. "I don't believe this. I really don't. I'm a true immortal. I was the obvious choice. You couldn't kill me, and I can regenerate blood faster than your most talented thrall. Even if you'd torn me in half, I'd have been fine in ten minutes. Less, even. It's the least—" She caught herself, but it was too late.

"The least you could do?" I dug around in my pants for my wallet and found it under the edge of the bed.

"Eric." She wouldn't hold her hands out to me, like Tabitha might have; nor would she put a hand on my shoulder and try to calm me down, like Nancy. "You know what I meant." Marilyn's hands were on her hips.

"Yeah." I fumbled for an envelope inside the wallet and unfolded it. "Yeah, I do. You think you owe me."

"You brought me back from the dead, Eric. Rescued me from hell and—"

"And you don't owe me shit!" My voice was hard-edged and sharp, like I wanted it to be. "I won't take a pity fuck, M. Maybe I should. Maybe that's the best I can expect after all that's happened. And maybe that doesn't make any sense." The envelope had Marilyn's name printed on it in my handwriting. "But I'm good at not making sense. It's my superpower." I handed her the envelope.

"What's this?" She tore it open. "A Dear John letter? You shouldn't have."

"It's a check for two million, four hundred sixty-nine thousand, nine hundred forty-two dollars and sixty-three cents." The note line on the check read "back salary."

She stared at the check and then at me. "What is this?"

"Magbidion and Beatrice helped me pull the numbers based on the files you had in your old apartment before you died." I looked at her feet, not able to meet her gaze. "It should be right. According to the records, Roger never paid you, so this is what you're owed, plus six months of termination pay."

"Explain it to me slowly, Eric." The set of her mouth made it clear that I'd gone past any thin veneer of amusement. She was angry. "Pretend you're trying to explain it to some really dumb animal, like . . . I don't know . . . a man."

"You need time," I said. "Whether you know it or not. You do. If we get together again now, after this, it will never work. If you feel like you owe me because I got you out of hell or if, I don't know, if you feel responsible for the stuff I'm having to do to pay that off." Our eyes met, but it was her turn to look away. I could see what she saw. She saw me strangling Father Ike in her name, and it was a wall between us. It needn't have been, but she didn't know that. "You didn't get to lead the rest of your life, Marilyn. I ate it up with my bullshit, and then Roger stole what was left. You used to want to go to college. Business or something.

"Do it.

"You have forever to figure out what it is you want to do with your life, and then you have forever to do it. I've made arrangements with the Iversonian . . . or rather, Talbot did. He's going to teach you how to use your powers and about how true immortal society works without letting you wind up in some of the weird soul-bondage serfdom crap that tends to happen to newbie immortals."

"Eric," she interrupted, but I barreled on.

"The girls will help you pack your stuff and get settled in a new place."

"Eric," she broke in again.

"If you think I owe you more money . . ." I kept on talking. If I stopped, I'd never get it out, and I'd never be strong enough to say it all again. "I'll give you whatever you want, but I knew you'd probably be offended if it seemed like I was just trying to thoughtlessly throw cash at you."

"Eric," Marilyn tried a third time, her voice growing louder.

"There's a bigger mix of supernatural types hanging out at the Iversonian, so if you want to work there for a while to get exposure, I've made sure you can do that, too."

"Eric!" The fourth time, she slapped me, but I barely felt it.

"What?"

"I love you." She said the words plaintively, like an excuse, an accusation, or the answer to a riddle. I needed it to be true. It was true.

"I know that, dumbass. I love you, too." I turned around and grabbed my shirt off the floor on my way into the bowling alley proper. "But for this to work, it has to be about that and only that. You can't be with me out of guilt or habit or because you think it's expected of you. I love you, and you're the only woman I've ever said that to in a romantic way."

I looked over my shoulder at her, from my position in the doorway. She wasn't listening anymore. Like mine, her anger is prone to take hold and block out reason. My girl has a will like the edge of a samurai sword. You could cut steel with it.

"Fine." Her fingers curled around the check.

"Once you've lived some and had a chance to be who you want to be . . ." I trailed off. "Then maybe you can come back, but until then, I can't look at you every day, do what I have to do to pay my debt, and smell your vomit from how sick what I've done has made you. I can't look at the pity in your eyes."

Her will softened and I almost caved. I caught a twitch of movement from her hand. She'd almost reached out for me. If she had, it would have all been over.

"Get the hell out of my bowling alley." I was halfway down the hall when she threw the brick at my head, but it was daytime, so I caught it easy. "I left you a present parked outside."

Well, I told myself, *there's step seven of the Marilyn portion of The Plan. Better late than never.*

My cell phone chirped. When I unlocked it, it opened directly to my Plan app.

DAYTIME SUPPORT: *That went well.*

If you say so.

DAYTIME SUPPORT: *I'm supposed to tell you that Code name Garnier is in play.*

Yeah. That's good, I guess.

DAYTIME SUPPORT: *Shock and awe.*

"Shock and awe." I thumbed the app closed. "Time was, when supernatural folks in Void City said those words, they'd be talking about the über vamp."

19

EVELYN

A BRIEF INTERLUDE, 1 OF 3

The sheriff was fast asleep and tucked into the trunk of her dad's car when the woman she'd called Mom walked out of the bowling alley and into the sun, all red hair, curves, and the kind of smolder most women have to work hard for. I could see why Eric found her so attractive. She was very much his era, transplanted into the modern age. She wasn't a vampire, but she was something magic. When I focused on her, a tinge of blue flared around the edges, soul magic of some kind. Maybe a sign of immortality. Hard to know from this far away. Following her would be easier if I could use the car, but it doesn't seem to like me. On the rooftop of the parking garage, a thrall with binoculars watched everything but the birds. Specifically, he was watching the woman, too.

She strode up to a classic bike, an old Harley-Davidson Duo-Glide, a 1963, if I recalled correctly. I did a story on classic bikes once, and it seemed familiar, not one of the bikes from the story but the same family. I forget what the difference is between a hog and a normal motorcycle.

Eric didn't come outside with her, and I felt torn between my two goals. I wanted to kill the son of a bitch so badly, I felt like a tightly strung cello whose metal strings might snap at the lightest touch of the bow. But I liked the sheriff. I couldn't say why, but when she did the whole monster thing, it wasn't as shocking as it should have been. It seemed natural when she did it.

Okay. Maybe this is just something that happens once you're a vampire. One day you're all hot for revenge, and the next, people start to look like menu options.

The woman carried only one bag, an army duffel. She wore an old leather jacket that had been well maintained. A scent of Old Spice and sweat, beer, and good times clung to it. She walked around the bike one time and snorted in either derision or amusement before climbing on and riding off. There was an energy to the bike, and I wondered if that was what caused her reaction. I could wait for Eric, but my instincts told me she was the real story, so I followed her.

Even without the magic in the city, no one stared up at the rooftops, checking for *nukekubi* gliding from roof to roof. Her trail led to the Void City Trust. While she did her thing inside, I dug out my e-reader and tried to settle back into my book. I'd been rereading *Don Quixote* back at Pythagoras's hideout, before the attack on Eric, before they all pulled out, but the section where I'd stopped reading vexed me:

"And do the enchanted eat?" said the cousin.

"They neither eat," said Don Quixote; "nor are they subject to the greater excrements, though it is thought that their nails, beards, and hair grow."

After my fifth time rereading the line, I scrolled through my books and found the next Rob Thurman book on my list and bought it. It had just finished downloading when my target came back out. Her gait was lighter, less concerned. Either she'd just paid something off or deposited a large sum of money she wasn't comfortable carrying around. I slid the e-reader back into my bag and slung it onto my back. Backpacks may be out of style, but nothing beats them for roof hopping. I can scarcely imagine trying it with a normal purse in tow.

Marilyn drove over to the Iversonian club, the magic there so obvious it would be hard not to notice it. I don't do spells, but I've seen enough of them over the last few years to know that those were there to say, "Hello! I'm a magic freaking ward, and if you mess with me, you will have no way to claim you didn't know about me because I have a giant backlit sign declaring MAGIC FREAKING WARD in forty-point type. So don't make me tell on you. Capiche?"

I wished she'd move again, because gliding from rooftop to rooftop tailing her had been the best fun I'd had in a long time. She didn't, though. The mnemonic device I used to remember her name and her face ran through my head over and over until I was sorry I thought it up: Marilyn was marry'n the man I want to kill. / Once I've gone and murdered him, she'll be his lover still.

It's a habit I picked up as a reporter, before I got in front of the camera. It's amazing how much leverage remembering a name can get you. I tried everything. Mentally spelling out a name in my head in all sorts of different ways . . . picturing a face on a name tag next to a name . . .

but the silly rhyme thing is what works for me, even if it does have a few disadvantages.

Marilyn went through half a pack of Marlboro Reds before she walked up to the front door of the club and knocked. A troll with mottled gray-green skin, rootlike fingers, and a suit I might have admired if there hadn't been a troll in it let her inside the bar. *Huh. Trolls. It doesn't seem real.* I took a moment to text my location to the sheriff, even though I knew she wouldn't get it until dark, then settled back into my book. Or tried to. My brain kept screwing with me, taking me back to that section of *Don Quixote*, those next few lines, before Sancho decides that Don Quixote is insane:

"And do the enchanted sleep, now, señor?" asked Sancho.

"Certainly not," replied Don Quixote, "at least during those three days I was with them not one of them closed an eye, nor did I either."

I quoted the proverb that was Sancho's reply to that from memory—"Tell me what company thou keepest and I'll tell thee what thou art"—and sighed.

My dad quoted it at me when I told him I was going into journalism and moving to Void City. He'd been a high school English teacher before he retired, but he was a preacher off and on for my entire life and most of his. When quoting the Bible didn't work on me, he quoted the classics.

Being a vampire gives you a world of time to play the what-if game: "if" I hadn't left home, "if" I hadn't stopped to get coffee, "if" I'd worn different perfume.

Dad was right, though. It had been so easy for Eric to lure me in. He hadn't even been trying. It took no effort on his part at all, and bam, he had the upper hand. It seemed like such a good idea, too. When he told me he'd let me try and kill him, I'd thought, *This idiot will stand still for it? Sure. Whatever. I agree.*

There'd been a nobility in the way he let himself burn. The pain must have been incredible. But when it was over, he hadn't snapped at me, or yelled, or laughed . . . He hadn't even bragged. He'd said, "That's your shot at killing me this year, okay? Now go help my little girl."

And so I was keeping company with vampires. According to the classics, that made me just like them—just like any other vampire. I didn't like the proverb, but when I tried to disagree, I had no words to make a liar of them. No logical words. My little brother would always counter Dad's quotes with references from cartoons. Old ones. New ones. It could come from anywhere, but his favorites were lines from Looney Tunes characters. I knew what he would have said in response to Sancho or to my dad: "Well, you know what they say: If you can't beat 'em, join 'em."

Maybe there was something more to this guy and the people who followed him than I first suspected. My instincts seemed to think so. I let my head detach from my body, the tattoos on my neck stinging like blue blazes as they lit up, the copper plate at my neck cold against me as I levitated. My senses are better when I'm just a head. Inside the club, I sensed power. It felt blue, electric, and alive. I heard a man with a stern voice saying, "Again. I cannot train you if you cannot perform the simplest step of spiritual empowerment."

Marilyn made a noise that sounded like anything but defeat, and I let myself be whole again, felt the shock of reconnection, a jolt of electricity up and down my spine, one to which I'd never become accustomed. My e-reader was still clutched in the viselike grip that my body takes on when I'm not one with it. The gnawing thirst of bloodlust curled more in my teeth than in my belly, a desire to coat my tongue and slosh the precious red liquid across my gums, swirl it around in my mouth. I took a thermos of goat's blood and milk from my backpack, poured myself a full cup, and slugged it down, pretending I was on assignment in some Arab country where this was what they drank crossing the desert.

The blood tasted better than the milk. That's something I didn't like to admit to myself. Not like Greta. Greta loved the blood and didn't care who knew it. I was still pretending that I didn't, that I was something more than a monster.

I dropped my e-reader and the empty thermos lid to the concrete rooftop, scarcely caring that the e-reader didn't break and not jumping in surprise when the fans from the building's rooftop ventilation system kicked on. It didn't matter what I told myself or what my brother might have said to make me feel better. Sancho was right. The quote was right. Had I run back to the vampire hunters? No. I'd cut a deal with the vampires and started making friends.

"Jesus Christ." I ground my fist into my forehead, eyes closed tightly, teeth clenched. "I'm a damned vampire."

With perfect timing, my cell went off. The caller ID listed the number as Pythagoras, the wheelchair-bound vampire hunter who headed up the Pythagorean Theorem, a group of vampire hunters hell-bent on destroying vampires, demons, and whatever other supernatural monsters they encountered that couldn't prove themselves friendly to humankind. They knew what they were, and I wasn't one of them. Never had been. I thought of Greta, eyes blazing red, fangs out, reveling in her monstrosity. Were those the only two choices? Monster or hero?

I answered the phone. "What?"

"You're working with Courtney's daughter now?"

"You're the asshole who bailed in the middle of a fight, Pythagoras," I snapped. "What the hell was that?" The anger felt good.

"My attack orders were countermanded by a higher power."

"Who?"

"I'm not at liberty to say."

"Of all the—"

"I'm sorry about that." In the background on his end, people were doing combat drills, their shouts making the signal warble. "What I am at liberty to say is that we owe you a debt. Don't let them suck you in. Courtney and his daughter are monsters. The daughter more so than the father."

"No shit, Sherlock."

"If you need us, call us. We owe you a debt. If you need information or if you feel lost and need us to end you"—his voice dropped low, intense—"you know where to find us."

I ended the call and stared back over at the club and watched the cars go by. All those people going about their lives, not knowing that at any moment, a monster could sweep down and tear their world to ribbons.

"I am not a monster," I said under my breath. "I am not a monster."

MARILYN

MY UNFAIR LADY—
A BRIEF INTERLUDE, 2 OF 3

Can you really not sense it all?" the angry bald man asked.

"You suck at this." I fished a cigarette out of my purse and lit up. As much as I hate the damn things, I'm addicted. When I was a thrall, each one was a victory over Roger. Each step took me closer to death and escape. It was the same way with alcohol and anything that did long-term damage in subtle ways. With faster methods unavailable to me, I didn't care what killed me first. I wanted out. With me gone, I thought Roger would screw up, try to take someone Eric cared about and be caught at it, or cross Greta, try to force his way into her pants . . . and then either Eric or Greta would put an end to his evil ass.

"You can't smoke in here," the Iversonian snapped.

I answered him with two careful rings of smoke, one inside the other, both of them aimed at his face. "I can smoke where I damn well please."

"Do not test me, Marilyn." The Iversonian gestured as if drawing a sword from midair, and *bam*, there it was in his hand. It would have been more impressive if I hadn't seen it several times already. I'd been here, what, an hour? The man sure liked to whip it out.

"What are you going to do?" I asked. "Kill me?"

"No." He spun the sword in a practiced arc. "But you are wrong if you think death is beyond you."

"So the 'true' part of 'true immortal' is a load of crap?" To be honest, it was the first interesting thing the man had said since I walked in. He was a guy, but not in the same way as Eric. The Iversonian liked to have his way, and he liked to be a big man. Showing off was so important to him that he collected things and people, not because he cared about them but because he wanted to keep others from possessing them. A trophy hound. A trophy hound who thought the fighting part was important. Inside, I was too busy alternately mooning over and being pissed at Eric to care about boys and their toys.

"As a true immortal, your energy may never be destroyed, but that does not mean it can't be absorbed and repurposed by another."

"I already told you, I'm not going to suck it." I was this close to stubbing my cigarette out on his nice dance floor, but he wasn't doing anything wrong, so I ground it out on my palm instead. The pain was disappointing and brief. Probably like the Iversonian in bed. Not that I knew for sure, but it was an educated guess. For the first time in many years, the smell of cigarette smoke didn't smell so sweet. *Maybe I should try those darned electronic cigarettes.* I looked up to see the Iversonian staring at me. "Okay. Sorry. Tell me again."

"Close your eyes and concentrate," the Iversonian said without missing a beat.

"Do you know how hard it is to take a man seriously when he expects to be addressed with a definite article in front of his name?"

"Then call me Iver," he snapped. "Now concentrate."

I closed my eyes but not all the way. Not in the presence of any man I don't trust. He closed his eyes and started talking about breathing and breath control. I didn't have the heart to tell him that yoga hadn't worked for me when I was alive, either. I'm strong as an ox, and I can work all day long and still have plenty of fire left in my tank to—

Right. Enough of that, Marilyn. A younger body came with a libido I hadn't gotten used to having back yet.

"Anything?" asked Iver.

"No." My mind was too busy. I was looking at the second floor and wondering why there wasn't a satellite bar up there. When this place was busy, it had to be a pain in the ass to get to the club's lone bar. It was a waste of space. He could probably get away with only stocking more expensive liquor at the upstairs bar, forcing clientele to choose between the long trek down to the main bar or spending a few bucks extra.

It was an otherwise impressive club. High-end lighting and sound system. Oval central bar. The decor was a bit mod, but in a good way. I caught myself wondering how much he pulled down on Friday and Saturday nights.

"So how does that work, then?"

"What?" he asked.

I was thinking more about the staffing but decided I'd antagonized him enough and made it about something he thought of import. "The dying-but-not-dying thing."

"True immortals may kill other true immortals," he began, "by bringing their souls or life forces into direct opposition. They extend their personal spirit into their weapons and use them to sever the connection between an immortal and his or her body; then they clash, soul against soul, the stronger soul defeating the weaker and assimilating it into his or her own energy."

"How do you know who wins?"

"It can be a game of inches." He smiled, and for the first time since I'd met him, he looked vaguely attractive. I think it was the humility. He knew all too well. I didn't know how, but there was loss in his eyes, things he could never get back. Not possessions but something else. "The largest factor is will, force of personality, but experience plays into it also." He dismissed his sword, a short utilitarian blade that I thought looked Roman or Greek. It vanished in a swirl of blue that sank into the Iversonian, merging with the subtle yet ever-present glow he seemed to have lurking just under his skin.

"The most intriguing part of any immortal conflict is the Soul Battle. There's no telling what it's going to be like until the combatants are truly committed."

"The winner gets the loser's energy?"

"Something like that, but it's more complex." He gestured for me to follow him, and we walked toward the back office. All the shallowness fell away from him, leaving behind a gravity that got my full attention. "Take me, for example."

"No, thanks," I mouthed to myself.

His office was impressive, if a bit tacky. I don't know what it is with guys in this town and having living quarters in their offices, but his was basically a two-room apartment with a bathroom and kitchenette. It was shelves to hell and back, with various antique-looking knick-knacks (some labeled, others not) covering every inch. The lone exception was a painting against the far wall that seemed to depict a Roman general with Timothy Dalton's eyes, Pierce Brosnan's hair, and Daniel Craig's rugged good looks.

"Who's the guy?"

"Me," he said softly. "As I was when I first became immortal."

"I thought immortals were changeless."

"We are." He stood in front of the painting so I could compare. "After a fashion. When the Soul Battle is close . . . well, the closer the battle is, the greater the influence the loser's energy may have over the victor."

"What sort of influence?" It wasn't a good likeness. The nose was wrong; Iver's nose was too rounded and pronounced. The jawline was wrong. Even the skin tone was wrong.

"Oh, anything, likes . . . dislikes . . . even, as you no doubt noticed, physical changes. I"—he paused as if he found that "I" ironic—"lost my hair in a battle with an immortal known only as the Old Man in the Monastery." He chuckled. "He even stayed around for a bit, haunting me, as it were, until his energy could be processed . . . absorbed. If I'd been smart, I would have put up with his presence, let him erode over time, taking only the pieces of his knowledge that I wanted, but it's a long process. There are those we hate with such passion that we must eradicate them from existence."

"I don't understand why you wouldn't always do that. Just put up with the haunting, I mean."

He sighed. "Well, self-control is usually hard to maintain when the one you hate is forever at your side, nattering in your ear, ready to take up the fight again. And haunting isn't always all there is to it. Sometimes the weight of an enemy spirit is enough to cause other problems: hallucinations, fever, confusion, the sense of being unstuck in time."

"Remind me to never kill another true immortal," I said.

"It's not all bad," he continued. "I gained an unrivaled knowledge of wines from Emile, the bastard, and it's not uncommon to learn languages that your opponent speaks, or to gain other tidbits of knowledge."

"You get an unwanted face-lift in the bargain?"

He nodded. "From time to time. There is a reason true immortals rarely risk . . . confrontations of such . . . finality."

"That's the first intelligent thing I've heard you say all night."

"Of course it is." Iver winked. "You have the wrong impression of me."

"I do?"

"Of course you do." He closed his eyes, a slow smile spreading across his lips, warming his features. "It is to be expected in one so young."

"Young? I'm—" I caught myself.

"Under a century, yes?"

I nodded.

"To someone your age, a woman in particular, I would believe you think me a . . . trophy hound. You think I care about possessing . . . people and things . . . to an extent that is . . ." He touched his chin thoughtfully. "You are probably right. But you should not let that keep you from learning what I have to teach you. After all, despite what you may have heard, my obsession with collecting is relatively recent and . . . not entirely of my own making, if you follow?"

"No, I don't. Oh, you mean it was part of a Soul Burn?"

"Yes." He shook his head again. "Or maybe no."

"Well, which is it?"

"It is hard to quantify." He held up a hand, warding off further comment. "I have slain other immortals over the years. Many, actually—don't take that as bragging, it simply is. As a result, a true immortal can reach a sort of tipping point where cumulative Soul Burns begin to add up, and each additional Burn, despite the insignificance to the whole being, can make a tremendous difference when weighed against the original whole."

"The core becomes . . . what? Diluted?"

"There are certain special talents some possess to minimize the effect or limit it, but"—and he seemed proud of this—"I possess none of them."

"You had one too many?"

"You could say that." He looked at the painting again and smiled vacantly as if momentarily somewhere else, then led me over to a tablet computer framed on the wall. The resolution was so high that at first I mistook it for an actual painting, until the image changed. Old photos appeared on the large surface. He touched it and typed in a code on the keypad that appeared. A few folders later, and a new slide show ran across the screen. The Iversonian wasn't in all of the pictures, but the ones in which he featured showed him as very much the same man physically as the man with whom I now spoke. He looked dapper and happy and—

"Is that Talbot?"" I reached out tentatively, pausing the stream of captured images.

Talbot, looking very much the same as modern-day Talbot, stood smiling next to the Iversonian. They were linked arm in arm with another man, a man with sullen eyes and thin severe lips who smiled as well, though the smile didn't reach his eyes. They stood in front of a building—

"Is that the Lovett Building?"

"Yes and yes," he answered. "The other man is Isaiah Emmanuel Lovett."

"You and Talbot look pretty chummy for a white and a black during Prohibition."

"There are very few things in true immortal society that have progressed so far in advance of mortal society as have race relations. Another . . . ah . . . benefit of absorbing the ones you kill as literally as we do.

"There are exceptions," he continued, "among those of us whose talent or will is so strong that the effects of Soul Burning are negligible . . .

or, as I mentioned before, those who allow themselves to be haunted by their victims long enough for each persona to surrender to the inevitable slow ebb. Though I think you have mistaken me again."

"Really?"

"Yes." He pointed to the figure who resembled him. "That man is Lovett. He and Talbot were very fond of each other, and I am the one who came between them. I killed Lovett, and the Burn was so shocking, so intense, that Talbot thought I'd been completely overwhelmed and that I was Lovett. And we were happy for a while."

"You . . . and Talbot? But I thought he was strictly a skirt chaser."

"Talbot chases whatever interests him, Marilyn." Iver looked at the picture again. "The parts attached to the individual rarely enter the equation once his interest is piqued. Though I believe his wife would say he's just being eccentric."

"Talbot's married?"

"Indeed he is." Iver touched my shoulder. "Dezbah is an impressive creature, as, I suspect, are you." He pulled me to him and forced me into an embrace, his mouth on mine.

The explosion of power came instinctively. I needed to be stronger, and I was. *He* flew across the room before I realized I intended to throw him. I charged after him, but the expression on his face—a knowing amusement—and the laughter caught me short. "You did that on purpose to make me tap in to my power!"

"Of course." And then I saw his power. Flowing around him and through him like a billowing cloud of azure blue, his soul roiled about him, tendrils reaching out in all directions, extending out of sight through the floor, the walls, the ceiling. "I had to find out how to reach you, and the more I stood here and read your mind, the clearer it became: You are a fighter. I never intended to hurt you, so your essence never felt the need to respond."

"You can read my mind?"

"Why else would I have agreed to train you?" Iver did a standing kip-up like you see in the movies. "The man you love has taken the attention of the mouser who was once mine. Through you, I can get a sense of the man and perhaps understand what fascinates my blackbird so utterly. Is this going to be a problem?"

"Are you going to stop reading my mind?"

"Of course not. You will stop me from reading it when you are able." The blue cloud of energy rolled around him again, leaving some sort of Roman legionnaire's armor in its wake. I knew the sword was next, and I didn't like the idea of him being armed and me defenseless. Running might have been smarter, but I've never liked to run. I charged in and grabbed at the energy, the part that felt like a sword to me, and that gladius was in my hand instead of his.

"Excellent." He slapped his hands together. "Now give it back or I shall be forced to take it back."

"Stop reading my mind," I repeated.

"No," he said softly.

"Then I think I'll hang on to the sword."

He gestured again, drawing a spear out of his cloud of energy.

"How many weapons do you have in there?" I asked.

"Only the ones I cherish." He lunged, and I barely managed to bat the spear away. "Defend yourself."

I should have simply handed his sword back, but let's face it. I'm too damn stubborn.

✦ 21 ✦

TABITHA

A BRIEF INTERLUDE, 3 OF 3

Just as I was thinking there was nothing more pathetic than a vampire browsing through a course catalog for her local college, *TMZ* came on. I had no intention of listening to celeb babble, so I shut it off with the remote. The course catalog glared up at me from my little glass table, and I snatched it up again.

Go to college. Me. Why on earth would I ever want to do that? That was one response. The other made me feel even worse. *Maybe,* the other part of me thought, *maybe if I go to college and get a degree in something really impressive, he'll want me back.* There was another thought, though, so I guess there were three. *What if I? I mean . . . Grrr . . .*

"Stupid." I banged my palm against my forehead. "Stupid!" And again. "Stupid!" The third time, I hit myself hard enough that I saw sparks in front of my eyes.

Why the hell did what he said matter so much?

"Eric Courtney is a no-good, lying, cheating piece of shit."

On the coffee table, my cell vibrated as it received a text. I got up out of my chair, dropping the course catalog on the glass table in my breakfast nook. I won't say this apartment was better than the suite of rooms I had at the Highland Towers before Eric totaled the building, but it was nice.

I was still downtown, so hunting was easy, and there was plenty of space for one. The kitchen I rarely used had all-new stainless-steel appliances and opened onto a breakfast nook, which was where I liked to read. Even now my e-reader was plugged in to charge. I wasn't sure whether I liked it enough to do most of my reading on it, but Talbot had given it to me (he called it a late wedding present), so I was trying to deal with it.

Rounding my couch to reach the cell, I caught sight of the city outside my window and sighed, wishing I had a deck or a balcony. Instead, there was a ledge running around the outside of each floor of the complex. Pigeons seemed to like it, but I don't know that anyone else got any use out of it.

He's certainly a cheater, but I disagree about the rest.

It was from Talbot. I looked around the room, listening hard for the sound of his breath or his heartbeat.

Where R U?

Close

What do U wnt?

I brought the rest of your things.

What things?

I'd had a lot of clothes, but that had basically been it. I hadn't even owned a computer, though I bought one when I got my cable and Internet hooked up. The laptop was in my bedroom. Eric owned a PC, so I went with a Mac just to annoy him, even though, in retrospect, I'm not sure how something he didn't and wouldn't know about could accomplish that.

Can I come in?

I saw him waving at me from the ledge outside my window, and I smiled. We'd had a thing, Talbot and me. It had been short but fun and had demonstrated why mousers make bad boyfriends. Everything went along just swimmingly until he decided he had somewhere else to be.

"These windows don't open," I said, raising my voice to make sure he could hear me.

I can't come in through the door, Greta's sitting out there waiting to kill you.

"You've got to be kidding me."

Nope. Never mind. I'll just leave it out here.

Reaching into the pocket of his charcoal-gray suit, Talbot withdrew a sock, a thong, and a piece of paper. The wind picked up, momentarily causing the items to flutter and flap. When it died back down, he reached into his other pocket and pulled out a metallic paperweight in the likeness of a cat. Gingerly crouching on the narrow ledge, he placed the cat atop the thong, sock, and . . . was that a check?

It's a check. Best of luck with Her Slaughterness.

Pausing only long enough to give me a wink, he leaped upward, vanishing into the night. God, that mouser is a great lay! Check. Check. Check. A check from Eric, no doubt. The so-called divorce settlement. I walked across to the window to peek down at the rectangular promissory note and counted the zeroes I could see. How much did Eric think our time together had been worth? What price did he put on our—
I must have read that wrong.
Four.
Zero.
Zero.
Zero.
Zero.
Zero.
Zero.
Decimal point.
Zero.
One.
Four million dollars and one cent.
Vampire speed has its drawbacks. One of them is how easy it can be to punch through a window to grab something you want. You decide you want it. You think about it. And you do it. Sometimes before you've even realized that maybe it would be just as effective to turn into a bird or cat, sneak out through the ventilation ducts, and then (in bird form) fly down to get the check.
In the "for" space, Eric had written simply *The Only Apology You Get.*
It was over. Really over. In the absence of Eric, of the hope of Eric, the real problem that had been haunting me came through loud and clear. It wasn't a fear of Greta but of . . . I looked back at the course catalog for Void City University. What if I was too dumb to go to col-

lege? High school seemed so far away. And what the hell use was a degree in dance? I . . .

"Crap."

The wind blew as I gathered up the thong, sock, check, and paperweight. I carried them into my bedroom, down the short hall, past the economy washer and dryer concealed in the hall closet—devices I doubted I'd ever personally use.

Lying on the king-size bed, what's-his-name looked peaceful. His breath came in light shallow puffs. His skin was pale but not vampire pale. I wanted a thrall, someone to force me awake in the morning so I didn't waste my days, someone like Eric's whores, who cared even if it wasn't a romantic thing. This guy wasn't it. He was nice in bed, and his abs were fine, as was the rest of him, but— I walked back down the hall and looked out the spy hole in my front door. There was Greta, sitting patiently next to a headless body.

"Greta," I called through the door, "what's the penalty for a vampire killing a human in the comfort of the vampire's own lair?"

"That's not a lair," Greta grumbled. "It's more an abode."

"Okay." I scoffed. "Abode, then."

"You're not spooky enough to have a lair."

"Fine. Abode."

"Dracula would have a lair."

"For Christ's sake, Greta." My hands clenched into fists involuntarily. "I agree with you. It's not a lair. My apartment counts as a fucking abode."

Then I sensed the other vampire. The power level felt squirrelly, and instead of my usual sensation, kind of a 3-D hologram effect, all I saw was a floating head and the name "Evelyn." She felt like she hadn't been a vampire much longer than I had.

"What the—?" I turned in time to see the floating head with blond hair coast in through the window.

"So you're Tabitha," Evelyn said after a moment. "We sensed each other earlier, near the Demon Heart, but you were preoccupied."

"What?" I asked. "Are you the new mom now?"

"I don't even know what you're talking about."

"You haven't heard her do the 'One Mom, Two Mom, Red Mom, Blue Mom' crap?"

"Shut up, Tabitha," Greta growled through the door. "I sent her to pick up your crap up off the ledge, but then you already did that, and instead of coming back, like a good deputy, LEGO-Head took it upon herself to investigate."

"LEGO-head?" I asked.

"Because my head comes off," Evelyn explained. "It's a whole thing."

"I want to talk to you about something," Greta called. "Let me in."

"You're here to kill me?"

"No." She sounded disappointed. "Dad told me not to kill you. I just want to talk."

"And you didn't just kick in the door?" That seemed incredibly polite for Greta. Maybe she really did want to talk.

"Do you want me to kick the door in?"

"No," I said quickly. I let her in, and Evelyn flew out past me to reconnect to her body.

Greta surveyed the room as if cataloging possible weapons before she walked over to my sofa and plopped down on it. Her "deputy" came in a few moments later, glowing marks on her neck fading from red to black, then pale, as she wrapped a black scarf around it to cover the marks and what looked like a thin line of copper. Then she walked over to the window and stood in the breeze.

"Call the window people and have them fix the window, Evie," Greta said imperiously.

Evelyn rolled her eyes but whipped out her smartphone and began scrolling through listings.

"Bill it to My Dad Killed Your Dad Web Designs," Greta continued. "I have an account with almost everybody in town."

"Web design?" Evelyn and I asked.

Greta scowled. "What, did you think I sponged off my dad for money?" She eyed my check. "Jobs are like humans: stupid but necessary. I picked one that let me work really hard upfront and in spurts but could be set on autopilot if something came up."

No one knew what to say to that, so we all stared at one another uncomfortably. "I didn't know that," I said, more to break the silence than anything else.

"So now you know." Greta put her feet up on my coffee table. "Now I want to know. Did you teach Dad anything?"

"Yeah," I said, "I taught him what a clitoris was. All those women before"—I clucked my tongue—"and he'd never figured it out."

Evelyn snorted, but Greta vanished from her position on the couch, reappearing in front of me. I expected glowing eyes and fangs, but instead, she smiled her bright, happy little-girl smile, and the fear that hadn't quite managed to rear its ugly head when I'd found out she was waiting outside my door came in waves so fierce that I felt sick to my stomach.

"How's the arm?" Her hand touched my shoulder, and it took all my self-control reserves not to jump out the window and run away or pop my claws and attack. Neither was the right move. Me snarking at Greta hadn't been the right move, either. I've never met another being like Greta; not even Eric's hose-bag ex–sex bomb Irene was close. Greta's particular brand of crazy was rarefied and fierce.

"It's fine now." I rolled my shoulder as if to demonstrate.

"Good." Greta sat back down. "I'll ask again. Did you teach Dad anything and"—she held up a finger—"I don't mean sexual. Something with his powers? Something unique?"

"What? You mean my special power?" I started to sit down but caught myself. I didn't want to sit that close to her. I needed to be able to move and react. She may be faster than me, but I'm no slouch. I wouldn't go down without a fight. "My seeming human?"

"Okay," Greta said. "Yeah. Sure. That. Or anything else, really."

I thought back on our time together. Had I ever taught Eric anything? I didn't think I had. What was it he'd said about my powers that time? I opened my mouth, hesitating before speaking.

"He once told me that any power I had, he—" The memory washed over me. I had just been turned into a vampire, and Eric was being such an asshat about everything. I know now why he did that. He did it to push me away because he was afraid of hurting me any more than he already had. It's how he operates. "He was yelling at me shortly after I turned. He said something about being the biggest, baddest motherfucker on the planet and that any vampire power I had, he either had it and could use it better or he didn't need to use it, because he had a stronger power or a better way of doing the same thing."

"Did you ever see him do it?" Greta asked. "Seem human better than you?"

"No," I answered, "no, I think he was just talking big and trying to keep me in line. When he found out I was a Living Doll, it seemed to impress him, and he never said anything about the power thing again. Why?"

"No reason." Greta got up, joining Evelyn at the window. "I think that's everything. You can kill the guy in your bedroom as long as you dispose of the body or pay someone to do it for you."

"One more question," Evelyn said, "if you don't mind."

"Sure." I shrugged. "Why would I mind a little more interrogation in my evening?"

"Have you noticed anything different about the way you sense Eric at night recently?"

"What do you mean?" Greta asked.

"You do the same thing," Evelyn said. "Sometimes I can detect you, like I do other vampires, and sometimes not. I assume that's a special power you have, but Eric . . . during the day, I sense him just as I would any other Vlad, but at night"—she shook her head—"not once."

"I didn't notice," I told her. "He's spoken in my head, but it might have been different. I don't remember."

"I'm going to see if I can get out the same way Talbot did," Greta said, directing her statement more to Evelyn than to me. With her questions answered and no permission to kill me, I was little more than furniture to Greta. "I'll meet you back at Fang."

We watched as Greta crept out on to the ledge, following Talbot's method of egress.

Evelyn stayed long enough to arrange for my window to be repaired, pausing to confirm when would be a good time. Before she left, she offered her hand, and I shook it.

"Sorry about the circumstances," she said with a smile, "but it was nice meeting you."

"Yeah." I thought that over and realized it actually had been nice to meet her. "Nice meeting you, too. Are you sure you're not Eric's new girl?"

"I'm his cousin," Evelyn said. "He murdered me a few years ago, and the Courtney Family Curse brought me back." She touched the scarf with her hand. "Like this."

"Did"—I paused again—"did you used to be on television or something? You look familiar."

"Guilty as charged," she said. "Former news anchor."

"Hard to do that as a . . . what did you say you are?"

"*Nukekubi*," she said. "Not really. We still show up in mirrors and on camera. It's the whole having-been-very-publicly-murdered thing that's the real problem." Evelyn looked over at my course catalog and weighed whether or not she should say anything. "You want a little free advice?"

"Why not?"

"If you're thinking about it, going to college, then go. List yourself as undecided and take classes that interest you until you figure out what you want to do." She picked up the catalog and tapped biology and chemistry, some of the hard sciences. "And try some of the stuff you assume you won't be any good at. I had no idea journalism was my thing until I took a course on a whim. I thought I was going to be a computer programmer. I have a niece who didn't realize how good at biology she was until she took a freshman-level course. Now she's a research scientist."

"Seriously?"

She nodded. "You're in a world where all the older male vampires are going to assume that all you're good for is what's below your neck and above your knees. It's up to you to remember that's your least important aspect."

"Thanks, Mom."

"You're welcome, dear." Evelyn patted my shoulder. "Do we need to talk about tampons next?"

"Ugh, no."

Evelyn laughed. "Good." She picked up my cell and started keying something in. "My cell is programmed into your cell now. If you need to talk, call me." She stepped backward out the window, and my jaw dropped open when she hovered there.

"That," I said, "is so unfucking fair."

✦ 22 ✦

ERIC

HARD TASKS

The hardest thing for me was waiting a week. I'd never gone without Marilyn for so long, not since the Courtney Family Curse (and a healthy dose of stubbornness) had brought me back from the dead as a vampire/revenant. Not while she was alive.

When she died the first time, it was hard, so hard I almost blocked it out. I got busy, and I had things to do. I had stuff to do now, too, but the plans I'd made, I wished I could go over with her. I wanted her advice and her approval. I needed her to hate my plans or love them, or slap me in the face, or laugh. I wanted her to blow smoke in my face and tell me to go to hell. Instead, I tried to keep everything going according to The Plan without her. I made myself stick to the regimen Magbidion had helped me work out. He still looked bad, but the artificial locus point did seem to help. It brought in the customers, too.

Supernatural types liked being around it, like freezing Boy Scouts crowding around a bonfire on a cold camping trip. We had to keep them out of the street, they loved the damn thing so much. That was part of the plan, too. N_CASE_ OF_HUNTERS1 called to let me know the face-to-face with Pythagoras and his loonies had gone well. They were all on board. All I had to do was not screw it up. That can be hard to do when screwing up is your single greatest talent.

By Friday, though, it was either go see Marilyn (which would royally screw up The Plan) or follow up with "Popsie" and find out exactly what Greta had agreed to with regard to the Population Control issue. After her few sentences the night of the chupacabra, I'd done some asking around. Turned out Talbot wasn't the right being to ask about

Population Control. Magbidion knew all about it. At Mags's insistence, I made my visit during the day, when things were easier on him.

It wasn't the first time I'd been to the Lovett Building, but I hoped this time I'd get out without punching through walls or getting shot. The last time I'd been there was to visit a demon who'd had Marilyn's soul. It had been a trap, but then again, isn't it always?

This time, rather than riding in a purse, I came in via Beatrice's ample bosom. Nestled there, I was warm and could easily poke my mousy noggin out to see or smell better what was going on. Bea wore a woman's business suit with a blue suit jacket, matching skirt, and a cream-colored silk blouse.

"It's fine." She pushed open one of the multiple glass doors in the lobby. "You're warming up now."

She sounded awfully chipper for a woman with a dead mouse down her blouse. Her hair was in an attractive updo with ringlets to straddle the line between businesslike and sexy. Jewelry-wise, she wore two golden ear studs and a tiny golden padlock on a short gold chain around her neck—it had become a sign, to those who knew to look for it, of a thrall going about her vampire's business.

I smelled melons, strawberries, oranges, and lemons, each mixed with water but in a separate carafe. "The fruit wasn't here last time," I squeaked.

"They've redone the lobby," she said softly. "Higher security. It looks like a hotel lobby, and now you have to walk past two guards to get into the complex proper. I think they're demons. And there's something like a metal detector, but it feels . . . off."

"What about the glass?"

"I don't know if it's safe for vampires or not." She chewed her lip. "It wasn't last time."

I thought I'd be fine going through the detectors, but I couldn't be certain without Magbidion or Talbot there to verify what they detected. Daytime should have been relatively safe, but—

"Lord Eric?" I heard the shuffle of robes accompanied by the arrival of someone who smelled of sulfur and lime. Whoever it was, he moved wrong, and the heartbeat was thready at best.

"I bear Lord Eric." Beatrice's breasts swelled (maybe with pride, maybe with something else) when she said that. Her high-heeled shoes clicked against the floor as she walked across the room to meet the new arrival.

"This way, please." Soft but firm, the voice sounded of confidence tainted by obedience.

"No." Beatrice shifted.

Glancing toward the detectors, I guessed.

"Ma'am?"

"Lord Eric doesn't walk through any mystical detection system without a Mages Guild rep or his own personal mage on hand to verify the purpose and extent of the scrying capacity. It's a rule."

He hesitated.

"Fine." Beatrice's heels clacked firmly on the floor. She was heading for the door. "Tell Popsie that he is to report to Lord Eric at the Demon Heart within the hour, and arrange to have yourself punished appropriately."

"That's a little much, don't you think?" I squeaked.

"Lord Eric says an hour is too much time," Beatrice said, deliberately misunderstanding me. "He would like Popsie to be waiting at the Demon Heart when we arrive."

"It's . . . it's okay, ma'am. Please." I expected fear, but this guy was more angry than afraid; the stammer came not from hesitance but a restrained desire to commit violence. "Please bear the Lord Eric this way. Around the detectors."

Beatrice paused but didn't turn. Her head cocked to one side, like she was listening to instructions.

"Please," the lime-and-sulfur-scented man added. That "please" hurt him deep down, and I knew instantly he'd never like me. He'd do as he was told, maybe, but not because he wanted to do it. I hated that. He hadn't even met me.

"Very well." Beatrice allowed herself a reluctant reverse course. This part, the High Society bullshit, she knew how to do quite well. She'd done it before she'd been my thrall, back when Lady Gabriella had been her vampire. With Rachel gone, Bea was my most experienced thrall. All the stuff other vampires do to prove to each other whose penis truly is the longest . . . I hate that stuff, too, as surely as I despise the idea of anyone's being forced to obey me for no better reason than that I can kill him. I felt like a monster. Monster mouse.

We made it to the bay of elevators. If I recalled correctly, there were eight, four on each side of the corridor. The *click-clack* of Beatrice's heels acted almost like sonar (which only gives me a headache when, as a bat, I try to use it) but even when I was a mouse, it revealed certain things about my surroundings. The corridor sounded the same shape and size. The soft metallic click of a panel being opened and gloved fingers punching in numbers on a keypad. Up above us, the drive motors began moving immediately. In the food court, farther into the interior area of the lobby than the bank of elevators, someone ordered Szechuan beef with double fried rice and a spring roll instead of an egg roll.

People laughed, conversed, ate, and watched the news and weather scroll by on what sounded like five or six different televisions. Even farther inside, it sounded like a book fair of sorts was under way. Normal people in an abnormal building. I flashed back to my memory, the one that had messed me up earlier, about the Murcheson case. The wolf had said: "That fat bastard." It had all felt wrong. Gritting my tiny mouse teeth, I closed my eyes.

I like to bury my head in the sand, to ignore things that are going on around me. If my girlfriend is cheating on me, I'd rather not know. If my best friend is robbing me blind, I'd rather not know that, either. I prefer the lie. But once I know, once I can't ignore it any longer, then I act, with finality.

Back then, the magic that was used to control more honest members of the police force had erased my memory and made me forget about the talking wolf. I snorted as the elevator doors opened and we went inside.

"If you don't mind my asking—" said the man.

"Yes?" Beatrice said quickly, to trip the guy up and put him off guard.

"Where is Lord Eric?"

Beatrice laughed at that. It was the same laugh you give someone who's just asked you an impertinent personal question that you have no intention of answering.

"Sorry." His voice, more muffled than usual, told me he'd looked down and away, so I used the opportunity to mist free of Beatrice's blouse, my eyes closed against the vertigo that such a transformation normally induced. Not staying mist for long seemed to help. Beatrice breathed out loudly as I coalesced in front of her, making it look like I'd been hiding within her and had erupted as mist rather than being a mouse and jumping out of her bra. Hot-out-of-the-dryer warmth wrapped itself around me, and my clothes re-formed . . . only this time I'd manifested not just in a WELCOME TO THE VOID shirt, jeans, combat boots, etc., but with three Swatches on my left arm and sand on my boots. WTF?

The night I turned Greta rolled back over me, and I shuddered, the smell of the sea air near the beach where I'd done the deed and turned her on her twenty-first birthday filling my nostrils. What was going on with my brain? Well, okay, Alzheimer's, true, but still . . .

"What's the sunlight situation upstairs?" I asked Beatrice instead of leper boy because apparently, that was how this worked.

"Lady Greta informed me that it was quite safe." She looked at hooded-robe guy.

"Yes, there is no danger of sunlight exposure," he said.

"What's your name?" I asked.

"I'm Todd."

"Todd?" I raised an eyebrow.

"Yes."

"And you're a chupacabra, Todd?"

He nodded.

"I didn't think you guys were real." The doors opened, unleashing the scents of sulfur and lime, and vanilla-scented candles meant to mask more unpleasant odors. Things smelled old and sick. Dried blood odors weren't immediately recognizable, because the blood was filled with taint. "Being a vampire may have its drawbacks, but being a chupacabra must really suck."

Heartbeats came from all directions, each with a thready beat similar to Todd's. Hundreds of heartbeats but no voices other than mine. I walked down a row of ledger-covered tables. Cracked and drying wallpaper covered the walls, the burgundy color of the paper faded, adding to the appearance of decay. Mange-ridden canines rested in dilapidated doggie beds, opening their eyes long enough to view and dismiss me as I passed. Robed figures, like Todd, moved about the place, creating a susurrus of swishing cloaks. Yes, susurrus. Remember, I was educated long before No Child Left Behind. Hell, I even know what "opprobrious" means.

"You guys must hate noise." I watched for signs of flinching when I spoke and caught a few robed dudes doing it.

"Our hearing is very sensitive," Popsie said as Todd broke away from us. I don't know how I knew it was Popsie, but he was obviously the guy. Face blackened and skull-like, he reminded me of the "Masque of the Red Death" outfit the Phantom wore in Andrew Lloyd Webber's *Phantom of the Opera*. His clothes and surroundings showed fewer signs of wear, tear, and decay.

I held out my hand, and he shook it with a firm (if brief) grip. As he released my hand, the air grew stale and oppressive. The back of my throat tickled. Popsie watched me with steely, sunken eyes. So I announced myself, forcing my mystical presence out into the surrounding area: a mental roar. I don't do it a lot, but it's a way to demonstrate one's level of power to other vampires. I'd learned that there are other supernaturals who feel it, too. Popsie and his ilk counted among them.

The oppression faded only slightly, so I roared again, pushing my mental shout farther and louder, again and again, until Popsie took a step back and the dogs in the hall whined in their sleep.

"You screwing with me, Popsie?" I growled the words, fangs out, eyes flashing red, their light turning his robes the color of blood. Outside, I felt a patrol car stop. *It's okay, Sal,* I said mentally, and the car rolled on.

"I'm the Prime Contagion, Lord Eric." He bowed stiffly. "I must make the challenge, and you must answer it, so that my outbreak understands that you are exactly what we fear you are. That we may accept you as our better, as stronger than we."

"Well, whoopty-doo." I touched Beatrice on the arm and pulled her a little closer to stave off the cold. "Looks like I'm the biggest badass at the Ugly Motherfuckers Convention. Are we good now?"

"I concede your power and authority." He spoke like he was transferring command of the *Enterprise* to me, all formal and brisk. "We must, however, still discuss the matter of the culling of the humans. I had not planned for such a marked decrease in the death rate, Lord Eric."

"Just Eric," I corrected.

"Very well, then . . . Eric. What would you have us do about the population? I can run you through the bulk-population-increase plans we have slated for the next few decades—"

"Nope." I shoved a pile of papers to one side and leaned on the table. "First, tell me this. Do chupacabra have to feed from humans?"

"We prefer livestock, as a general rule." Popsie cleared his throat. "Cows, goats, large mammals. Feeding . . ." He trailed off, averting his gaze in a look I'd seen on Greta's face when she had something to confess that she didn't want to tell.

"Feeding?" I prompted.

"Feeding." He crossed to sit in a large overstuffed chair upholstered in crushed velvet, but stopped himself as if he were loath to sit while I was still standing. "It's a communal thing for us. We still live, so we don't require as large a quantity of liquid sustenance as do vampires. Also, feeding on livestock keeps us out of the way of the more aggressive predators. We can fight them, but we prefer not to do so."

"Good." I nodded. "Go ahead and sit if you want. I don't care."

Popsie gathered his robes, lifting them slightly, and sat.

"What happens if we don't increase the culling to previous levels?"

"Then the population of the city would rise by as much as ten thousand mortals a year." He gripped the arms of the chair. "A disaster."

"Why exactly is this a disaster?"

"It would violate our treaties with the surrounding territories."

One of the benefits of being as powerful as I've been in the past is what I call the eight-hundred-pound-gorilla syndrome. Like that old joke: Where does an eight-hundred-pound gorilla sit? Anywhere he wants. It's the same with Emperor vampires. Where do Emperor vampires go? Wherever the Emperor vampires want to go. That's mostly true with Vlads, too. As a result, there were lots of rules I'd never had to learn, systems of checks and balances, because nobody wanted to come by and try to enforce them on me. I've been all over the country, and no vampire has ever shown up to ask me to leave or check in with someone or follow guidelines. I did get assessed the occasional Fang fee, but that made a lot more sense now that I remembered more of my life. Even that was only in or around Void City.

Elsewhere, vampires tended to stay the hell out of my way.

"What treaties?" I sat down on Popsie's desk. Eight-hundred-pound-gorilla syndrome.

Popsie laughed. "The nonaggression pacts with our surrounding territories." He waved his hand absently in the air as if I should have seen a mental chart or a map.

"Okay." I nodded. "What territories?"

Even Beatrice scoffed at that one, but she covered it well, pretending she'd swallowed wrong.

"Surely you know about—"

"Pretend I don't," I interrupted.

"The United States of America and most of Canada and Mexico are divided into territories of various sizes and shapes."

"What, like Balkanized states or something?" I asked.

"Exactly. Each one is ruled by a supernatural group or individual, some by vampires, some by Shifters, others by immortals; it varies. Void City is one of the smaller ones, but it has historically been one of the most stable, too."

"So what do these treaties have to do with the population?" I rubbed my eyes and took a deep breath just to feel my lungs expand. This wasn't part of The Plan—how could it be when I hadn't seen it coming?—but I knew what I was going to do. My cell vibrated in my pocket, but I ignored it.

Places like the former Soviet Union and Czechoslovakia were broken up into squabbling little states, but not my country. My country was one people. We disagreed. We fought. We acted stupid together, and we were a political nightmare, but the United States, in my day, when I was alive, when I fought in World War II and Korea, we were the best damn country on the planet. Human, revenant, vampire, immortal, half-n-half . . . whatever else I am, I'm proud as hell to be an American.

"We keep the size of our territory within certain pre-agreed-upon parameters. Our neighbors do the same, and we all agree not to encroach on one another," Popsie said.

"Fuck that." I got off the desk. "Are you in the mood for a change?"

"Perhaps." Popsie leaned forward, the light of my glowing eyes casting his face in bronze.

"You make this the best city you can." I slapped the top of the desk, and everyone jumped. "I want this place to be prosperous and growing. I want Void City to be a place where the American dream comes true."

"That will surely antagonize—"

"Yeah." I nodded. "Let's do that. Let's antagonize the fuck out of them."

"But it will cause a new blood war."

"Good." I looked him in the eye. "Then let's do that. I fought in two wars when I was alive. My side won both. Let's act like the good old U.S. of A. and throw our weight around."

"But the humans," Popsie said, rising to his feet. "They might notice."

"Good." I turned, taking Beatrice's hand and heading for the elevator. All the chupacabras stared at me as I passed. "It's about damn time."

◆ 23 ◆

ERIC
CRAZY THEY CALL ME

By the end of the next month, it was clear people thought I'd lost my mind. And maybe they were right. Magbidion sat on my bed at the Pollux, eyes closed but still talking. I'd stopped listening a while ago, though he wasn't trying to convince me of anything. It was all venting, and if it made him feel better, I saw no reason to shut him down. My tie had my full attention, anyway.

Since turning into a vampire, I'd been unable to tie my own tie. I've always had to watch myself in a mirror to do it correctly. As a result, for the few occasions I've had to wear one, one of the girls (or Marilyn) has tied the darn thing for me, but not at night. Then I tie it myself, looking at my reflection in the mirror. If I'm not careful, I find myself staring in the mirror each evening after I change. Since I haven't seen myself in so many years, my mental self-image has degraded, colored by years of killing. I expect to see a hideous beast when I look in the mirror. When I don't, it surprises me.

The suit was a shock, too. I looked good in it. The suit was for the annual Master/Thrall Social at the Irons Club. I'd never heard of the damn thing before, but Beatrice had informed me that, as head honcho of Void City, I absolutely had to show up, and I had to bring the thrall I wanted others to view as my "most valuable and important thrall." Doing so would announce that person as my majordomo or chief executive assistant or number one slave, allowing the thrall to deliver instructions to other vampires on my behalf and marking the thrall as inviolate, for the purposes of vampiric political games and attacks.

What it reminded me of was the prom.

The door opened, and the scents of lilac and honeysuckle filled the room. "Why, don't you look all dolled up and ready for prom."

I looked away from the mirror in the restroom at Dad's five-and-dime, then shook my head when I saw Betty Lou. She wasn't even dressed yet. Hadn't started. "And you know what happens after the prom, right?" Betty Lou said with a smile, and I blushed. I felt indecent with her standing next to me as I tried to tie my tie. The restroom wasn't a place for women; well, not women and men together. Unmarried men and women.

"Could you please wait outside, Betty?"

"So I'm Betty now, huh?" She moved in close, her hands teasing the tie out of mine. "Okay, sugar. I can be Betty if you want. Do you want to try that taste thing I've been working on?" She licked her lips and patted the inside of her thigh.

"It wouldn't be right," I said, trying to keep my eyes off of her legs. She was wearing a pair of really tight pants, and I wondered why her mother had let her out of the house in them. Then again, maybe she'd sewed them herself and her mother didn't know. "Even if I weren't leaving tomorrow—"

"Leaving? Where you going to, honey? Ain't nobody said a word to me about you going on a trip."

Roger sat up from where he'd been lying down on some old piece of furniture, a bed or something. I couldn't understand why a bed would be back here, but maybe Dad thought he could sell it. Or maybe it was a special order . . .

I rubbed my eyes. When had Betty and I walked out into the stockroom? It was more appropriate, but I didn't remember moving . . .

"Yes," Roger said shakily, "where are you going tomorrow, Eric?"

"Come on, Betty." She snugged up my tie even though she wasn't paying attention to it anymore. I went on, "We've talked about this. I'm going to enlist. Fight the Nazis and the Japs. I have to do it. I can't hide behind the seminary while brave men are out there fighting! I can't do it, I tell ya. My country needs me, and I can't turn a deaf ear to her call."

"Oh, fuck me running," Betty Lou said. "He's doing it again."

"Betty." My chest hurt, and I looked at Roger, not for help but for things I couldn't think of, so I turned back to Betty Lou. "What's gotten into you? You shouldn't be talking like that, not in front of Roger. Or at all." I took her hands in mine. They felt cold to the touch. "And I told you, we can't. We just . . ." Sweat, real sweat, I don't know why, but in the back of my head, it seemed wrong. Shouldn't it have been red?

"You can't be Betty Lou," I said, squeezing her hands. "Where are we, really?"

"The Pollux." Betty Lou frowned. "You're getting ready for the vampire/thrall dance."

"That doesn't make any sense to me." I pulled her close, clinging to her like I had the real Betty Lou that night after the prom, when both of us had let things go too far. Betty Lou had been the first woman I'd slept with, though I definitely hadn't been her first . . . and . . . the memory of the two of us awkwardly fumbling at each other flushed through me. Betty's voice, when I was spent: "That was nice."

"Which part felt best to you?" I'd asked.

"I can't talk about that, I—"

But she had talked, and after a little experimentation, we'd managed better than nice.

Then I was elsewhere, elsewhen, a letter in my pocket from Betty. She was pregnant, and I was in a war zone. I looked up at my buddy Carmichael and knew he wouldn't make it through the war, because he hadn't, and as if following a thread, I remembered another letter, bittersweet, from Betty, letting me know that she'd lost the baby, that everything was okay. She hadn't said anything to anyone, and no one needed to know.

I remembered writing a letter back home to Marilyn and asking her to check on Betty Lou. Marilyn, eternally ten years my senior. I had never kept secrets from her. Marilyn would know what to say. If my emotions were anywhere close to as complicated as Betty Lou's . . .

"I'm sorry about the baby, Betty Lou," I said now. "You know I would have done right by you. But by the time I got back, you'd already married Roger and—"

Time marched on. Fast. Painful. And it took me with it.

I was outside on a beautiful summer day, standing at Betty Lou's funeral. I'd been dating Sheila at the time. She stood next to me all in black, her blond hair in a perfect wave. It was over and done. Marilyn stood to the side, comforting Betty Lou's mother, and Roger stood off by himself. I remembered seeing him smile and wondering what he had to smile about. It was later than that when I finally started dating Marilyn.

"It's so tragic," Sheila whispered in my ear. "Things like this are exactly why women shouldn't be allowed to drive. How are we supposed to know when the brakes—?"

"Roger killed Betty Lou." I whispered the words. "How did I never realize it?"

And then I was somewhere else again, in Fang before he was Fang, going off the cliff. But that wasn't right, because I hadn't been driving Fang the first time. I'd been driving Roger's car. I'd relived my death inside Fang, later . . . The inconsistency didn't matter. The memory swept me on, and I remembered the instant I knew I was going to die.

The freedom I felt. I gunned the gas one last time and smiled to hear the engine roar. I'd been so happy in that moment. I . . .

I died and came back. Another memory come to life, and I remembered tears. Hearing them from a long way off, somewhere far below me, like someone crying underwater. In this last memory, there was no visual component other than whiteness and the sound. I remember knowing that I shouldn't go toward the tears but not being able to stop myself.

"Eric," said a voice, "for what are you waiting?" At the time, I don't know to whom I'd thought that voice belonged . . . God? Saint Peter? But now I recognized it all too well. It was the voice that had let me through the wards at the Highland Towers when I went to steal the Stone of Aeternum from Lord Phil. Later, in Paris, I'd heard it when I entered Le Château de Vincennes and set eyes on the alien-looking decapitated head of the demon Scrythax.

"That's Marilyn," I remembered saying. "Something's wrong. I gotta make sure she's okay."

"Eric," Scrythax said again, "for what are you waiting?"

"Will she be okay if I don't go to her?"

"No," Scrythax told the newly dead me.

"And if I do?"

"Eventually." Scrythax laughed when he said that, because I was already on way back to her. Was he laughing because I'd almost gotten away, escaped the Courtney curse? Was it because he was looking forward to playing games with me? I don't know. Maybe one day I'll ask him.

Next came pain and fire and a grave. I'd never remembered it clearly, my return from the dead, but now I did. The memory of a true immortal, though fouled up by my Alzheimer's, finally brought it back. I knew what was happening to me then. I think I could have stopped the flow and regained control, but I wanted to know. I wanted to see. To feel. To remember after all these years.

The stink of rotted flesh in my nose and chemicals beneath that smell. The scrape of wood against my fingernails. Pain as my fingernails lengthened into claws. Dirt filling my mouth as I fought my way toward the sound and scent of Marilyn. Hearing her heartbeat, her lungs gasping those little gasps between sobs.

"I'm coming," I tried to say, but the dirt stopped my words, and then the sun set me on fire. I ran to the cemetery chapel for cover, and sizzling in the shade, I asked one question before passing out. "Am I late for something?" The clock struck two. I was late for something, all right. My wedding day.

I closed my eyes, and when they opened again, I was lying in the middle of the road in front of the Demon Heart, the hard metal of the artificial locus point jabbing into my back. Cheryl, Erin, Magbidion, Beatrice, Talbot, and Greta were all standing over me.

"Can I be Claude Rains?" Greta asked.

"What?" My skin felt cool again. The moon was high, full and orange in the sky.

"If you're going to hallucinate some more," Greta clarified. "Let's do *Casablanca*. You be Humphrey Bogart and I'll be Claude Rains and we can do the part where they're sitting out front and I say, 'Waters? What waters? We're in the desert.' And you say—"

"'I was misinformed,'" I quoted. And I was, fundamentally. My information about how I came back from the dead had always been from Marilyn's point of view. She'd seen it firsthand, and she'd thought she knew what she'd seen. It didn't change a thing about the last half a century, but in a way it changed everything. I didn't come back as an angry ghost—a revenant—because I was murdered and I wanted revenge. I hadn't even known it was murder at the time.

I came back as an angry ghost because Marilyn was crying over my grave. She needed me, so I came back . . . and then the Courtney Family Curse (administered by freaky demon head) had its way with me and made me a vampire as well . . . the two-for-one-undead deal making me an Emperor-level vampire in the process.

Fumbling for my cell, I brought up my special app and typed in what I'd just figured out. The only response:

NIGHTTIME SUPPORT: I'm aware.

Which just goes to show you, even when I'm being a sneaky son of a bitch, I'm always the last to know.

24

GRETA

VAMPIRE BUDDY COP MOVIE?

Are you sure it's Friday?" The vampire I held aloft was too scared to comment sensibly. I wasn't asking him anyway. He's one of those vampires I hate. Chicken vampires (fraidy-cats, not vampires who are chickens, cuz that would be cool) piss me off. Pudgy ones piss me off more. Fat boy wore belted gray slacks with a white dress shirt and a plaid sweater vest. He smelled like Old Spice and pig blood. Worse, his BMI had to be at least twenty-five.

"I—I—I—" he babbled.

"Shut it, fat ass!" We stood on the edge of a butcher shop's rooftop. He was dangling over the side. I don't know why he let that scare him. Maybe he sucked at flying. "Evelyn?" I asked.

"It's Friday, Sheriff." Evelyn stood off to the side, holding up a digital tablet with the calendar app open.

"And vampires are immune to curfew on Mondays, Wednesdays, and Fridays?" I asked, even though I already knew.

"I'm pretty sure."

"Oh." I looked back to Fat Ass and frowned. "Then you can go." I opened my hand and let him fall. Flailing, he grabbed for me, but I slapped him instead, the sharp blow carrying enough strength to knock him farther past the edge of the rooftop. He yelled all the way down, even though it was only a one-story. When he hit the ground, he grunted in pain and fell over.

"Pathetic."

The corner of Evelyn's lips turned down in a grimace. "Was that absolutely necessary?"

"Public Safety Tip number four: The sheriff doesn't like fat vampires." I shrugged.

"Fat?" she mouthed. Evelyn's perceptions of who was and wasn't fat were totally out of whack. Sure, she was skinny, but most people aren't.

"And he took up valuable solving-the-mystery-of-what-Dad-is-hiding-from-me time by breaking curfew."

"Which," Evelyn said pointedly, "he didn't actually do."

"I'm hungry," I said, ignoring her. "Are you?"

"We just ate." This was a conversation Evelyn and I were beginning to have a lot. She tended to eat once a night and then not eat again, treating blood like medicine instead of something to be wallowed in and played with and imbibed at every available opportunity.

"Does that mean you aren't hungry?" I drew my Glock and kneecapped Fat Ass as he ran. He rolled into the street, avoiding being struck by traffic with the judicious application of vampiric speed and reflexes.

Evelyn flinched. "Yes."

"I could always feed off of you, and then you would be hungry, and we could go get someone to eat—"

"I don't think so." Evelyn was already gliding down to street level. It is totally not fair that she can fly—like real Peter Pan flying.

"I still haven't tested that theory I need a church for," I said, looking toward Void City Episcopalian. "We could do it now. Don't they have Friday-night Mass or—"

"Sheriff Courtney?" My cell chirped, interrupting me.

"What?" I replied, clicking and releasing the transmit button.

"We need an SC to assist with a domestic disturbance on Third and Midnight."

"Is this Kat?" I asked.

"Yes, ma'am. This is Captain Marx."

"Does 'SC' stand for 'supernatural citizen'?"

"Yes, ma'am." I liked to keep Marx talking until I could clearly hear agitation in her voice.

"Can we change it to Salacious Crumb?" Evelyn got the *Return of the Jedi* reference, which impressed me, but it was lost on Marx.

"Will that make you respond to the call?"

"I am responding to the call, Kat."

I heard her sigh, but she wasn't quite there yet. "I mean, show up and assist us."

"Oh." I thought for a moment. "Can I call you Kit Kat?"

Evelyn's head shook in perpetual disapproval with my teasing of

Captain Marx. I didn't understand. Why shouldn't I tease her? She was the one who dared to speak with me.

"Can I call you Slaughterhouse?" the reply crackled back.

"Nope." *Not bad, Kat.*

"Then no, ma'am." I heard another sigh. The edge to her voice was ragged and worn, tired beyond belief.

"Why do you need help with a domestic disturbance, Kit Kat?" Evelyn rolled her eyes at me, silently disapproving of my continued antics and disrespect.

"Because the domestics involved are both demons, Sheriff, and—"

"Cool!" I jumped off the building, going into a roll as I hit the pavement and came up minimally injured and already healing. I passed Deputy LEGO-Noggin on my way to Fang. He was parked around the corner from the butcher shop, waiting as patiently as a moray eel while a stray cat sniffed at his tire. I wanted to stop and watch, to see if the cat would be dumb enough to crawl under the car, but we didn't have time, so I kicked it underneath. There was only a brief yowl before its bones tinkled down atop the others in Fang's trunk.

"We have a domestic disturbance!" I told the car as I jumped into the driver's seat. Fright Ranger's "Oh Oh Oh Sexy Vampire" began playing over the Mustang's speaker, and I gave his steering wheel a good thump. "Would you stop being silly?"

Fang's left-turn indicator flashed, so I looked that way and caught a glimpse of a chupacabra teen in ratty jeans, gloves, and a gray hoodie, watching me from the shadows of a closed-down bar. He'd positioned himself downwind so I couldn't smell the sulfur-lime mixture. He couldn't have been older than nineteen or twenty, and he had a thin rangy look. The disfigurement wasn't so bad on him, maybe because he was so young: little more than reddish blotches on his skin that could have passed for eczema or maybe acne scars. Our gazes met and he looked away first, but not before I saw longing in those brown eyes.

I tossed him the universal "What?" gesture, and he opened his mouth to speak, then lost his nerve and looked away. Evelyn climbed into the passenger seat. Fang's engine roared to life, but I put my foot on the brake.

"What?" I shouted across the street. "You need something?"

Shoving his gloved hands awkwardly in the pockets of his hoodie, he turned and dashed down the sidewalk, but not before I saw what he'd stenciled on the back of his hoodie in bright red paint:

SHE'S THE BOSS, APPLESAUCE

"Ha," Evelyn snarked, "looks like you have a fan."

"Shut up." I raised my hand to knock her head off, but something stopped me. It could have been that I didn't want to annoy her, but more likely, I was just tired from holding Fat Ass over the edge of the roof for so long. "Third and Midnight," I instructed Fang as I took my foot off the brake pedal. He pulled away from the curb and let the music change to Megadeth's "Sweating Bullets," but I wasn't in the mood. Folding my arms under my breasts, I slunk down in the seat and closed my eyes.

"Um?" Evelyn said.

"What?"

"Won't people think *Knight Rider?* Oh. Right. Never mind. You have the little bag thingy."

I dug it out of my pocket and held it up. "Yep. Portable short-range Veil of Scrythax and, like Tigger, it's the only one."

"So what do you think the mortals who notice that you aren't driving will see?"

I closed my eyes, putting the gris-gris bag back in my jeans. "Maybe they'll be too busy looking at you?"

"Oh." I could hear her blushing, her hand touching her hair. "I'm not that—"

"Nope." I knocked her head off with an absentminded swat. "You're not."

I didn't even have to hit the gas myself. Fang was in on the joke now and knew exactly what to do. With wind blowing through my hair and the sound of heavy metal (and my deputy's curses) in my ears, I felt better again. Besides, it's not like it took Evelyn's head more than a few blocks to catch up with the car and reattach to her body. Where's the harm in that?

25

GRETA

BAD COP/WORSE COP

Third and Midnight took us close to the Episcopal church. I studied the stone architecture, wondering when it had been built and whether I'd catch fire if I walked inside. It smelled, even from a block over, of candles and hopeful people. The flashing red and blue lights of the VCPD squad cars parked in front of a multistory high-rise drew my attention back to the matter at hand as surely as my deputy's hand on my shoulder did.

"We're here."

"I know." I glanced back at the church. The sounds of a hymn cut through the night and reminded me of a thing so long gone and well forgotten that only the ache of its absence was left—the final twinge of remembrance. Long before foster care . . . I think I'd been to church.

"You still aren't thinking of trying out some plan involving a priest, are you?"

"Hmmm?" Dad stood in my mind's eye larger than life, as I remembered watching him strangling Father Ike, standing in the shadows like a child on the stairs eavesdropping on the grown-up conversations she's not supposed to hear. I understood most of it. I knew why he'd strangled Father Ike. He'd been ordered to do it, but the second part . . . that made no sense.

"The priest thing," Evelyn repeated. "You're not thinking about—"

"No." I climbed out of the car and headed for the officer who looked like he was in charge. "Not until after this demon thing."

The SWAT team stood outside looking conspicuous as hell, but passersby weren't paying them much attention. They had the front of the building cordoned off, with less combat-ready cops moving along the few mortals who thought to stop and stare. It was almost like the olden days . . . of several hundred days ago.

"Distraction screen," I said, mildly impressed.

Four mages stood one at each corner of the building. I could see only three of them, but I knew the fourth was there. Properly trained mages could set up a field like the one the Veil of Scrythax used to give off, but only on a smaller scale, and they aren't capable of keeping it going indefinitely. From what I understand, it takes a lot out of a mage to keep any kind of enchantment running long-term.

"I'd say so," Evelyn said. "You see them a lot in Atlanta."

"You spent a lot of time in Atlanta?"

"Sure." She looked down and away, which she'd been doing a lot. I didn't understand quite why. "I did. Yeah. The vampire hunter presence is pretty strong in Georgia, what with the Lycan Diocese being based in Rome."

"You hung out with humans?" I raised an eyebrow and squinched my mouth.

"As a rule, yes. I . . . I hunted vampires."

"Me, too!" I knew I liked Evelyn for some reason. "I mean the vampires, not Atlanta. Though Dad and I went to Dragon*Con once. We both went as Ghostbusters. How long did it take you to figure out the heart thing?"

"Ghostbusters?" I could see she had trouble picturing that, so she swallowed the mental image and moved on to the next query in the queue. "Heart thing?"

"Sure." One of the cops tried to wave me over, but I was in no hurry. Demons can be fun to fight, but their blood isn't always edible, so I was trying not to get too excited. I gave Evelyn my full attention, turning my back on the cops. "In higher-power vamps, most of the blood is in the heart. There's a spot—"

"Sheriff?" Captain Marx interrupted me, and I was going to snap at her for it, but instead, I stared straight at her chest.

"Holy crap! Your sweater puppies are growing out of control!"

"It's a side effect," she said, flatly meeting my gaze (though I guess it should have been impossible for her to do anything flatly now).

"Of what?" Evelyn asked.

Wait a minute!

I narrowed my gaze, trying to spot whether she was a thrall. I'd never made a thrall, so I couldn't just sense one; it was on my to-do list, though. I'd just never found the right person. Even so, I could usually guess by the evidence—stronger heartbeat, enhanced attributes—but I'd have to see the mark to be sure.

Each thrall bears a mark, a blood tattoo, bestowed upon them by their vampiric "master." Dad uses a butterfly, but it can be anything. Uncle Percy uses an ankh. Lady Gabriella, a rose. Of course, nothing would keep a vampire from changing things up. I think if I make a thrall, I'm going to use a little heart with demon wings. That or an upside-down Mary Poppins silhouette.

"Turn around," I said abruptly. When Captain Marx responded too slowly, I spun her in a circle, eyeing her for traces of a butterfly, but I didn't find anything. Very powerful vampires influence their opposite-gender (or gender of sexual preference) thrall's physical appearance subconsciously. Dad's thralls tend to get very busty and curvy, like, well, like Mom.

"What the—?" Marx said.

"Nope, no blood tattoo," I said. Did I smell Dad on her, though? A trace? Perhaps . . . hmmm. "Sorry, for a minute I wondered if you were Dad's thrall."

Her pulse quickened at that, but she obviously didn't have a tattoo (I should have been able to sense it even if it was someplace out of sight), and the Dad smell was faint enough that it could have been from one of the meetings he'd been having with the reps from the VCPD, the Mages Guild, the Orchard Lake Pack, and the Sable Oaks Vampires. I had a mind to go back and put on Percy's glasses to get his opinion, but I didn't want to read snark and fight a demon at the same time.

"Can you please see what you can do?" Kit Kat gestured at the building. "We've got two Khan Canis tearing the place apart because one of them has apparently been spending way too much time around a Gallus and—"

I held my hand up.

Kit Kat paused. "Yes?"

"Khan Canis?"

"Dog-headed ones with leathery wings." She cracked a smile. "They tend to use melee weapons. Some enchanted. Some not."

"Oh, that's what those are called." I nudged Evelyn. "I didn't know that. Did you know that?"

"I've never fought a demon," Evelyn said softly.

"Really?" I clasped my hands together. "This will be awesome. Big doggies are fun to fight! You basically just hit them over and over again until they stop moving."

"Oh." Her eyes sparkled with inner crimson, the *kanji* on her neck pulsing red to match the glow. "That I can manage. What's a Gallus?"

"Who cares?"

"Do we have a plan?"

"Let me demonstrate." I checked my Glock to make sure I'd re-loaded the clip, reholstered it, and looked at the building. "Which floor?"

"Twelve."

I nodded, grinned at Evelyn, reached out, and popped Kit Kat's uniform shirt open just to make sure there wasn't a tattoo hiding under there, and charged.

26

ERIC

I'M NOT WEARING A FEZ OR A MOOSE HAT

As far as I could tell, the Irons Club had once been a country club. Maybe it still counted as one. If it had been my club, I've have done something about the roads. We'd driven round and round on a winding road up the non–state park section of Bald Mountain, and it seemed as if the road's planners had gone out of their way to make it seem like Bald Mountain was more of a mountain than it is. It's big enough, but these aren't the damn Smokies.

In Fang, the drive might have been fun, but in the back of a limo, it had me wanting to throw my chauffeur out the window and drive myself (and my chauffeur weighed half a ton). Houses became more and more expensive as we entered the Sanguine Hills area. There were a fair number of for-sale signs posted, the owners having died when I knocked down the Highland Towers (of which Vampire High Society highly approved) or when Winter trapped them in the Artiste Unknown with a glorified death trap (on which Vampire High Society frowned).

Finally, the pricey houses gave way to a long stretch of well-manicured cherry trees and boxwoods. As we neared the gates, the bushes took on a topiary aspect: lions, tigers, and (bears!) other predators rendered in living plants stalked the massive iron gates. We stopped at the granite-hewn guard shack where some douche in a burgundy security uniform looked out. He walked up to the limo, bypassing the chauffeur's window and heading straight to mine.

"I'm terribly sorry to delay you—" His eyes widened. "Lord Eric. I—"

Beatrice leaned forward so she could be easily seen around me. If I thought I looked good in a suit, she put me to shame in her dress.

Green is her color, and she'd worn a strapless green thing that was all mountains and no molehills. It hugged everything it ought to hug and flowed and folded where a man might hope it would. Her red hair was done up, with ringlets hanging down to accent her cheeks. Those storm-cloud eyes of hers twinkled with mischief as she spoke for me.

I'd already been warned that even though I didn't give a damn about propriety, I should do my best not to talk to the staff. I didn't care about the rules, but apparently, they might wind up in hot water (real hot water) over it, so I decided to be a good little Emperor and let her talk.

"These aren't the droids you're looking for," she said, following his gaze to her chest. If he'd been awestruck by me, he was even more awestruck by Beatrice.

"I'm . . . I'm sorry, Lady Beatrice."

She smiled, cutting her eyes pointedly at the gate. "Should I get out and open that myself?"

"Invi—" He almost got out the entire word before deciding that whether we had my invitation with us or not, he wasn't going to get in trouble for letting us in. At least not as much trouble as he might find himself in if he offended me. Stupid vampire groupies. You gotta love 'em. "Ah. Ahem." He straightened and bowed so low, he missed hitting the door with his forehead by only a few centimeters. "Welcome. We are honored by the presence of your power."

"Weird," said Magbidion from the front passenger's seat. We'd weighed leaving him close to the artificial locus point against being that far away from him at night and decided it was less of a risk to bring him along.

"What's weird?" I asked.

"I half expected him to offer himself to you on the spot," Mags said.

Beatrice spoke up. "Oh, he wouldn't dare. Not in front of me. It's presumptuous, and I gained a reputation for frowning on that sort of thing when I was with Gabriella, or he might have risked it anyway."

"Mortals," our driver scoffed. Tiko was an Oni, and limo service was just one of the many enterprises that the brothers at Triple-T had gotten into. Normally, he was horned and strangely colored, but to-night he appeared to be a middle-aged Asian man. I'd seen him stick a piece of paper with strange writing on it to his forehead to enact the transformation, but I had no idea how it worked on a mystical me-chanics level.

Through the gates, the drive transitioned from asphalt to cobble-stone, and the ride got bumpy.

"That'll do wonders for my hairdo," Beatrice complained.

"You weren't getting lucky anyway," I said with a smile. "Besides, it isn't like there will be any pictures."

"You don't understand. It looks old, but it's newly done. Someone, possibly Piotr, wants those of us who weren't expecting it to look bad in front of our vampires." Withdrawing a compact from her tiny green handbag, Beatrice inspected her hair as best she could when we rolled to a stop in the entry circle. A huge building, the Irons Club looked from without as if it were once a small civic center but had gotten a growth spurt designed by someone who would have been cutting-edge however long ago they'd built the place. I had no idea where to park, but Tiko seemed to know, so when a uniformed valet came to the door, Tiko waved him away. Before he could open my door, I'd already done it.

When I opened Beatrice's door for her and offered my hand, she quirked a smile at me and let me help her from the limo. "Now everyone thinks we're sleeping together," she whispered in my ear in as she rose.

"Because I helped you out of the car?"

She nodded. "Welcome to the Lion's Den, Master." She composed herself, and I took her arm in mine. "These people read layers of intent and meaning into the smallest detail."

"Fuck 'em." I failed to suppress a sneer.

"Oh, they'd let you make them airtight and brag about it to all of their friends." She plastered on a smile. "Don't be surprised when we walk in the door."

"What's going to happen?" I did a double take. "Airtight?"

"If you don't know, you don't need to know." Her tone, a mixture of pleasant surprise and condescension, let me know I'd passed one of those pop quizzes that ladies throw at vampires from time to time to see if we really are better than the other men.

"Tiko?" I said softly.

"I'll keep an eye on your mage," he said pleasantly. "I've got three brothers on telepathic speed dial if I need them, and the mouser I wasn't supposed to notice is tailing us on that hot-shit motorcycle. Your mage will be fine."

Magbidion closed his eyes, already asleep. The wear on him worried me. I didn't have any other mage I could trust.

"Good." Beatrice and I were ushered through the grandest of three glass double doors into a hall with a grand chandelier and a boatload of undead assholes and their dates. What got my attention was the full orchestra playing incidental music to an empty room down the end of one long hallway. They were in a small theater that appeared to have been built for just such a purpose, the volume controlled (for our sensitive vampiric ears) by a series of sliding glass panels.

Waiters and waitresses in various states and styles of dress carried platters of food and beverages about the checkered tile. Plenty of room for dancing was unoccupied in the middle of the hall under the chandelier, and tables and chairs had been artfully arranged around the edges. Each had a little placard denoting who was to sit where once the more formal portion got under way. Apparently, there was to be a speaker, your basic socialite verbal masturbation and ego stroke. All of which I had expected. What I hadn't known was that when I walked in, everything would stop.

Everyone turned to face me. It was a High Society thing I'd seen before, reorienting one's self to face the most powerful and/or influential person in the room. Up until that very moment, that person had never been me. It had always been Phil or Winter. Beatrice's hand tightened around my biceps.

"Acknowledge them whenever and however you wish, Master," Beatrice said.

The "Master" thing grated like hell, but I'd been warned about that, too, so I let it slide, knowing that she'd back off as soon as she could without appearing to disrespect me. Maybe that's why I opted to "acknowledge" them all with a middle finger and my general disdain. I scanned the crowd in a 180, then flipped off the people behind me at the door just to make sure I got everybody.

They ate it up. My middle finger was met with applause, catcalls, wolf whistles, and bemused laughter like some bad-boy celebrity showing off at the Oscars. Everyone bowed, and I escorted Beatrice toward the Orchestra Hallway. Each glass pane was controlled by a volume knob set into a lacquered panel on the right side of the hallway.

"Is the music too loud, Lord Eric?" called a thin voice. Truth be told, I could barely hear it, my senses being what they are at night. "Or not loud enough?"

I'd expected a Peter Lorre–looking little sycophant and was surprised to find a very manly-looking guy in the kind of shape actors complain about having to work so hard to get into. He had a disarming smile, and I shook his hand without thinking about it. A lot of thralls seem not to know how to give a good handshake, letting their hand rest in mine like a dead fish. Manly Guy matched the firmness of my grip, smiled, and met my gaze.

"Forgive me for speaking out of turn, Lord Eric, but our music system is unique."

"Just Eric," I said. "And don't read anything into that. I don't like titles."

I didn't expect a thing when Beatrice laid him out. I don't think I'd even seen her throw a punch before, but she opened with a forearm to the jaw, or was it an elbow? Before I could decide, he lay sprawled on the tile, blood dappling his dress shirt, trying his best to dodge a high heel to the crotch. Emphasis on the word "trying." "Back off, Piotr!"

"You seem to have that covered," I said, not knowing what else to say. I reached over and slowly turned the volume higher until, one by one, all the panes of glass between us and the orchestra stood open and I could hear the music. When I looked back, it was to see Piotr catching Bea's leg.

I growled, and the room stopped again.

"I don't know what you did, Handshake." I rubbed my fingers together as if they felt oily. "Probably you shouldn't have shaken hands with me or engaged me in conversation without Bea's permission. I don't know, because I don't care about all the froufrou societal bullcrap you people get up to. But whatever it was, I can tell you this much: You knew, and you knew it would piss Beatrice off, and that's why you did it."

I focused my gaze, and a symbol, something like a V within a V, although they intersected, appeared plain as day over Piotr's head. I didn't know who belonged to that symbol, so I asked: "Where's your vampire, Piotr?"

He let go of Beatrice's leg. "Each Irons Club is managed by a thrall of Duke Gornsvalt. I—"

I shushed him. That name rang a bell. If I remembered correctly, he specialized in making blood wine and other beverages that could inebriate vampires. Lord Phillip had him do steaks once. Before I killed Phil, of course.

"Oh," I said softly. "I like him."

Beatrice paled. Piotr let a hint of smug grin creep onto his face and he looked like every bully you've ever met. He thought he'd won, and he had his victory speech all ready.

"I was going to destroy him," I continued. "But not just now." I looked around. "Is he here?"

An older gentleman got up from a table in the corner. "Yes, Eric."

I crossed the room in my own time and shook Duke Gornsvalt's hand. This was where Piotr had learned that handshake and the smile. It was pure good-old-boy network. I bet all the thralls he counted as friends were men, and any female thralls he had were for housework, bedroom work, or both. "Release Piotr from your thralldom," I said.

"For what offense?" Duke Gornsvalt asked.

"Annoying my thrall and daring to touch her." Arms spread, I gestured to the room as a whole. "That's how you do things, isn't it? That's the vampire way? Right? You make me mad, and in order to prove I'm head leech, I have to come down on you with hellfire and brimstone and scorch the earth! And if"—I straightened Gornsvalt's tie for effect, even though it wasn't mussed—"if I don't, then you stop respecting me."

My pocket started vibrating, but I couldn't remember why. My hand went out, and Beatrice took it. Handshake's blood had spattered her bare arm, and I plucked the handkerchief out of Gornsvalt's suit jacket to wipe it away. I spat with real saliva and realized my mistake as I made it. They gasped as one. My pocket stopped vibrating and chirped once.

"Impressed?" I laughed. "A parlor trick. I told my last vampiric girlfriend"—I mimed my apologies—"we'll get back to the chewing-out part, but I'm getting old, and I have to tell these little stories when they occur to me, or I won't remember. I told her once that there was no power she possessed that I couldn't do better."

Even Beatrice hadn't seen this; her surprise aided the illusion. "Tabitha's a Living Doll." I held my hand out level, then waggled it from side to side, one side lower, then back up. My pocket vibrated again, but I still had no clue. "It's cute, but she loses her vampiric powers, whereas I"—I tapped in to my strength and felt it flow, hoisted Duke Gornsvalt into the air with one hand, and slowly tucked the bloodstained handkerchief into his mouth—"don't. That's yours."

With my spare hand I beckoned a waiter carrying a plate of appetizers, selected a small hors d'oeuvre, and bit into it. It was a stuffed mushroom, but the meat inside wasn't meat, it was . . . I spat it out. "What the hell is that? Boca burger? That ain't meat, gentlemen. It never was, nor will it ever be."

I looked up at Gornsvalt as if I had forgotten him, and there was another chirp from my pocket. I needed to hold him up there long enough to make sure everyone saw it as a feat of supernatural strength, just in case anyone was putting two and two together and realizing that someone had poured Liquid Paper over the real problem and that their Emperor vampire, the one they all feared because he could go all über vamp and kill them, couldn't do so. Well, at least not at night. Selling them on the idea that I had even more powers than they thought seemed like the best idea for keeping the wool pulled firmly over their beady little eyes.

"I . . ." Real problem. Plan. Phone. Shit!

I looked back up at Gornsvalt and couldn't remember why he was there. I saw Beatrice and couldn't recall why she was important. I knew she was . . . was . . .

"And to think you started without me," called a musical voice from the entryway. I turned. There stood a vampire whose force of character could cut through even my bad memory. Ebon Winter wore a formal kimono in white, blue, and silver, his bleached white hair pulled back in a long ponytail. "I called to ask you all to wait, but no one"—he looked right at me—"answered the phone. How rude."

Was that a samurai sword? He drew it. Tapping in to my power as I was, I could just make out the blue tinge of enchantment on the blade.

"I think," he said, slicing the air with his katana in a downward arc, "that I shall be quite wroth."

27

GRETA

FIGHT, DEMON, FIGHT!

How is it that you only bleed hot pink?" I asked the bleeding doggie-headed demon. One wing torn, the other coated in her own gore flapping uselessly against a wall-mounted poster of *Night of the Lepus*. Yowling in unison with its injured mate, the pink-blooded one threw another ax at my head.

"Where do you keep getting those?" Evelyn asked as she snagged it out of the air and slammed the double-bladed ax home in the other doggie-headed demon with a loud *kathwack*.

"And can you throw them faster?" I pointed at Pink Blood's mate. "Because my deputy needs a few more."

A geyser of green blood erupted from the newest ax wound, and I wished someone were running around with us videotaping. True, I wouldn't show up (probably Evelyn wouldn't, either, but who knows with *nukekubi*), but I'd never fought demons who bled rainbow colors. Blood in all colors of the rainbow dripped from the multiple ax wounds, streaming down the demon's lightly furred skin and dyeing the carpet in patches of color that did not mix and blend.

It had been a nice apartment before we started wrecking it. Very fifties-retro, which made me suspect the two lovebirds would really dig the Sci-Fi Drive-in Café at Disney World. I mean, seriously, *Night of the Lepus*? I like bad movies as much as the next psychopath, but . . .

"Why won't you leave us alone?" Rainbow Blood screeched.

"I don't know," I said, sinking my claws into Pink Blood's biceps. She hurled me against the wall, and I laughed at the crack of my own bones, the twist and tear of muscle and ligament. "Marx called me and I came."

"Marx?" Rainbow Blood howled again. "Marx, you bitch! Marx!"

He turned for the door, heedless of the five axes sprouting from his back, torso, and shoulders. Evelyn backed away, unwilling to follow through.

"Kill it!" I shouted, and when she didn't react, I added, "Bread and butter!"

Jumping over the broken sectional sofa, I rolled past Pink Blood and grabbed her mate by an ax lodged in his back. It popped loose, and I licked the yellow iridescent blood as it oozed from the wound, only to take an ax in my own back, chunking into my spine. The pain roared bright and hot, then dimmed like it ought to dim. Then . . . nothing.

Special though its color may have been, the demon's blood tasted plain and ordinary. Still, there is pleasure in eating funny-colored ice cream, even if it tastes like vanilla. Life has many simple pleasures. Murder is my favorite.

"Where do you get these?" I pulled the ax from my back and decapitated Rainbow with it. His head rose ceiling-ward on a fountain right out of a Skittles commercial. "And how did he do that?"

Pink Blood screamed unintelligibly instead of answering. It may have been a "no." Hard to say.

"What the hell is going on in here?" Kit Kat picked then to intervene. Dressed in full supernatural-suppression gear, she strode in, aghast. "This is how you resolve a domestic dispute?"

"Well, you brought a SWAT team!" I turned to Kit Kat, and Pink Blood grabbed my arm.

"Why?" the doggie demon screamed. "Our blood is a dye. We make clothes. We were only—" Her ax vanished when I tried to chop her with it.

"A clever defense mechanism." I tried to hurl her across the room, but she was bigger than me, the mass more than I could overcome at such a strained angle.

Evelyn mouthed "Oh my God" and stepped back, her shoe slipping in the blood of many hues. She caught herself on the wall-mounted flatscreen.

Pink Blood pulled and wrenched at my left arm in an emotional attempt to pull it off. She did it wrong, so it only came loose at the elbow.

"That's not how you do it!" A few drops of blood leaked from the wound, but not much. My free hand found my Glock, and I fired all seventeen rounds into Pinkie's face. All the sound went away, replaced by the whine of ringing ears and damaged hearing. It's hard to behead a demon one-handed, but you can do it if you get her in a headlock first. A muzzle helps. It makes for a better grip.

Pinkie's headless corpse bled the color of her namesake in such quantities that I thought it might flood the floor. Gallons and gallons flowed out. Her lifeless claw held my dismembered forearm, so I pried it loose, turning to show Kit Kat as I touched the wounds together, skin, bones, and muscle reknitting in seconds.

"Why? You?" Katherine opened her mouth wide to make her ears pop, but she could hear again normally already, like I could. Too fast for a human but just right for a vampire . . . or a thrall. "I—"

"Spit it out, Kit Kat." I knelt in the rainbow-colored blood, which hadn't mixed with the other colors, tasting each color in turn and trying to imagine that each hue bore a minuscule variation in flavor. "I won't hurt you. I'm the sheriff." It had come off during the fight, but I found my old-timey sheriff's star and pinned it back on my shirt.

"Every few months," Kit Kat began carefully, "we get a call to break up a fight between those two. They almost always send a few good VCPD police officers to the hospital. But Captain Stacey would come in after the fight and calm them down and get them to shell out a large Fang fee and . . . I thought if I called you, I could avoid some banged-up cops."

"And you did." All the colors tasted the same. I dipped one finger into yellow, another into blue, and dribbled them together in my palm, but they still wouldn't mix.

"You killed them." Kit Kat breathed in a ragged sigh, reaching out to me as if I could return her wacko sense of outrage. "They run a huge fabric operation, with dyes that never run or bleed together. They employ four hundred people."

"Not anymore." I lapped up the blood in my palm and frowned. *I wonder if the colors mix inside of me* . . .

"Greta—" Evelyn started, but I silenced her with a look.

"Do you have a knife?" Neither woman responded, so I picked my way through to the kitchen and found a set of Shenzhen ceramic knives. Taking the six-inch blade, I rejoined the others. "I found one."

Cutting barely even hurts properly with a sharp enough blade, like getting a shot when you're a kid. "Ouch then over," as Marilyn used to say when she'd take me to get my boosters, vaccinations, and immunizations. Inside me, the blood dye failed, assuming the familiar red of my favorite and only beverage. I flung some of it on Kit Kat, and she flinched.

"Want to be my thrall, Kit Kat?" I dropped the knife. "You might understand me better. My blood's already on you."

"How would your dad feel about you forcing—"

"Forcing?" I barked. "I asked. I made an offer." Red light poured out of my flaring angry eyes, and I wanted to rip open the world and drink it down. "You threaten to tattle on me and lie on me to MY DADDY?"

Evelyn touched my arm. "You just scared her, Greta. She understands now. She won't tattle."

"You won't?" My fangs were out, and I slurred my words, but she understood.

"No." Kit Kat took a deep breath, looking over the damage. "I misunderstood. I . . . when your father said you'd work with us, I assumed you could help fill part of the role Captain Stacey used to fill before your dad got rid of him."

"That's police work." I tapped her badge. "I'm the sheriff." I tapped my badge. "When the bad guys ride into town and they're shooting up the place or harassing the locals, you call me up and I'll do some real sheriff'n." I kicked my foot through the room-wide puddle of blood. "The police'n is up to you."

She nodded. "Understood."

"Good." I was all chipper again. "Then I have to go across the street and strangle a priest."

Cops were chatting on their way up in the elevators, so Evelyn and I took the stairs. When we got to the bottom, there was no sign of Fang.

"Did any of you see what happened to my car?" I asked the uniforms securing the area.

"It drove off," one of them answered.

I frowned. "I wonder where he went," I said to no one in particular, then, "Oh well, Dad must have needed him." Eyes on the prize, I headed across the street for the Episcopal church to finally test my theory.

28

ERIC

SAMURAI SHOWDOWN

Nice sword," I told Ebon Winter. His grin deepened unpleasantly, no sense of mirth reflected in his eyes—those demonstrated frustration and concern. For half a second, they reminded me of the look I'd seen in the eyes of any number of women I'd dated . . . right after they'd realized I wasn't just saying that stuff about how I can never love them in order to be dramatic, and that I do truly love Marilyn, and all they are is an enjoyable way to pass the time.

"Does complimenting another man's sword sound queer to you?" I asked Beatrice.

"You really are a card." Winter never took his eyes from mine. He made contact, but it wasn't the mind-to-mind contact of two vampires fighting for supremacy, it was something else, and it contained vital information. I didn't understand it all, but it definitely seemed vital. "Though the leftover-remnant-from-the-Greatest-Generation bit is wearing a trifle thin. Gornsvalt there"—he nodded to the vampire I still held aloft in one hand—"fought in the Crusades, and you don't hear him going on and on about it."

"The Crusades," I said, lowering Gornsvalt. "Those were like the Dark Ages version of Vietnam, right?"

"Bravo." Winter tittered. "For a brain-addled simpleton, you are almost charming in a *Flowers for Algernon* way . . . when you aren't being odious, arrogant, and disrespectful."

"I wasn't aware that anyone in this room deserved my respect. After all, we won the two wars I fought in."

What was the other thing I was supposed to be doing? Fang. Right. If in trouble, try to summon Fang. Concentrating on seeing the world of the magical brought a display of energy strands into view. Some of them were connected to me. Others were connected to the thralls in the room, but not the vampires, except for wavering ones running between thrall and master.

A red line ran between me and Beatrice, so hard to see that I could barely make it out and then only because I'd caught it at the right angle. Trying to find the one between me and Fang was like being at one of those damn Harry Potter movies and trying to spot the golden whositz. Fang had grown more powerful after Greta and he destroyed my pseudo sire Lisette's memento mori by essentially feeding the squidlike golden travesty to Fang. Now, when Fang did his equivalent of my über vamp, gold detailing appeared on the car, even on the knockoff hubs.

Fang's connection to me was also gold. I found it and concentrated on it. Moments later, I felt a sensation as if someone had injected pure adrenaline straight into the old heart box. It shot blood through my veins like a nitro boost.

In my mind's eye, I saw Fang burn rubber out of downtown, right up the side of a high-rise near the old Episcopal church, and launch into the air. To be honest, when Talbot told me Fang could drive up walls and glide now, I thought he'd been fibbing. Apparently, not so much.

"You stole credit for Lord Phillip's death," Winter continued. "I planned for years to execute that fat, twisted mass of fecundity, and you ruined it all." He gestured at the assembled vampires and their dates. "All of you did. The so-called Vampiric Elite failed to comprehend the marvel of my plan and viewed you as a murderer rather than the mere implement of destruction. You"—he leveled his sword at me—"took credit for the kill and left me with no choice but the rather brutish display I delivered at the Artiste Unknown."

I ran my thumb across my middle finger and forefinger in imitation of the world's smallest violin playing the world's saddest song, "My Heart Bleeds for You," and ignored Winter.

"You're being awfully quiet." Duke Gornsvalt had been in my hand for a while, so I gave him my attention and dropped him unceremoniously. "Are you going to withdraw your whatchamajigger from Handshake or what?"

Gornsvalt looked at Winter. "If there were some other way—"

I grabbed Gornsvalt by the chin. "He ain't helping you, asshole. He's whining about how I stole his kill and walked off with his unique drop."

A surprising number of vampires got that joke. Frick'n *World of Warcraft* junkies. Duke Gornsvalt wasn't one of them. "He's been with me centuries, Eric. Please."

"I—" Winter's katana burst through my shoulder at an angle cutting down into my heart. Have I mentioned I heal very quickly? At night it's even faster. Not that it felt great. I sagged against the duke. "Tell me something. Did that prince wannabe just stab me?"

"Lord Winter?" the duke asked.

"Yep." My wounds closed around the blade. "That's the one."

A heart can't beat with a blade in it. If my heart's not beating . . . I'm . . . dead? But a funky little side effect of my condition is: I can't be dead, only ever-living or undead. I wondered which way my condition was going to deal with this one. I suspected Ebon Winter already knew and had bet on it.

A coil of wrongness twined through me, the enchantment on the blade pulling me down to the edge of unconsciousness. Fang's engine roared. I felt myself growing cold. Undead. I guessed Winter had arranged this as a little demonstration. Nice. Painful but nice. If all went well, I'd be able to manage the über vamp.

Fangs tore through the roof of my mouth, uppers and lowers sliding jaggedly into place, but not before they rent the inside of my mouth. My eyes flashed red, then purple. My ghosts came along, too, even though I was the only one who could see them.

"The Master/Thrall Social?" Phillip said with a tut-tut in his glare. "You're shouldn't have." He gestured at his dressing gown. "I'm not even dressed for it."

Roger opened his mouth to say something, but blue light washed him away. I screamed in unison with the phantasms of Lisette and Suzie Hu as the light took them as well.

When it came for Phillip, he responded with a complex gesture that my eyes couldn't follow. The blue light shattered off him in millions of tiny shards, and when it cleared, he wore a WELCOME TO THE VOID T-shirt and blue jeans under his dressing gown.

"How?" I asked.

"You took a thought from me"—his grin grew to Grinchy proportions—"a quote I knew and you wanted to know. That's when I realized we weren't ghosts. When Talbot couldn't see us but we could touch. I don't understand. What have you become, my boy?"

"That," I growled at him mentally, "would be telling!"

"If you can take things from my mind, boy, then I assure you I can read what you're hiding inside yours." He grabbed my head in his hands, and I felt like an open book.

"What is Operation Let's All Get Drunk and Screw?" he snapped.

"As Edmund Burke put it," I said, stealing another quote as Fang crashed through the glass doors, his tires squealing on the marble, "'Reading without reflecting is like eating without digestion.'"

I love my car. Fang always seems to know when to show up and what to do. But I guess there always has to be an exception to the rule. As Fang raced across the marble, I expected him to spin out around me and crash into something important, then eat a vampire or two. He didn't.

Note to self: Sometimes magic vampire convertibles don't roll with changes in the plan. I don't know exactly why Fang did what he did. Maybe he was trying to help hide my secret. But as I opened my mouth to shout, "No. No, stupid car," Fang ran me over, tore the flesh from my bones, and deposited them in his trunk. I heard Phillip say, "Of course." I hate it when evil asswipes figure things out.

Pain wiped out any reply I might have had. Re-forming is something I've done loads of times, but never as an immortal, from just bones, and never after having been eaten by Fang. Blue light washed over my body, coming in from the lines I'd seen all around, and powered my regeneration, converting the energy to matter like a damn *Star Trek* episode.

Through the trunk, Fang's radio blared "This Town Ain't Big Enough for Both of Us" by the Sparks. Cloth moved across my skin. Was Fang dressing me? Could he do that? As if in answer to my question, the trunk sprang open, and an unseen force tossed me out of the back like toast from a toaster, clad in my usual WELCOME TO THE VOID T-shirt and ensemble. The katana stayed in the trunk. I was afraid to mess with it, anyway.

Winter glared at me. "What," I asked, "you gonna stand out here and not kill me some more?"

"Be as glib as you wish, Eric." He waved away my comment, then snatched at the air as to grasp more words out of it. "Yet, I'll remind you of this. I may not have killed Lord Phillip with my own hands, but I arranged his death. Whether you give me credit or not, I marched you down the path and handed you the motive after ensuring that, having already defeated Lisette's memento mori, Fang would have the power to assist you. It took time, but as a vampire, I have plenty of that particular commodity."

"And so you're going to kill me?"

"Oh yes."

"But you're not going to kill my daughter or blow up my business or set fire to my movie palace or kill Marilyn or frame me for murder or wipe my brain with magic, right?" I folded my arms across my chest and watched him bristle. "Because all that's been done already."

Winter remained silent.

"No." My voice told those gathered that I couldn't believe such a thing. "You weren't planning on staging a repeat and calling it an encore?"

"Of course not."

I indicated him with both arms like Vanna White showcasing a brand-new car or a trip for eight to Disneyland. "Not Ebon G. D. Winter, artiste of bullshit and treachery and seven shades of I-told-you-so. Not him."

"I said I wasn't," Winter maintained.

"Good." I turned back to the duke. "Then fuck off, would ya? The big kids are having a dick contest, and we know you don't like to use yours for anything . . ."

Winter stalked from the room and misted through the shattered glass from Fang's arrival off into the night. As he left, I couldn't help but notice that none of the attending vampires shifted to follow his exit. Their attention and their directional disposition were squarely on me. *You win again,* I thought after him, *and they have no idea.*

"Beatrice," I called over the murmur of vampiric congratulations from the suddenly vociferous crowd.

"Yes, Master." She appeared at my side in a flash from wherever she'd run when Fang barged in.

"What was I talking about?"

"You were explaining to Duke Gornsvalt and those assembled that you hate Vampire Politics and hope that we can move toward a new level of civility."

"I was?" I raised an eyebrow.

"I could be wrong, Master. I am merely human, but I thought that's what you were doing." She batted her lashes at me.

"Wait." I pulled her close, as if greedily hoarding her warmth, and continued in a stage whisper. "Is this the thing where I was going to wait until someone pissed me off, act like I was playing hardball, and then be magnanimous to prove a point?"

"That is what you talked about in the car."

I leaned in and kissed her on the cheek. "Well," I said, looking right at Duke Gornsvalt, "if I was already talking about it in the car . . ."

29

GRETA

LOSING MY RELIGION
(OR THIS PARTICULAR PRIEST, ANYWAY)

Stained-glass images of scenes from the New Testament framed both sides of the church as Evelyn and I walked in. On my right, Jesus fed the five thousand. On my left, He walked on water. Farther down, He turned water to wine, healed the lame, and made Lazarus rise from the dead. I didn't know what all of them represented, but the ones with Jesus I knew from Sunday school, from a time before foster care and vampire dads.

The pipe organ played, and it was a bigger, better one than Father Ike's church had before Dad burned it down. I wasn't going to burn this one down, not unless I had to do it. No, my business was almost certainly restricted to the priest.

Wisps of smoke curled up from my shoes and off my shoulders as the strength of the beliefs of those present and engaging in active worship tried to force me out and destroy me . . . but not Evelyn. Religion is fickle.

"What are we doing here?" Evelyn whispered a step behind and to the right of me.

"I told you," I whispered back. "I have to strangle a priest and see if I understand why Dad did what he did. Give me your scarf."

"I'm not letting you strangle a priest with my scarf." Her voice got louder, and the ushers at the back moved toward us.

"That's not what I want it for, you goof," I replied, exasperation clear in my tone. "Just give it to me."

Reluctantly, Evelyn unwound the scarf, and I draped it around my own neck. The scant flock seemed to take no notice of us as we walked down the center aisle. The building was laid out like a cross, a long central section with pews on either side, then more pews to the right and left of the altar. Behind the altar, a huge stained-glass image of a resurrected Jesus ruling over the cosmos (or I think that's what He was doing) loomed over the priest and the altar. Atop the altar, a golden cross caught the overhead light shining brightly.

At the podium in front of the altar, a priest in a cassock and purple scarfy thing went through some sort of call-and-response deal with the parishioners. He'd say a long passage, and they would all respond in unison, standing, kneeling, standing, kneeling. It reminded me of an aerobics class, except I think most of it was in Latin.

"Thank you for joining us," the first usher said. He was a tall, pale-skinned food with blond hair. He blanched when he saw my fangs but kept on with his spiel. "There are plenty of seats in the empty pews . . ." He let the words trail off as he noticed the smoke rising off of me.

"Cool," I said, snapping his neck, "I see a spot."

He fell down like they all do, a marionette with cut strings.

"Was that really necessary?" Evelyn hissed. "We can't just murder people."

"Maybe you can't." I caught the other usher, a bald food with dark skin, and hurled him over my shoulder to where the organist sat amid his controls and pipes. "But I can do whatever I want."

"What in God's name?" the priest asked.

"I want to try something with you, Father." I had to shout to be heard over the commotion near the front. Then Evelyn came at me with a stake, one of those customized jobs that had a combat-knife handle. I spun to the right, grabbing the stake, and she nailed me in the side with a second one I hadn't spotted. It missed the mark, though, puncturing my lung and not my heart.

"I won't let you do this," Evelyn said, struggling to drive the stake farther home, to nick my heart. Her fangs sank into my neck, and I twirled free, letting go of her arm but shoving her through the nearest pew in an explosion of wood.

"Don't you be a bad deputy, Evelyn," I chastised her. "I like you, and I don't want to have to kill you."

"I told you, Greta." Evelyn pulled herself up, holding the stake point up, warding me off. "You can't just keep killing people in front of me. I'm not one of you. I can't sit back and—"

"Everyone please, remain calm," the priest was saying, "come this way and get clear of the rogue elephant. If anyone has a cell phone, please dial 911."

"Rogue elephant." I laughed. "I don't think the old Veil ever made anyone think I was a pachyderm. This is awesome!"

"Why are you doing this, Greta?" Evelyn floated over the broken pew, interposing herself between me and the priest, directly in the middle of the center aisle. "You didn't even eat those two men."

"I need to understand." If Evelyn kept this up, she was going to really annoy me.

"Understand what?" Evelyn looked back over her shoulder. "What it's like to kill a priest?"

"No, stupid." I heard two heartbeats behind me in the organ loft. "Besides, I only killed the one whose neck I broke. The other food still has a heartbeat."

"They're not food, Greta." Evelyn drifted back to the ground. "They're people. Humans. Like you and I were before we were turned into vampires by your father."

"Daddy didn't make you." I dropped low, into a crouch, like a linebacker getting ready to sack the other team's quarterback. "Daddy made me. You just happened. I was on purpose." I broke left and charged through the stained-glass depiction of Jesus walking on water, landing in the holly bushes that flanked the building. Slowing as little as possible, I cut back around the entrance and burst back in through the image of Lazarus rising from the dead on the right.

"Damn it, Greta! No!" Evelyn caught me less than a hand's breadth from the priest, my claws closing the gap enough that a single drop of blood rolled off his nose where she made me nick him.

Hands full of me meant she didn't have the stakes anymore. When had she dropped them? Oh. Just before grabbing me. I reached for the floor, snatched up a stake, and stabbed her through the eye. Her scream let me know she felt that more than I would have. I grabbed for my Glock, forgetting that I'd already emptied it into a demon until the lightness of the empty clip reminded me.

I didn't spot the other stake before it was piercing my chest—barely enough time for me to catch Evie's hand and keep her from actually staking me. "If you want to play, we can wrestle later! This is serious!"

"So am I!" she spat. We rolled on the ground, scrabbling for control of the stakes. When Kit Kat and several members of the VCPD hit the door, it brought a smile to my face.

"Thank God," Evelyn said as she struggled to hold me in place.

Kit Kat drew a crossbow and fired.

It *thunk*ed home.

I don't know why Evelyn thought Kit Kat would choose to shoot me. Maybe she thought it would be like the song and that Kit Kat would sing a verse about whom she shot and whom she didn't, but I didn't see how lyrical correctness would get Kit Kat to shoot this sheriff.

"Nice job, Kit Kat," I said, pushing Evelyn off of me. "Now take

these nice people outside to safety and leave me alone with the priest."
My shoulder caught fire, but I patted it out. I was running out of time.

"I—" Kit Kat opened her mouth.

"Don't make me quote the Incredible Hulk at you." I drew myself
up to my full height. "You wouldn't like me when I quote the Incredible Hulk at you."

She nodded before giving orders to the other officers. "Get all the
parishioners out of here, but keep the good reverend inside. Our sheriff would like a word with him."

A confused padre sat in the front pew while his flock was escorted
out, some sure they'd seen a Bengal tiger, others an elephant or a
group of gangbangers. I sat on the carpet patiently, with my staked
deputy. It was funny to listen to them babbling about what they'd
seen, all having seen something different.

"What about this one?" Kit Kat nudged Evelyn with her boot.

"I want her to see this," I said softly, "but you wait outside."

Kit Kat left without another word.

"Now, I don't know why you're so upset about all this." I detached
Evie's head and walked toward the good reverend with my best friend's
head under my arm. I wondered why the staking had disabled her
whole self, head and body and not just neck and below, like it had
when Dad staked her. Was that the effect the church had on her? She
couldn't detach naturally? "I don't understand why you have this perverse need to keep me from testing my theory, but I want you to see
this, to help me interpret it."

I sat her head on the pew next to the priest, and smoke began to
rise from her neck. I looked back to see that the body was doing the
same thing. Yep, it had to be all the holiness and stuff messing with her.

"Boo," I said, snatching up the head and thrusting it at the priest,
but he didn't react. I set it back down, and he jumped when I let go of
it, as if seeing me for the first time.

"What are you?"

"Don't be afraid, Father . . . ?"

"Paul," he said.

"Don't be afraid, Father Paul," I said. "It's true, I'm a vampire, but I
don't want to eat you. I need you to help me understand something.
Can you do that?" My left shoulder chose that moment to ignite, but
patting it out worked again. A red rash was slowly working its way
across my skin, a first-degree burn in progress.

"A vampire?" His eyes were unfocused. I'd lost him. All of this was
beyond him, not the kind of up-close-and-personal encounter with the
supernatural to which he'd been looking forward all of his life.

"Maybe it's better if I show you?" I asked.

He may have nodded slightly, I don't know, but I decided to interpret it that way. I wrapped my hands around his neck, and as slowly and gently as I could, I choked the life out of him. Eyes bulging, face turning purple, he asphyxiated. I eased him to the ground, not letting up even when his priest's alb began to make my skin smolder faster than the belief surrounding the place.

Flutter as it might, his heart could not keep beating without oxygen in his lungs circulating through his bloodstream and on to the brain and back. I listened carefully for the last beat of his heart as he pounded on me with his fists until they fell limply to either side.

I stepped back and watched him for a count of three before wrapping my borrowed scarf around his neck and beginning CPR, just like my dad had done with Father Ike.

"C'mon, you bastard, c'mon," I said, repeating Daddy's words. "I killed you fair and square, but nobody specified how long you had to stay that way." One moment Father Paul was dead, and then he was alive again and coughing on the floor of his church.

"Did that make any sense to you?" I asked the priest. He rolled away from me in fear, and I gathered up Evelyn's head, reattached it to her body, pulled the stake from her eye, then jerked out the crossbow bolt. She stopped smoldering, but I did not, which is a total rip-off, if you ask me.

"I don't think he gets it any more than I did," I told her.

"You wanted to strangle him just so you could resuscitate him?"

Like that wasn't totally frick'n obvious. I scoffed. "Duh!"

We walked past Kit Kat on the way out. "Thanks, Kit Kat. That's all I needed from him."

Evelyn and I stood out in the night air, both of us as befuddled as could be. My skin was bright pink, like a bad sunburn. In places, I had black spots where I'd burst into flames.

"Are you still my deputy?" I asked. "Or do I have to end you?"

"You don't know how," she said. "Keeping my head separated from my body during the day is extremely uncomfortable, and it causes serious damage that takes a long time to heal, but it doesn't end me."

"Trust me," I said, patting her on the back. "With as much time as we've spent together, I know exactly what it takes to end you, but I'd rather not."

"Thanks," she said.

"Now if we could only get you over this weirdo 'it's bad to kill' thing you have going on . . . ."

30

GRETA
INSPECTOR GRETA

A re you sure we're going to learn anything this way?" Evelyn asked. "What if he isn't really hiding anything?"

"He's meeting with Rachel again," I hissed. "Is that the one who used to be human and was Tabitha's sister?"

"Yes." I pointed at my laptop screen and maximized the feed from the bedroom cam over at the Pollux. Dad appeared on it, though the image of him shook and stuttered. I still hadn't been able to figure out what made the sound so wonky. I had it cranked up to the maximum, and Dad barely came through.

"Another task?" It had been a month since the last one, and that one had come a month after the fiasco at the Irons Club. At least I knew where Fang had run off to. "Have some pictures that need hanging down at the old Demonic Humpatorium?"

"Why is the sound so bad?" Evelyn asked. "Vampires use the phone with no trouble."

"When you figure it out," I snapped, "let me know."

Evelyn wandered around my apartment. It was a five-bedroom on Eighth Avenue, but I hadn't put much effort into it. Mostly, it was a place to keep stuff that wouldn't fit in my tiny room at the Pollux. I'd had to hock a lot back when Roger had blown up Dad, Marilyn, and the Demon Heart. I'd been desperate for liquidity just to keep Dad's business properties from being bought up and auctioned off. In my new role as sheriff, though, I'd wanted a place to serve as my office, so I'd started stockpiling things in the apartment: stakes, guns, ammo, and computers, though the computers were mainly for my other business. Two of the bedrooms had been turned into server rooms. There was a mattress in one of the others, but no bed frame or box springs.

I tracked my deputy's movements by sound. Ending her had shown up on my mental to-do list immediately after she attacked me at the church, but I'd put it off because I didn't want to do it. She couldn't be Mom, but I'd never had a vampire friend who was a girl, and I enjoyed it. If I was to learn anything from Dad's example, I supposed that what I ought to do was find a same-sex shapeshifter friend. Maybe a were-raven or a weresnake? Could a *nukekubi* count?

I reached down into the bucket of gerbils I had sitting in my extra chair, grabbed one, and drained it, holding the corpse against my cheek to feel the fur and fading warmth. Evelyn didn't seem to like being in the room when I killed one. She was awfully squeamish for a vampire. Then again, maybe that was a side effect of being able to point at blood and have it fly into her mouth. It gave her distance from the act. Even so, she could have sat down and watched with me . . . I would have moved the bucket. I mean, sheesh, I went out and bought a second chair because Evelyn had mentioned it might be nice to have a place to sit down.

"Couldn't you have gotten space at the Lovett Building or police headquarters?" she asked. Another cool thing about being friends with a vampire was that even when we were in different parts of the apartment or out and about, we didn't have to shout. We could talk in normal tones (whispers, even) and carry on a conversation.

"Maybe," I answered, fiddling with the audio filters, "but I don't know how much they know, and I don't want to put him at risk."

"What's in here?"

"The file room?" I thought that's where she was, but I'd been distracted by something Auntie Rachel had said about oral sex, and wasn't Dad curious about something called a Blood Dragon? I looked it up on my tablet and found a reference to something called a White Dragon and sighed at the mental image: Why would any man be stupid enough to hit a woman in the back of the head while she was in a bite-it-off stance . . . and why did she think Dad would want to see blood shoot out her nose? Wasn't that a waste of blood?

"The one with all the boxes?" Evelyn asked.

"Yup, it's from Marilyn's old apartment. I cleaned it out and stored the stuff until I could afford a place to put it. I kept meaning to have Dad go through it to see what he wanted, but . . ."

The screen stole my attention and my words. Auntie Rachel gave Dad the hard sell, sliding his hand beneath her dress to demonstrate her inability to find clean underwear when she got up in the morning. He didn't pull away, but he didn't respond, either. Her eyes half closed, and as she moved his hand, she whispered suggestions about where he might put his Daddy parts and how and with what frequency. Her tail slid down his pants, and my fangs burst through my gums.

"That's new," I said in reference to the tail.

"So," Evelyn said, making me jump, "what do we call this, then? A tail job or a skank wank?"

"A Bill Clinton," I said, "'cause it's not technically sex, but it sooo totally counts."

"What's she doing with her hands?" Evelyn asked. "Oh. Never mind."

I felt a flush throughout my body, the desire to feed rising like a wave. I wanted to grab a man, any man, and ride him like Rachel wanted to ride Dad, and then tear out the stranger's throat as he sullied me, then start over, going through his friends and neighbors one by one. I remembered sex with Telly, the parking attendant who used to watch me hunt vampires, the smell of him, the touch of him. I missed his skull, wanted to cradle it to my chest and think of blood.

The skin at my nipples tightened, and for just a moment, I considered how much easier life would be if I were Mom. My chest heaved, my lungs springing into action as being that in touch with my body's carnal desires stirred them to life.

I sniffed the air and caught the odors of sulfur, lime, and maleness. Had the chupacabra boy in the hoodie who was dedicated to me found my house? Followed me here? If so, I wanted him. I wanted anyone. I . . .

Evelyn.

I kissed her, my tongue exploring her fangs. She returned the kiss hesitantly, the scrapbook she'd held dropping to the floor, but she absolutely wasn't into me. There was no arousal. I would have smelled it. She simply didn't know what would happen if she pushed me away. Her fear tinted my vision red, increasing the lust for blood. I didn't want her . . . or any woman.

Experiment over.

"Sorry," I said before I could remember not to apologize. Daddy doesn't. I shouldn't, but the rules are so hard to remember, and sometimes they change, or maybe I never understood them correctly in the first place. The boy in the hall? His heartbeat sang to me, low and thready, not quite human, because he wasn't. To screw him would be to kill him, but I didn't want to kill him . . . he put my words on a hoodie, wore them like an echo of me, a mark, and I wanted him to be, to exist, not to die.

Frustrated, I turned back to Evelyn. She stood, hands raised at shoulder level, as lost as I was about what to do.

"Um . . . hell-o," she said as I kissed her again, letting my hands find her breasts, cold beneath my touch. I grabbed her groin and she took my wrist, gently pushing me away. "What the fuck, Greta?"

"No," I growled. "You're not. I . . . don't . . . Rrr." I backed away. "Sorry. Sorry. I—" I hate apologies, but I like Evelyn, and she deserved them.

My front door exploded as I went through it. My own mewling hit my ears along with the sound of Dad extricating himself from Rachel's grasp. He had self-control. Dad did, but not me. I was lost somewhere in the confusion of trying to understand his newest set of unspoken rules. Why was his heart beating but his skin cold? Why did he breathe even more than usual? Why was there blood, his blood, in all those apartments for retired cops? What was he doing during the day? How did Kit Kat seem like a thrall without being one? Why did he kill and resuscitate Father Ike, then hide what he had done rather than rubbing those demons' noses in it?

I wanted to ask him, but I wasn't sure whether I was supposed to figure it out myself. I really didn't want to seem stupid for not knowing. Stupid people annoy Dad. He doesn't respect them. He sends them away. And even though he's promised never to send me away again, knowing that he wants to but can't because he promised not to would be even worse.

I kicked in the door of what would have been my next-door neighbors' apartment if I hadn't slowly killed them all and taken over their spaces. Mrs. Rosetti's lonely apartment still looked clean and tidy, like I'd had the Mages Guild leave it. Throw rugs covered the floor, and my feet tangled in them as I moved too fast, crashing down in front of her old boxy cathode-ray-tube television set.

Shelf after shelf of her Russian stacking dolls stared down at where I lay on the floor, and I leaped to my feet, seizing the television with which to smash them to bits.

"I DON'T UNDERSTAND!" The TV exploded with more smoke and sizzle than flash and bang, and it wasn't enough.

"Tell me what's happening, Greta." Evelyn arrived in the doorway with vampire speed but came no farther.

"Why can't you be Mom?" I asked, blood tears streaming down my cheeks. "If you're Mom, then liking you, being friends with you, makes sense, and then Dad will have someone to fuck and the world will be right." The pain in my hands didn't even register, so I clawed them, each with the other, to make sure they still could. Why was I sobbing?

"If you were Mom, I could ask you to explain Dad, and you would have to do it." I clapped my hands together, rubbing the blood into my skin as the greedy flesh sucked it back in. "He's good in bed. He always makes them come." I nodded at her as if willing her to agree. "Even when he's preoccupied with Marilyn, he's not a selfish lover. And if he's not big enough in human form, the über vamp has a really really big—"

Sulfur. The odor had grown, was closer. It was not alone. It was listening at the wall and at the floor. There was more than one heartbeat now, but only one that I recognized. He was overhead, in the Martinezes' former residence.

I leaped through the Sheetrock between the joists, claws first like a diver, tearing my way through carpet, falling down on the first attempt but making it all the way through on the second. Hoodie boy was halfway out the door when I grabbed him and forced him onto the carpet of the now-sagging floor.

"Why are you following me?" I rolled him over so I could see his face and pinned his arms down on either side of his head. "What do you want?"

When he spoke, his accent reminded me of Telly's. English was a second language for him. The first sounded like it might have been Spanish. "I want to be yours," he said, eyes alive with passion. "To be near you. My kind, the older ones, they are afraid of the loud . . . of the noise, but I saw you conquer the Prime Contagion with your fury, and I want that. You bring the noise, and I want to bring it, too."

Three other chupacabras: an Asian boy, a Latina, and a heavyset African-American—all young, like him, but all old enough to eat by Daddy's rules—peeked in through the front door from the hall. There were more out there with them. They all wore my words on their clothes: SHE'S THE BOSS, APPLESAUCE.

"I want to have you and then kill you." My fangs were at his throat.

"Do what you want," he whispered. "I don't want to die in silence."

"Make us scream," said the girl. She could have been his sister; her skin was marred by the same eczema-like blotchy patches.

"All we know is quiet," said the heavyset boy. "Life in the plague is about silence. Keeping ours, enforcing it on others."

"You're the opposite," said the girl. "When you rage, you howl and growl and flaunt it. When you hurt, you scream."

"Teach us how," said the boy beneath me, his rigid manhood pressing against me through his jeans, "and we will go where you want during the day, when you can't, and be quiet there and listen and see. If you choose it, we will die for you. Just give us voice."

I sank my teeth into his jugular, and his blood had taste, sour, tart, and bitter, like lime. I kissed him then, his own blood slicking his lips, and if I hadn't taken so much, I would have mounted him and had to kill him after, but he was flaccid, not from lack of will but from lack of blood. That impotence saved him. He was the one. The right person to be my first thrall.

Clawing the shirt from his back, I rolled him over and spat dark red onto golden-brown skin, willing the blood into a tattoo, a badge of words on the back of his neck:

TEAM
GRETA

"I mark thee and bind thee." I said the words of thralldom without officially asking, but his smile let me know there was nothing he wanted more in the entire world than to belong to me. "Master to servant. Servant to master. You are mine until I set you free. You are mine. So mote it be."

Dad had said the experience was pleasurable when he made Rachel his thrall, but with the nameless chupacabra boy, it was more than that. Sparks lit up in my brain, and my legs buckled as I bucked against him, grinding his face into the carpet. All of the pain and confusion washed away on the wave of orgasm and my pants were wet with the scent of blood.

"I'm the boss, Applesauce," I said as I bit through his earlobe and opened wounds in his back with my claws. I watched as the skin flowed back together, then I parted it again, and he bit back a scream. "No!" I shouted, swatting the back of his head hard enough to concuss him. "Scream for me. I command it!" I drove my foreclaws knuckle-deep into his shoulders, and the howl that ripped free of his lungs was a primal thing beyond pain, a letting go of whispers, a surrender to noise. The wounds knit back together quickly, and his eczema was completely gone.

"Me next?" the female chupacabra asked.

"I decide who gets to be my next thrall." My eyes flashed crimson, and she responded to the anger with a smile. My breath no longer came in ragged jags. My lungs were still, my chest quiet. I was centered. Powerful. At peace. My body, once more only an interface.

"I don't understand everything that just happened," Evelyn said from the apartment below, "but can I say that if this is going to happen every time you get horny and frustrated, I'm buying you the biggest damn selection of vibrators and sex toys known to man."

"Why?" I asked, but Evie never answered.

"What's your name?" I asked the chupacabra boy.

"I wouldn't know," he answered. "You haven't named me yet."

Very good. What sort of fruit would fit him? But no, not a fruit.

He was nothing like those rejects Apples and Oranges. A noise. A
noise that was a triumph over silence . . . What was the name of that
Spanish metal band I'd heard Telly listening to from time to time? I
remembered.

31

GRETA

THE METAL'S GONNA GET YOU

Warcry walked up to the rear of the McDonald's, cutting right through the breakfast drive-through traffic. A padlocked metal grid blocked off the ladder providing rooftop access, but he didn't slow. His body, lean and well maintained, coiled and leaped, easily bringing the lowest exposed rung within reach, the rest accomplished by easy traction from the charcoal FiveFinger TrekSports he wore.

The smells of cooking meat and brewing coffee reached him even on the roof, and I smelled them through him in a dreamlike haze, lying in Fang's trunk, fast asleep and wearing Percy's glasses.

This is how you do it? I asked Percy, envisioning my words as blocks of red text.

I cannot see exactly what you're experiencing, Greta, but I imagine it's similar. How many senses do you get? His answer appeared in the air above Warcry, strokes of a golden pen writing in the air.

Three that I've noticed. I thought back. *Smell, sight, and hearing . . . but no touch or taste.*

Those two are the rarest of all, Percy wrote. *A lost opportunity, perhaps, but the three you have are typical of Vlads.*

Just as well, I thought to myself. *Warcry touches his face so much, it would have given me the creeps to have to feel it all the time.*

Can they hear you? Percy wrote.

No. The admission stirred resentment chased by self-loathing and inadequacy in my belly. Warcry paused, questioning wordlessly. *They seem to pick up on my emotions, but apparently, that's the best I can do when I'm asleep.*

Deciding to keep going with the plan, Warcry settled in next to the edge of the rooftop, mostly out of sight, and pulled out his smart-phone, flipping through the photos I'd scanned in from the scrapbooks Evelyn had found.

My three thralls perched on breakfast stops nearest the Void City police station downtown: McDonald's, Krispy Kreme, and Arby's. I could have used a fourth thrall to cover the Waffle House, but I didn't want to enthrall the fat one until he lost weight. The others in the hallway weren't in the running. They hadn't been brave enough to come walking in the door of the Martinezes' apartment, and I couldn't see myself joined to fraidycats.

Moving from one thrall's perceptions to another felt less like changing channels than rolling out of bed early in the morning and hitting the snooze button. It took time, and for random intervals, I dropped contact completely, sleeping the sleep of the dead until an-other dream cycle got me close enough to consciousness to reconnect.

While Warcry couldn't stop touching the now-smooth skin on his face, Nightwish obsessed over her legs, running her hands over her shins and thighs, then hugging her arms. I hoped she just looked cold to anyone who saw her. No one would be watching her up on the roof of the . . . But she wasn't on the roof.

Nightwish sat bold as brass in the dining area of the Arby's, eating a croissant and sipping at a cola. Two cops walked in through side doors, and she took a long hard look at them as if it were more natural than breathing to notice them and watch them. I couldn't compare them to the pictures from the scrapbook, but she could. Images flipped past on the smartphone's touch display like slides on an auto-advancing carousel, with the plus button stuck.

I watched for hours, sleeping on and off, until, through Chthonic's eyes, I saw Evelyn sit down at the table where Chthonic had made himself comfortable.

"What are you looking for, Greta?" she asked, directing the question half to herself, half to my thrall.

I couldn't answer, but Chthonic did. He passed her his phone.

"What?" She studied them. "These are the pictures from the photo albums I found? They're all cops."

He nodded. "Some. The ones she wants us to examine."

"Why?"

"I don't know."

"Why?" She looked at me, through his eyes, and her mind touched my mind . . . barely. Archives of horror, those things at which other Vlads quake, waited to be shared with her, but not through Chthonic's mind. He might break. I wasn't ready to give up my new toys and throw away the pieces yet. I settled for sending words rather than pictures. Safer.

Speaking, even telepathically, felt like shouting into a bucket of syrup . . . which . . . I've done, actually. My verdict? Sticky and hard to get out of your hair. I finally gave up and used acid.

When Dad was human, after Korea, Marilyn convinced him to try being a cop. They didn't know how the world worked. They didn't know that all the good cops were puppets.

I follow you so far, Evelyn thought back at me.

I . . . Dad's nostalgic. I struggled to remain close to consciousness. *And . . . I was remembering how, when he made his current thralls, some of them got younger, more attractive, even. He . . . deaged them.*

And you—Evelyn chewed her lip—*thought he might have enthralled . . . What? Some of the cops from the old folks' home?*

Yes. Why else would I have smelled his blood in every room?

Blood tattoos? Then why look here?

Breakfast places, I thought. *It's not just doughnuts that cops like.*

Evelyn yawned widely, giving me an excellent shot of her uvula. "Your brain is so slow during the day, it's making me sleepy."

Evie rubbed her eyes and took a sip of Chthonic's Coke.

Caffeine worked on her? That bitch!

"You're pissing her off," Chthonic whispered. "Best get to the point, neh?"

"Oh." She handed the Coke back to Chthonic. "Sorry. Marilyn."

"She feels confused," Chthonic said before I had to try to put it into words.

"Greta, Eric didn't tell you to watch Marilyn," Evelyn said. "You had me tail her the other day, to see where she went and make sure she was okay, but Eric didn't say anything about watching her. If he made a deal with the devil to get her back, do you really think he's going to turn her over to some unknown quantity without keeping a weather eye on the horizon?"

Gears turned and clicked into place. I smiled in my sleep.

"She likes that idea." Chthonic grabbed up his phone and started texting. "Where did this Marilyn get sent?"

"The Iversonian."

"Cool."

An hour later, Team Greta had the Iversonian and his club of the same name under surveillance. By the time the sun set and I woke up for the evening, they'd spotted nine different cops who looked like they might be men from the photo album. Whether doing a drive-by in a VCPD squad car, on foot, or in one case, on mounted patrol, one of the nine passed by the club every ten minutes.

"He's definitely keeping an eye on her," I said, standing next to Nightwish. She rubbed at her elbows, where I'd just fed off her ulnar artery, ignoring the healing wounds at her throat and femoral artery. Thralls heal fast, but she looked weak and pale, which made me want to feed again.

Evelyn saw the look in my eye and touched my shoulder. "Don't you think she's had enough?" She added an emphatic nod as if that would lend weight to her statement. "Give her a rest. You have other thralls."

"I like you, Evie." It was my turn to put a hand on her shoulder. "Do you like me?"

"This isn't a prelude to another weird kiss thing, is it?"

"No."

"Then sure." Her eyes unfocused slightly. "I can't explain it, but I think you're a nice person trapped inside this whole vampire mind trip. I think maybe I understand why . . . a little. Something horrible must have—"

"Don't talk about it unless you want to see it." I looked into her eyes. "Because I can show you, but I don't like it when people talk like they understand me when they don't know shit."

"Right."

"Can I kill you, Nightwish?" I asked the question of my thrall, but my eyes never left Evie. "If I want?"

"Yesss." Nightwish's answer, small and reminiscent of a chupacabra's hiss, hurt Evie more than I could on my own without getting inventive.

"What the hell?" Evie tried to turn to Nightwish, but I held her in place by the shoulder. "Why?"

"Because she's an unwanted thing," I said. "They all are, the chupacabras who want me to lead them. Their parents and fellow uggos probably say they want them around, want them to be happy, but then . . . why make them stay chupacabra? 'Cause that sucks, and Popsie could cure any of them . . . let them go, let them heal, but he doesn't want to. He just wants them to do as they're told and not ask any questions and pretend to be happy."

Nightwish was nodding.

"They say they want noise, but what they want is difference. Change. To feel. And good or bad, I can make them feel something.

It's what I do. Dad was lost when he rescued me, but I rescued him, too. Just a little."

Nightwish held her wrist out, and I sank my fangs into the radial artery and let her drop when she fainted. Warcry and Chthonic ran over, each taking a shoulder, and pulled her up.

"Sheriff," Evie said. "Can we not let ourselves get distracted?"

The "Sheriff" got my attention. I like respect.

"I don't want to step out of line, but is showing me how badass you can be really how we want to spend our time?" She nodded at the Iversonian. The club was just now opening. Cars were queuing up, and a redcap in a dirty leather jacket was parking cars. "I've seen all your forms. I know how scary you are, Sheriff. What I don't know is what Eric Courtney is up to, and I thought that was the important thing."

"You're right, Deputy." A squad car with two of the men from the scrapbook pulled around the corner, driving slowly in front of the Iversonian. As it neared us, I let my claws slide out, my eyes go red, and all my vampiric speed come out to play. Daddy said I couldn't kill the VCPD, but he never said I couldn't carjack and waterboard them.

Public Safety Tip #5: I have no accord with Geneva, I've never met anyone named Miranda, and "due process" is a misspelled discussion topic for why grass is wet in the morning.

32

MARILYN

MAYBE THERE'S SOMETHING TO ALL THIS STUFF AFTER ALL

Tending bar takes more skill than some give credit for, and I don't mean that in a Tom-Cruise-in-the-movie-*Cocktail* way. It also kills me that for some people, that reference is to a classic movie from a time gone by. To me, Tom Cruise is just a baby, and that movie was yesterday, but there are kids old enough to drink who come into the Iversonian, and to them, Tom Cruise is a punch line on some cartoon I've never watched.

Worse, to the Iversonian himself, I'm the same way. And for the record, whoever invented the damn apple mojito should be shot in the face twelve times and then run over. In a busy bar, there simply isn't enough time to mix the damn thing. I don't think it's worth the money in the ingredients, either.

"I said, 'Go fuck yourself, blue eyes.'" The twentysomething at the bar I'd convinced the Iversonian to let me open in his upstairs area didn't seem to understand that I wasn't going to fill his drink order.

"I just want an apple mojito," Blue Eyes repeated. "What's the problem?"

"Fine." The three-deep crowd at the bar all wanted my attention. "Twenty bucks, then."

"But they're only ten downstairs."

The urge to throw the guy across the room slid up my spine and sat on my shoulder like a tiny demon urging me to give in. All I had to do was tap in to the ambient life force around me, and I'd have the strength to do it. Knowing how true immortal powers work makes it clear why a guy like the Iversonian would want to run a club. More lives meant more life force, and more life force meant that if I wanted to throw my strength around, I didn't run the risk of killing plants and animals or giving people cancer by drawing too much and confusing their immune system or mutating cells.

His girlfriend cringed apologetically. "Geez, Dylan. Just order something simple, like a lemon drop."

I laughed, one explosive burst of air. Lemon drops are almost as bad, and they leave me with sticky fingers.

"Chelsea," I said to the bartender next to me, "my tips are yours. I'm out."

Chelsea glared at me with purple-accented eyes of pink, and the air around her sparkled. I forget what kind of an elf she is, but she's good at her job and three times as patient as I am. She says the patience comes with age. Ha!

Bass thumped in time to the beat of a song I'd heard, but never with the mix that had been applied to it now. Humans danced with fae and a few vampires, but mainly the fae folk, since most of them could disguise themselves enough to pass for human. Especially with the amount of body modification some of the Iversonian's clientele had undergone.

Headed out? the Iversonian asked telepathically from a spot at his favorite table.

I'll be back for my lesson.

Paying a visit to Greta?

Why do you ask? I thought as I shoved my way between two idiots.

She's outside. He raised his glass at me as I caught a glimpse of him through the crowd. *I thought you might have sensed her. Most true immortals learn to do that eventually, at least with Masters and Vlads: pick up on the energy that lets them sense each other.*

Nope, I thought back.

And now she appears to be stealing a police car.

What? I squinted, and the little blue lines of life force (or soul energy, as the Iversonian liked to call it) popped into view. I drew in little sparks of it to feed my speed and muscles. Stronger and faster, I elbowed my way through a sea of bruises and bumps, then out the front door.

33

GRETA
THE WORLD ACCORDING TO APPLESAUCE

Marilyn charged out the door of the Iversonian wearing a low-cut purple silk top and black leather pants with straps running up the sides. The boots and jacket I recognized, but she wore makeup . . . She never used to wear makeup. Or . . . maybe . . . a little, but not like this. Not since I'd known her. A leather cord dangling around her neck caught my eye, and I thought I saw a hint of gold: a ring through which the cord had been threaded, peeking out between her breasts.

Her engagement ring, I thought, *but are you Mom or an imposter with that makeup and those clothes?*

She waved.

I looked away, punching the cop in the face again and forcing him into the back of his squad car with his buddy. *Screw the not-Mom.*

"Officers Salvadore Donatello and Carl Vicks, you're coming with me." They were a lot quieter unconscious. Bruises turned purple, then yellowish, and started to fade. If they weren't somebody's thralls, they were missing a great opportunity. Either way, they were hiding something, because they looked and smelled like normal humans. I'd made three thralls now, and I thought I should be able to tell if these guys were thralls, but I wasn't getting anything. Maybe I was doing it wrong. Even with Uncle Percy's glasses on my face, I didn't see anything to explain the healing.

His words appeared in a golden script across the lenses. *I'll check again when we have more time, but I don't see any magic.*

"This is so wrong." Evelyn put a hand over her eyes.

"Start the car, Deputy."

"We're not going to kill them, right?" She opened the driver's door. It had slammed shut in the struggle.

"I'm not allowed to kill them." I handcuffed Sal's hands behind his back and slammed the rear door. "Duh!"

"Greta!" Marilyn shouted as she darted across the street between cars. "Greta! Wait!"

"Go on ahead." I shut the passenger door, which hung open, the window shattered where I'd punched through it and dragged Carl out of the vehicle. "Take them to my place. I'll catch up later."

"You're the boss," Evelyn said as she pulled away.

Marilyn met me at the sidewalk. I don't think she noticed Chthonic and Warcry watching her, one from the alley and the other from a nearby parking deck. Nightwish was even harder to spot, mixed in with the hopefuls waiting in line to get into the Iversonian.

"What's going on?" I hugged Marilyn begrudgingly. Mom or not, I still liked her, loved her even, maybe. She was familiar, and a person who'd always tried to be nice to me, cared for me—unless she'd misled me about being Mom.

"Were those cops?" Her eyes searched mine, and I wondered what she hoped or feared to find there. Her eyes widened in an expression of . . . something.

"Maybe."

"Please don't be cute, Greta." What did that look in her eyes mean? I'm better with negative emotions than positive ones, for the most part. Compensation comes in the forms of other people's reactions or by monitoring subtle changes in pulse and pupil dilation. Reading Marilyn should have been easy, but my fundamental confusion about her status and mine added to the existing difficulty in a way I don't think I'd experienced since my first few years of undeath.

"I wasn't." I ran my hand along her throat, closing it just enough to feel her breath and pulse together beneath my palm. "I don't know what they are. They used to be cops, but I don't think they are who they say they are, so I'm going to question them."

"Does Eric know what you're doing?"

"I don't know." My left hand went to my pocket, and I traced the edges of my badge through my jeans as my right hand felt her false mortality. "I'm the sheriff, though. So I can do what I want."

She's learning, Uncle Percy wrote. *I see things hanging in her soul matrix already: weapons, some sort of armor. The Iversonian is keeping his word to your father; he's teaching her. But I don't see a tithing cord or soul tap. It's surprising.*

"Greta . . ." She pulled away from my hand, and I fought the urge to tighten my grip and not let her go, to cling to that illusion of normal life. Hers, I mean. I didn't know how to feel about an i-Mom-mortal.

"Sorry." I jerked my hand away as if I'd been stung by a wasp. "I like to feel your heartbeat and your lungs moving air. I'm glad you're young again. Is the Iversonian nice?" *Are you fucking him?* I shifted to put her upwind of me and sniffed for man smells but found only the scents of sweat and alcohol and cleaning products that I expected if she was being faithful to Dad.

"If you want," she said reproachfully, "we'll go rent a room, and I can strip down so you can get a really thorough whiff."

I would have liked that, but I didn't think it was a real offer, so I apologized again. I still don't like to apologize, but Mom or not, I like Marilyn. She deserves an apology sometimes, too. She understands me better than anybody else.

"You're only looking out for your dad," she acknowledged. "Here, put your head to my chest so you can have a good listen." I did as she asked. "I'm not having sex with anyone, and I'm not dating anyone, and I'm not interested in dating anyone, not even your dad, until I sort some things out."

It was the truth, and it earned her another hug. Maybe she wasn't Mom, but she had so much potential to be Mom again, or still be Mom, that I couldn't hurt her or be too mean to her.

"Okay . . ." I couldn't *call* her Mom, though. It wouldn't come out. "I have to go . . ."

"One thing," Marilyn added. "That other vampire who was with you. That's Evelyn, right?"

"Yes." I clapped my hands, not knowing what else to do with them that didn't involve claws, squeezing, or more hugs. "She's my deputy, and her head comes off and then goes right back on again with no trouble. She's Dad's second cousin a few times removed, so technically, they could fuck and it wouldn't be weird or anything."

"Ha!" Marilyn brayed, then coughed. "They're not, though, right?"

"Nope." This was dangerous territory for me. Like the reason I've been trying to stay out of rooms with Dad and High Society vampires in them. I don't like it when people deny Dad what he wants or what he deserves. My eyes flashed red, and the diamond from Marilyn's engagement ring caught the rays, bent them, and refracted them as dots of red so that it looked like fireworks going off in her décolletage. "He only wants you, and you won't let him have you."

She sighed. "I guess I—"

But I was gone. I couldn't listen to her anymore without wanting to hit her and open her up to see what needed fixing. Why didn't she want Dad? What was wrong with her? Why couldn't I cut it out and feed it to Talbot like a demon?

I met Chthonic, Warcry, and Nightwish three blocks over in front of Query's Quick Pawn, and the three of us climbed into Nightwish's 2000-model Cadillac. Parts of its metal body were rusted through, and the paint job was a muddle of blue and primer gray, but it ran. Nightwish drove while both Chthonic and Warcry squeezed into the back with me.

"I'm cold." At once, they pressed against me, their body heat a shield against the ever-present chill. I excited them, but they didn't have the same effect on me. I wanted to eat them, kill them, tear them apart, but then they wouldn't be able to keep me warm. I've grown up a lot . . . I'm learning to take better care of my things. I will say this, though: Erections make damn good hand warmers.

"Turn on the radio," I said, wanting noise but not conversation. "And stop moving around, you two. If I get anything sticky on my hands, I'm going to wash it off with your blood."

"How can she just do that?" a whiny male voice was saying. "I was just out minding my own business on one of the nights when vampires are allowed to be out, and then the fucking sheriff and her lesbo side-kick are beating the hell out of me and dangling me off a rooftop. This shit never used to happen under Phillip."

"Thanks for your call, Travis." Sly Imp's voice came in a beat later, with Gorillaz bed music playing underneath. Was that "Revolving Doors"? "What do you think, Void City? Does Eric Courtney need to rein in his daughter, our Sheriff of Slaughter? Hello, you're in league with Sly Imp."

"Yeah." The voice sounded young and angry. "What the hell, man? E'rbody says Er'c is tough an' all, but I ain't seen him do shit that she ain't done her damn self if it need doin'. We only have her word that he saved her at all. I think she killed Lord Fat Ass and gave her pops the credit cuz she got crazy daddy issues. Know what ah'm sayn'?"

Whimpers came to my attention from close by, and when I noticed the sounds were coming from Chthonic and Warcry, I let go, wiping my hands on their pants. "You two are lucky that's blood." Neither thrall spoke, eyes wide, looking straight ahead. For a brief second I played with the notion of resuming my grip and seeing whether their eyes would actually pop out of their heads if I applied more pressure.

Annoyed with them both, I climbed into the passenger seat and got out my cell. Four callers later, I could see my apartment building, and Sly Imp finally gave the number to call in again. While Nightwish pulled in through the automated security gates (using my code and parking pass), I dialed the number.

To my astonishment, Sly Imp himself answered. "You're in league with Sly Imp."

"No." My voice shook. "I'm not."

"Be that way, caller. I—"

"If you hang up on me, I'm killing you and everyone in your building."

Sly Imp laughed nervously. "There are six different radio stations operating out of this one building, caller. And we have excellent guard demons. Gyre, run the mystic ID on this caller and let's—"

Gyre, his sidekick of the airwaves, came on next. "It's Greta Courtney."

"What?"

"It's the sheriff."

Silence.

All of his listeners heard more dead air in that pause than they probably had in the last year of broadcasting.

"So glad to find out you're a fan of the show, Your Slaughterness." I'd shaken him, but his chutzpah was back. Faked or not, I liked the recovery.

"I'm not."

"A new listener, then. I—"

"Find something else to talk about," I said. Nightwish turned off the car and slumped down in the seat. She looked tired. "But stop talking about my dad."

"Sheriff Courtney," Sly Imp began, "surely you must understand the supernatural community's interest in your adopted father."

"Adopted?"

"Well"—Sly Imp was nervous again, clearing his throat—"I . . . assumed. You know what? Forget about that. What my listeners would just love is to hear your side of everything. Tell us your history with Eric Courtney and how you came to be our resident lawperson."

"Do a lot of vampires listen to your show?"

"This is the most popular talk show in the greater Void City area," he said. "I have a huge vampire and demon listenership."

"Good." I got out of the car and cocked my head; I couldn't hear the two cops. "Tell them that my daddy is the biggest, baddest vampire in this town, and he will be treated as such. He will be respected and well treated or the perpetrators will answer to me."

"Up close and personal?"

"Up close and 'Oh no, I hope Greta doesn't know the one secret way to end me forever, oh, fuck, she does. Ack. Thud. Slurp. Poof.'"

The night air picked up, blowing over me, and I luxuriated in it despite the perceived chill. This at least I could do. Dad kept stopping me from killing people I needed to kill, but I could threaten these people and make them respect him or pretend to, and he didn't care about the difference. Dad is all about perception. If they seemed to respect him, that would be good enough for Dad.

"I have a bank full of callers that say otherwise."

"One word," I said, "and I'll be listening for their voices in the night. They may be fine for a while, but eventually, I'll find them or Fang will. Good night, demon." I hung up.

"Caller, you're in league with Sly Imp. Go ahead." Nothing. "Let's try line two, Gyre." Nothing. "And line four?" Nothing there, either.

My smile grew large enough to qualify for lying-Grinch status.

"Sheriff Slaughterhouse has made her point, folks," Sly Imp said. "Enough politics, but don't tune out. Next hour I'll have Rolfindorf Rottingham, the new power forward for the Void City Howlers. He's a Norse werewolf. We'll ask how he thinks the team is shaping up after all the recent changeups, and does the new coach, Carmen Samburro, have what it takes? Can a female hockey coach make it in Void City?"

My smile vanished when I saw Evelyn standing empty-handed in my apartment without the cops.

"I'm sorry, Sheriff." She held out a note. "Captain Marx delivered it herself."

> *Dear Greta,*
> *Please leave the cops alone. You can help them. You can ask for their help; you may not hurt them. Otherwise, you've been doing a great job.*
>
> > *Love,*
> > *Dad*

Damn. Thwarted again.

"What do you think?" I asked, aiming the query at both Evelyn and Percy (via his memento mori glasses, which were still on my face).

"I think we'll have to explore another lead," Evelyn said. "We'll need to steer clear of anything involving people who may or may not be his secret thralls. Can you think of anyone or anything else we might try?"

I think you're very close, my dear, Percy penned.

Maybe. I chewed my lip. "We got the names of those cops, though, didn't we?"

"Yes," Evelyn answered. I snapped my fingers, and my three thralls were at my side. "First," I said, "I want you to turn into dogs so I can pet you, because it's just occurred to me that you can. And second, we have the cops' names. Now let's find out who they are and what they mean to Dad."

34

ERIC

I NEVER LIE . . . TO HER

"N o."

"No?" Talbot held up the newest set of bills, watching me from across my desk. "If you don't do something, she's going to figure it out."

"So what?"

"So what?" Talbot put down the bills and looked at Magbidion, who was sitting in the recliner I'd bought for the office but rarely sat in. Mags looked half asleep. "You've put that one through an awful lot of trouble for 'So what.'"

"That's true."

Magbidion smiled. "I'm okay with whatever, boss." His speech was slurred. "We can rest up and try again or . . . something."

"No." I knew it, and Magbidion knew it, too. This was a one-shot plan. If I screwed the pooch, The Plan or this version of it would never work again.

"You could try ordering her not to interfere." Talbot leaned over the desk and took the checkbook from me. "And writing these checks yourself."

"I think that's the one order I could give her that she wouldn't follow, Talbot."

"I thought she'd do anything for you."

"Anything except let me get hurt." I powered down the computer and leaned back in my desk chair, watching him flawlessly fill out checks in my handwriting. "I could tell her to rob banks, kill women, children, and puppies, or even ask her for sex, and she'd probably go along with it, but can I get Greta to let some demon that I can't fight beat the hell out of me? I don't see that happening."

"True enough." Talbot looked up from signing my name. "I could always—"

"Not this time."

"Mind if I write myself a big fat check while I'm forging sigs?"

"If you think I owe it to you, take it all." Nervous, I got to my feet and started wearing a path in the carpet. My nighttime secret camped at the edges of my memory, messing with my brain. Familiar things woke memories that were prone—if I was too distracted—to turn into full-blown hallucinations.

"A cargo container shipped all the way from France on an otherwise empty sailing vessel, at vampire safety rates," Talbot commented as he wrote a check for a particularly large bill.

"Garnier," I said, using the code name for a being with whom I'd tussled back in Paris on my honeymoon. "Doesn't come cheap. I gotta grab some air."

"Go ahead, old man," Talbot said. "Try not to get lost on the way across the street."

"Yeah, right." I stepped out into the hallway.

"Oh, and watch out for the weregecko assassins in the hall."

"The wha?"

I looked up and marveled at the wonder and complexity of the universe. I knew there were all kinds of therianthropes, but fucking weregeckos? Six of them clung to the ceiling, bedecked in bandoliers of stakes and throwing stars, each wearing a dark-colored gi. The one closest to me looked for all world like a giant version of the Geico gecko, but with leopard markings and all ninja'd out, his toes and fingers bending backward at strange angles as he clung to the ceiling in the hall. As he opened his mouth with a hiss, his tongue darted at my head like a thick pink blackjack.

I dodged left as throwing stars rained down from above and the geckos attacked.

"You've got to be shitting me."

35

EVELYN
CHASING LEADS

Greta had her own ideas about research, but my methods needed neither thralls nor supernatural abilities. My ways were as simple and old as my mortal profession, even if the tech changed as the news media itself mutated and grew.

Sitting at Eric's desk, I slid open the lap drawer. His passwords were there on a Post-it note, but I could have guessed them easily enough. They weren't quite as bad as "password" or "123456," but they were still things you aren't ever supposed to use: Greta's birthday, Marilyn's birthday, Fang's license plate—which says FANG.

Eric's e-mails didn't tell me much. He'd been corresponding with someone in Europe about demons. How their chains of command worked. How their power levels worked. What was the difference between a Nefario and an Infernatti? Was Magbidion right about someone called Lady Scrytha? There were other questions, too, about things called Soul Bonding and Soul Burn.

I plugged in a thumb drive, set his PC to making an archive copy of his e-mail, and wrote down his settings so I could set up his account as an alternate on my own PC. As much as I liked Greta (despite my better judgment), I wanted to keep the option of killing this guy.

Leaving that process running, I locked the desktop and walked out into the hall. I'd seen Eric head over to the club, even said hello to him, but he wasn't suspicious enough to ask me what I was doing at the Pollux. I was his daughter's deputy, and he took that at face value in a naive way that would have made me feel guilty for sneaking around if he hadn't been the guy who'd torn off my head and thrown it down a manhole.

Padding down the hallway to Eric's bedroom, I heard Erin and

Cheryl talking downstairs but couldn't make out what they were say-ing. To add an extra layer of quiet to my creeping, I let myself drift away from the ground, floating down the hall. His bedroom door stood open, but inside, there wasn't much of interest: clothes, a new television, a refrigerator.

"I wonder how much blood an Emperor keeps on hand," I asked myself as I opened the fridge. The six bags surprised me, but not as much as the leftover steak from Outback, the half-six-pack of Coke in glass bottles, and the Tatsu 7 Go Gurt. And I opened the styrene con-tainer and balked: a piece of birthday cake?

Something else weird ran up the side of the fridge interior. Be-cause it was empty, I needed a few moments to identify it, but it was either a very strange beer-bong attachment or a scabbard.

I took a picture with my phone's camera and moved on to the bathroom. Kneeling close to the floor revealed some sort of powdery residue. My senses are better with my head detached, but I went mun-dane tech first. I pulled a UV penlight out of my bag and, after I flipped off the bathroom lights, let it play across the floor.

The magic circle it revealed got photographed, too. That had to be Magbidion's doing. I didn't know enough about magic to tell what it meant or implied. Like a good reporter, though, I knew who did.

A couple hours later, I was pulling off I-65 in Pelham, Alabama, with huge white natural-gas tanks looming large to my right. I turned right again before Highway 31 and wended my way along the heavily forested back roads so common in Alabama. Five more minutes, and I pulled up to a small square building behind a high chain-link fence. I parked my Harley on the grass next to the fence, not wanting to drive it on the gravel, and flew up and over the fence.

Unlike other vampires, *nukekubi* show up on camera unless our heads are detached (or that's how it works for me), so when the large metal garage-style door rolled up and the men with guns, crossbows, and crosses stepped out, I wasn't surprised.

"I want to talk to Pythagoras."

Wood, a heavyset man with long stringy unwashed hair, headed up the pack. As I settled to the ground, he spat. Wood has never liked or trusted me. "Maybe he doesn't want to talk to you, leech."

"And maybe he does." Pythagoras rolled out of the shadowy re-cesses of the building, stopping at the concrete edge of the Golden Triangle's safe house. "It all depends on what you have to tell me."

"Call off the ghostbusters here, and I'll be happy to tell you a lot of things."

"Very well." Pythagoras tipped the control of his electric wheel-chair back, and I walked in after him.

Pythagoras isn't a magician himself, but he's used mages from time to time to hunt vampires, to level the playing field. When I stepped into the warehouse, for example, I obviously tripped some sort of ward or barrier, because the symbols on my neck lit up, my fangs came out, and my eyes began to glow. Wood and his boys got spooked, but Pythagoras rolled on without comment.

Holy symbols bedecked the interior walls, but aside from that, it looked like I'd walked into a low-tech Batman's version of a weapons locker. Weapons ranging from swords and crossbows to AK-47s and bazookas lined the walls. At the center of the back wall, a Mac and a PC sat side by side. At the back left, on a mat, a one-armed man was demonstrating staking techniques on a high-tech dummy while a real (and totally staked) vampire lay next to it on the mat.

Wood and his buddies rejoined the class as I followed Pythagoras over to the computers.

"How are you getting along with the Courtney family?" he asked.

"It's weird." I set my thumb drive on the computer hutch. "I haven't seen the father make a live kill since I got there—like he's trying to quit—but the daughter kills easy as breathing."

"Breathing is easier for some than it is for others." Pythagoras took the thumb drive and plugged it in. "What am I looking at?"

"Courtney's e-mail archive and some pictures I took while snooping around."

His PC screen filled with thumbnails. He clicked on the black-light mystical symbols, and I caught a twitch at the corner of his mouth. The hint of a smile. "Where did you find this?"

"His bathroom floor."

"I'll send the images to Iso, but this is a multipurpose construction of some kind. It's related to concealment with the power created in the circle but focused through something else—I'd guess the caster, him- or herself—but Iso will know for sure."

"Iso?"

"Isosceles," he said. "He's my contact in the Mages Guild. And that's all you need to know about her."

It's always bugged me, the way Pythagoras swaps gender pronouns when discussing a resource he'd like to keep under wraps, but I let it go.

"What are these?" He clicked on the scanned images of the cops from Marilyn's scrapbooks.

"The sheriff—" Pythagoras started violently when I said the word.

"The daughter," I corrected, "has her new chupacabra thralls looking into that."

"Why?"

"One of the clues we followed led us to a home for retired Void City police officers. Courtney had trashed the records, and there was a residual scent of what the daughter seemed certain was Courtney's blood."

"Interesting." He twitched the joystick on the arm of his chair, rotating back for a better view of my face. "What else?"

"Some of the cops we've seen around town." I tapped the screen over one of the faces. "They're these men, and they have quick healing, but—"

"But aren't detectable as thralls?"

"Yes."

"They're thralls," Pythagoras said, "which is curious."

"Why?" I asked.

"Because I have it on good authority that Eric Courtney is no longer as he appears to be."

"What is he?"

"There's one way to find out." Pythagoras waved a hand at one of his troops. "Get her the katana I was prepping for her."

Wood walked over to a sealed case and typed numbers into a keypad. "We only have one more of these, Pyth."

"Thank you for the reminder, Woodroe." He directed the next bit directly to me. "We gave the other one to John Hawkes, and it wound up in Ebon Winter's hands."

A sapphire nimbus clung to the edge of the blade when Wood drew it. The cloud of magic was slight but obvious.

"What does it do?"

"It's a sword," Wood snapped. "It cuts things." He sheathed it again and handed the sword and scabbard over to me.

"Okay, so how am I going to use it to determine what Eric Courtney is or isn't?"

"You aren't," Pythagoras said. His software ejected my thumb drive. "I just wanted you to have it."

"Unh." I coughed, exasperated. "Then how do I do that?"

He clicked back to the image of the magic circle. "Simple. Courtney is working with a mage. A soulless one, yes?"

I nodded.

"He's the one powering the magic, whatever it is. Kill him." He made an "easy as that" gesture. "Kill him and the spells will drop, then whatever he's hiding will be out in the open. Can you do that?"

"I've never killed a human like that, just murdered—"

"The man sold his soul to a devil, Evelyn." Pythagoras touched my hand. "He doesn't count as human anymore. He abandoned us and sided with the monsters of his own free will."

"Yeah." I nodded, trying to convince myself. "I guess so."

"Know so," Pythagoras said, "and choose your time wisely. Courtney is planning something. Wait until he's at his most exposed, and then kill the mage."

✦ 36 ✦

ERIC

OLD FRIENDS WITH NEW CAUSES

A week after the fight with the weregecko assassins that Winter sent me as an I-still-publicly-hate-you present, I was still in the habit of checking the ceiling when I entered a room. Magbidion lay on my bed again, his face so white, I was afraid things might already have gone too far. My special invisibility-to-demons necklace, the Blind Eye of Scrythax (which I'd gotten back only a week or two before), moved up and down with each ragged breath. Talbot stood over him like one of those cats in old wives' tales who steal the breath of babies.

"How bad?"

"You can't wait any longer," Talbot said.

My cell vibrated.

DAYTIME SUPPORT: *not yet—the plan app* was displayed on the touch screen.

"Give me a timetable," I ordered, as if Talbot had a magic chart of how long Magbidion could continue to maintain all the spells and enchantments I had him running before he finally died of exhaustion. To his credit, Talbot's eyes changed from normal to glowing star emeralds without comment or objection. Maybe he'd become fond of my mage. Or maybe such abject loyalty fascinated him.

"He might make it to morning." Talbot touched Magbidion's forehead, his hand coming away wet with sweat. "He might not. It's a close thing."

"Mags?" I asked. He didn't answer. His lips were moving too soft, slow, and slurred for me to have a chance of reading them. His hands twitched occasionally as if completing portions of a mystic gesture in his semiconscious state . . . still maintaining the spells.

How much longer? I typed into my cell.

DAYTIME SUPPORT: *Rockstar says at least three more days.*

Too long, I typed back. *Get everyone into position. I'm calling a friend.*

DAYTIME SUPPORT: *Eric, if you do it this early, the Marilyn portion of the plan may fail completely.*

C'est la vie, I typed back. I had hope. Hope would have to be enough.

I closed the app, sent one text, and then walked down to the street. Fang's radio blared 100.6 FM (WVCT—Void City Talk Radio). Sly Imp was interviewing a local demon who claimed to be upset about the exclusivity of Orchard Lake and Sable Oaks, the local werewolf- and vampire-only neighborhoods just outside of Void City proper.

"Just because I'm a demon doesn't mean I don't like to fish and swim or drive a pontoon boat around a lake, but the parasites and the monthlies have all the best lake property sewed up tight."

"Now," Sly Imp cut in, "all that's true, Diaxicrotioush'nar, but can you honestly tell me that part of this, even if it's only a little bit, is not about property rights but about the contract you have on Eric Courtney's thrall Magbidion?"

"I'll admit the little greaser is overdue for collection, but that's a separate topic. I—"

"I hate to cut you off, but Gyre just handed me a note that—well, if it's true, then I expect our fearless fucktard of a vampiric lord and master"—he switched into a Ricky Ricardo impression—"has some 'splaining to do. Caller?"

"Hello, Sly." The lingering trace of hoarseness wasn't enough to obscure the words or disguise him at all. Talbot nodded to me on the way to his motorcycle.

"You certainly sound like the man, but that doesn't mean you're him."

"Some in my place might quote Mark Twain, but I find that cliché." The warmth in Father Ike's voice was a narcotic to some, a balm to others. Hell, even I was glad to hear him speak. "Others might quote Scripture. I can think of several passages that would be easily misused. John 11:25 might be misappropriated to claim biblical power and authority or intervention: 'Jesus said unto to her, I am the resurrection, and the life: he that believeth in me, though he were dead, yet shall he live.' First Corinthians 15:22. 'For as in Adam all die, so also in Christ shall all be made alive.'"

"That definitely sounds like you, Father, but even I can quote Scripture."

"Of course you can, Sly. James 2:19," Ike cited. "'For it is written that demons believe and shudder.' But your listeners don't really want to hear me preach, do they? If so, I have several sermons . . ."

I laughed, and so did Sly Imp. "No, thank you, Father, but if you could do me a favor and pass the Jude test?"

"Come now, Sly," the voice said, so softly that the roar of Talbot's bike almost drowned him out as my favorite mouser shot by on his way to the VCU campus. "'Thou shall not test the *Lord* thy God.' Faith is not a parlor trick—while I'm afraid my survival very much is. Well, that and a testament to the usefulness of CPR training."

"C'mon, Father. If you're really who I think you are, you can bind a demon like me with one specific quote."

"I know the passage of which you speak, Sly." Ike took a long breath, and I wondered what was going through his mind. This kind of up-front showy thing is something Ike has always disliked. He's more comfortable working with people on a personal level, but with what I offered him to help me after I strangled and resuscitated him . . . let's just say I understand why he was willing to comply. "You want me to bind you, but I think that's foolish. Why would any Christian want to bind a demon on earth?"

"Waitwaitwait—" Sly cut in. I guess he saw what was coming next. You see, vampires tend to steer clear of Ike because merely touching him can set us on fire, but when confronted with demons, if he wants to, if he feels it's the right time, Father Ike can—

"In the name of Christ Jesus, I cast you out."

I guess I'd expected a scream or *kaboom*, but the silence spoke volumes.

Gyre, Sly's sound tech, came over the air next.

"Thanks for the call, Father Ike," he said, "and I hope you don't mind me ending your call, but I don't have any desire to join Sly in the Pit just now." He cleared his throat and stepped up to the plate with a passable imitation of his former boss's jaunty style. "So . . . what do you think, Void City? Father Ike is revealed to be not only among the living but actively casting demonic shock jocks into hell? Who knew priests could pull that shit via telephone? Can all priests do it, or just badass soldiers for the Big Sky Bully, like Father Ike? Call in and speak your piece on the Widening Gyre."

I was tempted to call in myself and take Gyre to task for stealing the name of his show from the title of a Kevin Smith *Batman* limited series, but there was no time after the moment Father Ike's voice came over Fang's car speakers. The opening volley was out and fired across Scrytha's bow. Father Ike was alive, and boy, was Scrytha going to be pissed. The Plan was in full swing, and the only two people who could make it succeed or fail were the women I loved most.

For once in my life, there was nothing I could do to save myself. The fight was coming, and there was no way on earth I could win it alone.

37

MARILYN

OLD DOG NEW TRICKS

Void City University abuts the northwest side of the city, its high brick walls drawing a demarcation that says clearly to all: Void City Ends Here. The last time I'd set foot on campus had been for the graduation ceremony of one of Eric's former strippers. Bethany, I think her name was. I can't even remember what degree she was working on, only that she graduated magna cum laude and Eric was so proud that he bought her a car.

I pulled up to the gate on my Harley and waited while the guard walked out. A middle-aged man with balding hair and a paunchy waist, the guard didn't look that threatening unless you happened to see his supernatural side: an anthropomorphized rat clad in black armor dotted with cruel-looking spikes that glimmered with a hint of magic. Maybe it's that I've never liked rats. His security badge said NIMH, and despite my nerves, it gave me a slight chuckle.

"Nimh?" I handed him my student ID.

"S'ironic." He took my badge and gave it a sniff. The accent was one of the British ones, but I didn't know them well enough to tell which.

"Yeah."

On the other side of the iron gates, students went about their business, heading to class or their dorms or wherever. I wasn't sure I belonged with them, but Eric had been right about one thing. There were all kinds of things in this world I wished I knew more about, and wasting the time I had now would be crazy. I'd decided to start with a business degree, because in the back of my head, there was a little dream Eric and I had talked about back when we were engaged:

a bar I wanted to open. Not a strip club or a bowling alley but a real . . . joint. No dancing or loud music, just a few pool tables and—

"Mind's a terrible thing," he said, handing me back the ID.

"To waste?" I looked at him.

"That, too." He waved, and the gates opened to let me in.

"How long before I get to use the automated gate?" All the supernatural students had to come in the front gate, past the wererats, but I hoped that wasn't a permanent thing.

"After the appropriate, miss."

"Appropriate what?" I slid my ID back in my leather jacket. "Amount of time?"

"Could be, miss."

Finding a place to park took less time than I'd thought and gave me a chance to wander about campus. The army-surplus duffel on my shoulder weighed me down enough that I decided to carry it up to my dorm room. Dorm room. I sniffed. The very idea of a dorm room still cracked me up, but the Iversonian had insisted. "It will help you remember how young you look on the outside, to remind yourself that you are forever changed."

"'Besides,'" I quoted him under my breath, "'everyone needs a college experience, to be on one's own amongst strangers. Of course, I had mine when we were just inventing the concept. If yours involves a healthy fraction of the sex and vomiting mine did, I shall be impressed . . . and appalled.'"

After dropping things off, I checked my schedule. I didn't know why I'd signed up for a night class. Maybe I hoped there would be more people closer to my real age in it. Ten minutes later, I was seated in Accounting 101, waiting for Professor Duncan to come in and bore me. I had a thin tablet computer with a touch screen that I'd been assured all the kids craved and used for notes, though I'd yet to manage more than buying my textbooks on it. I fumbled with the stylus, trying to get it in a comfortable writing position, then gave up and reached into my messenger bag for the pen and notebook I'd packed just in case.

"You've got to be fucking kidding me," came a voice from the door.

"Hello to you, too, Tabitha." I left the pen and notebook where they were.

Tabitha dressed like some damn sluppie (slut + yuppie), all designer labels and accessories, making me momentarily self-conscious in my white T-shirt and jeans. I'm still getting used to not wearing granny panties and Depends. Given Tabitha's relationship with Eric, I felt particularly self-conscious about the engagement ring that hung on a leather cord around my neck, hiding in my cleavage.

"So?" She sat down next to me.

"So . . . ?"

"Did he give you the same talk he gave me?"

"Given that we're both here, I'd guess there were similarities." *Except he loves me and he doesn't love you.*

"Accounting 101?" Tabitha took a long break before she said that. I didn't know what was going through her head, but I imagined it couldn't have been fun to sit next to the woman whom the man she loved cared for more than he cared for her. It took a lot of guts to sit down next to me and be civil. Then again, Tabitha never lacked guts.

"I know a lot about running a bar, but not all of it comes from the correct way of doing things."

"What? You mean Fang fees and vampires?"

"Yeah." I looked down at my tablet. "I'm not sure I'm going to stay in town, and I don't want there to be any surprises. Plus, I have to admit I like the idea of being able to say I went to college, that I have a degree in something. What about you?"

"Eric gave me a lot of money in the divorce settlement, and I don't want to get screwed out of it or wake up one morning to find I squandered it all without realizing it." She looked at her hands, at some spot of paint on the cream-colored walls, and then at the door. "Are we the only students?"

I checked my watch. "They've still got twenty minutes."

"I guess we are early." Small talk was killing her. Vampires have little tells: Her nails were longer than they had been upon entering the room . . . not claws but longer. Her eyes had brightened in color, not glowing, exactly, but a color shift toward red. Her enunciation was more formal—clipped, preparing to speak around fangs without lisping.

"I can drop the class if you want, Tabitha," I offered.

"No," she said too quickly and too loudly. "It's fine."

It wasn't, but I took her at her word, because going into it further served no purpose other than to increase her discomfort and my own.

"Why—" She cut herself off, touching her hand to her lips, the poster child for Was That My Out-Loud Voice.

"Go ahead." I tapped my tablet and entered the pin. "Ask it."

"It's personal."

"Ha!" My laugh made her blink. "I've fed you blood, seen you naked, and staked you through the heart. Even if I hadn't, your sense of smell is strong enough that you can smell what color my panties are, so personal is fine."

"That last part sounded like Eric."

"We've known each other a long damn time." I flipped through screens until I found the note app I wanted, the one that looked like a yellow legal pad. "How do you know it's not Eric who sounds a lot like me? I'm older than he is."

"You are?"

"Yep." I typed "Acunting 101" at the top of the page, noticed my mistake, and added the missing C and O. "So what's twisted your nipples, honey?"

"Why didn't you let Eric turn you?"

"I was Roger's thrall, Tabitha." Immortal memories can be tricky things. It was as if I were in two places: sitting in the classroom and standing over Eric's grave simultaneously. "When Eric came back, I missed my window of opportunity, just like I did when he was alive. We were always in the wrong place at the wrong time. At first it was that I was older. Then it was Betty Lou. Then the war. The VCPD. Roger. It was such a different time. I don't think you can really even understand how different."

"Like what?"

"Well . . ." I watched her eyes. Did I want to try and explain it to her? I thought about how hard she'd tried to keep Eric, and how much of that was her getting caught up in the mess between Eric and me, and thought, *It's the least I can do.* "Maybe you know it, maybe you don't, but I cheated on Eric with Roger."

She nodded.

"But back then. God. Today you would have called it rape. Eric, Roger, and I were going to a Halloween party, but Eric got called in to work. He insisted Roger and I go on. I was mad at him, and I drank too much at the party, and somewhere between helping me home and making sure I got into the house safely, Roger had me bent over the kitchen counter, telling me how we were meant to be together. How he'd always loved me."

"Shit." Tabitha put her hand on mine, and I couldn't tell if it was sympathy or a vampire's natural urge to be warm.

"After that, I tried to make sure I kept away from him, but whenever Eric was on a late shift, Roger would try to find some reason to come over." My tablet blinked off, and it startled me to suddenly see my very young reflection in the black screen. "Or he'd come out to the bar I was working at, and he'd play nice and respectful, and I'd think everything was fine . . . until the next time. After a while, I almost looked forward to it. I didn't know what they were doing to Eric at work, the magic brainwashing and forgetting and all of that. I just knew that he was changing, becoming more distant and quiet and angry."

"Why didn't you tell Eric?"

"I should have," I said, nodding, "but he didn't have many friends back then. A lot of his old buddies were doing the hippie thing, and they didn't like him anymore because he was patriotic, pro-military, and a policeman. They were trying to speak truth to power. As a result, they hated The Man, and Eric was doing his damnedest to be The Man. When I didn't tell him at first, after a certain point, it was all too late, because Roger would tell him about all the earlier times and—"

"And you thought Eric would blame you?"

"No." I took a breath, waking my tablet and reentering the pin. "I knew he would believe me and forgive me, do his best to understand or forget, but . . . the timing was always wrong. It sounds stupid now, knowing what I know, but I did the same things when Eric rose. I thought everything would be okay, that he'd come back to rescue me. I thought that having returned from the dead, he'd automatically know everything, and it would all be okay, but he didn't remember dying, much less possess some secret knowledge from the grave, and I waited too long. By then I was a thrall. Roger had literally compelled me not to say anything or tell anyone."

"Wow." The voice came from behind us. "That's absolutely tragic."

Talbot perched in the row behind us, his chin resting on his hands.

Tabitha asked, "Talbot, what are you doing here?" at the same time I asked, "What do you want, cat?"

"Just checking in." He rolled his neck, the sound of deep pops clear even to my nonenhanced senses.

"Ha!"

"You wound me deeply, Marilyn." His voice sounded hurt, but his expression colored him amused. "Aren't I allowed to look in on old friends from time to time?"

"You looked in," I said. "Now, unless you're actually taking Accounting 101—"

"Oh, I'm auditing the class," Talbot added quickly. "It seems campus security is so tight all of a sudden that the only way a supernatural can get on campus without fighting a plague of wererats is if he has a valid student ID."

"I wondered what was going on with that," Tabitha said in a voice that suggested: "Look, I have boobies!" Had they slept together, or did she just want to bang the kitty?

"It seems they have a new student whose protection they have been ordered to assure at the peril of total annihilation." He smirked and met my gaze. "Not that anyone here would know anything about that."

"If they ever have a supernatural version of *TMZ*"—I turned back around to face the front of the class and my tablet—"you have a career waiting for you."

"Don't worry," Talbot said. "After she kills him, the new management will leave you to your own devices."

"She?" Tabitha asked (and if she hadn't, I would have, just to be clear).

"Scrytha," Talbot said.

"The demon he made the deal with?" Tabitha asked.

"No shit, Sherlock." I packed my tablet back into my messenger bag and slung it over my shoulder. "When is this happening, Talbot?"

As if on cue (and knowing Talbot, it may well have been), his cell chirped. He flashed it in my direction: 911 was all it said on the text he'd received.

"Now."

"Then get off your ass—" Tabitha started.

"He's not going, or he wouldn't have come," I interrupted. "He's here to make sure I know."

"And not me?" Tabitha got to her feet, claws out.

I didn't have time for her shit. "Why would he want you to know?"

"I can help," Tabitha snarled. "This isn't all about you, Marilyn. You aren't the only woman Eric's ever loved."

"Yeah." I sighed. "I'm pretty sure I am."

"You bitch!" Tabitha coiled to jump.

"This"—I tapped into the surrounding energy, since Talbot was full of it, with extra to spare, and activated my speed—"is not"—in my mind's eye, I could see the things I'd stored in energy form hanging about my person like accessories I could click on or off like a digital paper doll—"about"—I clicked on the loaded crossbow and poured more energy in to make it real again—"you"—and fired, staking her through the heart with a crossbow bolt. "It never was."

I didn't even watch her body thud to the ground. My eyes were on Talbot. "Just say it, cat."

"Say what?" He held up his hands. "Don't shoot?"

"Whatever you came here to say." I stepped over Tabitha's prone form and felt guilty about putting a crossbow bolt through her top. All her clothes were so expensive, there was no telling how much she'd paid for the thing, and it looked like silk.

"Demons can be like vampires." Talbot scratched his nose. "Different power levels, social responsibilities, even unique kill conditions. Scrytha made the move from Nefario to Infernatti when she signed Eric up and made a deal. Unlike vampiric power levels, though, demonic advancements can be taken away."

"And?"

"Eric called her out. He's not being a good little servant, and she just found out."

"So she has to make an example of him?"

"You could say that."

"Why aren't you helping him?"

"I helped him kill Captain Stacey," Talbot said. "If I help him kill the Infernatti . . . That's two big ones close together. If it comes down to it, I might be willing to incur a longer exile for him, but not if I don't have to. In El Segundo, I was the only one who could help him. I accepted the exile for my actions. But what he needs now, you can do."

"Really? What the hell can I do in a fight that he can't?" I looked at the accessories I'd bonded to my spirit, all items the Iversonian had suggested: a pair of crossbows, three stakes, a long knife, a bastard sword, some body armor, and a change of clothes. "Eric is like Godzilla compared to me."

"Demons tend toward old-fashioned weaknesses. The more powerful the demon, the more old-fashioned the weakness. Almost anything can be killed if I eat it, for mine is the power to devour. Really, though, if anyone can fit the whole being inside herself all at one time, that's the real trick. More to the point, Scrytha's weakness now that she's an Infernatti is based on the virtue she abused to make her first deal."

"Love?" I asked.

"Unconditional love," Talbot clarified.

"But Eric—"

"Eric made the deal," Talbot interrupted. "No matter what he does, he can never win. He can't hurt her. Can't bruise her. He can't even bloody her nose. Why do you think Magbidion needs Eric to defend him against a demon? Like Eric, he shook a devil's hand.

Once you do that to seal a deal, the demon is immune to you forever."

"Where is he?" I asked, running for the door.

"Where do you think?" Talbot asked.

And I knew. So much for my first day of class.

38

GRETA

WHO RUNS BARTER TOWN?

This is Percy," I told Evelyn.

As a sign of trust, I'd let her look inside my closet. I don't think she understood all the chains, the leather straps, or the duct tape. Unlike Uncle Phil, I knew that a stake through Uncle Percy's heart did nothing but suspend his need for blood, kind of putting the vampire side of him on hold and letting the mummy side become dominant. His mummy side didn't need to eat or sleep, and it didn't show up on vampiric mental radar, either.

Uncle Phil had displayed Percy in a glass box in the middle of his living area, like a giant Ken doll with a plaque under him that read: *My dear Percy, who serves as a remembrance to all that I do not bluff, I do not make empty threats, and there are indeed worse fates than death.*

I'd put Percy in a case, too, but mine was made of an airtight box within a box constructed of bulletproof glass and hand-etched with holy symbols by William, the Alpha of the Orchard Lake werewolf pack. Also, as Uncle Phil had before me, I staked him, but unlike my nefarious dead uncle, I'd taken the further precaution of wrapping Percy from head to toe in duct tape, leather, and the Infernal Chains of Sarno Rayus, which had been used on Talbot by Lord Phillip a while back when they tried to steal Dad's soul. Just because Uncle Percy likes our arrangement and agreed to it doesn't mean I trust him during the day, when I'm asleep.

"Is that water between the two layers of glass?" Evelyn asked.

"Holy water," I answered gleefully.

"And those little boxes with the blinking lights at each corner?"

"Blessed shaped charges of C4," I said. "If the glass breaks, Percy go boom. He'd probably survive it. He's an Emperor-level vampire,

like Dad, but I'm pretty sure this whole arrangement will decorporeal-
ize him long enough for me to feed his memento mori to Fang and get
my mummy kit."

"You know how to kill a mummy?"

"Oh." My eyes flashed red, bathing Uncle in the light of my killy-
killy gaze. "Given enough time and exposure, I know how to kill anything and anyone. It's my thing. Dad may be the über vamp, but I'm
the Omega vamp, the über killer. Anything short of a true immortal, I
can end forever."

"Including me?"

"I haven't checked." My eyes closed, and I thought about killing
my deputy, wanting her ended. "Keep your head separate from your
body for seventy-two hours, then when your body rots, dissolve the
remains in holy water. Once that's done, your head will combust in
sunlight. Expose it to sunlight, let it burn, then bury the ashes of your
head on holy ground, and you'll be dead forever. It's complicated and
time-consuming but easily done."

"Oh." Evelyn blanched, taking an unconscious step away from me.
"I . . . uh . . . good to know."

"I guess." I closed my closet door. "What I'd like to know is what
would happen if we pulled off your head and put it on the body of a
decapitated animal. Like, could I put your head on a horse's body and
have an Evie-corn? Or would that be an Evie-taur?"

"Can we please never try those things?"

"I guess I can live with the curiosity," I said with a sly smile, "as
long as you're a good deputy."

I felt Warcry, Nightwish, and Chthonic trying to tell me something, but I ignored them. My chat with Evie was way more fun. I noticed Nightwish's heartbeat out in the parking lot when she pulled up
in her battered old car, and I frowned.

"That's not a bad-deputy smile, is it?" Evie asked.

"Nightwish just pulled up, and her heart is racing."

"You can hear her heart from here?"

"Can't you?" I walked to the front door and opened it.

"Maybe vampire hearing is more acute than *nukekubi* hearing?"

"Duh," I said. "I'm always cuter than you."

Evie froze, trapped by that feeling I get a lot from people who
can't tell whether I'm joking or whether I really didn't understand what
they said. I could have let her in on the joke, but I like the way it keeps
people off balance not to know the whole of me.

"Mistress!" Nightwish shouted when she saw me. "It's all over
town. Lord Eric didn't kill Father Ike."

"Duh!" I said again. "I knew that. I was spying on him when he strangled Ike and set the church on fire. I was there even before then, when he fought Winter on the steps of the church. I almost jumped in to kick Winter's ass, but I was afraid it would embarrass Dad."

Nightwish stared at me blankly.

"So?" I wanted her to elaborate.

"The demon," she said, though she was clearly out of breath. "Reviving the priest and hiding it from her . . . It broke your dad's deal with some demon . . . and now she's going to show up in person to punish him."

Oh, please, like Dad and Talbot can't handle a demon.

"She who?"

"The demon."

"Which demon?"

"Someone called Scrytha."

"As long as Talbot's there—"

"But Talbot's not there," Nightwish blurted. "Chthonic tried to tell you mentally, but you were busy. Talbot rode off. Warcry tried to follow him but got stopped by the security guard at the college."

"Do you smell that?" I asked Evelyn.

"No." She sniffed the air. "What am I supposed to be smelling?"

"Dead cat." I thought back to the fight when Dad's sire had come to town, when Talbot left me to be kidnapped and tormented by Uncle Phil. I thought of what Phil would have done to me if my control over the connection to my body hadn't been as strong as it is. My eyes went red again, catching Nightwish in their red light.

"I'm sorry. I'm sorry. I'm sorry." She crumpled under my ire. I stepped over her on my way out the door.

"Wasn't Fang in the parking lot?" I asked.

"Your dad has him," Evelyn answered, keeping step with me.

I broke into a run.

Top vampire speed.

Nobody hurts my dad!

39

ERIC

MY COMEUPPANCE

And there she was, Lady Scrytha: ex-Nefario, full Infernatti, and (according to her) the being who writes my honey-do list until the end of time. For once, I'd come face-to-face with my chief irritant while none of my family was being held hostage. My club wasn't torched or rigged to explode, and my movie theater wasn't on fire.

Scrytha looked as alien as her father, plus had an extra set of breasts I didn't think she'd had the last time we met. Precious and semi-precious jewels studded twin pairs of ram's horns jutting from her skull. The jewels sparkled in the greenish light from two sets of eyes (one set normal-sized, the other small and round, like evil doll eyes). Her dress was tanned hide of some kind, though it didn't look like leather to me. It gripped her tightly, dual keyholes highlighting cleavage from both sets of breasts, making me uncomfortable.

"Mr. Courtney, to what are you up?" When she spoke, a spotlight from beyond the sight of us nondemons (or at least me) lit her up, and I couldn't help but notice that the tail snaking its way from beneath the hem of her dress cast three shadows.

"To what am I up?" I climbed out of Fang, leaving the driver's-side door open. The car's metal felt cool under my skin, and I traced the lines of his hood. I stopped when I got to his front bumper and leaned against him, the light from his headlights picking out the edge of my jeans and casting Scrytha's right side in shadow. "Is this English as a second language? Next shall I inform you that I'm a person with whom you ought not fuck?"

"Words are important, Mr. Courtney." Her cloven-hoofed high heels conjured sparks of blue flame from the street as she walked closer.

"So is the right lube," Rachel said as she poofed into existence next to her boss. She'd replaced the blue dress with a rubber bodysuit, thigh-high boots, gloves, and a leather duster. She would have looked great in or out of them, but in them, with her tail curling about, making shadows on the street, and those little red horns, she took on the appearance of danger, too.

"Do we call that a non sexquitur?" I punned.

Rachel smiled. Scrytha did not.

"You're hiding something from me, Mr. Courtney, and I want to know what it is." It's always unnerved me, the way her two sets of teeth move out of sync with each other, the inner set of jagged fangs snapping to a beat of its own.

"No, you don't." I patted Fang's hood, looking down with a half smile on my face, hoping that my visual verification that Fang was parked over the artificial locus point would be interpreted as nostalgia or cockiness.

"And why is that?"

"Because . . ." I let my eyes close, one last check to make sure everyone was ready. "Because"—I opened my eyes again—"you remember what it did to the cat?"

If my vampire hearing had worked properly at night, I might have heard a helicopter taking off from a private hangar at the airport. I might have heard a lot of things. I might have heard squad cars rolling this way, their sirens as silent as my grave in Valhalla Cemetery . . . just as soon as I said the code phrase . . . and I was pretty sure it was . . .

"Of what are you speaking, Mr. Courtney?"

"Curiosity."

"And satisfying mine would be dangerous in some way?" Scrytha examined the lacquered claws on her left hand, eyes cutting down at them and then back at me. "I find that highly doubtful. Now answer my question."

"Curiosity," I said again, louder. That was still the code word, wasn't it? Scrytha snapped her fingers, and six more demons poofed in. Large angry demons, three with black chitinous exoskeletons, each one at least as big as the über vamp, the other three sporting grasping gray tentacles and squidlike heads.

Did we have two code words? I know "curiosity" was the code word when we took out Captain Stacey. I could have sworn it was just the one. *You have an app for that, dumbass*, I thought to myself.

"Give me a second." I reached for my phone only to watch it rise out of my hand and roll into a ruined ball of tech.

"No." Scrytha's left hand was curled into a fist. When she opened it, the dead cell phone fell back into my hand. "Right now, Mr. Court-ney."

"Telekinesis, huh? Cute." I let the remains of my cell phone drop into the road. "I bet that comes in handy on long lonely nights."

"Yes." Scrytha smiled, the inner set of fangs clenched tightly, the outer set open. "I imagine you would. Is there any other lewd comment you'd like to make before I have my hounds"—she gestured at the chitin-covered demons—"practice tearing you apart?"

"Um?" I opened my mouth to say something clever, but instead, a demon hit me in the face. I don't know which one it was, probably one of the chitin-covered ones, but I wouldn't rule out Scrytha as the cul-prit. As I flew backward into the street, I heard Rachel pay me the best compliment I think she was capable of giving:

"We'd have had so much more fun if we just slept with him."

Under the circumstances, I agreed.

40

GRETA
MIGHTY MOUSE STYLE

Dad. Dad. Dad. Dad. Dad."
The word a mantra on my lips, I announced myself to Void City the way a policeman might call ahead to clear traffic lights in the movies. I wanted all greens, and I was going to get them.

Public Safety Tip #6: "Hot pursuit" means stay out of my way, or you might get dead.

"Greta?" Maybe-Mom's voice touched my mind, but not the kind of contact I could push my will across, that funky thing true immortals do—telepathy.

I dashed in and out amid the traffic, cars swerving and honking. What did my portable version of the Veil of Scrythax make them see? A crazed biker weaving in and out on a Harley? A deer? An escaped animal? I couldn't know. Vampires I passed, Masters and Vlads, bounced against my mind, but I dismissed them without heed.

"Greta?" Marilyn said again.

"I'm busy."

A street back, Evelyn rode down the sidewalk on a motorcycle I didn't know she owned . . . and maybe she didn't own it. I didn't care about that, either.

"Call Marx and tell her I want every cop in Void City at the Demon Heart and Pollux yesterday!" I shouted over my shoulder.

"What?" she shouted back.

I dropped back, running alongside her bike. She yelped, and I grabbed the handlebars, straightening her up, and repeated myself.

"Okay," she said.

"Then get your ass to—" There was a katana scabbard on her back that I hadn't noticed before. "Where the hell did you get that?"

"I mugged Toshirō Mifune's American like-a-look."

I smiled at the Marx Brothers reference. I like my deputy. I wonder if she knows I LoJacked her.

"I want you cutting up demons with it in front of the Demon Heart ASAP."

Hunger filled my gut like it always does, growing worse with each moment of superspeed, each drawn-out second I wasn't helping Dad.

I took the turn from Second Street onto Fifth Avenue, sideswiping a station wagon, its driver's-side door crumpling under the force of my impact. The driver lost control, rammed a parked car, and shot head-first through the windshield. A spray of blood and glass exploded next to me—a rain of orderly chaos in predictable patterns I had no time to appreciate or enjoy.

"Dad. Dad. Dad. Dad. Dad. Dad."

I did a forward somersault over a Void City Metro bus crossing Fifth and Midnight. My shoulder clipped the frame, and the bus tipped, following me over onto its side. Screams filled my ears like the roar of a crowd, like twenty dying cheerleaders urging me on. No looking back. Even if it means I miss the blood, fire, and Jell-O.

"Jesus Christ," Evelyn's voice said from far off.

Thuds and impacts from behind stirred me on.

Running down the center lane, white lines blurred into one line of white, a track to lead me straight to Dad.

Marilyn's 1200-cc two-cylinder engine caught my attention a block before she turned onto Fifth Avenue ahead of me on Sixth Street.

Greta, she said in my mind again.

How are you doing that? I thought at her.

Practice, she thought back. *You announcing yourself like your father does makes it pretty easy to connect.*

I'm busy, I thought back. *I have to help Dad.*

Then help me get there, she thought. *I'm the one he needs.*

I stopped dead still in the street, cars zooming past me. Why the hell does she get to be the one he needs?

Why do you get to be the one he needs?

The demon he's fighting, Marilyn thought back. *She can only be defeated by someone who loves Eric unconditionally . . . or something that can ingest her entire being all at once.*

But you don't meet either of those criteria. I sped up, pulling even with Marilyn.

Of course I do!

You can fit the whole demon in your mouth? I asked, running up and over a Datsun that was changing lanes. *Is she a tiny demon?*

"I love your father unconditionally, too!" she shouted.

"Bullshit!" I was right behind her.

"Greta, no!" Marilyn screeched as I grabbed the back of her leather jacket and threw her through the front window of Carl's Diner.

"You cheated." I ran alongside the Harley, quickstepping it to a halt because I knew how I would feel if someone wrecked something Dad gave me as a present. "Dad loves *you* unconditionally." I put the kickstand down and left the bike on the sidewalk. "You're fickle," I shouted back at Marilyn, "just like the rest of them! Just like everyone but me!"

Overhead, a VCPD helicopter cut through the night, circling but doing nothing: a holding pattern. Why was it waiting? Where were my sirens? Why weren't my thralls charging in to help? Where was my army of chupacabra? Okay, most of the chupacabra were too pussy to come charging down to fight a demon, but still, it made me mad.

"Fine," I growled as I passed Thirteenth Street, hitting the three-blocks-from-home demarcation, "I'll do it myself."

41

EVELYN

MAGBIDION'S LAMENT

The shortest distance between two points is a straight line (or . . . okay, technically, in a three-dimensional space, it's a geodesic, but that's pretty much the same thing, and I know that only because of the obnoxious math nerd I interviewed once for an episode of *Good Morning, Void City*). Abandoning the bike, I took to the air, like a busty animé version of *Peter Pan Versus the Vampires*. Flying up over the city, I could see the Pollux in the distance. Heading in a straight-ish line instead of the jagged L Greta's use of the city streets forced her to take, I might get there first.

I dialed the Void City Police Department, so the number would show up in my call log in case I had to prove it to Greta, then hung up before anyone answered. While Greta was wrecking half the city and trashing metro buses, I landed on the parking deck connected to the Pollux and peered over the edge.

On his own, Eric wasn't doing well. Demons with shiny black carapaces took turns holding him and pounding his skull while a female-ish-looking escapee from a *Hellraiser/ Aliens* crossover and her smaller, more attractively humanoid counterpart looked on. The big one shouted questions at Eric, but I couldn't make out what she was saying, and if he answered her, that was lost to me as well.

Flying down would have been faster, but I wanted clear of the fight for now. If that was the demon with whom Eric had made a deal, then I saw no better time to end Magbidion, and every instinct told me that the demon, whoever she was, was the one from whom Eric most wanted to hide whatever it was he was hiding.

I flung open the stairwell door, leaping from one concrete landing to the next until I reached the first-floor connection to the Pollux. Two of Eric's thralls watched the fight from the glass double doors, and I slid past them.

"You gonna go help him?" asked the thrall with the purple hair, without even looking my way.

Shit!

"Greta's on her way," I said. *Think. Think. Think!* "We're worried somebody might make a move on Magbidion." The truth.

"Shit!" Cheryl. Her name was Cheryl. She took her eyes off the fight outside. "We left him all alone up there!"

"I've got it," I said, rushing up the stairs. "Keep an eye out for Greta. I called the VCPD for backup but couldn't get through. Can one of you try from the landline?"

I didn't exactly lie. "I've got it" could be taken any which way. Lies have always astonished me, the way the first one comes hard, and then each successive deception falls more easily than the first. They gain momentum like dominoes in a line. A quick run up the marble steps, a dash down the hall, and I was alone with Magbidion. Locking the door behind me, I stalked to the side of the bed.

Eyes closed, chapped lips moving softly, he reeked of sweat and sickness.

"Did he say the code phrase?" Magbidion asked.

His head lay on one of the two pillows on the bed. I grabbed the blue pillow and jerked it off the bed. I'd planned to behead him, but the notion of cutting off someone else's head made me sick to my stomach.

"I know . . . that look." His eyes opened lazily, as if he had all the time in the world to act, not just a few more seconds. "That's death. Wanna hear the story of why I sold my soul to a demon, death lady?"

"Yes." I hesitated.

He drew in a wheezing breath. "Too bad." He closed his eyes, resigned to whatever I decided, so I covered his face with the pillow and watched him stop.

42

ERIC

THAT'S NOT GOOD!

Swordfish!" I shouted in desperation.

Scrytha raised a hand, and the two demons holding my arms kept right on holding them, but the four demons who were taking turns pummeling my face let up for a moment.

"Are you ready to explain yourself?" Scrytha loomed over me, drool from her lower lip bridging the space between her flesh and mine.

"Klaatu Barada Nicto?"

"What language is that?" Scrytha sneered.

"Geekanese," I answered.

Rachel giggled. "Oh, baby. Just answer her question."

The bones in my face slid back into place, my vision clearing. Teeth that had been knocked out regrew. "I'll answer a question if she'll answer one of mine."

"Done," Scrytha said. "Name your question."

"Do you speak pig latin?"

"What?"

"Just answer the question."

"I've never even heard of pig latin."

"How can you never have heard of pig latin?"

"Now you answer my question." Lady Scrytha raised me to her eye level (the big ones, not the evil round ones) and snarled.

"Nope." If I could have laughed in pig latin, I would have. "I said that I'd answer a question if you answered mine. I didn't say whose question I'd answer, and you didn't specify, so I pick mine."

Rachel stared at me as if I'd lost my mind. Lady Scrytha slapped me so hard that blood poured out of my mouth, and my eyes crossed.

"Indeed," I said as soon as my mouth would respond properly, "I do speak pig latin."

"You cheat!" Scrytha snapped, and something clicked. That's what this part of The Plan had been all about, or a portion of it. Cheating. The letter of the law versus the spirit of an agreement.

"No." I leered, adrenaline pumping, heat flushing through my body. My heart beat in my ears, and it felt like home. "You're the cheater. You abused the terms of our deal. And I'm gonna call you on it. I—"

Scrytha had stopped listening and began sniffing me like a dog.

"Why are you breathing?" Her forked black tongue lapped at my neck. "Why are you warm?" She slashed my throat clear through my voice box with her claws. Arterial spray splattered her. "What is this? What have you done, Mr. Courtney?"

Oh, fuck! I tried to speak, but it came out as a gurgle. *Magbidion!*

Behind her, I heard a solid thump as Rachel went facedown into the concrete; her attacker had long blond hair and wore a hot-pink baby-doll T-shirt that read, IF IT BLEEDS, I CAN EAT IT. Her low-cut jeans were ripped and torn, her tennis shoes scuffed, abraded, and smoking. Clipped through a belt loop, her sheriff's star dangled at a loose angle. On her face, she wore a pair of sunglasses that looked familiar. Behind the tinted lenses, her eyes were glowing the brightest red I'd ever seen.

"What the fuck do you think you're doing with my daddy?"

43

GRETA

I AM THE LAW

I stomped Rachel's head another good time to make sure she wouldn't be setting fire to me in the near future. I would have ripped off her head, too, but I didn't like the look of the big black rhino-beetle-looking demons (does that make them BBRBDs?) flanking Frankenskank. Lemmy Kilmister's vocal line from "Bye Bye Bitch Bye Bye" blared from Fang's speakers, but the car stayed put, parked directly over the artificial-locus thingy Dad and Auntie Rachel had put in.

I frowned at the Mustang. "You're just going to sit there?"

Fang flashed his high beams twice, as if signaling another car to turn in front of him or merge into his lane.

"Are you sure you aren't an import?" I said, sticking out my tongue in the car's general direction.

Fang revved but stayed put.

Three of the BBRBDs moved to protect Lady Scrytha. The light from the sign of the Pollux competed with the angry light of my eyes for reflective purchase on their shiny chitin.

"Greta." Dad coughed. "Don't."

"Don't what?"

"Don't get involved," Dad said. His heart beat loudly in my ears. His lungs moved. I closed myself off to other vampires, hiding my presence, then revealed it again, but I got no contact from him. Evelyn was in the Pollux. I sensed her, but not Dad.

"Dad?" I asked.

"It's me," he said. "And I'm telling you—"

"To let these demons beat you up in the middle of Thirteenth Street?"

"Yes. Please."

The big black rhino-beetle-looking demons lined up like Spartans, a wall of chitin-covered abs between me, the Frankenskank, and Dad.

"You'd best listen to your daddy," Frankenskank purred. "This does not concern you. This is between your father and I."

"Me," I said, taking a step forward.

"Excuse me?" Scrytha said.

"'This is between your father and me,' not 'your father and I'... object fucking pronoun." I rolled my neck, popping it. My shoulders were next, then my back, as I stretched my muscles.

"And here I thought the proper words were so important to demons," Daddy said.

"English is a changing language." Scrytha scowled. "That's how they say it on television and in the movies."

"You should watch more *Sesame Street*," I said. "Let me tell you how to get there." Most big bruisers expect you to try and go around them when you're smaller. I charged right up the middle because I don't care. Pain doesn't matter. The body is an interface, and I'd bet my interface against any Kafka-style demon. "That's it," I said as my claws raked along the carapace of the middle big black rhino-beetle-looking demon, "we can call you Kafka's Horned Unitards." Two of my claws snapped on its armor. It didn't even react, but one of its buddies clipped me in the shoulder, sending me across the street into the wall. Ow. Kafkas. A much better name than BBRBDs.

I ran down the street, looking for something heavy. The Kafkas didn't give chase so much as alter direction to keep themselves aimed at me.

Building—too big.

Puppy—too squishy.

Human—too fat and too squishy.

It occurred to me a little too late to grab the tire iron or samurai sword out of Fang's trunk. If I didn't come back with something useful, I'd look stupid in front of Dad.

Fire hydrant ... metal park bench ... or big blue mailbox?

Hmmm.

Then I had it. Epiphany! The right weapon was obvious and I only had to double back a little bit. I cut right on Seventh Avenue and right again on Fourteenth, approaching the Demon Heart from behind and coming in the back way. When I came out the front, I had a sixteen-pound bowling ball in each hand, and Gladys was queuing more of them up by the front door.

"Hello, roaches!" I said, throwing balls. I caught the first one in the shoulder, overcorrected, and hit the second in the thigh. Shards of carapace and polyurethane punched into the wounds, which leaked a pus-like substance instead of blood.

"I'm not drinking that," I said, on my way back for more bowling balls.

"If you cannot stop your offspring, Mr. Courtney," Scrytha said angrily, "I will."

"You?" I laughed. "I'm not scared of you. Daddy can't hurt you because he made a deal with you, but I didn't."

I landed body shots with two more bowling balls before the other Kafkas could get close enough to touch me, hate filling their beady little insect eyes as their buddies squealed and went down, more pus leaking from the holes my makeshift projectiles had punched in their torsos.

"Idiots," Scrytha shouted. "You are not fast enough. Watch Mr. Courtney." She blurred, and only by moving on instinct did I dodge her first strike. "I will handle the daughter."

✦ 44 ✦

EVELYN

SECOND THOUGHTS ON MURDER

Murdering Magbidion didn't feel like I'd hoped. The instant I did it, I heard Dad's voice in my head quoting *Don Quixote* at me, telling me that I was as bad as the company I kept . . . as bad as Eric or Greta . . . and he was wrong. I was worse. As far as I'd seen, Eric killed out of need. He hunted. Greta, too, in her own twisted way, had a morality. She fed on the people she killed. True, she fed too much and far too capriciously, but I had a theory about that. Suppose she had to sate an Appalachiosaurus-sized appetite? If the size of her largest form tied in to her need for blood, her constant hunger made perfect sense. But I . . . I had no such excuse. I neither needed nor wanted to eat the mage.

"I guess it's my turn to try CPR," I muttered to myself.

"Oh, I wouldn't bother," said a smooth-sounding voice. "I've already come to collect him."

A shadow stepped clear of the bed, as if the shadows gathered there had given birth to a charcoal-colored demon, soot drifting from his skin as he moved, leaving dirty trails along the sheets and floor. Eyes like black pits marked his face, but there seemed to be no mouth. In his right hand, he clutched a semitransparent version of Magbidion, rendered in Force-Ghost blue.

"Jesus." I took a step back. All the demons I'd seen before had at least resembled flesh-and-blood animals.

"Diaxicrotioush'nar," his voice crooned, "but that's a common mistake. I'd lost track of him thanks to that little Blind Eye toy of Courtney's, but the moment his soul left his body," he exulted, "I saw him clear as midnight to the eyes of the blind."

"Let him go." I drew my katana, its edge luminescing.

"But you just killed him." The demon gestured at the body. "Second thoughts? I'll sell him back to you. Regret isn't as impressive as other emotions, but I'm not intent on becoming an Infernatti. I'll leave that to Scrytha. Besides, a Courtney's regret? Your souls are trending hot right now."

"You aren't getting my soul, demon."

"I thought not." The indentation of black that served as his eyes seemed to narrow. "Good evening to you then."

Flowing like cloud, his soot billowed toward the edge of the bed. "But—"

Panic gripped my tongue, stilled it, and filled my mind with everything I'd ever done wrong. Like stage fright. Frozen, I couldn't move, couldn't react. I stared as that demon dragged Magbidion under the bed. *I've got to stop him,* I told myself. *I can't let him under the bed. If he goes under the bed, then he'll be gone to whatever place monsters go to once they've done all their scaring and—*

Dropping my katana, I grabbed the edge of the bed closest to me, trying not to think about the soot and the billowing cloud of demon moving through and around my feet. In one smooth motion, I gripped the bed frame and lifted with all my strength. As the bed tilted up, the soot cloud became demon once more. Magbidion's lifeless body tumbled to the floor.

I had no idea if there was time to save the mage, but I was sure that if I didn't try something, I'd always regret it. I grabbed my katana and slashed down into the demon.

"Very well," Diaxicrotioush'nar said, re-forming at my feet. "If we must." And then the soot flowed over me, and all I could see was black; the sound of powdery soot whirling through the air replaced all sound, and I was engulfed.

✦ 45 ✦

ERIC

ALL THE SINGLE LADIES

Rumpelstiltskin," I said, still trying to think of the code word. "Wankel rotary engine!"

"Maybe it's not something so obvious," said the Kafkaesque demon holding my right arm.

"Die! Die! The sheriff bids you die!" Greta shouted at Lady Scrytha as they threw down away from me and my retinue of insectoid demon detainers—over closer to the bowling alley. I chuckled. Even in a pitched battle with an Infernatti, Greta was trying to amuse me, this time with old pulp-era references.

Scrytha raked Greta's back with her claws, but Greta left a matching trail of wounds on Scrytha's legs, rolling between them and coming up behind her. A cloud of green vapor sprayed from Scrytha's back, driving Greta away from the demon's exposed posterior.

The fight between Lady Scrytha and Greta seemed to be pretty evenly matched when I could actually see it. They kept moving to one side or the other of my viewing area, which was significantly limited, I should add, by the big black carapaces of Scrytha's demonic hench-bugs.

Scrytha swung wide, claws extended. Her center claw nicked Greta as she dodged, and for the first time, I got a good look at the puff of smoke, the sizzle of flesh, that happened when Scrytha wounded Greta. Greta hissed as the wound failed to heal. I'd never seen her affected by a demon before. Demon magic, yes, but not tooth and claw. I guessed Scrytha's Infernatti-ness was enough to put Greta's natural defenses in the same category as Rachel's infernal fire.

Likewise, Scrytha burned where Greta injured her. The wounds didn't seem to be healing quickly for her, either, which I guess must have had something to do with Scrytha's whole special-weakness thing. If the universe ever needs any proof that my girl loves her dad, I offer Scrytha's burn-stained skin as evidence.

"What if it was a poem?" asked the one on my left. "Do you like William Blake?"

The demon on my right tutted. "He prefers Carl Sandburg. You can see it in his aura that's he's a Sandburg type of person."

"That's stupid," said a third demon. "With his memory? With the Alzheimer's and everything? There's no way he'd have memorized a bloody poem."

Greta became momentarily visible above the fight as she flew through the air, hurled by one of Scrytha's tremendous blows. Judging from the smile on her face, despite the burns dotting her cheek, hands, and chest, Greta still enjoyed every moment of it. The horn she'd ripped from the side of Scrytha's head contributed to that glee, I was certain.

"Try closing your eyes and thinking about something else," the one on the right said. "That helps me when I can't remember the current pass phrase in the Pit."

"They have pass phrases in the Pit?" I asked.

"For certain areas," the one on the left said.

"I'm talking with beetle demons," I muttered. "And they're apparently trying to help. What the hell? Now I don't even remember why it was important that Greta not fight Scrytha." Without my stupid app, I was screwed.

"Fang!" I shouted. "A little help?" But the Mustang didn't budge. Apparently, he knew what he was supposed to be doing, and he was going to stick to the program.

A Harley engine cut through the sound of the fight. Marilyn tore in, holding a sword outstretched and parallel to the ground. It glanced off the carapace of one of my guards, and the jolt sent her struggling with the bike to the sidewalk. She rolled free, pulling off her helmet and throwing it to the ground. When she came up, she was holding the sword again, even though I could have sworn she'd dropped it somewhere in there.

"True immortal mojo," I said once I realized how she'd grabbed it. "I see the Iversonian has been teaching you a few things."

"Oh." Marilyn glared up at me. "Are you here, too? I heard Greta was in trouble and came running."

I laughed. "Don't let me distract you."

"If you'll excuse us," said the two beetle demons who weren't holding me as they moved to intercept Marilyn.

"Leave her alone," I shouted.

"I'm a big girl, dumbass." Marilyn pulsed with blue energy as her biker gear vanished and was replaced with modern combat armor. It wasn't as sexy, but she still looked badass. "I can stomp a few bugs."

"Nobody said you couldn't."

"Ha!" She moved to engage the advancing demons. "You just sit pretty and let the girls who love you do the rescuing."

"Now, don't get riled up and go über vamp on us," said the demon on my left. I don't know why he thought the comment would annoy me. I was overjoyed. Marilyn had come to help, and she was happy to be helping. If she wasn't, there was no way she'd be cracking jokes with me. Wait . . . was that part of the plan?

"Come to think of it," said the one on my right, "I would have expected you to do that already. Why haven't you?"

"This would be a good time, Dad," Greta shouted at me from the other side of the fight.

"Yeah. About that. It's the wrong time of . . ." I realized that I wasn't cold to the touch and remembered Magbidion's enchantment was down, which meant the fact that I'm not a vampire at night anymore was just one perceptive demon away from being public knowledge. ". . . day. Shit!" Thank goodness the beetles were dense.

Marilyn clashed with the demons, her sword glancing off their armor as she rolled and spun to avoid their claws. Each attack she made came from a different angle, with a new attempt at penetrating their carapaces. She needed a better bug squasher.

"Damn it, Fang!" I said.

Marilyn dove under a massive claw from the beetle demon and tried hacking at its joints with her blade. Given time, that might work. I watched as she drew in strands of soul energy and channeled them into her strength and speed. She moved like a whirlwind, her shots to the joints slowly having an effect. Marilyn let loose a "ha" of triumph as she took one down. One bug demon hit the ground, but the other crushed Marilyn's arm with a lucky blow, then pinned her to the ground with the follow-up.

"Mistress," it squeaked as Marilyn kept fighting against it. "Perhaps a few more reinforcements?"

"Of course," Scrytha said. "This fight is no longer as amusing as it once was." She snapped her fingers, and dozens of demons appeared like renegades from a *Star Trek* movie, beaming in to join the away team.

Amid the assortment of Khan Canis demons, beetle demons, and other more human-looking demons like Rachel, five hooded demons in blue robes manifested in the middle of our brawl.

"Is this level of incursion into the human realms truly justified?" one of them asked.

"Wow, Fair Standards and Equitability," the demon on my right said. "You don't see *them* every day in the mortal realm."

"I'm an Infernatti," Scrytha snarled. "I am well within my rights to have an escort." Greta took the opportunity to get in a claw swipe across Scrytha's chest, opening her top and sending smoke from the lower set of breasts.

"Perhaps we should discuss your definition of an escort," said one of the other blue-cloaked figures. As one, they vanished and reappeared around her, a floating cloud of blue cloaks that reminded me of the ghosts in Pac-Man right after he eats a power pellet.

"Yes," said another as Greta stabbed Scrytha in the shoulder with her own horn. "In fact, if I may be so bold, you are allowed to travel with your Infernal Guard and one lieutenant, but that would be no more than nine demons. This is an entire cohort."

"And," interjected another as Scrytha jerked the horn out of her shoulder while dodging one more flurry of attacks, "though it might be reasonable for you to travel with as many as an entire retinue were you to impress your need to do so," snapped the horn back into place, "in advance upon the Council of Vices, a cohort is out of the question," and sent Greta sideways with a snapkick to the face, "so we must ask you to dismiss all of the current demons in excess of nine immediately or risk sanction by our august body."

That sounded familiar, too.

Something Magbidion had said. It rumbled around in the back of my head, and the memory was there, almost as if I were in two places at once: my room upstairs at the Pollux, talking to Magbidion, Winter, and Talbot, yet also down on the street in front of the building, being held captive by the Kafka twins. True immortal memory. I love it when it works.

Fang's engine revved to life. Clouds of smoke from burning rubber rose off his wheels in thick choking clouds, and his tires spun. Flame details rolled up the side of his body. His headlights filled with purple light. Beneath his undercarriage, the metallic symbol that represented the artificial locus point ripped free of its asphalt home, slamming into Fang's undercarriage with a resounding clang.

Purple smoke and blue sparks shot out of Fang's tailpipe, and the whole world vibrated like a window shaken in its frame by overdone bass on a ridiculously loud stereo system. Scrytha held up her hand to make some sort of gesture, but Greta caught her wrist and snapped it, using the purchase to send them both to the ground in a pile of claws and screaming.

Marilyn's eyes lit up with blue light as soul energy from the resulting explosion supercharged her . . . and me and . . . to be honest . . .

I remembered.

46

ERIC

LOVE IS PATIENT

My memory of events came back to me all at once, but to tell you exactly what happened, I have to let you in on The Plan. The night I'd forgotten, had known I would undoubtedly forget, had happened months ago, shortly after I made the deal with Scrytha.

I remember Winter was wearing a They Might Be Giants *Mesopotamians* T-shirt paired with salsa pajama bottoms and a pair of Crocs with socks.

"Fashion statement?" I asked.

"Compromise," he said irritably. "The gift of miraculously manifesting new outfits is not one I possess. You'll need both of us for this to work."

His skin went tan, eyes shifting to a preternaturally striking shade of blue, his stance shifting from rock-star swagger to that of a man so comfortable in his own skin, it made me want to smile and shake his hand.

"And I," said John Hawkes, "am not wearing all that crap he wears all the time. It's enough having his beauty products take up all the counter space in the bathroom when I'm trying to get ready for work in the morning."

Don't ask me how that all works. I have my own special brand of how-the-fuck-did-that-happen, so I can't act like weird shit doesn't go down in Void City.

John shook everyone's hand except for Talbot's. Talbot, he hugged.

"You guys know each other?" I asked.

"Hey." Talbot winked. "I get around."

"I don't," Magbidion put in.

"I know you've got the whole demon thing hanging over your head, Mags," I told him, "but don't worry. As soon as this is all done, we'll take care of it. You'll be fine. No worries."

"Okay." Magbidion nodded slowly, crossing his arms. "Okay. No worries. You do realize he's a full Nefario?"

"Big demon thing," I said. "Got it. Talbot, you eat the demon."

"If you can get it all the way here, then I'll do my best," Talbot agreed. "But Nefario can be almost as bad as Infernatti about not spending a lot of time in the mortal world. Now that Scrytha has the bump, she might be a problem, too."

"Bump?" John asked.

"Promotion," Winter clarified, the change so fast it made me blink. "A travesty for which the universe has you to thank."

"Father Ike." Talbot coughed. "Pot meet kettle."

"I recant my complaint," Winter said with a bow. "What *is* the name of the demon with whom you dealt, Magbidion?"

"Diaxicrotioush'nar."

"Shit," Talbot breathed, sucking in air through his teeth.

"The Prince of Shadow and Ash." Winter sounded impressed, going so far as to look Magbidion up and down as if reevaluating him. "You don't do things by half measures, do you?"

"I already had magic and didn't know it," Magbidion said. "It was the wrong kind, though."

"What were you?" Talbot asked.

"Zaomancer," he said softly.

"Those the guys who raise the dead?" I asked.

"Resurrect them," Winter clarified. "You'd have been quite sought after."

"And rich," Talbot said.

"And died very old at a very young age if I hadn't been enslaved, entrapped, or murdered first," Magbidion said. "And I would never have shaped fire with my own magic, or made lightning dance in the sky, or seen—"

"We get it," I said. "You dig your new powers better. So what are we going to do about my shit?"

"You shook her hand to seal the deal?" It felt weird to see Magbidion take the lead, but as far as I knew, he was the only one of us who'd ever sold his soul.

"Yep."

"And you never signed anything?"

"She asked me to when she showed up with Marilyn," I said as Mags sat down in a folding chair we'd hastily dragged into the room, "but we'd already talked, so I told her to go fuck herself."

"Good." Magbidion smiled, and it reminded me of the look Talbot gets when he sees a demon he's going to eat, or a mouse. "That means the deal is bound by exactly what you said."

"I don't remember exactly—"

"Yes, you do," Magbidion cut in. "You shook a devil's hand. You can never forget what you said. It's impossible. A law of magic. If you were brain-dead, you'd repeat the words you said until the day your body died or until someone gagged you or knocked you out, so you couldn't say them anymore, and you'd do it in tongues so that anyone in any language knew what you'd done."

"Shit." I looked at Talbot, and he nodded.

"The serious kind," Talbot said.

"Repeat the words," Winter ordered.

"Try not to think about it," John said. "Just say the first thing that comes to mind, and that will be it."

"'I'll do it,'" I repeated. "'Whatever it is. I'll do it.'"

"And she accepted that?" Magbidion asked.

"Yep."

"Then you have a shot," Magbidion said. "What she should have done was call in Fair Standards and Equitability, and they would have insisted that the contract be clarified. You didn't sign anything, and this is pitifully unclear. She'll wait at least six months to try to get you to do anything."

"Why six months?" I asked.

"Because if she can fly under the FS and E's radar for that long, the deal can't be nullified. Then it would be seen as unfair to her, because you enjoyed the fruits of the deal for six months, and for that, she'd have to be compensated." He chuckled. "And FS and E never want to do the compensating."

"Did anything else happen?" Magbidion asked. "Any other demons?"

"A couple of dudes in robes showed up and asked if I'd made a deal with Scrytha of my own free will, and I said that I had and they could screw off, because I wasn't making any deals with them."

"What color were the robes?"

"Blue," I said.

"They were FS and E, then," Magbidion said. "Probably Evaluators checking in on the validity of her claim to Infernatti status. Did they ask you about the deal?"

"I was uncooperative."

"Which was a good thing for once," Magbidion said. "They can't force you to answer questions unless they decide the deal is invalid, and Scrytha must have been calling in every favor she had to get her status confirmed."

"So what are we going to do to get me out of this?" I asked. "How does any of this help?"

"We aren't," Winter said. "Scrytha is going to tell you that her 'it' is going to be that you become her eternal slave."

I looked at Magbidion.

"But she can't do that," Magbidion said. "Eternal slavery has to be spelled out now. Too many deals have been overturned by vaguely defined terms. You have human lawyers to thank for that. She'll probably send someone she thinks you'd really like to work with, but Scrytha was never human, so she'll send someone you want to sleep with. She used to be a madame over a succubi den, so her thoughts are probably a little hardwired in that regard."

"She'll send Rachel," Winter said.

"How do you know?" Talbot and I asked together.

"You had the Eye of Scrythax that can grant eternal life or transfer power," Winter said. "I have the one that sees the future."

"But Courtneys can change prophecy and—" Talbot began.

"Oh," Winter crowed. "It hasn't been right about a damn thing yet where our Eric is concerned, but I can read him like a book. What the Eye does is give me enough of what might happen for me to deduce the rest."

"You're a creepy bastard," I said.

He took it as a compliment and unlimbered another bow. When he came back up, he was John again.

"He so totally is," said John.

"So why are you willing to help?" I asked John/Winter.

"Isn't it perfectly obvious?" Winter said, looking away, and bared his fangs like some wack-job version of a vampire coquette.

"Not to me."

"Then you didn't read the epilogue of the last book," Talbot said.

"What the fuck are you talking about, cat?" I asked.

Talbot batted his eyes at us all, the perfect picture of innocence. "Winter killed a whole lot of vampires?" He waited to see if that rang a bell. It didn't.

"Why?"

"I hate them," Winter said with a golden laugh. "I only worked with them because I needed you in place to kill Phillip."

"I'm a vampire," I said. "Why work with me?"

"You hate vampires." Winter laughed again. "And you're you, Eric." His tone indicated that was all the explanation I was going to get.

"Right." I looked at Talbot again, and he shrugged as if to say: "He's got you there, boss."

An hour later, we were still talking and working things through. Just before dawn, Magbidion excused himself and came back with two blood bags and chalk, then excused himself to the bathroom and started drawing a magic circle on the floor.

"What's this?" Winter asked.

"You mean Mr. Know-It-All doesn't already know?" I asked. "Magbidion, it looks like your enchantment is working better than we thought."

"What enchantment?" Winter asked again. When dawn came, Mags and I let Talbot and Winter watch me make the change from ever-living to undead, from true immortal with a pulse and a reflection to a bloodsucker with neither. I like to think it was at least half as unpleasant for them as it was for me. Just after sunrise, I walked out of the shower, drying my hair and sucking on a blood bag.

"So . . ."

It was awesome to see Winter at a loss for words.

"So?" I asked.

Magbidion took his turn in the shower, and I kept an ear out. I had to remember to watch him right after. Each time seemed to hit him a little harder, and I didn't want him to slip and break his neck or anything.

"So, during the day?" Winter asked.

"Yup." I flashed him my fangs.

"But at night?"

I shook my head, finished off the first bag, and started on the second. "It's not a problem, but if I'm going to take over control of the vampire population . . ." I let my sentence hang.

"Then they can't know," he said, "not until you are already so entrenched that removing you would be more trouble than it's worth."

"And," I said, lowering the blood bag for a moment, "whatever I do can't mess shit up with Marilyn. I want The Plan to help me win her back, not push her further away."

"That could be problematic," Winter said, "but I'm a sucker for long shots and making them into sure things. Give me a week, and let me involve Melvin. I'll come up with something. In the meantime, I want you to start reaching out to some allies I know you have. Tell them you want to kill an Infernatti. Have that one"—he indicated

Magbidion with a tilt of the head—"make sure no one overhears the calls who shouldn't. I'll get you an approximate date by tomorrow night."

"And there's my memory thing," I added. "Whatever we come up with and agree to, I won't be able to remember it. Not for as long as this plan is going to take. I'm pretty sure it really is Alzheimer's. Otherwise, the true immortal mojo should have cleared it up."

"We'll get you a workaround," John said. "Do you have a smartphone?"

"Um . . ." I felt like an idiot. "How smart does it have to be?"

"I'll handle that," Talbot offered.

Over the next three weeks, we worked out The Plan. A month later, John and Melvin delivered the app. After that, all conversation about The Plan was restricted to my bathroom, when I was wearing the Blind Eye of Scrythax, or via The Plan's app.

In one of those last face-to-faces, Winter/John, Magbidion, and I were all crammed into the bathroom at the Pollux. I was sitting in the shower, shirtless in my boxers, wearing the Blind Eye of Scrythax and waiting for my sunset transformation.

"I'm not happy about the thrall thing," I said.

Winter sat on the edge of the bathroom counter, which made it doubly strange when he shifted back and forth to John, since John had a reflection and Winter didn't. Magbidion, as usual, sat on the toilet, lid down, and looked tired.

"Eric," John said. He'd let Winter wear his rock-star clothes, so he seemed self-conscious in leather pants, high-heeled boots, a lacy blue shirt, and funky Goth eye makeup. "Think of it this way. You'll be giving most of these guys a shot at revenge. It's payback big-time for the guys who were on the force with you. And for the new guys, you're saving them a bout with Alzheimer's and a sad lonely end in a damn retirement home where they have nightmares about what sick, twisted vampire freaks made them do and/or cover up, then wiped from their superficial memories. And with you in charge, if they want to quit one day and lead a normal life, you'll let them."

Magbidion tapped the shower-stall glass. "Being your thrall is not a hardship, boss."

"Do it during the day—" Winter instructed.

"No shit, Sherlock."

"—around noon," Winter continued. "I'll warn Melvin, and he'll keep the area clear of thralls." He tapped the Blind Eye of Scrythax. "Wear that."

"What about the Ike thing?"

"I don't like the Ike thing, either, Winter," John put in.

"She's going to order Eric to kill him." Winter rubbed at his temple and frowned when his fingertips came away black. "I'm not picking the target, I'm just telling you whom she's going to pick. By having her first command be something so objectionable to Eric, she will believe he won't even second-guess other commands. She thinks he'll be broken and tractable, and he might be, except he has us. How's the CPR certification coming?"

"Greta was curious about why I had her go drop three thousand dollars on a CPR training doll, but when I let her learn with me, she just took it as a weird father/daughter activity and let it go," I said. "It's fine. Suzie lives every time now."

"Good," John said. "Strangle him, revive him, and get him to my place."

"He'll be wearing that"—Winter tapped the Blind Eye of Scrythax—"before you start CPR. And you won't see it again until he makes the call for us and reveals he's alive—unless Magbidion needs it."

"The Blind Eye will hide the wearer from any demon?" I asked. "Even Scrytha?"

"Any demon," Winter agreed. "Scrythax. His daughter. Even the demons from Fair Standards and Equitability."

"And you think that when everyone knows Father Ike is alive and that I cheated, it will bring Scrytha running?" I asked.

"It will enrage her," Magbidion said. "An Infernatti cannot afford to be embarrassed like that without reacting immediately. By not acting, she'd risk being bumped down to Nefario status, and the FS and E will be watching her like a hawk, waiting for her to screw up so they can demote her."

"That's where the . . . What did you call it?"

"Artificial locus point," Mags and Winter both answered.

"Yeah, that." I nodded, feeling the beginning of my change coming on. "That's where that comes in?"

"Yes," Winter agreed. "You'll need Fang parked directly over it and ready to destroy it."

I flashed out of the memory and smiled, looking at all of the demons around me on the street. It felt good to know The Plan had mostly worked. Greta being here may have screwed up the Marilyn part, but I didn't like manipulating Marilyn with some kind of plan anyway. If I had to win her back without Winter playing Cyrano to my Christian, that was fine.

"Breaking an artificial locus point," I said to myself while I could still remember it, "blows all the natural ones for most of a day." I looked out at Scrytha and her horde of demons, at Fair Standards and Equitability, and realized that they were all trapped in the mortal world. Even a powerful Infernatti like Scrytha couldn't go back and forth, not until the effect wore off or she traveled to a natural locus point far enough away.

I laughed out loud. I was trapped in their trap, and they, in turn, were trapped in mine. But even better than that . . .

"And for my next trick," I said to the demons holding me prisoner, "I will remember the fucking code phrase. I can't believe it didn't come out before now, when I was talking about pig latin. I think I must have almost remembered it." We'd picked something I wasn't likely to forget to say, then put it into pig latin so I wouldn't say it accidentally.

"Hey, Scrytha," I shouted. "Uck-fay ou-yay!"

As soon as the words left my mouth, the world went wild. Sirens pealed as the VCPD SWAT team rolled into action. Spotlights flashed from helicopters overhead; the magic that had been muting the baffle of their rotors surrendered to the noise. From one of them—a large military-style transport with two sets of chopper blades—a giant fucking werewolf the size of a horse plummeted to the sidewalk, forcing the concrete to crack and buckle upon impact.

"Bonjour," said La Bête du Gévaudan, code name Garnier (I think I'll still call him Megawolf). "Took you long enough." Back in Paris on my honeymoon, things got really screwed up, and part of it was indirectly his fault, so when I called in a favor and asked him to make a little road trip, he'd been very quick with the "oui."

"I was being all dramatic and shit," I said. "It was a caesura."

"Oh, please." Megawolf turned to fight part of the demonic horde. "Your language is far from poetry, and if that was any sort of a purposeful pause, it was Shatnerian at best." He took one long stride away from me before I realized he was really going to leave me imprisoned by my buggy captors.

"A little help here, dude?" I shouted.

"Let him go," Megawolf growled, looking back over one fur-covered shoulder. "That he may go forth and never again refer to me as 'dude.'"

They let me go.

And I never called him "dude" again.

Well . . . not that I recall.

47

EVELYN

LOVE IS KIND

Diaxicrotioush'nar bellowed and collapsed, releasing his grip on Magbidion and on me. Coughing and wiping the soot from my eyes, I was trying to find some explanation for what had happened when I heard sirens and a helicopter.

"What the hell?" I asked.

Magbidion's ghost spoke softly. "Eric just destroyed the artificial locus point. Diaxicrotioush'nar didn't come through to the mortal realm himself; he projected his power. When the gates between worlds slammed shut—"

"He lost control," I said.

"Yes," Magbidion agreed. "Now could you please try to resuscitate me? It might not work, but I'd appreciate the effort."

Sparks and wisps of white popped at the edge of his being. Peering into his soul, I didn't see a monster. I saw a person who could face the woman who murdered him and be hopeful, ask for help with a smile and a kind word. There was no reproach.

"Damn," I said as I rolled his body over and tried to get the soot and ash clear of his airway. "Let's hope I remember how to do this."

48

MARILYN

LOVE DOES NOT ENVY

Thanks, guys," Eric said to the beetle demons who'd been holding him hostage. "Have you seen my magic ice sword?"

I'd have felt bad ignoring my own fight to watch him, but the beetle I was fighting had the same idea. I knew what was coming even if the demons didn't. Eric has a swagger unlike any other and a smile that says, "Everything's gonna be all right."

"No," said the demon on his left.

"Sorry," said the demon on his right.

"Never mind," Eric said with his trademark smile. As I watched him reach into the cloud of spiritual energy around him, my mouth dropped open. In the sweet spot between heartbeats, his clothes were replaced by VCPD SWAT gear, and in his hand he held the hilt of a sword whose blade was wrapped in or perhaps composed entirely of ice. "I see it."

You're alive? I thought at him. *Immortal?*

"It's complicated," he said aloud.

Eyes flashing blue as he tapped in to the energy around him, he amped up his strength and speed, and I matched him. Lines of blue flowed through the fight, over and across, between him and me and even the giant wolf thing. Eric stabbed the beetle demon on his right through the center thorax, and it stared down at the wound in shock.

To be truly dashing, I thought at him, one true immortal telepathically to another, *you'd need a flaming sword.*

This can be a flaming sword, he thought back.

Forgetting about me, the demon I'd been fighting turned to attack Eric, but I reminded him of my presence with a stab to the joint where his head met his neck, sinking my blade in as far as it would go, then applying leverage like a crowbar.

Oh, really? I thought back.

Yep. He was too busy smiling at me and acting cool to dodge the attack from the demon on his left. It stabbed its pincer-like claws into his back, blood spattering. Eric laughed, and I couldn't help joining in as I finished off the demon I was fighting, sending his mono-horned head toppling free of his body.

On the Eighth Avenue side of the fight, the VCPD swerved in, blocking off the street with armored cars, cops pouring out like marines, shotguns firing and flamethrowers blazing. On the Seventh Avenue side, Eric's old flames (Tabitha excluded) charged in, claws out and fangs at the ready with a passel of werewolves in tow. Some of the demons tried to take to the air when it burst into flame-licked lightning as representatives of the Mages Guild appeared, manning the roofline.

Fang's tires kept on screeching, and P!nk's rendition of "Bohemian Rhapsody" blared over the din of battle, kick-starting directly into the pseudo-operatic portion of the song.

"This is going to reflect very badly on your review, Daughter of Scrythax," shouted one of the blue robes.

"And you, Eric Courtney," another shouted, "will immediately provide all representatives of Fair Standards and Equitability safe passage from this combat zone or—"

The "or" was as far as he got. Greta came out of nowhere, her skin pockmarked and smoking, covered in smoldering lacerations, and ripped its lower jaw free with a roar. "Watch how you talk to my dad!"

Scrytha rose up over Greta from behind, extra arms sprouting from her sides, claws extending to the size of machetes.

"No!" Eric and I shouted. Eric and I ran toward them, dodging Khan Canis demons and beetles alike. Flame scorched the ground in front of me, and I rolled along the asphalt to avoid it, cuts and abrasions healing as quickly as they opened on my road-rashed skin. For two heartbeats, Scrytha and Greta vanished from my vision. Eric decapitated the flame-breathing thing—a half-naked male with wings and tail (an Incubus, maybe?)—growling as two Khan Canis demons caught him from either side with massive ax blows to the back and shoulders.

I turned to help him, slashing the exposed arm of a Khan Canis.

"No," Eric shouted. "Help Greta!"

"Greta?" When I turned back, it was to the sound of primordial fury, a roar out of time. Where Greta had stood, there was now a dragon or . . . a dinosaur. Its eyes flashed red in the lightning and flame. From one of its claws dangled a scrap of blue hood and an ocher-coated jawbone. It was huge, twenty feet or more, and Greta's sunglasses clung to the end of its snout, while her badge and gris-gris bag hung from a cord pulled tight around its neck.

"Greta?"

49

GRETA

LOVE DOES NOT BOAST

Fang played a threatening excerpt from Dr. Horrible's Sing-Along Blog, but no one else cared. Scrytha shouted for her demons to concentrate on me. The blue-hooded demons shouted the same thing. Infernal magic blazed through me, taking chunks out of my thick leathery hide, but that's the thing about being willing to die or be destroyed for something. As long as the goal is within reach, nothing else matters. Being the one to save Dad was all that mattered.

"So you love him," Scrytha shouted. "Unconditionally. So what! Love does not conquer all!"

But I didn't need love to conquer all. I only needed love to conquer her.

A cloud of green vapor rose from Scrytha's back, but I bit down anyway, my maw alive with pain. Marilyn stumbled back. I guess she'd never seen an Appalachiosaurus in person. A clawing, scratching, burning thing, Scrytha went down hard, but I focused through the pain, forcing myself to swallow again and again until my belly was full and sick and quivering. I'd never eaten a whole demon before, but this just had to be how Talbot managed it.

Dad battled free of the Khan Canis demons that had engaged him. He and Maybe-Mom were fighting their way to my feet.

"Greta?" Maybe-Mom asked.

I nodded as best I could, managing more of a predatory bob as smoke escaped my throat from deep inside. Scrytha burned, but so did I.

It didn't matter who won now. Whether or not Scrytha burned her way out of me before I managed to dissolve her to death, I'd proved who loved Dad more.

Not Maybe-Mom.

Not Tabitha.
Not Talbot.
Me.
Nothing needed to be said.
Actions . . .
Speak . . .

50

ERIC

LOVE IS NOT PROUD

Damn it!" Greta (assuming it was Greta who had turned into a relatively obscure dinosaur she'd seen in an Alabama children's museum) sagged to her right, then fell like old timber. I dismissed my ice sword, snatching a combat knife from my gear and slashing open my wrist, spilling the blood onto her prone form.

"Cover me," I yelled to Marilyn, Fang, and any of my crew who could hear. Lisa, her long blond hair tinged with blood, led my offspring to my side to protect Greta. I couldn't help but notice that Lisa wore a flannel shirt cinched up under her breasts and a pair of Bedazzled capris. She was swinging an aluminum baseball bat more often than she used her claws.

"First favor you ever ask me for," Lisa said, "and it's 'Help me fight off a demonic army.' You don't go for in for half measures, do you, Master?"

Nancy didn't say a word. Her chestnut-colored hair up in a bun, she wore a tight-fitting catsuit as if she were in an action movie. She fired round after round from twin MAC-10s, one in each hand.

Irene danced in and around the demons, her pink pixie-cut hair twitching to the left and right across her eyes, telegraphing her motions. She fought with tooth and claw, delivering no single telling blow but a cascade of wounds on multiple opponents, doing damage over time to a group of foes, slowing them down, weakening them.

No one was more shocked than I (with the possible exception of Evelyn herself) when Cousin Evie dashed out of the front doors of the Pollux, katana in hand, and sheared a Khan Canis demon completely in twain from the tip of its Doberman-like snout to the crack in its puppy-dog butt.

"Sorry I'm late," she said. "Magbidion—"

"Nice of you to have second thoughts there," I cut her off. "We'll talk later. Right now I need to get more blood out."

"I—" Evelyn hesitated.

"Irene," I shouted, "you're the fastest, I need you to sever all my major arteries and keep them severed."

"Sire's blood," Irene said as she appeared next to me in a blink of vampiric speed. "What an annoying weakness. Won't you run out?"

"Not tonight."

Leave it to Irene to be the world's most capable vampire when it comes to turning me into a human spigot. With her help, I drenched Appalachiosaurus-Greta in my blood. To the world around us, it must have seemed like an endless supply, but I knew all too well from whence the reserves came. Blue lines of spirit energy flowed to me from all of the living things around me. Bacteria died. Animals beneath the streets and in the walls of the surrounding buildings were diminished, cells breaking down or mutating, the bodies' immune systems overreacting to an attack the body had no hope of fighting.

It hit my thralls as well, sapping them of the edge their thralldom granted them. The werewolves slowed, still fighting, but at a speed equal to rather than in excess of their opponents. Greta improved, but the belly of the beast twisted and turned as Scrytha fought.

"Help her, Marilyn!" I croaked.

Marilyn dropped back, leaving Nancy and Lisa to take up the slack in our defenses on that side, while Evelyn twisted and whirled with her blade in a whirlwind of death that made me glad I hadn't had to fight her without access to the über vamp.

"Do I just—?" Marilyn plunged her sword into Greta's belly, trying to aim her strikes where the skin pulsed and stretched the most. In the end, even with all the help, I don't think we would have managed it without the chupacabra. Megawolf seemed wholly occupied containing the blue-robed representatives of Fair Standards and Equitability, even though their fight didn't look like much more than the Clydesdale-sized dark-furred wolf pacing around the little demons.

Popsie's spine-backed beasties rushed in just as it looked like the VCPD line might break down. Quills flew, punching through armor and cars and walls, but demons, too, the screams of the dying and damned subsumed by the incessant hiss of the chupacabra.

Acrid fumes escaping Greta's stomach singed my eyes and made me nauseous, but I didn't have Irene stop until I noticed I was sinking. Greta shrank beneath me until I stood astride her human form.

"Enough!" shouted Megawolf and the blue robes in one voice.

More than fifty demons lay dead in the street with more than a few chupacabra and thralls alongside. I turned to thank my girls only to find Lisa lying decapitated on the ground, torn limb from limb. I hadn't even felt it. Marilyn and I recovered faster than the rest, and we wasted no time putting Greta's unconscious body safely in Fang's trunk.

"Is she okay?" Talbot asked.

"Now?" I asked, not sure where he'd come from or when he'd gotten here. "You show up now?"

"Class is over," he said, jacket over one shoulder, revealing the forest-green dress shirt and yellow tie underneath. "I e-mailed you and Tabitha a copy of my notes," he said to Marilyn.

"Ha!"

"She okay?" Talbot asked again.

"I think so," I said, "but I suspect we might not know anything for certain until she rises tomorrow."

"Eric Courtney," one of the blue-robed guys said.

"You have much," added another.

"For which to answer," completed a third.

A thump and a growl from Fang's trunk made the little dudes in robes flinch. The trunk latch popped and, weakly, Greta leaned up. Her eyes failed to glow, and only one fang managed to pop through her gums.

"It's okay, honey," Marilyn said. "We've got him covered. You can rest."

"Fugg'n," Greta mumbled as she slumped back down inside the trunk, "kill all you m'rfuggers. Mess . . . my . . . dad."

"Talbot, can you go check on Magbidion?" I asked. "The Decapa-Muppet thought the middle of the fight would be a great time to strangle and revive him."

"A lot of that going around," Talbot said as he headed to do as I asked.

I left the blue boys and Megawolf standing around and went up to the rooftop to confer with Paula, the pyromantic head of our local Mages Guild. Covered head to toe in sweat, she still had twice the sex appeal of most women twice her size.

"You okay?"

"We'll be okay," she said, "depending on how it goes with those guys." She pointed at the FS&E reps.

"It'll work out," I said. The other mages with her sat or leaned exhaustedly, a few smoking, others tweeting, Facebooking, or catching their breath. Back down on the street, I touched base with Popsie and his crew, who agreed to assist the Mages Guild in their cleanup efforts. I assured Captain Marx that I'd be by the station in the morning to talk to her, compare notes, and fill her in on whatever else went down.

It was strange to see the faces of fellow officers from my era, men I'd rescued from senility and retirement with nothing more than blood, words, and will. We chatted inconsequentially, shook hands, hugged, and eventually, after touching base with the werewolves William had sent and making sure my other thralls were okay and didn't need help, getting the bowling alley and the Pollux secured, I said my thanks to the vampires I'd created and once dated, and told them they were free of me. No need to answer my call should I call again, unless they so desired.

"Okay," I said, walking back over to Marilyn, Megawolf, and the FS&E reps. "Let's take this thing inside."

51

ERIC

ALL YOU NEED IS LOVE

W e adjourned to the Pollux. Ironically, to the theater portion itself—the very stage where I'd made the deal to bring Marilyn back. I also insisted on a shower and change of clothes for both of us. I wasn't going to die all sticky and covered in blood. On the other hand, if I was going to choose a place to die, it would be there, under the mystically simulated stars that displayed the real constellations above our heads, but as they might appear in a world without light pollution. We walked out under the mezzanine, and I stared up at those stars, happy to see them and even more overjoyed to see them with Marilyn at my side, even if it also felt as though we were walking into the principal's office to get spanked.

My Mighty Wurlitzer organ was below stage, and the blue curtain hung closed, the movie screen rolled up to the ceiling. The über vamps depicted on the panels masking the organ pipes were newly cleaned, and the ensconced wall lamps flickered as they had when they were gas lamps, even though they'd long been electric. I sat down in the front row and smiled inside when Marilyn sat next to me and took my hand.

Talbot walked down the aisle and touched me on the shoulder. "Weak," he whispered his report on Magbidion, "but fine. " Paula had taken him to the Mages Guild for treatment, and Talbot had ridden with him. "Evelyn is staying with him until I get back."

Marilyn laughed at that, and so did I. "I guess if she wanted him dead . . ."

"Yeah," Talbot agreed. He took a sidelong glance at the FS&E reps gathering onstage. "Let me know how this turns out?"

"Sure."

Talbot walked back down the aisle. I craned around, looking for La Bête du Gévaudan, but didn't see him.

"He," said one of the demons, "has agreed to."

"Wait outside," completed a second.

"Can I wait outside, too?" I asked. "And can I take Marilyn with me? Can we wait upstairs in my bedroom?"

Marilyn squeezed my hand. Without saying anything, in the middle of the fighting, working together to save Greta, we'd come back to a place long gone. I wasn't sure if we were together yet, but it was a touchstone, a starting point. I could handle that. I didn't need an easy fix. I could put in the time. She was worth it. Always had been. Always would be.

"We must discuss your deal," said all four of them in unison. I clapped one-handed, banging my palm on the cushioned armrest.

"Now sing something," I said, "barbershop-quartet-style. Can you do 'Raise Your Glass' like the Warblers, with all the ching-chikka-ching-chikkas? I know it's old, but I keep meaning to buy it on iTunes."

"No," they said in unison.

"Then hurry it up, assholes, because I'm tired of your demon bullshit."

"That demon 'bullshit,' as you put it," one of them said, "returned your Marilyn to you and—"

"And I paid that debt."

"Almost," said one.

"Nearly," said another.

"On the brink of," said the third.

"Not quite," inserted the fourth.

"It is not your fault that the agreement was not clearly defined," said the first.

"But the same," said the second.

"Good faith," supplied the third.

"That kept Scrytha from forever enslaving you with the deal," the second continued, "forces us to conclude that you dealt . . ."

"Dishonestly," supplied the fourth.

"With Lady Scrytha," continued the first, "when you slew and then revived Father Isaac. It was understood that you should leave him dead."

"Yet you did not," said the third.

"So . . . what?" I asked. "You guys—"

"You expect him to kill Ike again?" Marilyn jumped in. "That's not going to happen. I—"

"No," the fourth interrupted. "To settle this matter."

"And close the books on your deal," continued the second. "We request that you perform a service *for us*."

I opened my mouth to object.

"That or we will rule you willfully negligent and transfer your deal to another demon," said the first.

"One with whom your relationship might be more strained," said the second.

"Diaxicrotioush'nar, for example," added the fourth.

"Or someone with whom your relationship might become undesirably personal," said the third, "like the succubus you know as Rachel." Damn. I guess it was too much to hope that she'd died on the ground outside during the fight. Trust her to be the only demon smart enough to slip away unnoticed.

"So, because I obeyed the letter rather than the spirit of the agreement," I said, "you're objecting. I thought that's what demons were all about."

"You're confusing us with lawyers," said the first and third.

"Common mistake," added the second and fourth.

"What do you want me to do?"

"What you've been given," said the first, "the return of your lifelong love as a—"

"True immortal," picked up the fourth, "is very valuable. Your task should have been something equally valuable, not the death of just one."

"But the death of or the responsibility for many," the second chimed in. "Our command is simple, and it is one that many of your supporters already desire for you to perform."

"With the sole exception of yourself, your offspring, and those who expressly submit to your command," all four said in unison, "we order you to *destroy all vampires*."

"What?" Marilyn asked, coming out of her seat. "Destroy all the damn vampires? Why not just tell him to destroy all demons? Or destroy all wereleopards? What the hell? Hasn't he been through enough?"

"And if I say no?" I asked.

"Why would you refuse?" they asked together. "You despise vampires. You have often killed them."

"I'll answer that," I said, "if it fulfills the balance of my deal. Otherwise, you can just wonder."

"Then," said the first one.

"We," said the fourth one.

"Will," said the second one.

"Wonder," completed the third.

"What happens if I refuse?" I asked again. "Is it the weird painful feeling like I got when I was ordered to kill Father Ike? Because that I can deal with. You can't undo the deal and mess with Marilyn, because the time within which you could have done that has elapsed."

All four demons pulled back their hoods, and the robes fell away, revealing a single shape, a wrongness upon which I couldn't properly focus. It was just there. A blot, not black, not visible, but an unseen something that had filled those robes.

"On that subject," answered four voices joined as one, "we are content to let *you* wonder."

52

GRETA
SCHRÖDINGER'S VAMPIRE

Mom and I sat in the front row of the mezzanine, waiting for *Mr. Blandings Builds His Dream House* to start. We'd saved a seat for Dad between us (Mom likes to be on the end). Our kitties (both Kit Kat Marx and Talbot) sat across the aisle with some of Dad's police thralls. I guess Talbot wanted to seem all cool by staying in a different aisle. Who knows why cats do stuff?

My best friend sat next to me with her head on my shoulder, though I think she would have preferred if I let her head stay between her shoulders instead of balancing it on my left one. Down on the main floor, Dad's non-police thralls stood in the aisles being good little ushers, except for Cheryl, who'd opted to run the concession stand.

My thralls kept to the very back of the theater, I guess because they thought it was cool. I don't know. The smell of blood hovered over the theater, but that's to be expected when half your moviegoers are Vampire High Society. They'd expressly agreed to submit to his command. He had not ordered them to show up for a movie. I guessed they were attending because they wanted to make sure Dad knew they supported him—so he wouldn't kill them.

We heard the sound of the Mighty Wurlitzer as Dad rose up on it via the special lift built into the stage. After the first sing-along, I let Evelyn have her head back.

"Mom?" I said when Dad descended below the stage. I listened for his footsteps under the stage, up the stairs, around to the lobby, and up to the mezzanine.

"Yes?" Marilyn said.

"Just checking," I said.

"Ha!"

The cartoon started to play. It was one of my favorites, with Bugs Bunny and the Instant Martians. Dad joined us, and I took his hand, still weirded out by his heartbeat and body temperature.

"Dad?" I asked.

He held out his wrist, and I bit into the vein just to check. Yep, he still tasted like Dad. "So, during the day," I said.

"For the hundredth time, Greta," Dad said, "during the day, I'm a vampire."

"And at night?" I asked.

He sighed. "At night I'm a true immortal."

"But when you got stabbed through the heart . . ."

"I guess technically, I'm sort of like Schrödinger's Vampire," he said, clearly trying a new tactic. "If I'm dead, then I'm a vampire. Because I broke the Stone of Aeternum in the middle of Scrythax's trying to turn me into a true immortal, it worked halfway. So, normally, at night I'm a true immortal, but whenever I'm dead, I'm a vampire, even if it happens at night. But a true immortal's body doesn't stay dead long, so as soon as I'm not dead, then I'm a true immortal."

"Why?"

"Because Scrythax is a jackass."

"Shhh," said Mom. "The movie."

I enjoyed it more than I thought I would. Every time Tito Vuolo as Mr. Zucco would say "Yep," Dad would say it, too. After a couple of times, I joined in. After I did it twice, all the other vampires joined in. Evelyn glared at me, but I shook my head. I wouldn't say anything to them now, not in front of Dad—I don't think he noticed, and I didn't want him to—but the next time we had a council meeting, I'd have to address it. It had taken three meetings to get them all to stop reorienting themselves to face me whenever I walked into a room with other High Society vampires and Dad.

After the movie, Evelyn and I stalked my parents as Eric dropped Marilyn back by her dorm. (The wererats pretended to ignore us.) We watched through the window as they kissed on the love seat, and even Uncle Percy, who was watching through the glasses I wore, thought it was sweet when Daddy broke things off before they got too hot and heavy.

"I just don't want to screw things up this time around," he said.

"You won't," Mom said.

It was great just to see them talking. Mom made him coffee, and he drank it without vomiting blood or anything. That part was mildly disturbing, but I was willing to let it go if it meant I had Mom and Dad back and I knew who they were.

Chthonic signaled me, and I answered my cell. "Yeah?"

"They're here," he said.

"We'll be right down. I want to watch them a few more minutes."

"Eric?" Marilyn asked. "You still haven't felt anything strange?"

"Not even a twitch," he answered. "Maybe the demons were bluffing about the whole vampire thing."

"I don't think they were," Mom said. "We should look into it so it doesn't bite us in the ass. Tomorrow."

"Are you going to be with me tomorrow?" he asked.

She kissed him long and deep. I even heard mutual tongue action. *Go, Mom!* "You know I will."

"Then who gives a fuck about anything else?"

Evelyn and I made our way down to our motorcycles (I was trying to let Fang stay with Dad for his protection—he needed the car more than I did) and drove across town to my new offices. Evelyn had helped me pick out the fabric and the chairs to make it all very powerful-seeming, so everyone could tell I was in charge.

"Show them in," I said. Chthonic walked in wearing business-casual attire. With him were two Master-level vampires. I let them sense me, getting a sense of them at the same time. They were old but not that old, barely older than Dad. Both were hardworking, rugged-looking men who'd earned their money via hard labor before they'd become vampires.

The one on the left was Alan. He was in charge. The other was Brody.

I imagined Evelyn and I looked imposing. We'd been wearing jeans, T-shirts, and tennis shoes before, but we'd changed into our working clothes. I wore a custom-made suit in blacks and reds, the dress shirt unbuttoned three buttons, my sheriff star pinned to the breast pocket of my jacket. Evelyn's outfit was similar, but in crimson and white, and her star said "Deputy."

"Sheriff Courtney?" Alan said, offering me his hand. "I've been asked to touch base with your father about the territory renegotiation."

"You're mistaken," I said, ignoring the hand. "There is no negotiation. You're dealing with me, and this is how things are going to work: My dad is the King of the Damned, lord of all the world's vampires, and you either swear loyalty to him or my deputy and I pay you a visit and make an example of your thralls and your businesses."

Evelyn's head detached; her subtle way of grabbing the lip of the desk so her body would lock in place and not fall was getting even better.

"And you," she said, with her hair doing the slow-motion ripple it did when detached, as if she were being filmed underwater, "don't want that, now, do you?"

"I'm afraid that's unacceptable, ma'am," Alan said.

"Then in the name of my father, Eric Courtney, ruler of Void City . . ." My eyes flashed red as the stake I'd been holding darted lightning-fast into his heart and out again as he went poof and exploded into dust. ". . . I destroy you."

Evelyn staked Alan's partner, but he didn't dust, which meant that since he was a Master, we knew to which traditional method of vampire slaying he was immune; conversely, all the others, by definition, would work. Chthonic brought in a body bag, and we loaded Brody into it. "Ship him back to his home territory and let him give them one more chance to capitulate." I leaned menacingly over Brody. "We've got to destroy all the vampires who won't swear allegiance to Dad. They'd better get with the program and get with it fast, or Eric Courtney's little girl is coming for them. Every. Last. Fucking. One!"